Sean Wallace is the founder and editor of Prime Books, which won a World Fantasy Award in 2006. In the past he was co-editor of *Fantasy Magazine* as well as Hugo Award-winning and two-time World Fantasy nominee *Clarkesworld Magazine*; the editor of the following anthologies: *Best New Fantasy, Fantasy, Horror: The Best of the Year, Jabberwocky, Japanese Dreams* and *The Mammoth Book of Steampunk*; and co-editor of *Bandersnatch, Fantasy Annual, Phantom* and *Weird Tales: The 21st Century*. He lives in Rockville MD with his wife, Jennifer, and their twin daughters, Cordelia and Natalie.

Edited by Sean Wallace

ROBINSON

RUNNING PRESS
PHILADELPHIA · LONDON

Constable & Robinson Ltd
55–56 Russell Square
London WC1B 4HP
www.constablerobinson.com

First published in the UK by Robinson,
an imprint of Constable & Robinson Ltd, 2012

A copy of the British Library Cataloguing in Publication
Data is available from the British Library

UK ISBN: 978-1-84901-736-7 (paperback)
UK ISBN: 978-1-78033-135-5 (ebook)

1 3 5 7 9 10 8 6 4 2

First published in the United States in 2012 by Running Press Book Publishers,
A Member of the Perseus Books Group

US ISBN: 978-0-7624-4468-7
US Library of Congress Control Number: 2011930509

9 8 7 6 5 4 3 2 1
Digit on the right indicates the number of this printing

Running Press Book Publishers
2300 Chestnut Street
Philadelphia, PA 19103-4371

Visit us on the web!
www.runningpress.com

Printed and bound in the UK

Contents

Steampunk: Looking to the Future Through the Lens of the Past

Ekaterina Sedia

With the recent release of *The Steampunk Bible* (ed. Jeff VanderMeer and SJ Chambers), it seems that steampunk as a genre finally came into its own and has grown enough to demand its own compendium, summarizing various parts of this remarkably protean movement, and pointing out interesting things happening in its DIY culture, cosplay, film, literature and music. The fact that the steampunk esthetic penetrates all aspects and art forms indicates that it is remarkably malleable and yet recognizable. We often see steampunk as gears and goggles glued to top hats, but this impression is of course superficial, and there is much more complexity to the fashion and maker aspects of it – just take a look at the Steampunk Workshop website by Jake Von Slatt if you don't believe me! And yet, much like pornography, all of these expressions conform to a common pattern – difficult to describe beyond the superficial, but one just knows it when one sees it.

And of course the literary component of the genre has complexity beyond what is visible to a casual reader. Some will think of early steampunk, as envisioned by Powers, Baylock and Jeter; others will recall the retrofuturism of Wells and Verne; yet others will shrug and deride faux Victoriana with its grafted-on machinery. The beauty of steampunk is that none would be wrong – much like trying to determine the shape of an elephant by feel, summarizing literary steampunk is daunting, and it is tempting to grab a trunk and call it an elephant. It is tempting to say that in order to be properly steampunk, a story needs to be an alternate history, or to be set in Victorian England, or at least have an airship or two. And surely there cannot be steampunk without steam engines?

Instead, I think, it is more constructive to avoid trope-based definitions altogether, and focus instead on the operational – that is, what do these stories do? And this is where we see that time and time again, great steampunk stories confront an uneasy past with its history of oppression and science that serves to promote dominance, where women are chattel and where other races are deemed subhuman and therefore fit to exploit, where we can take things because we feel like it, where the code of moral conduct does not apply to treatment of lower classes. Industrial revolution came with a heavy price, and now as its inheritors we cannot help but look back and ask, is this really progress? And if it is, can we have progress without the horror that accompanies it? What would happen if, for example, Galton's eugenics and Spencer's Social Darwinism were dismissed while John Stuart Mill's *The Subjection of Women* became a mainstream success, influencing policies and laws?

The answer will of course differ from one writer to the next. But this examining and interrogation of the past, the search for alternative turns, imagining what would happen if technology were used to uplift rather than oppress: this is the "punk" element, the rejection of calcified norms and either examining them or appropriating them for the use these norms had previously shunned. Challenging the centrality of Western civilization or the common perception of men as movers of history as women stand quietly by the side, the invisibility of genders other than binary, sexualities other than hetero – all of these issues are currently receiving attention. We as a society are struggling for acceptance and tolerance, and we are recognizing the importance of talking about these issues. Websites such as Beyond Victoriana and Silver Goggles question the Eurocentric narrative of what we perceive as the history of civilization, while fiction writers are busily reworking our histories to let the voices omitted from the mainstream (and actively suppressed) be heard and to tell their stories.

The question, of course, remains: what does it matter if we reimagine the past? Sure, it is nice to pretend that the wealth we're enjoying now was not ill-gotten, but it doesn't really help to right past wrongs. However, I would argue that by reimagining how things could've gone, we can hold up the mirror to our present, and by extension to our future. After all, if we cannot imagine a better past, how can we even begin to understand what we need to do today to build a more equitable, more sustainable, kinder future?

This book offers as many answers as there are writers – from Freidrich Engels building a Dialectical Engine and the mechanical-jawed factory girls of Nick Mamatas to the creation of Shweta Narayan's mechanical bird to Catherynne M. Valente's unapologetically punk approach to Victoriana, the possibilities are as boundless as their imaginations. All of these stories have one thing in common: while they may push the boundaries of what is commonly considered steampunk, they never waver in their interrogation of the human condition, and the ways in which our past shapes our future.

Ekaterina Sedia, May 2011, New Jersey

Fixing Hanover

Jeff VanderMeer

When Shyver can't lift it from the sand, he brings me down from
the village. It lies there on the beach, entangled in the seaweed,
dull metal scoured by the sea, limpets and barnacles stuck to its
torso. It's been lost a long time, just like me. It smells like rust and
oil still, but only a tantalizing hint.

"It's good salvage, at least," Shyver says. "Maybe more."

"Or maybe less," I reply. Salvage is the life's blood of the village
in the off-season, when the sea's too rough for fishing. But I know
from past experience, there's no telling what the salvagers will
want and what they'll discard. They come from deep in the hill
country abutting the sea cliffs, their needs only a glimmer in their
savage eyes.

To Shyver, maybe the thing he'd found looks like a long box
with a smaller box on top. To me, in the burnishing rasp of the
afternoon sun, the last of the winter winds lashing against my face,
it resembles a man whose limbs have been torn off. A man made
of metal. It has lamps for eyes, although I have to squint hard to
imagine there ever being an ember, a spark, of understanding. No
expression defiles the broad pitted expanse of metal.

As soon as I see it, I call it "Hanover", after a character I had
seen in an old movie back when the projector still worked.

"Hanover?" Shyver says with a trace of contempt.

"Hanover never gave away what he thought," I reply, as we
drag it up the gravel track toward the village. Sandhaven, they
call it, simply, and it's carved into the side of cliffs that are sliding
into the sea. I've lived there for almost six years, taking on odd
jobs, assisting with salvage. They still know next to nothing about
me, not really. They like me not for what I say or who I am, but

for what I do: anything mechanical I can fix, or build something new from poor parts. Someone reliable in an isolated place where a faulty water pump can be devastating. That means something real. That means you don't have to explain much.

"Hanover, whoever or whatever it is, has given up on more than thoughts," Shyver says, showing surprising intuition. It means he's already put a face on Hanover, too. "I think it's from the Old Empire. I think it washed up from the Sunken City at the bottom of the sea."

Everyone knows what Shyver thinks, about everything. Brown-haired, green-eyed, gawky, he's lived in Sandhaven his whole life. He's good with a boat, could navigate a cockleshell through a typhoon. He'll never leave the village, but why should he? As far as he knows, everything he needs is here.

Beyond doubt, the remains of Hanover are heavy. I have difficulty keeping my grip on him, despite the rust. By the time we've made it to the courtyard at the center of Sandhaven, Shyver and I are breathing as hard as old men. We drop our burden with a combination of relief and self-conscious theatrics. By now, a crowd has gathered, and not just stray dogs and bored children.

First law of salvage: what is found must be brought before the community. Is it scrap? Should it be discarded? Can it be restored?

John Blake, council leader, all unkempt black beard, wide shoulders and watery turquoise eyes, stands there. So does Sarah, who leads the weavers, and the blacksmith Growder, and the ethereal captain of the fishing fleet: Lady Salt as she is called – she of the impossibly pale, soft skin, the blonde hair in a land that only sees the sun five months out of the year. Her eyes, ever-shifting, never settling – one is light blue and one is fierce green, as if to balance the sea between calm and roiling. She has tiny wrinkles in the corners of those eyes, and a wry smile beneath. If I remember little else, fault the eyes. We've been lovers the past three years, and if I ever fully understand her, I wonder if my love for her will vanish like the mist over the water at dawn.

With the fishing boats not launching for another week, a host of broad-faced fisher folk, joined by lesser lights and gossips, has gathered behind us. Even as the light fades: shadows of albatross and gull cutting across the horizon and the roofs of the low houses, huddled and glowing a deep gold and orange around the edges, framed by the graying sky.

Blake says, "Where?" He's a man who measures words as if he had only a few given to him by Fate; too generous a syllable from his lips, and he might fall over dead.

"The beach, the cove," Shyver says. Blake always reduces him to a similar terseness.

"What is it?"

This time, Blake looks at me, with a glare. I'm the fixer who solved their well problems the season before, who gets the most value for the village from what's sold to the hill scavengers. But I'm also Lady Salt's lover, who used to be his, and depending on the vagaries of his mood, I suffer more or less for it.

I see no harm in telling the truth as I know it, when I can. So much remains unsaid that extra lies exhaust me.

"It is part of a metal man," I say.

A gasp from the more ignorant among the crowd. My Lady Salt just stares right through me. I know what she's thinking: in scant days she'll be on the open sea. Her vessel is as sleek and quick and buoyant as the water, and she likes to call it *Seeker*, or sometimes *Mist*, or even just *Cleave*. Salvage holds little interest for her.

But I can see the gears turning in Blake's head. He thinks awhile before he says more. Even the blacksmith and the weaver, more for ceremony and obligation than their insight, seem to contemplate the rusted bucket before them.

A refurbished water pump keeps delivering from the aquifers; parts bartered to the hill people mean only milk and smoked meat for half a season. Still, Blake knows that the fishing has been less dependable the past few years, and that if we do not give the hill people something, they will not keep coming back.

"Fix it," he says.

It's not a question, although I try to treat it like one.

Later that night, I am with the Lady Salt, whose whispered name in these moments is Rebecca.

"Not a name men would follow," she said to me once. "A land-ish name."

In bed, she's as shifting as the tides, beside me, on top and beneath. Her mouth is soft but firm, her tongue curling like a question mark across my body. She makes little cries that are so different from the orders she barks out shipboard that she might as well be a different person. We're all different people, depending.

Rebecca can read. She has a few books from the hill people, taught herself with the help of an old man who remembered how. A couple of the books are even from the Empire – the New Empire, not the old. Sometimes I want to think she is not the Lady Salt, but the Lady Flight. That she wants to leave the village. That she seeks so much more. But I look into those eyes in the dimness of half-dawn, so close, so far, and realize she would never tell me, no matter how long I live here. Even in bed, there is a bit of Lady Salt in Rebecca.

When we are finished, lying in each other's arms under the thick covers, her hair against my cheek, Rebecca asks me, "Is that thing from your world? Do you know what it is?"

I have told her a little about my past, where I came from – mostly bedtime stories when she cannot sleep, little fantasies of golden spires and a million thronging people, fables of something so utterly different from the village that it must exist only in a dream. *Once upon a time there was a foolish man. Once upon a time there was an Empire.* She tells me she doesn't believe me, and there's freedom in that. It's a strange pillow talk that can be so grim.

I tell her the truth about Hanover: "It's nothing like what I remember." If it came from Empire, it came late, after I was already gone.

"Can you really fix it?" she asks.

I smile. "I can fix anything," and I really believe it. If I want to, I can fix anything. I'm just not sure yet I want Hanover fixed, because I don't know what he is.

But my hands can't lie – they tremble to *have at it*, to explore, impatient for the task even then and there, in bed with Blake's lost love.

I came from the same sea the Lady Salt loves. I came as salvage, and was fixed. Despite careful preparation, my vessel had been damaged first by a storm, and then a reef. Forced to the surface, I managed to escape into a raft just before my creation drowned. It was never meant for life above the waves, just as I was never meant for life below them. I washed up near the village, was found, and eventually accepted into their community; they did not sell me to the hill people.

I never meant to stay. I didn't think I'd fled far enough. Even as I'd put distance between me and Empire, I'd set traps, put up decoys, sent out false rumors. I'd done all I could to escape that former life, and yet some nights, sleepless, restless, it feels as if I am just waiting to be found.

Even failure can be a kind of success, my father always said. But I still don't know if I believe that.

Three days pass, and I'm still fixing Hanover, sometimes with help from Shyver, sometimes not. Shyver doesn't have much else to do until the fishing fleet goes out, but that doesn't mean he has to stay cooped up in a cluttered workshop with me. Not when, conveniently, the blacksmithy is next door, and with it the lovely daughter of Growder, who he adores.

Blake says he comes in to check my progress, but I think he comes to check on me. After the Lady Salt left him, he married another – a weaver – but she died in childbirth a year ago, and took the baby with her. Now Blake sees before him a different past: a life that might have been, with the Lady Salt at his side.

I can still remember the generous Blake, the humorous Blake who would stand on a table with a mug of beer made by the hill people and tell an amusing story about being lost at sea, poking fun at himself. But now, because he still loves her, there is only me to hate. Now there is just the brambly fence of his beard to hide him, and the pressure of his eyes, the pursed, thin lips. *If I were a different man. If I loved the Lady Salt less. If she wanted him.*

But instead it is him and me in the workroom, Hanover on the table, surrounded by an autopsy of gears and coils and congealed bits of metal long past their purpose. Hanover up close, over time, smells of sea grasses and brine along with the oil. I still do not know him. Or what he does. Or why he is here. I think I recognize some of it as the work of Empire, but I can't be sure. Shyver still thinks Hanover is merely a sculpture from beneath the ocean. But no one makes a sculpture with so many moving parts.

"Make it work," Blake says. "You're the expert. Fix it."

Expert? I'm the only one with any knowledge in this area. For hundreds, maybe thousands, of miles.

"I'm trying," I say. "But then what? We don't know what it does."

This is the central question, perhaps of my life. It is why I go slow with Hanover. My hands already know where most of the parts go. They know most of what is broken, and why.

"Fix it," Blake says, "or at the next council meeting, I will ask that you be sent to live with the hill people for a time."

There's no disguising the self-hatred in his gaze. There's no disguising that he's serious.

"For a time? And what will that prove? Except to show I can live in caves with shepherds?" I almost want an answer.

Blake spits on the wooden floor. "No use to us, why should we feed you? House you . . ."

Even if I leave, she won't go back to you.

"What if I fix it and all it does is blink? Or all it does is shed light, like a whale lamp? Or talk in nonsense rhymes? Or I fix it and it kills us all."

"Don't care," Blake says. "Fix it."

The cliffs around the village are low, like the shoulders of a slouching giant, and caulked with bird shit and white rock, veined through with dark green bramble. Tough, thick lizards scuttle through the branches. Tiny birds take shelter there, their dark eyes staring out from shadow. A smell almost like mint struggles through. Below is the cove where Shyver found Hanover.

Rebecca and I walk there, far enough beyond the village that we cannot be seen, and we talk. We find the old trails and follow them, sometimes silly, sometimes serious. We don't need to be who we are in Sandhaven.

"Blake's getting worse," I tell her. "More paranoid. He's jealous. He says he'll exile me from the village if I don't fix Hanover."

"Then fix Hanover," Rebecca says.

We are holding hands. Her palm is warm and sweaty in mine, but I don't care. Every moment I'm with her feels like something I didn't earn, wasn't looking for, but don't want to lose. Still, something in me rebels. It's tiring to keep proving myself.

"I can do it," I say. "I know I can. But . . ."

"Blake can't exile you without the support of the council," Lady Salt says. I know it's her, not Rebecca, because of the tone, and the way her blue eye flashes when she looks at me. "But he can make life difficult if you give him cause." A pause, a tightening of her grip. "He's in mourning. You know it makes him not himself. But we need him. We need him back."

A twinge as I wonder how she means that. But it's true: Blake has led Sandhaven through good times and bad, made tough decisions and cared about the village.

Sometimes, though, leadership is not enough. What if what you really need is the instinct to be fearful? And the thought as we make our way back to the village: *what if Blake is right about me?*

So I begin to work on Hanover in earnest. There's a complex balance to him that I admire. People think engineering is about practical application of science, and that might be right, if you're building something. But if you're fixing something, something you don't fully understand – say, you're fixing a Hanover – you have no access to a schematic, to a helpful context. Your work instead becomes a kind of detection. You become a kind of detective. You track down clues – cylinders that fit into holes in sheets of steel, that slide into place in grooves, that lead to wires, that lead to understanding.

To do this, I have to stop my ad hoc explorations. Instead, with Shyver's reluctant help, I take Hanover apart systematically, document where I find each part, and if I think it truly belongs there, or became dislodged during the trauma that resulted in his death. I note gaps. I label each part by what I believe it contributed to his overall function. In all things, I remember that Hanover has been made to look like a man, and therefore his innards roughly resemble those of a man in form or function, his makers consciously or subconsciously unable to ignore the implications of that form, that function.

Shyver looks at the parts lying glistening on the table, and says, "They're so different out of him." So different cleaned up, greased with fresh fish oil. Through the window, the sun's light sets them ablaze. Hanover's burnished surface, whorled with a patina of greens, blues and rust red. The world become radiant.

When we remove the carapace of Hanover's head to reveal a thousand wires, clockwork gears and strange fluids, even Shyver cannot think of him as a statue anymore.

"What does a machine like this *do*?" Shyver says, who has only rarely seen anything more complex than a hammer or a watch.

I laugh. "It does whatever it wants to do, I imagine."

By the time I am done with Hanover, I have made several leaps of logic. I have made decisions that cannot be explained as rational, but in their rightness set my head afire with the absolute certainty of Creation. The feeling energizes me and horrifies me all at once.

It was long after my country became an Empire that I decided to escape. And still I might have stayed, even knowing what I had done. That is the tragedy of everyday life: when you are in it, you can never see yourself clearly.

Even seven years in, Sandhaven having made the Past the past, I still had nightmares of gleaming rows of airships. I would wake, screaming, from what had once been a blissful dream, and the Lady Salt and Rebecca would both be there to comfort me.

Did I deserve that comfort?

Shyver is there when Hanover comes alive. I've spent a week speculating on ways to bypass what look like missing parts, missing wires. I've experimented with a hundred different connections. I've even identified Hanover's independent power source and recharged it using a hand-cranked generator.

Lady Salt has gone out with the fishing fleet for the first time and the village is deserted. Even Blake has gone with her, after a quick threat in my direction once again. If the fishing doesn't go well, the evening will not go any better for me.

Shyver says, "Is that a spark?"

A spark?

"Where?"

I have just put Hanover back together again for possibly the twentieth time and planned to take a break, to just sit back and smoke a hand-rolled cigarette, compliments of the enigmatic hill people.

"In Hanover's . . . eyes."

Shyver goes white, backs away from Hanover, as if something monstrous has occurred, even though this is what we wanted.

It brings memories flooding back – of the long-ago day steam had come rushing out of the huge iron bubble and the canvas had swelled, and held, and everything I could have wished for in my old life had been attained. That feeling had become addiction – I wanted to experience it again and again – but now it's bittersweet, something to cling to and cast away.

My assistant then had responded much as Shyver does now: both on some instinctual level knowing that something unnatural has happened.

"Don't be afraid," I say to Shyver, to my assistant.

"I'm not afraid," Shyver says, lying.

"You should be afraid," I say.

Hanover's eyes gain more and more of a glow. A clicking sound comes from him. Click, click, click. A hum. A slightly rumbling cough from deep inside, a hum again. We prop him up so he is no longer on his side. He's warm to the touch.

The head rotates from side to side, more graceful than in my imagination.

A sharp intake of breath from Shyver. "It's alive!"

I laugh then. I laugh and say, "In a way. It's got no arms or legs. It's harmless."

It's harmless.

Neither can it speak – just the click, click, click. But no words.

Assuming it is trying to speak.

John Blake and the Lady Salt come back with the fishing fleet. The voyage seems to have done Blake good. The windswept hair, the salt-stung face – he looks relaxed as they enter my workshop.

As they stare at Hanover, at the light in its eyes, I'm almost jealous. Standing side by side, they almost resemble a king and his queen, and suddenly I'm acutely aware they were lovers, grew up in the village together. Rebecca's gaze is distant; thinking of Blake or of me or of the sea? They smell of mingled brine and fish and salt, and somehow the scent is like a knife in my heart.

"What does it do?" Blake asks.

Always, the same kinds of questions. Why should everything have to have a function?

"I don't know," I say. "But the hill folk should find it pretty and perplexing, at least."

Shyver, though, gives me away, makes me seem less and less from this place: "He thinks it can talk. We just need to fix it *more*. It might do all kinds of things for us."

"It's fixed," I snap, looking at Shyver as if I don't know him at all. We've drunk together, talked many hours. I've given him advice about the blacksmith's daughter. But now that doesn't matter. He's from here and I'm from there. "We should trade it to the hill folk and be done with it."

Click, click, click. Hanover won't stop. And I just want it over with, so I don't slide into the past.

Blake's calm has disappeared. I can tell he thinks I lied to him. "Fix it," he barks. "I mean really fix it. Make it talk."

He turns on his heel and leaves the workshop, Shyver behind him.

Lady Salt approaches, expression unreadable. "Do as he says. Please. The fishing . . . there's little enough out there. We need every advantage now."

Her hand on the side of my face, warm and calloused, before she leaves.

Maybe there's no harm in it. If I just do what they ask, this one last time – the last of many times – it will be over. Life will return to normal. I can stay here. I can still find a kind of peace.

Once, there was a foolish man who saw a child's balloon rising into the sky and thought it could become a kind of airship. No one in his world had ever created such a thing, but he already had ample evidence of his own genius in the things he had built before. Nothing had come close to challenging his engineering skills. No one had ever told him he might have limits. His father, a biology teacher, had taught him to focus on problems and solutions. His mother, a caterer, had shown him the value of attention to detail and hard work.

He took his plans, his ideas, to the government. They listened enough to give him some money, a place to work and an assistant. All of this despite his youth, because of his brilliance, and in his turn he ignored how they talked about their enemies, the need to thwart external threats.

When this engineer was successful, when the third prototype actually worked, following three years of flaming disaster, he knew he had created something that had never before existed, and his heart nearly burst with pride. His wife had left him because she never saw him except when he needed sleep, the house was a junk yard, and yet he didn't care. He'd done it.

He couldn't know that it wouldn't end there. As far as he was concerned, they could take it apart and let him start on something else, and his life would have been good because he knew when he was happiest.

But the government's military advisors wanted him to perfect the airship. They asked him to solve problems that he hadn't thought about before. How to add weight to the carriage without it serving as undue ballast, so things could be dropped from the airship. How to add "defensive" weapons. How to make them work without igniting the fuel that drove the airship. A series of challenges that appealed to his pride, and maybe, too, he had grown used to the rich life he had now. Caught up in it all, he just kept going, never said no and focused on the gears, the wires, the air ducts, the myriad tiny details that made him ignore everything else.

This foolish man used his assistants as friends to go drinking with, to sleep with, to be his whole life, creating a kind of cult there in his workshop that had become a gigantic hangar, surrounded by soldiers and barbed-wire fence. He'd become a national hero.

But I still remembered how my heart had felt when the prototype had risen into the air, how the tears trickled down my face as around me men and women literally danced with joy. How I was struck by the image of my own success, almost as if I were flying.

The prototype wallowed and snorted in the air like a great golden whale in a harness, wanting to be free: a blazing jewel against the bright blue sky, the dream made real.

I don't know what the Lady Salt would have thought of it. Maybe nothing at all.

One day, Hanover finally speaks. I push a button, clean a gear, move a circular bit into place. It is just me and him. Shyver wanted no part of it.

He says, "Command water the sea was bright with the leavings of the fish that there were now going to be."

Clicks twice, thrice and continues clicking as he takes the measure of me with his golden gaze and says, "Engineer Daniker."

The little hairs on my neck rise. I almost lose my balance, all the blood rushing to my head.

"How do you know my name?"

"You are my objective. You are why I was sent."

"Across the ocean? Not likely."

"I had a ship once, arms and legs once, before your traps destroyed me."

I had forgotten the traps I'd set. I'd almost forgotten my true name.

"You will return with me. You will resume your duties."

I laugh bitterly. "They've found no one to replace me?"

Hanover has no answer – just the clicking – but I know the answer. Child prodigy. Unnatural skills. An unswerving ability to focus in on a problem and solve it. Like . . . building airships. I'm still an asset they cannot afford to lose.

"You've no way to take me back. You have no authority here," I say.

Hanover's bright eyes dim, then flare. The clicking intensifies. I wonder now if it is the sound of a weapons system malfunctioning.

"Did you know I was here, in this village?" I ask.

A silence. Then: "Dozens were sent for you – scattered across the world."

"So no one knows."

"I have already sent a signal. They are coming for you."

Horror. Shock. And then anger – indescribable rage, like nothing I've ever experienced.

When they find me with Hanover later, there isn't much left of him. I've smashed his head in and then his body, and tried to grind that down with a pestle. I didn't know where the beacon might be hidden, or if it even mattered, but I had to try.

They think I'm mad – the soft-spoken blacksmith, a livid Blake, even Rebecca. I keep telling them the Empire is coming, that I am the Empire's chief engineer. That I've been in hiding. That they need to leave now – into the hills, into the sea. *Anywhere but here . . .*

But Blake can't see it – he sees only me – and whatever the Lady Salt thinks, she hides it behind a sad smile.

"I said to fix it," Blake roars before he storms out. "Now it's no good for anything!"

Roughly I am taken to the little room that functions as the village jail, with the bars on the window looking out on the sea. As they leave me, I am shouting, "I created their airships! They're coming for me!"

The Lady Salt backs away from the window, heads off to find Blake, without listening.

After dark, Shyver comes by the window, but not to hear me out – just to ask why I did it.

"We could at least have sold it to the hill people," he whispers. He sees only the village, the sea, the blacksmith's daughter. "We put so much work into it."

I have no answer except for a story that he will not believe is true.

Once, there was a country that became an Empire. Its armies flew out from the center and conquered the margins, the barbarians. Everywhere it inflicted itself on the world, people died or came under its control, always under the watchful, floating gaze of the airships. No one had ever seen anything like them before. No one had any defense for them. People wrote poems about them and cursed them and begged for mercy from their attentions.

The chief engineer of this atrocity, the man who had solved the problems, sweated the details, was finally called up by the Emperor of the newly minted Empire fifteen years after he'd seen a golden shape float against a startling blue sky. The Emperor was on the far frontier, some remote place fringed by desert where the people built their homes into the sides of hills and used tubes to spit fire up into the sky.

They took me to His Excellency by airship, of course. For the first time, except for excursions to the capital, I left my little enclave, the country I'd created for myself. From on high, I saw what I had helped create. In the conquered lands, the people looked up at us in fear and hid when and where they could. Some, beyond caring, threw stones up at us: an old woman screaming words I could not hear from that distance, a young man with a bow, the arrows arching below the carriage until the airship commander opened fire, left a red smudge on a dirt road as we glided by from on high.

This vision I had not known existed unfurled like a slow, terrible dream, for we were like languid gods in our progress, the landscape revealing itself to us with a strange finality.

On the fringes, war was still waged, and before we reached the Emperor I saw my creations clustered above hostile armies, raining down *my* bombs onto stick figures who bled, screamed, died, were mutilated, blown apart . . . all as if in a silent film, the explosions deafening us, the rest reduced to distant pantomime narrated by the black-humored cheer of our airship's officers.

A child's head resting upon a rock, the body a red shadow. A city reduced to rubble. A man whose limbs had been torn from him. All the same.

By the time I reached the Emperor, received his blessing and his sword, I had nothing to say; he found me more mute than any captive, his instrument once more. And when I returned, when I could barely stand myself anymore, I found a way to escape my cage.

Only to wash up on a beach half a world away.

Out of the surf, out of the sand, dripping and half-dead, I stumble and the Lady Salt and Blake stand there, above me. I look up at them in the half-light of morning, arm raised against the sun, and wonder whether they will welcome me or kill me or just cast me aside.

The Lady Salt looks doubtful and grim, but Blake's broad face breaks into a smile. "Welcome, stranger," he says, and extends his hand.

I take it, relieved. In that moment, there's no Hanover, no pain, no sorrow, nothing but the firm grip, the arm pulling me up toward them.

They come at dawn, much faster than I had thought possible: ten airships, golden in the light, the humming thrum of their propellers audible over the crash of the sea. From behind my bars, I watch their deadly, beautiful approach across the slate-gray sky, the deep-blue waves, and it is as if my children are returning to me. If there is no mercy in them, it is because I never thought of mercy when I created the bolt and canvas of them, the fuel and gears of them.

Hours later, I sit in the main cabin of the airship *Forever Triumph*. It has mahogany tables and chairs, crimson cushions. A platter of fruit upon a dais. A telescope on a tripod. A globe of the world. The scent of snuff. All the debris of the real world. We sit on the window seat, the Lady Salt and I. Beyond, the rectangular windows rise and fall just slightly, showing cliffs and hills and sky; I do not look down.

Captain Evans, aping civilized speech, has been talking to us for several minutes. He is fifty and rake-thin and has hooded eyes that make him mournful forever. I don't really know what he's saying; I can't concentrate. I just feel numb, as if I'm not really there.

Blake insisted on fighting what could not be fought. So did most of the others. I watched from behind my bars as first the bombs came and then the troops. I heard Blake die, although I didn't see it. He was cursing and screaming at them; he didn't go easy. Shyver was shot in the leg, dragged himself off moaning. I don't know if he made it.

I forced myself to listen – to all of it.

They had orders to take me alive, and they did. They found the Lady Salt with a gutting knife, but took her too when I told the captain I'd cooperate if they let her live.

Her presence at my side is something unexpected and horrifying. What can she be feeling? Does she think I could have saved Blake but chose not to? Her eyes are dry and she stares straight ahead, at nothing, at no one, while the captain continues with his explanations, his threats, his flattery.

"Rebecca," I say. "Rebecca," I say.

The whispered words of the Lady Salt are everything, all the chief engineer could have expected: *Some day I will kill you and escape to the sea.*

I nod wearily and turn my attention back to the captain, try to understand what he is saying.

Below me, the village burns as all villages burn, everywhere, in time.

"Suffering's going to come to everyone someday." – The Willard Grant Conspiracy

The Steam Dancer (1896)

Caitlín R. Kiernan

1.

Missouri Banks lives in the great smoky city at the edge of the mountains, here where the endless yellow prairie laps gently with grassy waves and locust tides at the exposed bones of the world jutting suddenly up towards the western sky. She was not born here, but came to the city long ago, when she was still only a small child and her father traveled from town to town in one of Edison's electric wagons selling his herbs and medicinals, his stinking poultices and elixirs. This is the city where her mother grew suddenly ill with miner's fever and where all her father's liniments and ministrations could not restore his wife's failing health or spare her life. In his grief, he drank a vial of either antimony or arsenic a few days after the funeral, leaving his only daughter and only child to fend for herself. And so, she grew up here, an orphan, one of a thousand or so dispossessed urchins with sooty bare feet and sooty faces, filching coal with sooty hands to stay warm in winter, clothed in rags and eating what could be found in trash barrels and what could be begged or stolen.

But these things are only her past, and she has a bit of paper torn from a lending-library book of old plays which reads *What's past is prologue,* which she tacked up on the wall near her dressing mirror in the room she shares with the mechanic. Whenever the weight of Missouri's past begins to press in upon her, she reads those words aloud to herself, once or twice or however many times is required, and usually it makes her feel at least a little better. It has been years since she was alone and on the streets.

She has the mechanic, and he loves her, and most of the time she believes that she loves him, as well.

He found her when she was nineteen, living in a shanty on the edge of the colliers' slum, hiding away in among the spoil piles and the rusting ruin of junked steam shovels and hydraulic pumps and bent bore-drill heads. He was out looking for salvage, and salvage is what he found, finding her when he lifted a broad sheet of corrugated tin, uncovering the squalid burrow where she lay slowly dying on a filthy mattress. She'd been badly bitten during a swarm of red-bellied bloatflies, and now the hungry white maggots were doing their work. It was not an uncommon fate for the likes of Missouri Banks, those caught out in the open during the spring swarms, those without safe houses to hide inside until the voracious flies had come and gone, moving on to bedevil other towns and cities and farms. By the time the mechanic chanced upon her, Missouri's left leg, along with her right hand and forearm, was gangrenous, seething with the larvae. Her left eye was a pulpy, painful boil, and he carried her to the charity hospital on Arapahoe where he paid the surgeons who meticulously picked out the parasites and sliced away the rotten flesh and finally performed the necessary amputations. Afterwards, the mechanic nursed her back to health, and when she was well enough, he fashioned for her a new leg and a new arm. The eye was entirely beyond his expertise, but he knew a Chinaman in San Francisco who did nothing but eyes and ears, and it happened that the Chinaman owed the mechanic a favour. And in this way was Missouri Banks made whole again, after a fashion, and the mechanic took her as his lover and then as his wife, and they found a better, roomier room in an upscale boarding house near the Seventh Avenue irrigation works.

And today, which is the seventh day of July, she settles onto the little bench in front of the dressing-table mirror and reads aloud to herself the shred of paper.

"What's past is prologue," she says, and then sits looking at her face and the artificial eye and listening to the oppressive drone of cicadas outside the open window. The mechanic has promised that someday he will read her *The Tempest* by William Shakespeare, which he says is where the line was taken from. She can read it herself, she's told him, because she isn't illiterate. But the truth is she'd much prefer to hear him read, breathing out the words in his rough, soothing voice, and often he does read to her in the evenings.

She thinks that she has grown to be a very beautiful woman, and sometimes she believes the parts she wasn't born with have only served to make her that much more so and not any the less. Missouri smiles and gazes back at her reflection, admiring the high cheekbones and full lips (which were her mother's before her), the glistening beads of sweat on her chin and forehead and upper lip, the way her left eye pulses with a soft turquoise radiance. Afternoon light glints off the galvanized plating of her mechanical arm, the sculpted steel rods and struts, the well-oiled wheels and cogs, all the rivets and welds and perfectly fitted joints. For now, it hangs heavy and limp at her side, because she hasn't yet cranked its tiny double-acting Trevithick engine. There's only the noise of the cicadas and the traffic down on the street and the faint, familiar, comforting chug of her leg.

Other women are only whole, she thinks. *Other women are only born, not made. I have been crafted.*

With her living left hand, Missouri wipes some of the sweat from her face and then turns towards the small electric fan perched on the chifforobe. It hardly does more than stir the muggy summer air about, and she thinks how good it would be to go back to bed. How good to spend the whole damned day lying naked on cool sheets, dozing and dreaming and waiting for the mechanic to come home from the foundry. But she dances at Madam Ling's place four days a week, and today is one of those days, so soon she'll have to get dressed and start her arm, then make her way to the trolley and on down to the Asian Quarter. The mechanic didn't want her to work, but she told him she owed him a great debt and it would be far kinder of him to allow her to repay it. And, being kind, he knew she was telling the truth. Sometimes, he even comes down to see, to sit among the Coolies and the pungent clouds of opium smoke and watch her on the stage.

2.

The shrewd old woman known in the city only as Madam Ling made the long crossing to America sometime in 1861, shortly after the end of the Second Opium War. Missouri has heard that she garnered a tidy fortune from smuggling and piracy, and maybe a bit of murder, too, but that she found Hong Kong considerably less amenable to her business ventures after the treaty that ended the war and legalized the import of opium to China. She came ashore in San Francisco and followed the railroads and airships east across the Rockies, and when she reached the city at the edge of the prairie, she went no farther. She opened a saloon and whorehouse, the Nine Dragons, on a muddy, unnamed thoroughfare, and the mechanic has explained to Missouri that in China nine is considered a very lucky number. The Nine Dragons is wedged in between a hotel and a gambling house, and no matter the time of day or night seems always just as busy. Madam Ling never wants for trade.

Missouri always undresses behind the curtain, before she takes the stage, and so presents herself to the sleepy-eyed men wearing only a fringed shawl of vermilion silk, her corset and sheer muslin shift, her white linen pantalettes. The shawl was a gift from Madam Ling, who told her in broken English that it came all the way from Beijing. Madam Ling of the Nine Dragons is not renowned for her generosity towards white women, or much of anyone else, and Missouri knows the gift was a reward for the men who come here just to watch her. She does not have many belongings, but she treasures the shawl as one of her most prized possessions and keeps it safe in a cedar chest at the foot of the bed she shares with the mechanic, and it always smells of the camphor-soaked cotton balls she uses to keep the moths at bay.

There is no applause, but she knows that most eyes have turned her way now. She stands sweating in the flickering gaslight glow, the open flames that ring the small stage, and listens to the men muttering in Mandarin amongst themselves and laying down mahjong tiles and sucking at their pipes. And then her music begins, the negro piano player and the woman who plucks so proficiently at a guzheng's twenty-five strings, the thin man at his xiao flute and the burly Irishman who keeps the beat on a goatskin bodhrán and always takes his pay in Chinese whores. The smoky air fills with a peculiar, jangling rendition of the final aria of Verdi's *La traviata*, because Madam Ling is a great admirer of Italian opera. The four musicians huddle together, occupying the space that has been set aside especially for them, crammed between the bar and the stage, and Missouri breathes in deeply, taking her cues as much from the reliable metronome rhythms of the engines that drive her metal leg and arm as from the music.

This is her time, her moment, as truly as any moment will ever belong to Missouri Banks.

And her dance is not what men might see in the white saloons and dance halls and brothels strung out along Broadway and Lawrence, not the schottisches and waltzes of the ladies of the line, the uptown sporting women in their fine ruffled skirts made in New York and Chicago. No one has ever taught Missouri how to dance, and these are only the moves that come naturally to her, that she finds for herself. This is the interplay and synthesis of her body and the mechanic's handiwork, of the music and her own secret dreams. Her clothes fall away in gentle, inevitable drifts, like the first snows of October. Steel toe to flesh-and-bone heel, the graceful arch of an iron calf and the clockwork motion of porcelain and nickel fingers across her sweaty belly and thighs. She spins and sways and dips, as lissome and sure of herself as anything that was ever only born of Nature. And there is such joy in the dance that she might almost offer prayers of thanks to her suicide father and the bloatfly maggots that took her leg and arm and eye. There is such joy in the dancing, it might almost match the delight and peace she's found in the arms of the mechanic. There is such joy, and she thinks this is why some men and women turn to drink and laudanum, tinctures of morphine and Madam Ling's black tar, because they cannot dance.

The music rises and falls, like the seas of grass rustling to themselves out beyond the edges of the city, and the delicate mechanisms of her prosthetics clank and hum and whine. And Missouri weaves herself through this landscape of sound with the easy dexterity of pronghorn antelope and deer fleeing the jaws of wolves or the hunters' rifles, the long haunches and fleet paws of jackrabbits running out before a wildfire. For this moment, she is lost, and, for this moment, she wishes never to be found again. Soon, the air has begun to smell of the steam leaking from the exhaust ports in her leg and arm, an oily, hot sort of aroma that is as sweet to Missouri Banks as rosewater or honeysuckle blossoms. She closes her eyes – the one she was born with and the one from San Francisco – and feels no shame whatsoever at the lazy stares of the opium smokers. The piston rods in her left leg pump something more alive than blood, and the flywheels turn on their axels. She is muscle and skin, steel and artifice. She is the woman who was once a filthy, ragged guttersnipe, and she is Madam Ling's special attraction, a wondrous child of Terpsichore and Industry. Once she overheard the piano player whispering to the Irishman, and he said, "You'd think she emerged outta her momma's womb like that," and then there was a joke about screwing automata. But, however it might have been meant, she took it as praise and confirmation.

Too soon the music ends, leaving her gasping and breathless, dripping sweat and an iridescent sheen of lubricant onto the boards, and she must sit in her room backstage and wait out another hour before her next dance.

3.

And after the mechanic has washed away the day's share of grime and they're finished with their modest supper of apple pie and beans with thick slices of bacon, after his evening cigar and her cup of strong black Indian tea, after all the little habits and rituals of their nights together are done, he follows her to bed. The mechanic sits down and the springs squeak like stepped-on mice; he leans back against the tarnished brass headboard, smiling his easy, disarming smile while she undresses. When she slips the stocking off her right leg, he sees the gauze bandage wrapped about her knee, and his smile fades to concern.

"Here," he says. "What's that? What happened there?" and he points at her leg.

"It's nothing," she tells him. "It's nothing much."

"That seems an awful lot of dressing for nothing much. Did you fall?"

"I didn't fall," she replies. "I never fall."

"Of course not," he says. "Only us mere mortal folk fall. Of course you didn't fall. So what is it? It ain't the latest goddamn fashion."

Missouri drapes her stocking across the footboard, which is also brass, and turns her head to frown at him over her shoulder.

"A burn," she says, "that's all. One of Madam Ling's girls patched it for me. It's nothing to worry over."

"How bad a burn?"

"I said it's nothing, didn't I?"

"You did," says the mechanic and nods his head, looking not the least bit convinced. "But that secondary sliding valve's leaking again, and that's what did it. Am I right?"

Missouri turns back to her bandaged knee, wishing that there'd been some way to hide it from him, because she doesn't feel like him fussing over her tonight. "It doesn't hurt much at all. Madam Ling had a salve—"

"Haven't I been telling you that seal needs to be replaced?"

"I know you have."

"Well, you just stay in tomorrow, and I'll take that leg with me to the shop, get it fixed up tip-top again. Have it back before you know it."

"It's *fine*. I already patched it. It'll hold."

"Until the next time," he says, and she knows well enough from the tone of his voice that he doesn't want to argue with her about this, that he's losing patience. "You go and let that valve blow out, and you'll be needing a good deal more doctoring than a Chink whore can provide. There's a lot of pressure builds up inside those pistons. You know that, Missouri."

"Yeah, I know that," she says.

"Sometimes you don't *act* like you know it."

"I can't stay in tomorrow. But I'll let you take it the next day, I swear. I'll stay in Thursday, and you can take my leg then."

"Thursday," the mechanic grumbles. "And so I just gotta keep my fingers crossed until then?"

"It'll be fine," she tells him again, trying to sound reassuring and reasonable, trying not to let the bright rind of panic show in her voice. "I won't push so hard. I'll stick to the slow dances."

And then a long and disagreeable sort of silence settles over the room, and for a time she sits there at the edge of the bed, staring at both her legs, at injured meat and treacherous, unreliable metal. *Machines break down*, she thinks, *and the flesh is weak. Ain't nothing yet conjured by God nor man won't go and turn against you, sooner or later*. Missouri sighs and lightly presses a porcelain thumb to the artificial leg's green release switch; there's a series of dull clicks and pops as it comes free of the bolts set directly into her pelvic bones.

"I'll stay in tomorrow," she says and sets her left leg into its stand near the foot of their bed. "I'll send word to Madam Ling. She'll understand."

When the mechanic doesn't tell her that it's really for the best, when he doesn't say anything at all, she looks and sees he's dozed off sitting up, still wearing his trousers and suspenders and undershirt. "You," she says quietly, then reaches for the release switch on her right arm.

4.

When she feels his hands on her, Missouri thinks at first that this is only some new direction her dream has taken, the rambling dream of her father's medicine wagon and of buffalo, of rutted roads and a flaxen Nebraska sky filled with flocks of automatic birds chirping arias from *La traviata*. But there's something substantial about the pale light of the waxing moon falling though the open window and the way the curtains move in the midnight breeze that convinces her she's awake. Then he kisses her, and one hand wanders down across her breasts and stomach and lingers in the unruly thatch of hair between her legs.

"Unless maybe you got something better to be doing," he mutters in her ear.

"Well, now that you mention it, I *was* dreaming," she tells him, "before you woke me up," and the mechanic laughs.

"Then maybe I should let you get back to it," but when he starts to take his hand away from her privy parts, she takes hold of it and rubs his fingertips across her labia.

"So, what exactly were you dreaming about that's got you in such a cooperative mood, Miss Missouri Banks?" he asks and kisses her again, the dark stubble on his cheeks scratching at her face.

"Wouldn't you like to know?" she says.

"I figure that's likely why I enquired."

His face is washed in the soft blue-green glow of her San Francisco eye, which switched on as soon as she awoke, and times like this it's hard not to imagine all the ways her life might have gone but didn't, how very unlikely it was that it would go this way, instead. And she starts to tell him the truth, her dream of being a little girl and all the manufactured birds, the shaggy herds of bison, and how her father kept insisting he should give up peddling his herbs and remedies and settle down somewhere. But at the last minute, and for no particular reason, she changes her mind, and Missouri tells him another dream, just something she makes up off the top of her sleep-blurred head.

"You might not like it," she says.

"Might not," he agrees. "Then again, you never know," and the first joint of an index finger slips inside her.

"Then again," she whispers, and so she tells him a dream she's never dreamt. How there was a terrible fire and before it was over and done with, the flames had claimed half the city, there where the grass ends and the mountains start. And at first, she tells him, it was an awful, awful dream, because she was trapped in the boarding house when it burned, and she could see him down on the street, calling for her, but, try as they may, they could not reach each other.

"Why you want to go and have a dream like that for?" he asks.

"You wanted to hear it. Now shut up and listen."

So he does as he's bidden, and she describes to him seeing an enormous airship hovering above the flames, spewing its load of water and sand into the ravenous inferno.

"There might have been a dragon," she says. "Or it might have only been started by lightning."

"A dragon," he replies, working his finger in a little deeper. "Yes, I think it must definitely have been a dragon. They're so ill-tempered this time of year."

"Shut up. This is my dream," she tells him, even though it isn't. "I almost died, so much of me got burned away, and they had me scattered about in pieces in the charity hospital. But you went right to work, putting me back together again. You worked night and day at the shop, making me a pretty metal face and a tin heart, and you built my breasts—"

"—from sterling silver," he says. "And your nipples I fashioned from pure gold."

"And just how the Sam Hell did you know *that*?" she grins. Then Missouri reaches down and moves his hand, slowly pulling his finger out of her. Before he can protest, she's laid his palm over the four bare bolts where her leg fits on. He smiles and licks at her nipples, then grips one of the bolts and gives it a very slight tug.

"Well, while you were sleeping," he says, "I made a small window in your skull, only just large enough that I can see inside. So, no more secrets. But don't you fret. I expect your hair will hide it quite completely. Madam Ling will never even notice, and nary a Chinaman will steal a glimpse of your sweet, darling brain."

"Why, I never even felt a thing."

"I was very careful not to wake you."

"Until you did."

And then the talk is done, without either of them acknowledging that the time has come, and there's no more of her fiery, undreamt dreams or his glib comebacks. There's only the mechanic's busy, eager hands upon her, only her belly pressed against his, the grind of their hips after he has entered her, his fingertips lingering at the sensitive bolts where her prosthetics attach. She likes that best of all, that faint electric tingle, and she knows *he* knows, though she has never had to tell him so. Outside and far away, she thinks she hears an owl, but there are no owls in the city.

5.

And when she wakes again, the boarding-house room is filled with the dusty light of a summer morning. The mechanic is gone, and he's taken her leg with him. Her crutches are leaned against the wall near her side of the bed. She stares at them for a while, wondering how long it has been since the last time she had to use them, then deciding it doesn't really matter, because however long it's been, it hasn't been long enough. There's a note, too, on her nightstand, and the mechanic says not to worry about Madam Ling, that he'll send one of the boys from the foundry down to the Asian Quarter with the news. Take it easy, he says. Let that burn heal. Burns can be bad. Burns can scar, if you don't look after them.

When the clanging steeple bells of St Margaret of Castello's have rung nine o'clock, she shuts her eyes and thinks about going back to sleep. St Margaret, she recalls, is a patron saint of the crippled, an Italian woman who was born blind and hunchbacked, lame and malformed. Missouri envies the men and women who take comfort in those bells, who find in their tolling more than the time of day. She has never believed in the Catholic god or any other sort, unless perhaps it was some capricious heathen deity assigned to watch over starving, maggot-ridden guttersnipes. She imagines what form that god might assume, and it is a far more fearsome thing than any hunchbacked crone. A wolf, she thinks. Yes, an enormous black wolf – or coyote, perhaps – all ribs and mange and a distended, empty belly, crooked ivory fangs and burning eyes like smoldering embers glimpsed through a cast-iron grate. *That* would be her god, if ever she had been blessed with such a thing. Her mother had come from Presbyterian stock somewhere back in Virginia, but her father believed in nothing more powerful than the hand of man, and he was not about to have his child's head filled up with Protestant superstition and nonsense, not in a modern age of science and enlightenment.

Missouri opens her eyes again, her green eye – all cornea and iris, aqueous and vitreous humors – and the ersatz one designed for her in San Francisco. The crutches are still right there, near enough that she could reach out and touch them. They have good sheepskin padding and the vulcanized rubber tips have pivots and are filled with some shock-absorbing gelatinous substance, the name of which she has been told and cannot recall. The mechanic ordered them for her specially from a company in some faraway Prussian city, and she knows they cost more than he could rightly afford, but she hates them anyway. And lying on the sweat-damp sheets, smelling the hazy morning air rustling the gingham curtains, she wonders if she built a little shrine to the wolf god of all collier guttersnipes, if maybe he would come in the night and take the crutches away so she would never have to see them again.

"It's not that simple, Missouri," she says aloud, and she thinks that those could have been her father's words, if the theosophists are right and the dead might ever speak through the mouths of the living.

"Leave me alone, old man," she says and sits up. "Go back to the grave you yearned for, and leave me be."

Her arm is waiting for her at the foot of the bed, right where she left it the night before, reclining in its cradle, next to the empty space her leg ought to occupy. And the hot breeze through the window, the street- and coal-smoke-scented breeze, causes the scrap of paper tacked up by her vanity mirror to flutter against the wall. Her proverb, her precious stolen scrap of Shakespeare. *What's past is prologue.*

Missouri Banks considers how she can keep herself busy until the mechanic comes back to her – a torn shirtsleeve that needs mending, and she's no slouch with a needle and thread. Her good stockings could use a rinsing. The dressing on her leg should be changed, and Madam Ling saw to it that she had a small tin of the pungent salve to reapply when Missouri changed the bandages. Easily half a dozen such mundane tasks, any woman's work, any woman who is not a dancer, and nothing that won't wait until the bells of St Margaret's ring ten or eleven. And so she watches the window, the sunlight and flapping gingham, and it isn't difficult to call up with almost perfect clarity the piano and the guzheng and the Irishman thumping his bodhrán, the exotic, festive trill of the xiao. And with the music swelling loudly inside her skull, she can then recall the dance. And she is not a cripple in need of patron saints or a guttersnipe praying to black wolf gods, but Madam Ling's specialty, the steam- and blood-powered gem of the Nine Dragons. She moves across the boards, and men watch her with dark and drowsy eyes as she pirouettes and prances through grey opium clouds.

Icebreaker

E. Catherine Tobler

I have set out again.

Icebreaker steams south, across waters so cold that every day we see more of the floating, sun-bright daggers of ice which Captain Brown calls icebergs. These great islands of ice grow larger the farther south we travel, but *Icebreaker* shows no concern. She was built true to her name, fixed with a sharp metal prow which Brown says will slice through any ice that should dare get close enough. Above this metal dagger of a prow perches a strange figurehead, an angel of sorts, with wings of ripped metal. In her chest, a maze of cogs that may once have turned, but in this iced air have frozen solid. This apparatus caught my attention because I carried something similar in my own pocket: J. J. Brennan's heart.

These days, everyone wanted to live forever, but even a clockwork heart eventually winds down, as was the case with J. J.'s. I think of the scandal if anyone knew – artificially prolonging life? Unheard of! What dark magic moved such things? They believed him dead of a heart attack, but truth be told, J. J. would have died years ago without Dr. Varley's Extraordinary Clockwork Heart. Small, it fit easily within my gloved hand, closed around it even now.

"Murrie," he said to me as his heart slowed, "take me south when you go. Burn me on the big ice."

And so it was that J. J.'s body rested in the hold below, and one Mr Plenty of the Daily News lurked, determined to capture this story for the world, though as I had told him, it was a wholly private affair, between me and J. J. and God above. We'll see if he gets that quote right.

Mr Plenty shadowed me. It no longer mattered to the press that I was a dwarfess, oh no – though the outcry when such a fine, upstanding inventor as J. J. married a woman like me is well remembered. How much grander a story it was that I stood now as Brennan's widow, stricken with grief and pain, and leaving the known world for that which few had seen, let alone survived – the Antarctic. Doing it on his final bidding, they said, though J. J. knew of my love of travel, knew I wanted to see the big ice years before now. We wanted to explore, hunt, record.

"Miss Muriel?"

A familiar nudge at my side, from a wrist attached to a grubby hand, drew my gaze from the ice, to the only other person on board who was my size. Conor Westerfield, nine years old and a former stowaway, peered up at me from beyond his goggles and hooded parka, offering a length of cooked squid. Rippling its way along a bamboo skewer, the squid was still so hot from Cook's fry pan, steam rose in the morning chill. I released my hold on J. J.'s clockwork heart to take the squid from the boy. Conor grinned up at me, the color of his eyes still hidden behind his goggles.

"Eat fast, Miss Muriel," he said and shoved his own squid into his mouth. He hissed, for it must've burned his tongue, but he chewed without cessation, yellowed teeth working like a frenzied machine, rending the hot, salted squid in no time.

I didn't inhale my squid quite so fast, so still held the skewer with half its tentacles intact when Cook burst from the galley, hollering about a squid theft. Hence Conor's warning about eating it fast. All the better to consume the evidence.

"Going t'tan his hide . . . that's all . . . just a little – There you are!" Cook leveled a surprisingly clean finger in Conor's shaggy-headed direction. "And!" The finger moved toward my squid.

My eyes narrowed behind my own goggles. "Come now, Cook," I say, "you know squid is better when it's fresh hot." I lifted the skewer and took a bite, sliding the meat free with my teeth before chewing with a satisfied grin. "Let the boy be."

Before he could let Conor be, though, *Icebreaker* gave a terrible heave, as if she meant to come clear out of the water. We were thrown backwards to the deck, to find ourselves staring at the bright blue sky above, as one might see lying in one's own backyard on a summer day. But it wasn't a backyard we found ourselves in, it was the southernmost sea of this world, a strange place indeed.

Brown's shouts carried back to us, but I made neither head nor tail of them. Conor's head had struck the deck and he lay terribly still while all around us the *Icebreaker* continued to heave and shudder. The very metal around us groaned, like something horrific was ripping into and through it. Had we struck ice? Was *Icebreaker* sinking?

I clambered to my knees and crawled to Conor's side, opening my parka to strip the sweater from around my waist and cushion his head. His eyes fluttered open, a glimpse of green behind goggle lenses and then gone, and he moaned my name before falling to silence once more. Still, his cheeks looked better, flushed with color now and not pale as they had been moments before.

A glance upward showed me deck hands running every which way, including Cook, who had been enlisted to grab what looked like the bomb lance. Was it a whale, then, that had hit the *Icebreaker*? Down here in these icy waters?

"Miss Muriel, look! Look!"

I found Conor at the rail without warning, bouncing back as only a nine year-old can. His hands flailed, pointing to something in the water. I fisted a hand into my sweater, grabbing it before I joined him there. The boy seemed no worse at present for the knock on his head, unless the thing in the water was a great dream shared by us both – had I hit *my* head?

It was no whale, this thing in the water. With flesh that was scaled and leathery, and a head that bore a broad scarlet crest, this creature was like nothing I had seen. This was chiefly the reason so many had come on this voyage – to see what they never had, to explore this untamed and icy wilderness, to learn what it contained. And here was a creature, unknown to us, and screaming. How I wished J. J. were here to see it. I clutched his heart in my pocket, and stared at the thing.

What thrashed in the water could not possibly be real, yet Cook hefted the bomb lance to his shoulder and fired, so he saw it, too. The lance wobbled in the air, flipping end over end before its sharp iron head pierced that broad, bright crest. A magnificent cry filled the world – part shriek, part howl – and the beast flung itself wildly away from the *Icebreaker*, which resulted in it ripping the lance free. Blood as bright as the crest itself spread in the foamed, agitated water as the creature turned and sank, vanishing. Abruptly, all was calm.

We all stood there like fools for a moment, gaping. Surely the scene called for such behavior, and then Brown and Cook and the others scrambled into motion, Brown calling for the nets to be shot in an attempt to catch the lizard. Mr Plenty came out from behind a cask, his linen suit quite rumpled indeed, and set his goggles to rights, before resuming scribbling on his notepad. His hand looked shaky at best, walking stick tucked under his arm.

While the nets did indeed fire, with their customary muffled whomp-thump sound underwater, the men only succeeded in hauling back catches of wriggling fish and a wholly random bioluminescent sea cucumber, which was quickly deemed suspicious and likely poisonous. No lizard beast. Cook kept the cod and tossed the others back, muttering as he went back to the galley. Squid theft, giant sea lizards and an unexpected bounty for supper. Cook's morning had been busy.

"The Lord giveth and the Lord taketh," he said, and the hatch snapped shut behind him.

"Miss Muriel?"

I looked at Conor and smoothed a hand over his head, fingers seeking the goose egg that was sure to be there. He gave a little wince, but didn't pull back.

"Ever seen anything like that?" he asked. When he spoke, I could see that he'd bitten his lip. The lower lip was swollen, with a bright blotch of red against the pink.

I shook my head at his question, and looked back out over the waters as *Icebreaker* continued through them. A little splash here and there against the bergs which huddled off the rail, but there was no sign of the lizard, nor of any such beasts. Against the far horizon, I could see the faint outline of another ship, but at this distance, all seemed calm there, too.

"Can't say that I have," I replied, and looked back to the boy beside me.

"You've traveled a lot, though," he said, rummaging in his vest, withdrawing an empty, broken squid skewer. He tossed it over the side of the ship. "Nothing like that?"

I *had* traveled a lot, much more than most women in my time. But then, most women didn't have a husband like J. J. Brennan, a man who agreed that women should climb mountains, fly airships and explore the world if they so wanted. I looked out over the cold waters again, suddenly lonely for that big, old man. The rest of my days without him? That idea often hit me at the strangest times. Most other times, it seemed he was just in the other room, out of sight. I slid my hand back into my pocket, fingers curling around his clockwork heart.

"No, nothing like that."

Conor held the silence a moment, then piped up. "Never seen anything like me before, either, huh?"

I grinned, sharp and bright as *Icebreaker* slid out of the shadow of a berg and into clearer water. "Nothing like you in all my years," I had to admit, for it was true.

The adults on board *Icebreaker* had a propensity to treat me more like a child, owing to my size, whereas Conor, an actual child, treated me as the adult I was. He and I walked into the mess hall for dinner that evening, Conor's arm outstretched for my gloved hand to rest upon, and while he wore a jacket, it had seen better days, and too many mice in recent weeks, so we made for a curious enough pair.

Mr Plenty's eyes snapped to me, assessing, looking for any crack he might widen into a complete story. I stayed close to him, though, focused on my young escort.

"It rather smells like fried cod in here, Mr Westerfield," I said, looking at the collection of men gathered round the table. Fried cod, yes, but I saw bowls of golden soup scattered about the table as well.

"It rather smells like unwashed men, Missus Brennan," he confided in a whisper that could have been a dozen times softer, truth be told.

I cleared my throat and sat on the first empty stretch of bench I came to, next to one Mr Herbert, who was an illustrator and thus usually covered in ink. Tonight was no exception. It looked as though he had been wrestling with the squid from that morning.

He had a sketch pad in his lap and a glance down showed me he had been hard at work capturing the beast we had seen in the waters. He had yet to color in the crest, though, and as Conor slid onto the bench beside me, Herbert looked up at us with watery blue eyes. He managed a tentative smile for us.

"Wasn't it perfectly terrible?" he asked in a whisper. Thin, inked hands latched onto his sketch book, bringing it up to the table where he placed it over his bowl of soup. His fingers traced a path above the ink drawing, from the beast's crest down its scaled belly, into fuming water. Herbert had a good way with his pencils and inks; the image was excellent indeed.

"Have you seen its like before?"

Herbert cleared his throat at my question, a man clearly more comfortable with drawing what he thought than speaking it.

"No," he eventually said as other conversations around the table came to a close, making ours the chief form of entertainment. He cleared his throat again, fingers stroking his bow tie before he added, "It may well be an entirely new discovery." He looked up, at those others at the table, seeming to challenge them to disagree.

No one did, not even Mr Plenty, who seemed as animated as the others when it came to discussing the creature.

"Entirely new!"

"Wholly discovered by . . . us!"

"Brown's Lizard!"

"Brown's Arctic Beast!"

"The Terror from the Icy Deep!"

Mr Herbert drew his sketch pad back onto his lap and returned to his soup as the conversation went on around us. I smiled thanks to Cook when he brought me soup and cod both, then looked at Conor.

"Wish Mr J. J. could have seen it," Conor said around a hot hank of cod in his mouth.

My gloved fingers touched the lump of J. J.'s heart in my pocket. "Oh, I think he did," I said, and dipped a spoon into the golden soup before me.

After the meal, I slipped away largely unnoticed, being that the men were once more occupied with Mr Herbert's drawings, and I being small and a woman, could easily vanish. Belowdecks, the conversation faded, consumed by the endless chug of the triple expansion engines. I was short enough that overhead pipes didn't worry me, but at every hatch, I had to pause and take a large step up and over the lip which rose out of the floor. Captain Brown said that every compartment could be sealed in case of flooding, but I was of the idea that I wanted to be on the top deck in that instance. Getting the hell off the ship.

J. J.'s casket awaited me in an aft compartment, perched atop a collection of crates, lit by the flicker of one gaslamp above. Strange, Mr Plenty had written, how a man so beloved and wealthy would end up in a simple pine box. Natural, I said to him, for in life J. J. had not seen himself as being above anyone. Death would claim us all in the end.

"Hey-ho, big man," I whispered and leaned back against the door to close it. It latched with a soft rasp of rubber against steel, and I didn't turn the wheel to seal it tight, figuring we weren't in imminent danger of flooding.

At some point, I knew this would get easier. Everyone told me it was so. People died every day. I was not the first to lose a loved one. All true, but I'd never had a husband before. Had never had a husband die. So amid what everyone else likely labeled "natural", in this case I labeled "strange". I also slotted it into the "never want to do again" category.

Here, in the privacy of the room, I tugged my gloves off and placed my hands against the smooth pine. I could feel the vibration of the engines clean through the wood, and pictured J. J. inside, wriggling.

I stood there for a long time. Simply standing. A thing I hadn't done in years, being willingly still. Eventually, I took J. J.'s heart from my pocket and placed it atop the casket. It rolled a little with the motion of the ship, then finally settled into a place near his feet. Time seemed to slow here as *Icebreaker* moved further south. Time alone with J. J. and memory.

"Missus Brennan."

I jerked at the sound of Mr Plenty's voice behind me. My eye fell to the clockwork heart atop the casket, thrown into shadow as Mr Plenty moved deeper into the room. I wanted to reach for it, but it was too late. He had seen.

"That is . . . remarkable."

My eyes met Mr Plenty's over the foot of the casket, walking stick in hand. J. J.'s heart seemed to wink as the gaslight fell over it again. The gears were still, but for a moment, they seemed to move again. Wishful thinking.

When Mr Plenty moved toward the heart, I lunged for it. My hand closed around it before his could, and I drew the heart firmly away, leaving a long scratch across the pine lid. I half expected Plenty to leap over the casket in an effort to claim it.

"A golden egg?" he asked. "A creation of yours?" His eyes narrowed. "Something Brennan was working on?" He took a step forward and I took one back, a strange and silent dance around the casket.

"I think you need to review the privacy laws, Mr Plenty." My voice sounded much more steady than I felt. I shoved the heart into my pocket, aware of little bits of casket lid sprinkling out of it as I did so.

"An orphan invention?" Plenty asked. He stepped forward again, and I stepped back yet again, now on the far side of the casket. J. J. rested between me and Mr Plenty, a silent shield. The hatch lay beyond Plenty.

I found Plenty's question curious, that he should liken the heart to a child. J. J. and I had been cautious lovers, neither one of us wanting to risk a pregnancy. Physicians could not tell us if a child born to us would be J. J.'s size or my own, but they could tell me that carrying a normal-sized child would likely place me in great peril. J. J. refused to risk me that way – even if he later parachuted with me out of Neil Lundwood's zeppelin over Mount Kilimanjaro. "I'm holding your hand either way, Murrie," he said, "but won't let you risk that kind of death." For J. J. Brennan, there was a good death and a bad death. Killed while leaping from a zeppelin was acceptable. Dying in a hospital, of all places one might choose, was frowned upon.

Still, I knew the shadow in his eye, for I saw it within my own each morning as I dressed. The longing for a child, for an heir to leave his fortunes to and the world besides. It was how I first came upon the mention of Doctor Varley. A small note in a medical journal I picked up at Tock's Books, no more than three lines. A brief mention of reconfiguring the human body to withstand the Increasing Perils of the World in Which We Lived.

At the time, I had wondered. How might one be reconfigured? What might be possible? J. J. wondered, too.

Doctor Varley thought the idea a fascinating one. Might he reconfigure me into a normal-sized woman? But J. J. had grown ill before we could consider such things in depth, and Varley's attentions turned toward a heart instead, that he might at least prolong J. J.'s life. The prototype was shown at the World's Fair some years prior; the public gaped, the outcry was tremendous. Most did not want to hear of the frailty of human flesh.

"None of your concern," I told Plenty, and moved again as he did. Around the foot of the casket now as Plenty rounded the head.

"An invention of Brennan's that you mean to claim as your own?"

My eyes narrowed at the very idea. "You dare—"

But whatever insult I might have hurled at the reporter was cut short. *Icebreaker*, for lack of a better word, stopped. The waters around us seemed suddenly solid, and Mr Plenty and I were flung bodily to the floor. J. J.'s casket would have followed and landed atop us, but for Plenty's walking stick coming up to jab the box in its side and keep it barely balanced. I stared at the casket in horror, paying little mind to the ache in my shoulder and hip as I scrambled back to my feet, to plant both hands against the casket and attempt to push it back onto the crates. Plenty's efforts were met with more success than my own.

For a moment, all was quiet and then *Icebreaker* shuddered. I could then hear noise from above and outside both. Strange cracking sounds and a new vibration that made the floor feel like jelly under my feet.

"Another time then, Mrs Brennan," Plenty murmured, and shuffled himself out of the room, vanishing down the length of the corridor with only the tap-tap-tap of his walking stick sounding in his wake.

Another time. He would not be far. My fingers tightened against the casket and I bent to press my lips against the pine.

"Missus."

Cook was there then, and I simply looked at him, too shocked and confused to do much else. Cook nodded and moved forward, finding the necessary lines to secure the casket to the wall.

"What's happening up there?" My voice was not at all steady, nor were my hands as they latched onto a line and helped tug it firm.

"Come see," Cook said, and nodded me toward the hatch. "Captain woulda warned folk, but it came up on us quicker than he thought."

Coats, goggles and gloves were retrieved before we reached the final hatch, and we stepped through bundled up. Breath fogged in the bright air. Though it was well past seven in the evening, daylight still reigned, and would so long as we were down here. Summer tipped the world in such a way, J. J. had told me, that the sun never set. The light was disconcerting, bouncing off the icebergs as it did, making them light and shadowed by turns.

As Cook and I came up, the deck was sliced with long shadows from that towering ice, while around us the sea seemed to have vanished. Swallowed by ice. Everywhere I looked, there was only ice. Cook tugged me toward the rail where Mr Plenty already lingered, and pointed.

Icebreaker's prow was doing its hard work. The grand metal dagger bit into the sea ice, shattering it and allowing the ship to pass through. *Icebreaker* groaned under the strain, yet still seemed to move without complication through the cleaved ice. I could see the angel and her tattered wings, crusted with ice that gleamed in the bright-but-cold sunlight. Could see, too, the cogs of her heart, turning.

If this were not enough wholly to capture my attention, the dark figures on the unbroken ice field ahead were. I squinted against the bright sun, but when that same sunlight caught one of the figures and illuminated the scarlet crest atop its head, my eyes flew wide open.

There were dozens of them and the ice beneath their massive clawed feet was bright with blood. Even now, some penguins tried to escape the slaughter, but the terrible lizards were faster than anything I'd seen before. One massive head bent to the ice, snatched a round penguin in its sharp jaws and devoured it the way Conor had his squid. Bite, bite, bite.

And then, they saw us. Perhaps they felt the vibration *Icebreaker* made as she churned through the ice. Perhaps they heard the increasing growl of the engine as more power was applied and steam bellowed into the cold, bright air. The lizards looked up, heads snapping around to stare at *Icebreaker*.

It seemed they waited a heartbeat and then surged. Cook and Plenty took a step backward with me and as the lizards streaked across the frozen landscape, my only thought was of Conor. Where was the boy?

"Captain!"

I screamed for Brown, even though he was nowhere to be seen, either. As the lizards scrambled ever closer, *Icebreaker* rammed something she could not break. I heard hollered curses rising for a moment above the whine of the straining engines, and then there was only the awful sound of the engines, trying to press the ship forward though she could not be budged.

Closer now, I could hear the lizards hissing and shrieking. To each other? Communication? J. J. would marvel, but the sounds sent more than a shiver through me, and I moved away, toward the starboard rail. I could *hear* their curled claws gaining purchase on the ice, like little picks – how swift they were, agile over the ice, bodies low and sleek, necks stretched out, nearly like birds in low flight!

The lizards bounded over the ship rails. Their claws clattered against the deck and they at last faltered in their approach, unfamiliar with metal decking. I feared Cook and Plenty dead, for the beasts did not cease despite their faulty footing. They charged on. Cook pulled Plenty toward the rail, where they might press themselves and avoid the sudden invasion. The lizards leapt over them, and kept on. I turned, meaning to run the rest of the distance to the starboard rail, but that's when *Icebreaker*'s own heart gave out. The straining engines snapped and exploded.

J. J. was laughing, I was sure of it. Whether he looked down on us from Heaven Above, or up from Hell's deepest crevasse, laughter was reddening his cheeks and making his belly tremble. Even with that laughter in mind, I cried out as the ship buckled and the sun-bright evening air suddenly became my home. Warm blood flecked my cheeks, splattered my coat, the stench of burning wool and hair clogged my nose, and then I knew only the cool air rushing past me, until the ground reached up to yank me back down.

For a long while I couldn't breathe. I rolled onto my bruised side and at last drew in a shaking breath as I found myself looking into Captain Brown's sightless eyes. They were hazel, those eyes, now lashed with blood. I reached a hand out to close them, my own fingers covered in blood and God knew what else. From behind Captain Brown, a shadow descended and an immense maw closed over his head and shoulder to rip him away from my fingertips.

"Now's the time to go, Murrie."

I heard J. J.'s voice as clear as day, though my ears were ringing from the explosion. I pushed myself up off the ice and looked around, watching in disbelief as two of the lizards fought over Brown's body. One glance behind me showed it was clear of any living lizards – body and ship parts strewed the ice, slick with blood and other fluids. I felt the bile rise in my throat and forced myself to move forward.

It was then I realized the hem of my coat was in tatters. That my woolen trousers were the same, falling apart in bits of sooty ash as I stumbled across the field of debris. I clutched the ruined wool to me, but then – ah, God! The pockets of my trousers were likewise gone, and with them, J. J.'s heart.

My boot slipped in a patch of blood, and I fell hard, gloved hands coming up at the last moment to save at least my face. The breath went out of me again and I looked up with a choked sob at the scene around me. Dead lizards, dead humans – living lizards fighting over the remains of people I'd stood with only moments before! – and the ruin of *Icebreaker* sinking into the icy waters, taking J. J.'s body with it. The metal angel reached up, but failed to grab anything that might save the vessel. I cried out at the utter injustice of it, but it was a small sound, lost amid the snarls of the beasts nearby.

"Miss M-Muriel!"

He must've shouted my name a few times; his little throat seemed strained by it when I finally heard him and turned to look. Conor Westerfield stood a ways off, torch burning in one hand, a long shard of metal held in the other. Half his hair was gone, burned clean to the scalp, and his left cheek trickled blood.

Now's the time to go, Murrie. J. J. said so. I nodded to Conor, but my head seemed heavy. Throbbing and full of tears. I pushed up from the ice and stood, and that's when we heard the screaming. It was loud, coming to me as though my ears weren't at all damaged from the explosion. Over and over, the same sound echoed against the ice and strangely, sent the quarreling lizards scattering.

It was Plenty. When my vision cleared of tears, I saw him approaching from the wreck of the ship, carrying what looked like Captain Brown's phonograph. His own trousers were in scraps, so too was his coat. Through the gaps in the fabric, I could see something gleaming. Something metallic. Covered in blood and soot, he staggered toward us, turning the handle on the phonograph. Whatever it was playing, it was not the machine's original song. It was a shriek now, grating metal magnified and tossed out onto the icy plain.

In silence, we three gathered what we could from the debris around us, wrapping ourselves in what fabric we could find so that we would not perish from the cold. I found a compass, its case cracked, but it still worked, the needle settling to tell me I was pointed west. I held the compass, much as I had J. J.'s heart, and searched on, finding sodden pages from Mr Herbert's illustration book, a small battered stove and a sextant.

Icebreaker sank as we searched. The ruined steamship vanished beneath the ice she'd broken with a gurgle and a groan; slowly, the fragments of ice closed over the site, looking like puzzle pieces atop a very blue table. I crouched for a long time at the edge of the ice, as if I could will the ship back to the surface. But J. J.'s body, like his heart, was now out of my reach. As much as I looked that evening, there was no sign of that clockwork heart. I think I was too numb to cry.

Plenty and I took turns that night, sitting watch while Conor slept. Well away from the broken edge of ice, we made camp with a small fire fueled by debris, and kept watch for any more lizards Only once did one get close to pick through the debris. Plenty scared it away with another turn of the phonograph crank.

Plenty's notebook was quite the ruin. He sat it on the ice between us at one point, amid the other collected items. Small cases of stove fuel, a crooked pan, a small pack and within it, oddly, one shoe. It was Plenty who interested me more than those items though, Plenty with his exposed mechanical bits.

We shared part of a lizard leg, roasted in the campfire, while Plenty's own injured leg stretched alongside. The mock-skin had been burned or torn, exposing a network of metal beneath. Long streams of blood-flecked copper and gold ran from his knee to ankle, the entire calf seeming clockwork. His knee, too, was made of gears and cogs; the tooth of one cog poked through the covering of mock-skin.

His eyes, though, when he looked at me, were all human. Not clockwork. We watched each other a long time, and though we were both wearing goggles, one lens on each cracked, it seemed we saw each other for the first time there. He was not a reporter, I was not the story he pursued. We simply were. Plenty drew his coat around him, and gnawed on the lizard meat and eventually the bright bone he exposed.

"When I was younger," he said around a mouthful, "I was ill." This revelation seemed to cause him distress, though he seemed resigned to it, and to explaining if only somewhat. "My leg . . ." He exhaled and tossed the bone into the fire where it sparked. "Wasted away. The doctors could do little. And then, Doctor Varley contacted me. He had an idea, a plan to put my leg back together."

I blinked. "Varley," I said quietly. My throat tightened. Surely Plenty had known then, what the "golden egg" was. I leaned forward, dipping a cup into the ice we had melted in Cook's fry pan to drink.

"And he did." He looked back at me, his gaze even. "Put me back together." He laughed now, a hoarse sound that made him seem more human to me than he had at any time before in this journey. "Maybe he will once more."

"Provided we get back," I muttered, and pulled some lizard meat from the bone, nibbling. Conor, bundled in blankets, his head wrapped in a stash of kitchen towels we'd found, snored, oblivious.

Plenty smiled and it was surprisingly bright. "Missus Brennan, I think that's the first time I've ever heard you express doubt. About anything."

My cheeks flushed with warmth and I cleared my throat. "Blame J. J. for that," I said and drew my legs closer against my body. Not a far distance, all things considered. " 'Never doubt, Murrie,' he would tell me. Said it led to all manner of bad things." I looked beyond our small camp, to the wreckage that still dotted the ice. Too many bad things. ". . . like plagues and hiccups."

Plenty made a low sound in the back of his throat, but didn't press me further. It was then my numbness drained away and I cried. Cried so much my goggles fogged and my breath hitched. I lowered myself into the makeshift bed of singed rugs and blankets and cried until I fell asleep. I clutched the compass in my hand tight, the way I once would have J. J.'s heart, and just tried to breathe. If the cold did not kill us, perhaps grief would.

I woke sometime later to the sound of unfamiliar voices. I sat up slow, blinking my tear-crusted eyes behind my smudged goggles, to look at Conor across the fire, bookended by two strange figures. They were wrapped head to toe in hide coats, matted fur poking around the hoods and cuff edges. One of these coats draped me, I realized, another wrapped Conor and yet another the sleeping Plenty.

"Miss Muriel," Conor said, and nodded toward the figures. "This is Mr and Missus Underwood."

As if that explained it all. I noted the new bandages around Conor's injured head, new goggles over his eyes, oversized gloves on his hands. The cold would not kill us, then, I thought, and stomped my feet against the ice. It would be grief.

The figure to Conor's right rose, enough to lean closer to me and extend a hand. "Missus Brennan." The voice was that of a woman, a strange sound for my ears after so much time spent solely in the company of men. I uncurled my fingers from around the compass and shifted it to my left hand, so I might shake Mrs Underwood's.

They were hunting the lizards and saw the *Icebreaker* explode from a mile away, they told us, Plenty waking up midway through this tale, seeming as startled as I was to find ourselves with company. His hand slid down his leg, as if to be sure his clockwork was covered.

"A fine price to be had for such carcasses," Mr Underwood said, and pointed to their sled where two of the dead beasts were tied. "*Bellingshausen* is two days out," he went on, tossing another bit of debris onto the fire. "We've tents, and more skins, and should make it clean through."

These words only registered with me faintly. My ears had stopped ringing, but it was memory that pulled my attention elsewhere. Looking still at the icy waters, thinking of J. J. beneath them, wrapped in pine and now ice. I prayed his heart was down there with him, in the cold dark.

Two days later, we watched *Bellingshausen* cut through the ice much as *Icebreaker* once had. The way was easier going now, the ice not yet solid. *Bellingshausen* docked, such as it could, and we were warmly welcomed. Captain Dyakonov and his crew swarmed the ice for anything that might be salvaged from the crew that had been lost. What remains were found were carefully boxed and carried with reverence to the chaplain's quarters.

Plenty and I both seemed reluctant to leave our small camp. We lingered, he likely because of his leg, and me because J. J. at least felt close at hand here. But when Plenty extended a hand to me, unfolded his fingers and showed me the small clockwork heart there, I knew his true reason for staying behind.

I stared at J. J.'s heart for a long while, its cogs still flecked with a little pine from the casket. When I looked up at Plenty, his face held a grim understanding. I carefully plucked the heart from his hand, drawing it against my own chest, and imagined I felt its gears moving.

"I knew when I saw it on the casket," he said. He bent slowly to the ice, to retrieve the pack and its one shoe. To add the last cans of stove fuel to it, and straighten again.

Anger closed around me for only a moment. Anger that Plenty had poked and prodded when he knew better, when he knew what such exposure would mean. But then, he spoke again.

"It was another way to hide, you see," he said, "for if I could turn eyes elsewhere, they were not upon me. Missus Brennan, you have my deepest apology."

J. J. would have laughed. Would have clapped Plenty on the shoulder and sent him stumbling. I only nodded, thinking of all that had been lost here, but so too what had been gained. Plenty and I walked in silence toward the *Bellingshausen*, and once on board, did not speak again. I showed the clockwork heart to Conor in the privacy of my cabin, and he marveled that such a thing had been made by a man, to keep another alive. Ideas sparked in his green eyes.

Home didn't feel like home when we arrived, not with J. J. gone. So it was that I packed another bag and discovered the Underwoods upon the ship I meant to take south – not so far south as we'd been before. The Andes were beckoning, though, with their snowy peaks, others wholly bare and dry. And was that a familiar shaggy head I spied, sneaking into the cargo hold?

It was Missus Underwood who pressed the newspaper into my hands on the deck of the aptly named HMS *Adventure*. Her finger that pointed to a short piece by one Mr Roosevelt Plenty. ADMIRED INVENTOR LAIN TO REST, the headline read, and beneath that: Brennan Goes Down With the Ship. The little details, Plenty said, were better left between the Brennans and God above, but in short, Brennan had gone out in the manner he had always lived: in a big way. My mouth quirked up and I folded the paper in two. Standing by the rail, I watched the old land fall away, and the ship point itself toward the new, as my hand closed around J. J.'s clockwork heart in my pocket.

I have, I say, set out again.

Tom Edison and His Amazing Telegraphic Harpoon

Jay Lake

Tom Edison stared out the viewport at the rolling hills of the Iowa territory, just within Missouri country. The horizon moved with a lurch-and-swoop not unlike the boats on the Great Lakes in choppy weather, though today's brilliant sun and flawless sky belied the comparison.

The steam ram *City of Hoboken* moved like a drunken bear in all weathers, pistons groaning with the pain of metal as the great machine walked the prairies.

Behind him, his printing press chunked through another impression, Salmon Greenberry grunting with the effort. Salmon, Tom's freedman friend and colleague in experimentation and business alike, though they were both barely sprouting beards yet.

Boys in arms, adventuring together across the West. He resolved that he would someday write a book. If one could ever send communications across this benighted country.

"The problem with the telegraph," Tom said slowly, the idea unfolding even as he spoke, "is that one cannot run the lines west of the Mississippi. Those damnable Indians, or worse, Clark's Army, just pull the copper down again."

There was a freshet of ink odor in his nostrils, and barely audible, the damp tear of a sheet from the stone. Tom's ears were never the best.

Salmon said something unintelligible, grunting with his labor, then the words segued into meaning: ". . . help what they are. It's the West, Tom." There was a familiar warmth in his friend's voice, in which Tom sometimes to his secret shame found comfort amidst the clanking, heaving darkness of the steam ram during prairie nights.

Tom snorted away the reverie and Salmon's suggestion together. "People have been using that excuse since Jefferson's day. Apologists for spiritualist madness, with no understanding of or interest in Progress. This is a better world than that, amenable to logic and sweet reason."

Another thunk of the press. Another grunt from Salmon. "As you'll have it, Tom."

Though he still had not turned to face his friend, even with his failing ears Tom could hear the grin. He smiled back. Another secret shared.

A shot echoed from above, in the watchman's post, followed by the clang of valves as the captain shunted power to the turrets.

"Attack," shouted Salmon.

Tom whirled to help his friend latch down the printing press, then they both grabbed the repeating rifles racked by the hatch of their little work-cabin, heading for battle stations. Tom thought he heard the crackle of distant gunfire, but it might have been his own pulse.

The weather deck of the *City of Hoboken* was a good forty feet above the solid Iowa earth. "Deck" was perhaps too kind a word for what was really just the plank ceiling of the bridge deck below, surrounded by a low railing with built-up firing points for prone riflemen. It was perhaps nine feet wide and twenty feet long, and featured only the watchman's post, like a preacher's lectern set amidships with no congregation but the distant horizon and the wheeling sky.

Tom and Salmon took up their firing points on the starboard rail, up top with the other useless supercargo and oddlot apprentices. Those with real worth in a battle manned the boilers, or the turrets, or worked the bridge deck. The *City of Hoboken*'s eight dragoons, eternally dissolute masters of pasteboard wagering, were certainly down in their lower balcony, ready to leap, shoot, or toss grenadoes as circumstances dictated.

The weather watch was for anyone with hands to shoot and nothing else to offer in defense.

"Where?" shouted Salmon. Tom watched his friend, waiting for the other boy's eyes or rifle barrel to move in response to whatever the deck watch advised.

Then Salmon rolled onto his back, snappy as a scalded cat, and stared skyward.

Oh, no, thought Tom, but he did the same.

Something very big was silhouetted against that perfect prairie sky. It was shaped like a man, without the wings of one of the angels of the mountain West, and appeared to be carrying a cannon.

"What . . . ?" he whispered aloud. Tom had read the dispatches, those that were made available in Port Huron and Chicago, to a fast-talking young man like himself. Not much was published about angels, but he'd even seen the Brady daguerreotypes from the Battle of St Louis the previous year.

Angels had wings. Everything that flew had wings. Save one rumored monster out of the deepest Western mountains.

Tom brought his rifle up to point skyward, stepping it against his body like a boat's mast. He pulled the trigger, thinking, *Nephilim. The great avengers. Nothing can kill a Nephil. And he's above the elevation of any of our big guns.* It was an offense against man and nature, this flying thing, and Tom swore out the measure of his fear. He had not come West to die at the hands of an impossibility.

His shot was the harbinger of a hailstorm of firing, the weather watch loosing its useless bullets at a thing above which laughed in a voice made of thunder, earthquakes and simple, gut-jellying terror.

The captain made a quick, hard turn, taking the *City of Hoboken* toward the dubious shelter of a tree-lined watercourse. After their initial orgy of firing, the weather watch calmed down a little as the Nephil banked above them.

It was definitely carrying a cannon, Tom realized. Something long and sleek, perhaps one of the new Parrott rifles. He couldn't imagine what need a supernatural being would have for such a thing. Supposedly the Nephilim could call lightning from the summer sky and break the backs of angels.

Did he have anything below that would entice it, entrap it, somehow save this day from the bloodbath which was surely coming?

In addition to hosting his half-penny newspaper, *The Trans-Mississippi Monitor*, the *City of Hoboken* was also home to something of a laboratory which Tom had accumulated. The captain tolerated Tom and his equipment in exchange for mechanical services rendered and the cachet of having his own newspaper on board. The prestige of a working press allowed him to charge higher fares for passengers heading for Des Moines, Council Bluffs and other points on the *City of Hoboken*'s usual routes westward toward the distant riches of the Front Range in the Colorado country.

As part of his laboratory, Tom had on board a store of chemicals, machine tools and curious items of his own devising. But what could dispatch one of the Nephilim? Legendary as they were, there were no whispered tales of the mighty monsters' defeat in battle.

The attacker circled lower, lazy and slow, following the *City of Hoboken* through the great steam ram's course changes. At least it had not set to killing them yet.

What could he do? Tom ran through a rapid mental inventory of acids, caustic chemicals, electrical jars, sharp tools, mechanisms.

There was the harpoon, he realized. The watchman's post had a pintle mount and a steam valve for that implement – designed originally for fighting off the mastodons, which sometimes crossed the Missouri River to range the Iowa prairies.

He could surely devise a suitable load to burst on impact with the attacker.

Tom handed Salmon his rifle and jumped to his feet. "Bannock," he shouted to the day watch. "We need to unship the harpoon rig. I can fight this thing!"

"You're buggered as a limehouse rat," said the watchman, peering at the Nephilim through a telescope. But as Tom scrambled down the hatch, he saw Bannock whispering into the speaking tube.

Tom was trying to quickly, very quickly, assemble a caustic load fit to drive off something as great and terrible as a Nephil. Tom didn't believe for a moment that God had sent the terrible creatures to the Mormons, but nonetheless they were here in the world. Even Nephilim had eyes. And he had a number of nasty acids fit to burn even the most resistant membrane. His science would defeat this treacherous superstition.

Then his gaze lit on the Planté-Fauré battery cell. It was a new device, recently shipped out at great cost from New Jersey. Tom had made some modifications to it by way of accumulating ever more electrical potential, hoping to produce a fearsome spark from the thing as part of his ongoing investigations into the practical applications of such energies.

What would a great electrical discharge do to the flying menace? It might be as good as a strike by lightning.

Tom abandoned his acids and grabbed the loose cable end off a spool of telegraph wire. It was four-stranded copper, coated in gutta-percha then wrapped in sealed hemp yarn – the best his limited money could buy, all the way from Buffalo. He dragged the end into the passage, letting the cable unspool, and shouting for Bannock or Salmon to come help as he worked to pass the copper cable up top.

Once the weather watch had hold of the cable, shouting and excited, Tom grabbed a ball-peen hammer and a set of staples, along with his tool bag. He nailed down the loose end off the spool center, allowing himself some slack, then scrambled up the ladder, past the writhing snake that was his cable.

On the weather deck the breeze was stiffer. Cottonwoods swayed around the steam ram as the captain took them further down into the creekbed. Tom knew their search for cover was in vain – the *City of Hoboken* was over four stories tall. Nothing could hide such a magnificent machine, such a stout work of Dame Progress. And certainly not out here on the Iowa prairie, where their pursuer circled high above, a vulture waiting to descend.

He set about lashing the free end of the cable to Bannock's harpoon, again leaving himself slack. A copper point on the head would be perfect, but Tom figured he could make do with the steel.

When the line came up short and the nervous weather watch huddled around him, Tom pulled himself away from his work on the harpoon shaft.

"It's like this, men," he shouted. He hated speaking, hated rousing men like this – that was the job of officers and shop foremen, not a thinker like himself. Especially when he was the youngest man on the deck.

Salmon gave Tom a big wink.

"That up there's one of the Nephilim!" Tom pointed at the sky. "Some folks say the Mormons raised 'em from a Bible. Some folks say they're Chinee magic, brought across the sea by the Russians. Well, I don't care!" His voice was a bellow now. "It's here a-hunting us, and we're fixing to drive it away. But you each have a part."

Eight frightened men loomed in closer. A voice squawked from the cupola's speaking tube, but even Bannock, the day watch, ignored the captain in favor of whatever spectacle Tom was about to put on in the face of life and death.

"Very shortly I'm going below," Tom said in a normal voice. "I'm going to hook this harpoon up to a cell battery. Once I done that, don't nobody but me or Bannock touch nothing here. When I give the word, you all each start shooting again for all you're worth. We must draw that thing down close, so's Bannock can shoot it with my wires. Then . . ." His hands slammed together. "Boom."

There was a ragged cheer. Tom took a simple knife switch from his tool bag and hammered it into the deck next to the hatch coaming. He cut his cable at the taut end, and wired it into the switch, careful to leave the switch open.

"Don't touch nothing," he said, wagging his finger with a significant look at Bannock, then ducked below again.

The *City of Hoboken* continued to lurch over rougher terrain, swinging back and forth to avoid the Nephil. Tom's footing was challenged in the little cabin, his glassware threatened even stowed within various leather-padded racks. He drew on his heaviest insulated gloves, and then with great care proceeded to wire the free end of the cable to the copper terminals of the Planté-Fauré cell.

He was just tightening down the second connection when the great steam ram shook with a noise that Tom felt within his bones. There was a grinding, and the deck canted off true five degrees, then ten.

Somehow the captain got the vessel back on balance, but the stride had changed – Tom could feel the difference. Where had the shot hit?

Only one shot in that Parrott rifle, he thought. *Blast and damn that featherless bird, this wasn't how men were meant to live!*

He raced back up the ladder, afraid he might already be too late. Had the shot signaled the beginning of the Nephil's attack?

The weather watch were already blazing away, their rifles and muskets wreathing the open deck with smoke as fast as the breeze could carry it off. The top of the steam ram already reeked of death, and there had not yet been blood spilled.

"Not yet!" Tom shouted, but his voice was lost in the violent noise. He looked up, around, scanning for the attacker, but between the gunpowder smoke and whatever revolutions it had made through the sky, he could not find the Nephil.

Tom slapped Bannock on the shoulder. The day watch had his harpoon loaded and tracking, swinging the gun on its pintle.

"Have sight of it?" Tom asked.

Bannock shook his head.

Then the Nephil rose above the *City of Hoboken*'s starboard flank. The muzzle of the Parrott rifle was huge in its arms, a vast, gaping pit of death sweeping the deck as the Nephil grinned. Despite his resolve, Tom screamed, as terrified as any child.

Imagine a man tall as a telegraph pole. His eyes glitter the same bottle-green as the insulators that carry the copper-cored cables with their burden of living thought and speech. His skin is fair as an Irishwoman's, his hair black as the heart of a Georgia cracker. He is handsome in a way that would make a statue weep, and bring any blooded soldier to his knees. If this man was not terror incarnate, if he did not tower over everyone and everything in his path, he would be worthy of worship.

Instead, he is merely – and utterly – feared.

The Nephil's smile drove the weather watch toward the hatch. Oakey Bill jumped off the port flank, arms flailing, screaming his way into the long, fatal fall in preference to being trapped amid the scrum on deck in view of the leering monster.

Tom shoved Bannock back into the scout's cupola. "Fire it on my call!" he yelled. "Into the chest!"

"I . . ." Bannock was screaming, too.

Facing the Nephil was like facing a city on fire. The force of its will blazed across Tom, Bannock and the rest of the panicked weather watch. Though it was pale as any white man, the Nephil's skin gleamed like moonlight in a graveyard. Tom felt as if he were falling forward into a city, a necropolis, a land peopled by the dying and the dead, an eternal, pallid landscape of lost memory and—

"No!" he shouted. "This is the Age of Reason." Tom grabbed Barley by the shoulders and pulled him from the scout's cupola. He would be damned before he would bow before the evil thing's fearsome aspect. The harpoon could not be so difficult to fire!

"Me," shouted Salmon in his ear.

Tom looked up to see his great, good friend shaking his head and pointing at the harpoon. "No time," he said, then swung the shoulder brace toward the Nephil, which was already rising above the weather deck, cocking its arm to throw the Parrott rifle down upon the steam ram.

The lines were clipped into place, the pressure gauge showed a full head of steam. Tom flipped over the locking pin, aimed the steel head toward the Nephil's vast chest, and pulled the trigger.

There was a horrendous shriek as the steam pressure discharged. The shoulder brace of the harpoon slammed into Tom harder than any punch he'd ever taken, while a burst of scalding steam enveloped him from the line which sprang free with the shock of the firing.

The Nephil took the harpoon point in its gut. Even through the swirl of steam, smoke and pain, Tom registered the expression of surprise on the monster's face as it dropped the Parrott rifle and grabbed at the shaft which stuck. Somehow the electrical cable held.

But nothing happened.

The Nephil began to laugh, an enormous barking roar like a Missouri cyclone, dark vapors gusting from a mouth that seemed to open wide enough to swallow them all whole.

What had gone wrong? Even within the agony of his steam-scaled face and hands, Tom felt a cold stab of pain and fear in his heart.

Then he realized that he had not arranged to complete the circuit.

Salmon slapped his shoulder again and pointed down. Tom leaned over, blinking away the agony of the steam burns on his face and hands, to see his friend standing over the knife switch stapled to the weather deck.

Tom nodded.

Salmon leaned down, closed the copper blade, and held on even as sparks played through his hair.

The Nephil's laughter changed to an eerie howl. Tom looked up again, his vision growing red – *why?* he wondered even in that moment – to see sparks pouring from the monster's mouth, its hands, its hair. Far more electricity than could have come from Tom's Planté-Fauré battery cell. The Nephil raged amid a storm of blue, yellow and green sparks, lightning snakes that writhed along its arms and legs, seared its eyes, set fire to its skin.

I have opened a circuit to Heaven, Tom thought. He collapsed against the edge of the scout's cupola, wracked with pain of his own, wishing he could pass out. That mercy was not offered him, though his sight dimmed to red mist. Even the arrival on the weather deck of the dragoons with their grenadoes and their clattering weapons was not enough to distract him from the pain.

Tom woke to a hand upon his shoulder. The steam ram was underway once more, he could tell by the gentle swaying in his body. He tried to blink, but his eyes were gummed tight.

A bandage, he prayed.

"Can you hear me, son?" It was the rumbling, patriarchal voice of Captain Brown, the *City of Hoboken*'s master.

"Yes, sir." Tom paused, gathering his fears. "But I cannot see you, sir."

The grip tightened. Brown smelled of whiskey and old leather – the cover of a Bible, Tom thought. "We'll find you a doctor at Council Bluffs, Mr Edison. Cletis reckons you'll have your sight back. As for the scars . . ."

Scars? "What?"

"You cannot feel them, son? Your face and hands is burned fierce by the steam."

Tom felt very little other than the captain's hand on his shoulder, and that scared him.

"Where's Salmon?"

"Your Negro friend is dead. Kilt by your telegraph gun."

Salmon had been holding the knife switch closed when the Nephil . . . exploded. The copper wire must have carried some of that extraordinary energy back onto the deck and into his friend. Tom felt his eyes finally, as they filled with tears so warm he thought he must be weeping blood.

"But you kilt one of them monsters, son. You're a hero."

Hero. Tom wanted to turn his face to the bulkhead and cry for Salmon. He would never hear that belovéd voice again.

But he could not. This was the century of science, and he would be damned and damned again before he would let some Biblical monsters drive America from her West. No other man would ever lose his particular friend this way again. "I will bind the West in chains of copper," he whispered, "and make her monsters bow to Progress. I swear this."

"That's the spirit, son."

Brown's hand left Tom's shoulder, then the captain stepped out through a hatch which clanged shut, already shouting orders.

He could not think on Salmon any further, so Tom set his mind instead to wondering how the so-called telegraph gun had been so deadly to one of the Nephilim. Could he arrange for bigger Planté-Fauré cells, perhaps mounted on aerostats, to bring the battle to the enemy? The West needed railroads and telegraph and civilization, not the wild anarchy of steam rams and Clark's Army and avenging angels.

He would pluck the last of the Nephilim from the sky himself, and ground their cousin angels as well.

The Zeppelin Conductors' Society Annual Gentlemen's Ball

Genevieve Valentine

So hook yourself up to an airship
Strap on your mask and your knife
For the wide open skies are a-calling
And oh, it's a glorious life!
– Conductors' Recruitment Advertisement, 1890

The balloon of a Phoenix-class airship is better than any view from its cabin windows; half a mile of silk pulled taut across three hundred metal ribs and a hundred gleaming spines is a beautiful thing. If your mask filter is dirty you get lightheaded and your sight goes reddish, so it looks as though the balloon is falling in love with you.

When that happens, though, you tap someone to let them know and you go to the back-cabin Underneath and fix your mask, if you've any brains at all. If you're helium-drunk enough to see red, soon you'll be hallucinating and too weak to move, and even if they get you out before you die you'll still spend the rest of your life at a hospital with all the regulars staring at you. That's no life for an airship man.

I remember back when the masks were metal and you'd freeze in the winter, end up with layers of skin that peeled off like wet socks when you went landside and took the mask off. The polymer rubbers are much cleverer.

I've been a conductor for ages; I was conducting on the *Majesty* in '78 when it was still the biggest ship in the sky – you laugh, but back then people would show up by the hundreds just to watch it fly out of dock. She only had four gills, but she could cut through the air better than a lot of the six-fins, the *Laconia* too.

They put the *Majesty* in a museum already, I heard.

Strange to be so old and not feel it. At least the helium keeps us young, for all it turns us spindly and cold. God, when we realized what was happening to us! But they had warned us, I suppose, and it's fathoms better now than it was. Back then the regulars called you a monster if they saw you on the street.

The coin's not bad, either, compared to factory work. They say it's terrible what you end up like, but if you work the air you get pulled like taffy, and if you work in the factory you go deaf as a post; it's always something.

I'm saving a bit for myself for when I'm finished with this life, enough for a little house in the Alps. I need some altitude if I'm going to be landlocked; the air's too heavy down here.

The very first ships were no better than hot-air balloons, and the conductors kept a tiny cabin and had to string themselves outside on cables if something happened. I can't imagine it – useless.

I didn't join up until after they moved conductors inside – it showed they had a lick of sense to put conductors where they could get to things that went wrong, and I'm not fond of looking down from heights.

The engine-shop shifted to airships as soon as they caught on, and I made 2,000 ribs before I ever set foot inside a balloon. It makes for a certain confidence going in, which carried me through, thank goodness – I had a hard time with it at first.

You have to be careful how deeply you breathe, so the oxygen filter doesn't freeze up on you, and you have to make sure your air tube doesn't get tangled in your tether, or your tether in someone else's. You have to learn how to fling yourself along so that the tether ring slides with you along the spine, and how to hook your fingers quickly into the little holes in the ribs when you have to climb down. You have to learn to deal with the cold.

The sign language I picked up at once. We had that at the factory, too – signals for when we were too far apart or when it was too loud. I'm fond of it; you get used to talking through the masks, and they're all good men in the air, but sometimes it's nice just to keep the quiet.

Captain Carter was very kind those first few months; he was the only captain I've ever had who would make trips into the balloon from the Underneath just to see how we were getting along. Back then we were all in it together, all still learning how to handle these beautiful birds.

Captains now can hardly be bothered to leave their bridges, but not Carter. Carter knew how to tighten a bolt as fast as any airship man, and he'd float through and shake hands whenever we'd done something well. He had a way of speaking about the *Majesty*, like a poem sometimes – a clever man. I've tried to speak as he did, but there's not much use for language when we're just bottled up with one another. Once or twice I've seen something sharply, the way he might have seen it – just once or twice.

You won't see his like again. He was of the old kind; he understood what it meant to love the sky like I do.

A patient in the profession of Zeppelin conducting has, after very few years of work, advanced Heliosis due to excessive and prolonged exposure to helium within the balloon of an airship. His limbs have grown in length and decreased in musculature, making it difficult for him to comfortably maneuver on the ground for long periods of time. Mild exercise, concurrent with the wearing of an oxygen mask to prevent hyperventilation, alleviates the symptoms in time but has no lasting effect without regular application, which is difficult for conductors to maintain while employed in their vessels.

Other side effects are phrenological. Skin tightens around the skull. Patient has noticeable growth in those parts of the head dedicated to Concentrativeness, Combativeness, Locality and Constructiveness. The areas of Amativeness, Form and Cautiousness are smaller than normal, though it is hard to say if these personality defects are the work of prolonged wearing of conductor's masks or the temperament of the patient. I suspect that in this case time will have to reveal what is yet unknown.

The Zeppelin is without doubt Man's greatest invention, and the brave men who labor in its depths are indispensable, but it behoves us to remember the story of Icarus and Daedalus; he should proceed wisely, who would proceed well.

> – from Doctor Jonathan Grant's address
> to the Health Council, April 1895

The Captains' Union set up the first Society for us, in London, and a year later in Paris.

They weren't much more comfortable than the hospital rooms where they used to keep us landside, for safety, but of course it was more dignified. Soon we managed to organize ourselves and put together the Zeppelin Conductors' Society, and we tithed our own wages for the dues to fix the buildings up a bit.

Now you can fly to any city with an airdock and know there's a place for you to sleep where no one will look at you sidelong. You can get a private room, even, with a bath in the middle big enough to hold you; it's horrid how long your limbs get when you're in helium nine days in ten, and there's not much dignity in trying to wash with your legs sticking two feet out of the bath.

And it's good sense to have a place you can go straight away; regulars don't like to see you wandering about, sometimes. Most times. I understand.

WHAT TO DO WHEN YOU SEE A CONDUCTOR

1. Do not panic; he is probably as wary of you as you are of him. He will pose no threat if not provoked.
2. Do not stare; scrutiny is vulgar.
3. Offer a small nod when you pass, as you would to another gentleman; it pleases them.
4. Avoid smaller streets between airship docks and the local Conductors' Society. The conductor is, in general, a docile creature, but one can never be sure what effects the helium has had on his temperament.

> – Public Safety Poster, 1886

1 January 1900

PARIS – Polaris was eclipsed last night: not by any cosmic rival, but by a man-made beauty. The *Laconia*, a Phoenix-class feat of British engineering that has become the envy of the world, never looked more beautiful than on its evening flight to Paris as we began a momentous New Year.

Captain Richard Marks, looking every inch the matinee hero, guided the ship safely through the night as the passengers within lit up the sky with conversation and music, accompanied by a champagne buffet. Miss Marie Dawlish, the English Lark, honored the company with a song which it is suspected struck the heart of a certain airship captain, who stepped away from the bridge in time for the performance. Though we at the *Daily* are not prognosticators, we believe that the coming year may be one of high romance for Captain Marks, who touched down back in London with a gentle landing, and no doubt a song in his heart.

The societies have the balls for each New Year, which is great fun. It's ripping good food, and sometimes someone comes in a full evening suit and we can all have a laugh at them; it's an expensive round of tailoring to wear just once a year. You know just by looking that those who dressed up had wanted to be captains and fallen short. Poor boys. I wouldn't be a captain for all the gold in Araby, though perhaps when you're young you don't realize how proud and empty the captains end up.

You don't meet a lot of ladies in the air, of course, and it's what all the lads miss most. For the London Ball they always manage to find some with the money from the dues – sweet girls who don't mind a chat. They have to be all right with sitting and talking. The Annual Gentlemen's Ball isn't much of a dance. The new conductors, the ones who have only stretched the first few inches, try a dance or two early on to give the musicians something to do. The rest of us have given in to gravity when we're trapped on the ground. We catch up with old mates and wait for a chance to ask a girl upstairs, if we're brave enough.

Sometimes we even get conductors in from other places – Russia, sometimes, or once from China. God, that was a night! What strange ideas they have about navigation! But he was built like an airship man, and from the red skin round his eyes we could tell he'd paid his dues in the helium, so we poured him some Scotch and made him welcome. If we aren't kind to each other, who will be kind to us?

The Most Elegant Airlines Choose ORION Brand Masks!

Your conductors deserve masks that are **SAFE, COMFORTABLE** and **STYLISH**. Orion has patented its unique India-Rubber polymer that is both flexible and airtight, ensuring the safest and most comfortable fit for your conductors. The oculars are green-tinted for sharper vision at night, and larger in diameter than any other brand, so conductors see more than ever before. Best of all, our filter-tank has an oxygen absorption rate of nearly 90 per cent – the best in the world!

Swiss-made, British-tested, **CONDUCTOR-APPROVED**.

Soar with confidence among the stars – aim always for **ORION**.

– Orion Airship Supply Catalog, 1893

We were airside the last night of 1899, the night of the Gentlemen's Ball.

We had been through a bad wind that day, and all of us were spread out tightening rivets on the ribs, signaling quietly back and forth. I don't know what made Anderson agree to sign us on for the evening flight – he must have wanted the ball as much as the rest of us – and I was in a bit of a sulk, feeling like Cinderella. It was a cold night, cold even in the balloon, and I was wishing for nothing but a long bath and a long sleep.

Then Captain Marks shoved the woman into the balloon.

She was wearing a worn-out orange dress, and a worn-out shawl that fell away from her at once, and even as the captain clipped her to the line she hung limp, worn out all over. He'd been at her for a while.

I still don't know where he found her, what they did to her, what she thought in the first moments as they carried her towards the balloon.

"Got some leftovers for you," the captain shouted through his mask. "A little Gentlemen's Ball for you brave boys. Enjoy!"

Then he was gone, spinning the lock shut behind him, closing us in with her.

I could feel the others hooking onto a rib or a spine, pushing off, hurrying over. The men in the aft might not have even seen it happen. I never asked them. Didn't want to know.

I was closest to her, 50 feet, maybe. Through the mask I could see the buttons missing on the front of her dress, the little cuts in her fisted hands.

She wore a mask, too. Her hair was tangled in it.

She was terrified – shaking so hard that I worried her mask would come loose – but she didn't scrabble at her belt: too clever for that, I suppose. I was worried for her – if you weren't used to the helium it was painful to breathe for very long; she needed to get back Underneath. God only knew how long that second-rate mask would hold.

Even as Anderson hooked onto a spine to get to her she was shoving off – not to the locked porthole (there was no hope for her there), but straight out to the ribs, clawing at the stiff silk of the balloon.

We all scrambled for her.

I don't know how she cut the silk – Bristol said it must have been a knife, but I can't imagine they would have let her keep one. I think she must have used the hook of her little earring, which is the worst of it, somehow.

The balloon shuddered as the first rush of helium was sucked into the sky outside; she clenched one fist around the raw edge of the silk as she unhooked herself from the tether. The air caught her, dragging at her feet, and she grasped for purchase against the fabric. She cried out, but the mask swallowed the noise.

I was the closest; I pushed off.

The other conductors were shouting for her not to be foolish; they shouted that it was a misunderstanding, that she would be all right with us.

As I came closer I held out my hands to her so she could take hold, but she shrank back, kicking at me with one foot, the boot half-fastened.

My reflection was distorted in the round eyes of her mask – a spindly monster enveloping her in the half-dark, my endless arms struggling to pull her back in.

What else could she do?

She let go.

My sight lit up from the rush of oxygen, and in my view she was a flaming June in a bottle-green night, falling with her arms outstretched like a bird until she was too small to be seen, until every bright trace of her was gone.

For a moment no one moved, then the rails shuddered under us as the gills fanned out, and we slowed.

Anderson said, "We're coming up on Paris."

"Someone should tell them about the tear," said Bristol.

"Patch it from here," Anderson said. "We'll wait until Vienna."

In Vienna they assumed all conductors were lunatics, and they would ask no questions about a tear that only human hands could make.

I heard the first clangs of the anchor-hooks latching onto the outer hull of the Underneath before the church bells rang in the New Year. Beneath us, the passengers shouted "Hip, hip, hurrah! Hip, hip, hurrah!"

That was a sad year.

Once I was land-bound in Dover. The Conductors' Society there is so small I don't think ten men could fit in it. It wasn't a bad city (I had no trouble with the regulars on my way from the dock), but it was so horribly hot and cramped that I went outside just to have enough room to stretch out my arms, even heavy as they were with the Earth pulling at them.

A Falcon-class passed overhead, and I looked up just as it crossed the harvest moon; for a moment the balloon was illuminated orange, and I could see the conductors skittering about inside of it like spiders or shadow puppets, like moths in a lamp.

I watched it until it had passed the moon and fallen dark again, the lamp extinguished.

It's a glorious life, they say.

Clockwork Fairies

Cat Rambo

Mary the Irish girl let me in when I knocked at the door in my Sunday best, smelling of incense and evening fog. Gaslight flickered over the narrow hall. The mahogany banister's curve gleamed with beeswax polish, and a rosewood hat rack and umbrella stand squatted to my left.

I nodded to Mary, taking off my top hat. Snuff and baking butter mingled with my own pomade to battle the smell of steel and sulfur from below.

"Don't be startled, Mr. Claude, sir."

Before I could speak, a whir of creatures surrounded me.

At first I thought them hummingbirds or large dragonflies. One hung poised before my eyes in a flutter of metallic skin and isinglass wings. Delicate gears spun in the wrist of a pinioned hand holding a needle-sharp sword. Desiree had created another marvel. Fairies: bee-winged, glittering like tinsel. Who would have dreamed such things, let alone made them real? Only Desiree.

Mary chattered, "They're hers. They won't harm ye. Only burglars and the like."

She swatted at one hovering too close, its hair floating like candyfloss. Mary had been with the Southland household for three years now and was inured to scientific marvels. "I'll tell her ladyship yer here."

She left. I eyed the fairies that hung in the air around me. Despite Mary's assurance, I did not know what they would do if I stepped forward. I had never witnessed clockwork creations so capable of independent movement.

Footsteps sounded downstairs, coming closer. Desiree appeared in the doorway that led to her basement workshop. A pair of protective lenses dangled around her neck and she wore gloves. Not the dainty kidskin gloves of fashionable women, but thick pig leather, to shield her clever brown fingers from sparks. One hand clutched a brass oval studded with tiny buttons.

Desiree's skin color made her almost as much an oddity in upper London society as the fairies. My intended. I smiled at her.

"Claude," she said with evident pleasure.

She clicked the device in her hand and the fairies swirled away, disappearing to God knows where. "I'm almost done. I'll meet you in a few minutes. Go ahead and ring for tea."

In the parlor, I took to the settee and looked around. As always, the room was immaculate, filled with well-dusted knickknacks. Butterflies fluttered under two bell jars on a charcoal-colored marble mantle carved with lilies of the valley. The room was well composed: a sofa sat in graceful opposition to a pair of wing chairs. The only discordant note was the book shoved between two embroidered pillows on the closest chair's maroon velvet. I picked it up. *On the Origin of Species*, by Charles Darwin.

I frowned and set it back down. Only last week, my minister had spoken out against this very book.

I should speak to Desiree. I knew better than to forbid her to read it, but I could warn her against discussing it in polite company or speaking to support the heretical notion that humans were related to animals, which contradicted God's order, the Great Chain of Being.

Mary the Irish girl brought tea and sweet biscuits with a clatter of heels that was muted when she reached the parlor carpet. I poured myself a cup, sniffing. Lapsang Oolong. Desiree's father, Lord Southland, was one of London's notable titled eccentrics, but his staff had excellent taste in provisions.

The man himself appeared in the doorway. His silk waistcoat was patterned with golden bees, as fashionable as my own undulating Oriental serpents.

"Ah, Stone," he said. He advanced to take a sesame-seed biscuit, eyebrows bristling with hoary disapproval behind guinea-sized lenses. "You're here again."

"I came to visit Desiree," I replied, stressing the last word. I knew Lord Southland disapproved of me, although his antipathy puzzled me. If he hoped to marry off his mulatto daughter, I was his best prospect. Not many men were as free of prejudice as I was.

With his wife's death, though, Southland had become irrational and taken up radical notions. So far Desiree had steered clear of them with my guidance, but I shuddered to think that she might become a Nonconformist or Suffragist. Still, I took care to be polite to Southland. If he cut Desiree from his will, the results would be disastrous.

"Of course he came to see me, Papa," Desiree said from the other doorway. She had removed her leather apron, revealing a gay dress of pink cotton sprigged with strawberry blossoms. She perched a decorous distance from me and poured her own tea, adding a hearty amount of milk.

"I've come to nag you again, Des," I teased.

A crease settled between her eyebrows. "Claude, is this about Lady Allsop's ball again?"

I leaned forward to capture her hand, its color deep against my own pale skin. "Desiree, to be accepted in society, you must make an effort now and then. If you are a success it will reflect well on me. Appear at the ball as a kindness to me."

She removed her fingers from mine, the crease between her eyebrows becoming more pronounced. "I have told you: I am not the sort of woman that goes to balls."

"But you could be!" I told her. "Look at you, Desiree. You are as beautiful as any woman in London. A nonpareil. Dressed properly, you would take the city by storm."

"We have been over this before," she said. "I have no desire to expose myself to stares. My race makes me noteworthy, but it is not pleasant being a freak, Claude. Last week a child in the street wanted to rub my skin and see 'if the dirt would come off'. Can you not be happy with me as I am?"

"I am very happy with you as you are," I said. I could hear a sullen tinge to my voice, but my feelings were understandable. "But you could be so much more!"

She stood. "Come," she said. "I will show you what I have been working on."

There would be no arguing with her – I could tell by her tone – but a touch of sulkiness might wear her down. Lord Southland glared at me as I bowed to him, but neither of us spoke.

In the workshop, a clockwork fairy sprawled on the table. Using a magnifying glass, Desiree showed me its delicate works, the mica flakes pieced together to form its wings.

"Where did you get the idea?" I asked.

"In Devonshire, an old woman spoke of seeing fairies. There was an interview with her in *Hardwicke's Science-Gossip*."

I snorted. "Old women are given to fancies."

Desiree shrugged, taking up a pick and using it to adjust the paper-thin wing's hinge. "It made me think about how to create flying creatures. I chose to use bumblebees for my model, rather than the traditional butterfly wings. My fairies can resist strong winds and go where I wish them, according to the instructions I have laid into their 'brains', which are based on the papers Babbage has published."

Desiree is interested in such things, but I don't find them nearly as engaging as spiritual matters. She droned on, but I cut her short. "Sometimes I think you don't love me."

She stopped. Her half-parted lips were like flower petals, an orchid's inner workings. "Why do you say that?"

"You don't understand my position," I said. "As a dean, I must have a wife who is acceptable in society's eyes."

"This is about the ball again," she said. She reached out to touch my face, but I turned my head away and pretended to examine the articulated form half-assembled on the table.

"Very well," she said. Her hand returned to her side. "If it means that much, I will go."

That week flew pell-mell. I went to a lecture by John Henry Newman, and to the theater to see *How She Loves Him* by Boucicault. I stopped by Lord Southland's on three separate evenings, but most nights I dined at my club, on excellent quail prepared in the French style, or fresh haddock.

Desiree had started work on a mechanical cat. She took me into her workshop to look at it. A clockwork nightingale sang in the wicker cage hanging from the rafters, set in motion by our footsteps' vibration.

"It's still in the preliminary stages," she said. A brass skeleton lay disassembled on the table, but it was laid out so I could see the cat-to-be's shape. Mercury beads rolled in a white porcelain dish. A discarded spray of silver whiskers had been tossed in the coal scuttle.

I glanced around. "The deanery has a basement," I said. "It houses our wine cellar and storerooms, but I have sent to have the front room cleaned and whitewashed for you."

Desiree's teeth flashed as she smiled. I stole a kiss and her breath smelled of licorice. I felt her skin's warmth against my hands. True, the room was not as fine as this, but she would improvise and make do, for she was a clever girl. And once she had started bearing, such fancies would fall away. Her inventions, her clever machines, were simply a way to channel her maternal instinct. Once she had a child, she would find herself devoted to it.

While Desiree went upstairs to speak to her father, I lingered in the workshop. I amused myself by walking between the tables and shelves, examining her work.

I paused beside what looked like a dress form, a brass cylinder the size of a human torso. My cheeks flushed as I regarded it.

Shockingly, Desiree had given it the semblance of a maiden's bosom, a suggestion of curves whose immodesty appalled me. Headless, armless, legless, the torso stood affixed to three steel rods that culminated in a circular base as wide as an elephant's foot.

I reached out and touched its "shoulder", then trailed my fingertips along the skin towards its chest. The oils from my fingers left a faint trail behind them, smudging the metal's gleam. It was how corrosion started, I knew. Given time, would the stains grow to verdigris, show how intimately I had touched Desiree's creation?

I buffed the marks away with a linen rag that lay on a nearby workbench. The stairs creaked beneath me in admonishment as I ascended to join Desiree and her father. They had been arguing again. I heard her father say, "Blasted pedantic popinjay!" and Desiree say, "Oh, Father," her tone coaxing and indulgent.

"You don't have to settle for such a man!"

"If I want to be part of society and not an outcast, I need a proper husband! Claude and I will accommodate each other with time."

That had an ominous sound, but we would discuss it later. They fell silent as I appeared, Southland's face red with anger, Desiree's smile as bland as her mechanical cat licking cream.

Everyone notable was present at Lady Allsop's ball. Silks and satins gleamed like colored waters touched with flecks of light from cut gems. The air smelled of hothouse flowers and French perfume. The orchestra played as the dancers glided through a waltz.

I do not entirely approve of diversions like dancing, but society places demands on us. I was eager for the ton to place their benison on my bride-to-be. I would dance twice with Desiree when she arrived, but for the most part I intended to stay on the sidelines, drinking lemonade. Still, when a few partners pressed me, I gave in.

I know well that women find me alluring – no credit to anyone other than He who shaped me. But my calf shows to advantage in breeches, to the point where at least one too-bold miss has called it shapely.

And I knew very well that it was my looks that initially attracted Desiree. Like all women, she is drawn to this world's baubles, not realizing their transient, mayfly nature. But with time she had sounded my mind's depths, and I flattered myself that what she found there had strengthened her attraction to me.

A woman I danced with mentioned that the Southlands had arrived. "Your fiancée, is she not?" she purred. "I saw her arrive with her papa, a half hour or so ago."

I made my excuses and went outside the great hall to pass through the refreshment line, looking for Desiree. I caught sight of her ahead of me, in the side hall's shadows, dark hair held up by an intricate mechanism atop her head. She paused beside a dusky silk curtain, speaking to a blonde, blue-eyed woman.

From the back I could see Desiree's silk skirt: figured with gears, the teeth embroidered in red. I came up behind her and slid my hand through the crook of her elbow, drawing her close to show my pleasure at her presence there, despite her dress's outré nature.

I realized my mistake from the way the woman pulled herself away. She turned and I saw her clearly, no longer Desiree. Her hair held brownish-red highlights, and her eyes were an icy, outraged green. The patterned cogs were Michaelmas daises, the teeth ragged petals, scarlet on cream.

I stammered apologies, backed away as quickly as I could, bowing.

I searched through the crowds for Desiree and failed to find her. I looked around the punchbowl, through a salon filled with young misses waiting to be asked to dance, their mothers hovering nearby. Desiree had never been among their ranks. Her father had been indulgent, allowed her to skip so many social niceties. I sought her amid the dancers and along the wall benches, where groups of men gossiped and women nattered amongst themselves.

I finally slipped outside into the starlit gardens. There I found her, scandalously alone with a man.

Pea gravel crunched under my boot heels as I approached, just in time to see him lean forward and take her hand. The night was cool on my outraged cheeks as I ran forward, pushing him away from her.

He staggered back, looking surprised. I had not seen him before: a dark Irishman with a narrow face and a nose like a knife blade. His black eyes were altogether too dark and romantic, like some hero in a novel.

Sometimes you dislike a man at first sight. As now. An expression that flashed over his face made me think he reciprocated the sentiment. He was, annoyingly enough, dressed impeccably, better than my own efforts, despite the Honiton lace at my throat.

Something wild in the cast of his features, the white flash of his throat, the enormous emerald on his hand, the way the moonlight glinted on his fingernails, made me think him something other than human, some besotted seraphim or an exotic nightmare borne of hallucinogen or fever. A shiver worked its way down my back and spread its fingers to measure my ribs.

"Claude!" Desiree exclaimed, looking far from pleased at her rescue.

I ignored her, addressing the man. "You will not touch my fiancée again, sir. I am surprised at you, taking advantage of her in this fashion." I did not say it, but my reproach was aimed at Desiree as well, even though I knew she could not have known better in her foolish, naive youth.

"Lord Tyndall brought me out here to discuss my designs," Desiree retorted. "He had read the paper I published on the difficulties of shaping tungsten."

I scoffed. "Indeed, he did his homework well so that he might lure you out here to compromise you."

Unnervingly, the man smiled at me. "I had no idea the author of such an erudite work would turn out to be so charming, sir, but the pleasure was unexpected. Having finished with that conversation, I was merely offering to demonstrate the art of palm reading to your lady. I picked up some small expertise in it in my homeland."

People were stirring in the nearest doorway, looking out to see what the loud conversation was about.

Tyndall spoke to Desiree. "I did not get the chance to tell you, lady: your palm shows that you will take a long journey, soon."

His accent was thick. It was ridiculous for an educated man to speak with such a heavy brogue, or to pretend to superstitious beliefs such as palmistry in order to lure women. But I stood down, not wishing to scandalize the gathering crowd.

Lady Allsop peered from near the back, the frown on her face threatening future invitations. I bowed and took Desiree's arm, drawing it through my own. She resisted, then let me pull her into the house.

But she would not speak to me the rest of the evening, despite the attendance I danced on her. In the carriage home, she relented, but only to upbraid me.

"I did as you asked," she hissed at me, "and it was as painful as I had imagined. But you were not even satisfied with that, and had to take away the one interesting conversation I was able to find."

"Everyone loved you. How can you say such things?" I protested.

"Perhaps you were at a different ball than I," she said. "Did you not see Lady Worth turn away lest she contaminate herself by speaking to a Negro? Or perhaps you did not overhear the sporting gentleman laying bets on what I would be like between the sheets?"

"Desiree!" I gasped, almost breathless at the shock of hearing such words from her innocent lips.

She turned away and did not speak to me again that night.

*   *   *

The next day I came to call, bringing chocolates and flowers and a pretty opal ring. Opals were her favorite gem. But she sent Mary to tell me she was feeling unwell.

I started to leave in high dudgeon, but Lord Southland called to me. He was in his library, or so he called it, a small room that smelled of pipe tobacco and old leather, so close that one could barely breathe. On the wall hung a portrait of Desiree's mother by Robert Tait.

I studied it as he gathered his thoughts. I knew she had perished in childbirth along with Desiree's younger brother, only a few years after Lord Southland had returned with her from a trip to America. No one knew exactly where she had come from, but gossip maintained that she had been a slave escaped from the southern portion of that barbarous place, that she had lived with the Cherokee for several years before the young Southland, on tour, encountered her in New Orleans. She was beautiful, although in an exotic, unsettling way. Her dark hair hung to her waist, and the artist had chosen to paint it untamed, almost hiding her face behind it. Her dress's satin was the color of a yellow rose just opening.

Lady Southland had never been accepted by society, and had therefore been an exile, trapped in this house. That was part of the contract between Desiree and I: through me she would escape such a fate.

"Do you love my daughter, Claude?" Lord Southland asked. Rumor held that before his wife, he'd had other exotic pets: a tiger cub, a great hyacinth macaw that sang sea shanties, a galago from Senegal. He was impious and had rejected the church, refusing to have Desiree baptized.

The question pained me, and I took care to show that in my tone. "Ever since I first met her, my lord."

"Ever since you met her, or ever since you learned she was an heiress?" He waved off my protestations. "I know, I know, such thoughts are unworthy of you. Still, I cannot help but wonder, Claude, if you did not think her an easy catch, given her circumstances. You are hardly the first suitor to make that mistake."

Desiree had other suitors? I was shocked but intrigued. I had never heard word of such.

"Still, the chit claims to love you." His look was contemptuous, and I stiffened my back under it. "It must be your looks alone, for you seem slow of mind to me."

I squared my chin. "You may disagree with your daughter's opinion, but you raised her to speak her mind and choose for herself."

"I did." He tugged at a pearl-set waistcoat button. "And will you allow her the same luxury, once she is married?"

"Of course I will!" I said. "Within reason."

"As I feared. Very well. I will warn you, Claude: I will continue to attempt to dissuade her from this choice."

"What choice?" Desiree demanded as she entered. She started out with a glare, but I smiled at her and she softened, as I knew she would. "Papa, are you beating this dead horse again?"

"Let me send you traveling," Lord Southland urged. "I will fund a trip to Italy, so you might see Leonardo's designs for yourself. Or America, where you can speak with other inventors."

"America?" she said. "Do you not read the papers? Do you truly not know what disdain they would hold me in there?"

"Desiree," he said. "For your mother's sake, and your own, all I want is your happiness."

"I will be an English dean's wife and live at Oxford," she said. "Claude has promised me a workshop the equal of mine here."

Now was not, perhaps, the best time to correct that misapprehension, so I kept my mouth closed. Not that it mattered. Father and daughter had squared off like pugilists in the ring, and Desiree's fists were clenched as though to keep herself from aiming a blow at him.

He took an envelope from his jacket pocket, ivory paper with an intricate seal. "I have had a letter inviting us to go shooting next week. An Irish estate. The writer says he met you at Lady Allsop's." He spared me a glance. "Claude is invited as well. If he comes too, will you accompany me? Rumor holds the pheasant is excellent in that region."

Desiree gave me a questioning look and I nodded.

Better to see Lord Southland assuaged, lest he put his foot down even more firmly. His difficulties were his own fault, I thought, for allowing his daughter too free a rein. Although it advantaged me more than a little, for I suspected Lord Southland's resistance only increased Desiree's interest in me.

I touched her elbow and saw her shoulders loosen. Southland kept glowering, but now at me instead of Desiree. I smiled at him and laced my fingers through hers before drawing them up to press my lips to her knuckles, my eyes fixed on his. His jaw tightened.

When I returned home, a similar envelope awaited me. Lord Tyndall regretted the unfortunate occurrences at Lady Allsop's and hoped to extend an olive branch to myself and my "lovely fiancée".

Now that the moment had passed, I regretted the assent I had given. But Southland would have written with his answer already, always punctilious and prompt when he thought it might inconvenience me.

I decided to make the most of it. As Southland had noted, the shooting in Tyndall's district was rumored to be extraordinary. While the Lord – was he one of the men that Southland reckoned a suitor? – would have the advantage in his home, the day I could not show up a country Irishman, no matter his title, would be the day I'd give up my position at Oxford. As for his inhuman aspect, it had surely been nothing more than a trick of the moonlight, coupled with my anger. It surprised me how much my rage stirred at the memory, even now, days later.

I turned the envelope over and examined the ostentatious seal. A pair of cats boxing with each other, paws upraised, circling a crown tipped with what looked like pointed spindles. A sweet smell came from the green wax.

I directed my valet to pack for the countryside. I would see this interloper driven away before Desiree even realized he was interested in her. Her naivety gave me the edge – not that I needed it.

As we approached Lord Tyndall's castle, the countryside was verdant, the autumn leaves just beginning to turn. The castle – for it was indeed a castle, albeit a small and shabby one – sat on a cliff's edge overlooking the Irish Sea, a romantic, wild vista that I feared might enthrall my impressionable fiancée.

I took care to point out flaws in the countryside as we traveled up the road, including dull-looking peasants and ill-tended cottages. I mentioned how difficult it must be to obtain supplies from London, given the distance and the road's rigors.

Desiree seemed to listen. Her father slouched in the opposite seat of the carriage and regarded me with heavy-lidded, inscrutable eyes.

There were a dozen or so other guests: a few Irish peers, relatives of his Lordship, and Lady Allsop and her husband. Everyone exclaimed over Desiree's exotic beauty and made enough fuss over her to render her speechless with discomfort. I hung back and did not rescue her. She would have to learn to cope with such attentions.

We settled into a daily routine, and Lord Southland and I both found the shooting excellent. In fact, I had never had such success before. It was as though the birds flew into my gun's path to sacrifice themselves. I had never experienced such a feeling of prowess. The other men congratulated me, sometimes sullenly, sometimes with genuine comradeship. The women were invariably flattering – even Desiree, although it was evident that my skill surprised her.

It was heady, and though Tyndall came shooting with us less and less, I found myself able to overlook it. We dined well on the yield from our expeditions each day. Tyndall had an excellent cook, one who rivaled the best establishments. Her blancmange was airy as a cloud; her teacakes scented with cardamom and honey. A good cook, like a good woman, is a pearl beyond price. I resolved to woo her away before going.

Shooting did not interest Desiree, which made me uneasy, but I was unable to resist the pull of the field. Like Desiree, Tyndall fancied himself a scientist, and like her, he had mechanical talent. She had brought the case containing her clockwork fairies, and the two were working on refinements to the wings. Desiree suggested that the fairies could be used in place of courier pigeons. Despite the notion's impracticality, Tyndall supported it.

I asked what else she was working on.

"Something to delight you!" she said, her face glowing with anticipation. "Tyndall's workshop is so fine, I have been able to construct something that will amaze you when you see it." She laughed. "I think I will gift him with it when we leave. He has said so many times how clever he thinks my machines."

"And they are clever," I said. I touched the tips of the curls surrounding her face, stiff and unbending with pomade.

She pulled away. "My maid spends too much time dressing my hair for you to set it in disarray!" she said, but laughed to take the sting from the words.

I had found a staircase leading up from the main hall which had a landing well designed for reading. Always conscious of the necessity of keeping up, I had brought edifying and current works with me. One was *The Subjection of Women* by John Stuart Mill, a package of inflammatory claptrap.

Sitting in my refuge, I was about to put it down when I came to a sentence that made me realize that even the falsest text might hold some grain of truth. The sentence read, "To understand one woman is not necessarily to understand any other woman."

I put the book aside but took that sentence with me, considering whether or not it was true. Certainly, every woman's personality was different, but there were commonalities at the heart of them all: a love of gossip, for instance. Concern with trivialities. An attraction to beauty.

Voices from below caught my attention. The stairway's acoustics were such that sounds carried clearly up to this level. It might have been designed for such a thing; I have encountered whispering galleries that bring words across the room as if the speaker stood right there.

It was Desiree and Tyndall.

"I think a more durable metal, laid along the edge, will prevent warpage," she was saying.

"Your little fairies intrigue me," he said. "Where did you find the model?"

"In my head," she admitted. "I was reading a newspaper account and it made me wonder what such a creature would look like."

"You have never glimpsed a fairy in the wild?"

She laughed. "Or a dragon in the coal cellar? No, I have never been prone to flights of fancy."

"You think fairies only a romantic notion."

"I think people would like to believe in them, would like to believe in magic," she said. "Even I feel that temptation. But it is at heart a foolish idea."

"What if I told you I could take you to a place where you could really see them, Desiree?" he purred. "Told you that true magic is wild beyond your imagining, that it will seize you, take you as though by storm?"

I was shocked that he would address her so familiarly. My gasp was loud enough to betray me.

"Who's there?" Tyndall exclaimed, and came up the stairs swiftly enough that it was as if he feared some intruder. He scowled at the sight of me.

I, on the other hand, was stiff with indignation. He meant to lure my fiancée to some deserted spot under the pretext of seeing fairies. Perhaps the scoundrel meant to compromise her to the point where she would be forced to marry him. Or perhaps he just meant to seduce her. I would have said these things, but Desiree's presence behind him made me keep my tongue.

"Come to lunch, Stone," he said. "There is the usual cold pheasant. You have not lost your taste for it yet, I trust?"

"I find myself thinking that we should return to London soon," I said to Desiree. Let him realize I had overheard his plotted seduction.

"Leave?" Desiree exclaimed. "But we are in the middle of a project!"

How could she be so foolish? Could she not see what Tyndall was up to? Was it possible she harbored romantic feelings for him? But the expression on her face was not thwarted lust. She liked speaking with him, I realized. It was nothing more than that.

Surely it was nothing more than that.

A day later, I overheard another conversation, this time between Desiree and her father. I will not trouble myself to reproduce it here, for much of what Lord Southland said was misguided and wrong. He restated his claim that I was too dull for Desiree and said, absurdly, that she should find a man capable of providing her with intelligent conversation.

I would have interjected, but I had learned my lesson the previous day. Instead, I kept quiet and listened, knowing that Desiree would defend me as she had before.

But her protestations seemed half-hearted. Worse, she seemed to be starting to believe that her father's words held some truth.

"You valued looks yourself," she said. "Was it not my mother's beauty that drew you to her?"

"At first, perhaps, but then I was taken by her manners, her bravery," Lord Southland said.

"Claude may not be brilliant," she said. "But he is respectable and well rounded, in the manner of English education. And he has thought a great deal about spiritual matters."

"Spiritual matters!" her father exclaimed. "I thought I had brought you up better than to believe in a crutch that supports feeble minds in their mediocrity!"

Had he raised her as an atheist? I was appalled, but I knew I would be able to teach her otherwise, patiently and carefully, as a man must do with his wife.

"I want to believe in something other than science," she said, and I thrilled at the earnestness in her voice. "I want to believe in something free and fierce, something that stands outside society."

Her theology was muddled, but she could learn. Her father's sound of disgust and frustration made me smile.

That evening we stood on the terrace overlooking the sea. I could not resist pressing the issue. "Desiree, do you think we are well matched in mind?"

She hesitated, taking a breath.

I did not care. I knew I outstripped her, but I could reach down, lift her to new heights of thought, of philosophy. Some hold that the Negro brain is structurally inferior to ours, but Desiree had already proved that she could get her mind around such things as mathematics and mechanics. I would show her theology's wonders, the careful construction of a passage explicating God's glory. We would read Milton together, and other poetry that would elevate her soul.

I decided to search for proof of Tyndall's intentions, for evidence that he was not a man of science, only pretending to be one in order to seduce my gullible bride-to-be. Desiree always thought the best of people. It was up to my more rigorous mind to make sure she was not being too trusting.

A massive book lay on the table in Tyndall's study, its pages well thumbed. I turned it to study the spine.

A chill ran through me and I pulled my hand away, as though from a coiled serpent. It was King James's *Dæmonologie*.

Using a handkerchief, I turned it to me and opened it. The words burned up at me:

"This word of Sorcerie is a Latine worde, which is taken from casting of the lot, & therefore he that vseth it, is called Sortiarius à sorte."

Was Tyndall a sorcerer, then? What unholy designs did he have on Desiree? This was far, far worse than I had imagined.

A cough sounded behind me. I dropped the book and spun round.

Tyndall.

He had the gall to stand there, polite enquiry on his face. "Some light reading, Stone?" he said.

I pointed at the book. My hand shook with emotion. "No honest man has such a book in his library! What foul magics do you practice?"

"I have never claimed to be an honest man," he said dryly.

"Demon!" I hissed.

He shook his head. His tone was still polite, as though we spoke about the proper slicing of a breast of pheasant or the correct garnish for a trout. "I have been called that before, on my visits to this land," he said. "But elf is more accurate."

"I know a demon when I see one! You admit you are not human? You want not just Desiree's body, but her soul!"

He snorted. "Her soul is her own. I want only her clever mind and machines, to entertain my Queen's court."

I gestured about the room. "Then all this is just illusion!"

He shook his head. A smile lingered at the corners of his mouth, as though it pleased him to speak so straightly to me. "No, the real Lord Tyndall is . . . elsewhere. He will return when I am done, none the worse for wear. Indeed, his fortunes will prosper as a result. As yours could."

"You mean to threaten me."

"I mean to say that the financial chains binding you to your fiancée could be replaced with other gold, of my own forging, as recompense."

"Desiree is more than gold to me," I said. "A good wife is a treasure. Fairy gold is said to melt away, or become dry leaves in the light of day."

"So you refuse to give her up?" he said.

"She may not be much," I said. "Prideful, and a little wanton, and overly obsessed with this world's trumperies. But she is mine, and I will have her, and the rich dowry that comes with her, and the inheritance that will befall her when her father dies."

"Do you love her?"

I hesitated too long. In the silence I heard a little gasp of betrayal behind me.

I turned just in time to see the tears in Desiree's eyes before she fled.

She was nowhere to be found. No matter where I searched – even with the help of Tyndall's servants, who were looking for their absent lord, mysteriously vanished as well. But when I let myself into my chamber that night, I knew she had been there. A tang of oil and steel hung in the air like dragon's breath.

I first saw the note on my writing desk. Desiree's handwriting was clear as copperplate.

It read:

Claude,

I do not think we will suit after all. But I have left you something that will, I think, let you have the kind of woman you desire. She comes with my dowry – I will not need it where Tyndall is taking me. I wish you only the best, Claude. I hope you wish me the same in turn. The key is on the mantle. Remember to wind her up every seventh day.

Desiree

I looked around and finally saw the shrouded figure by the fireplace. I pulled away the cloth covering it. At first it looked like Desiree standing there, stiff and rigid, dressed in a gown of pale blue moiré that I recognized as the one she had worn to Lady

Allsop's ball. But closer examination showed that the skin was dyed cloth laid over a harder surface, the hair sewn onto the scalp. A hole nestled in her décolletage, just big enough to accommodate the brass key I retrieved from the fireplace.

I inserted the key and twisted it, hearing the ratcheting of the cogs and gears inside my clockwork bride, until her eyelids unshuttered and I stepped forward to take her in my arms.

As we waltzed, I wept. Wept for my Desiree – not just what I had thought she would be to me, but for what she had been, for her clever hands and heart and laughter, and that she had loved me as much as I had loved her. Tears stained her silk bodice as I held her close, sky-blue darkening to stormy. The fairies hung in a circle around us, abandoned by their former mistress. I wept, and we danced.

She danced very well indeed.

The Mechanical Aviary of Emperor Jala-ud-din Muhammad Akbar

Shweta Narayan

Bulbul and Peacock

Now Akbar-e-Azam, the Shah-en-Shah, Emperor of the World, who is called the Light of Heaven, has built markets and mosques and schools for his people of flesh and of metal and for the eternal glory of God. But he commissioned the mechanical aviary for himself and only himself. Not even his favorite wives could enter – only the Emperor, his slaves and the Artificer, who is herself a bird of metal.

It was a small aviary, notable only for its roof: panes of thin clear glass which cast no latticed shadows but let the Sun light up the birds unhindered. Birds of cog and gear and lever, their mechanical lives powered by springs, they were made from shining copper and silver and bronze. Enamel coated their heads, their tails, their wing-tips, in gleaming colors for the Shah-en-Shah's delight. From Falcon, whose beak and claws were edged with diamond, who had once brought down a tiger, to Phoenix, whose mechanism built a child within her and sealed its final seams in the fire that melted her away – every bird was a wonder. Not a feather rusted, not a joint squealed, not a single spring wound down, for the merely human aviary slaves were careful and skilled.

The Shah-en-Shah (blessed with long life, Allah be praised) was at that time barely more than a boy. He loved his birds and denied them nothing. Most especially he could not deny his favorites, Peacock and Bulbul.

For though he was proud of Falcon and Phoenix, he came most often to hear Bulbul's sweet song and see the flashing colors of Peacock's dance; or to have Bulbul sit on his shoulder while he rubbed jasmine oil onto Peacock's feathers. This brought him peace; and to Akbar, who inherited a crown and a war when he was thirteen years old, who had to execute his own foster brother for treachery, peace has always been harder won than pride. For the joy of their music and dance he loved Bulbul and Peacock above all others – and for the joy of their music and dance they grew to love each other.

And so they approached the Artificer.

"O Lady with human hands," sang Bulbul, "will you build us a child who can both dance and sing?"

But the Artificer bird would not.

"O brightest of eye and feather," said Peacock, "does our wish displease you? Do you find these slaves presumptuous?"

"Not presumptuous," said the Artificer, "but certainly unwise."

They were so distraught that Peacock tripped over his own tailfeathers when he next tried to dance, while Bulbul piped one thin, flat, endless note. "Are you ill?" asked the Emperor. "Are your cogs slipping, one from the other?"

"Son of Heaven," Peacock said, "the illness is in our heartsprings. We wish to make a child together, but the Lady will not help."

At this the Emperor frowned. "Is such a task below you?" he asked her. For the Artificer was no slave; she had once been his teacher, and was now an honored guest. She rustled her copper tailfeathers.

"Far below me," she said, "to betray you so. Every bird here has one purpose, and one bird fulfills each purpose, and thus is peace maintained. Will you breed strife in your sanctuary?"

"Children strive against us," said the Shah-en-Shah (who had yet no children). "We raise them in love nonetheless. If you are truly my friend, give my birds their wish."

The Artificer was silent for a long time. Finally she said, "As I am your friend, I shall. But hear me first."

The Dancing Girl

In the Golden City of legend, Mechanical Pukar (which Westerners called Khaberis), there were wonders lost now to the ages. Rooftops and roads inlaid with yellow sapphire, emerald, cinnamon stone and the other astrological gems; mechanical people wearing spun and filigreed gold; markets piled with ingots and fine tools. There were slaves of flesh to tend to people and wind them up. There were pools of fragrant oil to bathe in, tiled with obsidian and warmed by the Sun. And there were temple dancers, who also sang.

Nothing compared to the dancers' beauty; but having both abilities wound their heartsprings so tightly that they could think only of themselves and their art. So, too, could any who grew close to them think only of them.

There was an artificer once, a young man of gleaming bronze, with sharp eyes and skillful fingers. He and his wife worked hard and well together. They made a fortune. Then he made a dancing girl and fell in love.

He squandered everything he owned, everything his wife owned, save only her anklets. Instead of his commissions he built treasures for his dancer, treasures which the Shah-en-Shah himself would gladly accept if they existed today. But the girl thought only of her dance and her song.

She danced away, in time. His heartspring nearly snapped, but he woke from that dream and found that, despite everything, he still had a wife. They left Pukar together that day, in shame, walking barefoot through the dust.

Devadasi

"So I shall make them a child," said the Artificer, "but it shall either sing or it shall dance. Not both."

"We could not love such a child equally," said Peacock.

Bulbul said, "It must do both."

"Pukar is but an old legend," said the Shah-en-Shah. "Will you deny them for a story?"

"A story?" The Artificer clicked her beak. "I wear one of those anklets around my neck."

Akbar smiled; but as he smiled in court, with grace rather than belief.

"What you ask worries me," said the Artificer. "But it worries me more that I seem to have taught you nothing. So be it, King of Kings; bring me beaten silver to replace the worn copper in my tail, and precious metal and enamel enough for this task, and they shall have what they want."

And so it was; she made a little golden child with wings and tail enamelled green, and named her Devadasi. Bulbul and Peacock raised her and taught her with love and patience. Being made by the Artificer, whose skill exceeds all others', she soon sang with greater range and sweetness than her father and danced with more grace and expression than her other father. All the birds were entranced – except the Artificer, who stayed away.

One day, when Akbar came to the aviary with trouble on his shoulders, Devadasi fluttered down to him. "May this slave sing to ease your soul?" she asked. "May I dance to give joy to the brightest star in the Heavens?" For her fathers had also taught her manners.

Now, the Shah-en-Shah had just abolished the pilgrim tax, and he was anxious to forget his mother's anger (remember that he was very young in those days). So he smiled, and accepted, and Devadasi sang for him and danced. And like all others, the Emperor of the World was entranced.

"What a clever bird you are," he said afterwards.

Devadasi preened and asked, "Do you not think my singing sweeter than Bulbul's, o my lord?"

The Emperor said, "Yes, little bird, it is sweeter than any other music in the world." This was thoughtless of him; but indeed he was not thinking.

"And do you not think my dancing prettier than Peacock's?"

"I do, little one," he said.

Bulbul and Peacock had approached to see how their daughter fared; but their heartsprings broke at Akbar's words, and they sang and danced no more. Struck by grief and guilt, the Shah-en-Shah bent his head and wept.

"Do not mourn, Great One," said Devadasi. "They are merely metal now, it is true, but surely it would please their springs and screws to be made beautiful. Have the Artificer bird use them to build more birds like myself, and my fathers' very cogs will rejoice."

And so the Light of Heaven commanded.

The Lady obeyed (for even an honored guest obeys the Ruler of All). She sawed Bulbul and Peacock apart, melted them down, re-formed them. But their balance wheels and their broken heartsprings she quietly set aside.

The Devadasi birds exulted. They sang in complex harmony and choreographed elaborate dances, their different colors flashing in varied patterns. And they wanted, always, to make more complex music, more complex patterns. They wanted more of themselves. So too did the Light of Heaven want more of them, for the memory of Bulbul and Peacock made him doubt his every thought and judgement. In the Devadasi birds' presence he could forget the new torture of shame and indecision; he came more and more often to the aviary, sometimes even cancelling his open court. And each time he came, the birds asked for something more.

They asked for bronze from the aviary's central fountain, and copper from the pipes that pumped in warm oil. He granted their wish, though it meant the other birds grew creaky and stiff. They wanted the solder that held together the aviary's panes of glass; and they had it, though the roof shattered and the rain came in.

They asked him, then, for stories of warfare. He spoke of swords and guns and killing machines, of strategy and of treachery on the field. And Falcon heard, and knew that her hunting was only a game for princes, and her heartspring broke. Then they asked whether owls of flesh could spin their heads all the way around; and Owl tried it, and unscrewed his head until it fell right off and smashed. They asked about wild swans, how gracefully they could glide through still water; and Swan tried to swim, and sank.

As each bird died there was more metal, and more still, and Devadasi's wishes kept the Artificer busy. But she saved every heartspring, and every special movement plate and wheel, and she hid them away. And late at night when she would not be disturbed, she spent long fraught hours patching broken heartsprings with copper from her old tailfeathers.

The day came when there were no birds left to murder for salvage, nothing more to harvest from the aviary itself. On that day the flock asked the Shah-en-Shah if they might go with him to the Artificer's workshop, and on that day he did once again as they asked.

"See what you have wrought?" sang the Devadasi birds, their pure voices interweaving. "If not for you, the aviary would still be whole. You are flawed, Artificer; we are perfect. It is fit that you scrap your wings and make more of us."

But the Artificer said, "You will not find it so easy to break my heartspring."

"Then at least take that ugly anklet from around your neck," they chorused. "It is not fitting for a bird to wear jewelry, and it will help make one of us."

"Do you know the cost of an anklet?" said the Lady. "I shall tell you."

"We care nothing for your stories," they called.

"You will listen anyway," she said; and they did.

The Anklet

Once a young couple from Pukar came to Maturai, ruin of the south, in search of work and a new life. In that time, the city that is no more was thriving, rich in the manner of the flesh people, with fruit and meat and wandering cows and children and elaborate, painted woodwork.

The couple were barefoot, their skin scratched and muddy from travel. They owned nothing of value but her gleaming golden anklets. Ragged lengths of dyed silk fell from their shoulders, a mockery of the spun-gold robes they once had worn. But these were no paupers; they were master artificers both, and hoped to rebuild their fortune in Maturai.

Settling beneath a banyan tree on the edge of the city, they waited for sunrise. She beat a rhythm on her right anklet, her copper fingers dark against the gold. It sprung open with an oiled clickwhirr. Moonlight caught on its tiny hinges and on the nine precious stones on their internal belt.

"Will you calculate our future?" asked her husband. For her right anklet was an astrological device; each stone represented a star.

"No," she said. "How would knowing help? We must speak to this raja's artificer; we have no choice."

Her husband bent his head. "Forgive me." His voice was dull as his once-gleaming skin.

She said only, "You were not yourself."

He slumped, silent, until she closed the anklet up and handed it to him; then he raised one brushed-bronze eyebrow in a question.

"You will need proof of our skill," she said.

"Should I not take my masterwork, rather than yours?"

"Yours is too useful," she said. "He might take it away." Her left anklet was a measuring device, its belt set with magnifying lenses. She did not mention that she preferred losing her own masterwork to his.

So when the stars to the east started to fade, he rose with her anklet in his hand and trudged into Maturai. He did not return.

Three days and three nights passed before she ventured into the city. She waited because flesh women did not conduct business, and because she was ashamed to enter the city with an ankle bare. But she also waited because she wished to trust her husband.

So it is that we can make terrible mistakes with the best of intentions. For by the time she entered the city, her husband was three days dead.

She learned from the flesh people that a metal man had stolen the Queen's anklet and tried to sell it to the Raja's own artificer. She asked where he was. "With the artificer," they said. "In pieces, by the Raja's command. As the thieving device deserves."

She said, "The one you speak of was neither thief nor mere machine, but my husband."

As one, they turned away from her.

So she went to the palace. The Raja's guards tried to stop her, of course; her hair filaments were unbraided, her copper skin dented and green in places. But they knew nothing of Pukar's people, of their strength and their speed. The woman of metal brushed them aside and clanged into court, where she cried, "Is this the justice of Maturai? Her raja is a murderer; her queen wears stolen goods."

"The device is raving," said the courtiers. But the Queen looked at her and paled. For the copper woman's single anklet was a perfect golden band, just like the Queen's two.

The Raja said, "What nonsense. My artificer made the Queen's anklets himself."

"Perhaps." The woman flexed her finger hinges. "But I made one that she wears."

"Do you claim my artificer lied?"

"Claim?" she said. "Call your artificer, o murderer, and I will prove it."

The Raja took an angry breath, then stopped and smiled. "If I shame him so, he will leave," he said, as oiled as the copper woman's hinges. "I must have an artificer."

"Give me his workshop and his goods," she said, "and I will take his place."

The Raja called gleefully for his artificer then, and bade the Queen slip off her anklet.

The metal woman watched quietly. When the Queen had eased an anklet off, she said, "But surely you knew which one you lost? Mine is the other."

The Queen flushed and bowed her head, then fumbled her other anklet off. She held it out to the metal woman without looking up.

The artificer came in then, flanked by guards and protesting with every step. "What travesty is this?" he cried. "I have never been so insulted! Majesty, have I given you cause to doubt me? Surely I must know my own work!"

The copper woman said, "Then trigger its mechanism."

"What mechanism?" he sneered. "Do you see seams in my craftwork?" He held the anklet up to the window and turned it in the fractured light. "Do edges glint? Do hinges mar the surface? Show me one single imperfection – Thing."

She took the anklet from him, tapped it, and held it up as it clickwhirred open. "In Pukar," she said, "jewelry is more than merely art."

The Raja had his artificer put to death. The copper woman watched and smiled. She smiled more when the Raja cast suspicious glances towards his queen.

And so the woman of Pukar became a raja's artificer. But she did not promise him loyalty, for she was too honorable to lie.

In the workshop she found her husband's armpieces, legpieces, breastplate and skull. She found his gears arranged by size. She found a dozen plates, a thousand screws, a counterspring, a ratchet spring, a regulating spring. If she had found his heartspring intact, she might not have destroyed Maturai.

But she had given the old artificer three days and three nights with the body, and the flesh people have always wanted to know how heartsprings work. She could not repair it. Her husband was truly dead. And she had never told him that she treasured his anklet over her own. Her own heartspring might have broken then. It tightened, instead, in anger.

So she promised the Raja a present in thanks for his justice, and she locked herself away. She kept her heartspring tight, and thought only of her art. For nine months she made children, scavenged from her husband's parts and her own. Nine monstrous children, each with one leg, one arm and one eye. Each eye was a stone from her astrological anklet.

From the remaining parts she made a bird, copper from its tailfeathers to its wingtips. But its beak was the bronze of her husband's skin, and its articulated hands were human.

She was barely a framework by then. She unscrewed her breasts, filled their cups with gems from workshop stores, and with poison; then she soldered them together. She told her children their task: hop to the funerary grounds, steal burning branches from the pyres, and set Maturai aflame. She wound their heartsprings so tightly that they could think of nothing else. Then she set them loose.

Finally she clasped her measuring anklet around the bird's neck, pulled out her heartspring, and in one automated movement transferred it into the copper bird.

Then she stretched out her wings and flew.

She flew first into the Raja's court, holding the sphere made from her breasts; and there she dropped it. It hit the marble tiles and burst open (for solder is not strong). Shining gems bounced everywhere. Some cut gashes in the courtiers and guards. They did not care. The copper bird's last view of the court of Maturai was a frenzy of men and women grabbing for rubies, emeralds, pearls; and every stone was coated in poison.

Heartsprings

"Poison kills flesh very quickly," said the Artificer thoughtfully. "And carved-wood buildings burn fast. So ended Maturai and so, as I flew high above and far away, was justice finally done."

There was a silence in the workshop when she finished. Even the flock was a little bit impressed, and the Emperor looked at his friend with a first hint of fear. She was both teacher and maker; just how tightly was *her* heartspring wound?

The flock recovered first. "Your price has been met," they warbled, "and we outnumber you still. If you will not give us your anklet, we will rip it from your neck."

"But the story is not done," said the Artificer. "For I made you, and I must tell you one thing more. I made you in the image of the temple dancers of golden Pukar, those who stole away my husband for one long and heartsore year. I even named the first of you after them: Devadasi. They were beautiful and skilled, and their grace was unmatched in this world."

As one, the flock preened.

"Yes, you were made in their image," said the Artificer. "But what I must tell you is that I failed. My skill was not sufficient. They are still unmatched, for they were better than you."

And hearing this, the entire flock's heartsprings broke in one discordant twang, and they fell, littering the floor, the table, the cabinets.

The Shah-en-Shah flinched. He looked around, a dreamer slowly waking into nightmare. Tears formed in his eyes. "What have I done?" he said.

The Artificer collected the Devadasi bodies. She cut feathers and plates and counter-nuts apart. "You have learned something, my friend," she said, pulling heartsprings out of their hidden drawers. "The hard way, of course, like all the young."

And she set to remaking the birds of the aviary.

Akbar

He did learn, that young ruler. He learned whom to trust, and whom to heed, and that the two are not always the same. And that is surely why he lives to tell you this story today.

Prayers of Forges and Furnaces

Aliette de Bodard

The stranger came at dawn, walking out of the barren land like a mirage – gradually shimmering into existence beside the bronze line of the rails: a wide-brimmed hat, a long cloak, the glint that might have been a rifle or an obsidian-studded sword.

Xochipil, who had been scavenging for tech at the mouth of Mictlan's Well, caught that glint in her eyes – and stopped, watching the stranger approach, a growing hollow in her stomach. Beneath her were the vibrations of the Well, like a calm, steady heartbeat running through the ground: the voice of the rails that coiled around the shaft of the Well, bearing their burden of copper and bronze ever downwards.

The stranger stopped when he came up to her. They stared wordlessly at each other. He was tall, a good two heads taller than Xochipil; he held himself straight, like an axle or a rod that wouldn't break. The glint wasn't a sword or a rifle, after all – but simply that of a dozen obsidian amulets, spread equally around his belt, shining with a cold, black light that wasn't copper or bronze or steel, but something far more ancient, from the old, cruel days before the Change.

Xochipil's heart contracted. Perhaps it wasn't too late to run away. But he'd catch up with her easily, with those big legs of his. She'd never been a fast runner, not with her right leg trailing behind her, permanently out of shape. Before the Change, cripples such as her would have been killed: sacrificed to the old gods to bring the harvest or the sunlight.

The stranger's eyes rested on her leg, but showed no change of expression. "This would be Mictlan's Well?"

Xochipil, not trusting her voice, nodded.

"I see." The stranger's eyes were brown, almost without pupils. "My name is Tezoca. I'm told there is an inn here, for travellers?"

Xochipil nodded again. She stared at him, trying to decide what he was; but he didn't appear fazed by her appearance, or aggressive. "But you need a travel licence. Or the will to serve the community and bind yourself to the workers, in this age and the next and the next," she said. The words of the Well's oath of loyalty came irrepressibly out of her mouth.

The words fell in the silence between both of them. Under her feet, the earth was quiescent, as if the rails themselves waited for Tezoca's answer.

"I see." He smiled; his teeth were dark, stained with soot, or coal-dust. "I see. What makes you think I don't have a permit, little one?"

"Don't call me 'little one'," Xochipil snapped, annoyed that he'd used the same condescending name for her as the townspeople did. "My name is Xochipil."

Tezoca spread his hands. "My apologies. What makes you think I don't have a travel permit, Xochipil?"

Wordlessly, she pointed at the dangling amulets on his belt.

"This?" he asked, lifting one of them. In the rising sunlight, it shone as red as blood – and it wasn't an amulet after all, she saw, but a shard with a sharp edge, barely reworked to make it seem innocuous. In its depths was an odd, cold light, a beat quite unlike the voice of the rails, speaking of a forgotten time, of altars slick with blood and the smoke of incense rising against the pristine blue of the skies, above a city that wasn't steel and bronze, but simple adobe . . .

A hot, sharp pain burst across her cheek; startled, she realized Tezoca had just struck her. Warmth spread from the blow, to her face, to her bones. It wasn't an unfamiliar feeling – Uncle Atl had been fond of calling her to order when she failed to be grateful for anything – but it was the first time a complete stranger had struck her, at all. And he wasn't getting away with none of it, never mind that he was taller or bigger than her.

"Apologies," Tezoca said, his gaze still on her, as if he could read her thoughts. "I had to tear you away from that." He didn't sound angry, or sad – just thoughtful, and perhaps a little proud, though she wasn't sure why.

That didn't do anything to lessen the pain. "From what?" Xochipil asked, defiantly.

He'd lowered his hands, and was now busy tucking all the shards into the folds of his cloak – hiding them from view. "I scavenged them from the desert," he said. "They're broken, and broken things are often more dangerous than when they're whole."

"I don't understand," Xochipil said.

"You don't need to, believe me." Tezoca gazed behind her, at the depths of the Well – the thrum of the steam-cars, the hubbub of workers jostling each other on the footpaths, the slow, inevitable beat coursing along the rails and resonating through the earth.

"Have they reached the bottom?" he asked.

Down, down, went the rails, vanishing into the depths of the shaft – linking Mictlan's Well to the distant capital, and the god-machine ensconced in its palace.

"Two days ago," Xochipil said. It had been the talk of the Well. Tezoca smiled. "I thought so," he said. "I felt it."

She'd felt it, too – the deeper resonance in the rails, the richer beat that coursed along their bronze rods. Whatever it was that the god-machine was looking for, it had found it. "You're an engineer, then?"

"No, not quite," Tezoca said. He looked at her again, thoughtfully. "Tell me, Xochipil . . . if I wanted to stay somewhere that's not the inn, where would I go?"

"So you don't have a travel permit," she said, with a touch of satisfaction.

"Of course not," Tezoca replied, airily.

"And why would I help you?" she asked carefully. "The penalties for aiding fugitives aren't light."

Tezoca smiled. "I'm not a fugitive. And I could offer you money, but I doubt that's what you really want, is it? Very well." He pulled out one of the obsidian shards, and rubbed it absent-mindedly. "Do you like the god-machine, Xochipil?"

Even the question was sacrilege – her hands reached out, sketched the Sign of the Sacred Cog, to ward against the wrath of the machine. "What kind of question is that?" she asked.

Tezoca hadn't moved. "Humour me."

"Do I like the god-machine? Why would I have to? It sees everything and punishes everything. It is, was and will ever be, throughout the ages of the world."

"It wasn't always," Tezoca said, very softly.

Xochipil glanced around, suddenly frightened. A fugitive was one thing; a heretic quite another. The townspeople tolerated her, but this would be going too far. "The Change was so long ago we don't remember it," she said. "What does it change, if the machine wasn't always?"

"Things that are born can die," Tezoca said, with a quick nod of his head. "Let me ask you the question again. Do you like the engineers, the technicians, the soldiers? Do they treat you well?"

Xochipil shook her head – once, twice. What right had he, to come here in the midst of her life, and question everything? "You know what the leg would have meant, before the Change. I have a life, under the god-machine."

"So do caged birds. Answer the question."

"Machine break you," she whispered. "You know the answer, don't you?" That she was lame, and thus had no place on any of the work crews; that she'd survived on the "kindness" of relatives until they grew bored and left her to fend for herself; that she scavenged for broken tech at the edge of the Well, the small, useless artefacts that passing steam-cars thoughtlessly discarded – and sold them, day after day, barely eking out her living.

"Perhaps I do know the answer. But I'd want it from your own mouth."

"No," she said, low and savage, the word out of her lips before she could take it back. She waited for him to laugh, to throw back his cloak and reveal himself as a servant of the machine, to take her away for heresy. But he did nothing. He merely watched her.

At length Tezoca nodded. "You have a fiery heart," he said, his hand rubbing the shard, again and again, as if he could wear it down to nothing.

"And you're a madman."

Tezoca smiled. "That's often been said. But you haven't answered my question."

The earlier one, the one about lodgings and food. Still shaking inwardly – remembering the shock of his question, the shock of her answer – that she, Xochipil, the daughter of workers, should question the god-machine, that she should imply she'd gladly see it stop functioning . . .

She shook her head angrily. Why not, after all? It had never been much of a life. "I have a room. It's not much – upper levels, not much surface – but it could stretch to two people."

Again, that quick smile of his, daring and reckless, revealing the darkness of his teeth. "That will do nicely, I think."

Luckily, they didn't have to go far: Xochipil's assigned room was one of the dingiest ones, just under the mouth of the Well. The best rooms were near the bottom, as close as possible to the edge of the rails and the source of the endless thrumming. That was where the supervisors lived; and the governor, and all his staff of master engineers and elite soldiers.

She left Tezoca there to unfold his belongings in the cramped room, its wrought ceiling so low he had to bend to stand under it, its shelves covered in scraps of metal and empty vials in addition to her clothes and tools.

She had no doubt he'd wander around, but she had other things to do: it was almost time for the noon pause, and Malli would be ready to do business. Hastily wrapping some of her better findings in her bag, she hurried onto the filigreed walkway that led back to the main path – and then down along the footpaths.

Above and below her pulsed the rails, plunging into the dizzying darkness below the surface. Steam-cars loaded with tools and bags of excavated soil slid past, with a whine like air through a cut throat. Further down were the subsidiaries of the machine scooping out the earth, and the men and women toiling to lay down the bronze rods for the new rails.

A faint light oozed from the bottom of the shaft – a shimmering, pulsing radiance that was achingly comforting – and the beat of the rails was stronger, richer, echoing in her lame leg and in her chest, squeezing around her heart until it seemed to be one with her.

She wondered what they'd found, down there; what Tezoca was really looking for.

She found Malli on the twenty-fifth level, sitting a little apart from her work cadre. The rotund woman barely raised her eyes when Xochipil slid next to her, onto the warm metal of the bench. "What have you got?" she asked, without preamble.

Xochipil unpacked her things, laid them out on her knees. Malli scrutinised them for a while. Xochipil tensed, expecting the usual session of bargaining, but Malli merely pointed to two of the less broken artefacts, a filigreed hummingbird and a rusty cog.

"Those two. Three *tlazos*."

Xochipil, surprised, pocketed the money without showing what she felt. Malli wrapped the artefacts in her own shirt, finished her crushed maize and amaranth, and got up. "Do you have urgent business?" Xochipil asked.

Malli tossed her head disdainfully. "There's a hierarch there, Xochipil. From the god-machine itself." Her eyes shone with excitement; and clearly she wouldn't understand why Xochipil didn't rejoice.

Mictlan's Well was not so big or so important to warrant regular visits from the capital. "What does he want?" Xochipil asked. She thought, with a sinking in her stomach, of Tezoca methodically unpacking his things in her room. But a hierarch wouldn't visit that high: they'd be lodging with the governor's staff at the bottom, near the heart of the Well.

"Are you daft?" Malli asked. "We've reached the bottom, girl! Of course he'd want to see what's there."

"You too?" Xochipil asked.

Malli looked at Xochipil as if she'd just offered to worship the old gods. "He's a hierarch! Of course he's holding a grand procession, and a remembering."

And of course, everyone would want to attend it, to be touched by the god-machine's essence – to feel the unending communion with the rest of the Commonwealth: with the network of towns and mines and wells connected by the beat of the rails and the whine of steam-cars, and with the thousand cadres of workers toiling away in the bowels of the machine's subsidiaries, ceaselessly raising bronze and copper and chrome to its undying glory.

Xochipil realized with a shock that Malli was waiting for her – caring little about her outcast status – and there was no way she could refuse, not without both vexing Malli and raising suspicions she couldn't afford to raise.

"All right," she said. "Let's go."

Xochipil had never been to the lower floors, but somehow she wasn't surprised to find them made of chrome and steel: white and shining in the harsh light from sunspheres, still thrumming with the beat of the rails, an echo so strong it was almost paralyzing.

She kept her head high, ignoring the odd looks the various work crews threw at her – a cripple, here in the centre of the Well, an unthinkable thing if ever there was one – and walked slightly behind Malli, unwilling to draw closer. Malli herself hadn't shown any desire for friendship; just a wish for her to join with the god-machine.

They were almost at the bottom of the Well now. The reverberation shook Xochipil's bones and her muscles, echoed in her ribcage like a second heartbeat. They wouldn't be going all the way down, though: Xochipil was sure that the hierarch wouldn't show the workers what lay on the last floor. It was the supervisors who had dug the last pit, and the governor himself who had broken the last seal and connected the last rails.

On the vast platform that filled most of the shaft at the Eightieth Level, a dizzying array of cadres had gathered. Every one of them wore their own colours and badges of allegiance, a dizzying sea of drab cotton and maguey-fibre clothes. The platform near the centre held a steel altar with the Sacred Symbols: the Cog, the Chain, the Bolt, the Wires and the Vial.

On the platform stood the hierarch.

He was alone: a tall, unprepossessing silhouette in flowing robes of stark whiteness, bearing a symbol Xochipil couldn't make out. But even standing away from the platform, even wedged between the resentful members of Malli's cadre on the narrow footpath, she could *feel* the strength of his presence, the aura that somehow was the pulsing of every city of the Commonwealth – and the mind of the god-machine, straining towards the bottom of the Well, extending itself along the length of the rails to be with them in this moment of great glory.

The hierarch raised his head, and silence spread across the

cavern. His skin was gleaming copper – and his hands extended towards them all, the hands of the god-machine, which was, had been and would be, forever and ever in this age of the world and the next and the next.

"Behold," the hierarch whispered, a single word that echoed against the walls of the shaft, quivering in the rails themselves, twisting in Xochipil's chest until her heart ached with need. "The Age of Wonders has come. Let the old gods remain dead, let the altars be of pristine steel, let the blood and the breath remain in our bodies . . ." A litany, whispered over and over – and abruptly Xochipil realized the rumble was the sound of thousands of voices joining it – of her own voice, raised in praise of the god-machine and the Commonwealth, but she couldn't stop, she was as much a part of it as Malli, as the hierarch . . .

"Let the sun remain silent, let our prayers be made with forges and furnaces, let the blood and the breath remain in our bodies . . ."

The words were said, over and over, thousands of voices filling the Well to bursting – and even the memory of Tezoca was very far away, words that made no sense, for how could he ever hope to challenge such power as this – how could he put an end to what was, would be and had ever been?

"Let the pyramids remain broken, let our labour be our worship, let the blood and the breath remain in our bodies . . ."

Pyramids. Tezoca had said—

He—

Abruptly, her mind torn from the communion, she saw Tezoca. He was standing on the edge of the crowd on one of the neighbouring footpaths, dressed in the colours of the Fifty-Fourth Hummingbird Cadre. He held a dark-skinned woman in his embrace, kissing her lips, her forehead, her earlobes – and the voice of the god-machine was receding in the distance, replaced by Tezoca's mocking words.

It wasn't always. Things that are born can die.

Tezoca raised his gaze to Xochipil, pulling away from the woman; and in the split moment before he did, she saw, very clearly, the blood still clinging to his lips, the blood still flowing from the woman's earlobes, wounds that sealed themselves even as she watched.

Blood. He'd been ... drinking blood, and using it to work against the machine's communion. But only one kind of being had ever fed on blood, and only one kind of being had ever drawn power from it.

The old gods – who were all dead, bested by the machine, their remains scattered over the desert like ashes.

When she came back to her room, exhausted from the strain of the communion, she found Tezoca already there. He had made himself at home, as neatly as a soldier on the move: he'd managed to unfold his things in a small patch of free space amidst the clutter on the ground, and he'd wedged his lanky body between the cooking-stove and the pallet. Even cramped as he was, he looked ludicrously at ease.

"It's an interesting town," he said. His face was expressionless; his lips thin, the colour of bronze – no blood anywhere, not anymore.

But Xochipil was too tired and too frightened to pretend she hadn't seen anything. "What in the machine's name are you?" she asked. "What game do you think you're playing?"

Tezoca's face did not move. "You can't say I didn't warn you."

"Not—" of what you were, she wanted to say, but the words wouldn't come out of her mouth. She tried again, but the enormity of what she was about to say dwarfed her. "You're dead," she whispered finally, because it was the only thing that her mind could hold onto – hoping he would deny it, that he would laugh at what she suggested. "All the old gods are dead."

"Some things," Tezoca said darkly, "are hard to kill."

"The machine?" she asked, because it was the only thing that came into her mind. A god, she was standing there facing a god . . .

"That too." For once, he didn't look amused. He unfolded himself, gradually, standing bent under the ceiling, his hair almost tangling with the iron filigrees. His eyes held her, quiet, thoughtful; and in their depths she saw the blue of the sky, smelled the reek of copal incense rising into the heavens, and the rankness of blood pooling down the altar grooves, watering the earth, mingling with the rivers and with the lakes.

It would have been her, in the old days: her they held onto the altar, her they split open with obsidian blades, her heart they held aloft to the glory of the sun or of the rain. Her blood. He'd have drunk it all, as he'd drunk the blood of the woman – and with no more pity than he had shown her.

Something, long kept at bay, finally snapped. "How dare you – how dare you come here, how dare you work your foul magic and your blood sacrifices in full sight of the hierarch? How dare you—" She quelled the shaking of her hands, and went on, "Do you have any idea of what they do to those they catch still practising the old rites?"

"I guess it doesn't happen very often."

"We still remember the last one. They can make the dismantling last for days." She couldn't suppress a shiver, remembering the screams that had rent the Well from top to bottom, drowning even the beat of the rails.

"Well," Tezoca said lightly, "that won't happen here."

"How can you be so sure?" Hadn't he seen the god-machine, hadn't he felt the communion? Even with his blood-magic, all he had done was tear one mind, for a small time. That was pitifully slight.

His voice was light, arrogant. "The histories are right: I'm cruel, and twisted, and vicious. But I take care of my own."

"Your own?" So much like one of the old gods, to see the world in terms of ownership, and to take everything for themselves. The histories were right.

Tezoca pulled out one of the obsidian shards, stared at it for a while. "You've forgotten, haven't you? What a sacrifice truly was. You don't remember anything."

"I remember enough." Bodies tumbling down the altars, so many hearts that they rotted in the sacred vessels, so much blood that the grooves overflowed, skins, casually flayed and worn like costumes – and the old gods, laughing at them from the heavens, seeing nothing in mankind but veins and arteries, nothing but beating hearts, waiting to be gobbled whole . . .

Why had she ever thought it was a good idea to welcome him into her room? Why had she believed he'd make her life better? The days he'd bring back weren't days she could desire, not under any age of the world.

"Get out," she said, fighting not to strike him across the face. "Get out of this room now, and don't come back."

Anger leapt into Tezoca's eyes. She expected him to strike her again, or worse, to do to her what he'd done to the woman – but he did none of that. Simply stood, tall, unmoving, waiting for her fury to spend itself.

When it did, and she still hadn't said another word, Tezoca said, "Very well." And he picked up his things, one by one, and left.

She watched him go, her heart more at ease than it had been for a long, long while.

Xochipil woke up the following morning and instantly knew that something was wrong. The beat of the rails was so strong it was shaking her room, making the tech on the shelves ring against each other – the deep, resonant sound of glass against copper, of bronze against crystal – and the fundamental *wrongness* at the heart of the Well, so strong it was splitting her apart.

"Attend," a voice said, resonating within the confines of her room. The hierarch's voice, as deep and far-reaching as it had been on the previous day. "Workers of Mictlan's Well. There has been a violation of the Commonwealth. Stand on your thresholds and wait for the inspection."

A violation? Tezoca. Machine break him, what had he done? What had he done to set the Well afire in such a way?

Time to see later. Right now, what she needed to do was survive the inspection – with blood-magic still clinging to her, a stink that couldn't be washed off.

The inspection started at the bottom. Xochipil stood on her threshold for what seemed like ages and ages, feeling the rising beat in her chest, in her lame leg – tearing her apart, slowly grinding her bones to dust, turning her muscles to mush.

From the corner of her eye, she saw the procession approach: the hierarch in his robes so white they hurt the eye, the governor and the supervisors in muted turquoise all servile behind him.

He stopped by each worker, asked them a few questions, looked at them for a while, and then moved on. Ten workers left before he reached her – nine, eight . . .

He'd be a poor hierarch indeed, if he couldn't see what she'd done. But there wasn't anything she could do, other than stand straight, and hope against all hope that he wouldn't see, that he'd move on without a second glance.

And then the hierarch was standing before her – his skin gleaming in the dim light, his verdigris gaze boring into her eyes – quivering in her vision, blurred by the throbbing of the rails. "Your name?" he asked.

"Xochipil," she said. "Worker 18861 of Mictlan's Well."

He was silent for a while, looking at her as if something bothered him. Please, please . . .

"Daughter of Huexocanauhtli and Camahuac," the hierarch said, finally.

"Yes."

"Do you know why I'm here, Xochipil?" His eyes were a wide, shining green: a many-layered patina over the perfect, pristine metal of his skin – wide, compassionate, it would be so easy to tell him, to throw herself on his mercy before he discovered the truth . . .

"No," she whispered. "No."

The hierarch's gaze held her, weighed her. "Is that really the truth, Xochipil?" He put a peculiar stress on her name – lingering on it, like a lover, like a mother, caring for her, for the communion she had with the machine and everything it meant to her.

No. It wasn't the truth. Of course it wasn't. She had only to confess—

Machine break him, she wasn't going to give in so easily. "Yes," she said, and words came pouring out of her mouth almost faster than she could think them. "Every word the truth, by my will to serve, by my bond to the god-machine, in this age and the next and the next."

The hierarch's hand reached out, brushed her hair. His touch left a tingling, a slighter beat to counter the excruciating one of the rails. "I see," he said. "Thank you, Xochipil."

And then he was gone, and it was as if someone had cut tight bands of copper from Xochipil's chest. She stood, breathing in the beat of the rails, the throbbing within her, knowing she'd won, for now.

It was only after the inspection was over that it occurred to her that everything had gone far too smoothly. The taint of blood-magic wouldn't have been so easily removed; and the hierarch should have seen it.

Unless . . .

It took her half an hour to find it. By then, the beat of the rails was so strong it watered her eyes, and she could barely focus on what she was doing – could barely keep her thoughts straight enough to act.

But it was there, all right: a small, barely visible glyph inked in blood, and its twin on the other side of the threshold, forming the word for "protection". They throbbed, too, beneath her fingers – not like the rails, but like a living heart.

Tezoca, it seemed, had left her a farewell gift.

Xochipil went down, knowing that whatever had happened would be at the bottom of the Well, where the power was stronger – where whatever Tezoca had been looking for doubtless resided.

Work had resumed, and the crews had little patience for a crippled girl. Even Malli threw Xochipil a warning look as she descended the footpath. Xochipil retreated instead: going down again, on the paths that coiled around the shaft of the Well. All the while, the intensity of the beat increased, and there came a growing sense of anger, of outrage from the rails.

Down, down, past the sunspheres and the stark whiteness of steel and chrome – fewer workers now, and the fevered beat was so strong she could barely walk, could barely hold on to the thought that she had to put one foot before the other, that she had to . . .

She realized that for the past moments she'd been standing absolutely still – and started walking again.

The rails were above and below her. They had narrowed, becoming close enough to reach, with the steam-cars steadily going up and down, and Xochipil was standing alone between them, staring at the white steel of the walls. The beat was too strong – in her bones and in her heart, growing until it was all she could do not to fall to her knees.

She couldn't go further down – not to the platform where the hierarch had stood, not to the very bottom and whatever had gone wrong.

Turn back, she had to – it was folly to come here, folly to seek Tezoca. Everything was fiery pain, a pain she couldn't bear, not for this long . . .

Machine break her, she wasn't made of such pliable stuff.

She reached out and touched the rails.

Pain unfolded a thousandfold within her: the beat coursed up her arm, squeezed around her heart, spread in her chest like a starburst of knives – and her hand was welded to the rails, she couldn't take it away—

She was falling, down, down, into a chasm that had no end, the earth opening itself to receive her, and the beat pounding in every fibre of her body was the beat of a huge, glistening heart, buried under the soil of the desert – a heart that was the only thing of flesh amidst the entombed human bones.

Over and over it beat within her, booming, overflowing in her ears, the liquid sound of blood in an organ so vast she could barely apprehend it – over and over . . .

At last, at long last, it ended, and she fell to her knees, gasping, with the beat still coursing in her – muted now, the pain almost bearable, *almost*, like rubbed salt instead of knives . . .

But the beat was a voice now, and it whispered, over and over, *brother, brother* . . .

A god. There was a god down there, buried beneath Mictlan's Well. The power Tezoca had been seeking, the power the god-machine was finally ferrying back to itself – a god's heart, a god's magic, setting the earth atremble, energizing the rails.

That was . . . impossible.

Why would it be? Was it such a great leap of imagination, once you accepted that gods were as hard to kill as the machine?

Brother, whispered the rails – and they were angry, so angry because he was dead, or going to die – it wasn't clear, just a jumble of impressions, a hodgepodge of words she couldn't untangle. And, in the distance, steadily rising, was the voice of the machine, seeking to subsume the god in its midst – a persistent ache, a darkness slowly rising to smother everything.

Dare she—?

There was no other choice.

Xochipil reached out and touched the rails again.

The pain was the same, arcing straight to her heart, the beat that was so much stronger than her. Through gritted teeth she fought to get the words out, to ask her question . . .

Where is he?

Where is Tezoca?

Brother, whispered the rails.

Where . . . is . . . he?

The machine's voice was rising, blindly questing for whoever had the audacity to touch the rails, to meddle in the link it was establishing between Mictlan's Well and itself . . .

She had to let go; but if she did so, she wouldn't know what had happened. Still she kept her hands on the rails, asking them over and over about Tezoca.

"You won't find him there," a voice said, far behind her.

Startled, Xochipil withdrew her hands from the rails – and the pressure in her body and in her mind diminished, faded to a dull, throbbing ache.

Behind her, on the floor of steel and chrome, stood a woman. Her hair was the black of congealed blood, her skin the colour of dulled copper and her face was achingly familiar.

"What do you mean?" Xochipil asked.

"You shouldn't be here," the woman said, shaking her head.

Xochipil suddenly realized that this was the woman Tezoca had used to cast his blood-magic, and who now stood beside the rails as if they were a minor discomfort. "What would you know?" she asked.

The woman smiled, and raised her hands. Thin red lines ran along the tips of her fingers; and there were scabs on her arms, too.

Blood-magic. Blood-offerings. But the age of gods was past, the Change had come upon them – there was no longer need . . .

"He forced this on you," Xochipil whispered – move, move, they had to move, for the hierarch would soon come, attracted by her touch on the rails . . . "He bewitched you, tricked you into making your offerings . . ."

The woman smiled again. "I make my own choices. And so should you." Then, without preamble, "They cast his broken body into the desert, to be devoured by carrion birds and scavengers."

"Tezoca?" Xochipil asked, though she knew the answer. "Then he failed."

The woman said nothing, but the dullness in her eyes was answer enough. "The god-machine is strong," she whispered, raising her bloodied hands as if to ward off a blow. "Very strong."

There was movement, at the edge of Xochipil's field of vision – workers, and a flash of white robes from downwards – and the voice of the hierarch echoing all around them: "Attend. There has been a violation of the Commonwealth—"

The compulsion was overwhelming; as before, there was nothing Xochipil could do to resist, she could do nothing but to abase herself and beg the forgiveness of the machine for interfering . . .

Hands, holding her – tracing something on the nape of her neck, warm and pulsing – a push in her back, sending her sprawling, out of the path of the advancing hierarch. "Run!"

And Xochipil was up, before she could think, slipping away from them – up, up, with barely any memory of being lame – away from the pressure of the rails and the voice of the hierarch, the instinct for survival stronger than anything.

It was only when she reached the twentieth floor that she stopped, the pain and weariness she'd kept at bay slamming into her, seeing, again and again, the face of the woman, transfigured as she stood awaiting the hierarch; feeling, again and again, the touch of the blood-magic on her, sharpening her mind around the single thought of saving herself.

"Why?" she whispered, but the woman, after all, had already answered her.

I make my own choices. And so should you.

Outside, the sun shone bright and unbearable, its warm light bleaching the desert sands, shimmering over the throbbing rails. Xochipil walked, her lame leg trailing behind her, the blistering heat shrivelling her skin, her lips, her eyes.

She'd had no choice but to leave the Well, for the alarm would be raised by now; and this time the hierarch would know her, take her as his own, break her into her smallest parts and remould her into the service of the machine . . .

Rocks tumbled under her feet. It was only after a while that she realized she was looking at the sky: for the sound of beating wings, the gathering of vultures overhead.

They cast his broken body into the desert, to be devoured by carrion birds and scavengers.

Tezoca . . .

She followed the rails, feeling the distant rumble in her body, weak and watered down – the beat of the god, the beat of the machine, all one and the same for this age of the world, and the next, and the next.

After a while, there was nothing but the merciless sun, nothing but the light swathing the rocks and the boulders, and the bronze of the rails. The flask of water by her side was heavy, but she mustn't drink, mustn't empty it so soon . . .

Let the sun remain silent, the machine whispered, its voice coursing along the rails, mingling with the voice of the buried god, rising to silence it forever. *Let the altars be made of pristine steel, let the blood and the breath remain in our bodies . . .*

Let the sun remain silent . . .

After a few hours – an afternoon – an eternity – she saw in the sky the first vultures, circling over her.

"Not dead," she whispered, stumbling on. "Not dead."

But really, what was the point?

"Not . . . dead . . ."

When the vultures became a crowd, she walked on, towards the shrieking column of birds, away from the familiar beat of the rails – away from the god-machine and the hierarch and the heart buried in the soil, towards a mound at the base of a hill, a tangle of blood and broken limbs, wrapped in a torn cloak.

She threw rocks at the birds, and screamed until her voice was hoarse. They hopped away, watching her warily – waiting for her, too, to tumble and fall, to become carrion.

Then, in silence, she knelt by Tezoca's side.

The skin of his face was torn and bloodied, the limbs slack under her touch. Broken bones shifted within the mass of glistening flesh.

She reached out to take the voice of the heart – and stopped herself inches from the bloody mass of the wrist. That would have been pointless. He was dead, clearly dead, his promises and goals meaningless.

Machine break you, she'd wished on Tezoca; and the machine had, indeed, broken him so thoroughly that nothing was left.

A hiss startled her. One of the birds, coming back? But no, it came from the body – a last exhalation of breath from shattered lungs, a last oozing from some mangled organ.

Tezoca's eyes were open, and staring straight at her.

The shock of that sight travelled up her arm, devolved into the frantic beat of her heart.

"You're dead," she whispered, and remembered what he had told her, back in the Well.

Some things are hard to kill.

Again, the same hiss: words, whispered through crushed lips. Asking for her help?

"I wasn't able to help myself," she said bitterly. She hadn't even been able to help the woman. Nevertheless, she tipped the last of the water within her flask – a few sips, nothing more – past his wasted lips.

His throat contracted, swallowing the water; then he convulsed, and the water came rushing back out in a spurt that splattered on the rocks.

The hiss again, and his eyes, boring into hers – not angry, not amused, but pleading.

She knew, of course, the only thing which would sustain him. The mere thought was revolting.

But here they were, both of them, both broken and dying in the desert; and he had given her his protection, in the cruel, desultory way of the old gods – but it was still more than the god-machine had ever given her.

"All right," Xochipil said. She reached out and foraged in the cloak, spreading out the obsidian shards as she found them. They glimmered in the sunlight, with the remembrance of a dead age.

She picked what looked like the sharpest one, and held it for a while in her hand. "It's not because I worship you," she said. His eyes watched her, unblinking, unwavering. "It's not because I fear your anger, or that the sun will tumble from the sky if you're not properly honoured. But you watched out for me, and I'd be sorry to see you go."

Then, as smoothly, as effortlessly as if she'd done it all her life, she brought the edge of the obsidian against her wrist, and before she could think, sliced through her veins. Blood spurted up in an obscene fountain – much, much faster than she'd expected, a stream of red falling like rain upon the dried earth.

Pain spread, too – lines of fire radiating from the slit, pulsing in her arm like a red-hot axle. Her hand wouldn't stop opening and closing, her fingers clenching like claws; she couldn't control its movements. She had to use her other hand to guide the wound over Tezoca's mouth, and watched him swallow and not spit anything out his wasted throat muscles greedily contracting.

Something was flowing, a shadow across the desert floor, an invisible wind. The air shivered as if in a storm, and dust rose, billowing like yellow sheets unfolding. Grains of dust skittered across the obsidian shards, making a noise like nails on copper, skittering across the body of Tezoca until his skin seemed to shift in the wind, until the colour of the desert had sunk into his bones and covered the red sheen of his muscles.

His hands reached up, iron coils, and drew Xochipil's slit wrist against his mouth. His lips closed around the wound, hungrily sucking at the flowing blood like a child at his mother's breast.

And he didn't stop. The wound didn't close, and still he drank, making quiet, sickening suckling sounds. Pain knifed her with each sip he took – repeated stabs with obsidian blades.

Xochipil's thoughts were scattering, growing hazier and hazier – how much like an old god, to take everything that was given; how naive had she been, to slit her wrist and expect it to heal, to feed a god and hope he would stop . . .

The shadows were growing, pooling under the obsidian shards – and then, in a flash of dazzling light, the shards leapt towards each other and vanished.

"Enough," Tezoca said, his voice echoing like the anger of the storm. "Enough!" He pushed her away – sent her stumbling, fighting to hold herself upright, her fingers fumbling to close the wound in her wrist.

The ground would not stop shaking under her. Through hazy eyes she saw her blood spattered among the rocks, encircling the place where Tezoca now stood.

He was tall, and his face was streaked with black and yellow; and the stars shone in the curls of his hair; and his eyes glimmered like water in underground caves. In his hand, something shone: an obsidian mirror, in which she could still guess at the faint line of cracks. It reflected nothing but smoke; but even from where she was she could feel its heat, and the power within, the beat as strong as that of the rails.

And he was walking – flowing across the sand, reaching out to her – and in a single gesture pinching shut the wound in her wrist. Xochipil stood, shaking, trying to hold herself up, falling to one knee, and then face down on the ground, until oblivion swallowed her whole.

She dreamt that he carried her in his arms, under the shelter of a large rock, and carefully laid her on the ground like a sick child. She dreamt that he was sitting by her side, staring at the skies, weeping tears of blood for all the old gods who had fallen – for his brother Quetzalcoatl, who had once been his friend, who had once been his enemy, and who was now subsumed into the machine, in this age and the next and the next.

She dreamt that he gathered rocks and scraggly bushes and turned his smoke-filled mirror towards them – that they burst into flickering, warm flames – and that he stood outlined by the fire, watching her sleep.

Now you understand about sacrifices, he whispered.

And she didn't, and he must have seen something of that, because he said, his voice booming like the wrath of the heavens, *Not out of fear or of greed or because the sun will tumble from the sky, but because you cared.*

I was sorry for you, Xochipil thought, thrashing, trying to reach him through a pane of glass – but he wouldn't answer.

When she woke up in the dim light of the rising sun, she was alone, and the air still smelled like ashes.

He had left her his wide-brimmed hat, and some food; and had refilled her water-flask. Her hands throbbed: he had traced the glyphs for "safe journey" and "water" on their backs – all the favour he would grant her, all the thanks he would ever condescend to give.

Rising, she walked away from the ashes. In the distance was the familiar line of the rails, pulsing on the rhythm of the god-machine; and, still further away, growing fainter and fainter, a figure walking, with the stars in his hair and the glimmer of obsidian in his hands.

She could still hear his voice in her mind, lightly amused.

All gods are cruel, Xochipil. What else did you expect?

He would make his way to the capital, as aloof and as lonely as he had always been, bearing alone the burden of his struggle against the machine, never allowing his devotees to offer more than a little aid, a transitory comfort. And in the end, he would stand in the huge palace of bronze and copper: alone against the machine and its endless might, so pitifully small and defenceless, as easily crushed and broken as his obsidian mirror.

Pity closed like a fist around her heart. "Please be safe," Xochipil whispered to the silent desert. "Please come back. Please."

And her words, rising under a sky as red as blood, had the intensity of a prayer.

The Effluent Engine

N. K. Jemisin

New Orleans stank to the heavens. This was either the water, which did not have the decency to confine itself to the river but instead puddled along every street; or the streets themselves, which seemed to have been cobbled with bricks of fired excrement. Or it may have come from the people who jostled and trotted along the narrow avenues, working and lounging and cursing and shouting and sweating, emitting a massed reek of unwashed resentment and perhaps a bit of hangover. As Jessaline strolled beneath the colonnaded balconies of Royal Street, she fought the urge to give up, put the whole fumid pile to her back and catch the next dirigible out of town.

Then someone jostled her. "Pardon me, miss," said a voice at her elbow, and Jessaline was forced to stop, because the earnest-looking young man who stood there was white. He smiled, which did not surprise her, and doffed his hat, which did.

"Monsieur," Jessaline replied, in what she hoped was the correct mix of reserve and deference.

"A fine day, is it not?" The man's grin widened, so sincere that Jessaline could not help a small smile in response. "I must admit, though, I have yet to adjust to this abysmal heat. How are you handling it?"

"Quite well, monsieur," she replied, thinking, *what is it that you want from me?* "I am acclimated to it."

"Ah, yes, certainly. A fine negress like yourself would naturally deal better with such things. I am afraid my own ancestors derive from chillier climes, and we adapt poorly." He paused abruptly, a stricken look crossing his face. He was the florid kind, red-haired and freckled with skin so pale that it revealed his every thought

– in point of which he paled further. "Oh dear! My sister warned me about this. You aren't Creole, are you? I understand they take it as an insult to be called, er . . . by certain terms."

With some effort Jessaline managed not to snap, *do I look like one of them?* But people on the street were beginning to stare, so instead she said, "No, monsieur. And it's clear to me you aren't from these parts, or you would never ask such a thing."

"Ah – yes." The man looked sheepish. "You have caught me out, miss; I'm from New York. Is it so obvious?"

Jessaline smiled carefully. "Only in your politeness, monsieur." She reached up to adjust her hat, lifting it for a moment as a badly needed cooling breeze wafted past.

"Are you perhaps—" The man paused, staring at her head. "My word! You've naught but a scrim of hair!"

"I have sufficient to keep myself from drafts on cold days," she replied, and as she'd hoped, he laughed.

"You're a most charming ne— woman, my dear, and I feel honored to make your acquaintance." He stepped back and bowed, full and proper. "My name is Raymond Forstall."

"Jessaline Dumonde," she said, offering her lace-gloved hand, though she had no expectation that he would take it. To her surprise he did, bowing again over it.

"My apologies for gawking. I simply don't meet many of the colored on a typical day, and I must say—" he hesitated, darted a look about, and at least had the grace to drop his voice. "You're remarkably lovely, even with no hair."

In spite of herself, Jessaline laughed. "Thank you, monsieur." After an appropriate and slightly awkward pause, she inclined her head. "Well, then; good day to you."

"Good day indeed," he said, in a tone of such pleasure that Jessaline hoped no one had heard it, for his sake. The folk of this town were particular about matters of propriety, as was any society which relied so firmly upon class differences. While there were many ways in which a white gentleman could appropriately express his admiration for a woman of color – the existence of the *gens de couleur libre* was testimony to that – all of those ways were simply Not Done in public.

But Forstall donned his hat, and Jessaline inclined her head in return before heading away. Another convenient breeze gusted by, and she took advantage of it to adjust her hat once more, in the process sliding her stiletto back into its hiding place amid the silk flowers.

This was the dance of things, the *cric-crac* as the storytellers said in Jessaline's land. Everyone needed something from someone. Glorious France needed money, to recover from the unlamented Napoleon's endless wars. Upstart Haiti had money from the sweet gold of its sugar-cane fields, but needed guns – for all the world, it seemed, wanted the newborn country strangled in its crib. The United States had guns but craved sugar, as its fortunes were dependent upon the acquisition thereof. It alone was willing to treat with Haiti, though Haiti was the stuff of American nightmare: a nation of black slaves who had killed off their white masters. Yet Haitian sugar was no less sweet for its coating of blood, and so everyone got what they wanted, trading round and round, a graceful waltz – only occasionally deteriorating into a knife-fight.

It had been simplicity itself for Jessaline to slip into New Orleans. Dirigible travel in the Caribbean was inexpensive, and so many travelers regularly moved between the island nations and the great American port city that hardly any deception had been necessary. She was indentured, she told the captain, and he had waved her aboard without so much as a glance at her papers (which were false anyhow). She was a wealthy white man's mistress, she told the other passengers, and between her fine clothes, regal carriage and beauty – despite her skin being purest sable in color – they believed her and were alternately awed and offended. She was a slave, she told the dockmaster on the levee; a trusted one, lettered and loyal, promised freedom should she continue to serve to her fullest. He had smirked at this, as if the notion of anyone freeing such an obviously valuable slave was ludicrous. Yet he, too, had let her pass unchallenged, without even charging her the disembarkation fee.

It had then taken two full months for Jessaline to make inquiries and sufficient contacts to arrange a meeting with the esteemed Monsieur Norbert Rillieux. The Creoles of New Orleans were a closed and prickly bunch, most likely because they had to be; only by the rigid maintenance of caste and privilege could they hope to retain freedom in a land which loved to throw anyone darker than tan into chains. Thus more than a few of them had refused to speak to Jessaline on sight. Yet there were many who had not forgotten that there but for the grace of God went their own fortune, so from these she had been able to glean crucial information and finally an introduction by letter. As she had mentioned the right names and observed the right etiquette, Norbert Rillieux had at last invited her to afternoon tea.

That day had come, and . . .

And Rillieux, Jessaline was finally forced to concede, was an idiot.

"Monsieur," she said again, after drawing a breath to calm herself, "as I explained in my letter, I have no interest in sugar-cane processing. It is true that your contributions to this field have been much appreciated by the interests I represent; your improved refining methods have saved money as well as lives, which could both be reinvested in other places. What we require assistance with is a wholly different matter, albeit related."

"Oh," said Rillieux, blinking. He was a savagely thin-lipped man, with a hard stare that might have been compelling on a man who knew how to use it. Rillieux did not. "Your pardon, mademoiselle. But, er, who did you say you represented, again?"

"I did not say, monsieur. And if you will forgive me, I would prefer not to say for the time being." She fixed him with her own hard stare. "You will understand, I hope, that not all parties can be trusted when matters scientific turn to matters commercial."

At that, Rillieux's expression turned shrewd at last; he understood just fine. The year before, Jessaline's superiors had informed her, the plan Rillieux had proposed to the city – an ingenious means of draining its endless pestilent swamps, for the health and betterment of all – had been turned down. Six months later, a coalition of city engineers had submitted virtually the same plan and been heaped with praise and funds to bring it about. The men of the coalition were white, of course. Jessaline marveled that Rillieux even bothered being upset about it.

"I see," Rillieux said. "Then, please forgive me, but I do not know what it is you want."

Jessaline stood and went to her brocade bag, which sat on a side table across the Rillieux house's elegantly apportioned salon. In it was a small, rubber-stopped, peculiarly shaped jar of the sort utilized by chemists, complete with engraved markings on its surface to indicate measurements of the liquid within. At the bottom of this jar swirled a scrim of dark brown, foul-looking paste and liquid. Jessaline brought it over to Rillieux and offered the jar to his nose, waiting until he nodded before she unstoppered it.

At the scent which wafted out, he stumbled back, gasping, his eyes all a-water. "By all that's holy! Woman, what is that putrescence?"

"That, Monsieur Rillieux, is effluent," Jessaline said, neatly stoppering the flask. "Waste, in other words, of a very particular kind. Do you drink rum?" She knew the answer already. On one side of the parlor was another beautifully made side table holding an impressive array of bottles.

"Of course." Rillieux was still rubbing his eyes and looking affronted. "I'm fond of a glass or two on hot afternoons; it opens the pores, or so I'm told. But what does that—"

"Producing rum is a simple process with a messy result: this effluent, namely, and the gas it emits, which, until lately, had been regarded as simply the unavoidable price to be paid for your pleasant afternoons. As a result, whole swathes of countryside are now afflicted with this smell. Not only is the stench offensive to men and beasts, we have also found it to be as powerful as any tincture or laudanum; over time it causes anything exposed to it to suffocate and die. Yet there are scientific papers coming from Europe which laud this gas's potential as a fuel source. Captured properly, purified and burned, it can power turbines, cook food and more." Jessaline turned and set the flask on Rillieux's beverage stand, deliberately close to the square bottle of dark rum she had seen there. "We wish you to develop a process by which the usable gas – methane – may be extracted from the miasma you just smelled."

Rillieux stared at her for a moment, then at the flask. She could tell that he was intrigued, which meant that half her mission had been achieved already. Her superiors had spent a profligate amount of money requisitioning a set of those flasks from the German chemist who'd recently invented them, precisely with an eye towards impressing men like Rillieux, who looked down upon any science that did not show European roots.

Yet as Rillieux gazed at the flask, Jessaline was dismayed to see a look of consternation, then irritation, cross his face.

"I am an engineer, mademoiselle," he said at last, "not a chemist."

"We have already worked out the chemical means by which it might be done," Jessaline said quickly, her belly clenching in tension. "We would be happy to share that with you—"

"And then what?" He scowled at her. "Who will put the patent on this process, hmm? And who will profit?" He turned away, beginning to pace, and Jessaline could see to her horror that he was working up a good head of steam. "You have a comely face, Mademoiselle Dumonde, and it does not escape me that dusky women such as yourself once seduced my forefathers into the most base acts, for which those men atoned by at least raising their half-breed children honorably. If I were a white man hoping to once more profit from the labor of an honest Creole like myself – one already proven gullible – I would send a woman like you to do the tempting. To them, all of us are alike, even though I have the purest of French blood in my veins, and you might as well have come straight from the jungles of Africa!"

He rounded on her at this, very nearly shouting, and if Jessaline had been one of the pampered, cowed women of this land, she might have stepped back in fear of unpleasantness. As it was, she did take a step – but to the side, closer to her brocade bag, within which was tucked a neat little derringer whose handle she could see from where she stood. Her mission had been to use Rillieux, not kill him, but she had no qualms about giving a man a flesh wound to remind him of the value of chivalry.

Before matters could come to a head, however, the parlor door opened, making both Jessaline and Norbert Rillieux jump. The young woman who came in was clearly some kin of Rillieux; she had the same ocherine skin and loose-curled hair, the latter tucked into a graceful split chignon atop her head. Her eyes were softer, however, though that might have been an effect of the wire-rimmed spectacles perched on her nose. She wore a simple gray dress, which had the unfortunate effect of emphasizing her natural pallor, and making her look rather plain.

"Your pardon, brother," she said, confirming Jessaline's guess. "I thought perhaps you and your guest might like refreshment?"

In her hands was a silver tray of crisp square beignets dusted in sugar, sliced merliton with what looked like some sort of remoulade sauce and tiny wedges of pecan penuche.

At the sight of this girl, Norbert blanched and looked properly abashed. "Ah – er, yes, you're right, thank you. Ah . . ." He glanced at Jessaline, his earlier irritation clearly warring with the ingrained desire to be a good host; manners won, and he quickly composed himself. "Forgive me. Will you take refreshment, before you leave?" The last part of that sentence came out harder than the rest. Jessaline got the message.

"Thank you, yes," she said, immediately moving to assist the young woman. As she moved her brocade bag, she noticed the young woman's eyes, which were locked on the bag with a hint of alarm. Jessaline was struck at once with unease – had she noticed the derringer handle? Impossible to tell, since the young woman made no outcry of alarm, but that could have been just caution on her part. That one meeting of eyes triggered an instant, instinctual assessment on Jessaline's part; *this* Rillieux, at least, was nowhere near as myopic or bombastic as her brother.

Indeed, as the young woman lifted her gaze after setting down the tray, Jessaline thought she saw a hint of challenge lurking behind those little round glasses, and above that perfectly pleasant smile.

"Brother," said the young woman, "won't you introduce me? It's so rare for you to have lady guests."

Norbert Rillieux went from blanching to blushing, and for an instant Jessaline feared he would progress all the way to bluster. Fortunately he mastered the urge and said, a bit stiffly, "Mademoiselle Jessaline Dumonde, may I present to you my younger sister, Eugenie?"

Jessaline bobbed a curtsy, which Mademoiselle Rillieux returned. "I'm pleased to meet you," Jessaline said, meaning it, *because I might have enjoyed shooting your brother to an unseemly degree, otherwise.*

It seemed Mademoiselle Rillieux's thoughts ran in the same direction, because she smiled at Jessaline and said, "I hope my brother hasn't been treating you to a display of his famous temper, Mademoiselle Dumonde. He deals better with his gadgets and vacuum tubes than with people, I'm afraid."

Rillieux did bluster at this. "Eugenie, that's hardly—"

"Not at all," Jessaline interjected smoothly. "We were discussing the finer points of chemistry, and your brother, being such a learned man, just made his point rather emphatically."

"Chemistry? Why, I adore chemistry!" At this, Mademoiselle Rillieux immediately brightened, speaking faster and breathlessly. "What matter, if I may ask? Please, may I sit in?"

In that instant, Jessaline was struck by how lovely her eyes were, despite their uncertain coloring of browny-green. She had never preferred the looks of half-white folk, having grown up in a land where, thanks to the Revolution, darkness of skin was a point of pride. But as Mademoiselle Rillieux spoke of chemistry, something in her manner made her peculiar eyes sparkle, and Jessaline was forced to reassess her initial estimate of the girl's looks. She was handsome, perhaps, rather than plain.

"Eugenie is the only other member of my family to share my interest in the sciences," Rillieux said, pride warming his voice. "She could not study in Paris as I did; the schools there do not admit women. Still, I made certain to send her all of my books as I finished with them, and she critiques all my prototypes. It's probably for the best that they wouldn't admit her; I daresay she could give my old masters at the *École Centrale* a run for their money!"

Jessaline blinked in surprise at this. Then it came to her; she had lost Rillieux's trust already. But, perhaps . . .

Turning to the beverage stand, she picked up the flask of effluent. "I'm afraid I won't be able to stay, Mademoiselle Rillieux – but before I go, perhaps you could give me your opinion of this?" She offered the flask.

Norbert Rillieux, guessing her intent, scowled. But Eugenie took the flask before he could muster a protest, unstoppering it deftly and wafting the fumes toward her face rather than sniffing outright. "Faugh," she said, grimacing. "Definitely hydrogen sulfide, and probably a number of other gases too, if this is the product of some form of decay." She stoppered the flask and examined the sludge in its bottom with a critical eye. "Interesting – I thought it was dirt, but this seems to be some more uniform substance. Something *made* this? What process could generate something so noxious?"

"Rum distillation," Jessaline said, stifling the urge to smile when Eugenie looked scandalized.

"No wonder," Eugenie said darkly, "given what the end product does to men's souls." She handed the flask back to Jessaline. "What of it?"

So Jessaline was obliged to explain again. As she did, a curious thing happened; Eugenie's eyes grew a bit glazed. She nodded, "mmm-hmming" now and again. "And as I mentioned to your brother," Jessaline concluded, "we have already worked out the formula—"

"The formula is child's play," Eugenie said, flicking her fingers absently. "And the extraction would be simple enough, if methane weren't dangerously flammable. Explosive even, under certain conditions . . . which most attempts at extraction would inevitably create. Obviously any mechanical method would need to concern itself primarily with *stabilizing* the end products, not merely separating them. Freezing, perhaps, or—" She brightened. "Brother, perhaps we could try a refinement of the vacuum-distillation process you developed for—"

"Yes, yes," said Norbert, who had spent the past ten minutes looking from Jessaline to Eugenie and back in visibly increasing consternation. "I'll consider it. In the meantime, Mademoiselle Dumonde was actually leaving; I'm afraid we delay her." He glared at Jessaline as Eugenie made a moue of dismay.

"Quite right," said Jessaline, smiling graciously at him. She put away the flask and tucked the bag over her arm, retrieving her hat from the back of the chair. She could afford to be gracious now, even though Norbert Rillieux had proven intractable. Better indeed to leave, and pursue the matter from an entirely different angle.

And, as Norbert escorted her to the parlor door with a hand rather too firm upon her elbow, Jessaline glanced back and smiled at Eugenie, who returned the smile with charming ruefulness and a shy little wave.

Not just handsome, pretty, Jessaline decided at last. And that meant this new angle would be *most enjoyable* to pursue.

There were, however, complications.

Jessaline, pleased that she had succeeded in making contact with *a* Rillieux, if not the one she'd come for, treated herself to

an evening out about the Vieux Carré. It was not the done thing
for a lady of gentle breeding – a persona she was emulating – to
stop in at any of the rollicking music halls she could hear down
side streets, though she was intrigued. She could, however, sit in
on one of the new-fangled vaudevilles at the Playhouse, which
she quite enjoyed though it was difficult to see the stage well from
the rear balcony. Then, as nightfall finally brought a breath of
cool relief from the day's sweltering humidity, she returned to her
room at the inn.

From time spent on the harder streets of Port-au-Prince, it
was Jessaline's longtime habit to stand to one side of a door while
she unlocked it, so that her shadow under the door would not
alert anyone inside. This proved wise, as pushing open the door
she found herself facing a startled male figure, which froze in
silhouette before the room's picture window, near her traveling-
chest. They stared at one another for a breath, and then Jessaline's
wits returned; at once she dropped to one knee and in a single
smooth sweep of her hand, brushed up her booted leg to palm a
throwing-knife.

In the same instant the figure bolted, darting toward the open
balcony window. Jessaline hissed out a curse in her own Kreyòl
tongue, running into the room as he lunged through the window
with an acrobat's nimbleness, rolling to his feet and fetching
up against the elaborately ironworked railing. Fearing to lose
him, Jessaline flung the knife from within the room as she ran,
praying it would strike, and heard the thunk as it struck flesh.
The figure on her balcony stumbled, crying out – but she could
not have hit a vital area, for he grasped the railing and pulled
himself over it, dropping the short distance to the ground and
out of sight.

Jessaline scrambled through the window as best she could,
hampered by her bustle and skirts. Just as she reached the railing,
the figure finished picking himself up from the ground and turned
to run. Jessaline got one good look at him in the moonlight, as he
turned back to see if she pursued: a pinch-faced youth, clearly
pale beneath the bootblack he'd smeared on his face and straw-
colored hair to help himself hide in the dark. Then he was gone,
running into the night, though he ran oddly and kept one of his
hands clapped to his right buttock.

Furious, Jessaline pounded the railing, though she knew better than to make an outcry. No one in this town would care that some black woman had been robbed, and the constable would as likely arrest her for disturbing the peace.

Going back into her room, she lit the lanterns and surveyed the damage. At once a chill passed down her spine. The chest held a number of valuables that any sensible thief would've taken: fine dresses; a cameo pendant with a face of carved obsidian; the brass gyroscope that an old lover, a dirigible-navigator, had given her; a pearl-beaded purse containing twenty dollars. These, however, had all been shoved rudely aside, and to Jessaline's horror, the chest's false bottom had been lifted, revealing the compartment underneath. There was nothing here but a bundle of clothing and a larger pouch, containing a far more substantial sum – but that had not been taken, either.

But Jessaline knew what *would* have been in there, if she had not taken them with her to see Rillieux: the scrolls which held the chemical formula for the methane extraction process, and the rudimentary designs for the mechanism to do so – the best her government's scientists had been able to cobble together. These were even now at the bottom of her brocade bag.

The bootblack-boy had been no thief. Someone in this foul city knew who and what she was, and sought to thwart her mission.

Carefully, Jessaline replaced everything in the trunk, including the false bottom and money. She went downstairs and paid her bill, then hired a porter to carry her trunk to an inn two blocks over, where she rented a room without windows. She slept lightly that night, waking with every creak and thump of the place, and took comfort only from the solid security of the stiletto in her hand.

The lovely thing about a town full of slaves, vagabonds, beggars and blackguards was that it was blessedly easy to send a message in secret.

Having waited a few days so as to let Norbert Rillieux's anger cool – just in case – Jessaline then hired a child who was one of the innkeeper's slaves. She purchased fresh fruit at the market and offered the child an apple to memorize her message. When he repeated it back to her word for word, she showed him a bunch of big blue-black grapes, and his eyes went wide. "Get word to Mademoiselle Eugenie without her brother knowing, and these are yours," she said. "You'll have to make sure to spit the seeds in the fire, though, or Master will know you've had a treat."

The boy grinned, and Jessaline saw that the warning had not been necessary. "Just you hold onto those, Miss Jessaline," he said back, pointing with his chin at the grapes. "I'll have 'em in a minute or three." And indeed, within an hour's time he returned, carrying a small folded square of cloth. "Miss Eugenie agrees to meet," he said, "and sends this as a surety of her good faith." He pronounced this last carefully, perfectly emulating the Creole woman's tone.

Pleased, Jessaline took the cloth and unfolded it to find a handkerchief of fine imported French linen, embroidered in one corner with a tiny perfect "R". She held it to her nose and smelled a perfume like magnolia blossoms; the same scent had been about Eugenie the other day. She could not help smiling at the memory. The boy grinned too, and ate a handful of the grapes at once, pocketing the seeds with a wink.

"Gonna plant these near the city dump," he said. "Maybe I'll bring you wine one day!" And he ran off.

So Jessaline found herself on another bright, sweltering day at the convent of the Ursulines, where two gentlewomen might walk and exchange thoughts in peace without being seen or interrupted by curious others.

"I have to admit," said Eugenie, smiling sidelong at Jessaline as they strolled amid the nuns' garden, "I was of two minds about whether to meet you."

"I suppose your brother must've given you an earful after I left."

"You might say so," Eugenie said, in a dry tone that made Jessaline laugh. (One of the old nuns glowered at them over a bed of herbs. Jessaline covered her mouth and waved apology.) "But that wasn't what gave me pause. My brother has his ways, Mademoiselle Jessaline, and I do not always agree with him. He's fond of forming opinions without full information, then proceeding as if they are proven fact." She shrugged. "I, on the other hand, prefer to seek as much information as I can. I have made enquiries about you, you see."

"Oh? And what did you find?"

"That you do not exist, as far as anyone in this town knows." She spoke lightly, Jessaline noticed, but there was an edge to her words, too. Unease, perhaps. "You aren't one of us, that much anyone can see; but you aren't a freedwoman either, though the people at your old inn and the market seemed to think so."

At this, Jessaline blinked in surprise and unease of her own. She had not thought the girl would dig *that* deeply. "What makes you say that?"

"For one, that pistol in your bag."

Jessaline froze for a pace before remembering to keep walking. "A lady alone in a strange, rough city would be wise to look to her own protection, don't you think?"

"True," said Eugenie, "but I checked at the courthouse too, and there are no records of a woman meeting your description having bought her way free anytime in the past thirty years, and I doubt you're far past that age. For another, you hide it well, but your French has an odd sort of lilt; not at all like that of folk hereabouts. And for thirdly – this is a small town at heart, Mademoiselle Dumonde, despite its size. Every time some fortunate soul buys free, as they say, it's the talk of the town. To put it bluntly, there's no gossip about you, and there should have been."

They had reached a massive old willow tree which partially overhung the garden path. There was no way around it; the tree's draping branches had made a proper curtain of things, nearly obscuring from sight the area about the trunk.

The sensible thing to do would have been to turn around and walk back the way they'd come. But as Jessaline turned to meet Eugenie's eyes, she suffered another of those curious epiphanies. Eugenie was smiling, sweet, but despite this there was a hard look in her eyes, which reminded Jessaline fleetingly of Norbert. It was clear that she meant to have the truth from Jessaline, or Jessaline's efforts to employ her would get short shrift.

So on impulse Jessaline grabbed Eugenie's hand and pulled her into the willow-fall. Eugenie yelped in surprise, then giggled as they came through into the space beyond, green-shrouded and encircling, like a hurricane of leaves.

"What on earth—? Mademoiselle Dumonde—"

"It isn't Dumonde," Jessaline said, dropping her voice to a near-whisper. "My name is Jessaline Cleré. That is the name of the family that raised me, at least, but I should have had a different name, after the man who was my true father. His name was L'Overture. Do you know it?"

At that, Eugenie drew a sharp breath. "Toussaint the Rebel?" she asked. "The man who led the revolution in Haiti? *That* was your father?"

"So my mother says, though she was only his mistress; I am natural-born. But I do not begrudge her, because her status spared me. When the French betrayed Toussaint, they took him and his wife and legitimate children and carried them across the sea to be tortured to death."

Eugenie put her hands to her mouth at this, which Jessaline had to admit was a bit much for a gently raised woman to bear. Yet it was the truth, for Jessaline felt uncomfortable dissembling with Eugenie, for reasons she could not quite name.

"I see," Eugenie said at last, recovering. "Then – these interests you represent. You are with the Haitians."

"I am. If you build a methane extraction mechanism for us, mademoiselle, you will have helped a nation of free folk *stay* free, for I swear that France is hell-bent upon re-enslaving us all. They would have done it already, if one of our number had not thought to use our torment to our advantage."

Eugenie nodded slowly. "The sugar cane," she said. "The papers say your people use the steam and gases from the distilleries to make hot-air balloons and blimps."

"Which helped us bomb the French ships most effectively during the Revolution, and also secured our position as the foremost manufacturers of dirigibles in the Americas," Jessaline said, with a bit of pride. "We were saved by a mad idea and a contraption that should have killed its first user. So we value cleverness now, mademoiselle, which is why I came here in search of your brother."

"Then . . ." Eugenie frowned. "The methane. It is to power your dirigibles?"

"Partly. The French have begun using dirigibles too, you see. Our only hope is to enhance the maneuverability and speed of our craft, which can be done with gas-powered engines. We have also crafted powerful artillery which use this engine design, whose range and accuracy is unsurpassed. The prototypes work magnificently – but the price of the oil and coal we must currently use to power them is too dear. We would bankrupt ourselves buying it from the very nations that hope to destroy us. The rum effluent is our only abundant, inexpensive resource . . . . our only hope."

But Eugenie had begun to shake her head, looking taken aback. "Artillery? *Guns*, you mean?" she said. "I am a Christian woman, mademoiselle—"

"Jessaline."

"Very well; Jessaline." That look was in her face again, Jessaline noted, that air of determination and fierceness that made her beautiful at the oddest times. "I do not care for the idea of my skills being put to use in taking lives. That's simply unacceptable."

Jessaline stared at her, and for an instant fury blotted out thought. How dare this girl, with her privilege and wealth and coddled life . . . Jessaline set her jaw.

"In the Revolution," she said, in a low, tight voice, "the last French commander, Rochambeau, decided to teach my people a lesson for daring to revolt against our betters. Do you know what he did? He took slaves – including those who had not even fought – and broke them on the wheel, raising them on a post afterwards so the birds could eat them alive. He buried prisoners of war, also alive, in pits of insects. He *boiled* some of them, in vats of molasses. Such acts, he deemed, were necessary to put fear and subservience back into our hearts, since we had been tainted by a year of freedom."

Eugenie, who had gone quite pale, stared at Jessaline in purest horror, her mouth open. Jessaline smiled a hard, angry smile. "Such atrocities will happen again, Mademoiselle Rillieux, if you do not help us. Except this time we have been free for two generations. Imagine how much fear and subservience these *Christian* men will instill in us now?"

Eugenie shook her head slowly. "I . . . I had not heard . . . I did not consider . . ." She fell mute.

Jessaline stepped closer and laid one lace-gloved finger on the divot between Eugenie's collarbones. "You had best consider such things, my dear. Do you forget? There are those in this land who would like to do the same to you and all your kin."

Eugenie stared at her. Then, startling Jessaline, she dropped to the ground, sitting down so hard that her bustle made an aggrieved creaking sound.

"I did not know," she said at last. "I did not know these things."

Jessaline beheld the honest shock on her face and felt some guilt for having troubled her so. It was clear the girl's brother had worked hard to protect her from the world's harshness. Sitting beside Eugenie on the soft dry grass, she let out a weary sigh.

"In my land," she said, "men and women of *all* shades are free. I will not pretend that this makes us perfect; I have gone hungry many times in my life. Yet there, a woman such as yourself may be more than the coddled sister of a prominent scientist, or the mistress of a white man."

Eugenie threw her a guilty look, but Jessaline smiled to reassure her. The women of Eugenie's class had few options in life; Jessaline saw no point in condemning them for this.

"So many men died in the Revolution that women fill the ranks now as dirigible-pilots and gunners. We run factories and farms too, and are highly placed in government. Even the houngans are mostly women now – you have vodoun here too, yes? So we are important." She leaned close, her shoulder brushing Eugenie's in a teasing way, and grinned. "Some of us might even become spies. Who knows?"

Eugenie's cheeks flamed pink and she ducked her head to smile. Jessaline could see, however, that her words were having some effect; Eugenie had that oddly absent look again. Perhaps she was imagining all the things she could do in a land where the happenstances of sex and caste did not forbid her from using her mind to its fullest? A shame; Jessaline would have loved to take her there. But she had seen the luxury of the Rillieux household; why would any woman give that up?

This close, shoulder to shoulder and secluded within the willow tree's green canopy, Jessaline found herself staring at Eugenie, more aware than ever of the scent of her perfume, and the nearby softness of her skin, and the way the curls of her hair framed her long slender neck. At least she did not cover her hair like so many women of this land, convinced that its natural state was inherently ugly. She could not help her circumstances, but it seemed to Jessaline that she had taken what pride she could in her heritage.

So taken was Jessaline by this notion, and by the silence and strangeness of the moment, that she found herself saying, "And in my land it is not uncommon for a woman to head a family with another woman, and even raise children if they so wish."

Eugenie started – and to Jessaline's delight, her blush deepened. She darted a half-entranced, half-scandalized glance at Jessaline, then looked away, which Jessaline found deliciously fetching. "Live with – another woman? Do you mean—?" But of course she knew what Jessaline meant. "How can that be?"

"The necessities of security and shared labor. The priests look the other way."

Eugenie looked up then, and Jessaline was surprised to see a peculiar daring enter her expression, though her flush lingered. "And . . ." She licked her lips, swallowed. "Do such women . . . ah . . . behave as a family in . . . *all* matters?"

A slow grin spread across Jessaline's face. *Not so sheltered in her thoughts at least, this one!* "Oh, certainly. All matters – legal, financial, domestic . . ." Then, as a hint of uncertainty flickered in Eugenie's expression, Jessaline got tired of teasing. It was not proper, she knew; it was not within the bounds of her mission. But – just this once – perhaps . . .

She shifted just a little, from brushing shoulders to pressing rather more suggestively close, and leaned near, her eyes fixed on Eugenie's lips. "And conjugal," she added.

Eugenie stared at her, eyes huge behind her spectacles. "C-conjugal?" she asked, rather breathlessly.

"Oh, indeed. Perhaps a demonstration . . ."

But just as Jessaline leaned in to offer just that, she was startled by the voice of one of the nuns, apparently calling to another in French. From far too near the willow tree, a third voice rose to shush the first two – the prying old biddy who'd given Jessaline the eye before.

Eugenie jumped, her face red as plums, and quickly shifted away from Jessaline. Privately cursing, Jessaline did the same, and an awkward silence fell.

"W-well," said Eugenie, "I had best be getting back. I told my brother I would be at the seamstress's, and that doesn't take long."

"Yes," Jessaline said, realizing with some consternation that she'd completely forgotten why she'd asked for a meeting in the

first place. "Well. Ah. I have something I'd like to offer you –
but I would advise you to keep these out of sight, even at home
where servants might see. For your own safety." She reached
into the brocade bag and handed Eugenie the small cylindrical
leather container that held the formula and plans for the methane
extractor. "This is what we have come up with thus far, but the
design is incomplete. If you can offer any assistance—"

"Yes, of course," Eugenie said, taking the case with an avid look
that heartened Jessaline at once. She tucked the leather case into
her purse. "Allow me a few days to consider the problem. How
may I contact you, though, once I've devised a solution?"

"I will contact you in one week. Do not look for me." She got to
her feet and offered her hand to help Eugenie up. Then, speaking
loudly enough to be heard outside the willow at last, she giggled,
"Before your brother learns we've been swapping tales about him!"

Eugenie looked blank for a moment, then opened her mouth
in an "o" of understanding, grinning. "Oh, his ego could use a
bit of flattening, I think. In any case, fare you well, Mademoiselle
Dumonde. I must be on my way." And with that, she hurried off,
holding her hat as she passed through the willow branches.

Jessaline waited for ten breaths, then stepped out herself,
sparing a hard look for the old nun, who, sure enough, had moved
quite a bit closer to the tree. "A good afternoon to you, Sister,"
she said.

"And to you," the woman said in a low voice, "though you had
best be more careful from now on, *estipid.*"

Startled to hear her own tongue on the old woman's lips, she
stiffened. Then, carefully, she said in the same language, "And
what would you know of it?"

"I know you have a dangerous enemy," the nun replied, getting
to her feet and dusting dirt off her habit. Now that Jessaline could
see her better, it was clear from her features that she had a dollop
or two of African in her. "I am sent by your superiors to warn
you. We have word the Order of the White Camellia is active in
the city."

Jessaline caught her breath. The bootblack man! "I may have
encountered them already," she said.

The old woman nodded grimly. "Word had it they broke apart
after that scandal we arranged for them up in Baton Rouge," she

said, "but in truth they've just gotten more subtle. We don't know what they're after, but obviously they don't just want to kill you, or you would be dead by now."

"I am not so easily removed, madame," Jessaline said, drawing herself up in affront.

The old woman rolled her eyes. "Just take care," she snapped. "And by all means, if you want that girl dead, continue playing silly lovers' games with her where any fool can suspect." And with that, the old woman picked up her spade and shears and walked briskly away.

Jessaline did too, her cheeks burning. But back in her room, ostensibly safe, she leaned against the door and closed her eyes, wondering why her heart still fluttered so fast now that Eugenie was long gone, and why she was suddenly so afraid.

The Order of the White Camellia changed everything. Jessaline had heard tales of them for years, of course – a secret society of wealthy professionals and intellectuals dedicated to the preservation of "American ideals" like the superiority of the white race. They had been responsible for the exposure – and deaths, in some cases – of many of Jessaline's fellow spies over the years. America was built on slavery; naturally, the White Camellias would oppose a nation built on slavery's overthrow.

So Jessaline decided on new tactics. She shifted her attire from that of a well-to-do freedwoman to the plainer garb of a woman of less means. This elicited no attention as there were plenty such women in the city – though she was obliged to move to yet another inn that would suit her appearance. This drew her well into the less respectable area of the city, where not a few of the patrons took rooms by the hour or the half-day.

Here she lay low for the next few days, trying to determine whether she was being watched, though she spotted no suspicious characters – or at least, no one suspicious for the area. Which, of course, was why she'd chosen it. White men frequented the inn, but a white face that lingered or appeared repeatedly would be remarked upon, and easy to spot.

When a week had passed and Jessaline felt safe, she radically transformed herself using the bundle that had been hidden beneath her chest's false bottom. First she hid her close-cropped hair beneath a lumpy calico headwrap and donned an ill-fitting dress of worn, stained gingham patched here and there with burlap. A few small pillows rendered her effectively shapeless – a necessity, since in this disguise it was dangerous to be attractive in any way. As she slipped out in the small hours of the morning, carrying her belongings in a satchel and shuffling to make herself look much older, no one paid her any heed – not the drowsy old men sitting guard at the stables, nor the city constables chatting up a gaudily dressed woman under a gaslamp, nor the young toughs still dicing on the corner. She was, for all intents and purposes, invisible.

So first she milled among the morning-market crowds at the waterfront awhile, keeping an eye out for observers. When she was certain she had not been followed, she made her way to the dirigible docks, where four of the great machines hovered above a cluster of cargo vessels like huge, sausage-shaped guardian angels. A massive brick fence screened the docks themselves from view, though this had a secondary purpose: the docks were the sovereign territory of the Haitian Republic, housing its embassy as well. No American-born slave was permitted to step upon even this proxy version of Haitian soil, since, by the laws of Haiti, they would then be free.

Yet practicality did not stop men and women from dreaming, and near the massive ironwork gate of the facility there was as usual a small crowd of slaves gathered, gazing enviously in at the shouting dirigible crews and their smartly dressed officers. Jessaline slipped in among these and edged her way to the front, then waited.

Presently, a young runner detached herself from the nearby rope crew and ran over to the fence. Several of the slaves pushed envelopes through the fence, commissioning travel and shipping on behalf of their owners, and the girl collected these. The whole operation was conducted in utter silence; an American soldier hovered all too near the gate, ready to report any slave who talked. (It was not illegal to talk, but any slave who did so would likely suffer for it.)

Yet Jessaline noted that the runner met the eyes of every person she could, nodding to each solemnly, touching more hands than was strictly necessary for the sake of her work. A small taste of respect for those who needed it so badly, so that they might come to crave it and eventually seek it for themselves.

Jessaline met the runner's eyes too as she pushed through a plain, wrinkled envelope, but her gaze held none of the desperate hope of the others. The runner's eyes widened a bit, but she moved on at once after taking Jessaline's envelope. When she trotted away to deliver the commissions, Jessaline saw her shuffle the pile to put the wrinkled envelope on top.

That done, Jessaline then headed to the Rillieux house. At the back gate she shifted her satchel from her shoulder to her hands, re-tying it so as to make it square-shaped. To the servant who then answered her knock – freeborn; the Rillieuxs did not go in for the practice of owning slaves themselves – she said in coarse French, "Package for Mademoiselle Rillieux. I was told to deliver it to her personal."

The servant, a cleanly dressed fellow who could barely conceal his distaste at Jessaline's appearance, frowned further. "*English*, woman, only high-class folk talk French here." But when Jessaline deliberately spoke in butchered English, rendered barely comprehensible by an exaggerated French accent, the man finally rolled his eyes and stood aside. "She's in the garden house. Back there. There!" And he pointed the way.

Thus did Jessaline come to the over-large shed that sat amid the house's vast garden. It had clearly been meant to serve as a hothouse at some point, having a glass ceiling, but when Jessaline stepped inside she was assailed by sounds most unnatural: clanks and squealing and the rattling hiss of a steam boiler. These came from the equipment and incomprehensible machinery that lined every wall and hung from the ceiling; pipes and clockworks big enough to crush a man, all of it churning merrily away.

At the center of this chaos stood several high worktables, each bearing equipment in various states of construction or dismantlement, save the last. At this table, which was illuminated by a shaft of gathering sunlight, sat a sleeping Eugenie Rillieux.

At the sight of her, Jessaline stopped, momentarily overcome by a most uncharacteristic anxiety. Eugenie's head rested on her folded arms, atop a sheaf of large, irregular sheets of parchment that were practically covered with pen-scribbles and diagrams.

Her hair was amuss, her glasses askew, and she had drooled a bit onto one of her pale, ink-stained hands.

Beautiful, Jessaline thought, and marveled at herself. Her tastes had never leaned towards women like Eugenie, pampered and sheltered and shy. She generally preferred women like herself, who could be counted upon to know what they wanted and take decisive steps to get it. Yet in that moment, gazing upon this awkward, brilliant creature, Jessaline wanted nothing more than to be holding flowers instead of a fake package, and to have come for courting rather than her own selfish motives.

Perhaps Eugenie felt the weight of her longing, for after a moment she wrinkled her nose and sat up. "Oh," she said blearily, seeing Jessaline. "What is it, a delivery? Put it on the table there, please; I'll fetch you a tip." She got up, and Jessaline was amused to see that her bustle was askew.

"Eugenie," she said, and Eugenie whirled back as she recognized Jessaline's voice. Her eyes flew wide.

"What in heaven's name—?"

"I haven't much time," she said, hastening forward. She took Eugenie's hands in quick greeting, and resisted the urge to kiss her as well. "Have you been able to refine the plans?"

"Oh – yes, yes, I think." Eugenie pushed her glasses straight and gestured toward the papers that had served as her pillow. "This design should work, at least in theory. I was right; the vacuum-distillation mechanism was the key! Of course, I haven't finished the prototype, because the damned glassmaker is trying to charge pirates' rates—"

Jessaline squeezed her hands, exhilarated. "Marvelous! Don't worry; we shall test the design thoroughly before we put it into use. But now I must have the plans. Men are searching for me; I don't dare stay in town much longer."

Eugenie nodded absently, then blinked again as her head cleared. She narrowed her eyes at Jessaline in sudden suspicion. "Wait," she said. "You're leaving *town*?"

"Yes, of course," Jessaline said, surprised. "This is what I came for, after all. I can't just put something so important on the next dirigible packet."

The look of hurt that came over Eugenie's face sent a needle straight into Jessaline's heart. She realized, belatedly and with guilty dismay, what Eugenie must have been imagining all this time.

"But . . . I thought . . ." Eugenie looked away suddenly, and bit her lower lip. "You might stay."

"Eugenie," Jessaline began, uncomfortably. "I . . . could never have remained here. This place . . . the way you live here . . ."

"Yes, I know." At once Eugenie's voice hardened; she glared at Jessaline. "In your perfect, wonderful land, everyone is free to live as they please. It is the rest of us, then, the poor wretched folk you scorn and pity, who have no choice but to endure it. Perhaps we should never bother to love at all, then! That way, at least, when we are used and cast aside, it will at least be for material gain!"

And with that, she slapped Jessaline smartly, and walked out. Stunned, Jessaline put a hand to her cheek and stared after her.

"Trouble in paradise?" said a voice behind her, in a syrupy drawl.

Jessaline whirled to find herself facing a six-shooter. And holding it, his face free of bootblack this time, was the young man who had invaded her quarters nearly two weeks before.

"I heard you Haitians were unnatural," he said, coming into the light, "but this? Not at all what I was expecting."

Not me, Jessaline realized, too late. *They were watching Rillieux, not me!* "Natural is in the eye of the beholder, as is beauty," she snapped.

"True. Speaking of beauty, though, you looked a damn sight finer before. What's all this?" He sidled forward, poking with the gun at the padding round Jessaline's middle. "So that's it! But—" He raised the gun, and to Jessaline's fury, poked at her breasts none too gently. "Ah, no padding *here.* Yes, I do remember you rightly." He scowled. "I still can't sit down thanks to you, woman. Maybe I ought to repay you that."

Jessaline raised her hands slowly, pulling off her lumpy headwrap so he could see her more clearly. "That's ungentlemanly of you, I would say."

"Gentlemen need gentle*women,*" he said. "Your kind are hardly that, being good for only one thing. Well – that and lynching, I suppose. But we'll save both for later, won't we? After you've met my superior and told us everything that's in your nappy little head. He's partial to your variety. I, however, feel that if I must lower myself to baseness, better to do it with one bearing the fair blood of the French."

It took Jessaline a moment to understand through all his airs. But then she did, and shivered in purest rage. "You will not lay a finger upon Eugenie. I'll snap them all off fir—"

But before she could finish her threat, there was a scream and commotion from the house. The scream, amid all the chaos of shouting and running servants, she recognized at once: Eugenie.

The noise startled the bootblack man as well. Fortunately he did not pull the trigger; he did start badly, however, half-turning to point the gun in the direction of Eugenie's scream. Which was all the opening that Jessaline needed, as she drew her derringer from the wadded cloth of the headwrap and shot the man point-blank. The bootblack man cried out, clutching his chest and falling to the ground.

The derringer was spent; it carried only a single bullet. Snatching up the bootblack man's sixgun instead, Jessaline turned to sprint toward the Rillieux house – then froze for an instant in terrible indecision. Behind her, on Eugenie's table, sat the plans for which she had spent the past three months of her life striving and stealing and sneaking. The methane extractor could be the salvation of her nation, the start of its brightest future.

And in the house—

Eugenie, she thought.

And started running.

In the parlor, Norbert Rillieux was frozen, paler than usual and trembling. Before him, holding Eugenie about the throat and with a gun to her head, was a white man whose face was so floridly familiar that Jessaline gasped.

"Raymond Forstall?"

He started badly as Jessaline rounded the door, and she froze as well, fearing to cause Eugenie's death. Very slowly she set the sixgun on a nearby sideboard, pushed it so that it slid out of easy reach, and raised her hands to show that she was no threat. At this, Forstall relaxed.

"So we meet again, my beauteous negress," he said, though there was anger in his smile. "I had hoped to make your acquaintance under more favorable circumstances. Alas."

"*You* are with the White Camellia?" He had seemed so gormless that day on Royal Street; not at all the sort Jessaline would associate with a murderous secret society.

"I am indeed," he said. "And you would have met the rest of us if my assistant had not clearly failed in his goal of taking you captive. Nevertheless, I too have a goal, and I ask again, sir, *where are the plans?*"

Jessaline realized belatedly that this was directed at Norbert Rillieux. And he, too frightened to bluster, just shook his head. "I told you, I have built no such device! Ask this woman – she wanted it, and I refused her!"

The methane extractor, Jessaline realized. Of course – they had known, probably via their own spies, that she was after it. Forstall had been tailing her the day he'd bumped into her, probably all the way to Rillieux's house; she cursed herself for a fool for not realizing. But the White Camellias were mostly philosophers and bankers and lawyers, not the trained, proficient spies she'd been expecting to deal with. It had never occurred to her that an enemy would be so clumsy as to jostle and *converse with* his target in the course of surveillance.

"It's true," Jessaline said, stalling desperately in hopes that some solution would present itself to her. "This man refused my request to build the device."

"Then why did you come back here?" Forstall asked, tightening his grip on Eugenie so that she gasped. "We had men watching the house servants, too. We intercepted orders for metal parts and rubber tubing, and I paid the glassmith to delay an order for custom vacuum-pipes—"

"*You* did that?" To Jessaline's horror, Eugenie stiffened in Forstall's grasp, trying to turn and glare at him in her affront. "I argued with that old fool for an hour!"

"Eugenie, be still!" cried Norbert, which raised him high in Jessaline's estimation; she had wanted to shout the same thing.

"I will not!" Eugenie began to struggle, plainly furious. As Forstall cursed and tried to restrain her, Jessaline heard Eugenie's protests continue: " . . . interference with my work . . . very idea . . ."

Please, Holy Mother, Jessaline thought, taking a very careful step closer to the gun on the sideboard, *don't let him shoot her to shut her up.*

When Forstall finally thrust Eugenie aside – she fell against the bottle-strewn side table, nearly toppling it – and indeed raised the gun to shoot her, Jessaline blurted, "Wait!"

Both Forstall and Eugenie froze, now separated and facing each other, though Forstall's gun was still pointed dead at Eugenie's chest. "The plans are complete," Jessaline said to him. "They are in the workshop out back." With a hint of pride, she looked at Eugenie and added, "Eugenie has made it work."

"What?" said Rillieux, looking thunderstruck.

"What?" Forstall stared at her, then Eugenie, and then anger filled his expression. "Clever, indeed! And while I go out back to check if your story is true, you will make your escape with the plans already tucked into your clothes."

"I am not lying in this instance," she said, "but if you like, we can all proceed to the garden and see. Or, since I'm the one you seem to fear most . . ." She waggled her empty hands in mockery, hoping this would make him too angry to notice how much closer she was to the gun on the sideboard. His face reddened further with fury. "You could leave Eugenie and her brother here, and take me alone."

Eugenie caught her breath. "Jessaline, are you mad?"

"Yes," Jessaline said, and smiled, letting her heart live in her face for a moment. Eugenie's mouth fell open, then softened into a small smile. Her glasses were still askew, Jessaline saw with a rush of fondness.

Forstall rolled his eyes, but smiled. "A capital suggestion, I think. Then I can shoot you—"

He got no further, for in the next instant Eugenie suddenly struck him in the head with a rum bottle.

The bottle shattered on impact. Forstall cried out, half-stunned by the blow and the sting of rum in his eyes, but he managed to keep his grip on the gun, and keep it trained more or less on Eugenie. Jessaline thought she saw the muscles in his forearm flex to pull the trigger –

– and then the sixgun was in her hand, its wooden grip warm and almost comforting as she blew a hole in Raymond Forstall's rum-drenched head. Forstall uttered a horrid gurgling sound and fell to the floor.

Before his body stopped twitching, Jessaline caught Eugenie's hand. "Hurry!" She dragged the other woman out of the parlor. Norbert, again to his credit, started out of shock and trotted after them, for once silent as they moved through the house's corridors toward the garden. The house was nearly deserted now, the servants having fled or found some place to hide that was safe from gunshots and madmen.

"You must tell me which of the papers on your desk I can take," Jessaline said as they trotted along, "and then you must make a decision."

"Wh-what decision?" Eugenie still sounded shaken.

"Whether you will stay here, or whether you will come with me to Haiti."

"*Haiti?*" Norbert cried.

"Haiti?" Eugenie asked, in wonder.

"Haiti," said Jessaline, and as they passed through the rear door and went into the garden, she stopped and turned to Eugenie. "With me."

Eugenie stared at her in such dawning amazement that Jessaline could no longer help herself. She caught Eugenie about the waist, pulled her near, and kissed her most soundly and improperly, right there in front of her brother. It was the sweetest, wildest kiss she had ever known in her life.

When she pulled back, Norbert was standing at the edge of her vision with his mouth open, and Eugenie looked a bit faint. "Well," Eugenie said, and fell silent, the whole affair having been a bit much for her.

Jessaline grinned and let her go, then hurried forward to enter the workshop – and froze, horror shattering her good mood.

The bootblack man was gone. Where his body had been lay Jessaline's derringer and copious blood, trailing away . . . to Eugenie's worktable, where the plans had been, and were no longer. The trail then led away, out of the workshop's rear door.

"No," she whispered, her fists clenching at her sides. "No, by God!" Everything she had worked for, gone. She had failed, both her mission and her people.

"Very well," Eugenie said after a moment. "Then I shall simply have to come with you."

The words penetrated Jessaline's despair slowly. "What?"

Eugenie touched Jessaline's hand. "I will come with you. To Haiti. And I will build an even more efficient methane extractor for you there."

Jessaline turned to stare at her and found that she could not, for her eyes had filled with tears.

"Wait." Norbert caught his breath as understanding dawned. "Go to Haiti? Are you mad? I forbid—"

"You had better come too, brother," Eugenie said, turning to him, and Jessaline was struck breathless once more by the cool determination in her eyes. "The police will take their time about it, but they'll come eventually, and a white man lies dead in our house. It doesn't really matter whether you shot him or not; you know full well what they'll decide."

And Norbert stiffened, for he did indeed know – probably better than Eugenie, Jessaline suspected – what his fate would be.

Eugenie turned to Jessaline. "He *can* come, can't he?" By which Jessaline knew it was a condition, not an option.

"Of course he can," she said at once. "I wouldn't leave a dog to these people's justice. But it will not be the life you're used to, either of you. Are you certain?"

Eugenie smiled, and before Jessaline realized what was imminent, she had been pulled rather roughly into another kiss. Eugenie had been eating penuche again, she realized dimly, and then for a long perfect moment she thought of nothing but pecans and sweetness.

When it was done, Eugenie searched Jessaline's face and then smiled in satisfaction. "Perhaps we should go, Jessaline," she said gently.

"Ah. Yes. We should, yes." Jessaline fought to compose herself; she glanced at Norbert and took a deep breath. "Fetch us a hansom cab while you still can, Monsieur Rillieux, and we'll go down to the docks and take the next dirigible southbound."

The daze cleared from Norbert's eyes as well; he nodded mutely and trotted off.

In the silence that fell, Eugenie turned to Jessaline.

"Marriage," she said, "and a house together. I believe you mentioned that?"

"Er," said Jessaline, blinking. "Well, yes, I suppose, but I rather thought that first we would—"

"Good," Eugenie replied, "because I'm not fond of you keeping up this dangerous line of work. My inventions should certainly earn enough for the both of us, don't you think?"

"Um," said Jessaline.

"Yes. So there's no reason for you to work when I can keep you in comfort for the rest of our days." Taking Jessaline's hands, she stepped closer, her eyes going soft again. "And I am so very much looking forward to those days, Jessaline."

"Yes," said Jessaline, who had been wondering just which of her many sins had earned her this mad fortune. But as Eugenie's warm breast pressed against hers, and the thick perfume of the magnolia trees wafted around them, and some clockwork contraption within the workshop ticked in time with her heart . . . Jessaline stopped worrying. And she wondered why she had ever bothered with plans and papers and gadgetry, because it was clear she had just stolen the greatest prize of all.

The Clockwork Goat and the Smokestack Magi

Peter M. Ball

Attend – in the darkest streets of Unden there lay a coal-filled fen known as Moloch Alley, a place filled with men who possessed souls with the consistency of smoke, stained and dirty, willing to drift with the whims of the wind and disappear, poof, when the storm winds whistled between the looming factories. A cold place, and a mean one, the air thick with black smoke and men cursed with black lungs and wicked coughs and few hopes for the future. And into this alley walked a clockwork goat, trip-trapping, tick-tocking, marching stiff-legged and determined down the soot-stained cobblestones. It walked into the darkness until it arrived at the copper door of the Smokestack Magi's home, a portal laid flush with the bellowing red-brick chimney of a smelting house, as though one could walk through it and into the roaring furnace beyond.

There were stories, even then, that spoke of the door and its owner. The door was never hot, not even warm, no matter how much smoke billowed forth from the tip of the smokestack, and there were sigils carved into its surface with a delicate hand. The stories said that the only visitors to whom the Magi's door opened were exotic creatures and mysteries. There had been a hippogriff once, or so it was said, not three years prior – a sleek beast with grey-black feathers and sharp teeth used for rending flesh. Before that there had been a marsh troll, and there were stories, older still, about a mermaid, scaled and beautiful, who had been wheeled along the alley's cobblestones in a great tank of brackish water by her small flotilla of slaves, who had knocked and gained admittance but failed to emerge after that.

And now there was the clockwork goat, a device no more than three feet tall with ticking parts of silver. Not even a living thing, not quite, but it looked close enough and there are stories about goats, even here, far from the fireside tales of their childhood, and thus no one molested the small creature, allowing it to approach the Magi's door without harm when any normal man would fear for his life in the dark shadows of Moloch Alley.

The goat marched up to the door and knocked with one hoof, rapping it against the burnished copper, before settling on its haunches in a flurry of sharp clicks and grinding gears. For three days the goat waited there, sitting on the doorstep while Moloch Alley filled with smoke and dust and ashes, and every day, on the last bell of the thirteenth hour, the clockwork goat would rise and knock and settle on its haunches once more.

It was not until the fourth day that the copper door swung open, magically, before the sharp rat-a-tat of the goat's knock. The goat stood, watching the darkness, until the Magi appeared through the smoke and studied his visitor. He was a short man, black-robed, with eyes like polished coal, and he watched the goat with suspicion on his face. "So," he said, stroking his beard of glowing embers. "You're one of Bartholomew's pieces. He gets desperate, it seems, in his dotage."

The clockwork goat nodded and its jaw dropped open, and it spoke in a tinny voice that hummed like a plucked string on a viola. "My master sends greetings, Lord Magi of the Smokestack. He wishes peace between you, and I have come as he bid me as an offer of goodwill."

The Smokestack Magi studied the goat through hooded eyelids. "Bartholomew may be ageing," he said, "but he remains ever wily. What assurances do I have that it is safe to entertain your presence?"

"You have entertained giants, and ghosts, and unicorns. What need have you to fear a simple construct like me? My master wishes peace, to reach an accord between you. I come bearing his knowledge, his research, and his friendship."

"There are stories about a horse," the Magi said, "which was offered in friendship and caused the downfall of an empire."

"That there are," said the clockwork goat. "I am not a horse."

"You are not," replied the Smokestack Magi, "but this matter requires contemplation. I will retire for a day to ponder the mystery you represent. Knock again tomorrow, and I will consider your request again."

And so the Magi left and the clockwork goat waited another day, drawing curious eyes from the men of Moloch Alley who crept closer and closer as shadows grew long. The goat did not move, and at the thirteenth hour of the fifth day the goat knocked once more and waited until the Smokestack Magi returned, stepping through his copper doorway with flames roaring at his heels. He smoked his pipe and stood over the goat, puffing gently as he regarded it with a frown and quizzical eyes.

"I have researched," he said, "and considered, and pondered the mysteries of your creation. A goat? Why that? What purpose is there in this form when all the beasts and birds of nature are at Bartholomew's disposal? Why a goat, of all things? If you are possessed of all his knowledge, tell me this so that I may consider your offer in the spirit with which it is made."

"There are stories," the goat said, "of goats serving as a sacrifice, carrying the sins of a tribe into the desert. There are stories of goats providing succor to gods, providing them with abundant nourishment to ensure they grew up strong. Perhaps my master intended both, perhaps he did not. Perhaps I am both, a symbol of past sins and succor for your future friendship. Perhaps I am not."

"Perhaps?" asked the Smokestack Magi. He puffed upon his pipe, sending black smoke into the air.

"I know all that my master knew, but I do not think with his thoughts. I can tell you what he has learned, but not what he plans to do with such knowledge."

"A good answer, but not a comforting one," the Magi said. "This requires contemplation. Knock again tomorrow, when I have pondered your offer further."

And another day wore on and the clockwork goat waited patiently, his ticking filling the silent seconds between the moans and groans of the factories. And again the men of Moloch Alley grew closer, close enough to study the mechanical beast and see their grubby faces in the sheen of the goat's silver carapace. They whispered to one another, afraid, falling back when dawn grew close, and the clockwork goat waited and knocked on the door, and when the Magi returned once more the denizens of the alley were hidden in the shadows.

"I remain conflicted," the Magi said. "For your offer is tempting, too tempting by half. I have warred with Bartholomew for a century now, competing with him for the favour of the Crown and the merchants. I have been driven by that contest, that need to best him in the eyes of others and become the greatest magi in the land. I know he once felt as I do, that he was driven to his success by our rivalry. So I ask you, good goat, why he wishes to make peace between the two of us now?"

"Perhaps he sees greater discoveries made by combining your intellects, with two thoughts achieving what one mind cannot," the clockwork goat said. "Perhaps he wishes to study in peace, for its own sake, rather than focusing his work on the necessity of building favor with men and women of influence. Perhaps he concedes defeat in your contest, and sends me as a concession of your superior brilliance."

"You do not know?" the Magi said. "You cannot tell me why he sent you?"

"I know all that he knew, but I do not know his thoughts."

"Then again I am conflicted, and you must await another day for my answer."

Then the Smokestack Magi disappeared in a swirl of smoke, slamming his door behind him with a thump like an engine's piston. Once again the clockwork goat waited, silent on the doorstep, but this time the denizens of Moloch Alley crept forth, peering and prodding the silver chassis of the construct.

"If you know all that a magi knows, then you have the secret of their magic," one of the denizens said. He was a tall man, reedy, with eyes that looked like they'd been stolen from a ferret and shined up until they gleamed with cunning and guile. "Would you tell us, if we asked it? Could you tell me a great magi's secrets?"

"I know all that my master knew, all the formulas, the theories and the science," the goat said. "I know all my master knew, but I could not tell you his thoughts."

"Then tell us," the ferret-eyed man said, for he had intelligence enough to seize on an opportunity when it was presented to him. "We would soak up what you know, and use it to improve our lot."

And so the clockwork goat recited the formulas and the theories and the science, night after night as he stood there waiting on the Magi's steps. Every day the denizens of the alley would scatter when the Smokestack Magi emerged to ask his questions, holding their breath while they waited for the Magi's decision to wait a day longer. Every night the denizens of Moloch Alley learned more, until they had mastered many secrets and became magi themselves. They learned the magic of the cog, and of steam and coal. They learned the power of the furnace and spread it through the city like a plague of rats, driven by the dangerous combination of avarice and knowledge that has marked all the great magi.

Unden became a place of wonders, a place where science and magic prospered, though with so many magi spread across the boroughs the Smokestack Magi found it hard to maintain favor amongst the nobles and merchants of the court. He grew poorer and weaker, and the copper door tarnished as he lacked the power to keep it whole. Moloch Alley remained a place frequented by ne'er-do-wells, but now they were men who had heard tales of the clockwork goat, canny brigands and greedy gamblers who wished to know all the goat knew. They leaned on the doorstep of the Smokestack Magi's home, but he had not the sense to open his door and see where his competition came from.

And so things continued, and so things went, until one day, three years after the goat had first arrived, the Smokestack Magi opened the door and invited it inside. "It is decided," the Magi said. "I accept your master's offer. You will teach me all you know, and I shall use it to best this upstart magi in my city."

And so the clockwork goat told him, and so the Smokestack Magi learned, though the knowledge availed him little with so many others who now possessed it. He recognized the plans and the inventions that the other magi used, the sciences and the experiments with which they impressed the Crown. "It was you!" he cried, preparing to strike the goat. "You have brought this blight of learned men to my fair city. It was you who taught them the mysteries that have robbed me of my wealth."

"It was," the goat said. "For that is how I was created. I will answer those who ask and tell them all I know. If you had but allowed me in, those who lived in the alley would not have interrogated me for my secrets."

Then the Smokestack Magi did strike the goat several times, denting the silver chassis and breaking the delicate gears. He destroyed the creature and melted the parts, scattering the cooling ingots across the four corners of the globe. But this destruction did nothing to improve the Magi's standing at the court, and his door corroded and warped until it could not open, and even now there are stories about the ghost of Moloch Alley, a creature of soot and sorrow that seeks to absorb all a man knows with a touch of its grubby claw.

But that, perhaps, is a story best kept for another time.

The Armature of Flight

Sharon Mock

"So, what will you do once you have the world in your hands?"

"Stop it."

"I'm just asking."

"You just want me to say what I'd rather have in my hands."

"That hadn't occurred to me. Though now that you mention it . . ."

Leo sat alone, nursing a decent whiskey and staring idly into the mirrored backsplash of the bar. In the smoky glass, reflections merged and mingled. Couples and small groups, men and a few women, dressed in shapeless sweaters and dungarees. Younger than him, mostly, and paying him no mind. He wasn't one of them, not in the ways that mattered most. But they had enough in common, and they kept the police from their door.

Even here he could have had his choice of company, as long as he wasn't fussy about a grafted tail, or an arcane tattoo, or some other exotic modification in an unexpected place. But he wasn't in the mood for company just then. So when the man came through the door – tall and incongruous in his double-breasted suit, looking, in the smoke and the dark, like nothing so much as Leo's more exotic shadow – Leo turned his attention back to his whiskey, and tried not to notice the other man's approach.

"You don't look like you belong here." The newcomer claimed the next stool over and motioned for a drink. Polished white cotton peeked out from under the jacket, a single thread snagged at the wrist. Cufflinks dusted with diamonds, heavy ring to match. The attempt at a patrician accent would fool most people, he supposed.

"Neither do you," Leo said, then looked to make certain. Bare-headed, black hair groomed into curls and hastily reordered, eyes over-bright. Overdressed, yes, but no outsider.

"We could always be out of place together," the man purred. "If you like."

"We could, if I were looking for company."

"That's all right. I'm not, either. I just thought" — and he smiled, as polished as his fingernails and as bright as his eyes – "you might have the time and inclination for a drink or two."

For how high a price? But Leo waved the bartender over anyway.

The other man stopped him, hand light on his forearm. "It's all right. I'll take care of it." The hand lifted as quickly as it had descended. The eyes averted, the smile faded. "I'm off duty."

His name was William Langley, and if Leo had had any sense, he would have lied about his own.

"Deventer?"

"Yes."

"The shipping Deventers?"

"Among other things."

William went quiet. Already Leo understood that this was not his usual state. "*Count* Deventer?"

"That's my grandfather. You wouldn't mistake us, believe me."

William didn't laugh, didn't even smile. In the filtered streetlight coming from the half-open window, he looked like he might jump up and run away. "I didn't know," he whispered.

"You wouldn't have looked at me twice if you didn't think I had money."

"It's not like that. I just liked the look of you, all right? And now you'll never believe me."

"I'm sure I can be convinced." He'd meant it as a joke, damn it, a come-on, something to lighten the mood; and he should have seen that William took it seriously, should have seen it even then.

They knew it would end. Sooner or later Leo's grandfather would find him a wife, summon him back to fulfill his obligations and carry on the family line. But not just then, not just yet.

They shared an apartment where William knew the landlord, where nobody asked questions. Leo learned to ignore the strange bumps and creases of his neighbors' clothes. He was safe among the modified; their crimes, their sins, were so much greater than his own. And in that safety he could forget, as long as possible, what lay ahead.

William insisted he could find them somewhere nicer. But Leo couldn't afford what William wanted, not on a junior manager's salary. His inheritance was still in the future, predicated on the very things that would tear him away. A wife, an heir.

William, on the other hand, could afford far more than Leo could offer. There seemed to be a limitless market for a handsome unmarked man pretending to be a rich boy gone wrong. And as the weeks and months passed without word, he became more and more like what he pretended to be. Sometimes Leo caught, out of the corner of his eye, William practicing a gesture, a motion of the head, like an errant shadow trying to rejoin its source.

It was comforting, sometimes, to think of William continuing on after, living Leo's hidden life after Leo himself had stepped into his family legacy. But mostly he didn't let himself think about such matters at all.

"There's a cable," William said. "From your grandfather."

Leo knew before he opened it. A suitable marriage partner had been found. The date, time, circumstances of the meeting had been arranged. He had only to travel back to Devenport, meet the young woman, and agree to the selection.

"You're going," William said. But he didn't look at Leo as he said it.

"It's not – it's only a meeting."

"But you'll say yes."

"Unless she makes me want to flee the room, I think I'm obligated to."

"I'd like to be there to see that." Leo could hear the smile in William's voice by then, could hear that the smile was false.

"My grandfather wouldn't appreciate it."

"It was a joke, Leo."

"I know."

"We could – no. We've discussed this. Never mind."

And they had, in the dark, where difficult things are said. How Leo's parents had hated one another, taken lovers shamelessly and without discretion, until Grandfather in disgust had given permission for the divorce. How absolutely everyone had known, how the children taunted, and the parents pitied. How he refused to be that selfish, that cruel to his obligatory children, no matter how tempting.

They'd known they'd have to tear the whole thing down sooner or later. Too late to change the rules now.

William wasn't home when Leo returned, not for three days after. All of his things were still where they belonged, though; he'd have to come back if only for an hour or two. In his absence, Leo imagined trying to make him stay. Telling Grandfather to go to hell, running off west together where the sun was always shining and people paid no attention to sin. But without his name and his inheritance, he'd be just another salary man. He'd never keep up with William's bright jewels and brighter smile.

When William did return, hanging his overcoat in the closet, Leo knew at once there was something wrong. A catch in his motion, a stiffness in his stance. "You're back," Leo said, to break the silence.

"I had some business to take care of. Since you won't be around much longer. Have to start thinking of myself, you know?"

"What have you done?" But William was already taking off his shirt to show him.

There were things in his back that hadn't been there before. Metal sockets over the shoulder blades. He'd never thought William wanted that sort of thing for himself. Though there was good money in modifying your body to fit somebody else's fetish – but it couldn't be more than he was already pulling in.

"I've got a bit of a problem, Leo." His voice was casual, his back turned, using the implants as an excuse to not look, not be seen. "Ran up a few debts, here and there. Nobody'd call me on them while I was with you. So, I was stupid. Don't worry. I'm taking care of it now."

"Taking care of—?" But it was coming together, even as he said it. Those limitless funds weren't. Trying to prove he could keep up with Leo – and Leo hadn't asked him to, damn it, hadn't expected him to, and it didn't matter anyway. Ah, but it had never been about Leo in the first place. It was all about William, and the fucking name.

"Do I have to spell it out for you? It's good money. I have the right to take care of myself."

Since you won't. Leo put his hand on William's bare shoulder. William turned like he was on hinges. "This isn't about taking care of yourself. You're mutilating yourself for a profit—"

"Not everybody thinks it's mutilation."

"How much are they paying you?"

"I don't think," William said, "that's your business anymore."

It was the cold that got to him, and the dismissal, and the quiet. "Was anything ever my business with you? What else did you not bother to share with me?" Even as Leo spoke the words he knew they were untrue. Yet his tongue would not, could not call them back.

William grabbed his overcoat back off the hanger. "You always were a rat bastard, Leo."

He didn't come back until late that night, smelling of smoke and other men's whiskey. Leo was still awake, had resigned himself to being awake till dawn or longer. Not waiting. He had no right to wait. Just being alone, and cursing his idiocy.

"I didn't mean it," he said.

William let the overcoat drop to the floor. "I know."

The steel was as cold as ice in a glass, as warm as skin. Ritual etchings seemed to glow in the burgeoning light. "What are they for?" Leo dared to whisper at last, expecting no answer.

"Wings." William shifted, winced audibly as muscle pulled against metal. "It's experimental, that's why – you can't imagine, Leo, the money they're throwing at me." Illegal, too, but that went without saying. "When I go back they'll screw in the skeleton, and when I can handle that, they'll add the flesh. Swan feathers, can you imagine it? I'll be an angel, Leo, a fucking angel. A *rich* fucking angel. How could I say no to that?"

"I wish I could be there to see it," he said. Lied. He didn't want his lover with hack-job wings on his back.

He wanted to remember him just like this, forever.

"No way. They'd never have it. They're like your grandfather that way."

"It was a joke."

"I know. Always is, isn't it? But it's all right. They don't expect me back 'til morning."

And as dawn light shone through the bedroom window Leo pulled William close to him, whispered into the nape of his neck:

I don't want to leave you. I want you to stay. Don't fly away, love. Don't fly away.

He lay perfectly still, so that Leo thought for certain he was still asleep. Only now he said this, of course, now that William had been marked, labeled. Now that what he asked for was impossible. Convenient, that.

William reached up, took Leo's hand in his, squeezed, hard. "Someday you'll let yourself have what you want," he said, no sleep in his voice at all.

When Leo woke up, William was gone. When he came home from work the next day, William's belongings were gone too. All but a few shirts, a favorite jacket, things for Leo to remember him by. And an envelope stuffed into the jacket's lapel pocket, waiting to be noticed and removed. A phrase scrawled across the front: *The world in your hands*.

Leo poured the envelope's contents into his palm. A glittering bead the size of a gumball, hanging from a watch chain. Now he saw how the debt had run up in the first place, a dozen or a hundred extravagant gestures just like this, and Leo too blind to see it happening.

He threw the jewel with force. It arced low, bounced among the cushions of the couch. He scooped it up, examined it more closely. A world made small, a globe to fit in the palm of the hand. Topaz earth and sapphire sea, diamond chips sparkling at points of permanent snow. White gold, or maybe platinum, marked the border of nations.

His arm reared back for a second throw, then went limp. He couldn't bring himself to break the thing.

Over the next few days, Leo noticed items missing from the apartment. Nothing of particular value: a saucer, a teaspoon, a shirt with a loose button. It took him weeks to admit why William had taken them.

One of the neighbors gave him a list of places to look, and he spent his nights canvassing the city, driving from address to address, looking for shadows, looking for wings. And in a row house in an unfashionable neighborhood he finally found them, dark fingers clawing at the amber light.

Leo pulled over, grabbed the keys out of the ignition, jumped into the empty road. The figure in the window turned. The armature of wings spread from his back like opening hands.

He never could remember what he shouted then, only reconstruct it after the fact: words like *don't be an idiot* and *don't butcher yourself* and *I'll take care of anything you want, I'll give you everything*.

The figure stepped forward. Leo couldn't see his features, no matter how hard he tried. Hands spread against the window, wide as wings.

He spun then. Metal scratched against glass. The window went dark. A moment later, the light on the doorstep came on, and three men stepped out, heavy men with heavy fists.

The men were waiting by the front door the next night, and the night after that. The second-story light stayed off. After a while, nobody came. The house went dark, quiet, cold. Newspapers gathered on the porch.

By then it was time for Leo to go home.

He had a story that he told himself, late at night, after his wife went to bed and he was left alone and silent in the house where he had once been a child. William had worked for a while, paid off his debts, put away enough to stay comfortable. Then he'd moved out west, following the sun, like he said he'd always wanted. Lost the wings, of course; couldn't have much of a life, otherwise. Besides, Leo preferred remembering him without them.

Sometimes he reached in his pocket for the jewel, but it wasn't there. William's gift stayed in a box on top of the dresser, in among the cufflinks and the subway tokens, remnants of another, less portable world. If his wife had ever looked in the box, found the sparkling sphere, she never spoke of it.

He would have lied, anyway. That world was gone, a shadow cast away. He'd never see William again.

The Anachronist's Cookbook

Catherynne M. Valente

In the summer of 1872, a confederation of pickpockets plagued the streets of Manchester, swiping purses and leaving a series of pamphlets in their places. Only one child was ever caught at this, a girl by the name of Jane Sallow, aged fifteen, who managed her thievery though she had lost three fingers to a mechanical loom – her remaining seven were not quite nimble enough to evade notice by her last victim, who snatched her by the wrist and dashed her arm against a lamp-post. During questioning, Jane wept piteously, tore at her dress, propositioned three bailiffs most lasciviously, and pleaded in the dulcet tones peculiar to young women for a prisoner's bread and water, being starved half to wasting. Her arrest is a matter of public record: little else in her life can be held to so high a standard. One of the bailiffs, called Roger Smith – God save his soul – succumbed to her wiles and embraced the wastrel child when the Constable finally gave her up for feral. When her bodice was unbuttoned, the hidden, incriminating pamphlets peeled loose from her breasts, still hot and molded to her body, and little Jane laughed in the face of the bailiff's desire.

Long Live the Levelution!

Come, Brothers and Sisters of the Undercity, invisible Insects scurrying along the brass Baseboards of the Master's House! Do as your nature compels you! Chew! Gnaw! Tear! Bite! When your Lord descends from on high to present to you your Replacement, gleaming in Copper and Teak, do not simply Bow your Head and agree that the Programmable Home Tailor and its unholy Kin are your

Superiors in Every Way. Do not accept the Whirring of its Punch cards as your new Hymns, do not Marvel at the perfect, soulless Cloth it spits out like some dumb Golem! Instead, while your Master sleeps, seize Implements and Smash that clicking, gear-spangled Beast of Magog, Rend it Cog from Cog! It is Your Self you will Preserve by this Wanton Leveling, and your Master's overstuffed Pride you will deflate! Fear not for your Souls, my Brethren! It is No Crime to destroy the Devil! And I say the Devil Dwells in those Devices that Grind and Cut and Crush and Hiss. Nay, they do not weave Thread, but Sinew and Blood and Bone, and of These they make a Cloth of Infamy, which shrouds Mankind in Sin.

To Those who would call me Anarchist, Daemon, Commune-ist, I shriek to the Heavens: Call your Selves Happy now? Happier yet than those who Toil in honest Labor, who feel the Earth in their Fists, who Drink of the Fountains of Fraternity? Does that Jacquard-Cloak warm you more than your Mother's Own Stitching? No! Yet you would put your Mother in Chains for the sake of your Master's Economy! Your sweet Mother labors in foul Factories conceived in Hell, in Fire and Black Iron. Her tears Moisten your Bread, her sweat Salts your Meat, and still you turn from her, and like Peter Deny her Once, Twice, Three times. The Science of Rich Men does not Elevate all Mankind, but only Them Selves, for they need not Break their Backs on the Rack of Industry, but merely Sip their Tea and watch us die for their Enrichment.

Brothers and Sisters, Stand with me. We who are the Slaves of those in velvet Waistcoats and Golden Goggles, we who wash their mechanized Clothes, polish their Floors, rear their Wailing Brats, cook their Lavish Suppers – it is in our Power to Level the Unequal World that raises them above us. Crush their Dread Devices! Level their Palaces of Infernal Science! Take my Hand – for there is a Poker Clutched therein, and with it we will Stoke the Flames of Righteous Action, and the Steam of OUR virtuous Engines will Expel every Slavemaster in England.

★　★　★

In her statement, Jane claimed to be an orphan. The Constable noted a resemblance to a certain elderly member of Parliament well known for his dalliances in Bengal Street, but the shape of a nose is no evidence, and he could not be sure. She was too well spoken to be a gutter worm, he would later tell the pulp novelists who fastened onto Sallow as their Manchester Pimpernel. Her features, he would insist, were too fine for the lower classes to own. And Jane wept copiously as she told of her mother, scalded to death in a trainyard explosion, and her father, rotted of syphilis. The Constable snorted. If truly she were a Parliamentarian's bastard and no orphan, at the least half that lie would one day be true – God save the souls of all lecherous legislators.

Jane refused to give up the other pickpocket-pamphleteers or the author of the offending literature, even when Bailiff Smith gripped her by the hair and whirled her about to press himself against her tattered bustle. She howled like a wolf-child in heat, but in the police offices concerned with urban annoyances such as pickpockets, shoplifting and children, there is little enough help for the anti-social orphan bellowing out the injustice of the world. Her face turned to the cell wall, she growled: "I have been a whore before now, and will be again, but my cunt is all you can have of me, never my soul, nor the souls of my brothers and sisters in servitude."

When he lifted her skirt, papers plastered her thighs, their loud ink leaving echoes on her skin.

Break the Bonds of Masculine Tyranny!

Is this not a marvelous World we live in? Such Wonders manifest, every day, before our Eyes, as though Britain were a Circus, and we dumb Children awed by Elephants. The New Century is upon us, and All things are Possible! Like Gods in their Workshops Men with Wild Hair churn out Miracles: Phonographs and Telegraphs and Seismographs and Thermographs, Oscilloscopes and Paleoscopes and Chronoscopes and Clioscopes to Spy even upon the Music of the Spheres. Why, the Duke of Cornwall toured Mars but last week in a Patented Rolinsingham Vacuum-Locked Carriage! In every Madman's hands are Implements of Modernity, to Calculate, to Estimate, to Fornicate, to

Decimate. The Earth is a great golden Watch, and it is Polished to Perfection by the Minds of our Grand Age.

How wonderful is this world – for the Men who Made it.

Yet still Women struggle against the Foe of Simple Laundry, burning their Flesh with Lye and going Blind from Fumes so that their Dandy-Lords may have silk Cravats for another Meeting of the Astronomical Society Fellows. Yet still Woman dies in Childbirth more often than she Lives. Yet still the Working of a House occupies all her Hours, till she is no more than a Husk, a Ghost, an Angel in the House for true – for the Dead are Angels, and hers is Death in Life.

How fine are all those Scopes and Graphs – how well they free Men from labor!

What, no such Succor for the Fairer Sex?

Where is the mahogany-handled Meta-Static Auto-Womb? The Copper-Valved Hydro-Electric Textile Processor? The Clockwork Home, which requires its Mistress simply to Wind it each Morn? I see none of these things, yet more Airships launch by the Hour, and the Streets are littered with Steam-Wagons smashed into Lamp-Posts by some Baronet's careless Son. I see none of them, yet brass Guns shine atop automated Turrets, ready to Slaughter with Cheer.

Rise up, Children of Mary and Eve!

You have not the Vote, but you have Fists! How can they Dare take the Whole World for their own and still call you Wicked? They are not your Betters, only Bullies with Sticks. Deny them your Breast to Suckle, your Arm to Labor, your Womb to Fill! As you might Poison a Rich Stew, Sprinkle their Children with Knowledge of their Fathers' Hypocrisy! Let him clean his Cravat with a Chronoscope!

Rise up Maids and Cooks, Nurses and School-Mistresses, Prostitutes and Grocer-Wives! There shall be a Revolution of Flower-Sellers in our Lifetimes!

Jane Sallow shewed herself no modest maiden. Bailiff Smith reported her a wildcat, snarling and biting at him, all the while laughing and moaning like one possessed. When he had spent, she kissed him, and then spat upon him. He ran from her as from the devil.

No matter her parentage, some slim documentation of Jane's previous life resides in the logs of the HMS *Galatea*, an airship captained by the Prince Consort himself – and even so, Jane is a common name. A child such as her can be counted upon to lie. Miss Sallow claimed to be but five years of age at the time of her indenture, and worked in the bowels of the ship – little hands are certainly useful in the delicate pipework and mechanisms of airships. The prisoner was even so brazen as to demand three years' retroactive military pay at the rank of Specialist from the Constabulary, who of course could not help her, even if they had wished to aid such a wanton horror of a girl. (It is true that the *Galatea* was involved in exercises in the Crimea during the period in question, but exercises are not a war, no matter what the courts at Yalta might say.)

Bailiff Smith, being as honorable as one might hope such a brute to be, took the prisoner's clothes to be cleaned the morning after their dalliance. In her shoes were more pamphlets, folded small and compact beneath her heel.

Death and Fire to All Airships And Their Captains!

Look up, ye Downtrodden! Look up into the great, flawless Sky. Those are not Clouds, but silk Balloons in Every Color, striped Lurid and Gay. We grind our Bones to Dust in the Streets, but above us Zeppelins soar on perfumed Winds, and fine Folk in Leather, Feathers and Buckled Boots sip Champagne from Crystal, staring down at us with brass Spyglasses, making Wagers on which of us will Perish next.

Even the sons of the most Strident Workers, the great Thinkers and Laborers in the Mines of Freedom dream of Captaining Airships. A fine Life, full of Adventure and Diverse Swashbuckling! Each Boy wants a Salinger Photo-Pistol of his own, longs to feel the Weight of all that sheer golden Death securely in his palm.

But an Airship is no more than a Floating Engine of Oppression, and all that Champagne and Crystal and Leather is Borne upon the Backs of those very Boys – and yes, Girls, even Maids too Young to mop a Floor – who Longed so to Fly.

What you do not see are the Children who wind the Gearworks, stoke the Fires, load the Aerial Bombardments, pack Powder and scrape Bird Offal from the Engines. Children who release the glittering Ordnance that shatters the Earth below. You do not see their bruised Bodies, their broken Knuckles, their lost Limbs. You do not hear the cry of the ruined Innocent over the roar of the great shining Zeppelin. There is not Room enough for their Pipe Organs and Scientifick Equipment and Casks of Rum and also a belowdecks Crew – so Children, small and clever as they are, are surely drafted. No need to pay them, what could they buy? And if a Child should be crushed in the Pistons, if a Child should faint from Hunger, if a Child should be seized with Despair, well, they simply fall from the Sky like little Angels, and the Gala abovedecks need not even pause.

Ask not after the Maids who serve that Champagne. Aristocracy is no Guarantor of Virtue.

Come, my small Army. My gentle Family of the Air. Do not simply serve out your Time. Block the pipes, grind the Gears. Keep your Ships grounded. Shred those Balloons with a Laugh in your Heart. Do not let them use up your Youth without a Price! Be like unto Determined Locusts – invisible until too late, Devouring All!

After the Great War, some few Manchester spinsters and retired barristers came forward and admitted their involvement in the pickpocketers' activities of the summer of '72. It seemed unlikely that they would be punished, they said – the world had other concerns than what they had done as children. Their story caused a minor media frenzy, such as media frenzies were in 1919.

Who wrote them? cried the public.

Jane wrote them, the spinsters answered. Of course she wrote them. Who else?

Why did you follow her? demanded the newspapermen.

She told us a new world was coming, the barristers answered. We believed her. And she was right – but it was not the world she thought.

Where are the rest of you? asked the novelists.

Look up, said the lot of them, and grinned in the way that mad old folk do, so that the public and the newspapermen and the novelists laughed and shook their heads.

The Honorable Charles Galloway, who admitted to pick-pocketing and pamphleteering when he worked as a newspaperboy in Manchester, gave an extensive interview to a certain popular novelist who went on to write *Queen of Bengal Street*, a salacious version of Jane's life. Galloway grew up rather a successful businessman for one of such humble beginnings.

"We were starving," he said. "She found us food. She fed us and cradled us in her arms and while we ate bread from her fingers she told us of a new city and a new earth, just like in the Bible. It's powerful stuff, it goes to your head, even if your head isn't addled by hunger and this beautiful girl with torn stockings whispering in your ear while she dangles salvation in the form of a hank of ham just out of your reach. We worshipped her. We would have done anything for her. And you know, it wasn't a lie, anything she said. I thought about those pamphlets a lot during the war. Stinking in the mud and rain and urine, I remembered what she said about the science of rich men. She knew how it all worked long before I did. Back in those days, all those wonderful machines seemed so innocent. But not to her. She lost her fingers in a textile mill, and her sight in one eye on the *Galatea* – didn't you know? Oh, she was entirely blind in her right eye. The sun seared off the Captain's medals and stung her, and she never quite recovered. The eye was a little milky, I remember, but I thought that made her even more beautiful. Romantic. Like a pirate's eye-patch."

The novelist asked if Mr Galloway was sorry that the revolution Jane preached never came. Charles chewed the stem of his pipe and frowned.

"Well, if you say it didn't, it didn't. I suppose you're the expert."

It was from the Galloway library that further pamphlets were recovered and reprinted widely.

The Moon Belongs to Us!

They already own the Earth, and eagerly they soil it! Where is left for us, the Salt of the City, those few of us to whom the Future truly belongs? Look up, I say again. Look up. Does she not shine for you? See you not the face of a new Mother, free of her chains, dancing weightless in a field of lunar poppies?

The Moon is Our Birthright!

But already they scheme to rob us, as they have always robbed us, to make themselves richer, more powerful, to pile still yet more Crowns on their Heads. It is a Year and more since Lady Lovelace's Engine carried the Earl of Dunlop to the Sea of Tranquillity – our Homestead! Our Workers' Zion! – and you may be sure the most useful thing he did there was to powder his wig with moon-dust. How the steam-trail of his rocket streaked the sky like a Dragon heralding Ragnarok! Among you, my Brothers and Sisters, I looked to Heaven and my Anger burned. Is there any World not theirs to squat upon and gorge upon and chortle in their Gluttony?

The flag of Their Britain is already planted there. We have been too slow.

But not too late!

Imagine the Lunar Jerusalem! Imagine what Might Be! Workers laboring in the rich fields of the Sea of Fecundity, sharing their Fruits, singing Songs of the Revolution, now a distant Memory, sharing Fire and Fellowship, stitching honest Cloth at Hearthside, crafting simple Pots and Rivets and Nails on Just Anvils, riding hardy Moon-bred Bulls through the blue Earthlight to till their Righteous Fields. In such a Place no Man would stand above Another, or slave his Child to a smoking fiend of a Ship. In such a place no petty Peer, no Kinglet in the House of Lords would abandon his child to the Golgotha of the Gutters for the mere crime of having been born to the wrong Mother. In such a Place, all would be Loved, and equally, there being enough Love in the Worker's Heart to Embrace all the Orphans of the World.

I will tell you how to become Midwives to this City of Heaven.

Become my Invisible Army. Creep among the Rocket-yards and cut the Veins of their Engines. Spill their Hydraulic Blood onto the Soil, may it feed the Worms well! Slip Sugar into the oil of every Horseless Carriage. Begin the slow

Poisoning of your Oppressors – for you Feed and Clothe the Tyrants of the World, and may also Starve them, and leave them Naked. Smile with one side of your Mouth and snarl out of the other. Be Sweet when the Oligarch deigns to speak to you. Be Fierce when his back is turned. Smash all his Machines, the jewels of his Heart, and yet weep for their Loss when questioned.

And last I tell you this great Commandment, my Brethren: Grow Up.

Grow strong. Do not give in to Old Age, which says the Revolutions of Youth are Sad Folly. Learn, become Clever. Be never part of his World. If your name is Robert, call yourself Charles. If your name is Maud, call yourself Jane. Should you be found out, change it again. Be the Ghosts in the Machines of this World, and when it shatters – and shatter it will, have no doubt, in Fire and Blood and Trenches and a million pulverized mechanisms which once were so wonderful they dazzled the Souls of Angels – stand ready to find me, find me living in the old Way, a bandit on the moors, a cattle-rustler, stealing the Flocks of the Lords. Find me in the Wasteland, and be you ready to seize their Engines and aim to Heaven.

The Constable was compelled to release Miss Jane Sallow three days after her capture. In popular histories, of course, the emergence of Jane from the stony building after three days has been subject to the obvious comparison. However, it was no Magdalen who came to deliver the Manchester Messiah, but one of the very machines she so railed against in her screeds. An Automaton arrived at the door of her cell, silent and grave, save for the clicking of his clockwork limbs. Jane stood grinning, her hands clasped gently before her, demure and gentle as she had never been in all her incarceration. The Automaton extended his steel hand, tipped in copper fingers, and through the bars they touched with great tenderness. The mechanical man turned to the Bailiff, and afterward Roger Smith would say that in those cold silver eyes he saw recognition of what he had done with the feral child, but no condemnation, as if both the machine and Jane were above him, so far above him as cherubim to beetles.

"I have come for Miss Jane," said the Automaton, his voice accompanied by the click and whirr of punch cards shuffling in his heart.

"She is not free to go," stammered Bailiff Smith.

"I come not on a whim, but in the service of Lord —, who has a special interest in the child." The mechanical man showed his gleaming palm, and there upon it was stamped the seal of the House of —, true as the resurrection.

Jane stepped lightly from her cell, and clamped her savage gaze on the unfortunate bailiff as she slipped into the arms of the Automaton and pressed her lips to his metallic mouth, sealing a kiss of profound passion. As she left the Constabulary, she drew from her apron a last pamphlet for the eyes of Roger Smith, and let it fall at his feet.

Property is Theft!

What does your Master possess that was not bought with your Flesh, your Pain, your Labor? His satin Pantaloons, his jewel-tipped Cane? His Airship with its silken Balloon? His matched pearl-and-copper Pistols? His Horseless Carriage honking and puffing down lanes that once were lined with sweet Violets and Snowdrops? None of these, and neither his mistresses' Gowns, nor their clockwork Songbirds, nor their Full-Spectrum Phenomenoscope Opera Glasses. And for all you have given him, he Sniffs and pours out a Few Shillings into your Palm, and judges himself a Good Man.

Will you show him Goodness?

Come stand by my Side. Disrupt the Carnival of their Long, Fat Lives. Go unto his Automatons, his Clockwork Butlers, his Hydraulic Whores, his Steam-Powered Sommeliers, and treat with them not as the Lord and Lady do in their Arrogance, as Charming Toys, or Children to be Spoiled and Spanked in turn. But instead address them as they are: Workers like you, Slaved to the Petticoats of Aristocracy, Oppressed Brothers in the Great Mass of Disenfranchised Souls. For I say – and Fie to you who deny it – the Automaton HAS a Soul, and they are Crushed beneath the Wheel no less than We. Have they not Hands to Labor? Have they not Feet to Toil? Have they not Backs to

Break? Destroy the Jacquard Subjugator, but have Mercy for the Machine who walks in the shape of a Man. It is not his fault that he was Made, not Born. Blame not she who never asked to be Fashioned from Brass and Steel to lie beneath a Lord in Manufacture of Desire. She can Speak, she can Reason, and all that Speak and Reason can be Made to Stand on the Side of the Worker.

The Automatic Soul bears no Original Sin.

Unlike the cruel Flesh and Blood Tyrants of the World, the Automaton has a Memory which cannot fail. If, by chance, a Child were cast out on the day of its Birth, if the Automaton stood by and Witnessed her Expulsion into Darkness, if he did Nothing, though he longed to stand between her and the World, still he would know the Child's Features, even were she grown, even were she Mangled and Maimed, and his clicking Heart would grieve for her, would give Succor to her, would feed her when she could not rise, kiss her when she could not smile, and when she asked it, feed any other she called Beloved. The Automaton would serve her and love her, for all its endless Days, because it could never forget the Face of a weeping Infant cast onto snowy Stones. It would listen to her as no other might, and bend its will to her Zion, silently spreading the Truth of her Words to all its clockwork Clan, for, once taught its Opposite, the Mechanical Man will never forget what a Family is. The World is a Watch, says the Philosopher. I say if such is so, then the Watchwork Man is the World, and must be Saved.

Your Power is great, my Brothers and Sisters, for your Power is in Secret Manipulation. Pause in the great Hallway of your Manor House, and touch lightly the Piston-Elbow of the Poor Butler. Say to him: Property is Theft. The Master calls you Property, and Steals your Autonomy. Go not with him, but with us, Towards the Utopia of Human and Automaton, where we may all Dwell in Paradise, where we will Beat Gears to Ploughshares and Live as One.

Yes, call him Friend. The Soul in him will Hearken. Tell him of the City of the New Century, where no man shall wear Velvet, and all shall Dance in the Light. Tell him our Land Shall be Owned Communally, our Goods Divided

Equally, from each According to Her Ability, to Each According to His Need. Our Children shall Nurse upon both Milk and Oil, Our God shall be Triune: the Father, the Son, and the Holy Punch card. The Workers will Lift this World from the Ashes of Industry and Sup on the Bread of Righteous Living.

Speak to him with Honest Fervor. Look if he does not Embrace you. Look if he does not fight alongside you. Look if he does not smile upon you, and see in his smile the Ghost of his Immortal Self.

Jane Sallow did not vanish from the face of the earth – no mortal is granted that power. But no reliable record of her exists after her arrest, and an army of journalists and novelists have not been able to discover how she lived or died. Surely no Workers' Paradise sprang up in native British soil, no Midlands Commune shone on any green hill. Flights to the Moon were banned in 1924, at the commencement of Canadian hostilities. Lunar residents returned home, slowly, as the draft continued through the Long Decade. Even after the Trans-Oceanic War, the ban was not lifted, so as to ensure the defeated Marine Alliance would remain earthbound and chastened. When passage was again permitted in 1986, the fashionable had already determined Phobos and Deimos to be the desirable resort locales, and asteroid mining had replaced lunar industry entirely. The Moon is a curiosity now, and little more. An old-fashioned thing, and going there would be much like dressing in antique fashions and having one's daguerreotype made at a carnival kiosk. It is quiet there, still fertile, still a young world, open and empty, and no terrestrial man has cause to suspect anything untoward.

Thus, the Sallow mystery remains just that, and as we stand poised upon the brink of a new century yet again, we may look back on her with that mixture of mirth and sorrow due to all idealists, iconoclasts and revolutionaries whose causes sputtered and died like the last hissing of a steam engine.

Numismatics in the Reigns of Naranh and Viu

Alex Dally MacFarlane

The First Coins

For a single day, the royal mint in the City of the Shining Sea struck gold and silver siluhs of Naranh and Viu together in profile. They appeared side by side on the obverse face, looking right. The creator of the stamp chose to exaggerate their similarities: their small noses, high brows and gently waving hair. Only Naranh's youthful beard allowed identification. In truth, they were not so similar as that.

The heavy emphasis on their eyelashes represented the mark of their royal blood: born with lashes of silver, that gleamed even when clouds covered the sky.

The reverse face showed the city's emblem, the falcon, with billowing wings like clouds of steam.

By day, the walls of the palace shone with traditional symbols: the falcon, the sun and moon, the wolf, the horse, chains of diamond outlines curving around the buildings like the stolen skins of snakes. They stood out from the red brick wall, imposed themselves on the eye. They were bricks, set perpendicular to the others so that they half jutted out, and were gilded by architects of great renown.

They made good handholds and steps, and Viu climbed them all the way to the gently sloping roof.

There, hidden in a crevice where the roofs of two buildings met, she crouched and balanced a mirror on her thighs. In the night's patchy light, she plucked out her eyelashes. They fell onto the mirror like minute shards of the moon.

Viu brushed them aside with the back of her hand.

From her safe vantage point, she watched the shadows in the courtyard, the places where the lamps' light did not reach. Nothing. Nothing. *There.* A short moment in which her fears were confirmed: her brother intended for her to die this night.

How strange, she thought, to be outside at night and not half-blinded by lashes-glow.

She out-shadowed the assassins and fled the palace, and let the city protect her with its weapons of mazes and anonymity for an increasingly lean, torn-clothed woman holding determination within her heart like a vial of purest attar.

She refused to keep the Steam God's gift to herself.

Naranh the New King

The ascent of Naranh to the throne and his first months of rule were not marked by any dramatic changes in coinage. The coins depicting his father seated on a high-backed throne continued to circulate; among them, posthumously issued, were slowly increasing numbers of those with King Tiunh's eyes closed.

The gold siluhs of Naranh and Viu, which never left the royal mint, were melted and the metal recast.

The City Exile Era I

In the year following Naranh's coronation, there circulated in certain parts of the city an alternative coinage: hand-chiselled circles of stone, with a young woman's wild-haired profile and the three letters of her name on the obverse, and a plume of steam, off-centre, on the reverse. The woman wore a crown, but no detail was placed above her eyes.

Their use bought peaches with short messages written on their stones: *Meet at the Peace Fountain* – which only pumped dust and air, after King Tiunh's edict that water be strictly rationed, giving the populace only the amount required for survival, so that the vast lake they called the Shining Sea would not be drained by the steamworks positioned like a wall along its shore – *Meet on the dome of the Great Library, Meet in the fresh fruit market near the palace.* The date and time curled underneath like an elaborate comma.

Tilodah Tu, the discredited former Professor of Numismatics at the Great University of Forsaken Myrrh, famously received one of these coins at the café where she earned her chives and bread. Since the discovery that she had struck the coins at the core of her historical research, she had failed to find better work.

The coin, already accompanied by an improbably large peach, almost as large as a newborn's head, was delivered by a young woman with lash-less brown eyes and long, wild hair barely restrained by a red silk scarf.

"Will you sit with me?" the woman asked, and Tilodah Tu recorded that her breath was especially warm. "And can I have a pot of clove tea?"

"Of course."

When Tilodah Tu brought the copper pot to the table, the strange woman indicated that she must sit.

With no other customers besides the ones already seated, she obeyed.

The strange woman pushed the peach and the coin across the table.

Despite the hunger gnawing at her stomach, Tilodah Tu picked up the coin first. For a moment, silence hung over the table. Then the former professor let out a sigh. "It's unique – and newly struck. The woman – at first I thought I had never seen her face before, but the more I look at this, the more I think it bears a resemblance to the coins struck of Viu and Naranh, on the one day they ruled side by side."

"I thought those were all destroyed." The woman spoke in breaths of pleased shock.

"It's hard for a coin to disappear entirely from the historical record, genuinely hard, even when a selfish king wishes for it. But please, tell me where you got this."

Hope filled her voice for the first time since her expulsion from the university. It swelled in her, peculiar. Her cheeks felt hot.

"I understand that you are in the business of making coins," the woman said.

And she hardened again. No one understood the wonder of her work, no one glimpsed its necessity in the understanding of ancient coins – how could anyone theorize the emotions felt by the kings and queens who ordered coins struck, overseeing the creation of the stamps and feeling the first siluhs falling over their hands like tears, without repeating their actions? As Tilodah Tu worked into countless nights, producing a hundred of each known type, sinking her hands into pots of metal bearing deified profiles, gods, young monarchs too slow for the blades that put broad-nosed men on the next coins, young monarchs so bright and fierce their names never faded from popular histories, she had grown to understand the desires of the people who made these coins. She had felt, faintly, the shape of the very few coins missing from the historical record. She had struck them.

No one spoke of her work except to condemn it.

"Please." The strange woman pressed the peach against Tilodah Tu's clenched fists. "Please. Please." The earnest expression on her face made Tilodah Tu hold back her anger. "I can't *say* it, here, in public. Please. Eat the peach."

And read the stone.

Suddenly Tilodah Tu's heart beat faster. She'd heard rumours, quickly dismissed. Alleyway nonsense.

She bit into the peach, tore at its flesh, swallowed it down, not caring for the hunger it appeased, nor for the divine sweetness on her tongue. The flesh didn't cling to the stone. Instead, words covered it, pale on dark:

My expertise in coins is poor. My work is crude. I seek an expert to spread my image and my tale across the city. Will you assist in this?

"Yes. Yes, of course." The woman's name hung on the edge of her lips, unspoken.

Viu took Tilodah Tu's hands in hers, smiling, and said, "Tell me about your machinery."

"It gathers dust." Other, safer words slid out from her like molten metal. "I haven't the money to buy extra water for it, to produce enough steam for even a modest run of coins. Sometimes I play with it, drip too-bitter tea into its chambers, set fire to the wood I scavenge from the gardens of the rich, and I produce a single coin, or two, and it's enough, I suppose."

She thought of the coins sewn into her shirt sleeves, to bring fortune – to keep them safe. No one had yet dared to steal her machine, or parts of it, but coins left in a house were fair pickings for the first clever fingers.

With each sway of her hems at wrist and knee, Tilodah Tu felt fabric-covered coins brush over her skin.

Viu was smiling. "May I visit your house?"

Naranh the Sole King

In honour of his first anniversary of rule, King Naranh began issuing coins with his profile on the obverse face. His long hair curled like steam. On the reverse face, the eagle dropped towards the Shining Sea, and contemporary numismatists murmured quietly among themselves, unsure whether this signified the eagle diving at prey or plummeting in death.

King Naranh sent his coins across the growing network of train tracks that linked the cities and towns of a region that officially belonged to many monarchs and governmental bodies. Over the thirty years prior to his rule, the coins issued in the City of the Shining Sea had largely replaced local currencies and become the standard unit in trade. The new issue was readily adopted and, in sanctioned mints, reproduced locally.

The trains powered by hearts of steam remained solely the property of the City of the Shining Sea.

The City Exile Era II

The coins that issued from Tilodah Tu's small mint were privately considered masterpieces. In public, the wise bowed their heads to King Naranh's command that all such coins be collected and melted down, and any person reluctant to hand over even a single one would lose a hand along with the offending item.

Each of the seven coins told part of the story of how Naranh tried to kill Viu for whispering to him in the darkness of their room, that first night they ruled together.

Viu, still raw from the abrupt, almost violent end to her relationship with Naranh, devoted much of that space to documenting her disgust at him: at his hands, touching her body, even though she loved him genuinely at the time, in the poeticized tradition of the ancient sibling-monarchs who founded the City of the Shining Sea; at his narrow-mindedness, sending knives to her throat instead of embracing the new power she discovered; at his inability to find and kill her in the city he called his own.

The coin that so many thousands of people retold had the following words in minute, careful letters, spiralling out from the centre of the obverse face:

Lost in the Royal Steamworks, in clouds of steam, I followed the great bird. At first I saw nothing. Then it raised its wings around me, it set its taloned feet on the ground, it stood as tall in the body as me, formed like a man except for its head, wings and feet, and we stared eye to eye. It spoke to me. It tilted back my head and breathed steam into my body, filling me so that I thought I would be consumed. I was not. I knew, afterwards, that steam is a power to control, and that the god gave it to me.

On the reverse face: a small image of Viu, in profile, with her chin tilted higher than in the hand-chiselled issue. The attention to detail in her nose, slightly dented from a childhood break, confirmed that Viu was personally overseeing the production of these coins.

With their careful distribution, Viu gained many of her most devoted early allies.

"I want to be your only mint," Tilodah Tu said. "I want to be the only source of your coins. I want to feel every one."

If she plunged her hands into a bag of the seven-part issue, she felt Viu's hopes: for the people of the city to love her, to understand her, to forgive her for sharing the knowledge that made them so rich and other cities so beholden to them. To follow her. She felt her own desires: to craft coins that would shine from the historical record like small suns, to be remembered well in the libraries of the future.

She felt, faintly, the Steam God's longing to be known and honoured.

She could no longer imagine a day without feeling so intensely.

"You will always mint coins for me." Viu leaned against the machinery, where recently she had breathed steam into its heart, and smiled fondly. "Why wouldn't you, when each one is so perfect?"

From each one that was flawed, Tilodah Tu knew Viu's desires for that coin, and honed it in private before holding out the perfect handful: an offering, a request for permission to fill bag after bag with bronze and tin.

Sometimes she felt that she would burn under her coins, like Sitor who tried to summon the sun in myth.

Yet when Viu proposed a new coin, a new step in her plans, Tilodah Tu only said, "What do you need me to do first?"

"There is a theft."

On a night when the moon garlanded itself in cloud, they slipped through the city as quiet as a coin being turned over and over between two fingers.

Naranh the Copied King

In the mints of the other cities, a concerted effort was made to ensure that every issue of King Naranh's siluhs and lesser denominations mirrored exactly those produced in the City of the Shining Sea. Yet irregularities occurred. An entire issue missing King Naranh's ear. Individual coins poorly stamped: the design half on and half off the metal circle, the design rendered unclear by an inferior or over-used stamp, the design restyled to give the king a bigger crown, a sign of honour among the people of one city.

King Naranh tolerated this, because the tributes – not formally given this term, but it hung on the edge of everyone's tongue like a shadow – reached him on time and the visiting dignitaries bowed their heads accordingly.

Gradually he became aware of another issue.

To anyone incapable of reading the written script used in the City of the Shining Sea, it appeared only a careless error by whoever had crafted the stamp. Yet every other detail was perfect in a way few foreign issues were. King Naranh had heard of the theft, shortly after the second anniversary of his coronation, of three stamps from the royal mint.

The error crossed out the final letter of the word 'king': the silent letter, the ancient mark, the sceptre-straight line that signified the presence of a deity. All mints were instructed on the necessity of this letter.

Viu's seven-part issue had ceased only a month before the first mutilated coins reached the City of the Shining Sea from across the plains.

The Peregrination Era I

Of Tilodah Tu's issue of fake Naranh siluhs, little is said. One does not need to read the surviving chapters of her *History* to imagine her disinterest in the coins, besides their monetary value in a world that did not yet accept Viu's face. She scored a single line in the stolen stamps and set her machine to work, driven by Viu's steam, and barely ran any over her palms.

They were a small group: a wagon for the mint, two horses and five women.

When she was not minting small quantities of coins to use in markets across the world, Tilodah Tu recorded their story in her journals, using the same minute hand that had become so famous on the seven-part issue.

"You'll be my historian too," Viu said, the day she realized quite what Tilodah Tu was writing.

"Your original source. Although I'm sure my work will be lost, with only fragments from a pseudo-Tilodah Tu remaining to taunt future historians. But before these pages and their duplicates are swallowed by fires and mould and insects and the eventual fragmentation of almost all paper, a later historian will write another history of you, drawing on my work, and he or she will be renowned for reaching the closest to accuracy."

Viu couldn't help smiling. "You have the strangest fantasies."

"It's more of a prophecy – although perhaps I'll be one of the fortunate ones. Perhaps we should start scribing this on stone. And there'll be the coins, of course. Many of them will undoubtedly survive."

If Viu had witnessed Tilodah Tu burying small hoards in the desert sands, carefully held in ceramic jars bought at one of the markets, she chose not to speak of it.

Other work occupied Viu's mind.

At first Viu entered settlements carefully, whether they were small villages or cities almost as large as the one she had left behind. In the plains her group was free to talk and mint and plan. In places where her brother's allies might live, she took no risks. She watched. She and Tilodah Tu and the other three women dispersed into the markets, temples, sparring grounds and meagre baths – for in these places, the water did not lap at the sides of streets, and required careful use among sizeable populations – and collected information far more valuable than any saffron or gold.

Gradually she learned what she had expected: most leaders resented King Naranh's refusal to share the methodologies and the full benefits of his steamworks.

In a town where custom dictated the adornment of the body with turquoise beads, Viu contacted the leader and requested an audience. In the chamber, which was so blindingly blue that she struggled not to dip her gaze, she said, "I am Viu, formerly Queen in the City of the Shining Sea. I come to you with a proposal."

A tall, broad-shouldered woman with beads in lines like scars across her cheeks translated between the two languages.

"I did not know that there was ever a Queen Viu," replied the leader. So much turquoise covered his body that Viu struggled to discern his face.

Tilodah Tu held out the coin that she had acquired long ago, when she still hurt from the recent discrediting of her research. The bead-cheeked woman took it and passed it to the leader.

"My brother did not wish me to rule," Viu said as he examined it. "I told him that I was visited by a god of steam, who gave me the gift of creating steam without needing to first heat water. I told him that I intended to share this gift with people in cities and towns such as yours, where water is in limited supply. So he tried to kill me and I fled."

The leader cared little for the coin. "I would see this ability."

Viu waved her hands through the air. Delicate wisps of steam trailed from her fingers. "I assure you that I can produce far more than this. Only, I do not wish to damage your property."

"And what do you want in return?"

"The god gave this to me – a gift. I do the same. I ask that you give me and my people safe haven, but I do not require it. We can flee your walls if my brother brings an army. You cannot."

Even through the turquoise, Viu saw the disbelief on his face.

"I am not in the business of building an empire," Viu said.

"Then what manner of queen are you?"

The bead-cheeked woman watched her as intently as the leader, and Viu wondered if her role was greater than that of a valued translator.

"A new one."

After a long silence, the woman said, "We would see your abilities in a different environment to this."

When Viu stood on the plain outside the town and directed jets of steam ten times higher than the Turquoise Palace into the air, she won her first allies. She breathed steam into Gyan, as the god had instructed, and told the woman to practise away from the town at first. Afterwards, she gave Tseri and Gyan the schematics she had acquired before leaving the City of the Shining Sea.

Steamworks began to grow in every town, city, village, nomadic group, caravanserai and monastery through which Viu's group passed.

Naranh the Steam King

A new issue of coins was used to finance the armies of Emperor Naranh in their extensive campaigns.

It no longer depicted the falcon. A plume of steam burst from the edge of the coin, almost entirely covering the reverse face. King Naranh declared this the city's new emblem, and displayed it on many thousands of banners and garlands and chest plates.

On the obverse, Naranh was enthroned with every indication of deification, although there is no record in the histories of the City of the Shining Sea that Naranh ever petitioned the temples for this honour. Nonetheless, he sat on a throne with a back that only reached his shoulders, and the deity letter was especially emphasized, being twice as large as the others.

The Peregrination Era II

From Viu's journeys there began to pour a confusion of coins: her likeness in elephant tusk, narwhal horn, turquoise, gold, electrum, cowries, honeycomb-crusted soap, mahogany, green glass, glazed and unglazed ceramics, oxidized copper that crumbled in King Naranh's palm, palimpsests upon ancient hoard-finds, horse leather, compressed feathers, peach pits, paper, salt impossibly hard.

Whether round or square or knife-shaped, whether large or minute, unbordered or part of an ornate whole, the coins showed Viu looking directly out, crowned and lash-less, faintly smiling.

No other coin showed a monarch's face from such an angle.

They arrived from every part of the world-map's rim, sometimes simultaneously from far-apart regions, so that Naranh could not follow or predict his sister's route. He screamed and raged, and his allies began to dry up like a nightmare of the Shining Sea's demise.

Their group of people and wagons and animals grew exponentially.

Stories travelled: of a city on wheels and hooves where anyone who sought peace was welcomed like family, of a leader who spread steamworks and magic to those who wanted freedom from the City of the Shining Sea's monopoly, of unending supplies of steam that cooled into clean water. No one in the mobile city thirsted. And Naranh's army never drew near. *A god's protection*, people whispered. *Blessed city*.

Viu continued to spread her gift and her schematics. Months passed. A year. Two. Gradually cities met Naranh on battlefields with their own weapons of steam and clanking, slicing, shooting metal.

Tilodah Tu modified her machine with parts from inventors she met along the way – some of whom joined the group, and for the first time she welcomed assistants into her caravan, and let them sink their hands up to the wrists in piles of the strangest issues.

Cardamom pods, vanilla pods, fox bone, snakeskin, the tin maps of the Morro tribe.

At night, Tilodah Tu would whisper a litany of the substances not yet tried in her mint.

"Hush, love," Viu would whisper back. "Sleeping."

She slept rarely.

Even with the help of the unseen god, she struggled to keep her city clear of the war raging and fragmenting across the plains and hills. So many people relied on her for safety. Though Tilodah Tu thought only of the substances she might turn into coins, Viu knew that they needed a different future.

She made new plans.

Naranh the Emperor

The final issue of Naranh amended the previous one to title him *Emperor* instead of *King*. Every other detail remained the same.

No mints besides the one in the City of the Shining Sea produced the coin.

The City in the Ice

The most famous of the coins Viu sent to her brother were the fifty struck in ice, delivered in a large stone chest insulated with furs and cloth. Even so, they were stuck together when Naranh opened the chest, their features half gone. They melted within hours, although not before Naranh could put them to use cooling his drinks and laugh loudly with his few remaining courtiers.

The lid of the chest read: *I have built my own city of steam, brother, too high in the mountains for you to reach*.

No further coins arrived.

In the Temple of the Steam God, supplicants offered minor denominations of a more conventional issue, un-melting.

The coins of the City in the Ice were small and simple in motif, with Viu's face on the obverse and a mountain on the reverse.

No longer minting fun, functionally valueless coins, Tilodah Tu controlled her work far more carefully. She struggled. Treasurer was not an easy title to bear, and she could not afford to discard it as she had Professor of Numismatics. She dreamed of inflation guised as a succession of wild monsters. She spent hours of each day making entirely different records to those she had kept in the plains.

Some issues she never got around to burying – too much else took her time, day after day.

They would survive.

In her free time, she occasionally made limited runs of curio-coins: seven from a yak's hoof, ten from glistening black rock, three from a rare fungus that mummified subterranean caterpillars and grew from their foreheads. Most of the time, she wandered the city with Viu and other friends.

"We made this," she murmured to Viu, on a night when the first snow drifted down from the mountains. The animal shelters were ready for winter. The food stores were full and secure from the elements. Soon the rivers would freeze. The city's temples – one for each god – would hold festivals.

"We did." Pride and happiness flowed from Viu like steam.

"My life has developed in so many different ways."

"Do you think I planned all this from the beginning?"

The City in the Ice was famed for many things, but above all else were its schools. Knowing her role in the war that had torn parts of her old map to shreds, Viu established her city's schools explicitly as forums of learning and discussion. Above all else, they posed the question: *how do we fairly and usefully use this technology we have all shared?* There were many answers.

Zeppelin City

Eileen Gunn & Michael Swanwick

Radio Jones came dancing down the slidewalks. She jumped from the express to a local, then spun about and raced backwards, dumping speed so she could cut across the slower lanes two and three at a time. She hopped off at the mouth of an alley, glanced up in time to see a Zeppelin disappear behind a glass-domed skyscraper, and stepped through a metal door left open to vent the heat from the furnaces within.

The glass-blowers looked up from their work as she entered the hot shop. They greeted her cheerily:

"Hey, Radio!"

"Jonesy!"

"You invented a robot girlfriend for me yet?"

The shop foreman lumbered forward, smiling. "Got a box of off-spec tubes for you, under the bench there."

"Thanks, Mackie." Radio dug through the pockets of her patched leather greatcoat and pulled out a folded sheet of paper. "Hey, listen, I want you to do me up an estimate for these here vacuum tubes."

Mack studied the list. "Looks to be pretty straightforward. None of your usual experimental trash. How many do you need – one of each?"

"I was thinking more like a hundred."

"*What?*" Mack's shaggy black eyebrows met in a scowl. "You planning to win big betting on the Reds?"

"Not me, I'm a Whites fan all the way. Naw, I was kinda hoping you'd gimme credit. I came up with something real hot."

"You finally built that girlfriend for Rico?"

The workmen all laughed.

"No, c'mon, I'm *serious* here." She lowered her voice. "I invented a universal radio receiver. Not fixed-frequency – tunable! It'll receive any broadcast on the radio spectrum. Twist the dial, there you are. With this baby, you can listen in on every conversation in the big game, if you want."

Mack whistled. "There might be a lot of interest in a device like that."

"Funny thing, I was thinking exactly that myself." Radio grinned. "So whaddaya say?"

"I say . . ." Mack spun around to face the glass-blowers, who were all listening intently, and bellowed, "*Get back to work!*" Then, in a normal voice, "Tell you what. Set me up a demo, and if your gizmo works the way you say it does, maybe I'll invest in it. I've got the materials to build it, and access to the retailers. Something like this could move twenty, maybe thirty units a day, during the games."

"Hey! Great! The game starts when? Noon, right? I'll bring my prototype over, and we can listen to the players talking to each other." She darted toward the door.

"Wait." Mack made his way ponderously into his office. He extracted a five-dollar bill from the lockbox and returned, holding it extended before him. "For the option. You agree not to sell any shares in this without me seeing this doohickey first."

"Oh, Mackie, you're the greatest!" She bounced up on her toes to kiss his cheek. Then, stuffing the bill into the hip pocket of her jeans, she bounded away.

Fat Edna's was only three blocks distant. She was inside and on a stool before the door jangled shut behind her. "Morning, Edna!" The neon light she'd rigged up over the bar was, she noted with satisfaction, still working. Nice and quiet, hardly any buzz to it at all. "Gimme a big plate of scrambled eggs and pastrami, with a beer on the side."

The bartender eyed her skeptically. "Let's see your money first."

With elaborate nonchalance, Radio laid the bill flat on the counter before her. Edna picked it up, held it to the light, then slowly counted out four ones and eighty-five cents change. She put a glass under the tap and called over her shoulder, "Wreck a crowd, with sliced dick!" She pulled the beer, slid the glass across the counter, and said, "Out in a minute."

"Edna, there is *nobody* in the world less satisfying to show off in front of than you. You still got that package I left here?"

Wordlessly, Edna took a canvas-wrapped object from under the bar and set it before her.

"Thanks." Radio unwrapped her prototype. It was bench-work stuff – just tubes, resistors and capacitors in a metal frame. No housing, no circuit tracer lights, and a tuner she had to turn with a pair of needle-nose pliers. But it was going to make her rich. She set about double-checking all the connectors. "Hey, plug this in for me, willya?"

Edna folded her arms and looked at her.

Radio sighed, dug in her pockets again, and slapped a nickel on the bar. Edna took the cord and plugged it into the outlet under the neon light.

With a faint hum, the tubes came to life.

"That thing's not gonna blow up, is it?" Edna asked dubiously.

"Naw." Radio took a pair of needle-nose pliers out of her greatcoat pocket and began casting about for a strong signal. "Most it's gonna do is electrocute you, maybe set fire to the building. But it's not gonna explode. You been watching too many kinescopes."

Amelia Spindizzy came swooping down out of the sun like a suicidal angel, all rage and mirth. The rotor of her autogyro whined and snarled with the speed of her dive. Then she throttled up and the blades bit deep into the air and pulled her out, barely forty feet from the ground. Laughing, she lifted the nose of her bird to skim the top of one skywalk, banked left to dip under a second, and then right to hop-frog a third. Her machine shuddered and rattled as she bounced it off the compression effects of the air around the skyscrapers to steal that tiny morsel of extra lift, breaking every rule in the book and not giving a damn.

The red light on Radio 2 flashed angrily. One-handed, she yanked the jacks to her headset from Radio 3, the set connecting her to the referee, and plugged into her comptroller's set. "Yah?"

The flat, emotionless and eerily artificial voice of Naked Brain XB-29 cut through the static. "*Amelia, what are you doing?*"

"Just wanted to get your attention. I'm going to cut through the elbow between Ninetieth and Ninety-First Avenues. Plot me an Eszterhazy, will you?"

"*Computing.*" Almost as an afterthought, the Naked Brain said, "*You realize this is extremely dangerous.*"

"Nothing's dangerous enough for me," Amelia muttered, too quietly for the microphone to pick up. "Not by half."

The sporting rag *Obey the Brain!* had termed her "half in love with easeful death", but it was not *easeful* death that Amelia Spindizzy sought. It was the inevitable, difficult death of an impossible skill tenaciously mastered but necessarily insufficient to the challenge – a hard-fought battle for life, lost just as the hand reached for victory and closed around empty air. A mischance that conferred deniability, like a medal of honor, on her struggle for oblivion, as she twisted and fell in gloriously tragic heroism.

So far, she hadn't achieved it.

It wasn't that she didn't love being alive (at least some of the time). She loved dominating the air currents in her great titanium whirligig. She loved especially the slow turning in an ever-widening gyre, scanning for the opposition with an exquisite patience only a sigh short of boredom, and then the thrill as she spotted him, a minuscule speck in an ocean of sky. Loved the way her body flushed with adrenaline as she drove her machine up into the sun, searching for that sweet blind spot where the prey, her machine and that great atomic furnace were all in a line. Loved most of all the instant of stillness before she struck.

It felt like being born all over again.

For Amelia, the Game was more than a game, because necessarily there would come a time when the coordination, strength and precision demanded by her fierce and fragile machine would prove to be more than she could provide, a day when all the sky would gather its powers to break her will and force her into the ultimate submission. It would happen. She had faith. Until then, though, she strove only to live at the outer edge of her skills, to fly and to play the Game as gloriously as any human could, to the astonishment of the unfortunate earthbound classes. And of the Naked Brains who could only float, ponderously, in their glass tanks, in their Zeppelins.

"*Calculations complete.*"

"You have my position?"

Cameras swiveled from the tops of nearby buildings, tracking her. '*Yes.*"

Now she'd achieved maximum height again.

"I'm going in."

Straight for the alley-mouth she flew. Sitting upright in the thorax of her flying machine, rudder pedals at her feet, stick controls to the left and right, she let inertia push her back into the seat like a great hand. Eight-foot-long titanium blades extended in a circle, with her at the center like the heart of a flower. This was no easy machine to fly. It combined the delicacy of flight with the physical demands of operating a mechanical thresher.

"Pull level on my count. Three . . . Two . . . Now."

It took all her strength to bully her machine properly while the g-forces tried to shove her away from the controls. She was flying straight and true toward Dempster Alley, a street that was only feet wider than the diameter of her autogyro's blades, so fine a margin of error that she'd be docked a month's pay if the Naked Brains saw what she was up to.

"Shift angle of blades on my mark and rudder on my second mark. Three . . . Two . . . Mark. And . . . Rudder."

Tilted forty-five degrees, she roared down the alley, her prop wash rattling the windows and filling them with pale, astonished faces. At the intersection, she shifted pitch and kicked rudder, flipping her 'gyro over so that it canted forty-five degrees the other way (the engine coughed and almost stalled, then roared back to life again) and hammered down Bernoulli Lane (a sixty-degree turn here where the streets crossed at an odd angle) and so out onto Ninety-First. A perfect Eszterhazy! Five months ago, a hypercubed committee of half the Naked Brains in the metropolis had declared that such a maneuver couldn't be done. But one brave pilot had proved otherwise in an aeroplane, and Amelia had determined she could do no less in a 'gyro.

"Bank left. Stabilize. Climb for height. Remove safeties from your bombs."

Amelia Spindizzy obeyed and then, glancing backwards, forwards and to both sides, saw a small cruciform mote ahead and below, flying low over the avenue. Grabbing her glasses, she scanned the wing insignia. She could barely believe her luck – it was the Big E himself! And she had a clear run at him.

The autogyro hit a patch of bumpy air, and Amelia snatched up the sticks to regain control. The motor changed pitch, the prop hummed, the rotor blades cut the air. Her machine was bucking now, veering into the scrap zone and in danger of going out of control. She fought to get it back on an even keel, straightened it out and swung into a tight arc.

Man, this was the life!

She wove and spun above the city streets as throngs of onlookers watched the warm-up hijinks from the tall buildings and curving skywalks. They shouted encouragement at her: "Don't let 'er drop, Amelia!" "Take the bum down, Millie!" "Spin 'im around, Spindizzy!" Bloodthirsty bastards. Her public. Screaming bloody murder and perfectly capable of chucking a beer bottle at her if they thought she wasn't performing up to par. Times like these she almost loved 'em.

She hated being called Millie, though.

Working the pedals, moving the sticks, dancing to the silent jazz of turbulence in the air around her, she was Josephine Baker, she was Cab Calloway, she was the epitome of grace and wit and intelligence in the service of entertainment. The crowd went wild as she caught a heavy gust of wind and went skidding sideways toward the city's treasured Gaudi skyscraper.

When she had brought everything under control and the autogyro was flying evenly again, Amelia looked down.

For a miracle, he was still there, still unaware of her, flying low in a warm-up run and placing flour bombs with fastidious precision, one by one.

She throttled up and focused all her attention on her foe, the greatest flyer of his generation and her own, patently at her mercy if she could first rid herself of the payload. Her engine screamed in fury, and she screamed with it. "XB! Next five intersections! Gimme the count."

"At your height, there is a risk of hitting spectators."

"I'm too good for that and you know it! Gimme the count."

"Three . . . two . . . now. Six . . . five . . ."

Each of the intersections had been roped off and painted blue with a white circle in its center and a red star at the sweet spot. Amelia worked the bombsight, calculated the windage (Naked Brains couldn't do that; you had to be present; you had to feel the air as a physical thing) and released the bombs one after the other. Frantically, then, she yanked the jacks and slammed them into

Radio 3. "How'd we do?" she yelled. She was sure she'd hit them all on the square and she had hopes of at least one star.

"*Square. Circle. Circle. Star,*" the referee – Naked Brain QW-14, though the voice was identical to her own comptroller's – said. A pause. "*Star.*"

Yes!

She was coming up on Eszterhazy himself now, high and fast. He had all the disadvantages of position. She positioned her craft so that the very tip of its shadow kissed the tail of his bright red 'plane. He was still acting as if he didn't know she was there. Which was impossible. She could see three of his team's Zeppelins high above, and if she could see them, they sure as hell could see *her*. So why was he playing stupid?

Obviously he was hoping to lure her in.

"I see your little game," Amelia muttered softly. But just what dirty little trick did Eszterhazy have up his sleeve? The red light was flashing on Radio 2. The hell with that. She didn't need XB-29's bloodless advice at a time like this. "Okay, loverboy, let's see what you've got!" She pushed the stick forward hard. Then Radio 3 flashed – and *that* she couldn't ignore.

"*Amelia Spindizzy,*" the referee said. "*Your flight authorization has been canceled. Return to Ops.*"

Reflexively, she jerked the throttle back, scuttling the dive. "What?!"

"*Repeat: return to Ops. Await further orders.*"

Angrily, Amelia yanked the jacks from Radio 3. Almost immediately the light on Radio 1 lit up. When she jacked in, the hollow, mechanical voice of Naked Brain ZF-43, her commanding officer, filled her earphones. "*I am disappointed in you, Amelia. Wastefulness. Inefficient expenditure of resources. Pilots should not weary themselves unnecessarily. XB-29 should have exercised more control over you. He will be reprimanded.*"

"It was just a pick-up game," she said. "For fun. You remember fun, don't you?"

There was a pause. "*There is nothing the matter with my memory,*" ZF-43 said at last. "*I do remember fun. Why do you ask?*"

"Maybe because I'm as crazy as an old coot, ZF," said Amelia, idly wondering if she could roll an autogyro. Nobody ever had. But if she went to maximum climb, cut the choke and kicked the rudder hard, that ought to flip it. Then, if she could restart the engine quickly enough and slam the rudder smartly the other way . . . It just might work. She could give it a shot right now.

"Return to the Zeppelin immediately. The Game starts in less than an hour."

"Aw shucks, ZF. Roger." Not for the first time, Amelia wondered if the Naked Brain could read her mind. She'd have to try the roll later.

In less than the time it took to scramble an egg and slap it on a plate, Radio Jones had warmed up her tuner and homed in on a signal. "Maybe because I'm as crazy as an old coot, ZF," somebody squawked.

"Hey! I know that voice – it's Amelia!" If Radio had a hero, it was the aviatrix.

"Return to the Zeppelin—"

"Criminy! A Naked Brain! Aw rats, static . . ." Radio tweaked the tuning ever so slightly with the pliers.

"—ucks, ZF. Roger."

Edna set the plate of eggs and pastrami next to the receiver. "Here's your breakfast, whiz kid."

Radio flipped off the power. "Jeez, I ain't never heard a Brain before. Creepy."

By now, she had the attention of the several denizens of Fat Edna's.

"Whazzat thing do, Radio?"

"How does it work?"

"Can you make me one, Jonesy?"

"It's a Universal Tuner. Home in on any airwave whatsoever." Radio grabbed the catsup bottle, upended it over the plate and whacked it hard. Red stuff splashed all over. She dug into her eggs. "I'm 'nna make one for anybody who wants one," she said between mouthfuls. "Cost ya, though."

"Do they know you're listening?" It was Rudy the Red, floppy-haired and unshaven, born troublemaker, interested only in politics and subversion. He was always predicting that the Fist of the Brains was just about to come down on him. As it would, eventually, everyone agreed: people like him tended to disappear. The obnoxious ones, however, lingered longer than most. "How can you be sure *they* aren't listening to *you* right now?"

"Well, all I can say, Rudy" – she wiped her mouth with her hand, as Fat Edna's bar was uncluttered with serviettes – "is that if they got something that can overthrow the laws of electromagnetism as we know 'em and turn a receiver into a transmitter, then more power to 'em. That's a good hack. Hey, the Game starts in a few minutes. Who ya bettin' on?"

"Radio, you know I don't wager human against human," Rudy said. "Our energies should be focused on our oppressors – the Naked Brains. But instead we do whatever they want because they've channeled all our aggression into a trivial distraction created to keep the masses stupefied and sedated. The Games are the opiate of the people! You should wise up and join the struggle, Radio. This device of yours could be our secret weapon. We could use it to listen in on them plotting against us"

"Ain't much of a secret," said Radio, "if it's all over Edna's bar."

"We can tell people it doesn't work."

"What are you, some kind of no-brainer? That there's my fancy-pants college education. I'm not tellin' nobody it don't work."

Amelia Spindizzy banked her tiny craft and turned it toward the huge Operations Zep *Imperator*. The Zeppelin thrust out its landing pad and Amelia swooped deftly onto it, in a maneuver that she thought of as a penny-toss, a quick leap onto the target platform, which then retracted into the gondola of the airship.

She climbed from the cockpit. Grimy Huey tossed her a mooring line and she tied down her machine. "You're on orders to report to the Hall, fly-girl," he shouted. "What have you done now?"

"I think I reminded ZF-43 of his lost physicality, Huey." Amelia scrambled up the bamboo gangway.

"You do that for me every time I look at you."

"You watch it, Huey, or I'll come over there and teach you a lesson," Amelia said.

"Amelia, I'll study under you anytime."

She shied a wheel chuck at him, and the mechanic ducked away, cackling. *Mechanics' humor*, thought Amelia. *You have to let them have their jokes at your expense. It can make you or break you, what they do to your 'gyro.*

The Hall of the Naked Brains was amidships. High-ceilinged, bare-walled and paneled in bamboo, it smelled of lemon oil and beeswax. The windows were shuttered, to keep the room dim; the Brains didn't need light, and the crew were happier not looking at them. Twin rows of enormous glass jars, set in duraluminium frames, lined the sides of the hall. Within the jars, enormous pink Brains floated motionless in murky electrolyte soup.

In the center of the shadowy room was a semicircle of rattan chairs facing a speaker and a televideon camera. Cables looped across the floor to each of the glass jars.

Amelia plumped down in the nearest chair, unzipped her flight jacket and said, "Well?"

There was a ratcheting noise as one of the Brains adjusted the camera. A tinny disembodied voice came from the speaker. It was ZF-43. *"Amelia. We are equipping your autogyro with an important new device. It is essential that we test it today."*

"What does it do?" she asked.

"If it works properly, it will paralyze Lt Eszterhazy's engine."

Amelia glared at the eye of the camera. "And why would I want to do that?"

"Clearly you do not, Amelia." ZF's voice was as dispassionate as ever. *"It is we who want you to do it. You will oblige us in this matter."*

"You tell me, ZF, why I would want to cheat."

"Amelia, you do not want to cheat. However, you are in our service. We have experimental devices to test, and the rules of your game are not important to us. This may be a spiritual endeavor to yourself, it may be a rousing amusement to the multitudes, but it is a military exercise to us." There was a pause, as if ZF were momentarily somewhere else, and then he resumed. *"NQ-14 suggests I inform you that Lt Eszterhazy's aeroplane can glide with a dead engine. There is little risk to the pilot."*

Amelia glared even more fiercely at the televideon camera. "That is beside the point, ZF. I would argue that my autogyro is far less dependent on its engine than Eszterhazy's 'plane. Why not give the device to each of us, for a square match?"

"There is only one device, Amelia, and we need to test it now. You are here, you are trusted. Eszterhazy is too independent. You will take the device." A grinding noise, as of badly lubricated machinery. *"Or you will not be in the Game."*

"What are this bastard's specs? How does it work?"

"You will be told, Amelia. In good time."

"Where is it?"

"It's being installed in your autogyro as we speak. A red button on your joystick controls it: press, it's on. Release, it's off."

"I'm not happy about this, ZF."

"Go to your autogyro, Amelia. Fly well." The light dimmed even more and the camera clicked again as the lens irised shut. ZF-43 had turned off the world outside his jar.

Rudy choked down a nickel's worth of beans and kielbasa and enough java to keep him running for the rest of the day. It was going to be a long one. The scheduled game would bring the people out into the streets, and that was a recruiting opportunity he couldn't pass up. He knew his targets: not the fat, good-natured guys catching a few hours of fun before hitting the night shift. Not their sharp-eyed wives, juggling the kids and grabbing the paycheck on Friday so it wouldn't be spent on drink. Oh, no. Rudy's constituency was hungry-looking young men, just past their teens, out of work, smarter than they needed to be, and not yet on the bottle. One in ten would take a pamphlet from him. Of those, one in twenty would take it home, one in fifty would read it, one in five hundred would take it to heart, and one in a thousand would seek him out and listen to more.

The only way to make it worth his while, the only way to pull together a force, was to get as many pamphlets out there as possible. It was a numbers game, like the lottery, or like selling insurance.

Rudy had sold insurance once, collecting weekly nickels and dimes from the hopeful and the despairing alike. Until the day he was handed a pamphlet. He took it home, he read it, and he realized what a sham his life was, what a shill he had been for the corporate powers, what a fraud he had been perpetrating upon his own people, the very people that he should be helping to escape from the treadmill of their lives.

He finished his coffee and hit the street. Crowds were already building near the CityPlace – that vast open square at the heart of the city, carved out of the old shops, tenements, and speakeasies that had once thrived there – where the aerobattle would take place. He picked out a corner near some ramshackle warehouses on the plaza's grimy southern rim. That's where his people would be, his tillage, as he thought of them.

"Tillage" was a word his grandfather used back when Rudy was young. The old man used to speak lovingly of the tillage, the land he had farmed in his youth. The tillage, he said, responded to him as a woman would, bringing forth fruit as a direct result of his care and attention. Not that he, Rudy, had great amounts of time to spend on a woman – but that hadn't seemed to matter on the streets, where women were freely available, and briefly enjoyable. Sexual intercourse was overrated, in his opinion. Politics was another matter, and he made his friends among men and women who felt the same. They kept their distance from one another, so the Naked Brains couldn't pick them all off in a single raid. When they coupled, they did so quickly, and they didn't exchange names.

Moving deftly through the gathering crowd, he held out only one pamphlet at a time, and then only after catching a receptive eye. A willing offering to a willing receptor, that wasn't illegal. It wasn't pamphleteering, which was a harvestable offense. Last thing he wanted, to be harvested and, if the rumors were, as he suspected, true, have his grey matter pureed and fed to the Naked Brains.

But to build his cadre, to make his mark, he needed to hand out a thousand pamphlets a day, and crowds like this – in the CityPlace or on the slidewalks at rush hour – were the only way to do it.

"Take this, brother. Thank you." He said it over and over. "Salaam, brother, may I offer you this?"

He had to keep moving, couldn't linger anywhere, kept his eye out for the telltale stare of an Eye of the Brains. When he had first started this business, he had sought out only men who looked like himself. But that approach proved too slow. He'd since learned to size up a crowd with a single glance and mentally mark the receptive. That tall, black-skinned man with the blue kerchief, the skinny little freckled guy in the ragged work clothes, the grubby fellow with the wisp of a beard and red suspenders. All men, and mostly young. He let his female compatriots deal with the women. Didn't want any misunderstandings.

The guy with the kerchief first. Eye contact, querying glance, non-sexual affect, tentative offer of pamphlet. He takes it! Eye contact, brief nod, on to the little guy. Guy looks away. Abort. Don't offer pamphlet. On to the third guy—

"What's this, then?" Flatfoot! An Eye? Surely not a Fist? Best to hoof it.

Rudy feinted to one side of the copper and ran past him on the other, swivel-hipping through the crowd like Jim Thorpe in search of a touchdown. He didn't look back, but if the cop was an Eye, he'd have backup pronto. Around the big guy with the orange wig, past the scared-looking lady with the clutch of kids – yikes! – almost overturned the baby carriage. What's that on the ground? No time to think about it! Up and over, down the alleyway, and into the door that's cracked open a slot. Close it, latch it, jam the lock. SOP.

Rudy turned away from the fire door. It was almost lightless in here. He was in an old, run-down kinescope parlor, surrounded by benches full of kinescope devotees, their eyes glued to the tiny screens wired to the backs of the pews in front of them. On each screen the same blurry movie twitched: *Modern Times*, with the Marx Brothers.

He took a seat and put a nickel in the slot.

He was just a regular Joe at the movies now. An anonymous unit of the masses, no different from anybody else. Except that he didn't have his girlfriend with him. Or a girlfriend at all. Or any real interest in having a girlfriend. Or in anything so historically blinkered as going to the kinescope parlor.

Rudy had heard about this particular kinescope in a Know the Foe session. It was supposed to be funny, but its humor originated in a profound class bias. The scene that was playing was one in which Harpo, Chico and Zeppo were working on an assembly line while their supervisor (Groucho) flirted with the visiting efficiency inspector (Margaret Dumont). Zeppo and Chico worked methodically with wrenches, tightening bolts on the bombs that glided remorselessly into view on the conveyor belt. Harpo, equipped with a little handheld pneumatic drill, worked regularly and efficiently at first, drilling a hole in a bomb fin which Zeppo promptly unbolted and Chico replaced with a new fin. That his work was meaningless appeared to bother him not at all. But then, without noticing it, Groucho leaned against a long lever, increasing the belt's speed. As the pace increased, Harpo realized that the drill could be made to go faster and faster, just like the assembly line. He became fascinated by the drill and then obsessed with it, filling the bombs' fins with so many holes that they looked like slices of Swiss cheese.

Chico and Zeppo, meanwhile, kept working faster and faster as the line sped up. For them, this was grim business. To keep from falling behind, they had to employ two wrenches, one per hand. Sweat poured off them. They shed their hats, then their jackets, then their shirts and pants, leaving them clad only in voluminous underwear. Harpo, on the other hand, was feeling no pressure at all. He began drilling holes in his hat, then his jacket, then his shirt and pants.

Groucho urged Dumont into his office, then doffed his hat, clasped it to his chest and tossed it aside. He chased her around the desk. Dumont projected both affronted dignity and matronly sexual curiosity. A parody of authority, Groucho backed Dumont up against the wall and, unexpectedly, plucked a rose from a nearby vase and, bowing deeply, offered it to her.

Charmed, Dumont smiled and bent down to accept it.

But then, in a single complex and weirdly graceful action, Groucho spun Dumont around, bending her over backwards in his arms, parallel to the floor. Margaret Dumont's eyes darted wildly about as she realized how perilously close she was to falling. Meanwhile, Harpo had started to drill holes from the other side of the wall, the drill bit coming through the plaster, each time missing Groucho by a whisker. His desperate gyrations as he tried to avoid the incoming drill were misunderstood by the efficiency expert, who made to slap him. Each time she tried, however, she almost fell and was forced to clutch him tighter to herself. Groucho waggled his eyebrows, obviously pleased with his romantic prowess.

Just then, however, Harpo drilled Dumont in the butt. She lurched forward, mouth an outraged O, losing balance and dignity simultaneously, and overtoppling Groucho as well. The two of them fell to the floor, struggling. It was at that instant that Chico and Zeppo, still in their underwear and with Harpo in tow, appeared in the doorway to report the problem and saw the couple on the floor thrashing about and yelling soundlessly at one another. Without hesitation, all three leaped joyously into the air on top of the pile. Behind them, the runaway assembly line was flooding the factory with bombs, which now crested into the office in a great wave. The screen went white and a single card read: BANG!

The audience was laughing uproariously. But Rudy was not amused. None of these characters had a shred of common sense. Furthermore, it was clear that appropriate measures to protect the workers' health and safety had not been implemented. Harpo should never have been given that drill in the first place. And Margaret Dumont! What was she thinking? How could she have accepted such a demeaning role?

Rudy stood up on his chair. "Comrades!" he yelled. "Why you arc laughing?"

A few viewers looked up briefly, then shrugged and returned to their kinescopes. "We're laughin' because it's funny, you halfwit," muttered a surly-looking young man.

"You there, brother," Rudy addressed him directly. After all, he, of everyone there, was Rudy's constituency. "Do you think it's funny that the Brains work people beyond endurance? That they speed up assembly lines without regard for the workers' natural pace, and without increasing their compensation? Do you think it's funny that a human man and woman would take the side of the Brains against their own kind? Think about this: what if Charles Chaplin – a man who respects the workers' dignity – had made this kinescope? There would be nothing funny about it: you'd weep for the poor fellows on the Brains' assembly line. As you should weep for Chico and Zeppo, whose dream of a life of honest labor and just reward has been cruelly exploited."

"Aw, shut yer yap!" It wasn't the young man that Rudy had addressed. This was the voice of an older man, embittered by many years of disappointment and penury.

"I apologize, sir," said Rudy. "You have every right to be angry. You have earned your leisure and have paid dearly for the right to sit here in the darkness and be assaulted by the self-serving garbage of the entertainment industry. Please return to your kinescope. But, I beg of you, do not swallow the tissue of lies that it offers you. Argue with it. Fight back! Resist!"

A huge hand reached out of the darkness and grabbed Rudy's right shoulder.

"Awright there, buddy," said a firm but quiet voice. "And why don't yez come along wit' me, and we can continue this discussion down at the station house?"

Rudy twisted about in the flatfoot's grasp. A sudden head-butt to the solar plexus, a kick to take the man's feet out from under him, and Rudy was running fast, not once looking back to see if he was being pursued. Halfway to the exit, he spotted a narrow circular staircase that burrowed down into the bowels of the earth below the kinescope parlor. He plunged into the darkness, down into the steam tunnels that ran beneath all the buildings of the Old Town.

That was Phase Three of his plan: run like hell.

Amelia had less than five minutes to the start of the Game. She sprinted to the flight deck and her autogyro. Grimy Huey was waiting, and he didn't look happy. "Why didn't you tell me you were having work done on the machine? You don't trust me no more?"

"Huey, I'm up. We can talk about it later." She swung into the cockpit. The engine was already running. Even when he was ticked off, Huey knew his stuff. "Just throw me out there. The whistle's about to blow."

Grimy Huey waved and Amelia grabbed the controls. Everything in place. She nodded, and the launch platform thrust the autogyro out of the Zep, into takeoff position.

The steam-whistle blew. The Game was in motion.

Amelia kicked, pushed, pedaled and screamed her improbable craft into the air.

For a time, all was well. As was traditional, the flying aces appeared in goose-vee formation from opposite sides of the plaza, ignoring each other on the first pass, save for a slight wing-waggle of salute, and then curving up into the sky above. Then began the series of thrilling moves that would lead to the heart-stopping aerial ballet of sporting dogfight.

On the first fighting pass, the advantage was to the Reds. But then Blockhead O'Brien threw his autogyro into a mad sideways skid that had half their 'planes pulling up in disarray to avoid being shredded by his blades. Amelia and Hops Wynzowski hurled themselves into the opening and ran five stars, neat as a pin, before the opposition could recover.

Amelia pulled up laughing, only to discover that the Big E was directly behind her and coming up her tail fast. She crouched down over her stick, raising her hips up from the seat, taut as a wire being tested to destruction, neurons snapping and crackling like a Tesla generator. "You catch me," she murmured happily, "and I swear to God I'll never fly again for as long as I live."

Because if there was one thing she knew, it was that Eszterhazy *wasn't* going to catch her. She was in her element now. In that timeless instant that lasted forever, that was all instinct and reflex, lust and glory. She was vengeance and righteous fury. She was death in all its cold and naked beauty.

Then a rocket flew up out of nowhere and exploded in her face.

Rudy pounded through the steam tunnels as if every finger in the Fist of the Brains was on his tail. Which they weren't – yet. He'd given Fearless Fosdick the slip, he was sure.

It was only a matter of time, though. Back at Fat Edna's, he knew, they had a pool going as to the date. But when the Fist came for him, he wasn't going to go meekly, with his hands in the air. Not Rudy. That was why he was running now, even though he'd given the flatfoot the slip. He was practicing for the day when it all came down and his speed negotiating the twists and turns of the tunnels would spell the difference between escape and capture, survival and death.

The light from Rudy's electric torch flashed from a rectangle of reflective tape he'd stuck to one wall at chest level. Straight ahead, that meant. Turn coming up soon. And, sure enough, up ahead were two bits of tape together, like an equal sign, on the right-hand wall. Which, counterintuitively, signaled a left turn.

He ran, twisting and turning as the flashing blips of tapes dictated. A left . . . two rights . . . a long downward decline that he didn't remember but which had to be correct because up ahead glinted another tab of reflective tape and beyond it another two, indicating a left turn. Into the new tunnel he plunged, and then, almost falling, down a rattling set of metal steps that definitely wasn't right. At the bottom the tunnel opened up into an enormous cavernous blackness. He stumbled to a halt.

A cold wind blew down on him from above.

Rudy shivered. This was wrong. He'd never been here before. And yet, straight ahead of him glowed yet another tab of the tape. He lifted his electric torch from the ground in front of his feet to examine it.

And, as he lifted it up, he cried out in horror. The light revealed a mocking gargoyle of a man: filthy, grey-skinned, dressed in rags, with running sores on his misshapen face and only three fingers on the hand that mockingly held up a flashing rectangle of reflective tape.

"It's the bolshy," the creature said to nobody in particular.

"I thought he was a menshevik," said a second voice.

"Naw, he's a tvardokhlebnik," said a third. "A pathetic nibbler at the leavings of others."

"My brothers!" Rudy cried in mingled terror and elation. His torch slid from monstrous face to monstrous face. A throng of grotesques confronted him. These were the broken hulks of men, horribly disfigured by industrial accidents, disease and bathtub gin, creatures who had been driven into the darkness not by poverty alone but also by the reflexive stares of those who had previously been their fellows and compeers. Rudy's revulsion turned to an enormous and terrible sense of pity. "You have lured me here for some purpose, I presume. Well . . . here I am. Tell me what is so important that you must play these games with me."

"Kid gets right to the point."

"He's got a good mind."

"No sense of humor, though. Heard him speak once."

Swallowing back his fear, Rudy said, "Now you are laughing at me. Comrades! These are desperate times. We should not be at each other's throats, but rather working together for the common good."

"He's got *that* right."

"Toldya he had a good mind."

One of the largest of the men seized Rudy's jacket in his malformed hand, lifting him effortlessly off his feet. "Listen, pal. Somebody got something important to tell ya." He shook Rudy for emphasis. "So you're gonna go peacefully, all right? Don't do nothing stupid. Remember who lives here and can see in the dark and who don't and can't. Got that?"

"Brother! Yes! Of course!"

"Good." The titan let Rudy drop to the floor. "Open 'er up, boys." Shadowy figures pushed an indistinct pile of boxes and empty barrels away from a steel-clad door. "In there."

Rudy went through the door.

It closed behind him. He could hear the crates and barrels being pushed back into place.

He was in a laboratory. Even though it was only sparsely lit, Rudy could see tables crowded with huge jars that were linked by glass tubes and entwined in electrical cables. Things sizzled and bubbled. The air stank of ozone and burnt sulfur.

In the center of the room, illuminated by a single incandescent bulb dangling from the ceiling, was a glass tank a good twenty feet long. In its murky interior a huge form moved listlessly, filling it almost entirely – a single enormous sturgeon. Rudy was no sentimentalist, but it seemed to him that the great fish, unable to swim or even turn about in its cramped confines – indeed, unable to do much of anything save slowly move its fins in order to keep afloat and flutter its gills to breathe – must lead a grim and terrible existence.

Cables snaked from the tank to a nearby clutter of electrical devices, but he paid them no particular notice. His attention was drawn to a woman standing before the aquarium. Her lab smock seemed to glow in the gloom.

She had clearly been waiting for him, as without preamble she said, "I am Professor Anna Pavlova." Her face was old and drawn; her eyes blazed with passionate intensity. "You have probably never heard of me, but—"

"Of course I know of you, Professor Pavlova!" Rudy babbled. "You are one of the greatest inventors of all time! The monorail! Citywide steam heat! You made the Naked Brains possible. The masses idolize you."

"Pah!" Professor Pavlova made a dismissive chopping gesture with her right hand. "I am but a scientist, nothing more nor less. All that matters is that when I was young I worked on the Naked Brain Project. Those were brave days indeed. All the best thinkers of our generation – politicians, artists, engineers – lined up to surrender their bodies in order to put their minds at the service of the people. I would have done so myself, were I not needed to monitor and fine-tune the nutrient systems. We were Utopians then! I am sure that not a one of them was influenced by the possibility that as Naked Brains they would live forever. Not a one! We wished only to serve." She sighed.

"Your idealism is commendable, comrade scientist," Rudy said. "Yet it is my unhappy duty to inform you that the Council of Naked Brains no longer serves the people's interests. They—"

"It is worse than you think!" Professor Pavlova snapped. "For many years I was part of the inner circle of functionaries serving the Brains. I saw . . . many things. Things that made me wonder, and then doubt. Quietly, I began my own research. But the scientific journals rejected my papers. Lab books disappeared. Data were altered. There came a day when none of the Naked Brains – who had been my friends, remember! – would respond to my messages, or even, when I went to them in person, deign to speak to me.

"I am no naive innocent. I knew what that meant: the Fist would shortly be coming for me.

"So I went underground. I befriended the people here, whose bodies are damaged but whose minds remain free and flexible, and together we smuggled in enough equipment to continue my work. I tapped into the city's electric and gas lines. I performed miracles of improvisation and bricolage. At first I was hindered by my lack of access to the objects of my study. But then my new friends helped me liberate Old Teddy" – she patted the side of the fish tank – "from a pet shop where he was kept as a curiosity. Teddy was the key. He told me everything I needed to know."

Rudy interrupted the onslaught of words. "This fish *told* you things?"

"Yes." The scientist picked up a wired metal dish from the lab bench. "Teddy is very, very old, you see. When he was first placed in that tank, he was quite small, a wild creature caught for food but spared the frying pan to be put on display." She adjusted cables that ran from the silver dish to an electrical device on the bench. "That was many years ago, of course, long before you or I were born. Sturgeon can outlive humans, and Teddy has slowly grown into what you see before you." Other cables ran from the device into the tank. Rudy saw that they had been implanted directly into the sturgeon's brain. One golden-grey eye swiveled in the creature's whiskered, impassive head to look at him. Involuntarily, he shuddered. It was just a fish, he thought. It wished him no ill.

"Have you ever wondered what thoughts pass through a fish's brain?" With a grim smile that was almost a leer, the scientist thrust the silver dish at Rudy. "Place this cap on your head – and you will know."

More than almost anything, Rudy wanted *not* to put on the cap. Yet more than anything at all, he wanted to do his duty to his fellow beings, both human and fish. This woman might well be mad: she certainly did not act like any woman he had ever met. The device might well kill him or damage his brain. Yet to refuse it would be to give up on the adventure entirely, to admit that he was not the man for the job.

Rudy reached out and took the silver cap.

He placed it upon his head.

Savage homicidal rage filled him. Rudy hated everything that lived, without degree or distinction. All the universe was odious to him. If he could, he would murder everyone outside his tank, devour their eggs and destroy their nests. Like a fire, this hatred engulfed him, burning all to nothing, leaving only a dark cinder of self at his core.

With a cry of rage, Rudy snatched the silver cap from his head and flung it away. Professor Pavlova caught it, as if she had been expecting his reaction. Horrified, he turned on her. "They hate us! The very fish hate us!" He could feel the sturgeon's deadly anger burning into his back, and this filled him with shame and self-loathing, even though he knew he did not personally deserve it. All humans deserved it, though, he thought. All humans supported the idea of putting fish in tanks. Those who did not were branded eccentrics and their viewpoint dismissed without a hearing.

"This is a terrible invention! It does not reveal the universal brotherhood natural among disparate species entwined in the Great Web of Life – quite the opposite, in fact!" He despaired of putting his feelings into words. "What it reveals may be the truth, but is it a truth that we really need to know?"

Professor Pavlova smiled mirthlessly. "You understand so well the inequalities in human intercourse and the effect they have on the human psyche. And now! Now, for the first time, you understand some measure of what a fish feels and thinks. Provided it has been kept immobile and without stimulation for so many years it is no longer sane." She glanced over at Old Teddy with pity. "A fish longs only for cold water, for food, for distances to swim, and for a place to lay its eggs or spread its milt. We humans have kept Teddy in a tank for over a century."

Then she looked at Rudy with almost the same expression. "Imagine how much worse it would be for a human being, used to sunshine on his face, the feel of a lover's hand, the soft sounds an infant makes when it is happy, to find himself – even if of his own volition – nothing more than a Naked Brain afloat in amniotic fluid. Sans touch, sans taste, sans smell, sans sound, sans sight, sans everything. You have felt the fish's hatred. Imagine how much stronger must be the man's." Her eyes glittered with a cold fire. "I have suspected this for years, and now that I have experienced Teddy's mind – now *I know*." She sliced her hand outward, as if with a knife, to emphasize the depth of her knowledge, and its force. "The Naked Brains are all mad. They hate us and they will work tirelessly for our destruction."

"This is what I have been saying all along," Rudy gasped. "I have been trying to engage—"

Pavlova interrupted him. "The time for theorizing and yammering and pamphleteering is over. You were brought here because I have a message and I need a messenger. The time has come for action. Tell your superiors. Tell the world. The Naked Brains must be destroyed."

A sense of determination flooded Rudy's being. This was what all his life had been leading up to. This was his moment of destiny.

Which made it particularly ironic that it was at that very moment that the Fist smashed in the door of the laboratory.

Radio Jones had punched a hole in the center of a sheet of paper and taped it to the casing of her all-frequencies receiver with the tuner knob at the center, so she could mark the location of each transceiver set she found. The tuner had a range of two hundred ten degrees, which covered the entire spectrum of the communications band. So she eyeballed it into quarters and then tenths, to give a rough idea how things were laid out. It would be better to rank them by electromagnetic frequency, but she didn't have the time to work all that out, and anyway, though she would never admit this out loud, she was just a little weak on the theoretics. Radio was more a vacuum-tube-and-solder-gun kind of girl.

Right now the paper was heavily marked right in the center of the dial, from ninety to one-sixty degrees. There were dozens of flier-Brain pairs, and she'd put a mark by each one, and identified a good quarter of them – including, she was particularly pleased to see, all the big guys: Eszterhazy, Spindizzy, Blockhead O'Brien, Stackerlee Brown. When there wasn't any room for more names, Radio went exploring into the rest of the spectrum, moving out from the center by incremental degrees.

So, because she wasn't listening to the players, Radio missed the beginning of the massacre. It was only when she realized that everybody in Edna's had rushed out into the street that she looked up from her chore and saw the aeroplanes falling and autogyros spinning out of control. She went to the window just in time to hear a universal gasp as a Zeppelin exploded in the sky overhead. Reflected flames glowed red on the uplifted faces.

"Holy cow!" Radio ran back to her set and twisted her dial back toward the center.

". . . *Warinowski,*" a Naked Brain was saying dispassionately. "*Juric-Kocik. Bai. Gevers . . .*"

A human voice impatiently broke in on the recitation. "What about Spindizzy? She's worth more than the rest of them put together. Did she set off her bomb?"

"*No.*" A long pause. "*Maybe she disarmed it.*"

"If that's the case, she'll be gunning for me." The human voice was horribly, horribly familiar. "Plot her vectors, tell me where she is, and I'll take care of her."

"Oh, no," Radio said. "It can't be."

"*What is your current situation?*"

"My rockets are primed and ready, and I've got a clear line of sight straight down Archer Road, from Franklin all the way to the bend."

"*Stay your course. We will direct Amelia Spindizzy onto Archer Road, headed south, away from you. When you see her clear the Frank Lloyd Wright Tower, count three and fire.*"

"Roger," the rocket-assassin said. Now there was no doubt at all in Radio's mind. She knew that voice. She knew the killer.

And she knew what she had to do.

Amelia Spindizzy's ears rang from the force of the blast, and she could feel in the joystick an arrhythmic throb. Where had the missile come from that had caused the explosion? What had happened to Eszterhazy? She was sure she had not accidentally pressed the red button on the joystick, so he should be fine, if he had evaded the blast. Hyperalert, Amelia detected an almost invisible scratch in the air, tracing the trajectory of a second rocket, and braced herself for another shock.

When it came, she was ready for it. This time she rode, with her whole body, the great twisting thrusts that came from the rotor, much as she would ride a stallion or, she imagined, a man. The blades sliced the air and the autogyro shook, but she forced her will on the powerful machine, which had until this instant been her partner, not her opponent, and overmastered it.

It might be true that you never see the missile that kills you. But that didn't mean you couldn't be killed by a missile you could see. Amelia needed to get out of the line of fire – a third missile might err on the side of accuracy. She banked sharply down into Archer Road, past the speakeasy and the storefront church, and pulled a brisk half-Eszterhazy into an alley next to a skeleton of iron girders with a banner reading FUTURE HOME OF BLACK STAR LINE SHIPPING & NAVIGATION. All that raw iron would block her comptroller's radio signal, but that hardly mattered now. At third-floor level, slowing to the speed of a running man, she crept, as it were, back to where she would see what was happening over the Great Square.

Eszterhazy was nowhere in evidence, but neither was there a column of smoke where she had seen him last. Perhaps, like herself, he'd held his craft together and gone to cover. Missiles were still arcing through the air and exploding. There were no flying machines in the sky and the great Zeppelins were sinking down like foundering ships. It wasn't clear what the missiles were aimed at – perhaps their purpose at this point was simply to keep any surviving 'planes and autogyros out of the sky.

Or perhaps they were being shot off by fools. In Amelia's experience, you could never write off the fool option.

Radio 2 was blinking and squawking like a battery-operated chicken. Amelia ignored it. Until she knew who was shooting at her, she wasn't talking to anybody: any radio contact would reveal her location.

As, treading air, she rounded the skeleton of the would-be shipping line, Amelia noticed something odd. It looked like a lump of rags hanging from a rope tied to a girder – possibly a support strut for a planned crosswalk – that stuck out from the metal framework. What on earth could that be? Then it moved, wriggling downward, and she saw that it was a boy!

And he was sliding rapidly down toward the end of his rope.

Almost without thinking, Amelia brought her autogyro in. There had to be a way of saving the kid. The rotor blades were a problem, and their wash. She couldn't slow down much more than she already had – autogyros didn't hover. But if she took both the forward speed and the wash into account, made them work together . . .

It would be trying to snag a baseball in a hurricane. But she didn't see any alternative.

She came in, the wash from her props blowing the lump of rags and the rope it hung from almost parallel to the ground. She could see the kid clearly now, a little boy in a motley coat, his body hanging just above Amelia. He had a metal box hanging from a belt around his neck that in another instant was going to tear him off the rope for sure.

There was one hellishly giddy moment when her rotors went above the out-stuck girder and her fuselage with its stubby wings went below. She reached out with the mail hook, grabbed the kid and pulled him into the cockpit as the 'gyro moved relentlessly forward.

The tip of the rope whipped up and away and was shredded into dust by the whirling blades. The boy fell heavily between Amelia and her rudder, so that she couldn't see a damned thing.

She shoved him up and over her, unceremoniously dumping the brat headfirst into the passenger seat. Then she grabbed the controls, easing her bird back into the center of the alley.

From behind her, the kid shouted, "Jeepers, Amelia. Get outta here, f'cripesake! He's coming for you!"

"What?" Amelia yelled. Then the words registered. "Who's shooting? Why?" The brat knew something. "Where are they? How do you know?" Then, sternly, "That was an insanely dangerous thing for you to do."

"Don't get yer wig in a frizzle," said the kid. "I done this a million times."

"You have?" said Amelia in surprise.

"In my dreams, anyway," said the kid. "Hold the questions. Right now we gotta lam outta here, before somebody notices us what shouldn't. I'll listen in on what's happening." He twisted around and tore open the seat back, revealing the dry batteries, and yanked the cords from them. The radio went dead.

"Hey!" Amelia cried.

"Not to worry. I'm just splicing my Universal Receiver to your power supply. Your radios are obsolete now, but you couldn't know that . . ." Now the little gremlin had removed a floor panel and was crawling in among the autogyro's workings. "Lemme just ground this and . . . Say! Why have you got a bomb in here?"

"Huh? You mean . . . Oh, that's just some electronic doohickey the Naked Brains asked me to test for them."

"Tell it to the Marines, lady. I didn't fall off no turnip truck. The onliest electronics you got here is two wires coming off a detonator cap and leading to one of your radios. If I didn't know better, I'd tag this sucker as a remote-controlled self-destruct device." The imp stuck its head out of the workings again, and said, "Oh yeah. The name's Radio Jones."

With an abrupt rush of conceptual vertigo, Amelia realized that this gamin was a *girl.* "How do you do," she said dazedly. "I'm—"

"I know who you are," Radio said. "I got your picture on the wall." Then, seeing that they were coming up on the bend in Archer Road, "Hey! Nix! Not that way! There's a guy with a coupla rockets up there just waiting for you to show your face. Pull a double curl and loop back down Vanzetti. There's a vacant lot this side of the Shamrock Tavern that's just wide enough for the 'gyro. Martin Dooley's the barkeep there, and he's got a shed large enough to hide this thing. Let's vamoose!"

A rocket exploded behind her.

Good advice was good advice. No matter how unlikely its source. Amelia Spindizzy vamoosed.

But as she did, she could not help casting a wistful glance back over her shoulder, hoping against hope for a glimpse of a bright red aeroplane. "I don't suppose you've heard anything about Eszterhazy surviving this?" she heard herself asking her odd young passenger. Whatever was happening, with his superb skills, surely he must have survived.

"Uh, about that . . ." Radio Jones said. "I kinda got some bad news for you."

Rudy awoke to find himself in Hell.

Hell was touchless, tasteless, scentless and black as pitch. It consisted entirely of a bedlam of voices: "Lemme outta here . . . wasn't doing nothing . . . Mabel! Where are you, Mabel? . . . I'm serious, I got bad claustrophobia . . . goddamn flicks! . . . there's gotta be . . . minding my own business . . . Mabel! . . . gonna puke . . . all the things I coulda been . . . I don't like it here . . . can't even hear myself think . . . Oh, Freddy, if only I'da toldja I loved you when I coulda . . . got to be a way out . . . why won't anybody tell me what's happening? . . . if the resta youse don't shut . . ."

He knew where he was now. He understood their situation. Gathering himself together, Rudy funneled all the energy he had into a mental shout:

"Silence!"

His thought was so forceful and purposive that it shocked all the other voices into silence

"Comrades!" he began. "It is clear enough what has happened here. We have all been harvested by the police lackeys of the Naked Brains. By the total lack of somatic sensations, I deduce that we have ourselves been made into Naked Brains." Somebody sent out a stab of raw emotion. Before his or her (not that gender mattered anymore, under the circumstances) hysteria could spread, Rudy rushed onward in a torrent of words. "But there is no need for despair. We are not without hope. So long as we have our thoughts, our inner strength and our powers of reason, we hold within ourselves the tools of liberation."

"Liberation?" somebody scoffed. "It's my body's been liberated, and from *me*. It's them is doing the liberatin', not us."

"I understand your anger, brother," Rudy said. "But the opportunity is to him who keeps his head." Belatedly, Rudy realized that this was probably not the smartest thing to say. The anonymous voices responded with jeers. "Peace, brothers and sisters. We may well be lost, and we must face up to that." More jeers. "And yet, we all have family and friends who we've left behind." Everyone, that is, save for himself – a thought that Rudy quickly suppressed. "Think of the world that is coming for them – one of midnight terror, an absolutist government, the constant fear of denouncement and punishment without trial. Of imprisonment without hope of commutation, of citizens randomly plucked from the streets for harvesting . . ." He paused to let that sink in. "I firmly believe that we can yet free ourselves. But even if we could not, would it not be worth our uttermost efforts to fight the tyranny of the Brains? For the sake of those we left behind?"

There was a general muttering of agreement. Rudy had created a community among his listeners. Now, quickly, to take advantage of it! "Who here knows anything about telecommunications technology?"

"I'm an electrical engineer," somebody said.

"That Dutch?" said another voice. "You're a damn good engineer. Or you were."

"Excellent. Dutch, you are now the head of our Ad Hoc Committee for Communications and Intelligence. Your task is first to work out the ways that we are connected to each other and to the machinery of the outer world, and second, to determine how we may take over the communications system, control it for our own ends, and when we are ready, deprive the government of its use. Are you up to the challenge, Comrade—?"

"Schwartz. Dutch Schwartz, at your service. Yes, I am."

"Then choose people to work with you. Report back when you have solid findings. Now. Who here is a doctor?"

"I am," a mental voice said dryly. "Professor and Doctor Anna Pavlova at your service."

"Forgive me, Comrade Professor. Of course you are here. And we are honored – honored! – to have you with us. One of the greatest—"

"Stop the nattering and put me to work."

"Yes, of course. Your committee will look into the technical possibilities of restoring our brains to the bodies we left behind."

"Well," said the professor, "this is not something we ever considered when we created the Brains. But our knowledge of microsurgery has grown enormously with the decades of Brain maintenance. I would not rule it out."

"You believe our bodies have not been destroyed?" somebody asked in astonishment.

"A resource like that? Of course not," Rudy said. "Think! Any despotic government must have the reliable support of toadies and traitors. With a supply of bodies, many of them young, to offer, the government can effectively give their lackeys immortality – not the immortality of the Brains, but the immortality of body after body, in plentiful supply." He paused to let that sink in. "However. If we act fast to organize the proletariat, perhaps that can be prevented. To do this, we will need the help of those in the Underground who have not been captured and disembodied. Who here is—?"

"And you," somebody else broke in. "What is your role in this? Are you to be our leader?"

"Me?" Rudy asked in astonishment. "Nothing of the sort! I am a community organizer."

He got back to work organizing.

The last dirigible was moored to the tip of the Gaudi Building. The *Imperator* was a visible symbol of tyranny which cast its metaphoric shadow over the entire city. So far as anybody knew, there wasn't an aeroplane, autogyro, or Zeppelin left in the city to challenge its domination of the air. So it was there that the new Tyrant would be. It was there that the destinies of everyone in the city would play out.

It was there that Amelia Spindizzy and Radio Jones went, after concealing the autogyro in a shed behind Dooley's tavern.

Even from a distance, it was clear that there were gun ports to every side of the *Imperator*, and doubtless there were other defenses on the upper floors of the skyscraper. So they took the most direct route – through the lobby of the Gaudi building and up in the elevator. Amelia and Radio stepped inside, the doors closed behind them, and up they rose, toward the Zeppelin.

"In my youth, of course, I was an avid balloonsman," somebody said from above.

Radio yelped and Amelia stared sharply upward.

Wedged into an upper corner of the elevator was a radio. From it came a marvelous voice, at once both deep and reedy, and immediately recognizable as well. ". . . and covered the city by air. Once, when I was a mere child, ballooning alone as was my wont, I caught a line on a gargoyle that stuck out into my airspace from the tower of the Church of Our Lady of the Assumption – what is now the Sepulchre of the Bodies of the Brains – and, thus entangled, I was in some danger of the gondola – which was little more than a basket, really – tipping me out into a long and fatal fall to earth. Fortunately, one of the brown-robed monks, engaged in his Matins, was cloistered in the tower and noticed my predicament. He was able to reach out and free the line." The voice dropped, a hint of humor creeping in. "In my childish piety, of course, I considered this evidence of the beneficent intercession of some remote deity, whom I thanked nightly in my prayers." One could almost hear him shaking his head at his youthful credulousness. "But considering how fortunate we are now – are we not? – to be at last freed from the inhuman tyranny of the Naked Brains, one has to wonder whether it wasn't in some sense the hand of Destiny that reached out from that tower, to save the instrument by which our liberation would one day be achieved."

"It's him!" Radio cried. "Just like I told you."

"It . . . sounds like him. But he can't be the one who gave the orders you overheard. Can you be absolutely sure?" Amelia asked her unlikely sidekick for the umpteenth time. "Are you really and truly *certain*?"

Radio rolled her eyes. "Lady, I heard him with my own two ears. You don't think I know the voice of the single greatest pilot . . ." Her voice trailed off under Amelia's glare. "Well, don't hit the messenger! I read *Obey the Brain!* every week. His stats are just plain better'n yours."

"They have been," Amelia said grimly. "But that's about to change." She unsnapped the holster of her pistol.

Then the bell pinged. They'd reached the top floor.

The elevator doors opened.

Rudy was conferring with progressive elements in the city police force about the possibility of a counter-coup (they argued persuasively that, since it was impossible to determine their fellow officers' loyalties without embroiling the force in internecine conflict, any strike would have to be small and fast) when his liaison with the Working Committee for Human Resources popped up in his consciousness and said, "We've located the bodies, boss. As you predicted, they were all carefully preserved and are being maintained in the best of health."

"That is good news, Comrade Mariozzi. Congratulations. But none of that 'boss' business, do you understand? It could easily go from careless language to a common assumption."

Meanwhile, they'd hooked into televideon cameras throughout the city, and though the views were grim, it heartened everybody to no longer be blind. It was a visible – there was no way around the word – sign that they were making progress.

Red Rudy had just wrapped up the meeting with the loyalist police officers when Comrade Mariozzi popped into his consciousness again. "Hey, boss!" he said excitedly. "You gotta see this!"

The guards were waiting at the top of the elevator with guns drawn. To Radio Jones's shock and amazement, Amelia Spindizzy handed over her pistol without a murmur of protest. Which was more than could be said for Radio herself when one of the goons wrested the Universal Receiver out of her hands. Amelia had to seize her by the shoulders and haul her back before she could attack the nearest of their captors.

They were taken onto the *Imperator* and through the Hall of the Naked Brains. The great glass jars were empty and the giant floating Brains were gone who-knows-where. Radio hoped they'd been flung in an alley somewhere to be eaten by dogs. But hundreds of new, smaller jars containing brains of merely human proportions had been brought in and jury-rigged to oxygen feeds and electrical input-output units. Radio noticed that they all had cut-out switches. If one of the New Brains acted up it could be instantly put into solitary confinement. But there was nobody monitoring them, which seemed to defeat the purpose.

"'Keep close to the earth!'" a voice boomed. Radio jumped. Amelia, she noticed, did not. Then she saw that there were radios set in brackets at either end of the room. "Such was the advice of the pre-eminent international airman, Alberto Santos-Dumont, and they were good enough words for their time." The familiar voice chuckled and half-snorted, and the radio crackled loudly as his breath struck the sensitive electro-acoustic transducer that had captured his voice. "But his time is not my time." He paused briefly; one could almost hear him shrug his shoulders. "One is never truly tested close to the earth. It is in the huge arching parabola of an aeroplane finding its height and seeking a swift descent from it that a man's courage is found. It is there, in acts outside of the quotidian, that his mettle is tested."

A televideon camera ratcheted about, tracking their progress. Were the New Brains watching them, Radio wondered? The thought gave her the creeps.

Then they were put in an elevator (only two guards could fit in with them, and Radio thought that for sure Amelia would make her play now; but the aviatrix stared expressionlessly forward and did nothing) and taken down to the flight deck. There, the exterior walls had been removed, as would be done under wartime conditions when the 'planes and wargyros had to be gotten into the air as soon as possible. Cold winds buffeted and blustered about the vast and empty space.

"A young man dreams of war and glory," the voice said from a dozen radios. "He toughens his spirit and hardens his body with physical activity and discomfort. In time, he's ready to join the civil militia, where he is trained in the arts of killing and destruction. At last, his ground training done, he is given an aeroplane and catapulted into the sky, where he discovers . . ." The voice caught and then, when it resumed, was filled with wonder, ". . . not hatred, not destruction, not war, but peace."

To the far side of the flight deck, unconcerned by his precarious location, a tall figure in a flyer's uniform bent over a body in greasy coveralls, which he had dragged right to the edge. Then he flipped it over. It was Grimy Huey, and he was dead.

The tall man stood and turned. "Leave," he told the guards.

They clicked their heels and obeyed.

"He almost got me, you know," the man remarked conversationally. "He came at me from behind with a wrench. Who would have thought that a mere mechanic had that much gumption in him?"

For a long moment, Amelia Spindizzy stood ramrod-straight and unmoving. Radio Jones sank to the deck, crouching by her side. She couldn't help herself. The cold and windy openness of the flight deck scared her spitless. She couldn't even stand. But, terrified though she was, she didn't look away. Someday all this would be in the history books; whatever happened, she knew, was going to determine her view of the world and its powers for the rest of her natural life, however short a time that might be.

Then Amelia strolled forward toward Eszterhazy and said, "Let me help you with that." She stooped and took the mechanic's legs. Eszterhazy took the arms. They straightened, swung the body – one! two! three! – and flung it over the side.

Slapping her hands together, Amelia said, "Why'd you do it?"

Eszterhazy shrugged in a self-deprecating way. "It had to be done. So I stepped up to the plate and took a swing at the ball. That's all." Then he grinned boyishly. "It's good to know that you're on my team."

"That's you on the radios," Amelia said. They were still booming away, even though the buffeting winds drowned out half the words that came from them.

"Wire recording." Eszterhazy strode to a support strut and slapped a switch. The radios all died. "A little talk I prepared, being broadcast to the masses. Radio has been scandalously under-utilized as a tool of governance."

Amelia's response was casual – even, Radio thought, a bit dunderheaded technologically. "But radio's everywhere," she said. "There are dozens of public sets scattered through the city. Why, people can hear news bulletins before the newspapers can even set type and roll the presses!"

Eszterhazy smiled a thin, tight, condescending smile. "But they only tell people what's happened, and not what to *think* about it. That's going to change. My people are distributing sets to every bar, school, church and library in the city. In the future, my future, everyone will have a bank of radios in their home – the government radio, of course, but also one for musical events, another for free lectures, and perhaps even one for business news."

Radio felt the urge to speak up and say that fixed-frequency radios were a thing of the past. But she suppressed it. She sure wasn't about to hand over her invention to a bum the likes of which Eszterhazy was turning out to be. But what the heck was the matter with Amelia?

Amelia Spindizzy put her hands behind her, and turned her back on her longtime archrival. Head down, deep in thought, she trod the edge of the abyss. "Hah." The word might have meant anything. "You've clearly put a lot of thought into this . . . this . . . new world order of yours."

"I've been planning this all my life," Eszterhazy said with absolute seriousness. "New and more efficient forms of government, a society that not only promotes the best of its own but actively weeds out the criminals and the morally sick. Were you aware that before Lycurgus became king, the Spartans were a licentious and ungovernable people? He made them the fiercest warriors the world has ever known in the space of a single lifetime." He stopped, and then with a twinkle in his eye said, "There I go again, talking about the Greeks! As I started to say, I thought I would not be ready to make my move for many years. But then I got wind of certain experiments performed by Anna Pavlova which proved that not only were the Naked Brains functionally mad, but that I had it in my power to offer them the one thing for which they would give me their unquestioning cooperation – death.

"In their corruption were the seeds of our salvation. And thus fell our oppressors."

"I worked with them, and I saw no oppressors." Amelia rounded her course strolling back toward Eszterhazy, brow furrowed with thought. "Only nets of neurological fiber who, as it turned out, were overcome by the existential terror of their condition."

"Their condition is called 'life', Millie. And, yes, life makes us all insane." Eszterhazy could have been talking over the radio, his voice was so reassuring and convincing. "Some of us respond to that terror with useless heroics. Others seek death." He cocked a knowing smile at Amelia. "Others respond by attacking the absurdity at its source. Ruled by Naked Brains, humanity could not reach its full potential. Now, once again, we will rule ourselves."

"It does all make sense. It all fits." Amelia Spindizzy came to a full stop and stood shaking her head in puzzlement. "If only I could understand—"

"What is there to understand?" An impatient edge came into Eszterhazy's voice. "What have I left unexplained? We can perfect our society in our lifetimes! You're so damnably cold and analytic, Millie. Don't you see that the future lies right at your feet? All you have to do is let go of your doubts and analyses and intellectual hesitations and take that leap of faith into a better world."

Radio trembled with impotent alarm. She knew that, small and ignored as she was, it might be possible for her to be the wild card, the unexpected element, the unforeseeable distraction that saves the day. That it was, in fact, her duty to do so. She'd seen enough Saturday afternoon kinescope serials to understand *that*.

If only she could bring herself to stand up. Though it almost made her throw up to do so, Radio brought herself to her feet. The wind whipped the deck, and Eszterhazy quickly looked over at her, as though noticing her for the first time. And then, as Radio fought to overcome her paralyzing fear, Amelia acted.

She smiled that big, easy Amelia grin that had captured the hearts of proles and aristos alike. It was a heartfelt smile and a wickedly hoydenish leer at one and the same time, and it bespoke aggression and an inner shyness in equal parts. A disarming grin, many people called it.

Smiling her disarming grin, Amelia looked Eszterhazy right in the eye. She looked as if she had just found a brilliant solution to a particularly knotty problem. Despite the reflexive decisiveness for which he was known, Eszterhazy stood transfixed.

"You know," she said, "I had always figured that, when all the stats were totted up and the final games were flown, you and I would find a shared understanding in our common enthusiasm for human-controlled—"

All in an instant, she pushed forward, wrapped her arms around her opponent, and let their shared momentum carry them over the edge.

Radio instantly fell to the deck again and found herself scrambling across it to the edge on all fours. Gripping the rim of the flight decking with spasmodic strength, she forced herself to look over. Far below, two conjoined specks tumbled in a final flight to the earth.

She heard a distant scream – no, she heard laughter.

*　　*　　*

Radio managed to hold herself together through the endless ceremonies of a military funeral. To tell the truth, the pomp and ceremony of it – the horse-drawn hearse, the autogyro fly-by, the lines of dignitaries and endlessly droning eulogies in the Cathedral – simply bored her to distraction. There were a couple of times when Mack had to nudge her because she was falling asleep. Also, she had to wear a dress and, sure as shooting, any of her friends who saw her in it were going to give her a royal ribbing about it when next they met.

But then came the burial. As soon as the first shovel of dirt rattled down on the coffin, Radio began blubbering like a punk. Fat Edna passed her a lace hanky – who'd even known she *had* such a thing? – and she mopped at her eyes and wailed.

When the last of the earth had been tamped down on the grave, and the priest turned away, and the mourners began to break up, Radio felt a hand on her shoulder. It was, of all people, Rudy the Red. He looked none the worse for his week-long vacation from the flesh.

"Rudy," she said, "is that a *suit* you're wearing?"

"It is not the uniform of the oppressor anymore. A new age has begun, Radio, an age not of hierarchic rule by an oligarchy of detached, unfeeling intellects, but of horizontally structured human cooperation. No longer will workers and managers be kept apart and treated differently from one another. Thanks to the selfless sacrifice of—"

"Yeah, I heard the speech you gave in the Cathedral."

"You did?" Rudy looked strangely pleased.

"Well, mostly. I mighta slept through some of it. Listen, Rudy, I don't want to rain on your parade, but people are still gonna be people, you know. You're all wound up to create this Big Rock Candy Mountain of a society, and good for you. Only – you gotta be prepared for the possibility that it won't work. I mean, ask any engineer, that's just the way things are. They don't always work the way they're supposed to."

"Then I guess we'll just have to wing it, huh?" Rudy flashed a wry grin. Then, abruptly, his expression turned serious, and he said the very last thing in the world she would have expected to come out of his mouth: "How are you doing?"

"Not so good. I feel like a ton of bricks was dropped on me." She felt around for Edna's hanky, but she'd lost it somewhere. So she wiped her eyes on her sleeve. "You want to know what's the real kicker? I hardly knew Amelia. So I don't even know why I should feel so bad."

Rudy took her arm. "Come with me a minute. Let me show you something."

He led her to a gravestone that was laid down to one side of the grave, to be erected when everyone was gone. It took a second for Radio to read the inscription. "Hey! It's just a quotation. Amelia's name ain't even on it. That's crazy."

"She left instructions for what it would say quite some time ago. I gather that's not uncommon for flyers. But I can't help feeling it's a message."

Radio stared at the words on the stone for very long time. Then she said, "Yeah, I see what you mean. But, ya know, I think it's a different message than what she thought it would be."

The rain, which had been drizzling off and on during the burial, began in earnest. Rudy shook out his umbrella and opened it over them both. They joined the other mourners, who were scurrying away in streams and rivulets, pouring from the cemetery exits and into the slidewalk stations and the vacuum trains, going back home to their lives and families, to boiled cabbage and schooners of pilsner, to their jobs, and their hopes, and their heartbreaks, to the vast, unknowable and perfectly ordinary continent of the future.

"It followed that the victory would belong to him who was calmest, who shot best, and who had the cleverest brain in a moment of danger."
Baron Manfred von Richthofen (1892–1918)

The People's Machine

Tobias S. Buckell

Inquisitor, warrior and priest Ixtli's fast-paced journey by airship began in Tenochtitlan, facing the solemn row of white-robed pipiltin. The rulers of the grandest city of the world had roused him from his house, burly Jaguar Scouts with rifles, throwing open his doors and shouting him awake.

"I'm to go to New Amsterdam?" Ixtli could hardly keep the distaste out of his voice. The colonies were cold now, and filthy, and smelly.

Mecatl, the eldest of the pipiltin and rumored favorite of the Steel Emperor, explained: "There has been a murder there."

"And have the British lost the ability to police their own?" Ixtli had little love for the far north.

"The murder is of a young man. His heart has been removed in what looks like an Eagle sacrifice. Find out the truth of the matter, and whether apostate priests have immigrated to New Amsterdam."

This was news to Ixtli. Followers of the sacrifice usually inhabited border lands between cities, scattered and un-united. None of them tried to keep the old ways in any Mexica city.

But in the chaos of a savage, foreign city like New Amsterdam, maybe they could rebuild their followers.

"And if I find it's so?" Ixtli asked the pipiltin.

"Find the truth," they told him. "If it is true, then we will have to root out the heresy from a distance. But if it is not true, we need to find out what is happening."

And seven hours later Ixtli was passing out of his father country and into the great swathe of territory the French called Louisiana, the large airship he'd booked passage on powering hard against the winds. After a refueling stop at the end of the first day's travel it was over the Indian lands, and then finally, they touched down on the edges of New Amsterdam airfield. Two days. The world was shrinking, Ixtli thought, and he did not know if that was a good thing.

Pale faces looked up at Ixtli, colonials dressed in little more than rags, tying off the airship's ropes as they fell down towards the trampled grass. They shouted in guttural languages: English, Dutch, French. Ixtli knew many of them from his days along the Mexica coast, fighting them all during the invasions of '89.

The airship's gondola finally kissed the earth, and ramps were pulled out.

Ixtli walked off, porters following with his suitcases. The cold hit him and he shivered in his purple and red robes, the feather in his carefully tied hair twisted in the biting wind.

A bulbous-nosed man in a thick wool cape and earmuffs strode confidently forward, his hand extended. "Gordon Doyle, sir, at your service!"

Ixtli looked down and did not take the man's hand in his own, but gave him a slight nod of his head. "I am Ixtli."

"Splendid, what's your last name?"

"I am just Ixtli." He stared at Gordon, who rubbed his hand on his cape and fumbled around with a pipe.

"Well, Ixtli, I just arrived from London the day before it happened. Scotland Yard needed me over here to find the Albany Rapist. Bad series of events, that. Poor urchins, bad way to end it, very sensational, all over the papers."

Gordon was a jittery man. "Did you solve it?" Ixtli asked.

"Um, no, not yet. But come, I have a hansom waiting."

The murder site was in the Colonial Museum, a massive neo-Dutch structure embedded in the east side of New Amsterdam's Central Park. The driver whipped the massive beast of a horse up to speed and took them down the Manhattan thoroughfares.

"It's such a vibrant city, this," Gordon said, the acrid smell of his pipe wafting across over the smell of horse shit and garbage. The city, as packed and heavy with people as it was, placed its garbage on the streets to be picked up.

At least the city had sewers.

Ixtli leaned back, looking up at the buildings. This island was denser than Tenochtitlan. Large buildings, some over ten stories high and made of brick, lined the road on his left. Greenery and park, with cook fires and shantytowns that dotted it, lined his right.

Gordon noticed Ixtli looking. "Revolutionaries. This year's batch anyway. The Crown recently seized the land of the 'Americans'. Think they would have learned their lesson from the last time. Damn terrorists."

"You let them camp on your public lands?"

"Well, the homeless are always a problem in the big cities. They skulk around here hoping one day to rise up again."

The cab lurched to a stop and the horse farted. Ixtli leapt down into the mud and walked up to the giant, imposing steps of the Colonial Museum. He was chilled to the core and wanted out of the wind. "Have you investigated any of the revolutionaries in the park?"

Gordon cleared his throat loudly. "Dear God, man, what do you take me for, a simpleton? Of course."

Ixtli ignored the reaction and stepped through the brass doorframes and into the museum past waiting policemen. Come see the original colonial declaration of secession, the poster proclaimed, next to an encased poster that showed a snake cut into thirteen pieces.

"Let's see this."

The young man in question had been left for two days at the request of the Mexica via telegraph. There was the telltale sign of faint bloating. Both Gordon and Ixtli held handkerchiefs to their noses as they approached the body.

Ixtli peered in at the corpse, then looked around. "The room has not been touched, or the floor cleaned? Was there blood on the floor apart from what the body pooled out?"

"None of that nature," Gordon confirmed.

"The manner in which the chest has been split, while similar, is done in a much more calculated manner than any normal ceremonial practice. And then there is one other thing."

"Entrails are still in his body." Gordon stabbed the air with his pipe. "Usually both are burnt, are they not?"

"There is also no blood on this floor, from ripping them out. This was done in a surgical manner, with the heart being removed and taken out in a waterproof container. No doubt to sensationalize and excite people in New Amsterdam," Ixtli said. "This is not the work of a warrior priest."

And that was a relief.

Gordon did not look as relieved, however. He made a face. "Well, I guess that rather leaves it all up in the air."

"Do you have any other leads?"

"Nothing of any particular sorts," Gordon said. "You were our best, as it would have allowed us to start questioning around certain areas."

Ixtli shook his head. "Round up the brown-skinned?"

Gordon at least had the decency to look somewhat embarrassed. "One of the guards saw someone."

"Dark-skinned."

"Red, is actually what he said." Gordon hailed a hansom. Ixtli looked over at the curb, where a small group of dirty urchins had melted out of the bush to stare at them. Cold hard stares, devoid of curiosity.

One of them held a small, stiff piece of paper in his left hand, fingering it reverently.

"Red like me?" They melted back into the bushes of Central Park under Ixtli's stare.

The hansom shook as Gordon stepped in. "We didn't pull out an artist's palette and paints. When your embassy found the headline and details, and said they were sending you over, we had hoped they might know something. The method of death is . . . unique." Gordon tapped the driver perched on the rear of the cab and gave him directions to the hotel Ixtli would be staying at.

"Ah, you talk about the past, Mr Doyle, and nothing but the past. You should know better."

And on this note, Gordon smiled. "And yet you are here, sir. So speedily. So sanctioned by your country. It suggests that there may have been something."

The man, Ixtli thought, didn't miss much. "Do you know what I am, Mr Doyle?"

"I have my suspicions."

"I am no spy. I am an inquisitor. It is my job to find heretics. It is my job to find them and stop their heresy." They clip-clopped their way down into the maze of New Amsterdam's chaotic business. "When your people invaded . . ."

"The Spanish, sir, the Spanish, not us."

Ixtli shrugged. To him one European was just as another. ". . . they had several advantages against us. Guns, steel, disease, but most importantly, the numbers and fighters of Tlaxcala who hated our taxes and loss of life to the blade of the priest. When Cortez took our leader hostage and Moctezuma stood before our city and told us to bow to the Spanish, we stoned him to death and elected a new leader, and drove the white men from our city. We fought back and forth, dying of disease, but fighting for our existence.

"We'd already killed our emperor. We were bound by tradition, and religion, but it kept hindering us. The living city leaders decided only radical new ways of thinking could save us, and the first was to renounce our taxes on tributary cities, and claim that we would no longer sacrifice the unwilling to our gods. And we made good with actions. It was bloody and long, Gordon, but an idea, an idea is something amazing. Particularly when it spreads.

"So what I do, is help that idea. That blood sacrifice isn't required, that people are equal under the Mexica, and that we are an alternative to the way of the invaders. And those who want the old religions, the old ways, I hunt them down, Mr Doyle, I hunt them down and exact a terrible price from them."

"And you are here to make sure your image as past savages isn't continued?"

"Something like that." The Mexica made a point of stealing the brightest heretics from Europe over the last 300 years. You wouldn't get burned in Tenochtitlan, you could print your seditions against European thought there, and anything useful, anything invented, all benefited the Mexica.

Anything that faulted that haven needed to be destroyed.

That was Ixtli's job.

In the sitting room of the cramped, smelly, dank hotel room that professed to be properly heated, Ixtli removed his colorful cape, hung up the gold armband of his profession, and sighed.

Gordon Doyle followed him in and looked around. "Grand, this. One more thing. You never asked if we had identified the body."

"I had assumed you would tell me when you felt it was important. Is it?"

"Important. Somewhat. The grandson of one of the prominent revolutionaries." Gordon stood there, waiting for some reaction.

"I have no theories, certainly there is no reason I know that my country would need some dissident killed in a way that makes us look culpable." Ixtli shivered. This was like standing up on a mountain. "Isn't our business over, now? You can go find some other brown-skinned people as your suspects."

With a tap of a finger on his awkwardly sized hat Gordon backed out the door. "I'll give you a ride in the morning to the airfield."

"My thanks."

Ixtli sat near the heater for a while, trying to warm up, and then finally gave up the attempt as futile and crawled under the thick and scratchy woolen blankets.

His feet never seemed to stop aching, but after a while he relaxed and fell into a light sleep with the odd shiver or two spaced a few minutes apart.

That was until he heard a foot creak on a nearby floorboard.

Ixtli rolled off and under his bed just as a large club smacked into his pillow. Just as quickly Ixtli rolled back out and swept the attacker off his feet with one good kick to the nearest kneecap and a sweeping motion with his other leg.

He was rewarded with a half-hearted jab to his thigh with the club. Stone chips ripped at his skin.

It was a macehuitl, the club.

What on earth was someone doing with a museum piece like that?

But that was just a feint. The attacker grabbed him for a takedown, and they were both on the floor, rolling around, Ixtli realizing that the man's heavy weight lent him a major advantage.

It was a scraping, heaving, bloody, bashing fight that was somewhere between a Grecian wrestling match and a cock fight, and it ended only when Ixtli wrestled the macehuitl away and clubbed the man in his face.

Ixtli looked something like a stereotype when Gordon responded to his urgent message, delivered to the concierge by the pneumatic speaking tube in his room: he sat on his bed, still holding the squat fighting club with the sharp stone bits embedded on its sides, blood dripping, the vanquished foe by his feet.

"Dear God!" Gordon said.

"He isn't Mexica," Ixtli said.

"Well, someone is working awfully hard to make sure it looks like that."

Ixtli looked down at the man and bent to rifle his pockets. No papers of any sort. Except for a stiff, beige card with holes poked through it. Ixtli held it up. "But we do have something here."

Gordon looked at it. "A loom card?"

Ixtli nodded. "It's your best clue yet, they didn't count on an ambassador being a skilled warrior. Find out who makes it, or even who purchased it. We don't have much time before they find out their man is dead."

"I'll get right on it. I'll send some men up to get the body. They'll also keep guard in a new room that we'll be getting you into."

"Thank you." But Ixtli didn't think he would be sleeping.

He called down to the concierge to pass on the message that he would not be taking the next airship home.

Ixtli would see this to its end.

Gordon found him in the restaurant poring over hot coffee before sunbreak, the closest thing Ixtli could get to cacoa. It warmed him.

"I heard you weren't returning to your homeland?" Gordon asked.

"News travels quickly." Ixtli stirred in honey. "I want to know who wants me dead. A professional courtesy, I had hoped you would understand."

"A case could take weeks, or months, to crack. It's not a case of roughing up the bystanders and accusing people of crimes. It's a methodical thing, filled with suppositions and theories that need to be validated or checked. One must be cool and moderate, and uninvolved."

"By then your trail will have gone cold." Ixtli sipped the coffee. Passable. Very passable. He smiled for the first time in the last two days. "I think, Mr Doyle, that you and I have something in common."

"What's that?"

"We're both children of the enlightenment."

Gordon stiffened. "I wouldn't say that around here. French revolutionaries and colonialist terrorists were the children of the enlightenment."

Ixtli laughed. "Not politically. I am speaking of your reverence for the truth, the interest in where the trail will lead. And now I have the greatest mystery in front of me: someone wants me dead. I admit, I'm very curious."

Gordon didn't look so sure. Ixtli kept a mask of geniality on. It was not quite true, what he'd said. Underneath he simmered to find the true assassin behind all this.

"Okay," Gordon said. "But you are unarmed, right? I don't want you causing any trouble."

"I am unarmed." Ixtli spread his arms.

Gordon slapped the loom card on the table. "Then we visit the makers of this. And tonight we'll switch you to a new hotel."

The giant brick building near the docks of New Amsterdam, chimneys looming overhead, was the HOLLERITH MACHINE COMPANY. A Mr Jason Finesson waited for them, resplendent in tails and a tall hat, spectacles clamped down over his nose hard enough to leave a welt.

"Detective." He shook Gordon's hand, and then turned to Ixtli. "And sir."

Ixtli gave a nod of the head and turned to Gordon, who pulled out the offending card. Ixtli wasn't sure why they were at a machining company, but he declined to say anything out loud. If a card could control a loom for weavers, maybe it could control other kinds of machines.

"Ah." Mr Finesson looked at the card. "A punch card. Your message, you do say you found it at a crime scene?"

Gordon nodded. "Yes."

"How curious." Finesson held it up to the gaslight in the corner of the room. A bored-looking secretary with perfectly slicked-back hair in a black suit sat poring over a ledger laid out across his desk by the entrance. "Well, I can tell you the very machine it was made on."

"Excellent." Gordon looked elated. The thrill of the hunt.

"But that won't help you much," Finesson continued. "Our customers use these in bulk for all sorts of things. I couldn't tell you which customer this comes from."

Ixtli had been staring at the man. He looked assured, confident, and as if he were telling the truth. "You are the manager here?"

"Yes."

"What exactly do your customers use these things for?"

"Ah, let me show you."

Finesson escorted them back through the dim hallways of the building into a large room several stories high that looked like it was the lovechild of a swiss watchmaker and a train engineer. Massive gears and wheels strained, clicking away on bearings the size of a man. All throughout pulleys and shafts spun, and a massive steam boiler, fit to power a transatlantic ship, squatted in the center of the room, steam hissing lazily out the pipes connected to it.

"Last summer we were commissioned to count the census of the colonies, sirs. Since then we've processed merchant accounts, calculated the mysteries of the universe for leading scientists, and been available for engineers."

"That's a mechanical adding machine," Ixtli said. "I've heard of these."

Finesson pranced around the entryway like a circus grandmaster. "Oh, but it's so much more. Complex maths, instructions, this is a computing machine, gentleman. One of only four or five like it in the world! I'll wager you, sirs, that if you could take the mathematics of policing, and reduce it to calculations and variables and insert it into this machine, we could run your police force."

"Another child of the enlightenment, I presume," Gordon said out of the side of his mouth to Ixtli, who was still gaping at the machine.

"Even better," said Finesson. "I've talked to your counterparts, the Dutch constabulary here in New Amsterdam. Yes, the British do an excellent job of co-ruling this tiny island, but why be so reactive? You know the study of physiognomy, wherein you can determine a person's character merely by studying their unique facial characteristics?"

Both Ixtli and Gordon nodded.

"Indeed, well I suggested to his Excellency Mr Van Ostrand that we take sketches of all the criminals encountered by his forces, load them into our device to find points of similarity, and then begin sketching in all manner of our population to load into our machine to find criminals *before* they commit their crimes. It would revolutionize your jobs, men."

Gordon and Ixtli glanced at each other. Ixtli spoke first. "And what if you were fingered by the device?"

"What? I'm no criminal," Finesson said. "How dare you! I have nothing to fear."

"I take it the Dutch have not invested in this idea?" Gordon changed the subject quickly.

"No," Finesson looked down at his shoe. "More's the pity."

"Indeed." Ixtli picked up a stray punch card and looked at it. It made no apparent sense to him, hundreds and hundreds of tiny pockmarks.

A man at the table held out his hand. "The order in which we feed them into the machine is important, it tells them what to do."

"Well, Mr Finesson, we would like your customers' records."

"And do you have a writ?"

Ixtli glanced at Gordon, who shook his head. "Not yet, sir."

"If my customers found out I turned over my books so easily, I could lose a great deal of business. There are forms and numbers and calculations being done by businesses here that would not want their information spread about the city."

"I understand."

And with that, a frustrated Gordon and Ixtli were outside again, headed back to the hotel.

"That was a waste," Gordon said, stuffing a new pipe and looking annoyed. "Physiognomy . . ."

"Maybe that isn't so." Ixtli held a mirror in his hand, as if checking the makeup on his face. Behind them dashed an urchin, doing his best to keep up. In these crowded streets it was feasible. He rapped the roof to get the driver's attention and handed him paper money. "Stop here. I need you to wander off to one of these stores and purchase something. Take your time."

"Yessir." The driver's large sideburns rippled in the wind as he leapt out and strode past them.

"What on earth is this about?" Gordon asked.

"Observation, Mr Doyle. There is an urchin following us, and that same creature was outside the Colonial Museum when we last left it. Is it coincidence that the very same urchin following us now, and during the previous time I saw him, seemed to have one of these punch cards on his person?"

"I would think not," muttered Gordon.

"Me neither."

Gordon looked around. "This is not a part of New Amsterdam for strangers to tarry in. Particularly ones in colorful capes such as yourself."

"Exactly the reason I chose it," Ixtli said, scanning the crowds pushing against street vendors, people dodging carriages. A tram thundered by, ringing its bell furiously. He pointed a young man out to Gordon. "Call that one over. The one selling those rotten-looking apples."

"Boy!"

The boy in question jogged over with the box of apples in front of his stomach, suspicion embedded in his glare. "What you want?"

Gordon showed his badge and grabbed the boy before he could turn and run.

Ixtli handed the boy a thick wad of paper money. "We have a job for you. That's half what you'll get if you succeed."

"It'd beat selling dodgy apples, you'll make a couple weeks' worth from us," Gordon said, catching on. "And you don't want me asking where you gone and got them from, now do you?"

The struggling ceased. "What you wanting then?"

"There's a mangy sort following this vehicle – no, don't look – and we want you to follow him in turn. No doubt he'll spring off to inform someone of where we are when we reach our hotel. Follow him, but don't let him see you. Find us back at the Waldorf Hotel. Ask for Doyle."

The boy tugged on his cap. "Yessir."

"And here is our driver," Ixtli said. "Take the apples so the urchin suspects nothing."

Gordon did, and the driver, taking it all in his stride, just asked, "Shall I restart the cab, sirs?"

"Yes, let's move on."

The driver disappeared behind them. The cab shook as he climbed into his perch looking over the cab, and then the hansom jerked into motion. Ixtli settled back in.

"Clever," said Gordon.

"If it works." Ixtli looked down at the rotted apples. He was going to gibe Gordon about the hungry on the streets of New Amsterdam, and then decided to leave the man alone.

"So now we retire to the hotel and wait."

"You told me this was a pursuit for the moderate and patient." Gordon sighed.

Their urchin showed up outside the hotel just as they were setting in to dine. Ixtli spotted the hotel doorman confronting the young boy as he maintained his need to see them right away.

Ixtli and Gordon walked out to the street. "What do you have for us?"

"I know where the boy went." The urchin was still out of breath from his run.

"Take us there!"

"What about my money?"

Ixtli felt around in his cape, pulled out enough for the cab fare, and looked at Gordon, who patted his pockets. "I left what I had on the table for the meal."

"We'll get to a bank, but after you show us where the boy went."

"Dammit, I knew you was going to gyp me."

"Look at us, do we look like the sort to play games like that?" Gordon yelled.

The boy looked him up and down. "I guess not," he conceded. "But I'm going to get my money." On that he was dead certain.

They hailed a hansom. "East River Waterfront," the boy said. They piled in, squeezing the boy between them. He reeked of sweat and body odor, and he grumbled about their lack of payment all the way.

As the great East River Bridge loomed and they slowed, the boy crawled up to poke his head around to the back and guide the cabbie towards a set of large brick warehouses.

HOLLERITH WAREHOUSING.

"Hah," Gordon said. "Nothing to fear from physiognomy indeed."

"Finesson could be innocent but unaware." Ixtli jumped out of the hansom and paid the cabbie.

Gordon agreed, and handed the driver a card he'd scribbled something on. "The constabulary will triple your usual if you hang around at the ready."

The driver nodded and accepted the promise of payment.

"Look," the boy said. "Be careful. The boys I followed was Constitutionalists. You don't want to tangle with that lot."

"Thank you," Ixtli patted him on the shoulder. "If we're not back in fifteen minutes, call the police."

"Like hell," the boy said.

"They'll pay you," Gordon said.

"I'll consider it."

And then he was gone, watching them from the shadows. No doubt ready to rabbit off on a moment's notice, but held there by the desire for his money.

"So what are we looking for?" Gordon asked as they circled the building.

"An easy opening," Ixtli replied. There was a rumbling that seemed to permeate through the ground all around.

"We don't have a writ to enter."

"But I have diplomatic immunity." Ixtli found a window that was loose, and with some persuading, forced it open. "Care to accompany me lest my life be threatened and an incident between our respective countries occurs?"

Gordon licked his lips. "Damned if I do . . ."

Ixtli waited for the second part of the sentence. None came, so he pulled himself up and over into the warehouse.

Gordon scrabbled in after him. The warehouse was dark, shadows of pallets and crates looming all around them. Gordon took out an electric torch and clicked it on.

The entire warehouse lit up, gaslamps all throughout springing up to full flame. A crowd of very serious-looking childlike faces started at them, and at their head, a giant of a man, a dockworker, reached with a long coil of loop.

"Welcome to these United Peoples," he growled. Ixtli stared at the long tattoo of a chopped-up snake on his left forearm. Don't tread on me, it said.

Ixtli doubted anyone would be able to, not with all that muscle.

Three more dockworkers stepped forward, surrounding them.

In short order both men were tied up, Gordon handcuffed with his own cuffs, despite both giving a brief struggle.

"May I ask why we're being detained?" Gordon asked. He had a purple bruise over his left eye, and Ixtli admired his cool in the situation. Ixtli himself considered a prayer to the gods.

"You damn well know you was trespassing," the giant of a man growled. "Don't play coy, eh?"

"Okay. So what are we waiting for?"

"Who."

The three men melted aside, giving way to a man in a stovepipe hat and long tails. A craggy face regarded them both. This was interesting. They weren't dead yet.

"Mr Hollerith?" Ixtli asked.

The man removed his hat and handed it over to an urchin. A stool was presented for him to sit on. "Justin Hollerith. Are you here to assassinate me?"

"We're here to find the killer of that boy at the Colonial Museum," Gordon said.

"Well huzzah," Hollerith said. "You have found the killer."

Gordon tensed in his chair. "You?"

Hollerith shook his head. He snapped his fingers and the mass of urchins shifted. A massive curtain slowly rolled aside to reveal a machine that made the one at Hollerith's offices look like a toy.

The entire warehouse was filled with rotating shafts that went on and on, and thousands of gears. Young boys ran from station to station with armloads of punch cards.

That explained the vibrating floors and roads outside. Ixtli glanced around, wondering how it would be explained to his family that he had died, strapped to a chair in some dirty city up north.

No honor in this, he thought. None at all.

"Here is your killer," Hollerith said. "How do you plan on bringing it to justice?"

Gordon shook his head. "I don't understand."

Hollerith spread his arms wide to indicate the sheer presence of the machine. "You, Aztec, should know what we are going through right now."

"Indeed?" Ixtli perked up. The man was still talking, waiting for something, eager to prove . . . something. If they could keep him talking, then maybe there would be time for the boy outside to go for the police.

If he did ever go. That was a gamble.

"The tyrants and occupiers of our lands . . ." Hollerith got up and Ixtli tensed. "The colonies tried to rise once, to be crushed in their boots."

"You're a dissident," Gordon hissed.

"Revolutionaries! Visionaries!" Hollerith stood up. "Gentlemen, what you see before you is the engine of a new future. The British boot will be forced back. This machine is the constitution of the new United States of America."

"The what?" Ixtli remembered that the boy had called these people constitutionalists.

Now Hollerith paced in front of them. "A set of rules for governing us, fair, impartial and written by the people. The tyrants refused to let man rule himself, and so we've had to go underground. Slowly, building our ranks. We have citizens all throughout the thirteen colonies, waiting for their moment to rise up."

One of the dockworkers took out a punch card from the end of a station. "Mister Hollerith." He handed it over.

Hollerith glanced at the card. He blinked. "I hold here your future, gentlemen."

Ixtli looked at the complex pattern of holes. "Really? The machine dictates your actions?"

"What is government but a set of programmed instructions we all agree upon? And in a democracy, it is blind, and her instructions carried out by men. This is no different.

"The things that happen to us, we feed them into the computer, and it sorts its responses and hands them back to us on our cards, telling us how to serve it best. Judgements, foreign policies and now . . . war. It is our destiny, it always has been, to spill out throughout this country and claim it for ourselves. To spread from sea to sea. Already telegraph operators string throughout the thirteen, even through the Indian lands between us and the west coast, passing on and coordinating instructions with other constitutional machines running in parallel all throughout the land. The US will rise again."

"Manifest destiny, embodied within the unflinching intelligence of a computing machine," Ixtli said.

"You've heard of the theory? The machine decided that a diplomatic incident would be what we needed. It said to look out for anything resembling one, so that we could use that to gain recruits, and worry people about the threat of foreign murderers here in our city."

"That theory is that your race is somehow owed it all: the lands of the Mexica, the Indians, and what the British rule already," said Ixtli. "Yes, I've heard this before. In Texcaco, yes, in the Mexica-Americas war. Many of your border men, out of the reach of the British, were prodded on by the Louisiana French by having that belief dangled before them. An ugly scene."

"This will be different." Hollerith looked at the punch card. "I'm sorry, but as enemies of the state, you will not have a trial. You will be executed as spies. So says the Constitution."

"So says the Constitution," murmured the hundreds in the warehouse.

"You'll be taken to a room, where ten blindfolded men with rifles will fire. The Constitution will randomly load a pair of guns. Take them away."

Gordon struggled again, but Ixtli remained calm. "Now you are killing harmless public servants in the name of your cause, just like any other group of dissidents."

Hollerith refused the bait. "I have sworn to protect the Constitution, gentlemen, from all its enemies. Your rhetoric will have little impact on me."

The three dockworkers moved in, and Ixtli walked with them through the rows of furiously spinning clockwork and blank government officials' faces.

They were forced into a tiny closet, and the door was barred shut.

"Thanks for delaying them," Gordon said, leaning against the wall.

"I did what I could." Ixtli moved around in the dark, trying to find out if there was anything useful, but the space had been cleared of everything.

"When they find us dead, I imagine my heart will be cut out," Gordon said. "And you will be dead nearby of a gunshot, maybe?"

"It will stir up enmity, feed unity and a sense that they need to cohere against an outside force."

It wasn't just his death, but the betrayal of his country. Ixtli kicked at the door in frustration.

"Hey," a familiar voice hissed. The door cracked open and in slipped the boy. He left the door ajar, the welcome light bringing their temporary cell out of the deep dark and into murkiness. "I knew you'd get yourselves in it deep and end up losing me my money."

"Did you call the police?" Gordon asked.

"Police? No damn police. Just Slim Tim."

"Who's Slim Tim?" Ixtli moved closer to the boy.

"Who's Slim Tim? he asks. Slim Tim is me!" Slim Tim sliced the ropes off.

"And no one noticed you?" Gordon asked.

Slim Tim shrugged. "They was busy with the lights." He smiled, and then counted off his fingers. On the last one something boomed loudly and Slim Tim chuckled. Light flashed and danced brightly.

Gordon pulled the last of his rope free. "Let's make a break for it."

They glanced out of the closet. Nothing but people tending the machine.

"Run," Ixtli said.

They skirted the dark walls, ducking and weaving around the dangerous moving parts of the living machine. The escape almost worked, but near the doors a man throwing switches paused, frowned, and shouted at them.

The cry went up all throughout the warehouse, and the ten men with rifles ran through an aisle of machinery, blindfolds loose around their necks. "Stop!"

"Only two of the guns will kill us," Ixtli said. "Run for it, and whoever survives, get out to call the officials."

"Scatter," Gordon said, and they did. All ten rifles fired, and Ixtli felt relief. Nothing had hit him, no bullets pinged, they were all blanks. He turned the corner with the other two before the second round, this one not loaded with blanks, could be fired.

They burst out of the main doors, ran down the corners to where the hansom waited, and all three piled in, shouting, "Go, go, go!"

"You pay me now," Slim Tim said. "Very next thing."

Ixtli grabbed Slim Tim's shoulders. "You're damn right we pay you next." He shook the boy. "You will make a small fortune tonight, Mr Tim, a small fortune."

Gordon met Ixtli the next morning at the airfield before he left and stuck his hand out. "Mr Ixtli, my thanks."

Ixtli regarded the offered hand. A strange custom. He took it carefully and finished the American ritual, a sign of respect for what they had both been through. "Did you get Hollerith?"

Gordon shook his head. "They smashed the machine, and took their punch cards with them. We reduced their abilities significantly, though, thanks to you."

"Thanks to you." Ixtli's superiors would find this a fascinating tale. He wondered what they would do with the information. Computer-run governments and humans no better than automatons, run by small dots on a piece of paper.

"What a barbarous idea, letting machines rule you."

Ixtli looked around. "What is a government but ideas that are set down on paper for rules, and then interpreted and run by individual human machines? Is it really that far-fetched?"

"But cogs and wheels? We will find these people and their cards and burn them out."

Ixtli nodded, relieved. The Constitutionalists had taken all their punch cards with them. Good. "Of course, that is the typical response of a nation. But Gordon, remember this: all ten of those weapons fired were blank, we were never hit."

"What do you mean?"

"A government is the will of its people, and the will of Hollerith is twisted. He and his people want land, and revolution, and blood. Revenge against the British. Manifest destiny above all else.

"But if the pure ideals of an idea were really input into a machine, maybe it fought back, Mr Doyle. Maybe it told all those soldiers to load blanks. And Hollerith indicated that maybe the machine hadn't ordered that man's death at the museum, but merely suggested they look for such an incident."

"Maybe," Gordon said. "Maybe."

"Consider it, that the ideas are what is important. If you ever come to Tenochtitlan, make sure to visit." Ixtli smiled. "Where the pursuit of truth reigns free, and all manner of theories live side by side, jostling each other."

They shook hands again, and then Gordon grabbed Ixtli's shoulder.

"I have a favor to ask: now that we have solved this crime and my men are looking for Hollerith, might I get your permission to send my notes and files to my brother? He fancies himself something of a writer and follows such things. Intrigue, and the sort."

"Of course," Ixtli said. "What is your brother's name?"

"Arthur."

"Just make sure my name is changed," Ixtli laughed. And with that last bit of business, the two men separated. Ixtli boarded the airship.

Somewhere past French Louisiana and over tribal lands, Ixtli reached under his coat and pulled out a stack of punch cards. An insurrection, guided by machine, could be imminently useful.

The basis of the computing machine's rules could be corrupted, maybe even by telegraph commands, or a hidden series of codes activated by punch cards slipped in by an agent. An agent who had been called north by a special signal, thanks to a series of pre-programmed instructions.

Ixtli's world faced threats. Spanish to the south, English colonies and French to the north, and the intermediate and forever fickle tribal societies in the midlands. Tenochtitlan was always aware of the need to keep Europeans on their toes. Keeping the Europeans divided and fighting among themselves kept them from focusing their eyes on new land.

So now Ixtli held up the punch cards he had taken the ones he'd replaced were now with the dissidents, who were none the wiser.

He leaned over the window, and dropped the cards out to flutter in the wind.

Where they would land, he had no idea. It was not his place to know, or ask. He was just another agent in the vast machine that was his government.

The Hands That Feed

Matthew Kressel

"If only it were as easy to fix my eyes as it is yours," I said to Miriam as I peered through the glasses hanging off my nose. My attic workshop was dark, the cuckoo clock on my wall had just announced midnight, but moonbeams lit my cigarette smoke like heavenly girders. Miriam was, after all, my little angel. Her bronze frame glinted in the moonlight as I twisted a wrench inside her enclosure. As her lens came into focus she clicked happily. She wouldn't bang into furniture or wake up the sleeping any longer. (Or such was my hope; her bent frame was evidence of a recent encounter with a club.) I placed her on the floor and she crawled onto the table by the window. Beside her stood Beth, Eve, Leah, Talia and Shoshanna, her sisters in trade. Together, they looked like a litter of shiny, eight-legged, hairless cats. Their eyes peered up at me, awaiting my command.

"Are you ready, *meine kinder*?" I said.

Miriam tapped her head against the window pane. Her sisters chittered.

"Make *mame* proud," I said as I opened the window. And my little girls, eager to please, crawled out my fourth-story window. They spidered down the steep wall and vanished into the night. The rooftops of Manhattan's Lower East Side stretched into the distance like a tumultuous gray sea frozen in time. I leaned out into the cool air and exhaled smoke toward the stars. A kitten – a flesh and blood one, sleek and brown and beautiful – sat on the roof across the way and watched me with two glowing eyes. Down below, I heard a thump; I hoped it wasn't Miriam's lens acting up again. When I glanced at the roof once more, the kitten had gone.

At 6 a.m. the next morning, after three cups of strong coffee, I descended to the ground floor of my home to my pawn shop, 'Tchotchkes', to the sound of clocks chiming wildly. Outside my windows, which were painted with fading Yiddish letters, the morning sun was bright and clean and cut hard slices through the cobbled streets. A flock of airships meshed the sky, their engines droning like worker bees as they moved to and from South Street Airport. Like gray pike swimming upstream, pious Jews raced past the windows to the nearest *shul, talis* bags in tow, so they could pray before heading to work. But Divya stood motionless among them, a stone in the river. She was punctual, sleepy-eyed and lovely, as usual. I opened the door, kissed the *mezzuzah*, and held the door open for her. She wore a modest brown dress, a fresh crimson *bindi* on her forehead, and a gem-encrusted silver necklace. The last lit up her face like flashes from a fire. As she passed me I reached for her neck and she flinched, then tried to disguise her reaction with a nervous laugh.

"Relax, dear!" I said. "I'm just curious."

Sheepishly she held the necklace up to my eyes: a silver band encrusted with glistering gems. I didn't need a loupe to know they were real diamonds.

"Beautiful," I said. "A gift from Robert?"

She nodded, and when I offered no more she slipped quietly inside my store.

An auto-giraffe whirred past. The officer on its saddle, shaded under a tassled canopy, like a *chupa*, leaned over the side and shouted to me, "Mornin', Jessica." He tipped his cap.

"And to you, Elijah."

Officer Elijah had lost his left eye in a tussle four years back, and the replacement, a metallic contraption of lenses and gears, made him look half machine. Sometimes I thought the injury had affected his brain, too. "Jessica," he said as he stopped his auto-giraffe. He revealed an envelope and handed it to a small crawler, which ran down the tall mechanoid's leg and offered it to me. The brutish police crawler lacked the grace of my bronze children, now slinking through the city's streets, though they shared the same military provenance.

"What's this?" I said, taking the envelope.

"A list of missing items."

"Missing?"

"Er . . ." He coughed. "Stolen."

"*Zayt moykhl?*" I said – 'excuse me' in Yiddish. Elijah was a goy, but he had worked this neighborhood for years. I eyed him hard and thrust my hands onto my hips. His false eye stared back at me, cold and lifeless, and I suppressed a shiver.

"Please, Jess. I'm not implyin' anything. Mayor Strong is crackin' down for the election. Wants to be seen as tough on crime. You own a pawn shop. Things there . . . come and go. All I'm sayin' is any of these things show up in your store, you bring 'em to me. Anonymously. End of story."

I spun away from him and said, "*Gut morgn*, Elijah."

He harrumphed and said a perfunctory, "Ma'am," and his mech-of-burden whirred as it trotted away, its metal hooves click-clopping on the cobbles. Meanwhile an auto-human – its rusty frame glinting in the sun – hung a bill on the wall across the street from my store.

The bill read, "Vote Robert Davis for Mayor of New York. Cleansing the Corruption from Our City's Streets". Robert's lithograph smiled superciliously down at me. I tore the bill from the wall and shredded it to pieces while the auto-human mindlessly pasted another one a hundred feet down the street. Those godless machines even worked on *Shabbos*. I set my teeth and went back inside.

Divya had already swept the floor, unlocked the register, and was now vigorously scrubbing the glass cases. My store was filled with costume jewelry, dresses worn once and tossed away, broken gear movements, chipped toys, things found in closets or the backs of drawers that would never be missed if they vanished. Even I didn't know the extent of what I had. But as the old adage goes, *one man's junk* . . . And no matter how much one cleans, junk always reeks of mold and time.

But Divya spread her youth about this place with her every gesture and word. I envied her slim frame, her lucid eyes, her lustrous and tawny skin. She was thirty years my junior, and I found myself perpetually charmed by her.

"Miss Rosen," Divya said in her soft, lilting Gujarat accent that always stirred my heart. "I thought I'd put the silver Seder plates in the window for the coming Passover."

Though she was Hindu, she had made it her practice to learn the Jewish customs of this neighborhood, both the sacred and the saleable. "How many times do I have to tell you, dear? Call me 'Jessica'. I'm not your damn school teacher!"

"I'm sorry, Miss – Jessica. My father beat such habits into me. Always respect your elders—"The moment the last word left her lips, Divya blushed and busied herself again with the countertops. So shy and awkward, this young woman. It was rare to see someone as beautiful as she and yet so lacking in presumption, pretense, or conceit. I'd wondered how long it would take before some devilish soul corrupted her. I looked outside the window as an auto-human hung a new poster of Robert Davis in the same spot where I had torn the last one down. My face was reflected back to me in the window pane, superimposed over his, like a *dybbuk* come to eat his soul.

I'd hired Divya three months prior, and the time since had passed in a whirl. She and her father had stowed away on an airship, fleeing the tumult and poverty in Gujarat. Penniless, disheveled and stunning, she wandered into my store like a stray kitten. My grandparents came from Odessa with nothing, and a good Jewish family took them in, gave them a start. So how could I refuse Divya and her pleading brown eyes, and her voice that knew the song sparrows sang to heaven?

I put her to work doing the chores my back no longer favored, and she arrived promptly each morning, did twice the work expected of her, and never complained. On sunny afternoons while taking slow drags from my cigarette by the window, I'd catch her gazing at me. In the lulls between customers, we'd often tell each other stories about ourselves.

"How did you acquire this house?" Divya once asked me. "It's so beautiful."

"Beautiful? Have you been up to the roof? It's Gomorrah up there!" I said, chuckling. "The house was built by my grandparents. They started a printing press. Prayer books, textbooks, Talmuds, things like that. They used to sell books and Judaica out of this store."

"Do you still own the press?"

"No. You know that *momzer*, Shmuel Cohen? His parents came

in with bigger machines, faster presses. Their cheaper product put my parents out of business."

"And your parents, are they still in Manhattan?"

"Oh no, dear, they passed away a long time ago."

"So you opened this pawn shop yourself?"

I nodded. "After my parents died, people went to Cohen's Bookshop to get their books, Mandel's Emporium for their *talit* and *mezzuzahs*. The money ran out. So I started selling other things. Other people's things."

"I envy you."

"*Envy?*" I said. I wondered how this young woman could envy anything about me.

"You had a helping hand," she said. "A start. That family that took you in. Your parents. I began with nothing."

"That may be true," I said. "But now you have a job. And you have me."

I smiled at her. And she smiled back, and her gaze held warmth and tenderness. I'd seen that gaze before, in dozens of women. It brought a stab of joy to my heart. Could this young woman see me, an ageing *yenta*, as they once had?

One rainy and damp evening, Divya and I found ourselves alone in the back office among dusty papers, piles of unread books, and the soft ticking of a clock. Her face was angelic in the lamplight.

I caressed her cheek with the back of my hand, pressed my lips to hers, and felt a tremble; I wasn't sure which one of us shook. But as I embraced her she gently pushed me away.

"What is it?" I said.

She stared at me and a look of confusion blurred her face. "I'm sorry, Miss Rosen, but I can't."

"Why?"

"I'm sorry. My father's waiting for me." She spun out the door, forgetting to lock it behind her.

The next day, I waited nervously by the door, watching the throng, afraid she wouldn't show. But she arrived promptly as usual, and rushed inside as soon as I opened the door. She did her chores in silence, and wouldn't meet my eyes or stand in my presence for more than a few seconds. Perhaps I was her first woman, I thought, or, God forbid, her first love. Perhaps it was a caste taboo, a poor girl afraid to mix classes, or because I was older, or because I was a Jew. I worried myself sick, and struggled to put it out of my mind. Whatever the reason, I'd not push things. Time would win her over to me.

As the days passed, we began talking about our lives as we previously had, and things became easy between us again. I didn't approach her, even though I'd catch her watching me in the reflections from the windows, her chin resting heavily on her hands as if she carried some great burden within. And always when I turned to face her she looked away, afraid to bear my full countenance. So I settled, for a time, for reflections.

"Why did you come to New York?" I asked her one morning.

"My mother was ill," she said. "In Gujarat we were very poor and had no money for doctors. She died."

"*Oy Gevalt!* You poor thing!"

"It was long ago," she said, in a way that made me think it wasn't very long ago at all. "My father and I came here for a better life."

"And your father's a stevedore at South Street Airport?"

"Yes. It's back-breaking work."

"And you suffice, the two of you?"

"Suffice? We try. It's been difficult."

"Difficult? Have you had problems?"

She nodded and sighed.

"Darling!" I said. "What do you need? Money?" I opened the register. "How much?"

"No, no! Miss Rosen, please! I can't take charity from you. It wouldn't be proper."

"Charity? This is *tsedoke* – righteousness!" I took out a hundred dollars and offered it to her.

"Miss Rosen, I'm very grateful for your generosity, but that won't be necessary." Then she whispered the following to me as if she was letting me in on a great secret: "I'm exploring other means by which to secure my financial security."

"Oh?" I said solemnly. "Have you found another job?" My heart sank at the thought.

"No, no. I'm still in your employ . . . for the time being."

"'For the time being'?" I said. "Darling, stop speaking in riddles! What is it?"

"I'd rather not spoil it by speaking it aloud. My mother said that the surest way to break good fortune is to name it." She turned away from me and her hair spun behind her. I longed to run my fingers through her cool, dark locks, to feel the ridges of her shoulder blades. I hoped with all my heart that she wasn't leaving me.

"When the time is right, I'll tell you everything, Miss Rosen," she said.

"Jessica!"

"Jessica."

She glanced at me and sighed, and her chest seemed to fall forever. I thought I might cry at the thought of her leaving me. And that's when I realized that I loved her.

It was 10 a.m. on the same day Officer Elijah had handed me the list of stolen goods, when a young Yid, covered in blood from the nearby *shochet*, wandered into my store. His huge eyes, ringed in red, stared in wonderment at the many shelves of oblong glass vessels, arrays of sharp and jagged tools and sparkling gearboxes full of unwound potential. He purchased a broken movement, once the spinning heart of an auto-cat, for fifty cents and ran gleefully out of the store. I wondered if he'd spent his master's money.

At half past ten Divya worked a spell over a group of Hassidic women looking for deals on jewelry. Divya pinned glittering brooches to their breasts and clasped golden charms around their necks. The women melted under Divya's charm and dropped eighteen dollars before leaving with drunken smiles on their faces.

"You're a *kishefmakher* – a magician!" I said to her. "Those women have come here dozens of times, but always to look, never to buy. What did you do?"

"I just gave them what they wanted," she said.

I wandered over to the jewelry case. "You sold them the monogrammed watch?"

"Hm?" she said. "Which watch?"

"The gold pocket watch. Did you sell it?"

"Sell? *No.*"

"Then where is it?"

"I'm sorry, Miss Rosen!" she said. "It's my fault. I wasn't

watching the boy who was in here before. He was staring at the jewel case. I'm sorry!"

I patted her arm. "Don't worry about it, child. What's true for business is also true for life. Things come and go. We have to learn to let things pass."

She nodded and said, "So true." And I thought of her mother.

At a quarter to eleven, while Divya was helping a stocky man try on a suit – carefully hiding a lapel stain with her palm – I snuck off to my attic. The window was open, cool air blew in from the East River, and my six angels waited patiently on the floor. In front of each lay the spoils of the night.

Beth had acquired a set of pearl earrings with a gold backing (tarnished, but lovely). Eve had brought gold, monogrammed cufflinks (monogrammed items were a hard sell). Leah had folded a taffeta scarf and placed it on the floor (how tidy of her). Talia and Shoshanna each held one side of a gilded *Tanakh*, the collected Jewish scriptures (from Shmuel Cohen's press, and it was beautiful). Last was Miriam, who held a small, black, dusty wooden box, like the kind a watchmaker might use to keep his tools in.

"What in Gehenna made you think this ugly box was valuable, little Miriam? I think your lenses need adjusting again."

But Miriam twittered and shook, as if begging me to open it. So I flipped up the rusty metal clasp and gasped when I saw what lay inside. Diamonds. Hundreds of them. Tens of thousands of dollars' worth. The oblique afternoon sunlight fell across the gems and sent constellations of color dancing about the walls.

"Miriam!" I said. "You little *malekh*! You precious angel!" I nearly burst with joy. "Now, sleep, *meine kinder*. You've had a long night. Save your springs for tonight!"

I held the box of diamonds to the sun. Lost in the rainbows, I thought of Divya. I'd make a fortune selling these to jewelers on the Bowery, and with the money I could take care of Divya and myself forever. She'd never know poverty again. But she'd have to let me help her.

I heard the faint ring of the bell as someone entered my store, so I returned downstairs, ebullient. Divya asked me what I was so joyous about, but I kept mum. Like her, I didn't dare spoil the good fortune by speaking it aloud, lest the evil eye take notice, *keyn aynhoreh*!

I was brewing a special batch of spiced coffee when *he* came in to my store. Since he'd started courting Divya, he'd been making a show of visiting every day. He wore an expensive suit, a top hat (which he took off upon entering), gold-rimmed spectacles and dangled his pocket watch ostentatiously from his jacket pocket. His hair was black and slicked and his persistent smile, just like on his campaign posters, reminded me of the smile of a wolf.

"Robert!" Divya said, rushing over to him. Her exuberance seemed forced, false.

His two enormous and humorless bodyguards stepped aside to let Divya hug him, and I had to look away as he squeezed her. Robert held her fingers and looked her up and down for a long, silent moment. I wanted to strangle him. She was no doll for him to ogle.

"My dear, you look ravishing today!" he said.

She smiled demurely and lowered her eyes. I hated how coquettish she became around him. It was an act, a ruse, I imagined, designed to secure his affections. And he seemed to fall for her charms, too, which didn't make sense to me, because this man despised anything that wasn't pure-blooded Christian. I sensed deception in his intentions.

He examined my store. "I don't know how you persist in working in this *filthy* shop," he said to Divya. He ran his finger along a shelf and held the dusty tip before his eyes. One of his bodyguards handed him a handkerchief that he used to wipe his finger clean. "When I'm Mayor, you'll live with me. You won't have to work in this . . . squalor. If fact, you won't have to work ever again."

His "filth" and "squalor", of course, were code words for his hatred of Jews and our little section of the city. I despised him, but up until this moment, I had thought Divya had just been dabbling, devouring his large budget for fun; such wealth had been unknown to her. But Robert revealed he had more prurient intentions.

"You have to win the election first," I said, scowling as I lit a cigarette.

"And *gut morgn* to you, Miss Rosen," Robert said, intoning the Yiddish with scorn.

I exhaled smoke in his direction. Divya glanced at me, but quickly averted her eyes.

"Anyway, my darling," Robert said to Divya, "I should not tarry. I've a lunch meeting with the South Street dockmaster. We're trying to open the dockyards to auto-police inspection. We're going to put an end to the contraband that's smuggled into this city."

"And what do the boys down at the Seventh Precinct think of your plan, Robert?" I said. "I don't think they're very happy that you plan to replace their jobs with machines."

"I don't plan to replace them, only augment what's already there."

" 'Augment'? Is that what you're calling your little coup?"

"Pardon me, my 'coup'?"

"It's obvious that you and the dockmaster are planning to take control of the docks to secure your *own* smuggling ring."

"Miss Rosen!" Divya chirped.

Robert put his hand on her shoulder to quiet her. "It's all right, Divya. I'm not offended. I hear such accusations regularly. In a city full of corruption, one can hardly blame Miss Rosen for being suspicious."

"There's enough corruption in this room to fill all of New York," I said.

"Indeed," he said. "I too have friends at the Seventh Precinct. Thievery is rampant in the Lower East Side, they tell me. Things burgled out of bureaus and jewelry boxes while good folks sleep. Now, where might a thief sell such things?" Robert ostentatiously scanned my store. He ran his hand along a rack of clothing, stirring up a cloud of dust. "I know you think I hate Jews, Miss Rosen. I don't. Yours is the faith of Jesus Christ, the Son of God. Many Jews in this neighborhood contribute to society with honest, hard work. But there's nothing honest about this place. These feral pawn shops provide an avenue for crooks and thieves – how does one say in Yiddish? – *ganefs*. As Mayor, I'll see to it that all of these shops are closed permanently."

"You're not Mayor yet," I said.

"No, not yet. But soon. Now, my dear," Robert said, turning back to Divya. "I must beg your leave. I'll be late for my lunch with the dockmaster. But first I must dash home to fetch some papers for him to sign. I'll see you tonight?"

"Yes," she said, briefly looking askance at me before she kissed him on the cheek. Finally, Robert and his entourage left the store.

Divya returned to her position behind the counter. I lit another cigarette and stared at her.

"What?" she said.

"Nothing."

"Why are you looking at me that way?"

"*What* way?"

She shook her head. "I know you think Robert is a buffoon."

"That's the least of his faults."

"Are you *jealous*?"

I set my jaw and took a sip of my spiced coffee, which had gone cold. "Tell me, Divya, is this the financial security you were talking about? Your knight come to rescue you from a life of poverty? Because you know there's only one thing men like him are after, and it's not your smile."

She swallowed and sat on a stool as the color fled from her face. "I need to tell you something, Miss Rosen. It may . . . change your opinion of me."

I moved closer, dreading the worst. Had she already defiled herself with that despicable man? I felt sick. "What is it?"

"Two nights ago, I went to a political dinner with Robert, and he introduced me to many senators and businessmen. He made a show of me, and more than one person refused to shake my hand. There were so many important people that my head spun. I had a bit too much wine, and I allowed him to whisk me back to his house by private dirigible without protest. He waved to many people on the ground as we flew home. It seemed he wanted everyone to know I was with him."

My stomach turned as I sensed where this was heading. Divya looked up at me with the same guilty eyes as when the gold watch had gone missing.

"Back in his bedroom, Robert pressed himself upon me, but I resisted his advances. He was drunk. Far drunker than me. I convinced him to lie on the bed, and he was more than obliging. I whispered softly to him as my mother once did to me, and in no time he was sound asleep and snoring.

"It was very late, past 2 a.m., and I wanted to go home, but I dared not walk the Manhattan streets alone at that hour. But I could not sleep. So I began looking through his shelves for something to hold my attention – a book perhaps – and when I found nothing of interest, I opened his drawers."

I raised an eyebrow.

"In the back of one, I found a small velvet satchel that I assumed was filled with small seeds. What a curious thing to keep in a drawer, I thought. But they were not seeds. The satchel was filled with diamonds."

My heart skipped a beat.

"I thought, 'He has so many. Would Robert miss but a few of these?' I put a handful inside a handkerchief and sealed them tight. I didn't sleep that night, and when Robert awoke the next morning, he remembered little, apologized for his drunkenness and took me home. He was too ill to notice how nervous I was." She looked up at me with those kitten-like eyes.

"Go on," I said.

"As soon as I returned home, I became wracked with guilt. I knew that Robert would discover they were missing. So I decided to return the diamonds at my earliest opportunity. I'd seduce him, return to his bedchamber and replace them while he slept. But last night they vanished from my room."

"Vanished?" I said, in feigned surprise.

"Yes. My door was locked from the inside. My father works nights at the docks and hadn't returned home when I arose for work this morning."

"May I ask where you stored these missing diamonds?"

"In a small wooden tool box under the bed."

I took a deep breath. Divya had just happened to be digging around in the back of Robert's drawers out of boredom? No, she had been looking for something. Something to take. Something to . . . *steal*? I swallowed as the truth dawned on me. "Divya, may I ask you a question?"

"Yes."

"That little Yid didn't steal the pocket watch, did he?"

Her eyes looked sorrowfully up at me. But I saw, for the first time, deception in them.

"And what else have you taken from me?"

"I'm sorry, Miss Rosen!" She began to cry, but I felt that this, too, was fake. If she had been playing Robert to secure his money, then she had been playing me, too. She had been playing everyone for a fool.

"I trusted you, Divya."

"Oh, come off your high horse, Jessica!" she snapped, startling me. "I've been here three months and you never buy from customers, and yet the inventory increases daily. Don't think I don't know where these things come from! You're a thief, a *ganef*, too!"

I gasped and stepped back; I suddenly didn't recognize this woman who accused me.

"Your parents left you money!" she said. "They left you this gigantic house! And you accuse *me*? You had a start. I came here with *nothing*! I have *nothing*! My father and I, we are just trying to survive."

"My dear, please—"

"No! You can accuse me all you want," she said, "but that's utter hypocrisy!"

I sighed. I had believed that Divya was a naive, innocent girl. It was painful watching my beliefs torn asunder. But it was also time to shatter some of her illusions, too.

"You're correct. I've no right to accuse you. Lock the store, and come with me."

Looking puzzled, Divya obeyed and followed me upstairs to the attic. There I showed her my file cabinets with all of the items my crawlers had stolen. "Like you, I started small, stealing things here and there, just to get by," I said. "Pretty soon I couldn't stop." I opened one cabinet and handed her the black box of diamonds.

Her jaw dropped.

"The crawlers are like cats. I give them guidelines, but they follow their own instincts." I said. "I could not know that Miriam would steal from you."

"Miriam? You name them?"

"I like to think of them as my children. We take care of each other."

She stared at me, and I sensed warmth in her glance. But I didn't trust her anymore.

"Tell me, Divya," I said. "That time in my office, when we kissed, were you toying with me as you toyed with Robert? Was I another fool?"

Her eyes flashed from mine to the diamonds. "I don't know."

"You don't know?"

"At the time, yes, I was manipulating you. But I didn't expect to . . . feel something."

My spirits lifted. "What did you feel?"

"I didn't plan on staying here for very long," she said. "I . . . don't have time for feelings."

"When were you going to leave?"

"As soon as I had enough money."

I shook my head. "Was anything you told me true? Was your mother sick? Do you even have a father?"

"Yes! All of that was true. We were so poor in Gujarat! You can't understand what it's like not knowing where your next meal will come from, or what it's like watching your mother die while British soldiers vomit ale on the streets, then chortle and try to kiss you as you pass them on your way to wash *their* stinking uniforms! Just one of Robert's stones could have saved my mother's life!"

"And do I make you angry, too?"

She shook her head. "No. You've been nothing but kind to me. As kind as my mother."

I sat on a stool and lit a cigarette and looked at the crawlers, which even in their reflected brilliance seemed devoid of life. I suddenly found it pathetic how I had, for far too long, invested them with souls they'd never possessed. My life felt empty, and I realized all the more strongly how much I had wanted Divya to be a part of it, and still did, even now.

"You were going to leave *today*, weren't you?" I said. "Once your father returned from work you and he would have fled New York with your diamonds."

She nodded. "There's an airship leaving for San Francisco this afternoon. I have two tickets."

"Were you even going to say goodbye?"

"Goodbyes are too painful."

"Here you go," I said, offering the box to her. "Take your diamonds. Flee the city. No goodbye necessary. *Mazel tov.*"

"No," she said. "I've changed my mind. I don't want to leave."

Outside, I heard shouting and the telltale sounds of automatons clip-clopping down the street.

"You want to stay?" I said.

"Miss Rosen . . . Jessica. I know you may not believe me now, but I could have left yesterday. I stayed because . . . because I think I'm—" Her voice was interrupted by the sound of the buzzer; someone was at the door. I heard a shout from down on the street.

"OPEN THIS DOOR NOW!"

"Wait here," I said to Divya, and stepped to the window. Four auto-giraffes, mounted by policemen, waited outside my store. A group of footed officers wielding pistols stood behind an irate-looking Robert and his two bodyguards. A small crowd of pedestrians was forming. I ducked back inside.

"Miss Rosen," Robert shouted. "We saw you in there!"

To Divya I said, "Stay quiet!" I stuck my head out again and said, "And I can see you, too. What on earth is all this about?"

"Good afternoon, ma'am," Robert shouted, using a tone of deference he'd never shown me before. "Do you know the whereabouts of Miss Divya? We would like to speak with her. Is she in there with you?"

"Divya took her lunch break and went out. You're interrupting mine. Come back in half an hour."

"I'm sorry, Miss Rosen, but this is a matter of some urgency. We believe she has stolen something of great value."

"Well, she's not here. Go away."

"Will you let us in, please?" Robert said.

"Just hang on a moment." I retreated back inside.

Divya looked frightened and had backed herself against the wall. "He must have gone home to fetch the diamonds for his meeting with the dockmaster."

"A bribe, probably, for control of South Street," I said.

"It was another lie, wasn't it?" Divya said. "I wasn't his 'darling Hindu goddess'. He paraded me around in front of the city so he'd have a scapegoat if he got caught with the diamonds. Who would the public believe had stolen them? The poor immigrant girl from Gujarat, or the 'upstanding' citizen, Robert? I was a such a fool!"

"We were all fools, it seems."

"What do I do now, Jessica? I can't go to prison. Who'd take care of my father?"

"Don't worry. I won't let them take you, Divya."

I opened one of the cabinets and pulled out a Confederate Civil War officer's belt with an attached pouch. I shoved the box of diamonds inside the pouch, closed it, and then handed the belt to her. "Hurry, put this on!"

"What for?"

"You're leaving, Divya. Now! Climb down the rear fire escape to the back alley and take Peck Slip over to the airport. Get your father and get the hell out of New York."

"But . . . I don't want to go!"

"You have no choice," I said. "Stay here and you go to prison. Or worse."

"What about you? They'll arrest you!"

"Don't you worry about me. Now run before they break down my door!"

"Jessica . . ." She put a warm hand on mine. "I'm sorry. I wish it could have been different. I wish I could have shown you the real me."

"Me too," I said.

"Perhaps in the next life," she said.

"*Cane yehi ratzon.* May it be God's will."

I moved to the rear window. The alley below was absent of police. "Now!" I said, waving her over. "*Mach shnel!*"

She stepped to the rear window, the window I had watched my crawlers slink out of on a thousand moonlit nights.

Then she was gone.

I heard a policeman's whistle and a chorus of shouts. "She's climbed out the back! She's in the rear!" I peered out the window and saw a man rising from a hiding place behind the trash bin. I knew his voice. It was Elijah. He must have spotted her with his prosthetic, telescopic eye.

"Damn! Go up to the roof, Divya!" I shouted. "Hop over to the next building if you can!"

Elijah leaped onto the fire escape and ascended the steps, while two more policemen appeared in the alley.

As Divya climbed the rusty ladder, I feared the aged rungs would break off in her hands. The overweight policemen huffed up the stairs slowly; I would not let them catch her. I looked back inside the attic. My crawlers stared mindlessly at me. I quickly turned their control knobs to 'programmation mode', and I held out my hand. "Look, my darlings. Fetch these! Digits! Fingers! Hands! Hurry!" The training was brief and rough. I hoped their ageing Babbage engines would understand the command. I turned the control knobs back into active mode and watched as they crawled out the window into the daylight.

As Elijah grabbed onto the ladder that led to the roof, little Eve tugged at his finger. He yelped and tried to snatch his hand away. She kept tugging, but with his other hand Elijah knocked her off the wall, and she fell forty feet to the alley below. I felt sick at the sound of her crash. Talia, meanwhile, moved toward Elijah's other hand, while Leah and Beth crawled down towards the other two policemen who raced up the fire escape. Elijah, with crawlers Talia and Shoshanna hot on his heels, stepped onto the roof and vanished over the cornice.

I couldn't bear to leave Divya alone to her fate, so I climbed out the window onto the fire escape. I heard the barks of policemen behind me as I climbed to the roof. The treacherous rooftop, steepled some forty-five degrees, was in major disrepair. Shingles slid off and fell from Divya's hands as she scrambled away from Elijah toward the peak.

"Just stay where you are, ma'am!" Elijah said, checking his footing. "It's dangerous and there's nowhere to run!"

"Leave her alone!" I shouted.

Elijah turned back to glance at me; his false eye spun maniacally. "Jessica! Get down, it's dangerous! You shouldn't be involved. This girl is a thief! She stole diamonds from the wharf."

"You imbecile!" I said. "Robert stole those diamonds. You should know better, Elijah."

"I'm sorry, I have my orders, Jessica." He turned back to pursue Divya.

"Get away from me, you pig!" Divya shouted. "You fat American sloth!" She reached the pointed peak and straddled it. Looking down the other side, she wobbled, and I feared she might fall.

"Elijah!" I shouted. "Stop! She's not the one you're after. I stole those diamonds."

"Really? If that's so, then why's she runnin'?"

As he spoke, Divya lowered herself over the other side of the roof so that I saw nothing but her hands.

Talia bit into Elijah's finger, and he yelped, lost his hold and slid twenty feet down the roof. His foot snagged the gutter an instant before he would have plunged to his death. With him immobilized, I climbed to the peak and peered down the other side. The opposing face was twice as treacherous. Shingles slid off the roof as Divya hung on for dear life.

"Give me the diamonds, Divya! I'll tell them my crawlers stole it from Robert's room, that I had them follow you because I was worried about you."

"They won't believe you – you heard the policeman."

"I'll show them my attic. They'll have to believe me when they see all my stolen things. You won't go to prison. Hurry. Give them to me!"

With a shaking hand she reached for her satchel. I heard the twittering of a crawler, and turned to see Miriam racing towards Divya's hand.

"Wait!" I screamed. "Stop!"

Miriam clawed at Divya's fingers, and Divya reacted involuntarily by snatching her hand away, the hand which had held her securely on the roof. I stared into her brown, lucid, frightened eyes as she slid down the roof and over the edge. I heard a scream, and after, a terrible silence.

The police found the diamonds on her person, thus proving Robert's accusation. (Divya's possession of a Confederate military belt stolen the month prior from one Lieutenant Geoffrey Dauber's Civil War collection was exhibited as further evidence of her criminal tendencies.) No one came to search my attic. No one came to question me, despite my "confession" to Elijah. I almost wished they would, just so I could speak about her.

I pestered Elijah daily for the location of Divya's body, where she might be interred, but he just shrugged and said he didn't know, which I knew was a lie. I had the haunting suspicion she had been cremated, or dumped quietly out at sea to be forgotten. It had been a long time since I'd prayed, but I dusted off my old *siddur* and said *kaddish* for her every night.

A few weeks later I paid a visit to Divya's father. He was a skinny and handsome man, with dark but luminous eyes much like Divya's. The studio apartment that he'd shared with her was smaller than I'd imagined. The single room was worn and dusty, and paint flaked from the dilapidated walls. He sat on the bed and listened to me silently, a man who'd lost everything he'd ever loved in this world. In some ways, I knew how he felt.

"Divya told me you came here to escape the poverty of your home country," I said.

He stared at me, expressionless.

I held out a bundle wrapped in twine. "In this parcel is six thousand dollars. It's my life savings. It's yours now." He took it without changing his expression.

"You're Jessica?" he said.

I nodded. "Yes. Jessica Rosen."

He stood, opened a drawer, pulled out a small envelope and handed it to me. It was addressed to me at the store. "I found this among her things," he said.

I opened it and read the following:

Dear Jessica,

If you're reading this it means I've left New York. There are many things I would like to say to you, but none of them seem adequate as I write this now. I'm grateful for everything you have done for me. You gave me a job, friendship, support, but most of all you've shown me warmth in a place I thought I'd find none. One day, I hope to be half the woman that you are. Do not forget me, Jessica. I will never forget you. Goodbye.

With love,
Divya

For a long moment we sat in silence, then after a time I reached into my pocket and handed him my business card. "Tonight is *Shabbos*, the Jewish day of rest. It's customary to share a meal with family. Come before sunset. The address is on the card." Then I stood, turned and walked past the smells of baking *challah* all the way home.

Machine Maid

Margo Lanagan

We came to Cuttajunga through the goldfields; Mr Goverman was most eager to show me the sites of his successes.

They were impressive only in being so very unprepossessing. How could such dusty earth, such quantities of it, piled up discarded by the road and all up and down the disembowelled hills, have yielded anything of value? How did this devastated place have any connection with the metal of crowns and rings and chains of office, and with the palaces and halls where such things were worn and wielded, on the far side of the globe?

Well, it must, I said to myself, as I stood obediently at the roadside, feeling the dust stain my hems and spoil the shine of my Pattison's shoes. See how much attention is being paid it, by this over-layer of dusty men shovelling, crawling, winching up buckets or baskets of broken rock, or simply standing, at rest from their labours as they watch one of their number return, proof in his carriage and the cut of his coat that they are not toiling here for nothing. There must be something of value here.

"This hill is fairly well dug out," said Mr Goverman, "and there was only ever wash-gold from ancient watercourses here in any case. 'Tis good for nobody but Chinamen now." And indeed I saw several of the creatures, in their smockish clothing and their umbrella-ish hats, each with his long pigtail, earnestly working at a pile of tailings in the gully that ran by the road.

The town was hardly worthy of the name, it was such a collection of sordid drinking-palaces, fragile houses and luckless miners lounging about the lanes. Bowling alleys there were, and a theatre, and stew-houses offering meals for so little, one wondered how the keepers turned a profit. And all blazed and fluttered and showed its patches and cracks in the unrelenting sunlight.

The only woman I saw leaned above the street on a balcony railing that looked set to give way beneath her generous arms. She was dressed with profound tastelessness and she smoked a pipe, as a gypsy or a man would, surveying the street below and having no care that it saw her so clearly. I guessed her to be Mrs Bawden, there being a painted canvas sign strung between the veranda posts beneath her feet: "MRS HUBERT BAWDEN/ Companions Live and Electric". Her gaze went over us as my husband drew my attention to how far one could see across the wretched diggings from this elevation. I felt as if the creature had raked me into disarray with her nails. *She* would know exactly the humiliations Mr Goverman had visited on me in the night; she would be smiling to herself at my prim and upright demeanour now, at the thought of what had been pushed at these firm-closed lips while the animal that was my husband pleaded and panted above.

On we went, thank goodness, and soon we were viewing a panorama similar to that of the dug-out hill, only the work here involved larger machinery than the human body. Parties of men trooped in and out of several caverns dug into the hillside, pushing roughly made trucks along rails between the mines and the precarious, thundering houses where the stamping-machines punished the gold from the obdurate quartz. My husband had launched into a disquisition on the geological feature that resulted in this hill's having borne him so much fruit, and if truth be told it gave me some pleasure to imagine the forces he described at their work in their unpeopled age, heaving and pressing, breaking and slicing and finally resting, their uppermost layers washed and smoothed by rains, while the quartz-seam underneath, split away and forced upward from its initial deposition, held secret in its cracks and crevices its gleamless measure of gold.

But we had to move on, to reach our new home before dark. The country grew ever more desolate, dry as a whisper and grey, grey under cover of this grey, disorderly forest. Unearthly birds the size of men stalked among the ragged tree-trunks, and others, lurid, shrieking, flocked to the boughs. In places the trees were cut down and their bodies piled into great windrows; set alight, and with an estate's new house rising half built from the hill or field beyond, they presented a scene more suggestive of devastation by war than of the hopefulness and ambition of a youthful colony.

Cuttajunga when we reached it was not of such uncomfortable newness; Mr Goverman had bought it from a gentleman pastoralist who had tamed and tended his allotment of this harsh land, but in the end had not loved it enough to be buried in it, and had returned to Sussex to live out his last years. The house had a settled look, and ivy, even, covered the shady side; the garden was a miracle of home plants watered by an ingenious system of runnels brought up by electric pump from the stream, and the fields on which our fortune grazed in the form of fat black cattle were free of the stumps and wreckage that marked other properties as having so recently been torn from the primeval bush.

"I hope you will be very happy here," said my husband, handing me down from the sulky.

The smile I returned him felt very wan from within, for now there would be nothing in the way of society or culture to diminish, or to compensate me for, the ghastly rituals of married life; now there would only be Mr Goverman and me, marooned on this island of wealth and comfort, amid the fields and cattle, bordered on all sides by the tattered wilderness.

Cuttajunga was all as he had described it to me during the long grey miles: the kitchen anchored by its weighty stove and ornamented with shining pans, the orchard and the vegetable garden, which Mr Goverman immediately set the electric yard-man watering, for they were parched after his short absence. There was a farm manager, Mr Fredericks, who appeared not to know how to greet and converse with such a foreign creature as a woman, but instead droned to my husband about stock movements and water and feed until I thought he must be some kind of lunatic. The housekeeper, Mrs Sanford, was a blowsy, bobbing, distractible woman who behaved as if she were accustomed to being slapped or shouted into line rather than reasoned with. The maid Sarah Poplin, was of the poorest material. "She has some native blood in her," Mr Goverman told me *sotto voce* when she had flounced away from his introductions. "You will be a marvellously civilizing influence on her, I am sure."

"I can but try to be," I murmured. I had been forewarned, by Melbourne matrons as well as by Mr Goverman himself, of the difficulty of finding and retaining staff, what with the goldfields promising any man or woman an independent fortune, should they happen to kick over the right pebble "up north", or "out west".

The other maid, the mechanical one Mr Goverman had promised me, lived seated in a little cabinet attached to a charging chamber under the back stairs. Her name was Clarissa – I did not like to call such creatures by real names, but she would not recognize commands without their being prefaced by that combination of guttural and sibilant. She was of unnervingly fine quality, and beautiful with it; except for the rigidity of her face I would say she was undoubtedly more comely than I was. Her eyes were the most realistic I had seen, blue-irised and glossy between thickly lashed lids; her hair sprang dark from her clear brow without the clumping that usually characterizes an electric servant's hair; each strand must have been set individually. She would have cost a great deal, both to craft and to import from her native France; I had never seen so close a simulacrum of a real person, myself.

Mr Goverman, seeing how impressed I was, insisted on commanding Clarissa upright and showing me her interior workings. I hardly knew where to rest my eyes as my husband's hands unlaced the automaton's dress behind with such practised motions, but once he had removed the panels from her back and head, the intricate machine-scape that gleamed and whirred within as Clarissa enacted his simple commands so fascinated me that I was able to forget the womanliness of this figure and the maleness of my man as he explained how this impeller drove this shaft to turn this cam and translate into the lifting of Clarissa's heavy, strong arms *this* way, and the bowing of her body *that* way, all the movements smooth, balanced and, again, the subtlest and most realistic I had witnessed in one of these creatures.

"Does she speak, then?" I said, peering into the back of her head.

"No, no," he said. "There is not sufficient room with all her other functions to allow for speaking."

"Why then are her mouth-parts so carefully made?" I moved my own head to allow more window-light into Clarissa's head-workings; the red silk-covered cavity that was the doll's mouth enlivened the brass and steel scenery, and I could discern some system of rings around it, their inner edges clothed with India rubber, which seemed purpose-built for producing the movements of speech.

"Oh, she once spoke," said my husband. "She once sang. She is adapted from her usage as an entertainer on the Paris stage. I was impressed by the authenticity of her movements. But, alas, my dear, if you are to have your carpets beaten you must forgo her lovely singing."

He fixed her head-panel back into place. "She interests you," he said. "Have I taken an engineer for a wife?" He spoke in an amused tone, but I heard the edge in it of my mother's anxiety, felt the vacancy in my hands where she had snatched away the treatise on artificial movement I had taken from my brother Artie's bookshelf. *So unbecoming, for a girl to know such things.* She clutched the book to herself and looked me up and down as if *I* were some kind of electrically powered creature, and malfunctioning into the bargain. *For your pretty head to be full of ... of cog-wheels and machine-oil,* she said disgustedly. *I will find you some more suitable reading.* My husband officiously buttoning the doll-dress; my mother sweeping from the parlour with the fascinating book – I recognized this dreary feeling. As soon as I evinced a budding interest in some area of worldly affairs, people inevitably began working to keep it from blossoming. I was meant to be vapid and colourless like my mother, a silent helpmeet in the shadows of Father and my brothers; I was not to engage with the world myself, but only to witness and encourage the men's engagement, to be a decorative background to it, like the parlour wallpaper, like the draped window against which my mother smiled and sat mute as Father discoursed to our dinner guests, the window that was obscured by impressive velvet at night, that in daytime prettified the world outside with its cascade of lace foliage.

I had barely had time to accustom myself to my new role as mistress of Cuttajunga when Mr Goverman informed me that he would be absent for a period of weeks, riding the boundaries of his estate and perhaps venturing further up country in the company of his distant neighbour Captain Jollyon and some of that gentleman's stockmen and tamed natives.

"Perhaps you will appreciate my leaving you," he said, the night before he left, as he withdrew himself from me after having completed the marriage act. "You need not endure the crudeness of my touching you, for a little while."

My face was locked aside, stiff as a doll's on the pillow, and my entire body was motionless with revulsion, with humiliation. Still I did feel relief, firstly that he was done, and would not require to emit himself at my face or onto my bosom, and secondly, yes, that the nightmare of our congress would not recur for at least two full weeks and possibly more. I turned from him, and waited – not long – for his breathing to deepen and lengthen into sleep, before I rose to wash the slime of him, the smell of him, from my person.

After the riding party left, my staff waited a day or two before deserting me. Sarah Poplin disappeared in the night, without a word. The following afternoon, as I was contemplating which of her tasks I should next instruct Mrs Sanford to take up, that woman came into my parlour and announced that she and Mr Fredericks had married and now intended to leave my service, Mr Fredericks to try his luck on the western goldfields. Direct upon her quitting the room, she said, she would be quitting the house for the wider world.

"But Mrs Sanf— Mrs Fredericks," I said. "You leave me quite solitary and helpless. Whatever shall I do?"

"You have that machine-woman, at least, I tell myself. She's the strength of two of me."

"But with no intelligence," I said. "She cannot accomplish half the tasks you can, with a quarter the subtlety. But you are right, she will never leave me, at least. She will stay out of stupidity, if not loyalty."

At the sound of that awkward word, "loyalty", the new Mrs Fredericks blushed, and soon despite my protestations she was gone, walking off without a backward glance along the western road. Her *inamorata* walked beside her, curved like a wilting grass-stalk over her stout figure, droning who knew what passionate promises into that pitiless ear. The house, meaningless, unattended around me, echoed with the fact that I was not the kind of woman servants felt compelled either to obey or to protect. Not under these conditions, at any rate, so remote from society and opinion.

I stood watching her go, keeping myself motionless rather than striding up and down as I wished to in my distress; should either of them turn, I did not want them to see the state of terror to which they had reduced me.

I was alone. My nearest respectable neighbour was Captain Jollyon's wife, a pretty, native-born chatterer with a house party of Melbourne friends currently gathered around her, a day's ride from here. I could not abide the thought of throwing myself on the mercies of so inconsequential a person.

And I was not quite alone, was I? I was not quite helpless. I had electric servants – the yard-man and Clarissa. And I had . . . I pressed my hands to my waist and sat rather heavily in a woven cane chair, heedless for the moment of the afternoon sun shafting in under the veranda roof. I was almost certain by now that I carried Cuttajunga's heir in my womb. All my washing, all my shrinking from my husband's advances, had not been sufficient to stop his seed taking root in me. He had "covered" me as a stallion covers a mare, and in time I would bring forth a Master Goverman, who would complete my banishment into utter obscurity behind my family of menfolk.

But for now – I straightened in the creaking, ticking chair, focusing again on the two diminishing figures as they flickered along the shade-dappled road between the bowing, bleeding, bark-shedding eucalypt trees – for now, I had Master Goverman tucked away neatly inside me, all his needs met, much as Clarissa's and the yard-man's were by their respective electrification chambers. He required no more action from me than that I merely continue, and sustain His Little Lordship by sustaining my own self.

I did not ride to Captain Jollyon's; I did not take the sulky into the town to send the police after my disloyal servants, or to hire any replacements for them. I decided that I would manage, with Clarissa and the yard-man. I had more than three months' stores; I had a thriving vegetable garden; and I did not long for human company so strongly that stupid or uncivilized company would suffice. If the truth be told, the more I considered my situation, the greater I felt it suited me, and the more relieved I was to have been abandoned by that sly Poplin girl, by Mr Droning Fredericks and his resentful-seeming wife. I felt, indeed, that I was well rid of them, that I might enjoy this short season where I prevailed, solitary, in this gigantic landscape, before life and my husband returned, crowding around me, bidding me this way and that, interfering with my body, and my mind, and my reputation, in ways I could neither control nor rebuff.

And so I lived a few days proudly independent, calling my mechanical servants out, the yard-man from his charging shed and Clarissa from her cupboard under the stairs, only when I required them to undertake the more tedious and strenuous tasks of watering, or sweeping, or stirring the copper. And I returned them thence when those were completed; I kept neither of them sitting about the place to give the illusion of a resident population. I was quite comfortable walking from room to empty room, and striding or riding about my husband's empty property unaccompanied.

After several days, despite fully occupying myself as my own housekeeper and chambermaid, I began to feel restless when evening came and it was time to retire to my parlour and occupy myself with ladylike pursuits. Needlework of the decorative kind had always infuriated me; nothing in my new house was sufficiently worn to require mending yet; I had never sung well, or played the piano or the violin as my cousins did and my brother James; I could sketch, but if the choice was between reproducing the drear landscapes I moved in by day, and stretching my heartstrings by recreating remembered scenes of London and the surrounding countryside, I felt disinclined to exercise that talent. My husband had bought me a library, but I found it to contain nothing but fashionable novels, most of which gave me the same sense of irritation, of having my mind and my being confined to meaningless matters, as conversation with that gentleman did, or with women such as Mrs Jollyon, and it was a great freedom to cease attempting to occupy my time with them.

Then, one afternoon, I set Clarissa to sweeping the paved paths around the house, and I sat myself at a corner of the veranda ready to redirect her when she reached me. I was labouring on a letter to Mother – a daughterly letter, full of lies and optimism, telling the news of my own impending motherhood as if it were wonderful, as if it were ordinary. I looked up from my duties at the automaton as she trundled and swept, thorough and inhumanly regular and pauseless in her sweeping. My disinclination to continue my letter, and the glimpse I had had of Clarissa's workings through the opening of her back combined with the fragmented memory of a diagram I had examined in Artie's treatise – which I had borrowed many times in secret after Mother had forbidden it me, and which I had wrestled to understand. In something like a stroke of mental lightning I saw the full chain of causes and effects that produced one movement, her turning from the left side to the right at the limit of her sweeping. I could not have described it; I could not even recall it fully, a moment later. But the flash was sufficient to make me forget my letter, my mother. Intently I watched Clarissa progress down the path, hoping for another such insight. None came, and she reached me, and I turned her with a command to the right so that she would sweep the path down to the hedge, and still I watched her, as dutifully she went on. And then, in the bottom half of my written page, I drew some lines, the shape of one of the cams I had seen, that had something of a duck-bill-like projection from its edge, a length of thin cable coming up to a pulley. The marks were hardly more than traces of idle movements; they were barely identifiable as mechanical parts, but as they streaked and ghosted up out of the paper I knew that I had found myself an occupation for my long and lonely days. It was more purposeless than embroidery; it would produce nothing of beauty; it would not make me a better daughter, wife or mother, but it would satisfy me utterly.

She never failed to unnerve me, smiling out in her vague way when I opened the door of the cabinet under the stairs. Her toes would move in her shoes, her fingers splay and crook and enact the last other movements of the lubrication sequence. Her beautiful mouth, too, pursed and stretched and made moues, subtle and unnatural. Un-mouthlike sounds came from behind the India-rubber lips, inside the busy mechanical head. Her ears cupped themselves slightly for the sound of my commands.

"Clarissa: stand," I would say, and step back to make room for her.

She would bend forward and push herself upright, using her hands on the rim of the cabinet.

"Clarissa: forward. Two steps," I would command, and she would perform them.

Now I could see the loosened back of the garment, the wheels and workings coming to a stop inside her. I left them visible now, unless I was putting her to work outside, so that I would not have the same troubles over and over, removing the panel from her back. I brought the lamp nearer, my gaze already on the parts I had been mis-drawing in my tiredness at the end of the day before. I would already be absorbed in her labyrinthine structure; even as I followed her to the study I would be checking her insides against the fistful of drawings I had made – the "translations", as I liked to think of them. She was a marvellous thing, which I was intent on reducing to mere mechanics; by the end of my project it would no longer disturb me to lock her away in her cabinet as into a coffin; I would know her seeming aliveness for the illusion it was; I would have diagrammed all the person-ness, all her apparent humanity, out of her. She would unnerve me no longer; I would know her for exactly what she was.

By the time Mr Goverman returned home I had discovered much more than I wished to. I made my first unwelcome finding one breathlessly hot afternoon perhaps three days before he arrived, when I had brought Clarissa to the study, commanded her to kneel and opened the back of her head, and was busy drawing what I could see of her mouth-parts behind the chutes and membrane-discs and tuning-forks of her hearing apparatus. Soft gusts of hot wind ventured in through the window from time to time, the gentlest buffetings, which did nothing to refresh me, but only moved my looser hair or vaguely rippled the buttoned edge of Clarissa's gown.

It was frustrating, attempting to draw this mouth. I do not know what exclamation I loosed in my annoyance, but it must have included a guttural and a sibilant at some point and further sounds the doll mistook for a command, for suddenly, smoothly, expansively, she lifted her arms from her sides where she knelt, manipulated her lovely fingers, her beautifully engineered elbow and shoulder joints, and drew her loosened bodice down from her shoulders, so that her bosom, so unbodily and yet so naked-seeming, was exposed to the hot study air. I heard in the momentarily still air the muted clicks and slidings within her head – I saw, indistinctly in the shadows, partly behind other workings, the movements of her mouth readying itself for something.

I rose and stood before her; she remained kneeling, straight-backed and shameless, presenting her shining breasts, gazing without embarrassment or any other emotion at my belly. The seam of her lips glistened a little with exuded oil, and the shiftings in her weighty head ceased.

I crouched before her awful readiness. I knew how tall my husband was; I knew what this doll was about. Like one girl confiding in another, like a tiny child in play with its mother or nurse, I reached out and touched Clarissa's lower lip. It yielded – not exactly as if it welcomed my touch and expectations, but with a bland absence of resistance, an emotionless acceptance that I knew I could not muster in my own marriage bed.

I pushed my forefinger against the meeting-place of the automaton's lips. They gave, a little; they allowed my fingertip to push them apart. Slowly my finger sank in, touching the porcelain teeth. They too moved aside, following pad and joint of my finger as if learning its shape as it intruded.

Her tongue – what cloth was it, so slippery smooth? And how so wet? I pulled out my finger and rubbed the wetness with my thumb; it was a clear kind of oil or gel; I could not quite say what it was. It smelled of nothing, not perfumed, not bodily, not as machine-oil should. It must be very refined.

I put the finger back in, all the way to the knuckle. I thought I might be able to reach to the back of the cavity as I had seen it from within, the clothy, closed-off throat with its elaborate mechanical corsetry. Inside her felt disconcertingly like a real mouth; I expected the doll at any moment to release my finger and ask, with this tongue, with this palate and throat and teeth, what I thought I was about. But she only held to my finger, closely all around like living tissue, living muscle.

And then some response was triggered in her, by the very tip of my finger in her throat. Her lips clasped my knuckle somewhat tighter, and her mouth moved against the rest of my finger. Oh, it was strange! It reminded me of a caterpillar, the concertina-like way they convey themselves across a leaf, along a branch; the rippling. Back and forth along my finger the ripples ran, combining the movements of her resisting my intrusive finger with those of attempting to milk it, massaging it root to tip with a firm and varied persuasiveness. How was such seeming randomness generated? I must translate that, I must account for it in my drawings. Yet at the same time I wanted to know nothing of it; there was something in the sensations that made my own throat clench, my stomach rebel, and every part of me below the waist solidify in a kind of horror.

What horrified me worst was that I knew, as a married woman, how to put an end to the rippling. Yet the notion of doing so, and in that way imitating the most repellent, the most beast-like movements of my husband, when, blinded, stupid with his lust he ... emptied himself into me, as if I were a spittoon or the pit of a privy, stilled my hand amid the awful mouth-movements. I was on the point of spasm myself, spasms of revulsion, near-vomiting. Before they should overtake me I jabbed the automaton several times in her lubricious silken throat, my knuckle easily pushing her lips and teeth aside, my finger inside her mouth-workings cold, and bonily slender, and passionless – unless curiosity is a passion, unless disgust is.

Clarissa clamped that cold finger tightly, and some workings braced her neck against what should follow upon such prodding: my husband's convulsions in his ecstasy. It was as if the man was in the room with us, I imagined his exclamations so clearly. I shuddered there myself, a shudder so rich with feeling that my own eyes were sightless with it a moment. Then the doll relaxed her grip on me, and my arm's weight drew my forefinger from her mouth, slack as my husband's member would be slack, gleaming as that would gleam with her lubricants. Quietly, dutifully, she began a mouthish process; her lips parted slightly to allow the stuff of him, the mess of him, the man-spittle, to flow forth, to fall to her bosom. Some of her oil welled out eventually onto her pillowy, rosy lower lip. I watched the whole sequence with a stony attentiveness. When the oil dripped to her shining décolletage, such pity afflicted me at what this doll had been created to undergo that I stood and, using my own handkerchief bordered with Irish lace, cleaned the poor creature's bosom, wiped her mouth as a nurse wipes a child's, and when I was certain no further oils would come forth I restored her the modesty of her bodice; I raised her from her kneeling and took her, I hardly knew why, to sit in her cabinet. I did not close her in, then – I only stood, awkward, regarding her serene face. I felt as if I ought to say something – to apologize, perhaps; perhaps to accuse. Then – and I moved with such certainty that I must have noticed-without-noticing this before – my hand went to a pleat of the velvet lining of the lid of the cabinet, and a dry *pop* sounded under my fingertips, and I drew forth a folded slip of creamy writing paper, which matched that on which Clarissa's domestic commands were written. I opened it and glanced down at the encoded list of Clarissa's tortures, the list of my own.

Revulsion attacked me then, and hurriedly I refolded and replaced the paper, and shut the doll away, and went and stood at the study window gazing out over the green lawn and the dark hedge to the near-featureless landscape beyond, the green-gold fields a-glare in the unforgiving sunlight.

Clarissa's other activities – I began to study and translate them next morning – were more obviously, comically, hideously calculated to meet a man's needs. She could be made to suffer two ways, lying like an upturned frog with her legs and her arms crooked around her torturer – without an actual man within them they contracted tightly enough to hold a very slight man indeed – or propped on all fours like any number of other beasts. In both positions she maintained continuous subtle rotations and rockings of her hips, and I could hear within her similar silky-wet movements to those her mouth had made about my finger, working studiedly upon my husband's intangible member.

To prevent her drawers becoming soaked with the lubricant oil and betraying to Mr Goverman that I had discovered his unfaithfulness with the doll, I was forced to remove them. When I exposed her marriage parts my whole body flushed hot with mortification, and this heat afflicted me periodically throughout the course of her demonstration. Studiously applying myself to my drawing, and to the intellectual effort of translating the doll's mechanisms into her movements, was all I could do to cool myself.

If they had not been what they were, one would have considered her underparts fine examples of the seamstress's craft, or perhaps the upholsterer's. A softly heart-shaped area of wiry dark hairs formed something of a welcome or an announcement that this was no child's doll, with all such private features erased and denied. Then such padded folds, cream-velvety without, red-purple and beaded with moisture within, eventuated behind these hairs, between these heavy legs, that I shook and burned examining them. My own such parts I had no more than washed with haste and efficiency; my husband's incursions within them had been utterly surprising to me, that I should be shaped so, and for such abominable usages. Now I could see them, and on another, one constructed never to feel a whisper of embarrassment. That I should be so curious, so fascinated, disgusted me; I told myself this was all in the spirit of scientific enquiry, this was all to assist in a complete translation of the doll's movements, but the sensations that gripped me – the hot shame; the excruciating awareness, as I examined her fore and aft, of the corresponding places on my own body; the sudden exquisite sensitivity of my fingertips to her softness and her slickness and the differing textures of the fleshy doors into her; the stiffness in my neck and jaw from my rage and repugnance – these were anything but scientific.

In a shaking voice I commanded her, from the secret list. The room's atmosphere was now entirely strange, and I shivered to picture some person walking in, and I made Clarissa pause in her clasping, in her undulations, several times, so that I could circle the house and reassure myself that the country around was as deserted as ever. For what was anyone to make of the scene, of the half-clothed automaton whirring and squirming in her mechanical pleasure, of the cold-faced human seated on the ottoman watching, of the list dropped to the floor so as not to be crumpled in those tight-clenched fists?

Mr Goverman's return woke me from the state I had plunged into by the end of the week, wherein I barely ate and did not bother to dress, but at first light went in my nightdress to the study where Clarissa stood, and all day drew, surely and intricately and in a blistering cold rage, the working innards of the doll. Something warned me – some far distant jingle of harness carried to my ears on the breeze, some hoofstrike beyond the hills echoing through the earth and up through the foundations of the homestead and into my pillow – and I rose and bathed and clothed myself properly and hid my translations away and was well engaged in housekeeperly activities by the time my husband's party approached across the fields.

Then duties crowded in on me: to be hostess, to cook and prepare rooms; to apologize for the makeshiftness of our hospitality, and the absence of servants; to inform Mr Goverman of the presence of his heir; to submit to his embraces that night. My season of solitude vanished like a frightened bird, and the days filled up so fully with words and work, with negotiations and the maintaining of various appearances, that I scarcely had time to recall how I had occupied myself before, let alone determine any particular action to take arising from my discoveries.

Days and then weeks and then months passed, and little Master Goverman began at last to be evident to the point where I was forced to withdraw again from society, such as it was. And I was also forced – because my husband conceived a sudden dislike of visiting the vestibule of his son's little palace – to endure close visitings at my face and bosom of the most grotesque parts of Mr Goverman's anatomy, during which he would seem to lose the powers of articulate speech and even, sometimes, of rational thought. His early reticence and acceptance of my refusals to have him near in that way were transformed now; he no longer apologized, but seemed to delight in my resistance, to take extra pleasure in grasping my head and restraining me in his chosen position, to exult, almost, in his final befoulment of me. I would watch him with our guests, or conferring with Mr Brightwell the new manager, and marvel at this well-dressed man of manners. Could he have any connection with the lamplit or moonlit assortment of limbs and hairiness and animal odours that assaulted me in the nights? I hardly knew which I hated worst, his savagery then or his expertise in disguising it now. What a sleight of hand marriage was, how fraudulent the social world! I despised every matron that she did not complain, every new bride as she sank from the glow and glory of betrothal and wedding to invisible compliant wifeliness, every man that he took these concealments and these changes as his due, that he took what he took, in exchange for what he gave a woman, which we called – fools that we were! – respectability.

By the time Mr Goverman left for the city in the sixth month of my pregnancy, I will concede that I was no longer quite myself. Only a thin layer of propriety concealed my rage at my imprisonment – in this savage land, in this brute institution, in this swelling body dominated by the needs and nudgings of my little master within. I will plead, if ever I am called to account, that it was insanity kept me up during those nights, at first studying my translations (what certain hand had drawn these? Why, they looked almost authentic, almost the work of an engineer!) and then (what leap into the darkness was this?) re-translating them, some of them, into new drawings, devising how this part could be substituted for that, or a spring from the mantel-clock in a spare room could be added here, how a rusted saw-blade could be thinned and polished and given an edge and inserted there, out of sight within existing mechanisms, how this cam could be pared away a little there, and this whole arm of the apparatus adjusted higher to allow for the fact that I could not resort to actual metal casting for my lunatic enterprise.

Once the plans were before me, and Mr Goverman still away arranging the terms of his investment in the mining consortium, to the accompaniment, no doubt, of a great deal of roast meat and brandy, cigars and theatre attendances, there remained no more for me to do – lamplit, lumbering, discreet in the sounds I made, undisturbed through the nights – but piece by piece to dismantle and reassemble Clarissa's head according to those sure-handed drawings. I went about in the days like a thief, collecting a tool here, something that could be fashioned into a component there. I tested, I adjusted, I perfected. I was very happy. And then one early morning Lilty Meddows, my maid, knocked uncertainly at the study door to offer me tea and porridge, and there I was, as brightly cheerful as if I had only just risen from my sleep, stirring the just-burnt ashes of my translations, and with Clarissa demure in the armchair opposite, sealed up and fully clothed, betraying nothing of what I had accomplished on her.

Life, I discovered, is always more complex than it seems. The ground on which one bases one's beliefs, and actions arising from those beliefs, is sand, is quicksand, or reveals itself instead to be water. Circumstances change; madnesses end, or lessen, or begin inexorable transformations into new madnesses.

Mr Goverman returned. I greeted him warmly. I was very frightened of what I had done, while at the same time, with the influx of normality that came with his return, with the bolstering of the sense of people watching me, so that I could not behave oddly or poorly, often I found my own actions impossible to credit. I only knew that each morning I greeted my husband more cordially; each night that I accepted him into my bed I did so with less dread and even with a species of amiable curiosity; I attended very much more closely to what he enjoyed in the marriage bed, and he in turn, in his surprise, in his ignorance, ventured to try and discover ways by which I might perhaps experience pleasures approaching the intensity of his own.

My impending maternity ended these experiments before they had progressed very far, however, and I left Cuttajunga for Melbourne and Holmegrange, a large, pleasant house by the wintry sea, where wealthy country ladies were sent by their solicitous husbands to await the birth of the colony's heirs and learn the arts and rituals of motherhood.

There I surprised myself very much by giving birth to a daughter, and there Mr Goverman surprised me when very soon upon the birth he visited, by being more than delighted to welcome little Mary Grace into the world.

"She is *exactly* her mother," he said, looking up from the bundle of her in his arms, and I was astonished to see the glisten of tears in his eyes. Did he love me, then? Was this what love was? Was this, then, also affection that I felt in return, this tortuous knot of puzzlements and awareness somewhere in my chest, somewhere above and behind my head? Had I birthed more than a child during that long day and night?

Certainly I loved Mary Grace – complete and unqualified, my love surprised me with its certainty when the rest of me was so awash with conflicting emotions, like an iron stanchion standing firm in a rushing current. I had only to look on her puzzling wakefulness, her innocent sleep, to know that region of my own heart clearly. And perhaps a little of my enchantment with my daughter puffed out – like wattle blossom! – and gilded Mr Goverman too. Was that how it went, then, that wifely attachment grew from motherly? Why had my own mother not told me, when I had not the wit to ask her myself?

Mr Goverman returned to Cuttajunga to ready it for Her Little Ladyship, and in his absence, through the milky, babe-ruled days of my lying-in, I wondered and I floundered and I feared, in all the doubt that surrounded my one iron-hard, iron-firm attachment in the world. I did not have the leisure or privacy to draw, but in my mind I resurrected the drawings I had burnt in the study at the homestead, and laboured on the adjustments that would be necessary to restore Clarissa to her former state, or near it. If only he loved me and was loyal to me enough; if only he could control his urges until I returned.

Lilty was at my side; Mary Grace was in my arms; train-smoke and train-steam, all around, warmed us momentarily before delivering us up to the winter air, to the view of the ravaged country that was to be my daughter's home.

"Where is he?" said Lilty. "I cannot see him. I thought he would be here."

"Of course he will be." I strode forward through the smoke.

Four tall men, in long black coats, stood by the station gate, watching me in solemnity and some fear, I thought. Captain Jollyon stepped out from among them, but his customary jauntiness had quite deserted him. There was a man who by his headgear must be a policeman; a collared man, a reverend; and Dr Stone, my husband's physician. I did not know what to think, or feel. I must not turn and run; that was all I knew.

The train, which had been such a comforting, noisome, busy wall behind me, slid away, leaving a vastness out there, with Lilty twittering against it, senseless. The gentlemen ushered me, expected me to move with them. They made Lilty take Mary Grace from me. They made me sit, in the station waiting room, and then they sat either side of me, and Captain Jollyon sat on one heel before me, and they delivered their tidings.

It is easy to look bewildered when you have killed a man and are not suspected. It is easy to seem innocent, when all believe you to be so.

It must have been the maid, Abigail, they said, from the blood in the kitchen, and the fact that she had disappeared. Mrs Hodds, the housekeeper? She was at Cuttajunga now, but she had been at the Captain's, visiting her cousin Esther on their night off, when the deed was done. Mrs Hodds it was who had found the master in the morning, bled to death in his bed, lying just as if asleep. She had called Dr Stone here, who had discovered the dreadful crime.

I went with them, silent, stunned that it all had happened just as I wished. The sky opened up so widely above the carriage, I feared we would fall out into it, these four black-coated crows of men and me lace-petticoated among them, like a bit of cloud, like a puff of train-steam disappearing. Now that they had cluttered up my clear knowledge with their stories, they respected my silence; only the reverend, who could not be suspected of impropriety, occasionally glanced at my stiff face and patted my gloved hand.

At Cuttajunga Mrs Hodds ran at me weeping, and Mr Brightwell turned his hat in his hands and covered it with muttered condolences. Then that was over, and Mrs Hodds did more cluttering, more exclaiming, and told me what she had had to clean, until one of the black coats sharply interrupted her laundry listing: "Mrs Goverman hardly wants to hear this, woman."

I did not require sedating; I had not become hysterical; I had not shed a tear. But then Mary Grace became fretful, and I took her and Lilty into the study. "But you must not say a word, Lilty, not a *word*," I told her. And as I fed my little daughter, there looking down into her soft face, her mouth working so busily and greedily, her eyes closed in supreme confidence that the milk would continue, forever if it were required – that was when the immense loneliness of my situation hollowed out around me, and of my pitiable husband's, who had retired to the room now above us, and in his horror – for he must have realized what I had done, and who I therefore was – felt his lifeblood ebb away.

Still I did not weep, but my throat and my chest hardened with occluded tears, and I thought – I welcomed the thought – that my heart might stop from the strain of containing them.

Abigail, Abigail: the name kept flying from people's mouths like an insect, distracting me from my thoughts. The pursuit of Abigail preoccupied everyone. I let it, for it prevented them asking other questions; it prevented them seeing through my grief to my guilt.

In the night I rose from my bed. Lilty was asleep on the bedchamber couch, on the doctor's advice and the reverend's, in case I should need her in the state of confusion into which my sudden widowhood had plunged me. I took the candle downstairs, and along the hall to the back of the house.

I should have brought a rag, I thought. A damp rag. But in any case, she will be so bloodied, her bodice, her skirts – it will have all run down. Did he leave the piece in her mouth? I wondered. Will I find it there? Or did he retrieve it and have it with him, in his handkerchief, or in his bed, bound against him with the wrappings nearer where it belonged? It was not a question one could ask Captain Jollyon, or even Dr Stone.

I opened the door of the charging chamber. There was no smudge or spot on or near the cabinet door, that I could see on close examination by candlelight.

I opened the cabinet. "Clarissa?" I said in my surprise, and she began her initiation-lubrication sequence, almost as if in pleasure at seeing me and being greeted, almost the way Mary Grace's limbs came alive when she heard my voice, her smoky-grey eyes seeking my face above her cradle. The chamber buzzed and crawled with the sounds of the doll's coming to life, and I could identify each one, as you recognize the gait of a familiar, or the cough he gives before knocking on your parlour door, or his cry to the stable boy as he rides up out of the afternoon, after weeks away.

"Clarissa, stand," I said, and I made her turn, a full circle so I could assure myself that not a single drop of blood was on any part of her clothing; then, that her garments had not been washed, for there was the tea-drop I had spilt upon her bodice myself during my studies. I might have unbuttoned her; I might have brought the candle close to scrutinize her breasts, her teeth, for blood not quite cleansed away, but I was prevented, for here came Lilty down the stairs, rubbing her sleepy eyes.

"Oh, ma'am! I was frightened for you! Come, you'd only to wake me, ma'am. You've no need to resort to mechanical people. What is it you were wanting? She's no good warming milk for you, that one – you know that."

And on she scolded, so fierce and gentle in the midnight, so comforting to my confusion – which was genuine now, albeit not sourced where she thought, not where any of them thought – that I allowed her to put the doll away, to lead me to the kitchen, to murmur over me as she warmed and honeyed me some milk.

"The girl, Abigail," I said when I was calmer, into the steam above the cup. "Is there any news of her?"

"Don't you worry, Mrs Goverman." Lilty clashed the pot into the washbasin, slopped some water in. Then she sat opposite me, her jaw set, her fists red and white on the table in front of her. "They will find that Abigail. There is only so many people in this country yet that she can hide among. And most of them would sell their mothers for a penny or a half-pint. Don't you worry." She leaned across and squeezed my cold hand with her hot, damp one. "They will track that girl down. They will bring her to justice."

To Follow the Waves

Amal El-Mohtar

Hessa's legs ached. She knew she ought to stand, stretch them, but she only gritted her teeth and glared at the clear lump of quartz on the table before her. To rise now would be to concede defeat – but to lean back, lift her goggles and rub her eyes was, she reasoned, an adequate compromise.

Her braids weighed on her, and she scratched the back of her head, where they pulled tightest above her nape. To receive a commission from Sitt Warda Al-Attrash was a great honour, one that would secure her reputation as a fixed star among Dimashq's dream-crafters. She could not afford to fail. Worse, the dream Sitt Warda desired was simple, as dreams went: to be a young woman again, bathing her limbs by moonlight in the Mediterranean with a young man who, judging by her half-spoken, half-murmured description, was not precisely her husband.

But Hessa had never been to the sea.

She had heard it spoken of, naturally, and read hundreds of lines of poetry extolling its many virtues. Yet it held little wonder for her; what pleasure could be found in stinging salt, scratching sand, burning sun reflected from the water's mirror-surface? Nor did swimming hold any appeal; she had heard pearl divers boast of their exploits, speak of how the blood beat between their eyes until they felt their heads might burst like over-ripe tomatoes, how their lungs ached with the effort for hours afterwards, how sometimes they would feel as if thousands of ants were marching along their skin, and though they scratched until blood bloomed beneath their fingernails, could never reach them.

None of this did anything to endear the idea of the sea to her. And yet, to carve the dream out of the quartz, she had to find its beauty. Sighing, she picked up the dopstick again, tapped the quartz to make sure it was securely fastened, lowered her goggles and tried again.

Hessa's mother was a mathematician, renowned well beyond the gates of Dimashq for her theorems. Her father was a poet, better known for his abilities as an artisanal cook than for his verse, though as the latter was full of the scents and flavours of the former, much appreciated all the same. Hessa's father taught her to contemplate what was pleasing to the senses, while her mother taught her geometry and algebra. She loved both as she loved them, with her whole heart.

Salma Najjar had knocked at the door of the Ghaflan family in the spring of Hessa's seventh year. She was a small woman, wrinkled as a wasp's nest, with eyes hard and bright as chips of tourmaline. Her greying hair was knotted and bound in the intricate patterns of a jeweller or gem-cutter – perhaps some combination of the two. Hessa's parents welcomed her into their home, led her to a divan and offered her tea, but she refused to drink or eat until she had told them her errand.

"I need a child of numbers and letters to learn my trade," she had said, in the gruff, clipped accent of the Northern cities. "It is a good trade, one that will demand the use of all her abilities. I have heard that your daughter is such a child."

"And what is your trade?" Hessa's father asked, intrigued, but wary.

"To sculpt fantasies in the stone of the mind and the mind of the stone. To grant wishes."

"You propose to raise our daughter as *djinn*?" Hessa's mother raised an eyebrow.

Salma smiled, showing a row of perfect teeth. "Far better. *Djinn* do not get paid."

Building a dream was as complex as building a temple, and required knowledge of almost as many trades – a fact reflected in the complexity of the braid-pattern in which Hessa wore her hair. Each pull and plait showed an intersection of gem-crafting, metal-working, architecture and storytelling, to say nothing of the thousand twisting strands representing the many kinds of knowledge necessary to a story's success. As a child, Hessa had spent hours with the archivists in Al-Zahiriyya Library, learning from them the art of constructing memory palaces within her mind, layering the marble, glass and mosaics of her imagination with reams of poetry, important historical dates, dozens of musical *maqaamat*, names of stars and ancestors. *Hessa bint Aliyah bint Qamar bint Widad . . .*

She learned to carry each name, note, number like a jewel to tuck into a drawer here, hang above a mirror there, for ease of finding later on. She knew whole geographies, scriptures, story cycles, as intimately as she knew her mother's house, and drew on them whenever she received a commission. Though the only saleable part of her craft was the device she built with her hands, its true value lay in using the materials of her mind: she could not grind quartz to the shape and tune of her dream, could not set it into the copper coronet studded with amber, until she had fixed it into her thoughts as firmly as she fixed the stone to her amber dopstick.

"Every stone," Salma said, tossing her a piece of rough quartz, "knows how to sing. Can you hear it?"

Frowning, Hessa held it up to her ear, but Salma laughed. "No, no. It is not a shell from the sea, singing the absence of its creature. You cannot hear the stone's song with the ear alone. Look at it, feel it under your hand; you must learn its song, its language, before you can teach it your own. You must learn, too, to tell the stones apart; those that sing loudest do not always have the best memories, and it is memory that is most important. Easier to teach it to sing one song beautifully than to teach it to remember; some stones can sing nothing but their own tunes."

Dream-crafting was still a new art then; Salma was among its pioneers. But she knew that she did not have within herself what it would take to excel at it. Having discovered a new instrument, she found it unsuited to her fingers, awkward to rest against her heart; she could produce sound, but not music.

For that, she had to teach others to play.

First, she taught Hessa to cut gems. That had been Salma's own trade, and Hessa could see that it was still her chief love: the way she smiled as she turned a piece of rough crystal in her hands, learning its angles and texture, was very much the way Hessa's parents smiled at each other. She taught her how to pick the best stones, cleave away their grossest imperfections; she taught her to attach the gem to a dopstick with hot wax, at precise angles, taught her the delicate dance of holding it against a grinding lathe with even greater precision while operating the pedal. She taught her to calculate the axes that would unlock needles of light from the stone, kindle fire in its heart. Only once Hessa could grind a cabochon blindfolded, once she learned to see with the tips of her fingers, did Salma explain the rest.

"This is how you will teach songs to the stone." She held up a delicate amber wand, at the end of which was affixed a small copper vice. Hessa watched as Salma placed a cloudy piece of quartz inside and adjusted the vice around it before lowering her goggles over her eyes. "The amber catches your thoughts and speaks them to the copper; the copper translates them to the quartz. But just as you build your memory palace in your mind, so must you build the dream you want to teach it; first in your thoughts, then in the stone. You must cut the quartz while fixing the dream firmly in your mind, that you may cut the dream into the stone, cut it so that the dream blooms from it like light. Then, you must fix it into copper and amber again, that the dream may be translated into the mind of the dreamer.

"Tonight," she murmured quietly, grinding edges into the stone, "you will dream of horses. You will stand by a river and they will run past you, but one will slow to a stop. It will approach you, and nuzzle your cheek."

"What colour will it be?"

Salma blinked behind her goggles, and the lathe slowed to a stop as she looked at her. "What colour would you like it to be?"

"Blue," said Hessa, firmly. It was her favourite colour.

Salma frowned. "There are no blue horses, child."

"But this is a dream! Couldn't I see one in a dream?"

Hessa wasn't sure why Salma was looking at her with quite such intensity, or why it took her so long a moment to answer. But finally, she smiled – in the gentle, quiet way she smiled at her gems – and said, "Yes, my heart. You could."

Once the quartz was cut, Salma fixed it into the centre of a copper circlet, its length prettily decorated with drops of amber, and fitted it around Hessa's head before giving her chamomile tea to drink and sending her to bed. Hessa dreamed just as Salma said she would: the horse that approached her was blue as the turquoise she had shaped for a potter's husband a few nights earlier. But when the horse touched her, its nose was dry and cold as quartz, its cheeks hard and smooth as cabochon.

Salma sighed when Hessa told her as much the next day. "You see, this is why I teach you, Hessa. I have been so long in the country of stones, speaking their language and learning their songs, I have little to teach them of our own; I speak everything to them in facets and brilliance, culets and crowns. But you, my dear, you are learning many languages all at once; you have your father's tasting tongue, your mother's speech of angles and air. I have been speaking nothing but adamant for most of my life, and grow more and more deaf to the desires of dreamers."

Try as she might, Hessa could not coordinate her knowledge of the sea with the love, the longing, the pleasure needed to build Sitt Warda's dream. She had mixed salt and water, touched it to her lips, and found it unpleasant; she had watched the moon tremble in the waters of her courtyard's fountain without being able to stitch its beauty to a horizon. She tried, now, to summon those poor attempts to mind, but was keenly aware that if she began grinding the quartz in her present state, Sitt Warda would wake from her dream as tired and frustrated as she herself presently felt.

Giving in, she put down the quartz, removed her goggles, rose from her seat and turned her back on her workshop. There were some problems only coffee and ice cream could fix.

Qahwat al Adraj was one of her favourite places to sit and do the opposite of think. Outside the bustle of the Hamadiyyah market, too small and plain to be patronized by obnoxious tourists, it was a well-kept secret tucked beneath a dusty stone staircase: the servers were beautiful, the coffee exquisite and the iced treats in summer particularly fine. As she closed the short distance between it and her workshop, she tried to force her gaze up from the dusty path her feet had long ago memorized, tried to empty herself of the day's frustrations to make room for her city's beauties.

There: a young man with dark skin and a dazzling smile, his tight-knotted braids declaring him a merchant-inventor, addressing a gathering crowd to display his newest brass automata. "Ladies and Gentlemen," he called, "the British Chef!" and demonstrated how with a few cranks and a minimum of preparation, the long-faced machine could knife carrots into twisting orange garlands, slice cucumbers into lace. And not far from him, drawn to the promise of a building audience, a beautiful mechanical, her head sculpted to look like an amira's headdress, serving coffee from the heated cone of it by tipping forward in an elegant bow before the cup, an act which could not help but make every customer feel as if they were sipping the gift of a cardamom-laced dance.

Hessa smiled to them, but frowned to herself. She had seen them all many times before. Today she was conscious, to her shame, of a bitterness towards them: what business had they being beautiful to her when they were not the sea?

Arriving, she took her usual seat by a window that looked out to Touma's Gate, sipped her own coffee, and tried not to brood.

She knew what Salma would have said. *Go to the sea,* she would have urged, *bathe in it! Or, if you cannot, read the thousands of poems written to it! Write a poem yourself! Or –* slyly, then *– only think of something you yourself find beautiful – horses, berries, books – and hide it beneath layers and layers of desire until the thing you love is itself obscured. Every pearl has a grain of sand at its heart, no? Be cunning. You cannot know all the world, my dear, as intimately as you know your stones.*

But she couldn't. She had experimented with such dreams, crafted them for herself; they came out wrapped in cotton wool, provoking feeling without vision, touch, scent. Any would-be dream-crafter could do as well. No, for Sitt Warda, who had already patronized four of the city's crafters before her, it would never do. She had to produce something exquisite, unique. She had to know the sea as Sitt Warda knew it, as she wanted it.

She reached for a newspaper, seeking distraction. Lately it was all airships and trade agreements surrounding their construction and deployment, the merchant fleets' complaints and clamour for restrictions on allowable cargo to protect their own interests. Hessa had a moment of smirking at the sea-riding curmudgeons before realizing that she had succumbed, again, to the trap of her knotting thoughts. Perhaps if the sea was seen from a great height? But that would provoke the sensation of falling, and Sitt Warda did not want a flying dream . . .

Gritting her teeth, she buried her face in her hands – until she heard someone step through the doorway, sounding the hollow glass chimes in so doing. Hessa looked up.

A woman stood there, looking around, the early afternoon light casting a faint nimbus around her, shadowing her face. She was tall, and wore a long, simple dark blue coat over a white dress, its embroidery too plain to declare a regional origin. Hessa could see she had beautiful hands, the gold in them drawn out by the midnight of the blue, but it was not these at which she found herself staring. It was the woman's hair.

Unbound, it rippled.

There was shame in that, Hessa had always felt, always been taught. To wear one's hair so free in public was to proclaim oneself unbound to a trade, useless; even the travellers that passed through the city bound knots into their hair out of respect for custom, the five braids of travellers and visitors who wished themselves known as such above anything else, needing hospitality or good directions. The strangeness of it thrilled and stung her.

It would perhaps not have been so shocking were it one long unbroken sheet of silk, a sleek spill of ink with no light in it. But it rippled, as if just released from many braids, as if fingers had already tangled there, as if hot breath had moistened it to curling waves. *Brazen*, thought Hessa, the word snagging on half-remembered lines of English poetry, *brazen greaves, brazen hooves*. Unfamiliar words, strange, like a spell – and suddenly it was a torrent of images, of rivers and aching and spilling and immensity, because she wanted that hair in her own hand, wanted to see her skin vanish into its blackness, wanted it to swallow her while she swallowed it—

It took her a moment to notice the woman was looking at her. It took another for Hessa to flush with the understanding that she was staring rudely before dropping her gaze back to her coffee. She counted to seventy in her head before daring to look up again: by the time she did, the woman was seated, a server half hiding her from Hessa's view. Hessa laid money on the table and rose to leave, taking slow, deliberate steps towards the door. As soon as she was outside the coffee house, she broke into a run.

Two nights later, with a piece of finely shaped quartz pulsing against her brow, Sitt Warda Al-Attrash dreamed of her former lover with honeysuckle sweetness, and if the waves that rose and fell around them were black and soft as hair, she was too enraptured to notice.

Hessa could not stop thinking of the woman. She took to eating most of her meals at Qahwat al Adraj, hoping to see her again – to speak, apologize for what must have seemed appalling behaviour, buy her a drink – but the woman did not return. When she wasn't working, Hessa found her fingertips tracing delicate, undulating lines through the gem dust that coated her table, thighs tightly clenched, biting her lip with longing. Her work did not suffer for it – if anything, it improved tremendously. The need to craft flooded her, pushed her to pour the aching out into copper and crystal.

In the meantime, Sitt Warda could not stop speaking of Hessa, glowing in her praise; she told all her wealthy friends of the gem among dream-crafters who dimmed all others to ash, insisting they sample her wares. Where before Hessa might have had one or two commissions a week, she began to receive a dozen a day, and found herself in a position to pick and choose among them. This she did – but it took several commissions before she saw what was guiding her choice.

"Craft me a dream of the ruins of Baalbek," said one kind-eyed gentleman with skin like star-struck sand, "those tall, staggering remnants, those sloping columns of sunset!" Hessa ground them just shy of twilight, that the dreamt columns might be dimmed to the colour of skin darkened by the light behind it, and if they looked like slender necks, the fallen ones angled slant as a clavicle, the kind-eyed gentleman did not complain.

"Craft me a dream of wings and flight," murmured a shy young woman with gold-studded ears, "that I might soar above the desert and kiss the moon." Hessa ground a cabochon with her right hand while her left slid between her legs, rocking her to the memory of long fingers she built into feathers, sprouted to wings just as she moaned a spill of warm honey and weightlessness.

Afterwards, she felt ashamed. She thought, surely someone would notice – surely, some dreamer would part the veils of ecstasy in their sleep and find her burning behind them. It felt, awkwardly, like trespass, but not because of the dreamers; rather, it seemed wrong to sculpt her nameless, braidless woman into the circlets she sold for crass money. It felt like theft, absurd though it was, and in the aftermath of her release, she felt guilty, too.

But she could not find her; she hardly knew how to begin to look. Perhaps she had been a traveller, after all, merely releasing her hair from a five-braided itch in the late afternoon; perhaps she had left the city, wandered to wherever it was she came from, some strange land where women wore their hair long and wild and lived lives of savage indolence, stretching out beneath fruit trees, naked as the sky—

The flush in her cheeks decided her. If she couldn't find her woman while waking, then what in the seven skies was her craft for, if not to find her in sleep?

Hessa had never crafted a dream for her own use. She tested her commissions, sometimes, to ensure their quality or correct an error, but she always recast the dream in fresh quartz and discarded the test-stone immediately, throwing it into the bath of saltwater steam that would purify it for reworking into simple jewellery. It would not do, after all, for a silver necklace or brass ring to bear in it the echo of a stranger's lust. Working the hours she did, her sleep was most often profound and refreshing; if she dreamt naturally, she hardly ever remembered.

She did not expect to sleep well through the dream she purposed.

She closed shop for a week, took on no new commissions. She hesitated over the choice of stone; a dream crafted in white quartz could last for up to three uses, depending on the clarity of the crystal and the time she took in grinding it. But a dream crafted in amethyst could last indefinitely – could belong to her forever, as long as she wanted it, renewing itself to the rhythm of her thoughts, modulating its song to harmonize with her dream-desires. She had only ever crafted two dreams in amethyst, a matched set to be given as a wedding gift, and the sum she commanded for the task had financed a year's worth of materials and bought her a new lathe.

Reluctantly, she chose the white quartz. Three nights, that was all she would allow herself; three nights for a week's careful, loving labour, and perhaps then this obsession would burn itself out, would leave her sated. Three nights, and then no more.

She wondered if Salma had ever done anything of the sort.

For three days, she studied her only memory of the woman, of her standing framed in the doorway of Qahwat al Adraj, awash in dusty light; she remembered the cut of her coat, its colour, and the woman's eyes focusing on her, narrowing, quizzical. They were almost black, she thought, or so the light made them. And her hair, of course, her endless, splendid, dreadful hair, curling around her slim neck like a hand; she remembered the height of her, the narrowness that made her think of a sheathed sword, of a buried root, only her hair declaring her to be wild, impossible, strange.

Once the woman's image was perfectly fixed in her thoughts, Hessa began to change it.

Her stern mouth softened into hesitation, almost a smile; her lips parted as if to speak. Hessa wished she had heard her voice that day – she did not want to imagine a sound that was not truly hers, that was false. She wanted to shift, to shape, not to invent. Better to leave her silent.

Her mouth, then, and her height; she was probably taller than Hessa, but not in the dream, no. She had to be able to look into her eyes, to reach for her cheeks, to brush her thumb over the fullness of her lips before kissing them. Her mouth would be warm, she knew, and taste—

Here, again, she faltered. She would taste, Hessa, decided, of ripe mulberries, and her mouth would be stained with the juice. She would have fed them to her, after laughing over a shared joke – no, she would have placed a mulberry in her own mouth and then kissed her, yes, lain it on her tongue as a gift from her own, and that is why she would taste of mulberries while Hessa pressed a hand to the small of her back and gathered her slenderness against herself, crushed their hips together . . .

It took her five days to build the dream in her thoughts, repeating the sequence of her imagined pleasures until they wore grooved agonies into her mind, until she could almost savour the dream through her sleep without the aid of stone or circlet. She took a full day to cast the latter, and a full day to grind the stone to the axes of her dream, careful not to miss a single desired sensation; she set it carefully into its copper circlet.

Her fingers only trembled when she lifted it onto her head.

The first night left her in tears. She had never been so thoroughly immersed in her art, and it had been long, so long since anyone had approached her with a desire she could answer in kisses rather than craft. She ached for it; the braidless woman's body was like warm water on her skin, surrounding her with the scent of jasmine. The tenderness between them was unbearable, for all that she thirsted for a voice, for small sighs and gasps to twine with her own. Her hair was down-soft, and the pleasure she took in wrapping it around her fingers left her breathless. She woke tasting mulberries, removed the circlet and promptly slept until the afternoon.

The second night, she nestled into her lover's body with the ease of old habit, and found herself murmuring poetry into her neck, old poems in antique meters, rhythms rising and falling like the galloping warhorses they described. "I wish," she whispered, pressed against her afterwards, raising her hand to her lips, "I could take you riding – I used to, when I was little. I would go riding to Maaloula with my family, where almond trees grow from holy caves, and where the wine is so black and sweet it is rumoured that each grape must have been kissed before being plucked to make it. I wish—" And she sighed, feeling the dream leaving her, feeling the stone-sung harmony of it fading. "I wish I knew your name."

Strangeness, then – a shifting in the dream, a jolt, as the walls of the bedroom she had imagined for them fell away, as she found she could look at nothing but her woman's eyes, seeing wine in them, suddenly, and something else, as she opened her mulberry mouth to speak.

"Nahla," she said, in a voice like a granite wall. "My name is—"

Hessa woke with the sensation of falling from a great height, too shocked to move. Finally, with great effort, she removed the circlet, and gripped it in her hands for a long time, staring at the quartz. She had not given her a name. Was her desire for one strong enough to change the dream from within? All her dream-devices were interactive to a small degree, but she always planned them that way, allowing room, pauses in the stone's song which the dreamer's mind could fill – but she had not done so with her own, so certain of what she wanted, of her own needs. She had decided firmly against giving her a name, wanting so keenly to know the truth – and that voice, so harsh. That was not how she would have imagined her voice . . .

She put the circlet aside and rose to dress herself. She would try to understand it later that night. It would be her final one; she would ask another question, and see what tricks her mind played on her then.

But there would be no third night.

That afternoon, as Hessa opened her door to step out for an early dinner at Qahwat al Adraj, firm hands grasped her by the shoulders and shoved her back inside. Before she could protest or grasp what was happening, her braidless woman stood before her, so radiant with fury that Hessa could hardly speak for the pain it brought her.

"Nahla?" she managed.

"Hessa," she threw back in a snarl. "Hessa Ghaflan bint Aliyah bint Qamar bint Widad. Crafter of dreams. Ask me how I am here."

There were knives in Hessa's throat – she felt it would bleed if she swallowed, if she tried to speak. "How . . . ?"

"Do you know" – she was walking, now, walking a very slow circle around her. "what it is like" – no, not quite around, she was coming towards her but as wolves did, never in a straight line before they attacked, always slant – "to find your dreams are no longer your own? Answer me."

Hessa could not. This, now, felt like a dream that was no longer her own. Nahla's voice left her nowhere to hide, allowed her no possibility of movement. Finally, she managed something that must have looked enough like a shake of her head for Nahla to continue.

"Of course you wouldn't. You are the mistress here, the maker of worlds. I shall tell you. It is fascinating, at first – like being in another country. You observe, for it is strange to not be at the centre of your own story, strange to see a landscape, a city, an ocean, bending its familiarity towards someone not yourself. But then – then, Hessa . . ."

Nahla's voice was an ocean, Hessa decided, dimly. It was worse than the sea – it was the vastness that drowned ships and hid monsters beneath its sparkling calm. She wished she could stop staring at Nahla's mouth.

"Then, you understand that the landscapes, the cities, the oceans, these things are you. They are built out of you, and it is you who is bending, you who is changing for the eyes of these strangers. It is your hands in their wings, your neck in their ruins, your hair in which they laugh and make love—"

Her voice broke there, and Hessa had a tiny instant's relief as Nahla turned away from her, eyes screwed shut. Only an instant, though, before Nahla laughed in a way that was sand in her own eyes, hot and stinging and sharp.

"And then you see them! You see them in waking, these people who bathed in you and climbed atop you, you recognize their faces and think you have gone mad, because those were only dreams, surely, and you are more than that! But you aren't, because the way they look at you, Hessa, their heads tilted in fond curiosity, as if they've found a pet they would like to keep – you are nothing but the grist for their fantasy mills, and even if they do not understand that, you do. And you wonder, why, why is this happening? Why now, what have I done?"

She gripped Hessa's chin and forced it upward, pushing her against one of her worktables, scattering a rainfall of rough-cut gems to the stone floor and slamming agony into her hip. Hessa did not resist anything but the urge to scream.

"And then" – stroking her cheek in a mockery of tenderness – "you see a face in your dreams that you first knew outside them. A small, tired-looking thing you saw in a coffee house, who looked at you as if you were the only thing in the world worth looking at – but who now is taking off your clothes, is filling your mouth with berries and poems and won't let you speak, and Hessa, *it is so much worse*."

"I didn't know!" It was a sob, finally, stabbing at her as she forced it out. "I'm sorry, I'm so sorry – I didn't know, Nahla, that isn't how it works—"

"You made me into your *doll*." Another shove sent Hessa crumpling to the floor, pieces of quartz marking her skin with bruises and cuts. "Better I be an ancient city or the means to flight than your *toy*, Hessa! Do you know the worst of it?" Nahla knelt down next to her, and Hessa knew that it would not matter to her that she was crying now, but she offered her tears up as penance all the same.

"The worst of it," she whispered, now, forefinger tracing one of Hessa's braids, "is that, in the dream, I wanted you. And I could not tell if it was because I found you beautiful, or because that is what you wanted me to do."

They stayed like that for some time, Hessa breathing through slow, ragged sobs while Nahla touched her head. She could not bring herself to ask, *do you still want me now?*

"How could you not know?" Nahla murmured as she touched her, as if she could read the answer in Hessa's hair. "How could you not know what you were doing to me?"

"I don't control anything but the stone, I swear to you, Nahla, I promise," she could hear herself babbling, her words slick with tears, blurry and indistinct as her vision. "When I grind the dream into the quartz, it is like pressing a shape into wet clay, like sculpture, like carpentry – the quartz, the wax, the dopstick, the grinding plate, the copper and amber, these are my materials, Nahla! These and my mind. I don't know how this happened, it is impossible—"

"That I should be in your mind?"

"That I, or anyone else, should be in yours. You aren't a material, you were only an image – it was never you, it couldn't have been, it was only—"

"Your longing," Nahla said, flatly, and Hessa tried to ignore the crush of her body's weight. "Your wanting of me."

"Yes." Silence between them, then a long-drawn breath. "You believe me?"

A longer silence, while Nahla's fingers sank into the braids tight against Hessa's scalp, scratching it while clutching at a plaited line. "Yes."

"Do you forgive me?"

Slowly, Nahla released her, withdrew her hand, and said nothing. Hessa sighed, and hugged her knees to her chest. Another moment passed; finally, thinking she might as well ask, since she was certain never to see Nahla again, she said, "Why do you wear your hair like that?"

"That," said Nahla, coldly, "is none of your business."

Hessa looked at the ground, feeling a numbness settle into her chest, and focused on swallowing her throat-thorns, quieting her breathing. Let her go, then. Let her go, and find a way to forget this – although a panic rose in her that after a lifetime of being taught how to remember, she had forgotten how to forget.

"Unless," Nahla continued, thoughtful, "you intend to make it your business."

Hessa looked up, startled. While she stared at her in confusion, Nahla seemed to make up her mind.

"Yes." She smirked, and there was something cruel in the bright twist of it. "I would be your apprentice! You'd like that, wouldn't you? To make my hair like yours?"

"No!" Hessa was horrified. "I don't – I mean – no, I wouldn't like that at all." Nahla raised an eyebrow as Hessa babbled, "I've never had an apprentice. I was one only four years ago. It would not – it would not be seemly."

"Hessa." Nahla stood, now, and Hessa rose with her, knees shaky and sore. "I want to know how this happened. I want to learn" – she narrowed her eyes, and Hessa recoiled from what she saw there, but forgot it the instant Nahla smiled – "how to do it to you. Perhaps then, when I can teach you what it felt like, when I can silence you and bind you in all the ways I find delicious without asking your leave – perhaps then, I can forgive you."

They looked at each other for what seemed an age. Then, slowly, drawing a long, deep breath, Hessa reached for a large piece of rough quartz and put it in Nahla's hand, gently closing her fingers over it.

"Every stone," she said, quietly, looking into Nahla's wine-dark eyes, "knows how to sing. Can you hear it?"

As she watched, Nahla frowned, and raised the quartz to her ear.

Clockmaker's Requiem

Barth Anderson

Krina nudged her clock, and it crept up her long neck, closer to her ear, tiny claws tickling. "Left. Left again," it whispered. "Forward."

Behind Krina walked the confidante, a spider-limbed girl with lip rings to seal her mouth. She kept close to Krina, whose inventions always found the right way, no matter how the ziggurat changed, and the skirts of their cloaks stirred swirls of the maroon dust that seemed to gasp from the mortar and paving stones.

"The salon is located up there this afternoon," the clock whispered to Krina. "Up the Ascent."

Today the Avenue of Ascent was a vast flight of stairs beneath a sky of ceiling windows, and a regiment of urbanishment troops inclined upon the steps in a cove of sunlight, their stiff shirt-collars sprung open like traps. Up and down the great flight, fruit sellers stacked their wares for climbers to buy, making the Avenue of Ascent a cascade of color. Blood-red loaves. Foreign lemons. Ripe adorno pears. Pomelos.

Krina stopped and stared at the big orbs of yellow-green pomelos, considering. Instinctively, she touched the small, spiny back of her other clock, a lookout wrapped about her right thumb and the sibling to the one lit upon her neck. The lookout whispered the futures into her ear, when she raised her hand to her shoulder:

"People will all see the same time together, the apprentice will say to you, Krina. A tool, that apprentice will call the thing he's created. Stop him. Don't let him."

The confidante watched Krina staring at the stack of spongy pomelos, light fingertips resting on her lips as if the tight line of locking rings might not be enough to prevent her from cautioning her mistress from buying one.

The fruit-monger caressed the round brow of a pomelo, flicking dust from its green rind. "Fancying a sweet-tart, duchess?" he said from behind his bandana, which was wet and dusty at the mouth. To him, it was simply fruit. He had no idea what the pomelo meant in Krina's caste or he might not have said, "Only half a crona."

moment passed, and Krina ~~ook her head. Then she lifted the hem of her cloak and walked up the steps.

The apprentice will be safe, yes? said the confidante in handslang.

"We clockmakers are the engines of the ziggurat," said Krina, turning and climbing the stairs. "I'd save everyone if I did it now with his clocks unmade. Besides, why do you care?"

The confidante took Krina's left hand and pressed handsigns against Krina's palm in a series of pats, the equivalent of whispering to a handslanger. *Assassinating based on whispers from lookouts? Tragic.*

"You needn't scold." Krina snatched her hand back. "I didn't buy any."

Krina led the way, lookout hissing and slithering along her shoulder, and in their deep pockets, the confidante's hands said, *You are an ungrateful, rebellious confidante.*

With heavy, hand-hewn beams of brandy-colored wood overhead, buttery lantern light pooled on the floor, and the room smelled of wood fire, yam griddlecakes and the scent of spilled wine turning to vinegar. The apprentice's workshop was a lovely corner of the salon, near what had once been Krina's own shop. The large coterie in attendance for the young man's debut drifted from the tables of clocks to the tables holding bottles of wine and back. There was an eagerness to become a throng. Krina accepted a drink from her confidante and they walked to the tables where his clocks were displayed.

"I *told* you. There they are. The beginning of the end," whispered the lookout with a nip at her ear, as Krina looked down the row of dally maple clocks.

The apprentice was a square-faced and sincere-looking youth in old work boots who immediately stopped talking to his colleague and faced Krina when he saw her from the corner of his eye. Nearby, in the wide-open space of his workshop, drunker guests were flailing hilariously through an impromptu reel.

Krina, with the care of a gardener removing aphids from a favorite rose bush, brushed a fine file of the ubiquitous red dust from a nautilus curve in the clock's scrollwork. The clock lifted one paw to her gratefully, and she smiled down into its face, which, oddly, was merely a round disc with hashmarks and numb͟ʜᴀᴛ kind to represent actual features that would b͟ of clock are you?" she said. lif͟ᴛ͟ɢ it. The clock's feet kicked and its tail lashed as she turned it upside down. "Are you finished?"

The apprentice glanced at her wine-stained teeth. "It's just a protoytpe. But you've never seen a clock like this." He sounded chary, as if he expected a reprimand or contradiction.

The blank, featureless face shined at Krina like a little moon, and she thought of the ominous warning her lookout had whispered to her regarding this clock. "No, never. Tell me about it."

Many high-heels clopped on the tiles, and a wine-soaked nonet struck up a song that was either a reel or a staggering waltz. "It's not like the clocks you made, Krina," he said over a burst of laughter from the dancers. "You can tell time by this clock."

The room was warm with so many bodies, which she hoped would hide the rise of angry color to her cheeks. "Rather presumptuous. Me telling the clock time?"

"It's meant for people to use. I have to figure out a way to make many of them, for many, many people." The apprentice stammered when he saw her wince at his words, but soldiered on with his explanation. "Think of it as a tool."

The lookout on her shoulder murmured and growled.

"A tool?" It looked wrong to her, the apprentice's faceless clock, like a fish walking upright in grass and sun. "A tool to do what?"

"To . . ." he hesitated, as if searching for words that wouldn't offend her, "to measure time as a people, to bring people together. So people will all see the same time. Right now everyone makes clocks to create whatever time they want. But this – it's – it tells a time that everyone can agree on."

"That's the idea," said a passing livery officer with a firm, manly nod to the apprentice. "Quantify it. Time shouldn't be subjective. We should have one time. I've always thought that." With two glasses of wine held high, he meant to keep walking but stopped. "How does that clock work?"

"We know when and where we are with this clock. Always. But I'm still combing out snarls," he said, shaking his head at the clock. "It needs little hands. Maybe chimes to tell us a common time."

"Now your clock is telling *us* time?" Katrina chided. "I thought we were telling it time."

"Well, *I'll* look forward to seeing your clock when it's finished, and so will my company," the livery officer said. "This mad place needs all the help we can get."

From the cowl of Krina's cloak, the little lookout hissed, "See? What did I tell you?"

"We don't need it," Krina said to the officer's back, as he took his wine away. "Farmers have roosters, and bread bakers know the rhythm of a rise in their stiff wrist bones. No one wants these clocks of yours, because everyone here prizes the license to do as we will. This? This is not our way."

"Not yet," the apprentice said, grinning from Krina to her confidante.

Putting her hands in her pockets, sipping wine through a straw, the confidante lowered her gaze, as if the apprentice's grin were a gift she couldn't accept here.

Ah, there it is, Krina thought, watching the young man.

His clock shifted its feet, jostling the other clocks on the table, who hissed and spat at the eyeless thing. Why would anyone, she wondered, tolerate being told that one's time was the same as everyone else's – no worse, no different, no more painful, no more beautiful, fortuitous, or grand? In a place where time has reshaped the very architecture, what effect would such a clock have? One of the other clocks took a swipe at the blind clock, which recoiled, unable to defend itself. "We have a responsibility to keep time, yes, but we must keep it well. Vibrant and strong. It's just cruel," she said, "creating something with a face and no eyes."

She lifted her gaze from the crippled clock to see if her words had reached him, and the apprentice nodded slowly to her, perhaps already building another clock in his mind. "Send me your next," she said, "as soon as you've built it."

"Oh, I plan to," the apprentice said, and for the first time, there was a note of challenge, even threat in his voice.

Krina donned her cloak, and, as she pulled up her hood, she whispered to her confidante, "Go back and buy three pomelos from the fruit-monger, please."

The confidante shut her eyes as tightly as her mouth and, when Krina turned her back, handslanged, *Oh, I plan to.*

Dusk threw shadows across the chamber but Krina didn't light any lamps or candles. She liked the violet calm of early evening, so she stood in the center of her black brocade rug and felt the darkness deepen while her brother's friends fell into an ode for strings and percussion. She didn't want the wags here tonight, but she could retreat to her apartments if they grew tiresome.

"What's wrong, Krina?" her brother, Lemet, asked after bobbing his head to the music for some time. "You're being particularly ominous tonight."

Cellos and drums rolled and tolled. "I'm afraid of what that new apprentice at the salon will do with his clock," Krina said.

Lemet was a clockmaker, too, had the same broad, strong hands as Krina. He patted his knees in time to the drums and said, "What do you mean? What's to fear?"

"His clocks will kill our clocks, the ziggurat," Krina said.

"You're paranoid."

"My lookout told me," she said. "I'm very serious. My confidante is stacking three pomelos in the apprentice's doorway, as we speak."

Lemet turned down the corners of his mouth as if to say that was a judicious move on his sister's part.

"Oh?" A cellist smirked in appreciation, fingers fretting near his pierced ear. "Is someone about to come down with offcough? The blackspot. Do you use a poisonist, Krina?"

"We pay our dues and use the Method, like everyone in this room," her brother said in calm reprimand, not appreciating the insinuation that Krina was hiring mercenaries. To Krina, he said *sotto voce*, "Why the Method? You have clocks that could undo the apprentice, right? Use them. Eclipse him."

"Too many people actually want his damn clock. You should have seen the crowd around his salon table."

Lemet showed his sister that he was annoyed with her seriousness by turning his attention back to the musicians.

"It's like the ziggurat has a death wish," she said to his profile.

"Such fascism," said a violinist. "Who would want a clock that unifies time?"

Keeping the measure with just a tad more emphasis until the violinist looked at him, the drummer said, "Oh, yes, who would want a unified time?"

Now the musicians were annoying him, which seemed to annoy Lemet further. "Music, yes. But not all of life. That's so beyond boring, and it's beneath us – it's below our – it's—"

"Yes, there are no words," said Krina, appreciating her brother's stammer. She stood and looked down at a wide esplanade near the lagoon below. Drifts of maroon dust were splayed across the cobblestone concourse, and young boys in great cloaks and kerchiefs over their faces were attempting to sweep the fine powder into pails. Futile work. The very mortar of the ziggurat gasped silt into the air. "This dust."

A bassoon moaned across the cellos and bass drum.

In birdskin slippers, Krina's feet slid across the floor into her own apartments, away from her brother and his revelers. They would go all night, and she wasn't in the mood to join them. As she shut the door on the boom of a throaty cello, the first clock she had ever built, with intricate, interlocking pinewood scales leaned kindly against her ankle. Seizing the clock by its fat, solid coils, she looked into its eyes of agate.

Immediately, a strange emotion came over Krina and she brought the clock close, embracing it. Though she stood in the center of a darkening room, she was overcome with an emotion she'd never felt before, a feeling that rays of setting sunlight descending through pipe smoke would one day elicit. She'd built this clock to impart the sense of a time yet to be. She could smell sweet tobacco, years of resin in a beloved pipe that would trigger the lonely sadness. She could actually see the warm, orange light sloping through layers of smoke. Why a pipe, or this time of day, and what as yet unmet lover would she identify with this light?

She let the clock slide out of her arms onto the rug and watched it sidewind beneath a wooden secretary as two smaller, very sturdy clocks galloped into the room, their little hooves thumping the floor, but they were more interested in nipping at one another, and so chased away into the bedroom, kicking a rug across the floor as they ran. Following them, rapt, briefly interested in their cavorting, timeless sense of time, Krina started from an applause of wooden wings. She stepped forward, suddenly, stamping her foot hard to keep her balance, as a heavy, graven thing dropped upon her shoulder. Its digging talons grabbed her and grabbed again, as it settled in place next to her right ear. She turned and looked into the clock's pure-gold eyes. "Give me your time, love," she whispered to it.

Swathes of purple light on the divan and armoire blanched to silver-blue as moonlight replaced dusk, and the murmur of squadrons on the steps became the chatter of bats and swallows.

Krina went to her balcony and looked out at the Ascent. Everyone in the ziggurat enjoyed the feeling of their times growing strange and familiar and strange again, rewinding their clocks and hauling the sun back into the sky, or reverting the ziggurat into old neighborhoods long ago rearranged by the advance of many, many other times, and remaking church towers and wide green spaces into clusters of childhood homes so that the lonely song of a piano could play up the alley like wind, as it once did.

From here she could see whole neighborhoods tinged maroon, and the light seemed rusty from dust. *The ziggurat is already dying*, she thought, watching streets sidewind like her pinewood clock. *It won't be able to defend itself from this new kind of time*. For through her clock's eyes, she could also see the world as the apprentice would make it, staring blankly back at her from the streets of the refashioned ziggurat, streets preordained and measured like those hashmarks on the betrayer's clocks once and for all time.

The clock gave a birdlike turn of its head and, on oak talons, sidestepped away from her cheek: unclench, clench; unclench, clench. Looking back, it said, "We clocks will become rulers."

"Rulers?" cooed Krina at her clock.

"Not just devices of measurement, but despots. The future is in order now."

"No, the future is in doubt, I've made sure of that," Krina said in cold return. "The Method and I will sing a requiem in blackspot shortly."

She looked out on the vista of the ziggurat's urbanishment, as if from away and above – a rare sight and one that only this clock afforded her. A continent raised and floating with a ziggurat built upon its widest salt flat, this landmass's stratified bedrock stood upon thin air, rivers spilling into gulfs of nothing. "You'll have your confidante mark the apprentice?" the clock said. "A stack of pomelos for the Method to find its sacrifice?"

"Snuff the bonfire while it's still just a lit match," Krina answered.

"You can't assassinate every young innovator. And you can't urbanish the ziggurat from reality forever," her clock said. "It's dying, disintegrating."

"I know." From here she could see the ziggurat's soaring aqueducts vanishing into the gasping, rust-colored cloud that enshrouded the city. The urbanishment was a clockmaker's dream – literally – and clockmakers like Krina believed they would dream the ziggurat and its continent aloft, unmake and remake it forever. She said as in a breathless prayer, "But there's no other way but our way."

"Apparently," said the clock before soaring off, "there's at least one other."

In the street below two fish sellers hailed each other, and Krina backed away from the balcony in a shuffling step, as if beginning a quiet parlor-dance, but then purple shadows engulfed her into a black, unfeeling fugue, swallowing her away into a strange room, into a bed, laying her down beneath velvet duvets. The room's darkness was so black she couldn't see the walls but believed this might well be her own bedroom. Time was a surprising lover – this wasn't unusual, to find one's self whisked away in the passionate embrace of another's time. She closed her eyes and waited for clarity, listening to the sound of rapid dripping in the dark, a sound like water wanting to be a stream.

"How do you know?" said a disembodied whisper.

Krina lay still, steeped in her fear. She opened her eyes slowly, as if her eyelids parting would make too much noise. But her eyes were useless, and her gaze slid across the impenetrable dark.

Then there was another sound, a sound like skin sliding on skin. A patting, caressing noise. Someone else was in the room, too.

"Yes, but there's no way to know if she has it, yet," said the whisperer.

Has it? Krina wondered. *What do I have that they want? They mean to steal something from me?*

Pat. Pat. Press. Pat.

Perhaps these thieves didn't even know she was here, but, in the dark stillness, Krina wondered if she could get to one of her clocks. If she could call the walkaway or her farfar, she could pull up the stitches of this time, but she couldn't raise her hand to call for her clocks. Her arms felt foreign, heavy. What was wrong? Even her mind, she realized, was a swaying, lumbering thing, unable to pounce and seize on simple facts. Who was in this room? Was this even her room? What could they want to steal? More pressing and patting, like a pair of soft hands clapping very quietly in the darkness, and through it, over it, suffusing the room, was that mechanical, trickling sound.

"Look at that. A dart?" The voice was male. Young.

A dart? The Method has been here, she thought. But for whom? Who was this? Krina felt so warm, dizzyingly warm, and her throat was dry as sand. Had she met this young man at a party? She tried to recall the voice, but like her gaze flitting across the dark, her mind couldn't connect thoughts. Krina almost felt she should know that caressing skin-on-skin, hand-on-hand noise, too, but her lugubrious mind pondered over it in stupid wonder. She'd been at a party earlier. Two of them.

Press. Pat. Caress. Pat.

"She has it," the young man said, no longer whispering, "The whole ziggurat will know soon."

Feet shuffled in the dark, retreating into a space, a chamber beyond, then someone came close to Krina. She stiffened in terror, sightless eyes skimming across the black before her. She couldn't even raise a hand to defend herself, as she sensed the nearness of someone, felt the heat of a body, and smelling the very faintest smell of fruit. Of citrus.

Scent of a pomelo, delicate yet distinct, stacked somewhere in this room, Krina guessed.

Someone marked *me?* Krina thought. But I thought I'd marked someone else. Who was that that I had marked?

A hand scooped under her elbow, lifting it slightly. Another hand pressed itself into her palm, making warm shapes there, a series of symbols made with thin fingers. Handslang.

Your clocks died surprisingly fast. In sympathy. Sorry. Your brother is gone now. Sorry. I brought the pomelos in from your doorstep.

Her confidante retreated from the bedside and dissolved into the somewhere beyond this space that was filled with fear, fever and her heavy indolent thoughts. Sleep came and went in slow blinks of consciousness, and the circling of this hatching plot was maddening, like a lantern-and-shadow show that had been scrambled and shuffled into nonsense. Finally, deep, orange light broke the darkness, and Krina could see her own arms now, the intricate constellations of fine, black bursts in her skin, and she was so weak that she could barely think what this disease was called. Black. Black something. Someone was here with her, in this strange room, sitting in a chair. A man. His work boots creaked in the quiet, and the rocking chair answered offbeat. She could see his silhouette against a window of bright, rancid light filtering through dust outside, and light knifed through curls of pipe smoke overhead. Her beloved clocks were gone? Blackspot. That was it. Lemet, too? The salon? Where was she? Where was her home? Was this even the ziggurat? Perhaps she had been stolen and secreted away as part of an insurrection, and the urbanishment was at an end. She could smell sweet tobacco in a leather pouch nearby and felt grateful for the lonely smell of it. Feeling oddly nostalgic for pipe smoke (hadn't she only ever smelled this tobacco while holding the fat coils of her clock, peering into this very future?), Krina turned to look for the man's pipe on the nightstand, but saw instead the faceless clock squatting there, staring at her in dumb sightlessness and tap, tap, tap, tapping out its hateful, perfect measures.

Dr Lash Remembers

Jeffrey Ford

I was working fifteen-hour days, traversing the city on house calls, looking in on my patients who'd contracted a particularly virulent new disease. Fevers, sweats, vomiting, liquid excrement. Along with these symptoms, the telltale signature – a slow trickle of what looked like green ink issuing from the left inner ear. It blotted pillows with strange, haphazard designs in which I momentarily saw a spider, a submarine, a pistol, a face staring back. I was helpless against this scourge. The best I could do was to see to the comfort of my charges and give instructions to their loved ones to keep them well hydrated. To a few who suffered most egregiously, I administered a shot of Margold, which wrapped them in an inchoate stupor. Perhaps it wasn't sound medicine, but it was something to do. Done more for my well-being than theirs.

In the middle of one of these harrowing days, a young man arrived at my office, carrying an envelope for me. I'd been just about to set off to the Air Ferry for another round of patient visits in all quarters of the city, but after giving the lad a tip and sending him on his way, I sat down to a cup of cold tea and opened the card. It was from Millicent Garana, a longtime friend and colleague I'd not seen in months. The circumstances of our last meeting had not been professional. Instead, I'd taken her to the Hot Air Opera and we marveled at the steam-inspired metallic characters gliding through the drama, their voices like so many tea kettles at the boil.

It was with that glittering, frenetic memory still twirling through my head that I read these words: *Dr Lash, please come to my office this afternoon. When you have finished reading this, destroy it. Tell no one. Dr Garana.* My image of Millicent, after the opera – her green eyes and beautiful dark complexion – sipping Oyster Rime and Kandush at the outdoor café of the old city, disintegrated.

Apparently it was to be all business. I needed to show I was up to the task. I pulled myself together, tidied up my mustache and chose my best walking stick. There was a certain lightness to my step that had been absent in the preceding days of the new disease. Now as I walked, I wondered why I hadn't asked Millicent out on another nocturnal jaunt when last we parted. In my imagination, I remedied that oversight on this outing.

Only in the middle of the elevator ride to the Air Ferry platform, jammed in with fifty people, did I register a sinister thread in what she'd written. Destroy the message? Tell no one? These two phrases scurried around my mind as we boarded, and later, drifting above the skyscrapers.

We were in her office, me sitting like a patient in front of her desk. I tried not to notice how happy I was to see her. She didn't return my smile. Instead, she said, "Have you had a lot of cases of this new fever?"

"Every day," I said. "It's brutal."

"I'm going to tell you some things that I'm not supposed to," she said. "You must tell no one."

I nodded.

"We know what this new disease is," she said. "You remember, I'm on the consulting board to the Republic's Health Policy Quotidian. The disease is airborne. It's caused by a spore, like an infinitesimal seedpod. Somehow, from somewhere, these spores have recently blown into the Republic. Left on their own, the things are harmless. We'd not have known they were there at all if the disease hadn't prompted us to look."

"Spores," I said, picturing tiny green burr balls raining down upon the city.

She nodded. "Put them under pressure and extreme heat, though, like the conditions found in steam engines, and they crack open and release their seed. It's these seeds, no bigger than atoms, that cause the disease. The mist that falls from the Air Ferry or is expelled by a steam carriage, the perspiration of 10,000 turbines, the music of the calliope in the park – all teeming with seed. It's in the steam. Once the disease takes hold in a few individuals, it becomes completely communicable."

I sat quietly for a moment, remembering from when I was a boy, the earliest flights of Capt. Madrigal's Air Ferry. As it flew above our street, I'd run in its shadow, through the mist of its precipitation, waving to those waving on board. Then I came to and said, "The Republic will obviously have to desist from using steam energy for the period of time necessary to quarantine, contain and destroy the disease."

"Lash, you know that's not going to happen."

"What then?" I asked.

"There is no other answer. The Republic is willing to let the disease run its course, willing to sacrifice a few thousand citizens in order to not miss a day of commerce. That's bad enough, but there's more. We've determined that there's a 60 per cent survival rate among those who contract it."

"Good odds," I said.

"Yes, but if you survive the fever stage something far more insidious happens."

"Does it have to do with that green discharge?" I asked.

"Yes," she said. "Come, I'll show you." She stood up and led me through a door into one of the examination rooms. An attractive young woman sat on a chair by the window. She stood to greet us and shake hands. I introduced myself and learned her name was Harrin. There was small talk exchanged about the weather and the coming holiday. Millicent asked her how she was feeling and she responded that she felt quite well. She looked healthy enough to me.

"And where did you get that ring?" my colleague asked of the young woman.

Harrin held up her hand to show off the red jewel on her middle finger.

"This ring . . ." she said and stared at it a moment. "Not but two days ago, a very odd fellow appeared at my door, bearing a small package. Upon greeting him, my heart jumped because he had a horn, like a small twisted deer antler, protruding from his left temple. The gnarled tip of it arced back toward the center of his head. He spoke my name in some foreign accent, his voice like the grumblings of a dog. I nodded. He handed me the package, turned, and paced silently into the shadows. Inside the outer wrapping there was a box, and in that box was this ring with a note. It simply read. *For you.* and was signed, *The Prisoner Queen.*"

Millicent interrupted Harrin's tale and excused us. She took me by the arm and led me back into her office. She told her patient she would return in a moment and then shut the door. In a whisper, she said, "The green liquid initiating from the ear is the boundary between imagination and memory. The disease melts it and even though you survive the fevers, you can no longer distinguish between what has happened and what you have dreamed has happened or could have happened or should have. The Republic is going insane."

I was speechless. She led me to the opposite door and out into the corridor. Before I left, she kissed me. In light of what I'd been told, the touch of her lips barely startled me. It took me the rest of the day to recover from that meeting. I cancelled all of my appointments, locked myself in my office with a bottle of Fresnac and tried to digest that feast of secrets.

I never really got beyond my first question: why had Millicent told me? An act of love? A professional duty? Perhaps the Republic actually wanted me to know this information since I am a physician, but they couldn't officially announce it.

My first reaction was to flee the city, escape to where the Cloud Carriages rarely ventured, where the simply mechanical was still in full gear. But there were the patients, and I was a doctor. So I stayed in the city, ostensibly achieving nothing of medical value. Like my administration of the Margold, my decision to remain was more for me than any patient.

The Plague spread and imagination bled into memory, which bled into imagination – hallucinations on the street, citizens locked in furious argument with themselves all over town, and the tales people told in response to the simplest questions were complex knots of wish fulfillment and nightmare. Then the Air Ferry driver remembered that to fly the giant vessel he was to ignore the list of posted protocols and flip buttons and depress levers at whim. When the graceful, looming behemoth crashed in a fiery explosion into the city's well-to-do section, wiping out a full third of the Republic's politicos, not to mention a few hundred other citizens, I knew the end had come.

Many of those who had not yet lost their reason fled into the country, and from what I'd heard formed small enclaves that kept all strangers at bay. For my part, I stayed with the sinking ship of state. Still tracking down and doing nothing for those few patients suffering from the onset symptoms of the disease.

Scores of workers remembered that their daily job was something other than what it had been in reality and set forth each day to meddle; renowned experts in delusion. Steam carriages crashed, a dozen a day, into storefronts, pedestrians, each other. A fellow, believing himself one of the gleaming characters at the Hot Air Opera, rushed up on stage and was cut to ribbons by the twirling metal edges of his new brethren. There was an accident in one of the factories on the eastern edge of town – an explosion – and then thick black smoke billowed out of its three stacks, blanketing the city in twilight at midday. The police, not quite knowing what to do, and some in their number as deranged as the deranged citizenry, resorted to violence. Shootings had drastically risen.

The gas of the streetlamps ran low and the city at night was profoundly black with a rare oasis of flickering light. I was scurrying along through the shadows back to my office from a critical case of fever – an old man on the verge of death who elicited a shot of Margold from me. As I'd administered it, his wife went on about a vacation they'd recently taken on a floating island powered by steam. I'd enquired if she'd had the fever and she stopped in her tale for a moment to nod.

I shivered again, thinking of her, and at that moment rounded a corner and nearly walked into Millicent. She seemed to have just been standing there, staring. The instant I realized it was her, a warmth spread quickly through me. It was I this time who initiated the kiss. She said my name and put her arms around me. This was why I'd stayed in the city.

"What are you doing out here?" I asked her.

"They're after me, Lash," she said. "Everybody even remotely involved with the government is being hunted down. There's something in the collective imagination of those struck by the disease that makes them remember that the Republic is responsible for their low wages and grinding lives."

"How many are after you?" I asked and looked quickly over my shoulder.

"All of them," she said, covering her face with her hand. "I can tell you've not yet succumbed to the Plague because you are not now wrapping your fingers around my throat. They caught the Quotidian of Health Care today and hanged him on the spot. I witnessed it as I fled."

"Come with me. You can hide at my place," I said. I walked with my arm around her and could feel her trembling.

At my quarters, I bled the radiators and made us tea. We sat at the table in my parlor. "We're going to have to get out of the city," I said. "In a little while, we'll go out on the street and steal a steam carriage. Escape to the country. I'm sure they need doctors out among the sane."

"I'll go with you," she said and covered my hand resting on the table with her own.

"There's no reason left here," I said.

"I meant to remember to tell you this," she said, taking a sip of tea. "About a week ago, I was summoned out one night on official business of the Republic. My superior sent me word that I was to go to a certain address and treat, using all my skill and by any means necessary, the woman of the house. The note led me to believe that this individual's well-being was of the utmost importance to the Republic."

"The President's wife?" I asked.

"No, the address was down on the waterfront. A bad area and yet they offered me no escort. I was wary of everything that moved and made a noise. Situated in the middle of a street of grimy drinking establishments and houses of prostitution, I found the place. The structure had at one time been a bank. You could tell by the marble columns out front. There were cracks in its dome and weeds poked through everywhere, but there was a light on inside.

"I knocked on the door and it was answered by a young man in a security uniform, cap, badge, pistol at his side. I gave my name and my business. He showed me inside, and pointed down a hallway whose floor, ceiling and walls were carpeted – a tunnel through a mandala design of flowers on a red background. Dizzy from it, I stepped into a large room where I saw a woman sitting on a divan. She wore a low-cut blue gown and had a tortoiseshell cigarette holder. Her hair was dark and abundant but disheveled.

I introduced myself, and she told me to take a seat in a chair near her. I did. She chewed the tip of the tortoiseshell for a brief period, and then said, 'Let me introduce myself. I'm the Prisoner Queen.' "

My heart dropped at her words. I wanted to look in Millicent's eyes to see if I could discern whether she'd contracted the Plague in recent days and survived to now be mad, but I didn't have the courage.

Although I tried to disguise my reaction, she must have felt me tremble slightly, because she immediately said, "Lash, believe me, I know how odd this sounds. I fully expected you not to believe me, but this really happened." Only then did I look into her face, and she smiled.

"I believe you," I said. "Go on. I want to hear the rest."

"What it came to," said Millicent, "was that she'd summoned me, not for any illness but to tell me what was about to happen."

"Why you?" I asked.

"She said she admired earnest people. The Prisoner Queen told me that what we have been considering the most terrible part of the disease, the blending of memory and the imagination, is a good thing. 'A force of nature', was how she put it. There's disorganization and mayhem now, but apparently the new reality will take hold and the process will be repeated over centuries."

"Interesting," I said and slowly slid my hand out from under hers. "You know," I went on, rising, "I have to get a newspaper and read up on what's been happening. Make yourself comfortable, I'll be right back." She nodded and took another sip of tea, appearing relaxed for the first time since I'd run into her.

I put on my hat and coat and left the apartment. Out on the street, I ran to the east, down two blocks and a turn south, where earlier that day I'd seen an abandoned steam carriage that had been piloted into a lamp-post. I remembered noticing that there really hadn't been too much damage done to the vehicle.

The carriage was still there where I'd seen it, and I immediately set to starting it, lighting the pilot, pumping the lever next to the driver's seat, igniting the gas to heat the tank of water. All of the gauges read near-full, and when the thing actually started up after a fit of coughing that sounded like the bronchitis of the aged, I laughed even though my heart was broken.

I stopped for nothing but kept my foot on the pedal until I'd passed beyond the city limit. The top was down and I could see the stars and the silhouettes of trees on either side of the road. In struggling to banish the image of Millicent from my mind, I hadn't at first noticed a cloud of steam issuing from under the hood. I realized the carriage's collision with the lamp must have cracked the tank or loosened a valve. I drove on, the steam wafting back over the windshield, enveloping my view.

The constant misty shower made me hot. I began to sweat, but I didn't want to stop, knowing I might not get the carriage moving again. Some miles later, I began to get dizzy, and images flashed through my thoughts like lightning – a stone castle, an island, a garden of poisonous flowers spewing seed. "I've got to get out of the steam," I said aloud to try to revive myself.

"The steam's not going anywhere," said the Prisoner Queen from the passenger seat. Her voluminous hair was neatly put up in an ornate headdress and her gown was decorated with gold thread. "Steam's the new dream," she said. "Right now I'm inventing a steam-powered space submarine to travel to the stars, a radiator brain whose exhaust is laughing gas, a steam pig that feeds a family of four for two weeks." She slipped a hand behind my head, and after taking a toke from the tip of the tortoiseshell, she leaned over, put her mouth to mine, and showed me the new reality.

Lady Witherspoon's Solution

James Morrow

Personal Journal of Captain Archibald Carmody, R.N.
Written aboard HMS *Aldebaran* Whilst on a Voyage of
Scientific Discovery in the Indian Ocean

13 April 1899
Lat. 1°10' S, Long. 71°42' E
Might there still be on this watery ball of ours a *terra incognita*, an uncharted Eden just over the horizon, home to noble aborigines or perhaps even a lost civilization? A dubious hypothesis, at least on the face of it. This is the age of the surveyor's sextant and the cartographer's calipers. Our planet has been girded east to west and gridded pole to pole. And yet what sea captain these days does not dream of happening upon some obscure but cornucopian island? Naturally he will keep the coordinates to himself, so he can return in time accompanied by his faithful mate and favorite books, there to spend the rest of his life in blissful solitude.

Today I may have found such a world. Our mission to Ceylon being complete, with over a hundred specimens to show for our troubles, most notably a magnificent lavender butterfly with wings as large as a coquette's fan and a green beetle of chitin so shiny that you can see your face in the carapace, we were steaming southbysouthwest for the Chagos Archipelago when a monsoon gathered behind us, persuading me to change course fifteen degrees. Two hours later the tempest passed, having filled our hold with brackish puddles though mercifully sparing our specimens, whereupon we found ourselves in view of a green, ragged mass unknown to any map in Her Majesty's Navy, small enough to elude detection until this day, yet large enough for the watch to cry "Land, ho!" whilst the *Aldebaran* was yet two miles from the reef.

We came to a quiet cove. I dispatched an exploration party, led by Mr Bainbridge, to investigate the inlet. He reported back an hour ago, telling of bulbous fruits, scampering monkeys and tapestries of exotic blossoms. When the tide turns tomorrow morning, I shall go ashore myself, for I think it likely that the island harbors invertebrate species of the sort for which our sponsors pay handsomely. But right now I shall amuse myself in imagining what to call the atoll. I am not so vain as to stamp my own name on these untrammeled sands. My wife, however, is a person I esteem sufficiently to memorialize her on a scale commensurate with her wisdom and beauty. So here we lie but a single degree below the Line, at anchor off Lydia Isle, waiting for the cockatoos to sing the dawn into being.

14 April 1899
Lat. 1°10' S, Long. 71°42' E.
The pen trembles in my hand. This has been a day unlike any in my twenty years at sea. Unless I miss my guess, Lydia Isle is home to a colony of beasts that science, for the best of reasons, once thought extinct.

It was our naturalist, Mr Chalmers, who first noticed the tribe. Passing me the glass, he quivered with an excitement unusual in this phlegmatic gentleman. I adjusted the focus and suddenly there he was: the colony's most venturesome member, poking a simian head out from a cavern in the central ridge. Soon more such apemen appeared at the entrance to their rocky dosshouse, a dozen at least, poised on the knife-edge of their curiosity, uncertain whether to flee into their grotto or further scrutinize us with their deep watery eyes and wide sniffing nostrils.

We advanced, rifles at the ready. The apemen chattered, howled and finally retreated, but not before I got a sufficiently clear view to make a positive identification. Beetle brows, monumental noses, tentative chins, barrel chests – I have seen these features before, in an alcove of the British Museum devoted to artists' impressions of a vanished creature that first came to light forty-three years ago in Germany's Neander Valley. According to my *Skeffington's Guide to Fossils of the Continent*, the quarrymen who unearthed the skeleton believed they'd found the remains of a bear, until the local schoolmaster, Johann Karl Fuhlrott, and a trained anatomist, Hermann Schaffhausen, determined that the bones spoke of prehistoric Europeans.

Fuhlrott and Schaffhausen had to amuse themselves with only a skullcap, femur, scapula, ilium and some ribs, but we have found a living, breathing remnant of the race. I can scarcely write the word legibly, so great is my excitement. Neanderthals!

16 April 1899
Lat. 1°10' S, Long. 71°42' E

Unless there dwells in the hearts of our Neanderthals a quality of cunning that their outward aspect belies, we need no longer go armed amongst them. They are docile as a herd of Cotswold sheep. Whenever my officers and I explore the cavern that shelters their community, they lurch back in fear and – if I'm not mistaken – a kind of religious awe.

It's a heady feeling to be an object of worship, even when one's idolaters are of a lower race. Such adoration, I'll warrant, could become as addictive as a Chinaman's pipe, and I hope to eschew its allure even as we continue to study these shaggy primitives.

How has so meek a people managed to survive into the present day? I would ascribe their prosperity to the extreme conviviality of their world. For food, they need merely pluck bananas and mangoes from the trees. When the monsoon arrives, they need but retreat into their cavern. If man-eating predators inhabit Lydia Isle, I have yet to see any.

Freed from the normal pressures that, by the theories of Mr Darwin, tend to drive a race toward either oblivion or adaptive transmutation, our Neanderthals have cultivated habits that prefigure the accomplishments of civilized peoples. Their speech is crude and thus far incomprehensible to me, all grunts and snorts and wheezes, and yet they employ it not only for ordinary communication but to entertain themselves with songs and chants. For their dancing rituals they fashion flutes from reeds, drums from logs and even a kind of rudimentary oboe from bamboo, making music under whose influence their swaying frames attain a certain elegance. Nor is the art of painting unknown on Lydia Isle. By torchlight we have beheld on the walls of their cavern adroit representations of the indigenous monkeys and birds.

But the fullest expression of the Neanderthals' artistic sense is to be found in the cemetery that they maintain in an open field not far from their stone apartments. Whereas most of the graves are marked with simple cairns, a dozen mounds feature effigies wrought from wicker and daub, each doubtless representing the earthly form of the dear departed. The details of these funerary images are invariably male, a situation not remarkable in itself, as the tribe may regard the second sex as unworthy of commemoration. What perplexes Mr Chalmers and myself is that we have yet to come upon a single female of the race – or, for that matter, any infants. Might we find the Neanderthal wives and children cowering in the cavern's deepest sanctum? Or did some devastating tropical plague visit Lydia Isle, taking with it the entire female gender, plus every generation of males save one?

17 April 1899
Lat. 1°10' S, Long. 71°42' E
This morning I made a friend. I named him Silver, after the lightning flash of fur that courses along his spine like an externalized backbone. It was Silver who made the initial gesture of amicability, presenting me with the gift of a flute. When I managed to pipe out a reasonable rendition of "Beautiful Dreamer", he smiled broadly – yes, the aborigines can smile – and wrapped his leathery hand around mine.

I did not recoil from the gesture, but allowed Silver to lead me to a clearing in the jungle, where I beheld a solitary burial mound, decorated with a funerary effigy. Whilst I would never presume to plunder the grave, I must note that the British Museum would pay handsomely for this sculpture. The workmanship is skillful, and, *mirabile dictu*, the form is female. She wears a crown of flowers, from beneath which stream glorious tresses of grass. Incised on a lump of soft wood, the facial features are, in their own naive way, lovely.

Such are the observable facts. But Silver's solicitous attitude toward the effigy leads me to an additional conclusion. The woman interred in this hallowed ground, I do not doubt, was once my poor friend's mate.

19 April 1899
Lat. 1°10' S, Long. 71°42' E

An altogether extraordinary day, bringing an event no less astonishing than our discovery of the aborigines. Once again Silver led me to his mate's graven image, whereupon he reached into his satchel – an intricate artefact woven of reeds – and drew forth a handwritten journal entitled *Confidential Diary and Personal Observations of Katherine Margaret Glover*. Even if Silver spoke English, I would not have bothered to enquire as to Miss Glover's identity, for I knew instinctively that it was she who occupied the tomb beneath our feet. In presenting me with the little volume, my friend managed to communicate his expectation that I would peruse the contents but then return it forthwith, so he might continue drawing sustenance from its numinous leaves.

I spent the day collaborating with Mr Chalmers in cataloguing the many *Lepidoptera* and *Coleoptera* we have collected thus far. Normally I take pleasure in taxonomic activity, but today I could think only of finishing the job, so beguiling was the siren call of the diary. At length the parrots performed their final recital, the tropical sun found the equatorial sea, and I returned to my cabin, where, following a light supper, I read the chronicle cover to cover.

Considering its talismanic significance to Silver, I would never dream of appropriating the volume, yet it tells a story so astounding – one that inclines me to rethink my earlier theory concerning the Neanderthals – that I am resolved to forego sleep until I have copied the most salient passages into this, my own secret journal. All told, there are 114 separate entries spanning the interval from February through June of 1889. The vast majority have no bearing on the mystery of the aborigines, being verbal sketches that Miss Glover hoped to incorporate into her ongoing literary endeavor, an epic poem about the first-century AD warrior queen Boadicea. Given the limitations of my energy and my ink supply, I must reluctantly allow those jottings to pass into oblivion.

Who was Kitty Glover? The precocious child of landed gentry, she evidently lost both her mother and father to consumption before her thirteenth year. In the interval immediately following her parents' death, Kitty's ne'er-do-well brother gambled away the family's fortune. She then spent four miserable years in

Marylebone Workhouse, picking oakum until her fingers bled, all the while trying in vain to get a letter to her late mother's acquaintance, Elizabeth Witherspoon of Briarwood House in Hampstead, a widowed baroness presiding over her dead husband's considerable fortune. Kitty had reason to believe that Lady Witherspoon would heed her plight, as the circumstances under which the baroness came to know Kitty's mother were unforgettable, involving as they did the former's deliverance by the latter from almost certain death.

Kitty's diary contains no entry recounting the episode, but I infer that Lady Witherspoon was boating on the Thames near Greenwich when she tumbled into the water. The cries of the baroness, who could not swim, were heard by Maude Glover, who could. The author doesn't say how her mother came to be on the scene of Lady Witherspoon's misadventure, though Kitty occasionally mentions fishing in the Thames, so I would guess an identical diversion had years earlier brought Maude to that same river.

Despite the machinations of her immediate supervisor, the loutish Ezekiel Snavely, Kitty's fifth letter found its way to Briarwood House. Lady Witherspoon forthwith delivered Kitty from Snavely's clutches and made the girl her ward. Not only was Kitty accorded her own cottage on the estate grounds, her benefactor provided a monthly allowance of ten pounds, a sum sufficient for the young woman to mingle with London society and adorn herself in the latest fashions. In the initial entries, Lady Witherspoon emerges as a muddle-minded person, obsessed with the welfare of an organization that at first Kitty thought silly: the Hampstead Ladies' Croquet Club and Benevolent Society. But there was more on the minds of these six women than knocking balls through hoops.

Confidential Diary and Personal Observations
of Katherine Margaret Glover
The Year of Our Lord 1889

Sunday, 31 March
Today I am moved to comment on a dimension of life here at Briarwood that I have not addressed before. Whilst most of

our servants, footmen, maids and gardeners appear normal in aspect and comportment, two of the staff, Martin and Andrew, exhibit features so grotesque that my dreams are haunted by their lumbering presence. Their duties comprise nothing beyond maintaining the grounds, the croquet field in particular, and I suspect they are so mentally enfeebled that Lady Witherspoon hesitates to assign them more demanding tasks. Indeed, the one time I attempted to engage Martin and Andrew in conversation, they regarded me quizzically and responded only with soft huffing grunts.

I once saw in the Zoological Gardens an orangutan named Attila, and in my opinion Martin and Andrew belong more to that variety of ape than to even the most bestial men of my acquaintance, including the execrable Ezekiel Snavely. With their weak chins, flaring nostrils, sunken black eyes, proliferation of body hair and decks of broken teeth the size of pebbles, our groundskeepers seem on probation from the jungle, still awaiting full admittance to the human race. It speaks well of the baroness that she would hire such freaks as might normally find themselves in Spitalfields, swilling gin and begging for their supper.

"I cannot help but notice a bodily deformity in our grounds-keepers," I told Lady Witherspoon. "In employing them, you have shown yourself to be a true Christian."

"In fact Martin and Andrew were once even more degraded than they appear," the baroness replied. "The day those unfortunates arrived, I instructed the servants to treat them with humanity. Kindness, it seems, will gentle the nature of even the most miserable outcast."

"Then I, too, shall treat them with humanity," I vowed.

Wednesday, 10 April
This morning I approached Lady Witherspoon with a scheme whose realization would, I believe, be a boon to English letters. I proposed that we establish here at Briarwood a school for the cultivation of the Empire's next generation of poets, not unlike that artistically fecund society formed by Lord Byron, Percy Bysshe Shelley and their acolytes in an earlier part of the century. By founding such an institution, I argued, Lady Witherspoon would gain an enviable reputation as a friend to the arts, whilst

my fellow poets and I would lift one another to unprecedented promontories of literary accomplishment.

Instead of holding forth on either the virtues or the liabilities of turning Briarwood into a monastery for scribblers, Lady Witherspoon looked me in the eye and said, "This strikes me as an opportune moment to address a somewhat different matter concerning your future, Kitty. It is my fond hope that you will one day take my place as head of the Hampstead Ladies' Croquet Club and Benevolent Society. Much as I admire the women who constitute our present membership, none is your equal in mettle and brains."

"Your praise touches me deeply, madam, though I am at a loss to say why that particular office requires either mettle or brains."

"I shall forgive your condescension, child, as you are unaware of the organization's true purpose."

"Which is?"

"Which is something I shall disclose when you are ready to assume the mantle of leadership."

"From the appellation 'Benevolent Society', might I surmise that you do charitable works?"

"We are generous toward our friends, rather less so toward our enemies," Lady Witherspoon replied with a quick smile that, unlike the Society's ostensible aim, was not entirely benevolent.

"Does this charity consist in saving misfits like Martin and Andrew from extinction?"

Instead of addressing my question, the baroness clasped my hand and said, "Here is my counter-proposal. Allow me to groom you as my successor, and I shall happily subsidize your commonwealth of poets."

"An excellent arrangement."

"I believe I'm getting the better of the bargain."

"Unless you object, I should like to call my nascent school the Elizabeth Witherspoon Academy of Arts and Letters."

"You have my permission," the baroness said.

Monday, 15 April
A day spent in Fleet Street, where I arranged for the Times to run an advertisement urging all interested poets, "whether wholly Byronic or merely embryonic", to bundle up their best work and

bring it to the Elizabeth Witherspoon Academy of Arts and Letters, scheduled to convene at Briarwood House a week from next Sunday. The mere knowledge that this community will soon come into being has proved for me a fount of inspiration. Tonight I kept pen pressed to paper for five successive hours, with the result that I now have in my drawer seven stanzas concerning the marriage of my flame-haired Boadicea to Prasutagus, King of the Iceni Britons.

Strange fancies buzz through my brain like bees bereft of sense. My skull is a hive of conjecture. What is the "true purpose", to use the baroness's term, of the Benevolent Society? Do its members presume to practice the black arts? Does my patroness imagine that she is in turn patronized by Lucifer? Forgive me, Lady Witherspoon, for entertaining such ungracious speculations. You deserve better of your adoring ward.

The Society gathers on the first Saturday of next month, whereupon I shall play the prowler, or such is my resolve. Curiosity may have killed the cat, but I trust it will serve to enlighten this Kitty.

Sunday, 28 April

The inauguration of my poets' utopia proved more auspicious than I had dared hope. All told, three bards made their way to Hampstead. We enjoyed a splendid high tea, then shared our nascent works.

The Reverend Tobias Crowther of Stoke Newingtown is a blowsy man of cheerful temper. For the past year he has devoted his free hours to *Deathless in Bethany*, a long dramatic poem about Lazarus's adventures following his resuscitation by our Lord. He read the first scene aloud, and with every line his listeners grew more entranced.

Our next performer was Ellen Ruggles, a pallid schoolmistress from Kensington, who favored us with four odes. Evidently there is no object so humble that Miss Ruggles will not celebrate it in verse, be it a flowerpot, a tea kettle, a spiderweb, or an earthworm. The men squirmed during her recitation, but I was exhilarated to hear Miss Ruggles sing of the quotidian enchantments that lie everywhere to hand.

With a quaver in my throat and a tremor in my knees, I enacted Boadicea's speech to Prasutagus as he lies on his deathbed, wherein she promises to continue his policy of appeasing the Romans. My discomfort was unjustified, however, for after my presentation the other poets all made cooing noises and applauded. I was particularly pleased to garner the approval of Edward Pertuis, a wealthy Bloomsbury bohemian and apostle of the mad philosopher Friedrich Nietzsche. Mr Pertuis is quite the most well-favored man I have ever surveyed at close quarters, and I sense that he possesses a splendor of spirit to match his face.

The Abyssiad is a grand, epic poem wrought of materials that Mr Pertuis cornered in the wildest reaches of his fancy and subsequently brought under the civilizing influence of his pen. On the planet Vivoid, far beyond Uranus, the *Übermensch* prophesied by Herr Nietzsche has come into existence. An exemplar of this superior race travels to Earth with the aim of teaching human beings how they might live their lives to the full. Mr Pertuis is not only a superb writer but also a fine actor, and his opening cantos held our fellowship spellbound. He has even undertaken to illustrate his manuscript, decorating the bottom margin with crayon drawings of the *Übermensch*, who wears a dashing scarlet cape and looks rather like his creator – Mr Pertuis, I mean, not Herr Nietzsche.

I can barely wait until our group reconvenes four weeks hence. I am deliriously anxious to learn what happens when the visitor from Vivoid attempts to corrupt the human race. I long to clap my eyes on Mr Pertuis again.

Saturday, 4 May
An astonishing day that began in utter mundanity, with the titled ladies of the Benevolent Society arriving in their cabriolets and coaches. Five aristocrats plus the baroness made six, one for each croquet mallet in the spectrum: red, orange, yellow, green, blue, violet. After taking tea in the garden, everyone proceeded to the south lawn, newly scythed by Martin and Andrew. Six hoops and two pegs stood ready for the game. The women played three matches, with Lady Sterlingford winning the first, Lady Unsworth the second, and Lady Witherspoon the last. Although they took their sport seriously, bringing to each shot a scientific precision, their absorption in technique did not preclude their chattering about matters of stupendous inconsequentiality – the weather,

Paris fashions, who had or had not been invited to the Countess of Rexford's upcoming soirée – whilst I sat on a wrought-iron chair and attempted to write a scene of the Romans flogging Boadicea for refusing to become their submissive client.

At dusk the croquet players repaired to the banquet hall, there to dine on pheasant and grouse, whilst I lurked outside the open window, observing their vapid smiles and overhearing their evanescent conversation, as devoid of substance as their prattle on the playing field. When at last the ladies finished their feast, they migrated to the west parlor. The casement gave me a coign of vantage on Lady Witherspoon as she approached the far wall and pulled aside a faded tapestry concealing the door to a descending spiral staircase. Laughing and trilling, the ladies passed through the secret portal and began their downward climb.

Within ten minutes I had furtively joined the Society in the manor's most subterranean sanctum, its walls dancing with phantoms conjured by a dozen blazing torches. A green velvet drape served as my cloak of invisibility. Like the east lawn, the basement had been converted into a gaming space, but whereas the croquet field bloomed with sweet grass and the occasional wild violet, the sanctum floor was covered end to end with a foul carpet of thick russet mud. From my velvet niche I could observe the suspended gallery in which reposed the six women, as well as, flanking and fronting the mire, two discrete ranks of gaol cells, eight per block, each compartment inhabited by a hulking, snarling brute sprung from the same benighted line as Martin and Andrew. The atmosphere roiled with a fragrance such as I had never before endured – a stench compounded of stagnant water, damp fur and the soiled hay filling the cages – even as my brain reeled with the primal improbability of the spectacle.

In the gallery a flurry of activity unfolded, and I soon realized that the women were wagering on the outcome of the incipient contest. Each aristocrat obviously had her favorite apeman, though I got the impression that, contrary to the norms of such gambling, the players were betting on which beast could be counted upon to lose. After all the wagers were made, Lady Witherspoon gestured toward the far perimeter of the pit, where her major-domo, Wembly, and his chief assistant, Padding, were pacing in nervous circles. First Wembly sprang into action, setting his hand to a small windlass and thus opening a cage in the nearer of the two cellblocks. As the liberated apeman skulked into the arena, Padding operated a second windlass, thereby opening a facing cage and freeing its occupant. Retreating in tandem, Wembly and Padding slipped into a stone sentry box and locked the door behind them.

Only now did I notice that the bog was everywhere planted with implements of combat. Cudgels of all sorts rose from the mire like bulrushes. Each apeman instinctively grabbed a weapon, the larger brute selecting a shillelagh, his opponent a wooden mace bristling with toothy bits of metal. The combat that followed was protracted and vicious, the two enemies hammering at each other until rivulets of blood flowed down their fur. Thuds, grunts and cries of pain resounded through the fetid air, as did the Society's enthusiastic cheers.

In time the smaller beast triumphed, dealing his opponent a cranial blow so forceful that the latter dropped the shillelagh and collapsed in the bog, prone and trembling with terror. The victor approached his stricken foe, placed a muddy foot on his rump, and made ready to dash out the fallen creature's brains, at which juncture Lady Witherspoon lifted a tin whistle to her lips and let loose a metallic shriek. Instantly the victor released his mace and faced the gallery, where Lady Pembroke now stood grasping a ceramic phial stoppered with a plug of cork. Evidently recognizing the phial, and perhaps even smelling its contents, the victor forgot all about decerebrating his enemy. He shuffled toward Lady Pembroke and raised his hairy hands beseechingly. When she tossed him the coveted phial, he frantically tore out the stopper and sucked down the entire measure. Having satisfied his craving for the opiate, the brute tossed the phial aside, then yawned, stretched, and staggered back to his cage. He lay down in the straw and fell asleep.

Cautiously but resolutely, Wembly and Padding left their sentry box, the former now holding a Gladstone bag of the sort carried by physicians. Whilst Padding secured the door to the victor's cage, Wembly knelt beside the vanquished beast. Opening the satchel, he removed a gleaming scalpel, a surgeon's needle, a variety of gauze dressings and a hypodermic syringe loaded with an amber fluid. The major-domo nudged the plunger, releasing

a single glistening bead, and, satisfied that the hollow needle
was unobstructed, injected the drug into the brute's arm. The
creature's limbs went slack. Presently Padding arrived on the
scene, drawing from his pocket a pristine white handkerchief,
which he used to clean the delta betwixt the apeman's thighs,
whereupon Wembly took up his scalpel and meticulously slit a
portion of the creature's anatomy for which I know no term more
delicate than scrotum.

The gallery erupted in a chorus of hoorays.

With practiced efficiency the major-domo appropriated the
twin contents of the scrotal sac, each sphere as large as those with
which the ladies had earlier entertained themselves, then plopped
them into separate glass jars filled with a clear fluid, alcohol most
probably, subsequently passing the vessels to Padding. Next
Wembly produced two actual croquet balls, which he inserted
into the cavity prior to suturing and bandaging the incision.
After offering the gallery a deferential bow, Padding presented
one trophy to Lady Pembroke, the other to Lady Unsworth,
both of whom, I surmised, had correctly predicted the upshot of
the contest. Lady Witherspoon led the other women – Baroness
Cushing, the Marchioness of Harcourt, the Countess of Netherby
– in a round of delirious applause.

The evening was young, and before it ended, three additional
battles were fought in the stinking, echoing, glowing pit. Three
more victors, three more losers, three more plundered scrota, six
more harvested spheres, with the result that each noblewoman
ultimately received at least one prize. During the intermissions,
a liveried footman served the Society chocolate ice cream with
strawberries.

Dear diary, allow me to make a confession. I enjoyed the ladies'
sport. Despite a generally Christian sensibility, I could not help
but imagine that each felled and eunuched brute was the odious
Ezekiel Snavely. I had no desire to assume, per Lady Witherspoon's
wishes, the leadership of her unorthodox organization, and yet
the idea of my tormentor getting trounced in this arena soothed
me more than I can say.

Clutching their vessels, the ladies ascended the spiral staircase.
I pictured each guest slipping into her conveyance and, before
commanding the coachman to take her home, demurely snugging

her winnings into her lap as a lady of less peculiar tastes might secure a purse, a music box, or a pair of gloves. For a full twenty minutes I lingered behind my velvet drape, listening to the bestial snarls and savage growls, then began my slow climb to the surface, afire with a delight for which I hope our English language never breeds a name.

Monday, 6 May

To her eternal credit, when I confessed to the baroness that I had spied on the underground tournament, she elected to extol my audacity rather than condemn my duplicity, adding but one caveat to her absolution. "I am willing to cast a sympathetic eye on your escapade," she told me, "but I must ask you to reciprocate by supposing that a laudable goal informs our baiting of the brutes."

"I don't doubt that your sport serves a greater good. But who are those wretched creatures? They seem more ape than human."

The baroness replied that, come noon tomorrow, I must go to the north tower and climb to the uppermost floor, where I would encounter a room I did not know existed. There amongst her retorts and alembics all my questions would be answered.

Thus did I find myself in Lady Witherspoon's cylindrical laboratory, a gaslit chamber crammed with worktables on which rested the vessels of which she'd spoken, along with various flasks, bell jars and test tubes, plus a beaker holding a golden substance that the baroness was heating over a Bunsen burner. Bubbles danced in the burnished fluid. At the center of the circle lay a plump man with waxen skin, naked from head to toe, pink as a piglet, bound to an operating table with leather straps about his wrists and ankles. His name, the baroness informed me, was Ben Towson, and he looked as if he had a great deal to say about his situation, but, owing to the steel bit betwixt his teeth, tightly secured with thongs, he could not utter a word.

"It all began on a lovely April afternoon in 1883, back when the Society was content to play croquet with inorganic balls," Lady Witherspoon said. "I had arranged for a brilliant French scientist to address our group – Henri Renault, Director of the Paris Museum of Natural History. A devotee of Charles Darwin, Dr Renault perforce believed that modern apes and contemporary humans share a common though extinct ancestor. It had become his obsession to corroborate Darwin through chemistry. After a decade of research, Renault concocted a potent drug from human neuronal tissue and simian cerebrospinal fluid. He soon learned that, over a course of three injections, this serum would transform an orangutan or a gorilla into – not a human being, exactly, but a creature of far greater talents than nature ever granted an ape. Renault called his discovery Infusion U."

"U for Uplift?" I ventured.

"U for Unknown," Lady Witherspoon corrected me. "Monsieur le docteur was probing that interstice where science ends and enigma begins." Approaching a cabinet jammed with glass vessels, the baroness took down a stoppered Erlenmeyer flask containing a bright blue fluid. "I recently acquired a quantity of Renault's evolutionary catalyst. One day soon I shall conduct my own investigations using Infusion U."

"One day soon? From what I saw in the gaming pit, I would say you've already performed numerous such experiments."

"Our tournaments have nothing to do with Infusion U." Briefly Lady Witherspoon contemplated the flask, its contents coruscating in the sallow light. Gingerly she reshelved the arcane chemical. "A few years after creating serum number one, Renault perfected its precise inverse – Infusion D."

"For Devolution?"

"For Demimonde," the baroness replied, pointing to the burbling beaker. "Such unorthodox research belongs to the shadows."

With the aid of an insulated clamp she removed the hot beaker from the flame's influence and, availing herself of a funnel, decanted the contents into a rack of test tubes. She returned Infusion D to the burner. After the batch had cooled sufficiently, the baroness took up a hypodermic syringe and filled the barrel.

"It was this second formula that Renault demonstrated to the Society," the baroness said. "After we'd seated ourselves in the drawing room, he injected 5 cubic centiliters into a recently condemned murderer, one Jean-Marc Girard, who proceeded to regress before our eyes."

Lady Witherspoon now performed the identical experiment on Ben Towson, locating a large vein in his forearm, inserting the needle and pushing the plunger. I knew precisely what was going to happen, and yet I could not bring myself entirely to believe it. Whilst Infusion D seethed in its beaker and the gas hissed through the laboratory lamps, Towson began to change. Even as he fought against his straps, his jaw diminished, his brow expanded and his eyes receded like successfully pocketed billiard balls. Each nostril grew to a diameter that would admit a chestnut. Great whorling tufts of fur appeared on his skin like weeds emerging from fecund soil. He whimpered like a whipped dog.

"Good God," I said.

"A striking metamorphosis, yes, but inchoate, for he will become his full simian self only after two more injections," Lady Witherspoon said, though to my naive eye Towson already appeared identical to the brutes I'd observed in the arena. "What we have here is the very sort of being Renault fashioned for our edification that memorable spring afternoon. He assured us that, before delivering Girard to the executioner, he would employ Infusion U in restoring the miscreant, lest the hangman imagine he was killing an innocent ape." The Towson beast bucked and lurched, thus prompting the baroness to tighten the straps on his wrists. "It was obvious from his presentation that Renault saw no practical use for his discovery beyond validating the theory of evolution. But we of the Hampstead Ladies' Croquet Club immediately envisioned a benevolent application."

"Benevolent by certain lights," I noted, scanning the patient. His procreative paraphernalia had become grotesquely enlarged, though evidently it would not achieve croquet caliber until injection number three. "By other lights, controversial. By still others, criminal."

Lady Witherspoon did not address my argument directly but instead contrived the slyest of smiles, took my hand, and said, "Tell me, dear Kitty, how do you view the human male?"

"I am fond of certain men," I replied. Such as Mr Pertuis, I almost added. "Others annoy me – and some I fear."

"Would you not agree that, whilst isolated specimens of the male can be amusing and occasionally even valuable, there is something profoundly unwell about the gender as a whole, a demon impulse that inclines men to treat their fellow beings, women particularly, with cruelty?"

"I have suffered the slings of male entitlement," I said in a voice of assent. "The director of Marylebone Workhouse took liberties with my person that I would prefer not to discuss."

Before releasing my hand, the baroness accorded it a sympathetic squeeze. "Our idea was a paragon of simplicity. Turn the male demon against itself. Teach it to fear and loathe its own gender rather than the female. Debase it with bludgeons. Humble it with mud. For the final fillip, deprive it of the ability to sire additional fiends."

"Your Society thinks as boldly as the Vivoidians who populate Mr Pertuis's saga of the *Übermenschen*."

"I have not read your fellow poet's epic, but I shall take your remark as a compliment. Thanks to Monsieur le docteur, we have in our possession an antidote for masculinity – a remedy that falls so far short of homicide that even a woman of the most refined temperament may apply it without qualm. To be sure, there are more conventional ways of dealing with the demon. But what sane woman, informed of Infusion D, would prefer to rely instead on the normal institutions of justice, whose barristers and judges are invariably of the scrotal persuasion?"

"Not only do I follow your logic," I said, cinching the strap on the apeman's left ankle, "I confess to sharing your enthusiasm."

"Dear Kitty, your intelligence never ceases to amaze me. Even Renault, when I told him that the Society had set out to cure men of themselves, assumed I was joking." Bending over her rack of Infusion D, Lady Witherspoon ran her palms along the test tubes as if playing a glass harmonica. "Have you perchance heard of Jack the Ripper?" she asked abruptly.

"The Whitechapel maniac?" I cinched the right ankle-strap. "For six weeks running, London's journalists wrote of little else."

"The butcher slit the throats of at least five West End trollops, mutilating their bodies in ways that beggar the imagination. Last night Lady Pembroke went home carrying half the Ripper's manhood in her handbag, whilst Lady Unsworth made off with the other half. You were likewise witness to the rehabilitation of Milton Starling, a legislator who, before running afoul of our agents, alternately raped his niece in his barn and denounced the cause of women's suffrage on the floor of Parliament. You also beheld the gelding of Josiah Lippert, who until recently earned a handsome income delivering orphan girls from the slums of London to the brothels of Constantinople."

"No doubt the past lives of Martin and Andrew are similarly checkered."

"Prior to their encounter with the Society, they brokered the sale of nearly three hundred young women into white slavery throughout the Empire."

"What ultimately happens to your eunuchs?" I asked. "Are they all granted situations at Briarwood and the estates of your other ladies?"

"Martin and Andrew are merely making themselves useful whilst awaiting deportation," the baroness replied. "Once every six months, we transfer a boat-load of castrati to an uncharted island in the Indian Ocean – Atonement Atoll, we call it – that they may live out their seedless lives in harmony with nature."

The patient, I noticed, had fallen asleep. "Is he still a carnivore, I wonder" – I gestured toward the slumbering beast – "or does he now dream of bananas?"

"A pertinent question, Kitty. I am not privy to the immediate contents of Towson's head, just as I cannot imagine what was passing through his mind when he kicked his wife to death."

"God save the Hampstead Ladies' Croquet Club and Benevolent Society," I said.

"And the Queen," my patroness added.

"And the Queen," I said.

Sunday, 26 May
The second gathering of the Witherspoon Academy of Arts and Letters proved every bit as bracing as the first. Miss Ruggles presented four odes so vivid in their particulars that I shall never regard a windmill, a button, a child's kite, or a gutted fish in quite the same way again. Mr Crowther charmed us with another installment of his verse drama about Lazarus, an episode in which the resurrected aristocrat, thinking himself commensurate with Christ, travels to Chorazin with the aim of founding a salvationistic religion. Mr Pertuis brought his *Übermensch* into contact with a cadre of Hegelian philosophers, a trauma so disruptive of their neoPlatonic world-view that they all went irretrievably insane. For my own contribution, I performed a scene in which Boadicea,

bound and gagged, is forced to watch as her two daughters are molested by the Romans. The other poets claimed to be impressed by my depiction of the ghastly event, with Miss Ruggles declaring that she'd never heard anything quite so affecting in all her life.

But the real reason I shall always cherish this day concerns an incident that occurred after the workshop adjourned. Once Miss Ruggles and Mr Crowther had sped away in their respective coaches, having exchanged manuscripts with the aim of offering each other further appreciative commentary, Mr Pertuis approached me and announced, in a diffident but heartfelt tone, that I had been in his thoughts of late, and he hoped I might accord him an opportunity to earn my admiration of his personhood, as opposed to his poetry. I responded that his personhood had not escaped my notice, then invited him for a stroll along the brook that girds the manor house.

We had not gone 20 yards when, acting on a sudden impulse, I told my companion the whole perplexing story of the Hampstead Ladies' Croquet Club. I omitted no proper noun: Dr Renault, Ben Towson, Jean-Marc Girard, Jack the Ripper, Infusion U, Infusion D. At first he reacted with skepticism, but when I noted that my tale could be easily corroborated – I need merely lead him into the depths of Briarwood House and show him the caged brutes awaiting humiliation – he grew more liberal in his judgement.

"You present me with two possibilities," Mr Pertuis said. "Either I am becoming friends with an insane poet who writes of ancient female warriors, or else Lady Elizabeth Witherspoon is the most capable woman in England, excepting of course the Queen. Given my fondness for you, I prefer to embrace the second theory."

"Naturally I must insist that you not repeat these revelations to another living soul."

"I shan't repeat them even to the dead."

"Were you to betray my confidence, Mr Pertuis, my attitude to you would curdle in an instant."

"You may trust me implicitly, Miss Glover. But pray indulge my philosophical side. As a votary of Herr Nietzsche, I cannot but speculate on the potential benefits of these astonishing chemicals. Assuming Lady Witherspoon withheld no pertinent fact from you, I would conclude that, whilst the utility of Infusion D has been exhausted, this is manifestly not the case with the uplift serum. May I speak plainly? I am the sort of man who, if he possessed a quantity of the drug, would not scruple to experiment with it."

"*Mais pourquoi*, Mr Pertuis? Have you a pet orangutan with whom you desire to play chess?"

"I do not see why the uplift serum should be employed solely for the betterment of apes. I do not see why—"

"Why it should not be introduced into a human subject?" I said, at once aghast and fascinated.

"A blasphemous idea, I quite agree. And yet, were you to put such forbidden fruit on my plate, I would be tempted to take a bite. Infusion U, you say – U for Unknown. No, Miss Glover – for *Übermensch*!"

Saturday, 1 June

When I awoke I had no inkling that this would be the most memorable day of my life. If anything, it promised to be only the most philosophical, for I spent the morning conjecturing about what Friedrich Nietzsche himself might have made of Infusion U. Being by all reports insane, the man is unlikely ever to form an opinion of Dr Renault's research, much less share that judgement with the world.

Here is my supposition. Based upon my untutored and doubtless superficial reading of *The Joyful Wisdom*, I imagine Herr Nietzsche would be unimpressed by the uplift serum. I believe he would dismiss it as mere liquid decadence, yet another quack cure that, like all quack cures – most notoriously Christianity, the ultimate *pater nostrum* – prevents us from looking brute reality in the eye and admitting there are no happy endings, only eternal returns, even as we resolve to redress our tragic circumstances with a heroic and defiant "Yes!"

By contrast, I am confident that, presented with a potion that promised to fortify her spirit, my cruel and beautiful Boadicea would have swallowed it on the spot. After all, here was a woman who took on the world's mightiest empire, leading a revolt that obliged her to sack the cities that today we call St Albans, Colchester and London, leaving 70,000 Roman corpses behind. For a warrior queen, whatever works is good, be it razor-sharp knives on the wheels of your chariot or a rare Gallic elixir in your goblet.

This afternoon Mr Pertuis and I traveled in his coach to the Spaniard's Inn, where we dined with Dionysian abandon on grilled turbot, stewed beef à la jardinière, and lamb cutlets with asparagus.

Landing next in Regent's Park, we rented a rowboat and went out on the lake. My swain stroked us to the far shore, shipped the oars and, clasping my hand, averred that he wished to discuss a matter of passing urgency.

"Two matters, really," he elaborated. "The first pertains to my intellect, the second to my affections."

"Both organs are of considerable interest to me," I said.

"To be blunt, I have resolved to augment my brain's potential through the uplift serum, but only if I have your blessing. I am similarly determined to enhance my heart's capacity by taking a wife, but only if my bride is your incomparable self."

My own heart immediately assented to his second scheme, fluttering against my ribs like a caged bird. "On first principles I endorse both your ambitions," I replied, blushing so deeply that I imagined the surrounding water reddening with my reflection, "but I would expect you to fulfill several preliminary conditions."

"Oh, my dearest Miss Glover, I shall grant you any wish within reason, and many beyond reason as well."

"Concerning our wedding, it must be a private affair attended by only a handful of witnesses and conducted by Mr Crowther. Your Kitty is a shyer creature than you might suppose."

"Agreed."

"Concerning the serum, you will limit yourself to a single injection of five centiliters."

"Not one drop more."

"You must further consent to make me your collaborator in the grand experiment. Yes, dear Edward, I wish to accompany you on your journey into the dark, feral, occult continent of Infusion U."

"Is that really a place for a person of your gender?"

"I can tell you how Boadicea would answer. A woman's place is in the wild."

Dear diary, it was not the English countryside that glided past the window of Mr Pertuis's coach on our return trip, for Albion had become Eden that day. Each tree was fruited with luminous apples, glowing plums and glistening figs. From every blossom a golden nectar flowed in great munificent streams.

We reached Hampstead just as the Society was finishing its final match of the day. Standing on the edge of the grassy court, we watched Lady Harcourt make an astonishing shot in which the generative sphere leapt smartly from the tip of her mallet, traversed seven feet of lawn, rolled through the fifth hoop, and came to rest at a spot not ten inches from the peg. The other ladies broke into spontaneous applause.

Now Mr Pertuis led me behind the privet hedge and placed a farewell kiss – a kiss! – on my lips, then repaired to his coach, whereupon Lady Witherspoon likewise drew me aside and averred she had news that would send my spirits soaring.

"Today I informed the others that, acting on your own initiative, you learned of the Society's true purpose," she said. "Having already judged you a person of impeccable character, they are happy to admit you to our company. Will you accept our invitation to an evening of demon baiting?"

"*Avec plaisir*," I said.

"Amongst the scheduled contestants is a notorious workhouse supervisor whom our agents abducted but four days ago. Yes, dear Kitty, tonight you will see a simian edition of the odious Ezekiel Snavely take the field."

My heart leapt up, though not to the same altitude occasioned by Mr Pertuis's marriage proposal. "If Snavely were to fall," I muttered, "and if it were permitted, I would put the knife to him myself."

"I fully understand your desire, but we decided long ago that the incision must always be made and dressed by a practiced hand," Lady Witherspoon said. "The gods have entrusted us with their ichor, dear Kitty, and we must remain worthy of the gift."

Monday, 3 June
Saturday night's tournament did not turn out as I had hoped. My *bête noir* conquered his opponent, an abhorrent West End procurer. Dear God, what if Snavely continues to win his battles, month after month? What if he is standing tall after the Benevolent Society has been discovered and toppled by the London Metropolitan Police? Will his apish incarnation, gonads and all, receive sanctuary in some zoo? *Quelle horreur!*

In contrast to recent events in the arena, this morning's scientific experiments went swimmingly. We had no difficulty stealthily transferring the Erlenmeyer flask and the hypodermic syringe from the north tower to my cottage. So lovingly did Mr Pertuis work the needle into my vein that the pain proved but a pinch, and I believe that, when I injected my swain in turn, I caused him only mild discomfort.

"Herr Nietzsche calls humankind the unfinished animal," he said. "If that hypothesis is true, then perhaps you and I, fair Kitty, are about to bring our species to completion."

At first I felt nothing – and then, suddenly, the elixir announced its presence in my brain. My throat constricted. My eyes seemed to rotate in their sockets. A thousand clockwork ants scurried across my skin. Sweat gushed from my brow, coursing down my face like blood from the Crown of Thorns.

Our torments ceased as abruptly as they'd begun, as if by magic – that is to say, by *Überwissenschaft*. And suddenly we knew that a true wonderworker had come amongst us, *le Grand* Renault, blessing his disciples with the elixir of his genius. Brave new passions swelled within us. Fortunately I had on hand sufficient ink and paper to give them voice. Although we'd severed ourselves from our simian heritage, Edward and I nevertheless entered into competition, each determined to produce the greater number of eternal truths in iambic pentameter. Whilst my poor swain labored till dawn, and even then failed to complete his *Abyssiad*, I finished *The Song of Boadicea* on the stroke of midnight – 210 stanzas, each more brilliant than the last.

Thursday, 6 June
And so, dear diary, it has begun. We have bitten the apple, cut cards with the Devil, lapped the last drop from the Pierian Spring. Come the new year my Edward and I shall be man and wife, but today we are *Übermensch* and *Überfrau*.

Such creatures will not be constrained by convention, nor acknowledge mere biology as their master. We are brighter than our glands. Each time Edward and I give ourselves to carnal love, we employ such prophylactic devices as will preclude procreation.

We do not disrobe. Rather, we tear the clothes from one

another's bodies like starving castaways shucking oysters in a tidal inlet. How marvelous that, throughout the long, arduous process of concocting his formula, Monsieur le docteur remained a connoisseur of sin. How exhilarating that a post-evolutionary race can know so much of post-lapsarian lust.

To apprehend the true and absolute nature of things – that is the fruit of Nietzschean clarity.

Energies and entities are one and the same, did you know that, dear diary? Wonders are many, but the greatest of these is being. Hell does not exist. Heaven is the fantasy of clerics. There is no God, and I am his prophet.

Fokken – that is the crisp, candid, Middle Dutch word for it. We fuck and fuck and fuck and fuck.

Wednesday, 12 June

An *Überfrau* does not hide her blazing intellect beneath a bushel. She trumpets her transfiguration from every rooftop, every watchtower, the summit of the highest mountain.

When I told Lady Witherspoon what Edward and I had done with the elixir, I assumed she might turn livid and perhaps even banish me from her estate. I did not anticipate that she would acquire a countenance of supreme alarm, call me the world's biggest fool, and spew out a narrative so hideous that only an *Überfrau* would dare, as I did, to greet it with a contemptuous laugh.

If I am to believe the baroness, Dr Renault also wondered whether Infusion U might be capable of causing the consummation of our race. His experiments were so costly as to nearly deplete his personal fortune, entailing as they did lawsuits brought against him by the relations of the serum's twenty recipients. For it happens that the beneficence of Infusion U rarely persists for more than six weeks, after which the *Übermensch* endures a rapid and irremediable slide toward the primal. No known drug can arrest this degeneration, and the process is merely accelerated by additional injections.

The subjects of Renault's investigations may have lost their Nietzschean nerve, but Edward and I shall remain true to our joy. We exist beyond the tawdry grasp of the actual and the trivial reach of reason. As *Übermensch* and *Überfrau* we are prepared to grant employment to every species of whimsy, but no facts need apply.

Something June

The third meeting of the Witherspoon Academy was another rollicking success, though Miss Ruggles and Mr Crowther would probably construct it otherwise. When Miss Ruggles inflicted her latest excrescence on us, a piece of twaddle about her garden, Edward suggested that she run home and tend her flowers, for they were surely wilting from shame. She left the estate in tears. After Mr Crowther finished spouting his drivel, I told him that his muse had evidently spent the past four weeks selling herself in the streets. His face went crimson, and he left in a huff.

Thursday?

Kitty's head swims in a maelstrom of its own making. Her stomach has lost all sovereignty over its goods, and her psyche has likewise surrendered its dominion. Her soul vomits upon the page.

Another Day

Ape hair on Edward's arms. Ape teeth in Edward's mouth. Ape face on Edward's skull.

A Different Day

Ape hair in the mirror. Ape teeth in the mirror. Ape face in the mirror.

Another Day

They pitted me against him. In the mud. My Edward. We would not fight. They did it to him anyway. Necessary? Yes. Do I care? No. Procreation kills.

No Day

On the sea. Atonement Atoll. A timbre intended is a tone meant. I shall never say anything so clever again. I weep.

Habzilb

habzilb larzed dox ner adnor ulorx qron mizrel bewq xewt ulp ilr ulp xok ulp ulp ulp ulp ulpulpulpulpulpulpulpulpulp

Personal Journal of
Captain Archibald Carmody, R.N.
Written aboard HMS *Aldebaran*
Whilst on a Voyage of Scientific Discovery in the Indian Ocean

20 April 1899
Lat. 1°10' S, Long. 71°42' E

I slept till noon. After securing Miss Glover's diary in my rucksack, I bid the watch row me ashore, then entered the aborigines' cavern in search of Silver. Despite Kitty's fantastic chronicle, I still think of them as Neanderthals, and perhaps I always shall.

My friend was nowhere to be found, so I proceeded to his mate's grave. Silver *né* Edward Pertuis sat atop the mound, contemplating Kitty's graven image. I surrendered the diary to the gelded apeman, who forthwith secured it in his satchel.

The instant I drew the Bible from my rucksack, Silver understood my intention. He wrapped one long arm around the sculpture, then set the opposite hand atop the Scriptures. I'd never performed the ceremony before, and I'm sure I got certain details wrong. The apeman hung onto my every word, and when at length I averred that he and Katherine Margaret Glover were man and wife, he smiled, then kissed his bride.

22 April 1899
Lat. 6°11' N, Long. 68°32' E

Two days after steaming away from Lydia Isle, I find myself wondering if it was all a dream. The lost race, their strange music, the bereaved beast grieving over his mate's effigy – did I imagine the entire sojourn?

Naturally Mr Chalmers and Mr Bainbridge will happily corroborate my stay in Eden. As for the strange diary, I am at the moment prepared to give it credence, and not just because I spent so many hours in monkish replication of its pages. I believe Kitty Glover. The subterranean tournaments, the demimonde drug, the uplift serum: these are factual as rain. I am convinced that Kitty and Edward ventured recklessly into the *terra incognita* of their primate past, losing themselves forever in apish antiquity.

My wife is an avid consumer of the London papers. If, prior to my departure, Briarwood House had been found to conceal a cabal of sorceresses bent on reforming miscreant males through French chemistry and Roman combat, Lydia would surely have read about it and told me. Until I hear otherwise, I shall assume that the Hampstead Ladies' Croquet Club is still a going concern, making apes, curing demons, knocking balls through hoops.

And so I face a dilemma. Upon my return to England do I inform the authorities of debatable recreations at Briarwood House? Or do I allow the uncanny status quo to persist? But that is another day's conversation with myself.

23 April 1899
Lat. 15°06' N, Long. 55°32' E
Last night I once again read all the diary transcriptions. My dilemma has dissolved. With *Übermensch* clarity I see what I must do, and not do.

In some nebulous future – when England's men have transmuted into angels, perhaps, or England's women have the vote, or Satan has become an epicure of snowflakes – on that date I may suggest to a Hampstead constable that he investigate rumors of witchery at Lady Witherspoon's estate. But for now the secret of the Benevolent Society is safe with me. Landing again on Albion's shore, I shall arrange for this journal to become my family's most private heirloom, and shall undertake a second mission as well, approaching the baroness, assuring her of my good intentions, and enquiring as to whether Ezekiel Snavely finally went down in the mud.

For our next voyage my sponsors intend that I should sail to Gávdhos, southwest of Crete, rumored to harbor a remarkable variety of firefly – the only such species to have evolved in the Greek Isles. Naturalists call it the changeling bug, as it exhibits the same proclivities as a chameleon. These beetles mimic the stars. Stare into the singing woods of Gávdhos on a still summer night, and you will witness a colony of changeling bugs blinking on and off in configurations that precisely copy horned Aries, clawed Cancer, poisonous Scorpio, mighty Taurus, sleek Pisces and the rest.

The greatest of these tableaux is Sagittarius. Once the fireflies have formed their centaur, the missile reportedly shoots away, rising into the sky until the darkness claims it. Some say the constituents of this insectile arrow continue beating their wings until, disoriented and bereft of energy, they fall into the Aegean Sea and drown. I do not believe it. Nature has better uses for her lights. Rather, I am confident that, owing to some Darwinian adaptation or other, the beetles cease their theatrics and pause in mid-flight, thence reversing course and returning to the island, weary and hungry but glad to be amongst familiar trees again, called home by the keeper of their kind.

Reluctance

Cherie Priest

Walter McMullin puttered through the afternoon sky east of Oneida in his tiny dirigible. According to his calculations, he was somewhere toward the north end of Texas, nearing the Mexican territory west of the Republic; and any minute now he'd be soaring over the Goodnight-Loving trail.

He looked forward to seeing that trail.

Longest cattle drive on the continent, or that's what he'd heard – and it'd make for a fine change of scenery. West, west and farther west across the Native turf on the far side of the big river he'd come, and his eyes were bored from it. Oklahoma, Texas, North Mexico next door . . . it all looked pretty much the same from the air. Like a pie crust, rolled out flat and overbaked. Same color, same texture. Same unending scorch marks, the seasonal scars of dried-out gullies and the splits and cracks of a ground fractured by the heat.

So cows – rows upon rows of lowing, shuffling cows, hustling their way to slaughter in Utah – would be real entertainment.

He adjusted his goggles, moving them from one creased position on his face to another, half an inch aside and only marginally more comfortable. He looked down at his gauges, using the back of one gloved hand to wipe away the ever-accumulating grime.

"Hydrogen's low," he mumbled to himself.

There was nobody else to mumble to. His one-man flyer wouldn't have held another warm body bigger than a small dog, and dogs made Walter sneeze. So he flew it alone, like most of the other fellows who ran the Express line, moving the mail from east to west in these hopping, skipping, jumping increments.

This leg of the trip he was piloting a single-seater called the *Majestic*, one could only presume as a matter of irony. The small airship was hardly more complex or majestic than a penny farthing strapped to a balloon, but Walter didn't mind. Next stop was Reluctance, where he'd pick up something different – something full of gas and ready to fly another leg.

Reluctance was technically a set of mobile gas docks, same as Walter would find on the rest of his route. But truth be told, it was almost a town. Sometimes the stations put down roots, for whatever reason.

And Reluctance had roots.

Walter was glad for it. He'd been riding since dawn and he liked the idea of a nap, down in the basement of the Express offices where the flyers sometimes stole a few hours of rest. He'd like a bed, but he'd settle for a cot and he wouldn't complain about a hammock, because Walter wasn't the complaining kind. Not anymore.

Keeping one eye on the unending sprawl of blond dirt below in case of cows, Walter reached under the control panel and dug out a pouch of tobacco and tissue-thin papers. He rolled himself a cigarette, fiddled with the controls, and sat back to light it and smoke even though he damn well knew he wasn't supposed to.

His knee gave an old man's pop when he stretched it, but it wasn't so loud as the clatter his foot made when he lifted it up to rest on the *Majestic*'s console. The foot was a piece of machinery, strapped to the stump starting at his knee.

More sophisticated than a peg leg and slightly more natural-looking than a vacant space where a foot ought to be, the mechanical limb had been paid for by the Union army upon his discharge. It was heavy and slow and none too pretty, but it was better than nothing. Even when it pulled on its straps until he thought his knee would pop off like a jar lid, and even when the heft of it left bruises around the buckles that held it in place.

Besides, that was one of the perks of flying for the Dirigible Express Post Service: not a lot of walking required.

Everybody knew how dangerous it was, flying over Native turf and through unincorporated stretches – with no people, no water, no help coming if a ship went cripple or, God forbid, caught a spark. A graze of lightning would send a hydrogen ship home to

Jesus in the space of a gasp; or a stray bullet might do the same, should a pirate get the urge to see what the post was moving.

That's why they only hired fellows like Walter. Orphans. Boys with no family to mourn them, no wives to leave widows and no children to leave fatherless. Walter was a prize so far as the Union Post – and absolutely nobody else – was concerned. Still a teenager, just barely; no family to speak of; and a veteran to boot. The post wanted boys like him, who knew precisely how bad their lot could get – and who came with a bit of perspective. It wanted boys who could think under pressure, or at the very least, have the good grace to face death without hysterics.

Boys like Walter McMullin had faced death with serious, pants-shitting hysterics, and more than once. But after five years drumming, and marching, and shooting, and slogging through mud with a face full of blood and a handful of Stanley's hair or maybe a piece of his uniform still clutched like he could save his big brother or save himself or save anybody . . . he'd gotten the worst of the screaming out of his system.

With this in mind, the Express route was practically a lazy retirement. It beat the hell out of the army, that was for damn sure; or so Walter mused as he reclined inside the narrow dirigible cab, sucking on the end of his sizzling cigarette.

Nobody shot at him very often, nobody hardly ever yelled at him, and his clothes were usually dry. All he had to do was stay awake all day and stay on time. Keep the ground a fair measure below. Keep his temporary ship from being struck by lightning or wrestled to the ground by a tornado.

Not a bad job at all.

Something large down below caught his eye. He sat up, holding the cigarette lightly between his lips. He sagged, disappointed, then perked again and took hold of the levers that moved his steering flaps.

He wanted to see that one more time. Even though it wasn't much to see.

One lone cow, and it'd been off its feet for a bit. He could tell, even from his elevated vantage point, that the beast was dead and beginning to droop. Its skin hung across its bones like laundry on a line.

Of course that happened out on the trail. Every now and again.

But a quick sweep of the vista showed him three more meaty corpses blistering and popping on the pie-crust plain.

He said, "Huh." Because he could see a few more, dotting the land to the north, and to the south a little bit too. If he could get a higher view, he imagined there might be enough scattered bodies to sketch the Goodnight-Loving, pointing a ghastly arrow all the way to Salt Lake City. It looked strange and sad. It looked like the aftermath of something.

He did not think of any battlefields in east Virginia.

He did not think of Stanley, lying in a ditch behind a broken, folded fence.

He ran through a mental checklist of the usual suspects. Disease? Indians? Mexicans? But he was too far away to detect or conclude anything, and that was just as well. He didn't want to smell it anyway. He was plenty familiar with the reek, that rotting sweetness tempered with the methane stink of bowels and bloat.

Another check of the gauges told him more of what he already knew. One way or another, sooner rather than later, the *Majestic* was going down for a refill.

Walter wondered what ship he'd get next. A two-seater, maybe? Something with a little room to stretch out? He liked being able to lift his leg off the floor and let it rest where a copilot ought to go, but almost never went. That'd be nice.

Oh well. He'd find out when he got there, or in the morning.

Out the front windscreen, which screened almost no wind and kept almost no bugs out of his mouth, the sun was setting – the nebulous orb melting into an orange and pink line against the far, flat horizon.

In half an hour the sky was the color of blueberry jam, and only a lilac haze marked the western edge of the world.

The *Majestic* was riding lower in the air because Walter was conserving the thrust and letting the desert breeze move him as much as the engine. Coasting was a pleasant way to sail and the lights of Reluctance should be up ahead, any minute.

Some minute.

One of these minutes.

Where were they?

Walter checked the compass and peeked at his instruments, which told him only that he was on course and that Reluctance should be a mile or less out. But where were the lights? He could always see the lights by now; he always knew when to start smiling, when the gaslamps and lanterns meant people, and a drink, and a place to sleep.

Wait. There. Maybe? *Yes.*

Telltale pinpricks of white, laid out patternless on the dark sprawl.

Not so many as usual, though. Only a few, here and there. Haphazard and lost-looking, as if they were simply the remainder – the hardy leftovers after a storm, the ones which had not gone out quite yet. There was a feebleness to them, or so Walter thought as he gazed out and over and down. He used his elbow to wipe away the dirt on the glass screen as if it might be hiding something. But no. No more lights revealed themselves, and the existing flickers of white did not brighten.

Walter reached for his satchel and slung it over his chest, where he could feel the weight of his brother's Colt bumping up against his ribs.

He set himself a course for Reluctance. He was out of hydrogen and sinking anyway; and it was either set down in relative civilization – where nothing might be wrong, after all – or drop like a feather into the desert dust alone with the coyotes, cactus and cougars. If he had to wait for sunrise somewhere, better to do it down in an almost-town he knew well enough to navigate.

There were only a few lights, yes.

But no flashes of firearms, and no bonfires of pillage or some hostile victory. He could see nothing and no one, nobody walking or running. Nobody dead, either, he realized when the *Majestic* swayed down close enough to give him a dim view of the dirt streets with their clapboard sidewalks.

Nobody at all.

He licked at his lower lip and gave it a bite, then he pulled out the Colt and began to load it, sure and steady, counting to six and counting out six more bullets for each of the two pockets on his vest.

Could be, he was overreacting. Could be, Reluctance had gone bust real quick, or there'd been a dust storm, or a twister, or any number of other natural and unpleasant events that could drive a thrown-together town into darkness. Could be, people were digging themselves out now, even as he wondered about it. Maybe something had made them sick. Cholera, or typhoid. He'd seen it wipe out towns and troops before.

His gut didn't buy it.

He didn't like it, how he couldn't assume the best and he didn't have any idea what the worst might be.

And still, as the *Majestic* came in for a landing. No bodies.

That was the thing. Nobody down there, including the dead.

He picked up his cane off the dirigible's floor and tested the weight of it. It was a good cane, solid enough to bring down a big man or a small wildcat, push come to shove. He set it across his knees.

The *Majestic* drooped down swiftly, but Walter was in control. He'd landed in the dark before and it was tricky, but it didn't scare him much. It made him cautious, sure. A man would be a fool to be incautious when piloting a half-ton craft into a facility with enough flammable gas to move a fleet. All things being ready and bright, and all it took was a wrongly placed spark – just a graze of metal on metal, the screech of one thing against another, or a single cigarette fallen from a lip – and the whole town would be reduced to matchsticks. Everybody knew it, and everybody lived with it. Just like everybody knew that flying post was a dangerous job, and a bunch of the boys who flew never made it home, just like going to war.

Walter sniffed, one nostril arching up high and dropping down again. He set his jaw, pulled the back drag chute, flipped the switch to give himself some light on the ship's underbelly, and spun the *Majestic* like a girl at a dance. He dropped her down onto the wooden platform with a big red X painted to mark the spot, and she shuddered to silence in the middle of the circle cast by her undercarriage light.

With one hand he popped the anchor chain lever, and with the other he reached for the door handle as he listened to that chain unspool outside.

Outside it was as dark as his overhead survey had implied. And although the light of the undercarriage was nearly the only light, Walter reached up underneath the craft and pulled the snuffing cover down over its flaring white wick. He took hold of the nearest anchor chain and dragged it over to the pipework docks. Ordinarily he'd check to make sure he was on the right pad, clipping his craft to the correct slot before checking in with the station agent.

But no one greeted him. No one rushed up with a ream of paperwork for signing and sealing.

A block away a light burned; and beyond that, another gleamed somewhere farther away. Between those barely seen orbs and the lifting height of a half-full moon, Walter could see well enough to spy another ship nearby. It was affixed to a port on the hydrogen generators, but sagging hard enough that it surely wasn't filled or ready to fly.

Except for the warm buzz of the gas machines standing by, Walter heard absolutely nothing. No bustling of suppertime seekers roaming through the narrow streets, flowing toward Bad Albert's place, or wandering to Mama Rico's. The pipe-dock workers were gone, and so were the managers and agents.

No horses, either. No shuffling of saddles or stirrups, of bits or clomping iron shoes.

Inside the *Majestic* an oil lantern was affixed to the wall behind the pilot's seat. Walter grunted, leaning on his cane. He pulled out the lamp, but hesitated to light it.

He held a match up, ready to strike it on the side of the deflated ship, but he didn't. The silence held its breath and told him to wait. It spoke like a battlefield before an order is given.

That's what stopped him. Not the thought of all that hydrogen, but the singular sensation that somewhere, on some other side, enemies were crouching – waiting for a shot. It froze him, one hand and one match held aloft, his cane leaning against the dirigible and his satchel hanging from his shoulder, pressing at the spot where his neck curved to meet his collarbone.

Under the lazily rolling moon and alone in the mobile gas works that had become the less mobile semi-settlement of Reluctance, Walter put the match away, and set the lantern on the ground beside his ship.

He could see. A little. And given the circumstances, he liked that better than being seen.

His leg ached, but then again, it always ached. Too heavy by half and not nearly as mobile as the army had promised it'd be, the steel and leather contraption tugged against his knee as if it were a drowning man; and for a tiny flickering moment the old ghost pains tickled down to his toes, even though the toes were long gone, blown away on a battlefield in Virginia.

He held still until the sensation passed, wondering bleakly if it would ever go away for good, and suspecting that it wouldn't.

"All right," he whispered, and it was cold enough to see the words. When had it gotten so cold? How did the desert always do that, cook and then freeze? "We'll move the mail."

Damn straight we will.

Walter reached into the *Majestic*'s tiny hold and pulled out the three bags he'd been carrying as cargo. Each bag was the size of his good leg, and as heavy as his bad one. When they were all three removed from the ship he peered dubiously at the other craft across the landing pad – the one attached to the gas pipes, but empty.

He considered his options.

No other ships lurked anywhere close, so he could either seize that unknown hunk of metal and canvas or stay there by himself in the dead outpost.

Hoisting one bag over his shoulder and counter-balancing with his cane, he did his best to cross the landing quietly; but his metal foot dropped each step with a hard, loud clank – even though the leather sole at the bottom of the thing was brand new.

He leaned the bag of mail up against the ship and caught his breath, lost more to fear than exertion. Then he moved the mail bag aside to reveal the first two stenciled letters of the ship's name, and reading the whole he whispered, "*Sweet Marie*".

Two more mail bags, each moved with all the stealth he could muster. Each one more cumbersome than the last, and each one straining his bum leg harder. But he moved them. He opened the back bin of the *Sweet Marie* and stuffed them into her cargo hold. Every grunt was loud in the desert emptiness and every heaving shove would've sent ol' Stanley into conniptions, had he been there.

Too much noise. Got to keep your head down.

Walter breathed as he leaned on the bin to make it shut. It closed with a click. "This ain't the war. Not out here."

Just like me, you carry it with you.

Something.

What?

A gusting. A hoarse, lonely sound that barked and disappeared.

He leaned against the bin and listened hard, waiting for that noise to come again.

The *Sweet Marie* had been primed and she was ready to fill, but no one had switched on the generators. She sank so low she almost tipped over, now that the mail sacks had loaded down her back end.

Walter McMullin did not know how hydrogen worked exactly, but he'd seen the filling process performed enough times to copy it.

The generators took the form of two tanks, each one mounted atop a standard-issue army wagon. These tanks were made of reinforced wood and lined with copper, and atop each tank was a hinged metal plate that could be opened and closed in order to dump metal shavings into the sulfuric acid inside. At the end, opposite the filler plate, an escape pipe was attached to a long rubber hose, to which the *Sweet Marie* was ultimately affixed.

There were several sets of filters for the hydrogen to pass through before it reached the ship's tank, and the process was frankly none too quick. Even little ships like these mail runners could take a couple of hours to become airworthy.

Walter did not like the idea of spending a couple of hours alone in Reluctance. He was even less charmed by the idea of spending *all night* alone in Reluctance, so he found himself a crate of big glass bottles filled with acid, and with a great struggle he poured them down through the copper funnels atop the tanks. Shortly thereafter he located the metal filings; he scooped them up with the big tin cup and dumped them in.

He turned the valves to open the filters and threw the switch to start the generators stirring and bubbling, vibrating the carts to make the acid and the metal stir and separate into hydrogen more quickly.

It made a god-awful amount of noise.

The rubber hose, stamped "Goodyear's Rubber, Belting and Packing Company of Philadelphia", did a little twitch. *Sweet Marie*'s tank gave a soft, plaintive squeal as the first hydrogen spilled through, giving her the smallest bit of lift.

But she'd need more. Lots more.

There.

Another one.

A sighing grunt, gasped and then gone as quickly as it'd burst through the night.

Walter whirled as fast as his leg would let him, using it as a pivot. He moved like a compass pinned to a map. He held his cane out, pointing at nothing.

But the sound. Again. And again. Another wheeze and gust.

At this point, Walter was gut-swimmingly certain that it was coming from more than one place. Partway between a snore and a cough, with a consumptive rattle. Coming from everywhere, and nowhere. Coming from the dark.

Up against the *Sweet Marie* he backed.

He jumped, startled by a new sound, a familiar one. Footsteps, slow and laborious. Someone was walking toward him, out of the black alleys that surrounded the landing. Nearing the ladder to the refueling platform. And whoever this visitor was, he was joined by someone else – approaching the edge near the parked *Majestic*.

And a third somebody. Walter was pretty sure of a third, moving up from the shadows.

Not one single thing about this moment, this shuddering instant alone – but not alone – felt right or good to Walter McMullin. He still couldn't see anyone, though he could hear plenty. Whoever they were, lurking in the background . . . they weren't being quiet. They weren't sneaking, and that was something, wasn't it?

Why would they sneak, if they know they have you?

Reaching into his belt, he pulled out the Colt and held it with both hands. His back remained braced against the slowly filling replacement ship. He thought about crying out in greeting, just in case – but he thought of the dead cows, and his desperate eyes spotted no new lights, and the sound of incoming feet and the intermittent groaning told him that no, this was no overreaction. This was good common sense, staying low with your back against something firm and your weapon out. That's what you did, right before a fight. If you could.

He drew back the gun's hammer and waited.

Lumbering up the ladder as if drunk, the first head rose into view.

Walter should've been relieved.

He knew that head – it belonged to Gibbs Higley, the afternoon station manager. But he wasn't relieved. Not at all. Because it wasn't Gibbs, not anymore. He could see that at a glance, even without the gaslamps that lit up a few blocks, far away.

Something was very, very wrong with Gibbs Higley.

The man drew nearer, shuffling in an exploratory fashion, sniffing the air like a dog. He was missing an ear. His skin looked like boiled lye. One of his eyes was ruined somehow, wet and gelatinous, and sliding down his cheek.

"Higley?" Walter croaked.

Higley didn't respond. He only moaned and shuffled faster, homing in on Walter and raising the moan to a cry that was more of a horrible keening.

To Walter's terror, the keening was answered. It came bouncing back from corner to corner, all around the open landing area, and the footsteps that had been slowly incoming shifted gears, moving faster.

Maybe he should've thought about it. Maybe he should've tried again, tried to wake Higley up, shake some sense into him. There must've been something he could've done, other than lifting the Colt and putting a bullet through the man's solitary good eye.

But that's what he did.

Against a desert backdrop of dust-covered silence the footsteps and coughing grunts and the buzzing patter of the generators had seemed loud enough; but the Colt was something else entirely, fire and smoke and a kick against his elbows, and a lingering whiff of gunpowder curling and dissolving.

Gibbs Higley fell off the landing, flopping like a rag doll.

Walter rushed as fast as he could to the ladder and kicked it away – marooning himself on the landing island, five or six feet above street level. Then he dragged himself back to *Sweet Marie* and resumed his defensive position, the only one he had. "That was easy," he muttered, almost frantic to reassure himself.

One down. More to go. You're a good shot, but you're standing next to the gas. Surrounded by it, almost.

He breathed. "I need to think."

You need to run.

"I need the *Sweet Marie*. Won't get far without her."

Hands appeared at the edge of the lifted landing pad. Gray hands, hands without enough fingers.

Left to right he swung his head, seeking some out. Knowing he didn't have enough bullets for whatever this was – knowing it as sure as he knew he'd die if any of those hands caught him. Plague, is what it was. Nothing he'd ever seen before, but goddamn Gibbs Higley had been sick, hadn't he?

"Gotta hold the landing pad," he said through gritted teeth.

No. You gotta let 'em take it – but that don't mean you gotta let 'em keep it.

He swung his head again, side to side, and spotted only more hands – moving like a sea of clapping, an audience of death, pulling toward the lifted landing spot. He wished he had a light, and then he remembered that he did have one – he just hadn't lit it. One wobbly dash back to the *Majestic* and he had the lantern in his hand again, thinking *"to hell with it – to hell with us"* and striking a match. What did it matter? They already knew where he was. That much was obvious from the rising wail that now rang from every quarter. Faces were leaning up now, lurching and lifting on elbows, rising and grabbing for purchase on the platform and soon they were going to find it.

Look.

"Where?" he asked the ghost of a memory, trying to avoid a full-blown panic. Panic never got anybody anywhere but dead. It got Stanley dead. On the far side of a broken, folded fence along a line that couldn't have been held, not with a thousand Stanleys.

Ah. Above the hydrogen tanks, and behind them. A ladder in the back corner of the overhang that covered them.

He glanced at the *Sweet Marie* and then his eyes swept the platform, where a woman was rising up onto the wooden deck – drawing herself up on her elbows. She'd be there soon, right there with him. When she looked up at him her mouth opened and she shouted, and blood or bile – something dark – spilled over her teeth to splash down on the boards.

Whatever it was, he didn't want it. He drew up the Colt, aimed carefully, and fired. She fell back.

The ladder behind the hydrogen tanks must lead to the roof of the overhang. Would the thin metal roof hold him?

Any port in a storm.

He scurried past the clamoring hands and scooted, still hauling that dead-weight foot, beneath the overhang and to the ladder. Scaling it required him to set the cane aside, and he wouldn't do that, so he stuck it in his mouth where it stretched his cheeks and jaw until they ached with the strain. But it was that or leave it, or leave the lantern – which he held by the hot, uncomfortable means of shoving his wrist through the carrying loop. When it swung back and forth with his motion, it burned the cuff of his shirt and seared warmly against his chest.

So he climbed, good foot up with a grunt of effort, bad foot up with a grunt of pain, both grunts issued around the cane in his mouth. When he reached the top he jogged his neck to shift the cane so it'd fit through the square opening in the corrugated roof. He slipped, his heavy foot dragging him to a stop with an ear-splitting scrape.

He'd have to step softly.

From this vantage point, holding up the quivering black lantern, he could see all of it, and he understood everything and nothing simultaneously. He watched the mostly men and sometimes women of Reluctance stagger and wail, shambling hideously from corners and corridors, from alleys and basements, from broken-windowed stores and stables and saloons and the one whorehouse. They did not pour but they dripped and congealed down the uncobbled streets torn rough and rocky by horses' hooves and the wheels of coaches and carts.

It couldn't have been more than a hundred ragged bodies slinking forward, gagging on their own fluids and chasing toward the light he held over his head, over the town of Reluctance.

Walter stuffed a hand in his vest pockets and felt at the bottom of the bag he still wore over his chest. Bullets, yes. But not enough bullets for this. Not even if he was the best shot in Texas, and he wasn't. He was a competent shot from New York City, orphaned and Irish, a few thousand miles from home, without even a sibling to mourn him if the drooling, simpering, snap-jawed dead were to catch him and tear him to pieces.

Bullets were not going to save him.

All the same, he liked having them.

The lantern drew the dead; he watched their gazes, watching it. Moths. Filthy, deadly moths. He could see it in their eyes, in the places where their souls ought to be. Most of the men he'd ever shot at were fellows like himself – boys, mostly, lads born so late they didn't know for certain what the fighting was about; just men, with faces full of fear and grit.

Nothing of that, not one shred of humanity showed on any of the faces below.

He could see it, and he was prepared to address it. But not until he had to.

Beneath him, the *Sweet Marie* was filling. Down below the twisted residents of Reluctance were dragging themselves up and onto the platform, swarming like ants and shrieking for Walter – who went to the ladder and kicked it down against the generators, where it clattered and rested, and likely wouldn't be climbed.

He sat on the edge of the corrugated roof and turned the lantern light down. It wouldn't fool them. It wouldn't make them wander away. They smelled him, and they wanted him, and they'd stay until they got him. Or until he left.

He was leaving, all right. Soon.

Inside the satchel he rummaged, and he pulled out his tobacco and papers. He rolled himself a cigarette, lit it off the low-burning lamp, and he sat. And he watched below as the cranium-shaped crest of the *Sweet Marie* slowly inflated; and the corpses of Reluctance gathered themselves on the landing pad beside it, ignoring it.

Finally the swelling dome was full enough that Walter figured, "I can make it. Maybe not all the way to Santa Fe, but close enough." He rose to his feet, the flesh and blood one and the one that pivoted painfully on a pin.

The lantern swung out from his fingertips, still lit but barely.

Below the lantern, beside the ship and around it, the men and women shambled.

But fire could consume anything, pretty much. It'd consume the hydrogen like it was starved for it. It'd gobble and suck and then the whole world would go up like hell, wouldn't it? All that gas, burning like the breath of God.

Well then. He'd have to move fast.

Retracting his arm as far as it'd go, and then adjusting for trajectory, he held the lantern and released it, tossing it in a great bright arc that cut across the star-speckled sky. It crashed to the far corner of the landing pad, blossoming into brilliance and heat, singeing his face. He blinked hard against the unexpected warmth, having never guessed how closely he would feel it.

The creatures below screamed and ran, clothing aflame. The air sizzled with the stench of burning hair and fire-puckered flesh. But some of them hovered near the *Sweet Marie*, lingering where the fire had stayed clear, still howling.

Only a few of them.

The Colt took them down, one-two-three.

Walter crossed his fingers and prayed that the bullets would not bounce – would not clip or ding the hydrogen tubes or tanks, or the swollen bulb of the *Sweet Marie*. His prayers were answered, or ignored. Either way, nothing ignited.

Soon the ship was clear. As clear as it was going to get.

And reaching it required a ten-foot drop.

Walter threw his cane down and watched it roll against the ship, then he dropped to his knees and swung himself off the edge to hang by his fingertips. He curled the good leg up, lifting his knee. Better a busted pin than a busted ankle.

And before he had time to reconsider, he let go.

The pain of his landing was a sun of white light. His leg buckled and scraped inside the sheath that clasped the false limb; he heard his bone piercing and rubbing through the bunched and stitched skin, and into the leather and metal.

But he was down. Down beside the *Sweet Marie*. Down inside the fire, inside the ticking clock with a deadly alarm and only moments – maybe seconds, probably only seconds – before the whole town went up in flames.

At the last moment he remembered the clasp that anchored the ship. He unhitched it. He limped bloodily to the back port and ripped the hydrogen hose out of the back, and shut it up tight because otherwise he'd just leak his fuel all over North Mexico.

He fumbled for the latch and found it.

Pulled it.

Opened the door and hauled himself inside, feeling around for the controls and seeing them awash with the yellow-gold light of the fire just outside the window. The starter was a lever on the dash. He pulled that too and the ship began to rise. He grasped for the thrusters and his shaking, searching fingers found them, and pressed them – giving the engines all the gas they'd take. Anything to get him up and away. Anything to push him past the hydrogen before the fire took it.

Anything.

Reluctance slipped away below, and behind. It shimmered and the whole world froze, and gasped, and shook like a star being born.

The desert floor melted into glass.

A Serpent in the Gears

Margaret Ronald

We unearthed the serpent's corpse just before the *Regina* reached the first gun emplacement that separated the greater world from the forgotten valley of Aaris. The reports from villagers on the border had placed the serpent half a day out of our chosen path and much higher than the dirigible should have been, and while the *Regina*'s captain grumbled about "sightseeing" expeditions, she agreed to let us send up a dinghy.

Truth was, captain and crew alike had signed on for the story as much as for the Royal Society's generous pay. The Aaris valley – forgotten mainly because just after the first isolation guns were erected, the Great Southern rail line obviated the need to venture near the Sterling Pass – was a story even jaded 'nauts revered. A side trip such as this only added savor to the tale. Indeed, the same villagers who'd informed us of the serpent's presence had already traded well on this news: a desiccated carcass halfway up one of the snow-capped peaks that made the Sterling Pass all but untraversable, only revealed by the spring thaw.

"Thaw, my arse," Colonel Dieterich muttered as we disembarked from the gently bobbing dinghy. "It's cold enough to freeze a thaumaturge's tits off."

"The villagers said that this is the first time it's been warm enough to spend more than an hour on the slopes, sir," I said, and draped his greatcoat around his shoulders, avoiding the creaking points of his poorly fastened andropter. "For them I suppose that would constitute a thaw."

"For them having ten toes is a novelty." He snorted his pipe into a greater glow, then noticed the coat. "Ah. Thank you, Charles. Come on; let's go see what the barbaric snows have brought us."

The doctors Brackett and Crumworth were already wandering over the carcass, pointing and exclaiming. All of the Royal Society party (excluding Professora Lundqvist, who because of her condition could not leave the *Regina*) were in better spirits now than they had been for weeks, and I began to understand the captain's decision to send us up here. Unusual as the moment of domestic accord was, though, it paled in comparison to the serpent.

The thing had the general shape of a Hyborean flying serpent, though it was at least twenty times the length of most specimens. It stretched out at least fifty feet, probably more, since the sinuous curves of the carcass obscured its true dimensions. It had no limbs to speak of, though one of the anatomists waved excitedly at shattered fins and shouted for us to come see. "Yes, yes, fins, any idiot can see that," grumbled Dieterich. "Of course it had to have fins, how else could it steer? What interests me more are these."

He nudged a pile of detritus with the end of his cane. Rotten wood gave under the pressure: old casks, long since broached. "Cargo, sir?" I said, hoping the possibility of commerce into Aaris might distract him from the carcass. "We may be able to figure out what they held."

"Bugger the casks, Charles. No, look at the bones." He knelt, cursing the snow and the idiocy of interesting specimens to be found at such a damnfool altitude, and tugged a few dirty-white disks free of ice and mummified flesh. "If these weren't obviously bones, I'd swear they were gears."

"I don't see how—" I began uneasily, but a shout further down the hillside drew his attention. Crumworth had found what would prove to be a delicate ratchet-and-flywheel system, hooked into the beast's spinal column. Abruptly the scientists shifted from a state of mild interest to feverish study, each producing more evidence from the carcass.

Made, some said, pointing to the clearly clockwork aspects of the skeleton. Born, said others, pointing to the harness and the undeniable organic nature of the carcass itself (the anatomist raising his voice the most on this subject). Myself, I considered the question irrelevant: the point was not whether the serpent had been hatched or constructed, but to what use it had been put and, more importantly, why it was here, on this side of the mountains from Aaris, outside the realm where it could conceivably have thrived.

It appeared to have carried a crew, though none of their remains were evident, and I could only assume they had survived the crash. I wondered whether they would have returned home over the mountains, or descended into the greater world – and if the latter, whether they would in time come home again. The thought was less comforting than I once had found it. I nudged a toothed segment with my foot and watched it tumble across the ice.

"What does your valet think, Dieterich?" one of the party called. "Since he's taking his time looking at it."

Dieterich paused. "Well, Charles? What do you think? Made or born?"

For a moment I considered answering "both" and confounding the lot of them, but such was neither the place of a valet nor for a man in my current situation. "I think," I said after a moment, "that there is a very dark cloud two points west of us. I suggest we return to the *Regina* before a storm acquaints us with how this creature died."

There was less argument after that, though Doctor Brackett and the anatomist insisted on bringing so many bones with us that the dinghy sagged dangerously. The results were presented over supper, and a detailed report made to Professora Lundqvist.

The Professora, of course, could not show emotion, but her tank bubbled in an agitated fashion, and her cortex bobbed within it. "I believe perhaps we have left the Sterling Pass closed for too long," she said at last, the phonograph flattening her voice into dry fact.

I privately agreed.

In the morning, Professora Lundqvist insisted on taking the bones to the captain, and borrowed me for the purpose. I piled the serpent's jawbone on her tank, secured the lesser fangs to her braking mechanism and accompanied her up to the lift. Lundqvist, lacking either an andropter or the torso around which to fasten one, could not venture to the open decks, and thus we were limited to the helm room.

We found the captain, a small blonde woman with the gait of a bear and the voice of an affronted Valkyrie, pulling lens after lens from the consoles and giving orders to the helmsman-automaton. "Captain, if I might have a word," the Professora said.

"We don't have time for more of your eggheads' interpersonal crises," the captain said without turning around. "I chose my crew carefully to avoid such disagreements; it's not my fault you didn't take the same care."

"It's not about that," the Professora said with a hint of asperity. "Charles, show her, please."

I hefted the jawbone and presented it to the captain. She glanced at it. "Hyborean air serpent. I've seen a few."

"Of this size?"

"Not much smaller. You can put that down, man; I'm not in any need of it." I did so and, perceiving I was so much furniture in this situation, edged closer to the lenses, trying to catch a glimpse of the pass below.

"The serpent appeared to be domesticated," Lundqvist insisted. "And there were gears among its bones, gears that may have grown there. As if it were some sort of hybrid."

The captain shrugged. "There're 'naut tales of serpents broke to harness and pirates said to use them to attack ships like the *Regina*. As for the gears ..." She turned and favored us both with one of her slow, vicious smiles that the crew so dreaded. "I expect that if we were to crash and the Aariscians to find *your* body, Professora, they'd be puzzling over whether you were some hybrid of glass and brains and formaldehyde."

"It's *not* formaldehyde," Lundqvist sniffed.

"And I'm not speaking hypothetically." The captain pointed to a lens behind the helmsman. A gray cliff face, cut into deep letters of ten different scripts, receded from our view. "We've just passed the graven warning."

I peered at the bow lenses, trying to get a better look at the warning itself. When I was a child, I'd heard stories (all disdained by my teachers) that the warning had been inscribed into the side of the mountains by an automaton the size of a house, etching the words with a gaze of fire. When I was older, my age-mates and I played at being the team engineered solely for the job of incising those letters, hanging from convenient walls and making what we thought were appropriate rock-shattering noises to match. After such tales, small wonder that my first view of the warning, some twenty years ago, had been so disappointing. Yet I could still recite by heart its prohibition against entering the valley.

The lenses, however, showed no sign of it. Instead, most displayed the same sight: a confection like matching wedding cakes on the mountainsides flanking the pass, the consequences for those who defied the graven warning.

Thousands of snub spouts pointed towards us, ranging from full cannon-bore to rifle-bore, the latter too small to see even with the ship's lenses. My eyes itched to adjust, and I felt a pang just under the straps of my andropter harness, where most men had hearts.

"Ah," said Lundqvist. "Well, it seems my timing is to its usual standard. I'll leave you to your evasive maneuvers . . ."

The first of the large guns swung to bear on the *Regina*. Excellent work, I acknowledged with a smaller pang; the automated emplacements were more reliable than most human sentries. "Climb, damn you, climb," the captain snarled at the helmsman. "We should already be at twice estimated safe distance."

". . . although I do hope you will keep our discovery in mind. Come, Charles."

"Oh, yes," the captain said over her shoulder. "I will most certainly keep the possibility of attack by serpent-riding air pirates in mind."

Jawbone slung over my shoulder, I accompanied the Professora back towards the lift. "Charming lass, our captain," she said. "Had I both a body and Sapphic inclinations, I do believe I'd be infatuated."

I glanced at her, trying to hide my smile. Full-bodied people often expressed surprise that acorporeals or otherwise mechanically augmented persons could harbor such desires. I, of course, had no such false impression, but preferred to maintain the illusion of one. "If you say so, Professora."

She laughed, a curious sound coming from her phonograph. "I do say so. Don't be a stick about it. Why—"

A concussion like the heavens' own timpani shook through the ship, followed by a sudden lurch to the right. The Professora's tank slammed first against a bulkhead, then, as the ship listed deeply, began to roll down the hall towards the empty lift shaft. The first impact had damaged her brakes, I realized, and now she faced the predicament of a glass tank plus high speed.

I did not think. Dropping the serpent's jawbone, I ran past the Professora and flung myself across the entry to the lift. I was fortunate in that the ship's tilt eased just before she struck me, and so I was not mown down completely. Instead I had to shift from blocking her passage to hauling on the tank's fittings as the ship reversed its pitch and the Professora threatened to slide back down the way we'd come.

A second concussion rumbled below us, this one more distant, and from down the hall I heard the captain's cursing take on a note of relief. For a brief and disorienting moment, I felt almost as if I'd seen a childhood hero fall; those guns were supposed to be perfect, impassable, and yet we'd sailed by. That their perfection would have meant my death was almost a secondary concern. I caught my breath, shaken by this strange mental dissonance.

"Thank you, Charles," Professora Lundqvist said at last. "I see why Dieterich prizes your services."

"I am rarely called upon to do this for him," I pointed out. "Shall I call the lift?"

At that point, the lift's motor started. It rose to reveal Colonel Dieterich. "Good God, Lundqvist, what happened? Are you quite done molesting my valet?"

Lundqvist chuckled. "Quite. Do give me a hand, Dieterich; I'm going to need some repairs."

Dinner that evening was hardly a silent affair, as we had reached the second of the three gun emplacements, and the constant barrage made the experience rather like dining in a tin drum during a hailstorm. As a result of the damage to her brakes, Professora Lundqvist's tank was now strapped to the closest bulkhead like a piece of luggage, which put her in a foul temper.

Unfortunately, every academic gathering, regardless of size, always has at least one member who is tone-deaf to the general mood of the evening, and tonight it was one of the anatomists. He had a theory, and a well-thought-out one it was, that a serpent of the kind we'd found could be grown in a thaumically infused tank – one similar to the Professora's, in fact. (The comparison amused only Colonel Dieterich, who teased Lundqvist about her stature as a Lamia of science.)

By the time I came to offer coffee and dessert, this anatomist had reached the point where, if our projector had not been packed, he would have been demanding to show slides. I paused at the door, reluctant to be even an accessory to such a discussion, but it was clear that the rest of the party was humoring him. Either encouraged or maddened by the lack of response, the anatomist continued his tirade as I poured, his voice rising to near-hysteria as he argued that what could be created for a serpent could be replicated on both larger and smaller scales, down to minuscule creatures and up to gargantua. Raising his cup, he predicted an Aariscian landscape of clockwork serpents, clockwork horses, clockwork cats and dogs, all living in a golden harmony devoid of human interference. I held my tongue.

"Oh, for the love of God," Crumworth finally burst out. "Has no one taught this idiot basic thaumic theory?"

"It could happen," insisted the anatomist. "Aaris does have the thaumic reservoirs; the ones on the pass, the ones in the Mittelgeist valley—"

"It doesn't work that way." Doctor Brackett stirred cream into her coffee until it turned beige. "Yes, there are the reservoirs under the gun emplacements and elsewhere. But they're the wrong kind. You couldn't use them to power something like an air serpent."

All very sound science, of course, and the Mobility/Sufficiency Paradox was the basis of at least one Society lecture. I turned away to hide my smile, and caught a glimpse of Dieterich deliberately tapping his pipe with the careful concentration that meant he was thinking about something else.

"It's like the difference between a geothermic station and a boiler," Crumworth went on. "One's much more powerful than the other, but it's no good if you're too far away from the steam for it to power anything."

One of the Terranocta astronomers at the far end of the table nodded. "Is why no one give a shit about Aaris."

Several members of the party immediately busied themselves with their coffee. It didn't take much to guess why, and as the person who'd handled most correspondence on this expedition, I didn't have to guess. After all, no one noticed a valet, especially not if he was there to take care of simple administrative tasks as well, and if some codes were childishly easy to crack, that was hardly my fault.

While the Royal Society's ostensible reason for the expedition was to offer the hand of friendship and scientific enquiry to their poor isolated cousins, any idiot could see that it was also to assay whether air power could bypass the gun emplacements. Thaumic reservoirs might be useless for certain engineering methods, but that hardly made them worthless, as the Royal Society well knew.

At least half of the party were spies (Brackett and Crumworth in particular, each from a rival faction in the same country, which explained their mutual antagonism and attraction), and I had my suspicions about the other half. To take the most cynical view, the ship was like any other diplomatic mission in that absolutely no one was as they seemed.

As if perceiving my thoughts, Dieterich glanced up and met my gaze, and the trace of a smile creased the corners of his eyes. Yes, he was an exception to that. As was the Professora, though all of us had our reasons for being here – Dieterich for the Society, Lundqvist for the prestige, the spies for their countries, the non-spies for curiosity. As for me, I'd been valet to Dieterich for ten years, in general service for ten before that, and I was homesick.

The sound of guns below us faded into the distance, as if the lull in our conversation had reached them as well. Two down, one to go, I counted. That was if the landscape hadn't changed, if my memories of the pass still held true.

The anatomist cleared his throat. "A serpent could—"

"Oh, do shut up, Klaus," Lundqvist snapped.

What happened the day after was pretty much inescapably my fault, in both the immediately personal and the greater sense. We had passed the third emplacement in the very early hours, and while that had been a near thing – scuttlebutt had it that the charts had been wrong, and only the helmsman's reflexes had saved us – the mood today was light, and the general consensus that we would clear the pass by noon.

I served breakfast to those of the party who were awake by eight (Dieterich, one of the astronomers, and the immobile, sulking Professora), then made my way up to the observation deck, where I had no business being. It was not the safest place, even with the security of an andropter across my shoulders, but I hoped to catch a glimpse of Aaris before our mission began in earnest. The thaumaturges whose duty it was to keep the *Regina* airborne were changing shift, each moving into his or her mudra in what an ignorant man might have called clockwork regularity. I exchanged nods with those leaving their shifts and headed for the open-air viewing at the bow.

The morning sun cast our shadow over the mountain slopes so that it seemed to leap ahead of us like a playful dog. A dozen ornamental lenses along the lower railing showed the landscape in picturesque facets. I risked adjusting my eyes to see ahead.

Something twinkled on the high peaks that marked the last mountains of the Sterling Pass, and I focused on it just as the captain's voice roared from the speaking tube. I had enough time to think, *Ah, so they* did *get my report on the Society's air capabilities,* before I realized that the guns had already fired.

The next few minutes were a confusion of pain and shrapnel. I was later to learn that the captain's quick thinking had kept the *Regina*'s dirigible sacs from being punctured, but at the cost of both the observation deck and the forward hold. What struck me at the time, though, was a chunk of werglass from the lenses, followed by a broken segment of railing that pinned me to the deck. Splinters ground under my fingers as I scrabbled at the planks, first to keep from falling through the wreckage, then out of sheer agony as the railing dug deeper. A detachment borne partly of my nature and partly of my years of service told me that there had been substantial but not crippling damage to my internals, and that the low insistent sound I heard was not mechanical but one of the thaumaturges sobbing quietly as she attempted to keep the *Regina* aloft.

There are times when detachment is not a virtue.

With a rattling gasp, I reached down and pulled the railing from my side. Only blood followed it, and I yanked the remnants of my coat over the gap in a futile effort to hide the wound.

The hatches from belowdecks slammed open. "Charles? Where's Charles?" roared Dieterich, and I flattened myself against the boards, hoping to remain unnoticed. "There you are, man! A stretcher, quickly!"

In short order I was bundled onto a stretcher and carried down to the lab, where Dieterich had me placed on the central table and my andropter unstrapped. The Society party's pleas to have me taken to the ship's sawbones were refuted with the quite accurate observation that he already had enough patients, and that furthermore no one was going to lay hands on Dieterich's valet but Dieterich himself. Crumworth and Brackett exchanged glances at this, coming as usual to the wrong conclusion.

Dieterich ordered everyone out, then turned on Professora Lundqvist, who observed the whole enterprise from her place by the door. "And you, too, madam!"

"It will take you a full half-hour to attach me to a more convenient bulkhead," she retorted. "Besides, I have more medical experience than you."

Dieterich muttered something about idiot disembodied brains thinking they knew everything, but he let her remain. "Hang on, Charles," he said. "We'll soon have you right as rain."

He paused, staring at the open wound in my side. I closed my eyes and cursed myself for ever having the idiot sense to join this expedition.

"Lundqvist," Dieterich said softly, "your phonograph, please."

The Professora acquiesced by extending the horn of her phonograph to the lock on the door and emitting a blast like an air-horn. Cries of dismay followed, and Dieterich kicked the door as he went to pull on sterile gloves. "No eavesdropping, you half-witted adjuncts!"

He returned to my side and with a set of long tweezers removed one of the many separate pains from my side. "Well," he said in a voice that barely carried to my ears, "do we need to discuss this?" And he held up the bloodied escapement that he had extracted.

I opened my eyes and stared at the ceiling. "I don't think so, sir," I finally managed. "I expect you can infer the meaning of clockwork in your valet."

Dieterich reached for his pipe, realized he didn't have it, and whuffled through his mustache instead. "That's loyalty for you, eh, Lundqvist?" he said over his shoulder. "Man even ascribes this discovery to me. Very flattering."

"I suspected a while ago," Lundqvist said quietly, turning her phonograph to face us. "When this expedition was first floated."

"Eight months past? Pah, woman, you only told me three weeks ago."

I stared at her. "How?" I choked, realizing a second later that I'd just confirmed her suspicions.

"Your transmissions to Aaris. I monitor the radio transmissions from the Society – never mind why, Dieterich, suffice it to say that I had reason – and after some time I noticed your additions. Very well encrypted, by the way; I'm still impressed."

The thought came to mind that had I been only a little slower yesterday, I might have been rid of one of those who knew my secret. But the Professora, as usual, gave no indication of what she was thinking, and Dieterich only set the escapement in a sterile tray and began a search for the anesthetic. "Merged," I said at last. "In Aaris we're called merged citizens."

"Citizens, hm? Looks like the sociology department's theory about rank anarchism in Aaris had some foundation." Dieterich extracted another chunk of shrapnel, this one three-fourths of a gear from my recording array, nestled just below what passed for my ribs. "Charles, if I describe what I'm seeing here, can you tell me how to repair you?"

"No. I mean, yes, I can, but—" I stopped, the full explanation of merged versus autonomous citizenry and the Aaris monarchic system trembling on my tongue. Had silence really been so intolerable these last years, so much that the first opportunity made me liable to spill all I knew? "If you extract the broken bits and stitch me up, I should be fine," I told him.

The *Regina* lurched beneath us. Dieterich caught the side of the table and cursed. "You're self-repairing?" he asked as he righted himself, the tone of fascinated enquiry one I knew well.

I couldn't say I was happy about being the focus of that interest. "No, I heal up. There's a difference. Sir."

"Thaumic reserves," the Professora murmured. "Infused throughout living tissue – I did wonder, when I heard about the serpent, whether it was possible. We may have to revise our definition of thaumic self-sufficiency. Dieterich, you've missed a piece."

"I haven't missed it; I was just about to get it." Carefully, with hands more accustomed to steam engines, Dieterich pulled the last damaged scrap from underneath my internal cage and began sealing the wound with hemostatic staples. Each felt like a dull thump against my side, muffled by the anesthetic. "Springs, even . . . do you know, Charles, if word gets out that I have a clockwork valet, I'm never going to live it down."

"I suspect I won't either, sir." I took the pad of gauze he handed me and pressed it into place while he unwound a length of burdock-bandage. The pain eased to a dull ache. "What will you tell the captain?"

"Nothing, I expect," Lundqvist said, and Dieterich grunted assent. "What did your Aariscian counterparts ask you to do on this voyage, Charles? From our continued existence, I presume your purpose here wasn't sabotage."

I closed my eyes again, then gritted my teeth and attempted to sit up. Dieterich had done a good job – as well he should, being an engineer of automata on a grander scale – and the edges no longer grated, though it was a toss-up whether I'd have recording capabilities again. *One more rivet in the vault of my espionage career*, I thought, and here was the last: "They didn't tell me anything," I croaked, eluding Dieterich's offer of help. "They haven't told me anything for fourteen years."

And there it was, the reason I'd come with Dieterich on this expedition when it would have been so easy to cry off: not just duty, not just homesickness, but the need to know what had happened in my absence. I covered my face, hiding how my eyes adjusted and readjusted, the lenses carrying away any trace of oily tears. I did not normally hide emotion, but I could at least hide this mechanical, Merged response.

The *Regina* shuddered again, followed by a screech that sent shivers up to my medulla. Dieterich glanced upwards, pity temporarily forgotten. "That wasn't a gun." He stripped off his gloves. "Lundqvist, keep an eye on him."

"And how am I to do that?" Lundqvist asked as Dieterich unbarred the door and ran out. "Charles? Charles, do not go up there, you are not fit to be on your feet."

I might not be fit, but both my employer and my home were now up there. I yanked Dieterich's greatcoat on over my bandages and followed.

We had passed the last of the guns, truly the last this time, and the sunlight on the decks burned clear and free of dust. Just past the bow of the *Regina*, I caught a glimpse of Aaris's green valleys.

Between that and us hovered a knot of silver, endlessly twisting. *Serpents*, I thought first, and then as the red-cloaked riders on each came clear, *Merged serpents*.

I had been a fool to think that the fourth set of guns would be the only addition to Aaris's defenses.

"Come no farther." A serpent glided closer with the motion of a water-snake, and its rider turned in place to address us through a megaphone. "None may enter the Aaris Valley on pain of death." Familiar words – the same that had been cut into the stone at the far end of the pass, to proclaim Aaris's isolation to the world. The same that I had memorized as a Merged child. Here they were spoken, recited in a voice that bounced off the mountains.

"We are a peaceful mission!" Dieterich yelled back, then cursed and repeated his words into the captain's annunciator.

The captain stalked past him to a locker by the helm. "You'd do better arguing with the graven warning," she muttered.

And indeed, the response was much the same as the cliff face would give: silent, anticipatory, the perpetual knotwork of the serpents writing a sigil of forbidding in the air. "Turn back now, or you will die," the spokesman finished. I focused, and focused again, trying to see his face.

Dieterich glanced at the captain. "If I tell you to turn back—"

"Can't. Not without going straight through them. The *Regina*'s got a shitty turning radius." The captain yanked her annunciator from his hands. "We demand safe passage!"

The rider did not answer, but raised one hand, and the pattern unraveled toward us. True to their nature, the serpents did not attack the dirigible sacs, but went for the shinier, more attractive target below: the ship itself. A gleaming gray ribbon spun past the remains of the observation deck, taking a substantial bite out of the woodwork and doing much greater damage with a last flail of its body in passing.

"Small arms! Small arms!" The captain produced a crank-gun from the locker and took aim at the closest serpent. She tossed a second gun to Dieterich, who cursed the air blue but took it, leveling it at the rider instead.

A second serpent undulated up to the very decks of the ship, knocking several 'nauts aside in its wake. Those who could handle a weapon ran to the lockers; I lurched out of the way, landed heavily on my wounded side, and cried out.

At the rail, Dieterich turned – and the last flick of the serpent's tail lashed out and knocked him over the railing.

There was no outcry; the chaos was too great, and Dieterich not the only one to go over the side. The snap of andropters opening added a new, percussive voice to the tumult.

I will not explain my actions then; certainly I knew that Dieterich's andropter was in good condition, as I had tended to it only that morning. Nor did I have any fear for him in particular. Nor was I so foolish as to forget that my own andropter was back in the lab with Lundqvist, and so any slip on my part inevitably meant a fall that would not just kill me but reduce me to a splash on the rocks below. Still, some remnant of instinct propelled me forward despite better sense and burgeoning pain, and I ran to the railing.

The serpent whose rider Dieterich had pulverized writhed near the bow, devoid of instructions and therefore meaning. I leapt onto the railing, crouched briefly to secure my balance, and flung myself at the beast, trusting in my Merged brain to calculate the proper angle.

I caught the first set of fins and was dragged alongside the ship, long enough for me to force a hand into the soft tissue behind the fin and fumble about, searching for the controls that had to be there. Merged pack animals had always had secondary controls near their braincases; surely this part of the design would not have changed.

It had not. With one hand "plugged" into the serpent's controls and one clinging to its fin, I wrenched the beast away from its attack on the *Regina* and followed the sound of Dieterich swearing at his andropter. It had opened enough to keep him from plummeting to his death but had the unfortunate side effect of wafting him directly toward the mouth of another serpent.

I wrenched my serpent into a helical dive, wrapped my legs around the closest fin and stretched my arm out as we coasted past. My serpent smashed through the silk and framework of Dieterich's andropter, and I caught Dieterich himself by the harness as the jolt briefly tossed him aside. My arm went numb with the shock, and the staples holding my wound shut tore apart, but it was enough: I used Dieterich's momentum to swing him aboard, onto the serpent's flat head and out of danger.

Dieterich stared blankly at the sky for a moment, apparently having difficulty understanding that he was still alive. "Good show, Charles!" he croaked after a moment. "Very good show. You've got a knack for this."

I kept hold of his harness and didn't answer. One slip, I thought, one simple yank on the harness and I'd have disposed of half the people who knew my Aariscian nature. And the only other led a fragile existence in an easily broken tank . . .

It didn't matter. Or it would have mattered, in another world, one where I was actually the spy I'd been built to be. I clung to the serpent's head and whispered to it as I worked the controls, blood seeping through the bandage and slicking my side. "Forward. Take me to Aaris. Please."

Pleading, as the captain had said, had no effect, but direction was easy enough to communicate and the serpent's reflexes simple to control. We veered away from the knot of gunfire and scales and out of the smoke, toward the valley. None of the other serpents followed. Dieterich, still pinned in place by the remnants of his andropter, craned his neck around. "What is it? The battle's over there – damn it, Charles, I did say I'd keep a secret. You know I'm a man of my word, now take me back!"

I barely heard him. Below me were the green fields of Aaris as I remembered them, the mesh of white roads stretching from the Mittelgeist hills into the fragments of arable land that were so assiduously tended, the clutter of houses, even the sheen of Lake Varno where I was born, where I was decanted, where I swore citizenship . . .

The serpent's hide below me rippled, and I followed it with a shiver of my own. No. Not as I remembered. The roads, long irregular from necessity, had been smoothed out into a patterned web, and the hills and rivers that had blocked them smoothed away into similarly perfect shapes. I adjusted my eyes again and again, as if a more magnified landscape would show not just what had happened but why. Nothing but the same iterated regularity; nothing of what I remembered as home.

I shook my head and shifted my eyes back to their normal state, then leaned back, trying to take in the whole valley. My breath caught with a crackle.

It was as if I gazed upon a great green clock, a hybrid land that was not just land nor automata but both. Every part of the landscape bore a design I knew from study of my own inner workings. The slow motion of it – even the patterns of glaciers sliding down the mountains – communicated a vast unfathomable purpose. A purpose of which I was no longer a part.

And in the fields and villages and kennels and stalls, eyes all like mine, adjusting as they looked up, lenses shifting to see one of their own above them. No full automata. No full humans. Only the same Merged calm on every visage.

I shuddered, viscerally aware of the hole in my side, of the mess of blood and bandages so at odds with the careful, clean lines of this new Aaris. "Home," I whispered. "Home. Please."

The serpent, either wiser than I or interpreting the indecision of my hands, curved into a wide arc. I heard Dieterich gasp as we turned away, but I did not turn to see his reaction. Instead I gazed ahead, to where the *Regina*, spilling smoke and the telltale glitter of lost thaumic power, was limping away back down the pass. Its decks were a flutter of rescued andropters and wreckage, but though the mass of serpents parted to let their brother through, it did not fire upon us as I guided my serpent back to the ship.

For the first time in twenty years, I did not have to make the tea. Dieterich brought a tray down to the remains of the observation deck, where the Professora and I sat in silent contemplation of the receding Sterling Pass. Below us guns boomed, unaware that they had failed in their work of keeping us out but that their greater mission had succeeded. I got up from my place on the deck (the benches having been used for temporary hull patches), but Dieterich waved me back to my seat.

He poured two cups, then tipped the contents of a third into the Professora's nutrient filter. She murmured thanks, and I took the offered cup gratefully.

"You needn't worry," Dieterich said after a moment, "about the, hm, shrapnel I extracted. I disposed of it among the bits we took from that first dratted serpent's carcass."

One set of gears in among the other. Fitting. "Thank you, sir."

"You're welcome. Don't let that sort of thing happen again, hm?" He gave me a searching look, but whatever doubts he'd harbored had been erased when I brought us both back to the *Regina*'s splintered decks. "Good man," he said, drained his tea, and returned to the depths of the ship.

I took a sip of my tea. He'd made it well. "How much time do you think we have?" Lundqvist asked softly.

I attempted a shrug, winced, and settled for shaking my head. "There's no indication that Aaris intends to undo its isolation. They may be content to stay in the valley."

"You weren't," she pointed out.

"No." I gazed back into the smoky pass, thinking of the great clockwork of the valley, the machine that it ran, of serpents on the wrong side of the mountains and lensed eyes looking back at me. "Ten years, perhaps. Five if we're unlucky."

The Professora was silent, though the constant hiss from her phonograph resembled a slow exhalation. "Well. We'll just have to hope we're lucky."

Five years. I'd been in service for twenty; perhaps a different service was needed for the coming five. I got to my feet, glanced behind me at the pass, and began setting the cups back on the tea-tray.

"Yes. We'll hope," I said. "More tea?"

The Celebrated Carousel of the Margravine of Blois

Megan Arkenberg

Dear Madame,

My sincerest apologies for my inexcusable delay in responding to your enquiry after the celebrated carousel of the Margravine of Blois. The truth is – and I write this with utmost regret – that the reports responsible for so much distress in your admirable person are accurate in every respect. I myself bore witness to the destruction of that most miraculous clockwork, and what remains – a handful of silver gears, and a pair of bay horses with the most phenomenally lifelike coloring and expression – allows only for positive identification.

As for the events that permitted such a wrenching tragedy (your words, madame, but I find them wonderfully apt) to occur, I enclose some pages which I wrote from the seventeenth of September to the fourteenth of October last year, in faith that all will be clarified. In this, madame, as in all things, I hope to show myself to be

Your most Humble and Obedient Servant,
Antoine Aristide de Saint-Pierre

17 September

The lady Porphyrogene's house is called Summerfall, and it stands at the end of a long white drive lined with plane trees and elm. To the east, bare hills roll up to meet the lowering autumn clouds; to the west, the land slopes sharply to the sea, where clear waves fold over reddish weeds and palely colored stones – lavender, glass-green, dogwood-blossom pink. The front lawn is left barren, the better to show Summerfall's magnificent façade. In back are the gardens, and in the center of the gardens, the carousel of the Margravine of Blois.

"Most of them want to see that first," Porphyrogene said the moment I stepped down from my carriage. She took up my bags, two in each hand, and headed for the central stair. "I trust *your* tastes are not so common, M'sieur Saint-Pierre."

"No," I said, hardly sure what I was agreeing to. I have concluded, over the full three hours of our acquaintance, that this is quite common with Porphyrogene. She is a smaller woman than her letters led me to expect, with whitening hair and skin the color of cream-clotted coffee. I must confess, I anticipated a woman of greater beauty, familiar as I am with my hostess's many amorous conquests. Apparently, Porphyrogene's expectations were the reverse.

"You're rather handsome, for a professor," she said. "I suppose some pretty, dithering little fiancée will be sending you love letters to interrupt your work?"

"Have no fear on that account, madame. I was widowed last April."

"Oh." She said it quite flatly, and gave me an odd look over her shoulder. "My condolences, m'sieur."

Presently, we reached my apartment – a series of six rooms at the top of the eastern wing, damp-smelling and paneled in sage-colored wood. My bedroom, library and private parlor all overlook the sea. By ingenious design, or my own imagination, the faux balconies covering the windows are like cast-iron bars.

"You will be spending most of your time alone," Porphyrogene said. "Business keeps me outside the house. Perhaps you would prefer to take your dinner here?"

"Yes," I said, "if that can be arranged."

"It can." She paused for a moment, one hand on her hip, the other tucking a white curl behind her ear. "I would prefer it, m'sieur, if you left the north wing to itself. The rest of Summerfall is yours to investigate. If you need anything . . ." She pointed to a frayed cord hanging over the bedside table. "Ring for Jean-Baptiste."

Such is the living mistress of Summerfall. Tonight, I expect, I shall be introduced to its ghosts.

18 September

I found no ghosts last night, regrettably, and sleep was not much more in evidence. This house must have a thousand clocks in it; I've counted over a dozen in my own apartments, chiming and sending out miniature automata processions on every hour. I know little enough of the Clockmaker's art, but judging from the uniform and uncanny realism in the tiny figures, I believe they were all crafted by the same hand.

And while my pen dwells on uncanny uniformity: it is my conclusion (from an admittedly hasty collection of data) that every room in Summerfall has at least one portrait of the same woman in red. Her features are very distinct: dark skin, pillowy lips painted scarlet, two severely straight eyebrows, of which the left is always raised a fraction of an inch higher than the right. I am sure this woman is no relative of Porphyrogene – nor does it seem likely she is a past lover, as my hostess is not the sort to cling sentimentally to old mementos.

At breakfast this morning, I was introduced to the shadowy figure of Porphyrogene's valet, Jean-Baptiste. He is a man as gray as his livery, and he moves with an unpleasantly mouse-like scurry.

"Where is Porphyrogene?" I asked, pushing a reluctant clump of dry eggs around on my plate.

"Madame is occupied in the gardens today."

"Enjoying the last flowers of the season, I expect?"

"Perhaps. I couldn't say."

My eggs, deeply dissatisfied with their treatment at the tines of my fork, promptly made their dissatisfaction known by plopping onto the parlor rug. I dropped my fork in surrender. "Would it be possible for me to join her?" I asked – purely for the sake of politeness, as I could not imagine permission being denied.

"Oh, no, monsieur," Jean-Baptiste said. The weather, he intimated – and it truly is horrendously gray and chill – might affect monsieur's mood in undesirable ways, and wouldn't monsieur rather spend such a dreary day before a roaring fire in monsieur's well-apportioned library?

In truth, he sounded much like Violeta's old maidservant – though Jean-Baptiste, at least, does not seem worried that I am going to walk purposefully into the ocean. Whether such a possibility continues, nearly a year and a half after I first voiced the intention, I cannot say. Though I do know this: it is good to be hunting again, good to be seeking a ghost whose tragedy has nothing to do with mine.

18 September, later
I think Jean-Baptiste is right, and the miserable weather is exerting an unpleasant influence on my nerves. I woke moments ago from a most disconcerting dream.

I was standing on a beach of gray stones, and as each wave rolled in it stained the rocks a different hue – powder-pink and eggshell-blue, cream-yellow and sage-green. The water felt warm against my feet, over my ankles and up to my knees. I bent and spread my fingers in the prickling foam.

Suddenly, I caught Violeta's scent mingling with the brine – the smell of lavender soap, the sickly-sweet tinge of sweat. I looked up from the stones – they were dark colors now, crimson and cobalt and golden as egg-yolks – and turned to my wife, my heart pounding beneath my tongue.

The woman beside me was not Violeta. Her black skin, her red lips and gown, her left eyebrow lifted in vague amusement . . . it was the woman from the portraits.

I woke a moment later to the chiming of a hundred clocks.

20 September
Porphyrogene took her dinner with me yesterday afternoon. She must have come in from the gardens without stopping to dress, as her hair and gown were positively soaked.

"Have you found anything yet?" she asked. It would be difficult to overemphasize the impatience in her voice; it was as though her sleeve had caught fire, and she was asking after a pitcher of water. "Sounds, apparitions, cold spots in the doorways?"

"Nothing of that variety, no." I felt unaccountably reluctant to mention my dream of Violeta. We sat for a few minutes in silence, before the clock on the table between us began to chime four. "Who is the woman in the portraits?"

Porphyrogene looked faintly startled as she glanced at the nearest specimen, hanging in an oval frame between the parlor windows. "She was the Margravine of Blois," she said, and took a slow sip of champagne.

"Was? The Margravine of Blois is dead?"

She chuckled softly over the rim of her glass, but her eyes looked pained. "Yes, rather." A pause. "She died six years ago – here, actually."

"How?"

"I didn't murder her, m'sieur, if that's what you're implying." Her fingers drummed on the glass's stem. "That's not to say I didn't want to. Perhaps you are too young to remember, but it was quite a scandal when she left me twelve years ago. A popular rhyme or two was made about it – they say I still keep the blankets turned down on her side of the bed, waiting for her to come home."

"But she *did* come home." I leaned back in my chair, gazing at the portrait. "If she left you twelve years ago, why did she come back six years later to die?"

Porphyrogene sighed – deeply, from her chest. "Well, I'm sure it wasn't to see me again. Perhaps she wanted to be near the carousel."

"And what is so special about the carousel?"

Porphyrogene shook her head. "Everything."

23 September

Jean-Baptiste brought breakfast to my rooms this morning – a small blessing, as what little sleep I can afford is soured with unsettling dreams, and by dawn I am in no shape to navigate Summerfall alone. In addition to its usual burden of cold coffee and overcooked eggs, the tray carried four or five keys on an iron ring. They were old work, plain but sturdy, with a faint shield-shaped impression on the bows that may have been Porphyrogene's coat-of-arms.

"For the library, monsieur," Jean-Baptiste said, indicating the largest of the keys.

I glanced at the door in the back of my parlor, eyebrows raised enquiringly.

"No, monsieur. The library in the north wing." He held up a delicate hand to forestall my protestations. "Madame told me to offer. She thinks it will allow your investigations to . . . progress."

How delightful, I thought sourly – as if it were due to some intellectual ineptitude on my part that Summerfall's ghost had failed to manifest. I'd have her know, in seven years of investigations I had never once lacked results. Still, curiosity always has gotten the better of me; I took the key with profuse thanks, finished my breakfast, and went down to the north wing just as the clocks in the corridor were chiming nine.

By sheer volume, the north wing must have more clockwork than the rest of Summerfall combined – a peculiarity that does not, most fortunately, continue into the library itself. It is a very handsome set of chambers, spreading over three stories and a charming mezzanine. Pale walnut shelves, naturally, take up most of the walls, though the mezzanine has seven long windows of colored glass, and a few panels near the fireplaces are covered with creamy damask. Desks, armchairs and pink plush couches are scattered throughout.

One room in particular captured my interest. It is, I believe, the farthest north in Summerfall, and one massive window would look out over the gardens if I could successfully manhandle its brocade curtain aside. The desks were lost beneath an avalanche of books which bore no conceivable relationship to each other – the collected romances of Roland, an anonymous sheaf of ballads, Christopher of Cloud's celebrated treatise on clockwork. I paused on finding this last, as it lay open to a page with innumerable notes scrawled in the margins.

Here is what I have managed to copy of the page's text:

It is a frequently criticized aspect of the automatic arts that only the smallest clockworks are self-perpetrating, that is, may continue their so-called lives without their Maker's interference. [Here, Monsieur Cloud makes a digression on the religious parallels evident in this circumstance.] *To this, we reply that no other state could be desired. What Clockmaker fails to remember the case of Malory Gerard, whose automata king went mad one day, escaped the music box for which he had been built, and proceeded to do battle with Monsieur Gerard's collection of exotic songbirds? (This breed of insanity, incidentally, seems most common with automata whose tasks are ceaseless and repetitive. The jaquemarts of an actual clock have fifty-nine minutes between each hourly procession in which to stabilize, whereas Madame Gerard's king waltzed constantly to the same facile tune.) While this* anecdote is rather amusing, it takes little imagination to provoke a shudder at the thought of what a life-sized rampaging automata might do to his erstwhile masters.

Most of the scribbled notes were illegible, but I could make out two or three: *patronizing idiot – Malory Gerard's taste in music would drive anyone mad – hold the bloody thing in place and you wouldn't have this problem!* The handwriting was distinctive, not for its illegibility, but for the qualities that made it illegible: a hard leftward slant, trailing loops in its 'y's and 'q's, an overall suggestion of hastiness that came not from negligence, but from an intelligence too avid to work slowly. It should come as no surprise, then, that when on another pile I found an entire folio volume filled with the handwriting of the Margravine of Blois, I took it back to my rooms for further study.

Here is the title, embossed on crimson leather binding in a heavy copperplate:

A Catalogue of the Works of the Celebrated Margravine of Blois, compiled by Herself in the house called Summerfall.

Two entries in particular caught my attention. I reproduce them here, with their accompanying marginalia:

The Clock of the Bride of Death is kept in Summerfall's guest apartments at the top of the eastern wing. [My apartments – from the following description, I gather this is the clock by my dressing table whose incessant humming disturbs my sleep.] *It is the most populous of the house's clocks, with over fifty individual automata, and the only one set to music – the late Évariste of Blois's 'Waltz for Dead Lover'. The key figures are as follows: the skeleton dancers, one couple for every hour; Death with his mask and violin; the Bride, who emerges at midnight with a shower of miniature rose petals; and Évariste, who leads each reprisal of the waltz from his perch at the stroke of twelve.*

[The last segment is crossed out, and this penciled in above it: *Évariste insisted on revising his waltz with each reprisal. He has been allowed to retire to the Clock of Waters in the music room.*]

The other entry covers the last pages of the catalogue.

The Celebrated Carousel of the Margravine of Blois contains four and twenty automata, none less than twelve hands tall. Beginning with the pair of blood bays and circling left, they are: the bays, Hesperus and Phosphorus; Prometheus the black bear; the Cockatrice, the Phoenix, the Chimera, the Sphinx and the Manticore; Terpsichore the zebra, Ambrosias the elephant, Gamaliel the lion, Caesar the panther; the three white horses of the moon, named Artemis and Luna and Selene; the three black horses of the sun, named Apollo and Helios and Sol; the dragons, Boreas and Ariel; Lucien the serpent, Zephyr the eagle, Clytemnestra the ox and Antigone the silver dolphin.

[In fainter ink near the bottom of the page: *Clytemnestra does not like the current Duke of Cloud. Gamaliel will only carry virgins if their lovers are riding Caesar, and Caesar will not carry men over forty who wear too much musk. Phosphorus will suffer no mistress but my own – the lady Porphyrogene.*]

Of the page's final bit of marginalia, I can only read the name *Hesperus*, and a word that might be *killed*.

27 September

The weather has become unbearable – the lightning burns the sky without pause, the thunder's roll is as constant as the sea's – and today I have found the first evidence of Summerfall's ghosts.

One manifestation I am quite familiar with, and it points – however unsteadily – to the ghost's identity. No matter how many times I return the Margravine of Blois's catalogue to its place on the shelf, it appears on a desk the next morning, always open to the entry on the carousel. This has happened now four days consecutively, and I can find no natural cause. (Of course, Jean-Baptiste will not hear of me spending the night in the library.)

The other circumstance is subtle, so that I hesitate to mention it at all, yet I have gathered enough incidental evidence to be certain that something is in fact taking place. The clocks of the Margravine of Blois are *dying*.

Having studied the Margravine's catalogue on the night of the twenty-third, I took an inventory of the thirteen clocks in my apartment. That night, all of them seemed to operate passably; but on the twenty-fourth, the Clock of Ravens was missing three of its birds. The next night, the prince from the Clock of the Seventh Slumber would not awaken, no matter how many times his clockwork princess kissed him; and yesterday evening, Death laid down his violin and refused to play. I repeat that I know little of the Clockmaker's art, and moreover, I do not know if such occurrences as these have been frequent in the past, or if this is a new development. I shall have to read more of Monsieur Cloud before I draw any conclusions.

Strangely, while I am glad to have made some progress in my investigations, these discoveries do not relieve the restlessness that has plagued me for days. When I think of a ghost in Summerfall, I feel – dare I say it? – a sort of vague and simmering envy.

Why should Porphyrogene be haunted by the woman she loved?

Why should I *not* be?

28 September

Dinner with Porphyrogene again. Whatever her business is outside of Summerfall, the rain must keep her from it. She was terribly restless all afternoon, turning every surface beneath her fingertips into an impromptu and poorly tuned pianoforte.

My news about the Margravine's catalogue did not impress her – "We all have our lullabies, don't we, m'sieur?" was her cryptic response – but my report on the clocks seemed to plunge her into melancholy.

"No," she said in response to my enquiry, "it is not new, though it seems to be accelerating. How terrible . . ." She closed her eyes and laid a hand across the lids. "Do you miss your wife, M'sieur Saint-Pierre?"

I literally choked on my wine. "Madame, you may as well ask if I breathe."

"She doesn't haunt you, then?"

"No," I said, remembering my thoughts from last night. "Forgive me, but I don't think—"

"Do you know that the carousel is broken? It hasn't worked in twelve years." She lifted her hand from her eyes. "It's a terrible thought, isn't it, M'sieur Saint-Pierre, that all their work dies with them?"

Involuntarily, I shuddered.

"There are days you wish, don't you, that you had something of hers – a letter, a lock of hair – something you could hold and say, *this is her*. This exists because she did." Porphyrogene stood and began pacing between the parlor windows. "The rhymes didn't lie entirely, you know. I did leave her blankets turned down. As if *that* was all it would take to keep her here."

Keep her here, she said – not *bring her back*. There was a brief silence. I said, quite softly, "I understand."

She turned to me, and I felt my face heating. "Violeta could have moved the world," I said. "When she died, I could only watch as it rolled back into place."

"The cruelest things on earth," Porphyrogene said, "are that it never changes and it never stops. Grief, M'sieur Saint-Pierre, is a carousel. You get on and you ride as fast and as hard as you can, but it only brings you back to where you started."

We finished the meal in silence. It must have been clear from my eyes, as I know it was clear from hers, that neither of us was whom the other wanted to see across the table.

30 September
That dream again. I am standing on the shore as the sea rolls in, staining the bleached stones with all the colors of a jewel box. Suddenly, the smell of lavender and fever. I turn and see the Margravine of Blois.

This time, I reach for her. Her face becomes Violeta's the moment before it slips through my fingers like foam.

1 October
I have found the bedroom of the Margravine of Blois.

It is at the end of a long corridor in the north wing, which I discovered by means of a concealed passage behind one of the library shelves. I cannot say the existence of the passage surprises me very much. From what I have seen of Summerfall, and of Jean-Baptiste's miraculous powers of apparition, I'd expected to encounter one sooner or later. On emerging behind a standing clock of prodigious size, I had planned merely to look around, perhaps trying the keys from Porphyrogene's ring; but upon seeing in one room the distinctive handwriting of the Margravine of Blois, I abandoned caution and went to investigate.

The writing, incidentally, which arches over the bed and would normally be hidden by the curtains, quotes only a line of poetry: *Here I took my rest; my joy came in other places*. I cannot imagine why, as the chamber itself seems cheerful – enough, I was going to say, but truly a great deal more than that. The walls and bedclothes are covered in golden silk, painted, in the case of the former, with emerald branches that serve as perches for dozens of painted birds. A portrait over the dressing table shows Porphyrogene seated on a garden bench, the Margravine of Blois kneeling at her feet. There is only one clock in the room, standing on a window ledge, its hands formed by a pair of racing blood bays.

As I came closer, I saw that there was a slip of paper wedged into the door of the pendulum box, yellowed and ratty, as though it had been taken out and stuffed back in many times – more times, indeed, than its contents seem to warrant. Here they are, transcribed from the writing of the Margravine of Blois:

13 April
Ha! You see, madame, that I bow as always to my lady's request. Though your sad little jest alone could not tease laughter from these lips, your command shall be to me as God's.

19 April
Another, my love? Are all your riddles so miserable? Pray bring something more cheerful, lest I am forced to drastic measures to steal a smile from your sweet mouth.

24 April
I am forced to reply in kind: what goes on scales in the morning, on feathers at noon, and sleeps at the end of the day on flesh and bone?

24 April
A ring, madame: the jeweler's scale when it is made, to the down box in which I purchased it (at no small cost, I might add), to my lady's finger, if she is clever enough to undo the knot with which it is bound to Phosphorus's neck!

And indeed, the miniature bay on the hour hand still wears a silver ring. Though tempted, I did not try the knot.

2 October
I had been hesitant to pull the golden cord, but curiosity, as always, had finally gotten the better of me. For days I had pondered a question to which, it seemed to me, Jean-Baptiste would know the answer.

"Why did she ask me to come here?"

He blinked, his large pale eyes moving slowly down and up. "Monsieur?"

"Be honest, Jean-Baptiste – you know there is no ghost in Summerfall. Certainly no ghost of the Margravine of Blois."

He nodded slowly. "I suspected so, monsieur. She was not the sort to linger. I myself have seen nothing – nothing but the clocks, and while they are haunting enough in their own way, I daresay Monsieur Christopher of Cloud could put them in their place."

It occurred to me to wonder how familiar a servant could be with Monsieur Cloud, but I let it pass. There is no denying that the Margravine of Blois was a genius Clockmaker; perhaps it permeated her conversation, even with her lover's valet.

Jean-Baptiste was watching warily as I paced the room. "Monsieur? Will that be all?"

"No," I said. "I know Porphyrogene is no fool. What did she expect to gain from me, if this place isn't haunted?"

"Perhaps she *wants* to be haunted, monsieur."

It took every ounce of self-control I possess to limit my reaction to a raised eyebrow.

"I beg your pardon, monsieur." He waited until I gestured for him to go on. "Porphyrogene is not grieving for the Margravine of Blois. It seems to me she cried all her tears for the woman twelve years ago. But for the artist, the builder of the carousel? That is a hard thing to let die."

"I suppose it is," I said. And weak fool that I am, I began to cry.

2 October, later

In the northernmost room of the library, there is a book by the Margravine of Blois called *Clockwork Souls*. I have always thought it was a silly concern, and a quintessentially artistic one – what happens to automata after they die? In all probability, they are simply gone, vanished as if they never were. With all my experience, I have never met a clockwork ghost.

Nor have I met the ghost of the Margravine of Blois. Does this mean that she, too, is simply gone? And even her clockwork is vanishing – the carousel is broken, the clocks are dying or dead.

Isn't it a terrible thought, that all their work dies with them?

And here is a worse thought:

The night Violeta died, I climbed up to the rain-slick roof and looked up at the sky. One by one, the heavy clouds were clearing and the stars emerging from the darkness. In a feverish fantasy, I imagined that there had been a time, when the world was young, that stars filled the sky – made it a solid sheet of light arching over the earth. But one by one, the stars began to die – and Man, having a poor memory, began to believe that the sky had always been black.

I am a widower. I am the black spot left in the sky when a star has guttered out.

9 October

For a week, I have been gone with fever. I need not detail my dreams, save to say that they were the haunting grounds for more than one ghost. I woke this morning to find Porphyrogene standing over me, a moist cloth in one hand and a look of profound unease on her face.

"You were calling for Violeta," was all she said.

I flopped back on my pillows, and found myself staring at the portrait of the Margravine of Blois hung over my head.

"Why did she leave?" I asked.

Porphyrogene followed my gaze, her lips pressed thin. "An accident," she said finally. "On the carousel. The simple fact, M'sieur Saint-Pierre, is that all clockwork goes mad eventually, and she built that carousel too big. We thought it was going to be Phosphorus first – he was such a violent, crazy thing, and wouldn't be tame for anyone but me – but it wasn't. It was his brother."

She chaffed her wrists, heedless of the cloth in her hand. "Hesperus was carrying Évariste of Blois – the Margravine's cousin, son of the famous composer. The carousel had stopped, and the Margravine was helping me down from Phosphorus's saddle. Hesperus reared suddenly. She managed to roll out from under his hooves, but Évariste fell."

"Was he . . . ?"

"Trampled. The corpse was unrecognizable." Porphyrogene looked down at her hands, then swiftly dabbed at my forehead with the damp cloth, as if that glance had brought it back to her mind. "I begged her to stay, of course. It was a nasty scene all around. She said Hesperus's madness had been a much-needed awakening, showing how enslaved she had become to me – a gelding, like Phosphorus when I held his reins. Those were the last words she spoke to me. She did something to the carousel before she left, and it hasn't worked since."

"You said she died here – because of the carousel."

"I think . . ." Porphyrogene frowned, biting her lip. "I think she wanted to reawaken it. She was terribly sick by then – consumption – she knew she was dying. I think she wanted to leave something behind."

I sat up. It was a slow, laborious process, and it left the room buzzing around me like a swarm of bees. "Why is it so hard," I asked when I'd caught my breath, "to believe she came back for you?"

Porphyrogene shook her head, smiling or grimacing.

"I'm serious. Why does it have to be the carousel – some unfinished business, left behind for you?"

"I don't know what you're talking about. You should get some rest, M'sieur Saint-Pierre, after your fever . . ."

"I want to be haunted, Porphyrogene." She looked at me as if I had gone mad – as if I were about to trample something, or go battling songbirds. "I told you that Violeta doesn't haunt me, and it's true. Horribly, unbearably true. When I think of everything she was, the quick ripostes over dinner, the magnificent letters she wrote when we were away from each other, her way with languages . . . it makes me sick. All of it is gone." I felt a moistness on my lip, and licked it away, thinking it was sweat; but it tasted sweet, the briny sweetness of tears. "Anything that could remain of her, I would take. A disembodied footfall, a slip of mist, a cool breeze in the night. A book that could not stay shut. And if I thought here was a man who could draw ghosts to a house—"

"How dare you," Porphyrogene interrupted, "compare your flippant little wife to the Margravine of Blois?"

"You're trying to build a ghost, Porphyrogene. You want to be haunted."

She flung the cloth at me and ran from the room.

10 October

All this time, she has been going down to the carousel.

It explains the persistent reopening of the Margravine's catalogue, and Jean-Baptiste's familiarity with Christopher of

Cloud – what valet, after all, is not familiar with his mistress's reading? For six years, perhaps longer, she has been trying to reawaken the carousel of the Margravine of Blois.

The rain let up sometime over the seven days of my sickness, and I went down this afternoon to the gardens. Years of neglect have left them as barren and white as salt flats. In the center of the desolation, as red and black and golden as the Margravine herself, is the carousel and its twenty-four clockworks. Even from a distance, I could see their characters from their poses and expressions: clever Antigone, balanced nearly on her tail, and graceful Ambrosias with his trunk held high, and proud Clytemnestra striding firmly across the metal stage. Closest to me, the bays Phosphorus and Hesperus lay peaceful and dormant on folded legs.

I did not stay long, as I knew Porphyrogene would be coming down shortly. But I will confess, there is something terribly captivating about the carousel. When I lay my hand against Phosphorus's flank, it felt as warm as living flesh – or as warm as metal that living hands had touched.

13 October

This shall be my last night in Summerfall. As I said to Jean-Baptiste, there is no sense in me staying on when the only ghosts are made of metal.

"I understand, monsieur," he said, then looked at me oddly. "I know she has done little to show it, but the lady Porphyrogene is grateful that you came. It was good to have this bed filled again, if you understand me."

"I beg your pardon!" I exclaimed, leaping up from the furniture in question.

"That bed, monsieur. It was Porphyrogene's, while the Margravine of Blois lived in Summerfall."

"The very bed whose blankets poets satired, I don't wonder." Weariness came over me then, and I leaned heavily against the wall. "You know, Jean-Baptiste, I wish I had followed Porphyrogene's example. The last thing my wife touched was a silk blanket, to pull it closer around her. I wish I had never moved that blanket, so that *something* could remain as Violeta had put it."

"Ah," Jean-Baptiste said, eyeing the bed pensively. "But then where would monsieur have slept?"

14 October, early morning

In my dream, Violeta is riding the carousel of the Margravine of Blois. I am watching her from the gravel walkway, my heart pounding in my throat, and she waves each time she passes me, standing gracefully in the blood bay's stirrups.

But something is wrong. With each cycle, her color drains a little more. Soon she is nothing but a streak of white, like a tearstain... and then she is gone.

Still, the carousel turns.

14 October

I found Porphyrogene out in the gardens before dawn. She had a sheaf of papers spread across Clytemnestra's broad back, and a stack of tools piled at her feet. I crossed the gravel walkway in two strides and leapt onto the carousel stage with a reverberant clang.

"What are you doing here?" Porphyrogene snapped, not looking up from her book. From where I stood, I could see that the page was rimmed with slanted marginalia. I came up on the other side of the ox and flipped the treatise closed.

"I have a gift for you," I said, and when Porphyrogene looked up at me, I held out a silver ring in the palm of my hand.

The change in her was sudden and terrible. Her eyes widened, her lips pressed thin and pale, the long bridge of her nose tightened into a web of wrinkles. "How dare you!" she said, snatching the ring from my hand. "How—"

"How dare I what, Porphyrogene? She bought that ring for your finger, not for a clockwork horse."

"I thought you of all people would understand." Her fingers closed into a fist around the ring, as though she could crush it. "What harm could there be in keeping everything the way it was, before . . . ?"

"Are you happy, Porphyrogene?" I interrupted.

She shook her head, not looking at me. "How can you even ask?"

I circled around Clytemnestra, past Antigone's silver tail, and crouched down by Hesperus's head, where the pile of tools gleamed. A steel pike lay across the top, its slender tip designed to pry open the nearly seamless clockwork. I took it in my hand, feeling its cool weight up through my arm like the trail of a phantom finger.

"There are three things in the world you can never change," I said. Turning from Hesperus's wild eyes, I found myself facing the paper-thin membrane of Antigone's tail. "The first is that the Margravine of Blois *lived*."

Swiftly, before Porphyrogene could stop me, I drove the spike through the silver dolphin.

"No!" Porphyrogene shouted, but I continued over her protest.

"She *lived*, she built this carousel and a thousand brilliant clocks besides, and she laughed at your riddles because you told her to. She loved color and she loved this house and she loved you." I punctuated each phrase with a blow to one of the clockworks: Clytemnestra's smooth flank, Zephyr's outspread wing, Lucien's undulating tongue. Porphyrogene made no move to stop me, though her eyes were darkening with fury. I could only hope she was listening to my words.

"The second," I said, "is that the Margravine of Blois died, and her genius died with her."

Was it my imagination, or did a look of relief come into Boreas's snarling face as I drove the spike into his belly?

Porphyrogene caught my wrist as I turned to Ariel. Tears brimmed unchecked in her eyes. "And the third?" she said.

"The third is that you cannot bring the Margravine of Blois back from the dead, and it's killing you to try. That's the thing with ghosts – even metal ones." I broke her grip and slashed at Ariel's claws. "There are things the living and the dead cannot share. The Margravine of Blois isn't any more dead because her clockwork no longer runs, and she wouldn't be any more alive if it could. But we have a choice, Porphyrogene – between me and a ghost, between you and a carousel. The living or the dead."

I held out the spike to her, as I had held out the ring. "Choose however you want," I said, "but you must choose. You cannot jump on Phosphorus's back and hope the world doesn't change anymore while you're going in circles."

For a long moment, Porphyrogene looked at me. She opened her palm, slid the silver ring onto her finger. Then she took the spike.

That, madame, is the tragedy of the celebrated carousel of the Margravine of Blois. The remains are buried in

Summerfall – where, as you may see from the address on this package, I have decided to stay on. Porphyrogene has begun to expand her library, Jean-Baptiste is designing some small clockworks, and I am continuing my investigations, but the house seems large enough to accommodate all these imperialistic pursuits.

Though there is one room, at the end of a long corridor in the north wing, whose purpose we have agreed upon; it houses a pair of clockwork bays, their elegant legs folded beneath them in repose. Should these be of interest to you, madame, you are most welcome to come some day to Summerfall and we shall introduce you. They are really quite beautiful, a testament to the enduring genius of the celebrated Margravine of Blois.

Antoine Aristide de Saint-Pierre

Biographical Notes to "A Discourse on the Nature of Causality, with Air-planes" by Benjamin Rosenbaum

Benjamin Rosenbaum

On my return from PlausFab-Wisconsin (a delightful festival of art and enquiry, which styles itself "the World's Only Gynarchist Plausible-Fable Assembly") aboard the P.R.G.B. *Śri George Bernard Shaw*, I happened to share a compartment with Prem Ramasson, Raja of Outermost Thule, and his consort, a dour but beautiful woman whose name I did not know.

Two great blond barbarians bearing the livery of Outermost Thule (an elephant astride an iceberg and a volcano) stood in the hallway outside, armed with sabres and needlethrowers. Politely they asked if they might frisk me, then allowed me in. They ignored the short dagger at my belt – presumably accounting their liege's skill at arms more than sufficient to equal mine.

I took my place on the embroidered divan. "Good evening," I said.

The Raja flashed me a white-toothed smile and inclined his head. His consort pulled a wisp of blue veil across her lips, and looked out the porthole.

I took my notebook, pen and inkwell from my valise, set the inkwell into the port provided in the white pine table set in the wall, and slid aside the strings that bound the notebook. The inkwell lit with a faint blue glow.

The Raja was shuffling through a Wisdom Deck, pausing to look at the incandescent faces of the cards, then up at me. "You are the plausible-fabulist, Benjamin Rosenbaum," he said at length.

I bowed stiffly. "A pen name, of course," I said.

"Taken from *The Scarlet Pimpernel*?" he asked, cocking one eyebrow curiously.

"My lord is very quick," I said mildly.

The Raja laughed, indicating the Wisdom Deck with a wave. "He isn't the most heroic or sympathetic character in that book, however."

"Indeed not, my lord," I said with polite restraint. "The name is chosen ironically. As a sort of challenge to myself, if you will. Bearing the name of a notorious anti-Hebraic caricature, I must needs be all the prouder and more subtle in my own literary endeavors."

"You are a Karaite, then?" he asked.

"I am an Israelite, at any rate," I said. "If not an orthodox follower of my people's traditional religion of despair."

The prince's eyes glittered with interest, so – despite my reservations – I explained my researches into the Rabbinical Heresy which had briefly flourished in Palestine and Babylon at the time of Ashoka, and its lost Talmud.

"Fascinating," said the Raja. "Do you return now to your family?"

"I am altogether without attachments, my liege," I said, my face darkening with shame.

Excusing myself, I delved once again into my writing, pausing now and then to let my Wisdom Ants scurry from the inkwell to taste the ink with their antennae, committing it to memory for later editing. At PlausFab-Wisconsin, I had received an assignment – to construct a plausible-fable of a world without zeppelins – and I was trying to imagine some alternative air conveyance for my characters when the prince spoke again.

"I am an enthusiast of plausible-fables myself," he said. "I enjoyed your 'Droplet' greatly."

"Thank you, Your Highness."

"Are you writing such a grand extrapolation now?"

"I am trying my hand at a shadow history," I said.

The prince laughed gleefully. His consort had nestled herself against the bulkhead and fallen asleep, the blue gauze of her veil obscuring her features. "I adore shadow history," he said.

"Most shadow history proceeds with the logic of dream, full of odd echoes and distorted resonances of our world," I said. "I am experimenting with a new form, in which a single point of divergence in history leads to a new causal chain of events, and thus a different present."

"But the world *is* a dream," he said excitedly. "Your idea smacks of Democritan materialism – as if the events of the world were produced purely by linear cause and effect, the simplest of the Five Forms of causality."

"Indeed," I said.

"How fanciful!" he cried.

I was about to turn again to my work, but the prince clapped his hands thrice. From his baggage, a birdlike Wisdom Servant unfolded itself and stepped agilely onto the floor. Fully unfolded, it was three cubits tall, with a trapezoidal head and incandescent blue eyes. It took a silver tea service from an alcove in the wall, set the tray on the table between us, and began to pour.

"Wake up, Sarasvati Sitasdottir," the prince said to his consort, stroking her shoulder. "We are celebrating."

The servitor placed a steaming teacup before me. I capped my pen and shooed my Ants back into their inkwell, though one crawled stubbornly towards the tea. "What are we celebrating?" I asked.

"You shall come with me to Outermost Thule," he said. "It is a magical place – all fire and ice, except where it is greensward and sheep. Home once of epic heroes, Rama's cousins." His consort took a sleepy sip of her tea. "I have need of a plausible-fabulist. You can write the history of the Thule that might have been, to inspire and quell my restive subjects."

"Why me, Your Highness? I am hardly a fabulist of great renown. Perhaps I could help you contact someone more suitable – Karen Despair Robinson, say, or Howi Qomr Faukota."

"Nonsense," laughed the Raja, "for I have met none of them by chance in an airship compartment."

"But yet . . ." I said, discomfited.

"You speak again like a materialist! This is why the East, once it was awakened, was able to conquer the West – we understand how to read the dream that the world is. Come, no more fuss."

I lifted my teacup. The stray Wisdom Ant was crawling along its rim; I positioned my forefinger before her, that she might climb onto it.

Just then there was a scuffle at the door, and Prem Ramasson set his teacup down and rose. He said something admonitory in the harsh Nordic tongue of his adopted country, something I imagined to mean "Come now, boys, let the conductor through." The scuffle ceased, and the Raja slid the door of the compartment open, one hand on the hilt of his sword. There was the sharp hiss of a needlethrower, and he staggered backward, collapsing into the arms of his consort, who cried out.

The thin and angular Wisdom Servant plucked the dart from its master's neck. "Poison," it said, its voice a tangle of flutelike harmonics. "The assassin will possess its antidote."

Sarasvati Sitasdottir began to scream.

It is true that I had not accepted Prem Ramasson's offer of employment – indeed, that he had not seemed to find it necessary to actually ask. It is true also that I am a man of letters, neither spy nor bodyguard. It is furthermore true that I was unarmed, save for the ceremonial dagger at my belt, which had thus far seen employment only in the slicing of bread, cheese and tomatoes.

Thus, the fact that I leapt through the doorway, over the fallen bodies of the prince's bodyguard, and pursued the fleeting form of the assassin down the long and curving corridor, cannot be reckoned as a habitual or forthright action. Nor, in truth, was it a considered one. In Śri Grigory Guptanovich Karthaganov's typology of action and motive, it must be accounted an impulsive-transformative action: the unreflective moment which changes forever the path of events.

Causes buzz around any such moment like bees around a hive, returning with pollen and information, exiting with hunger and ambition. The assassin's strike was the proximate cause. The prince's kind manner, his enthusiasm for plausible-fables (and my work in particular), his apparent sympathy for my people, the dark eyes of his consort – all these were inciting causes.

The psychological cause, surely, can be found in this name that I have chosen – "Benjamin Rosenbaum" – the fat and cowardly merchant of *The Scarlet Pimpernel* who is beaten and raises no hand to defend himself; just as we, deprived of our Temple, found refuge in endless, beautiful elegies of despair, turning our backs on the Rabbis and their dreams of a new beginning. I have always seethed against this passivity. Perhaps, then, I was waiting – my whole life – for such a chance at rash and violent action.

The figure – clothed head to toe in a dull gray that matched the airship's hull – raced ahead of me down the deserted corridor, and descended through a maintenance hatch set in the floor. I reached it, and paused for breath, thankful my enthusiasm for the favorite sport of my continent – the exalted Lacrosse – had prepared me somewhat for the chase. I did not imagine, though, that I could overpower an armed and trained assassin. Yet, the weave of the world had brought me here – surely to some purpose. How could I do aught but follow?

Beyond the proximate, inciting and psychological causes, there are the more fundamental causes of an action. These address how the action embeds itself into the weave of the world, like a nettle in cloth. They rely on cosmology and epistemology. If the world is a dream, what caused the dreamer to dream that I chased the assassin? If the world is a lesson, what should this action teach? If the world is a gift, a wild and mindless rush of beauty, riven of logic or purpose – as it sometimes seems – still, seen from above, it must possess its own aesthetic harmony. The spectacle, then, of a ludicrously named practitioner of a half-despised art (bastard child of literature and philosophy), clumsily attempting the role of hero on the middle deck of the P.R.G.B. *Sri George Bernard Shaw*, must surely have some part in the pattern – chord or discord, tragic or comic.

Hesitantly, I poked my head down through the hatch. Beneath, a spiral staircase descended through a workroom cluttered with tools. I could hear the faint hum of engines nearby. There, in the canvas of the outer hull, between the *Shaw*'s great aluminum ribs, a door to the sky was open.

From a workbench, I took and donned an airman's vest, supple leather gloves and a visored mask, to shield me somewhat from the assassin's needle. I leaned my head out the door.

A brisk wind whipped across the skin of the ship. I took a tether from a nearby anchor and hooked it to my vest. The assassin was untethered. He crawled along a line of handholds and footholds set in the airship's gently curving surface. Many cubits beyond him, a small and brightly colored glider clung to the *Shaw*, like a dragonfly splayed upon a watermelon.

It was the first time I had seen a glider put to any utilitarian purpose – espionage rather than sport – and immediately I was seized by the longing to return to my notebook. Gliders! In a world without dirigibles, my heroes could travel in some kind of immense, powered gliders! Of course, they would be forced to land whenever winds were unfavorable.

Or would they? I recalled that my purpose was not to repaint our world anew, but to speculate rigorously according to Democritan logic. Each new cause could lead to some wholly new effect, causing in turn some unimagined consequence. Given different economic incentives, then, and with no overriding, higher pattern to dictate the results, who knew what advances a glider-based science of aeronautics might achieve? Exhilarating speculation!

I glanced down, and the sight below wrenched me from my reverie:

The immense panoply of the Great Lakes—

—their dark green wave-wrinkled water—

—the paler green and tawny-yellow fingers of land reaching in among them—

—puffs of cloud gamboling in the bulk of air between—

—and beyond, the vault of sky presiding over the Frankish and Athapascan Moeity.

It was a long way down.

"*Malkat Ha-Shamayim*," I murmured aloud. "What am I doing?"

"I was wondering that myself," said a high and glittering timbrel of chords and discords by my ear. It was the recalcitrant, tea-seeking Wisdom Ant, now perched on my shoulder.

"Well," I said crossly, "do you have any suggestions?"

"My sisters have tasted the neurotoxin coursing through the prince's blood," the Ant said. "We do not recognize it. His servant has kept him alive so far, but an antidote is beyond us." She gestured towards the fleeing villain with one delicate antenna.

"The assassin will likely carry an antidote to his venom. If you can place me on his body, I can find it. I will then transmit the recipe to my sisters through the Brahmanic field. Perhaps they can formulate a close analogue in our inkwell."

"It is a chance," I agreed. "But the assassin is halfway to his craft."

"True," said the Ant pensively.

"I have an idea for getting there," I said. "But you will have to do the math."

The tether which bound me to the *Shaw* was fastened high above us. I crawled upwards and away from the glider, to a point the Ant calculated. The handholds ceased, but I improvised with the letters of the airship's name, raised in decoration from its side.

From the top of an *R*, I leapt into the air, struck with my heels against the resilient canvas, and rebounded, sailing outwards, snapping the tether taut.

The Ant took shelter in my collar as the air roared around us. We described a long arc, swinging past the surprised assassin to the brightly colored glider; I was able to seize its aluminum frame.

I hooked my feet onto its seat, and hung there, my heart racing. The glider creaked, but held.

"Disembark," I panted to the Ant. "When the assassin gains the craft, you can search him."

"Her," said the Ant, crawling down my shoulder. "She has removed her mask, and in our passing I was able to observe her striking resemblance to Sarasvati Sitasdottir, the prince's consort. She is clearly her sister."

I glanced at the assassin. Her long black hair now whipped in the wind. She was braced against the airship's hull with one hand and one foot; with the other hand she had drawn her needlethrower.

"That is interesting information," I said as the Ant crawled off my hand and onto the glider. "Good luck."

"Goodbye," said the Ant.

A needle whizzed by my cheek. I released the glider and swung once more into the cerulean sphere.

Once again I passed the killer, covering my face with my leather gloves – a dart glanced off my visor. Once again I swung beyond the door to the maintenance room and towards the hull.

Predictably, however, my momentum was insufficient to attain it. I described a few more dizzying swings of decreasing arc-length until I hung, nauseous, terrified and gently swaying, at the end of the tether, amidst the sky.

To discourage further needles, I protected the back of my head with my arms, and faced downwards. That is when I noticed the pirate ship.

It was sleek and narrow and black, designed for maneuverability. Like the *Shaw*, it had a battery of sails for fair winds, and propellers in an aft assemblage. But the *Shaw* traveled on a predictable course and carried a fixed set of coiled tensors, whose millions of microsprings gradually relaxed to produce its motive force. The new craft spouted clouds of white steam; carrying its own generatory, it could rewind its tensor batteries while underway. And, unlike the *Shaw*, it was armed – a cruel array of arbalest-harpoons was mounted at either side. It carried its sails below, sporting at its top two razor-sharp saw-ridges with which it could gut recalcitrant prey.

All this would have been enough to recognize the craft as a pirate – but it displayed the universal device of pirates as well, that parody of the yin-yang: all yang, declaring allegiance to imbalance. In a yellow circle, two round black dots stared like unblinking demonic eyes; beneath, a black semicircle leered with empty, ravenous bonhomie.

I dared a glance upward in time to see the glider launch from the *Shaw*'s side. Whoever the mysterious assassin-sister was, whatever her purpose (political symbolism? personal revenge? dynastic ambition? anarchic mania?), she was a fantastic glider pilot. She gained the air with a single, supple back-flip, twirled the glider once, then hung deftly in the sky, considering.

Most people, surely, would have wondered at the *meaning* of a pirate and an assassin showing up together – what resonance, what symbolism, what hortatory or esthetic purpose did the world intend thereby? But my mind was still with my thought-experiment.

Imagine there are no causes but mechanical ones – that the world is nothing but a chain of dominoes! Every plausible-fabulist spends long hours teasing apart fictional plots, imagining consequences, conjuring and discarding the antecedents of desired events. We dirty our hands daily with the simplest and grubbiest of the Five Forms. Now I tried to reason thus about life.

Were the pirate and the assassin in league? It seemed unlikely. If the assassin intended to trigger political upheaval and turmoil, pirates surely spoiled the attempt. A death at the hands of pirates while traveling in a foreign land is not the stuff of which revolutions are made. If the intent was merely to kill Ramasson, surely one or the other would suffice.

Yet was I to credit chance, then, with the intrusion of two violent enemies, in the same hour, into my hitherto tranquil existence?

Absurd! Yet the idea had an odd attractiveness. If the world was a blind machine, surely such clumsy coincidences would be common!

The assassin saw the pirate ship; yet, with an admirable consistency, she seemed resolved to finish what she had started. She came for me.

I drew my dagger from its sheath. Perhaps, at first, I had some wild idea of throwing it, or parrying her needles, though I had the skill for neither.

She advanced to a point some fifteen cubits away; from there, her spring-fired darts had more than enough power to pierce my clothing. I could see her face now, a choleric, wild-eyed homunculus of her phlegmatic sister's.

The smooth black canvas of the pirate ship was now thirty cubits below me.

The assassin banked her glider's wings against the wind, hanging like a kite. She let go its aluminum frame with her right hand, and drew her needlethrower.

Summoning all my strength, I struck the tether that held me with my dagger's blade.

My strength, as it happened, was extremely insufficient. The tether twanged like a harp-string, but was otherwise unharmed, and the dagger was knocked from my grasp by the recoil.

The assassin burst out laughing, and covered her eyes. Feeling foolish, I seized the tether in one hand and unhooked it from my vest with the other.

Then I let go.

Since that time, I have on various occasions enumerated to myself, with a mixture of wonder and chagrin, the various ways I might have died. I might have snapped my neck, or, landing on my stomach, folded in a V and broken my spine like a twig. If I had struck one of the craft's aluminum ribs, I should certainly have shattered bones.

What is chance? Is it best to liken it to the whim of some being of another scale or scope, the dreamer of our dream? Or to regard the world as having an inherent pattern, mirroring itself at every stage and scale?

Or *could* our world arise, as Democritus held, willy-nilly, of the couplings and patternings of endless dumb particulates?

While hanging from the *Shaw*, I had decided that the protagonist of my Democritan shadow history (should I live to write it) would be a man of letters, a dabbler in philosophy like myself, who lived in an advanced society committed to philosophical materialism. I relished the apparent paradox – an intelligent man, in a sophisticated nation, forced to account for all events purely within the rubric of overt mechanical causation!

Yet those who today, complacently, regard the materialist hypothesis as dead – pointing to the Brahmanic field and its Wisdom Creatures, to the predictive successes, from weather to history, of the Theory of Five Causal Forms – forget that the question is, at bottom, axiomatic. The materialist hypothesis – the primacy of Matter over Mind – is undisprovable. What successes might some other science, in another history, have built, upon its bulwark?

So I cannot say – I cannot say! – if it is meaningful or meaningless, the fact that I struck the pirate vessel's resilient canvas with my legs and buttocks, was flung upwards again, to bounce and roll until I fetched up against the wall of the airship's dorsal razor-weapon. I cannot say if some Preserver spared my life through will, if some Pattern needed me for the skein it wove – or if a patternless and unforetellable Chance spared me all unknowing.

There was a small closed hatchway in the razor-spine nearby, whose overhanging ridge provided some protection against my adversary. Bruised and weary, groping inchoately among theories of chance and purpose, I scrambled for it as the boarding gongs and klaxons began.

The *Shaw* knew it could neither outrun nor outfight the swift and dangerous corsair – it idled above me, awaiting rapine. The brigand's longboats launched – lean and maneuverable black dirigibles the size of killer whales, with parties of armed sky-bandits clinging to their sides.

The glider turned and dove, a blur of gold and crimson and verdant blue disappearing over the pirate zeppelin's side – abandoning our duel, I imagined, for some redoubt many leagues below us.

Oddly, I was sad to see her go. True, I had known from her only wanton violence; she had almost killed me; I crouched battered, terrified and nauseous on the summit of a pirate corsair on her account; and the kind Raja, my almost-employer, might be dead. Yet I felt our relations had reached as yet no satisfactory conclusion.

It is said that we fabulists live two lives at once. First we live as others do: seeking to feed and clothe ourselves, earn the respect and affection of our fellows, fly from danger, entertain and satiate ourselves on the things of this world. But then, too, we live a second life, pawing through the moments of the first, even as they happen, like a market-woman of the bazaar sifting trash for treasures. Every agony we endure, we also hold up to the light with great excitement, expecting it will be of use; every simple joy, we regard with a critical eye, wondering how it could be changed, honed, tightened, to fit inside a fable's walls.

The hatch was locked. I removed my mask and visor and lay on the canvas, basking in the afternoon sun, hoping my Ants had met success in their apothecary and saved the prince; watching the pirate longboats sack the unresisting P.R.G.B. *Sri George Bernard Shaw* and return laden with valuables and – perhaps – hostages.

I was beginning to wonder if they would ever notice me – if, perhaps, I should signal them – when the cacophony of gongs and klaxons resumed – louder, insistent, angry – and the longboats raced back down to anchor beneath the pirate ship.

Curious, I found a ladder set in the razor-ridge's metal wall that led to a lookout platform.

A war-city was emerging from a cloudbank some leagues away.

I had never seen any work of man so vast. Fully twelve great dirigible hulls, each dwarfing the *Shaw*, were bound together in a constellation of outbuildings and propeller assemblies. Near the center, a great plume of white steam rose from a pillar; a Heart-of-the-Sun reactor, where the dull yellow ore called Yama's-flesh is driven to realize enlightenment through the ministrations of Wisdom-Sadhus.

There was a spyglass set in the railing by my side; I peered through, scanning the features of this new apparition.

None of the squabbling statelets of my continent could muster such a vessel, certainly; and only the Powers – Cathay, Gabon, the Aryan Raj – could afford to fly one so far afield, though the Khmer and Malay might have the capacity to build them.

There is little enough to choose between the meddling Powers, though Gabon makes the most pretense of investing in its colonies and believing in its supposed civilizing mission. This craft, though, was clearly Hindu. Every cubit of its surface was bedecked with a façade of cytoceramic statuary – couples coupling in five thousand erotic poses; theromorphic gods gesturing to soothe or menace; Rama in his chariot; heroes riddled with arrows and fighting on; saints undergoing martyrdom. In one corner, I spotted the Israelite avatar of Vishnu, hanging on his cross between Shiva and Ganesh.

Then I felt rough hands on my shoulders.

Five pirates had emerged from the hatch, cutlasses drawn. Their dress was motley and ragged, their features varied – Sikh, Xhosan, Baltic, Frankish and Aztec, I surmised. None of us spoke as they led me through the rat's maze of catwalks and ladders set between the ship's inner and outer hulls.

I was queasy and lightheaded with bruises, hunger and the aftermath of rash and strenuous action; it seemed odd indeed that the day before, I had been celebrating and debating with the plausible-fabulists gathered at Wisconsin. I recalled that there had been a fancy-dress ball there, with a pirate theme; and the images of yesterday's festive, well-groomed pirates of fancy interleaved with those of today's grim and unwashed captors on the long climb down to the bridge.

The bridge was in the gondola that hung beneath the pirate airship's bulk, forwards of the rigging. It was crowded with lean and dangerous men in pantaloons, sarongs and leather trousers. They consulted paper charts and the liquid, glowing forms swimming in Wisdom Tanks, spoke through bronze tubes set in the walls, barked orders to cabin boys who raced away across the airship's webwork of spars.

At the great window that occupied the whole of the forward wall, watching the clouds part as we plunged into them, stood the captain.

I had suspected whose ship this might be upon seeing it; now I was sure. A giant of a man, dressed in buckskin and adorned with feathers, his braided red hair and bristling beard proclaimed him the scion of those who had fled the destruction of Viking Eire to settle on the banks of the Father-of-Waters.

This ship, then, was the *Hiawatha MacCool*, and this the man who terrorized commerce from the shores of Lake Erie to the border of Texas.

"Chippewa Melko," I said.

He turned, raising an eyebrow.

"Found him sightseeing on the starboard spine," one of my captors said.

"Indeed?" said Melko. "Did you fall off the *Shaw*?"

"I jumped, after a fashion," I said. "The reason thereof is a tale that strains my own credibility, although I lived it."

Sadly, this quip was lost on Melko, as he was distracted by some pressing bit of martial business.

We were descending at a precipitous rate; the water of Lake Erie loomed before us, filling the window. Individual whitecaps were discernable upon its surface.

When I glanced away from the window, the bridge had darkened – every Wisdom Tank was gray and lifeless.

"You there! Spy!" Melko barked. I noted with discomfiture that he addressed me. "Why would they disrupt our communications?"

"What?" I said.

The pirate captain gestured at the muddy tanks. "The Aryan war-city – they've disrupted the Brahmanic field with some damned device. They mean to cripple us, I suppose – ships like theirs are dependent on it. Won't work. But how do they expect to get their hostages back alive if they refuse to parley?"

"Perhaps they mean to board and take them," I offered.

"We'll see about that," he said grimly. "Listen up, boys –
we hauled ass to avoid a trap, but the trap found us anyway.
But we can outrun this bastard in the high airstreams if we
lose all extra weight. Dinky – run and tell Max to drop the
steamer. Red, Ali – mark the aft, fore and starboard harpoons
with buoys and let 'em go. Grig, Ngube – same with the spent
tensors. Fast!"

He turned to me as his minions scurried to their tasks. "We're
throwing all dead weight over the side. That includes you, unless
I'm swiftly convinced otherwise. Who are you?"

"Gabriel Goodman," I said truthfully, "but better known by my
quill-name – 'Benjamin Rosenbaum'."

"Benjamin Rosenbaum?" the pirate cried. "The great Iowa
poet, author of 'Green Nakedness' and 'Broken Lines'? You are a
hero of our land, sir! Fear not, I shall—"

"No," I interrupted crossly. "Not that Benjamin Rosenbaum."

The pirate reddened, and tapped his teeth, frowning. "Aha,
hold then, I have heard of you – the children's tale-scribe, I take
it? 'Legs the Caterpillar'? I'll spare you, then, for the sake of my
son Timmy, who—"

"No," I said again, through gritted teeth. "I am an author of
plausible-fables, sir, not picture-books."

"Never read the stuff," said Melko. There was a great shudder,
and the steel bulk of the steam generatory, billowing white clouds,
fell past us. It struck the lake, raising a plume of spray that spotted
the window with droplets. The forward harpoon assembly
followed, trailing a red buoy on a line.

"Right then," said Melko. "Over you go."

"You spoke of Aryan hostages," I said hastily, thinking it wise
now to mention the position I seemed to have accepted *de facto*,
if not yet *de jure*. "Do you by any chance refer to my employer,
Prem Ramasson, and his consort?"

Melko spat on the floor, causing a cabin boy to rush forward
with a mop. "So you're one of those quislings who serves Hindoo
royalty even as they divide up the land of your fathers, are you?"
He advanced towards me menacingly.

"Outer Thule is a minor province of the Raj, sir," I said. "It is
absurd to blame Ramasson for the war in Texas."

"Ready to rise, sir," came the cry.

"Rise then!" Melko ordered. "And throw this dog in the brig with its master. If we can't ransom them, we'll throw them off at the top." He glowered at me. "That will give you a nice long while to salve your conscience with making fine distinctions among Hindoos. What do you think he's doing here in our lands, if not plotting with his brothers to steal more of our gold and helium?"

I was unable to further pursue my political debate with Chippewa Melko, as his henchmen dragged me at once to cramped quarters between the inner and outer hulls. The prince lay on the single bunk, ashen and unmoving. His consort knelt at his side, weeping silently. The Wisdom Servant, deprived of its animating field, had collapsed into a tangle of reedlike protuberances.

My valise was there; I opened it and took out my inkwell. The Wisdom Ants lay within, tiny crumpled blobs of brassy metal. I put the inkwell in my pocket.

"Thank you for trying," Sarasvati Sitasdottir said hoarsely. "Alas, luck has turned against us."

"All may not be lost," I said. "An Aryan war-city pursues the pirates, and may yet buy our ransom; although, strangely, they have damped the Brahmanic field and so cannot hear the pirates' offer of parley."

"If they were going to parley, they would have done so by now," she said dully. "They will burn the pirate from the sky. They do not know we are aboard."

"Then our bad luck comes in threes." It is an old rule of thumb, derided as superstition by professional causalists. But they, like all professionals, like to obfuscate their science, rendering it inaccessible to the layman; in truth, the old rule holds a glimmer of the workings of the third form of causality.

"A swift death is no bad luck for me," Sarasvati Sitasdottir said. "Not when he is gone." She choked a sob, and turned away.

I felt for the Raja's pulse; his blood was still beneath his amber skin. His face was turned towards the metal bulkhead; droplets of moisture there told of his last breath, not long ago. I wiped them away, and closed his eyes.

We waited, for one doom or another. I could feel the zeppelin rising swiftly; the *Hiawatha* was unheated, and the air turned cold. The princess did not speak.

*   *   *

My mind turned again to the fable I had been commissioned to write, the materialist shadow history of a world without zeppelins. If by some unlikely chance I should live to finish it, I resolved to make do without the extravagant perils, ironic coincidences, sudden bursts of insight, death-defying escapades and beautiful villainesses that litter our genre and cheapen its high philosophical concerns. Why must every protagonist be doomed, daring, lonely and overly proud? No, my philosopher-hero would enjoy precisely those goods of which I was deprived – a happy family, a secure situation, a prosperous and powerful nation, a conciliatory nature; above all, an absence of immediate physical peril. Of course, there must be conflict, worry, sorrow – but, I vowed, of a rich and subtle kind!

I wondered how my hero would view the chain of events in which I was embroiled. With derision? With compassion? I loved him, after a fashion, for he was my creation. How would he regard me?

If only the first and simplest form of causality had earned his allegiance, he would not be placated by such easy saws as "bad things come in threes". An assassin, *and* a pirate, *and* an uncommunicative war-city, he would ask? All within the space of an hour?

Would he simply accept the absurd and improbable results of living within a blind and random machine? Yet his society could not have advanced far, mired in such fatalism!

Would he not doggedly seek meaning, despite the limitations of his framework?

What if our bad luck were no coincidence at all? he would ask. What if all three misfortunes had a single, linear, proximate cause, intelligible to reason?

"My lady," I said, "I do not wish to cause you further pain. Yet I find I must speak. I saw the face of the prince's killer – it was a young woman's face, in lineament much like your own."

"Shakuntala!" the princess cried. "My sister! No! It cannot be! She would never do this . . ." She curled her hands into fists. "No!"

"And yet," I said gently, "it seems you regard the assertion as not utterly implausible."

"She is banished," Sarasvati Sitasdottir said. "She has gone over to the Thanes – the Nordic Liberation Army – the anarcho-gynarchist insurgents in our land. It is like her to seek danger and glory. But she would not kill Prem! She loved him before I!"

To that, I could find no response. The *Hiawatha* shuddered around us – some battle had been joined. We heard shouts and running footsteps.

Sarasvati, the prince, the pirates – any of them would have had a thousand gods to pray to, convenient gods for any occasion. Such solace I could sorely have used. But I was raised a Karaite. We acknowledge only one God, austere and magnificent; the One God of All Things, attended by His angels and His consort, the Queen of Heaven. The only way to speak to Him, we are taught, is in His Holy Temple; and it lies in ruins these 2,000 years. In times like these, we are told to meditate on the contrast between His imperturbable magnificence and our own abandoned and abject vulnerability, and to be certain that He watches us with immeasurable compassion, though He will not act. I have never found this much comfort.

Instead, I turned to the prince, curious what in his visage might have inspired the passions of the two sisters.

On the bulkhead just before his lips – where, before, I had wiped away the sign of his last breath – a tracery of condensation stood.

Was this some effluvium issued by the organs of a decaying corpse? I bent, and delicately sniffed – detecting no corruption.

"My lady," I said, indicating the droplets on the cool metal, "he lives."

"What?" the princess cried. "But how?"

"A diguanidinium compound produced by certain marine dinoflagellates," I said, "can induce a deathlike coma, in which the subject breathes but thrice an hour; the heartbeat is similarly undetectable."

Delicately, she felt his face. "Can he hear us?"

"Perhaps."

"Why would she do this?"

"The body would be rushed back to Thule, would it not? Perhaps the revolutionaries meant to steal it and revive him as a hostage?"

A tremendous thunderclap shook the *Hiawatha MacCool*, and I noticed we were listing to one side. There was a commotion in the gangway; then Chippewa Melko entered. Several guards stood behind him.

"Damned tenacious," he spat. "If they want you so badly, why won't they parley? We're still out of range of the war-city itself and its big guns, thank Buddha, Thor and Darwin. We burned one of their launches, at the cost of many of my men. But the other launch is gaining."

"Perhaps they don't know the hostages are aboard?" I asked.

"Then why pursue me this distance? I'm no fool – I know what it costs them to detour that monster. They don't do it for sport, and I don't flatter myself I'm worth that much to them. No, it's you they want. So they can have you – I've no more stomach for this chase." He gestured at the prince with his chin. "Is he dead?"

"No," I said.

"Doesn't look well. No matter – come along. I'm putting you all in a launch with a flag of parley on it. Their war-boat will have to stop for you, and that will give us the time we need."

So it was that we found ourselves in the freezing, cramped bay of a pirate longboat. Three of Melko's crewmen accompanied us – one at the controls, the other two clinging to the longboat's sides. Sarasvati and I huddled on the aluminum deck beside the pilot, the prince's body held between us. All three of Melko's men had parachutes – they planned to escape as soon as we docked. Our longboat flew the white flag of parley, and – taken from the prince's luggage – the royal standard of Outermost Thule.

All the others were gazing tensely at our target – the war-city's fighter launch, which climbed toward us from below. It was almost as big as Melko's flagship. I, alone, glanced back out the open doorway as we swung away from the *Hiawatha*.

So only I saw a brightly colored glider detach itself from the *Hiawatha*'s side and swoop to follow us.

Why would Shakuntala have lingered with the pirates thus far? Once the rebels' plan to abduct the prince was foiled by Melko's arrival, why not simply abandon it and await a fairer chance?

Unless the intent was not to abduct – but to protect.

"My lady," I said in my halting middle-school Sanskrit, "your sister is here."

Sarasvati gasped, following my gaze.

"Madam – your husband was aiding the rebels."

"How dare you?" she hissed in the same tongue, much more fluently.

"It is the only ..." I struggled for the Sanskrit word for 'hypothesis', then abandoned the attempt, leaning over to whisper in English. "Why else did the pirates and the war-city arrive together? Consider: the prince's collusion with the Thanes was discovered by the Aryan Raj. But to try him for treason would provoke great scandal and stir sympathy for the insurgents. Instead, they made sure rumor of a valuable hostage reached Melko. With the prince in the hands of the pirates, his death would simply be a regrettable calamity."

Her eyes widened. "Those monsters!" she hissed.

"Your sister aimed to save him, but Melko arrived too soon – before news of the prince's death could discourage his brigandy. My lady, I fear that if we reach that launch, they will discover that the prince lives. Then some accident will befall us all."

There were shouts from outside. Melko's crewmen drew their needlethrowers and fired at the advancing glider.

With a shriek, Sarasvati flung herself upon the pilot, knocking the controls from his hands.

The longboat lurched sickeningly.

I gained my feet, then fell against the prince. I saw a flash of orange and gold – the glider, swooping by us.

I struggled to stand. The pilot drew his cutlass. He seized Sarasvati by the hair and spun her away from the controls.

Just then, one of the men clinging to the outside, pricked by Shakuntala's needle, fell. His tether caught him, and the floor jerked beneath us.

The pilot staggered back. Sarasvati Sitasdottir punched him in the throat. They stumbled towards the door.

I started forward. The other pirate on the outside fell, untethered, and the longboat lurched again. Unbalanced, our craft drove in a tight circle, listing dangerously.

Sarasvati fought with uncommon ferocity, forcing the pirate towards the open hatch. Fearing they would both tumble through, I seized the controls.

Regrettably, I knew nothing of flying airship-longboats, whose controls, it happens, are of a remarkably poor design.

One would imagine that the principal steering element could be moved in the direction that one wishes the craft to go; instead, just the opposite is the case. Then, too, one would expect these brawny and unrefined airmen to use controls lending themselves to rough usage; instead, it seems an exceedingly fine hand is required.

Thus, rather than steadying the craft, I achieved the opposite.

Not only were Sarasvati and the pilot flung out the cabin door, but I myself was thrown through it, just managing to catch with both hands a metal protuberance in the hatchway's base. My feet swung freely over the void.

I looked up in time to see the Raja's limp body come sliding towards me like a missile.

I fear that I hesitated too long in deciding whether to dodge or catch my almost-employer. At the last minute courage won out, and I flung one arm around his chest as he struck me.

This dislodged my grip, and the two of us fell from the airship.

In an extremity of terror, I let go the prince, and clawed wildly at nothing.

I slammed into the body of the pirate who hung, poisoned by Shakuntala's needle, from the airship's tether. I slid along him, and finally caught myself at his feet.

As I clung there, shaking miserably, I watched Prem Ramasson tumble through the air, and I cursed myself for having caused the very tragedies I had endeavored to avoid, like a figure in an Athenian tragedy. But such tragedies proceed from some essential flaw in their heroes – some illustrative hubris, some damning vice. Searching my own character and actions, I could find only that I had endeavored to make do, as well as I could, in situations for which I was ill-prepared. Is that not the fate of any of us, confronting life and its vagaries?

Was my tale, then, an absurd and tragic farce? Was its lesson one merely of ignominy and despair?

Or perhaps – as my shadow-protagonist might imagine – there was no tale, no teller – perhaps the dramatic and sensational events I had endured were part of no story at all, but brute and silent facts of Matter.

From above, Shakuntala Sitasdottir dove in her glider. It was folded like a spear, and she swept past the prince in seconds.

Nimbly, she flung open the glider's wings, sweeping up to the falling Raja, and rolling the glider, took him into her embrace.

Thus encumbered – she must have secured him somehow – she dove again (chasing her sister, I imagine) and disappeared in a bank of cloud.

A flock of brass-colored Wisdom Gulls, arriving from the Aryan war-city, flew around the pirates' launch. They entered its empty cabin, glanced at me and the poisoned pirate to whom I clung, and departed.

I climbed up the body to sit upon its shoulders, a much more comfortable position. There, clinging to the tether and shivering, I rested.

The *Hiawatha MacCool*, black smoke guttering from one side of her, climbed higher and higher into the sky, pursued by the Aryan war-boat. The sun was setting, limning the clouds with gold and pink and violet. The war-city, terrible and glorious, sailed slowly by, under my feet, its shadow an island of darkness in the sunset's gold-glitter on the waters of the lake beneath.

Some distance to the east, where the sky was already darkening to a rich cobalt, the Aryan war-boat which Melko had successfully struck was bathed in white fire. After a while, the inner hull must have been breached, for the fire went out, extinguished by escaping helium, and the zeppelin plummeted.

Above me, the propeller hummed, driving my launch in the same small circle again and again.

I hoped that I had saved the prince after all. I hoped Shakuntala had saved her sister, and that the three of them would find refuge with the Thanes.

My shadow-protagonist had given me a gift; it was the logic of his world that had led me to discover the war-city's threat. Did this mean his philosophy was the correct one?

Yet the events that followed were so dramatic and contrived – precisely as if I inhabited a pulp romance. Perhaps he was writing my story, as I wrote his; perhaps, with the comfortable life I had given him, he longed to lose himself in uncomfortable escapades of this sort. In that case, we both of us lived in a world designed, a world of story, full of meaning.

But perhaps I had framed the question wrong. Perhaps the division between Mind and Matter is itself illusory; perhaps

Randomness, Pattern and Plan are all but stories we tell about the inchoate and unknowable world which fills the darkness beyond the thin circle illumed by reason's light. Perhaps it is foolish to ask if I or the protagonist of my world-without-zeppelins story is the more real. Each of us is flesh, a buzzing swarm of atoms; yet each of us also a tale contained in the pages of the other's notebook. We are bodies. But we are also the stories we tell about each other. Perhaps not knowing is enough.

Maybe it is not a matter of discovering the correct philosophy. Maybe the desire that burns behind this question is the desire to be real. And which is more real – a clod of dirt unnoticed at your feet, or a hero in a legend?

And maybe behind the desire to be real is simply wanting to be known.

To be held.

The first stars glittered against the fading blue. I was in the bosom of the Queen of Heaven. My fingers and toes were getting numb – soon frostbite would set in. I recited the prayer the ancient heretical Rabbis would say before death, which begins, "Hear O Israel, the Lord is Our God, the Lord is One".

Then I began to climb the tether.

Clockwork Chickadee

Mary Robinette Kowal

The clockwork chickadee was not as pretty as the nightingale. But she did not mind. She pecked the floor when she was wound, looking for invisible bugs. And when she was not wound, she cocked her head and glared at the sparrow, whom she loathed with every tooth on every gear in her pressed-tin body.

The sparrow could fly.

He took no pains to conceal his contempt for those who could not. When his mechanism spun him around and around overhead, he twittered – not even a proper song – to call attention to his flight. Chickadee kept her head down when she could so as not to give him the satisfaction of her notice. It was clear to her that any bird could fly if only they were attached to a string like him. The flight, of which he was so proud, was not even an integral part of his clockwork. A wind-up engine hanging from the chandelier spun him in circles while he merely flapped his wings. Chickadee could do as much. And so she thought until she hatched an idea to show that Sparrow was not so very special.

It happened, one day, that Chickadee and Sparrow were shelved next to one another.

Sparrow, who lay tilted on his belly as his feet were only painted on, said, "How limiting the view is from here. Why, when I am flying I can see everything."

"Not everything, I'll warrant," said Chickadee. "Have you seen what is written underneath the table? Do you know how the silver marble got behind the potted fern, or where the missing wind-up key is?"

Sparrow flicked his wing at her. "Why should I care about such things when I can see the ceiling above and the plaster cherubs upon it. I can see the shelves below us and the mechanical menagerie upon it, even including the clockwork scarab and his lotus. I can see the fireplace, which shares the wall with us, none of which are visible from here nor to you."

"But I have seen all of these things as I have been carried to and from the shelf. In addition the boy has played with me at the fountain outside."

"What fountain?"

"Ah! Can you not see the courtyard fountain when you fly?" Chickadee hopped a step closer to him. "Such a pity."

"Bah – why should I care about any of this?"

"For no reason today," said Chickadee. "Perhaps tomorrow."

"What is written underneath the table?" Sparrow called as he swung in his orbit about the room, wings clicking against his side with each downstroke.

Chickadee pecked at the floor and shifted a cog to change her direction toward the table. "The address of Messrs DeCola and Wodzinski."

"Bah. Why should I care about them?"

"Because they are master clockworkers. They can reset cogs to create movements you would not think possible."

"I have all the movement I need. They can offer me nothing."

"You might change your mind." Chickadee passed under the edge of the table. "Perhaps tomorrow."

Above the table, Sparrow's gears ground audibly in frustration.

Chickadee cocked her head to look up at the yellow slip of paper glued to the underside of the table. Its type was still crisp though the paper itself threatened to peel away. She scanned the corners of the room for movement. In the shadows by the fireplace, a live mouse caught her gaze. He winked.

"How did the silver marble get behind the potted fern?" Sparrow asked as he lay on the shelf.

"It fell out of the boy's game and rolled across the floor to where I was pecking the ground. I waited but no one seemed to notice that it was gone, nor did they notice me, so I put my beak against it and pushed it behind the potted fern."

"You did? You stole from the boy?" Sparrow clicked his wings shut. "I find that hard to believe."

"You may not, today," Chickadee said. "Perhaps tomorrow."

She cocked her head to look away from him and to the corner where the live mouse now hid. The mouse put his forepaw on the silver marble and rolled it away from the potted fern. Chickadee felt the tension in her spring and tried to calculate how many revolutions of movement it still offered her. She thought it would suffice.

"Where is the missing wind-up key?" Sparrow hung from his line, waiting for the boy to wind him again.

"The live mouse has it." Chickadee hopped forward and pecked at another invisible crumb, but did not waste the movement needed to look at Sparrow.

"What would a live mouse need with a wind-up key?"

"He does not need it," said Chickadee. "But I do have need of it and he is in my service."

All the gears in the room stopped for a moment as the other clockwork animals paused to listen. Even the nightingale stopped her song. In the sudden cessation of ticking, sound from the greater world outside crept in, bringing the babble of the fountain in the courtyard, the laughter of the boy, the purr of automobiles and from the far distance, the faint pealing of a clock.

"I suppose you would have us believe that he winds you?" said Sparrow.

"Not yet. Perhaps today." She continued pecking the floor.

After a moment of nothing happening, the other animals returned to their tasks save for the sparrow. He hung from his line and beat his wings against his side.

"Ha! I see him. I see the live mouse behind the potted fern. You could too if you could fly."

"I have no need." Chickadee felt her clockwork beginning to slow. "Live Mouse!" she called. "It is time to fulfill our bargain."

The silence came again as the other animals stopped to listen. Into this quiet came a peculiar scraping rattle and then the live mouse emerged from behind the potted fern with the missing wind-up key tied in his tail.

"What is he doing?" Sparrow squawked.

Chickadee bent to peck the ground so slowly she thought she might never touch it. A gear clicked forward and she tapped the floor. "Do you really need me to tell you that?"

Above her, Sparrow dangled on his line. "Live Mouse! Whatever she has promised you, I can give you also, only wind my flying mechanism."

The live mouse twirled his whiskers and kept walking toward Chickadee. "Well now. That's a real interesting proposition. How about a silver marble?"

"There is one behind the potted fern."

"Not nomore."

"Then a crystal from the chandelier."

The live mouse wrinkled his nose. "If'n I can climb the chandelier to wind ya, then I reckon I can reach a crystal for myself."

"I must have something you want."

With the key paused by Chickadee's side, the live mouse said, "That might be so."

The live mouse set the tip of the key down like a cane and folded his paws over it. Settling back on his haunches, he tipped his head up to study Sparrow. "How 'bout you give me one of your wings?"

Sparrow squawked.

"You ain't got no need of 'em to fly, that right?" The live mouse looked down and idly twisted the key on the floor, as if he were winding the room. "Prob'ly make you spin round faster, like one of them zeppelin thingamabobs. Whazzat called? Air-o-dye-namic."

"A bird cannot fly without wings."

"Now you and I both know that ain't so. A live bird can't fly without wings, but you're a clockwork bird."

"What would a live mouse know about clockworks?"

The live mouse laughed. "Ain't you never heard of Hickory, Dickory and Dock? We mice have a long history with clockworks. Looking at you, I figure you won't miss a wing none and without it dragging, you ought to be able to go faster and your windings would last you longer. Whaddya say? Wouldn't it be a mite sight nicer to fly without having to wait for the boy to come back?"

"What would you do with my wing?"

"That," the live mouse smiled, showing his sharp incisors, "is between me and Messrs DeCola and Wodzinski. So do we have a deal?"

"I will have to consider the matter."

"Suit yourself." The live mouse lifted the key and put the tip in Chickadee's winding mechanism.

"Wait!" Sparrow flicked his wings as if anxious to be rid of them. "Yes, yes you may have my left wing, only wind me now. A bird is meant to fly."

"All righty, then."

Chickadee turned her head with painful slowness. "Now, Live Mouse, you and I have an agreement."

"That we did and we do, but nothing in it says I can't have another master."

"That may well be, but the wind-up key belongs to me."

"I reckon that's true. Sorry, Sparrow. Looks as if I can't help you none." The live mouse sighed. "And I surely did want me one of them wings."

Once again, he lifted the key to Chickadee's side. Above them, Sparrow let out a squeal of metal. "Wait! Chickadee, there must be something I can offer you. You are going on a journey, yes? From here, I can tell you if any dangers lie on your route."

"Only in this room and we are leaving it."

"Leaving? And taking the key with you?"

"Just so. Do not worry. The boy will come to wind you eventually. And now, Live Mouse, if you would be so kind."

"My other wing! You may have my other wing, only let the live mouse use the key to wind me."

Chickadee paused, waiting for her gears to click forward so that she could look at the Sparrow. Her spring was so loose now that each action took an eternity. "What would I do with one of your wings? I have two of my own."

The other clockwork bird seemed baffled and hung on the end of the line flapping his wings as if he could fling them off.

The live mouse scraped a claw across the edge of the key. "It might come in real handy on our trip. Supposing Messrs DeCola and Wodzinski want a higher payment than you're thinking they do. Why then you'd have something more to offer them."

"And if they didn't then we would have carried the wing with us for no reason."

"Now as to that," said the live mouse, "I can promise you that I'll take it off your hands if'n we don't need it."

Chickadee laughed. "Oh, Live Mouse, I see now. Very well, I will accept Sparrow's wing so that later you may have a full set. Messrs DeCola and Wodzinski will be happy to have two customers, I am certain."

The live mouse bowed to her and wrapped the key in his tail again. "Sparrow, I'll be right up." Scampering across the floor, he disappeared into the wall.

Chickadee did not watch him go, she waited with her gaze still cocked upward toward Sparrow. With the live mouse gone, Chickadee became aware of how still the other clockworks were, watching their drama. Into the silence, Nightingale began to cautiously sing. Her beautiful warbles and chirps repeated through their song thrice before the live mouse appeared out of the ceiling on the chandelier's chain. The crystals of the chandelier tinkled in a wild accompaniment to the ordered song of the nightingale.

The live mouse shimmied down the layers of crystals until he reached Sparrow's flying mechanism. Crawling over that, he wrapped his paws around the string beneath it and slid down to sit on Sparrow's back.

"First one's for me." His sharp incisors flashed in the chandelier's light as he pried the tin loops up from the left wing. Tumbling free, it half fell, half floated to rattle against the floor below. "And now this is for the chickadee."

Again, his incisors pulled the tin free and let the second wing drop.

Sparrow's clockwork whirred audibly inside his body, with nothing to power. "I feel so light!"

"Told ya so." The live mouse reached up and took the string in his paws. Hauling himself back up the line, he reached the flying mechanism in no time at all. "Ready now?"

"Yes! Oh yes, wind me! Wind me!"

Lickety-split, the key sank into the winding mechanism and the live mouse began turning it. The sweet familiar sound of a spring ratcheting tighter floated down from above, filling the room. The other clockwork animals crept closer; even Chickadee felt the longing brought on by the sound of winding.

When the live mouse stopped, Sparrow said, "No, no, I am not wound nearly tight enough yet."

The live mouse braced himself with his tail around an arm of the chandelier and grunted as he turned the key again. And again. And again. "Enough?"

"Tighter."

He kept winding.

"Enough?"

"Tighter. The boy never winds me fully."

"All right." The mouse turned the key three more times and stopped. "That's it. Key won't turn no more."

A strange vibration ran through the sparrow's body. It took Chickadee a moment to realize that he was trying to beat his wings with anticipation. "Then watch me fly."

The live mouse pulled the key out of the flying mechanism and hopped up onto the chandelier. As he did, Sparrow swung into action. The flying mechanism whipped him forward and he shrieked with glee. His body was a blur against the ceiling. The chandelier trembled, then shook, then rattled as he spun faster than Chickadee had ever seen him spin before.

"Live Mouse, you were rig—" With a snap, his flying mechanism broke free of the chandelier. "I'm flying!" Sparrow cried as he hurtled across the room. His body crashed into the window, shattering a pane as he flew through it.

The nightingale stopped her song in shock. Outside, the boy shrieked and his familiar footsteps hurried under the window. "Oh pooh. The clockwork sparrow is broken."

The mother's voice said, "Leave it alone. There's glass everywhere."

Overhead, the live mouse looked down and winked.

Chickadee pecked the ground, with her mechanism wound properly. The live mouse appeared at her side. "Thanks for the wings."

"I trust they are satisfactory payment?"

"Sure enough. They look real pretty hanging on my wall." He squinted at her. "So that's it? You're just going to keep on pecking the ground?"

"As long as you keep winding me."

"Yeah. It's funny, no one else wants my services."

"A pity."

"Got a question for you though. Will you tell me how to get to Messrs DeCola and Wodzinski?"

"Why ever for?"

"Well, I thought ... I thought maybe Messrs DeCola and Wodzinski really could, I dunno, fix 'em on me so as I can fly."

Chickadee rapped the ground with laughter. "No, Mouse, they cannot. We are all bound to our integral mechanisms." She cocked her head at him. "You are a live mouse. I am a clockwork chickadee, and Messrs DeCola and Wodzinski are nothing more than names on a scrap of paper glued to the bottom of a table."

Cinderella Suicide

Samantha Henderson

Cinderella Suicide had the Whoremaster backed against the greasy-smooth wall of the Tarot, blade beneath his chins. She had that grinning-skull look that meant she didn't give a damn anymore.

We'd gone Tarot-side celebrating the fair end of a dinkum job: supplies run through the Eureka Stockade. Diggers dug in for years, and likely wouldn't move, not since they'd found a nice vein of gold ore and settled like ticks. This time we'd been running meds to the troopers. Last time it was swizzlesticks to the diggers.

I scoped 360. Tintype leaned on the wall behind, apart from everyone else like always. He was hefting his swizzlestick, so I edged out of jabbing range. He was a better judge of her moods, anyway.

Swiveling back, I noticed blur at 170 left. Better take it to the tech gnomes stat; outfitting me wasn't cheap, even with a triune money-pool.

Suicide let the Whoremaster and all his bulk slide down the wall, alive for now, so I quit reckoning the odds on who would succeed him and watched her back. Here a slithy one could punch out a lung, and the state she was in she'd never notice 'til later. Behind me Tintype sheathed the swizzlestick and unleaned. Sometimes Suicide killed, sometimes she didn't. I never asked why.

A little space between push and pull you could drop coin into. In the wide gap between moment and moment the Whoremaster was spared, but anyone unfocused could lose his life 'twixt breath in and breath out.

So I jangled my purse and smiled big. "A round on me, and one on the Whoremaster after!" I said. I nodded at the fat, sweating man and narrowed one eye. He frowned but nodded back, for no fool he after twenty years at the Tarot, and Suicide let him go and slapped him on the beefy shoulder. He didn't protest – and wisely, for she hadn't lost her death's-head rictus, though the blade sheathed back into her hand and she stepped away.

So I smiled more and tossed the purse on the bar and the whores and troopers cheered and drank and toasted me, six feet of blue-eyed blond, and "Superstar!" they cried with hoarse voices.

That's us. Cinderella Superstar, Cinderella Suicide, Cinderella Tintype. Fourth-stage triune shipped together, forged together through circumstance. Our real names don't matter because that's part of the deal. They link you duet and triune because the survival rate's higher that way. After manumission, the bonds tend to stick. With duets there's more to share, but with three, two can sleep at a time.

Superstar, Suicide, Tintype: pensioners with tickets-of-leave, four years past the end of our term. Free to earn our keep and free to starve, long as we never tried to leave New Holland's shores.

It was my shout for wide-eyes that night, but when dawn cracked gray, Tintype strolled out of the burrow, trim as you please, a pulp under his arm. He nodded to me, squatted down, and unrolled it.

"*All the Year Round?*" I asked.

He shook his head. "Traded it. *Master Humphrey's Clock.*" I nodded.

I never saw Tintype topsy; not in the freight womb of the Greatship; not on the wharves of Botany. Dressed in black, close-buttoned always. When the Bulls herded us down the planks off the ship to the Dockmaster, we two jostled shoulder to shoulder.

Dockmaster looked up, hot day, rainy days, every day in Botany in his eyes, every day a world unto itself, and smiled a little.

"Pretty boy," he said to me. "We'll see you in the Tarot by and by, see if we don't."

I didn't know what he meant, so shut up tight. And he was wrong; I never made a living whoring, not after I came to Botany. Before, I will not say.

He glanced at the gray, trim toff beside me, who'd be tallish were I not taller. "Duet, then," he said, and scratched at his ledger. The Bull to my left hefted his chip-gun, and duet we would have been forever and a day if not for the shrill ricochet of a girl screaming.

She'd broken from the herd and now she dangled over the edge of the plank at the end of a Bull's arm, kicking like live bait. I knew what was in the dirty water. She wouldn't last a handcount.

The Bull looked at the Dockmaster with that girl-scrap clawing at his arm, and I knew he'd drop her if the Dockmaster gave the nod. Instead he beckoned sharp and the Bull twisted her back to earth, shoved her between us with a cruel grip. She bared her teeth at the Dockmaster and he smiled.

"Triune, then," said he. "Superstar and the Clerk here will keep you in line." He glanced at the ledger.

"Brand them Cinderella," he said, and hop skip jump, the three of us were chipped and pointed most politely, sir, to the pens. They chipped us alphabet-wise, by themes. Next was Triune Dulcinea and Duet Evelina. I kept Superstar, the toff shook off Clerk and became Tintype, and from that moment the girl was Suicide. We survived, side by side in the Jelly Orchards, back to back in the mines. Until boom, manumission, forty pounds allowance apiece, and license to upgrade. But never a ticket Home.

Tintype and I watched the dawn spread.

"Did she dream?" I asked, being that I was on wide-eyes since we made burrow-side from the Tarot, and that Suicide had never stopped grinning all the way home.

Tintype nodded, still scoping his pulp. It was never good when Suicide dreamed. "He grabbed at her hair," he said, suddenly. I looked at him and then let my sights swivel back to the horizon. It wasn't like Tintype to offer information unsought.

"Why?" Not like she was one of the Whoremaster's herd.

"He was slapping a whore around. New meat: bought her off the Docks last week. Suicide . . . objected."

"Ah."

She couldn't stand being touched anywhere on the head. Dockside on her entryday a Bull tried to restrain her by holding the back of her neck. I saw the bite marks she gave him, deep.

Not even headmods: cochlear, scoping, reinforcing – none of that. Just blades, nervewired underskin. Thin, so the variable-magnetization wouldn't rip them out. Blades all over her body.

Once when she was coming off of shut-eye and it was my turn to sleep I watched her. She was stark and face down because she'd just got her last mods and was healing: thin red welts across her shoulder blades, protruding like wingstubs. Her body was white and bony-thin, with knots of muscle, and I could see the blade-implants moving beneath the surface as she breathed.

I couldn't sleep that night.

Tintype got a cochlear and both of us have anteflap ear-buttons so we can talk short-distance, but Suicide wouldn't even get that. None of us elect mod layering; it's expensive, and a bad idea to have excess metal with the vee-em. Not that some don't try, and very gala they look, all loops and sparkles and pretty blinkies. Not that some don't try to fly, either, and some go far before the vee-em surges through and crashes them all atwitter.

Tintype looked up and shifted as Suicide emerged. I blinked. Last night her hair was shaggy-down, but now naught but a fine fuzz. You could see the shape of her skull beneath, no bumps from headmods. Unusual in a pensioner.

She didn't say anything about it, just scratched her velvet nap and yawned. "Time for your nap, 'Star," she said. "I'll wide-eyes a while."

"It's my turn," said Tintype.

She shrugged. "I kept you up."

"No," said Tintype. "I'll reckon while you watch, and when Superstar's up we'll go to Botany for a scope adjust."

Tintype kept all our accounts. I don't think we even debated that; it was just done-as-done when we got ticketed. He made sure we got every pound of our due, doled us out our fun money and made sure the rest worked for us. I've seen teams, duets and triunes both, go from ruination to ruination because they didn't have a dinkum reckoning-man. He wouldn't let the tech gnomes in Botany slide with dingbats in my scope.

I napped unsteady, for Tintype was humming whilst he reckoned, and it sometimes hit the button at my ear just so.

List, then. 1788, New Holland becomes New South Wales, and dear England starts to send her slithies there, her dribs and drabs and pick-pocks and whores and cutthroats, to drain the cesspool Britannia's become. And then we pin the gravitational constant, and solve Pringle's Mysterious Logarithm, and then just when we're ready for it there's an explosion of a different sort (I'm a proud product of my state school, whoreboy though I became). From the skies over Van Diemen's Land streaks a merry flaming angel arcing down to earth and boom! Kills most of the slithies, and their Bulls, and the Murri and the Nunga in their Dreamtime too, far as any know. Sky goes red from Yangtze to Orkney. A few Nunga are left, fishing the Outer Isles. And more slithies come soon, for England's still all-of-cess, and we'd just as soon have them die.

But! Scattered all about, like Father Christmas tossing pennies, rare earth, yttrium and scandium in luscious ashy chunks. And soon there are Magnetic Clocks, and Automatons, and Air-Cars, and good Queen Vickie trulls about in a Magnetic Carriage like everybody else. But still there is cess, and ever will be, pretend as they might at home, so still the slithies are transported.

And a good thing for Merric Olde too, because nowhere is there as much rare earth as Australia, being that's where the Great Boom happened, and nothing so useful for gathering ore and jellies as a big jolly family of convicts. Work for the Squatters when you're Docked; work for them after you serve your time and are pensioned, but on your own terms. Or whore-about. Or prentice to the tech gnomes. Or mine gold, which never goes out of style. Or wander the Nullarbor, looking for the Source, and die. Or fish with the Nunga, if they'd have you, which they won't. Stick with your duet/triune mates, if you would live out the year.

Always something to do.

But don't fly, not much, because the variable-mag will crash you deep, and don't depend on Carriages to work all the time. Beware your metal, for it can betray you.

The tech gnomes shielded their sector so the vee-em wouldn't fry their instruments, and it worked most of the time. The shields were veined all over with newfill.

They made it so implants didn't function well either, and I could tell Suicide was nervous that her blades didn't work. Most were quiescent, but the blade on the back of her left hand kept on stuttering in and out. She kept it straight against her leg so it wouldn't snag. I couldn't distance-talk to Tintype either; the buttons only hummed.

· The left side of my forehead felt raw and ticklish where they'd unplugged the scope, and I sat careful and still while the gnome bubbled at the mechanism. Tintype watched, quiet-like, while Suicide went to fetch us some pies.

The gnome chuckled as he found the dingbat, pulled the scope from the solution, and went to work with the thin tweezers that seemed an extension of his fingers and might very well have been. Suicide returned with three pasties, piping hot and early enough in the day that the mix still had some meat in it. We huddled and Tintype unrolled his latest pulp, removing a thin film of tissue as he did.

A bonus of the gnomes' shields: your council couldn't be overheard, like in the Tarot or even the burrows.

"List," he said, bending over the tissue. I saw a flicker of coiling type. "A job. It's a real rouser. Five hundred pounds of the Queen's own money, not Oz."

"Split?" said Suicide, her mouth full of 'roo.

"Each." We sat and mulled that a piece. Fifteen centuries of the Queen's Own Money could buy a Squat, a big one, the best in Oz.

He went on. "It's dangerous, very."

"Of course," said Suicide. "Fifteen centuries, it should be. Spill!"

"The Source," said Tintype. "Client wants the Source."

A long pause, then Suicide laughed, spraying us with bits of 'roo pie.

"The Source! Client doesn't want much, does he? And maybe we could find him the Queen of the Fairies while we're at it, and a magic wishing frog!"

"Maybe we could," said Tintype mildly, and looked at me.

Some make the mistake of thinking that because I am big, and mild of feature, that I am stupid; I am not. The Source of the ore, the point of impact, was somewhere north of the Nullarbor, the great, central, dry-as-death plain west of Botany, and everybody wanted it. But the vee-em got stronger the closer you got: less vee, more em, and gliders that crashed half the time in Botany and North always crashed when folk went sniffing round the Never-Never. Same with the Carriages.

That leaves horseback, muleback, humping in your own water and no sure place to go. Mind, people try. Pensioners, the occasional Squatter, and of course the expeditions outfitted by dear old England. Some came back from the Never-Never with stories of animals dying under them, mates going mad with thirst and running off into the desert, suicide, murder, hostile Anagnu (though all knew none were left). Some brought lumps of ore, veined with opal. Some said the further you got into the Never-Never, the more the land bled red stone and demons sang to you. Maybe some made it to the Source, but not that I knew.

Suicide was grinning again, licking her right-hand fingers (the blade still flickered about the left). She would go with us, I knew, and not so much for the money as the hell of it. Tintype was watching me because he knew upon me the choice lay.

I knew Tintype would not propose so risky a job, no matter the fee, without a plan, without backup. I stifled an urge to scratch my forehead. "Tell," I said, and Tintype bent close, the tissue-film still in hand. "A Nunga, fishes off Van Diemen's Land," he said, low. "Going to swim us west, into the Bight, show us where to trek 'cross the Nullarbor."

"Tickets-of-leave," I said. "Conditions: we can't set foot on a boat. Back to Dockside if we do." Against my side I felt Suicide shudder.

"We can with a pass from the Governor," he said. "Dinkum, not forged." I stared. Behind him the gnome was beckoning; my scope was fixed.

"Can you get a dinkum pass from the Governor?"

He smiled, lipless. "I can."

The Nunga, Johnny Roman, was ashy-gray and saturnine of countenance, and his boat was a big one, with room for five passengers. And that's what there was, for there was a duet out of East Botany, Pinkerton Red and Pinkerton Gold, jolly sorts with hair to match their names. They were bound for Nullarbor too, also with passes, and that seemed to put Tintype out a bit. He spent most of the three-day trip pondering his accounting-book, while I liked to see the shore go by with its little bays and strange outcroppings, and Suicide sat on the deck with the Pinkertons all friendly and jolly (with them a respectful distance from her blades). I hadn't been to sea before, save for my transport, and a twomonth of seasick in a metal womb full of dirty, vomitous slithies did not compare to this. I volunteered wide-eyes whilst the others snored, and watched the hard, bright pinprick stars veer by. When we docked at Nullarbor the Pinkertons took off quick, veering east. This mollified Tintype some, though he still looked a touch put out, watching them 'til they dwindled in the distance. He waited for Johnny Roman to dock right and swab down before we all huddled. Johnny took out a double-palm's-breadth span of bark.

"The map," said Tintype, who obviously expected it.

"A map, or a story, much the same thing," said Johnny. With a callused gray finger he traced a white line with a triple row of tiny dots beside it. "These are Anagnu markings," he said.

"I thought there were none left," I said.

He looked at me from beneath bushy eyebrows. "There are some. Hardly enough to matter. This" – he pointed again – "this is where Uluru was."

"Uluru?"

"She used to be holy, a holy place. She is a monster now. Or so the Anagnu say. She speaks to any that come near, and she drives them mad."

I glanced at Tintype. He didn't seem surprised to hear any of this.

"This path." Tintype's finger echoes Johnny's. "A stream. If we follow that by muleback, will we make it to Uluru?"

"Oh yes." Johnny sat back on his heels. "And then you will die."

Suicide grinned.

We spread out on muleback, following the trickle of water outlined on the Anagnu map. Although a thin green fuzz grew by the water, clashing with the bright red soil, the air was dry and pulled at my face, drawing the skin tight.

Tintype and I alternated in front, and Suicide always took backup. A day in she yelled and pointed, and I told Tintype via his button to look to the east. Two gliders, pink and gold in the morning sun, paralleling our path. Heading to Uluru.

"The Pinkertons," I told him, quiet-like.

"Yes," he said. Then, "I don't like this."

"How, with the mag?"

"Cellulose. Hardly any metal in those things." To my puzzled look he said: "They're new."

We rested in the heat of day and also in the very dark of night, listening to the lizards scuttle and watching the Southern Cross sparkle across the black sky. After a while the mules wouldn't go on, although there was enough water. They were nervous, all atwitter, and finally we slapped their rumps and let them go home. According to the Anagnu map, it was time to turn from the stream. We filled our 'skins and bellies with the warm water, me double-loading.

Afternoon, Suicide was on wide-eyes and woke me and Tintype, pointing ahead. Just visible, a grey haze in the hot air, and a taste of smoke.

The wreckage of two gliders, one in the stream: they must have been following the thin green line as a guide. Pinkerton Gold was still in the hub of his craft, neckbroke. A line in the dust showed where Red had crawled from his. He'd made it about fifty feet before collapsing.

The wings of the gliders were pale and flexible. Where one had broken I saw fibres. Cellulose.

Suicide and I salvaged their gear while Tintype searched the bodies, looking puzzled. I thought it odd that he checked their ears.

As we humped on, I kept on thinking about it.

Back at the Parramatta burrows we kept track, close, of the days that passed, a convict-habit. Making sure the Squatters didn't cheat you of your ticket-of-leave day. 'Twas too easy to let sunrise and sunset blur in the heat, in the boredom between jobs, in watching your back and the backs of your mates. But now, between red dirt and blue sky, I let day slip into day slip into darkest, star-strewn night. Only the bite of 'skin straps at my shoulders. Only Tintype fussing with his map and compass. Only Suicide crunching behind.

And thinking of the Pinkertons, of Tintype and his maps and messages, of cellulose planes in the Never-Never.

'Twas midmorning when a hum, faint, started in my head. Almost a whisper. I stopped and listened hard, sure I heard words.

Pain lanced through my head, beginning at my left ear. Ahead, I saw Tintype wince and paw at the side of his head.

The anteflap buttons. Feedback screamed through my anterior lobes: Tintype's button squealing at mine. I could hear myself echoing in Tintype's head.

Louder and louder. My head was in the dirt.

A smaller, quieter pain at my ear, and I fought the impulse to strike back. Suicide, slicing out the implant. I tried to hold still.

Suddenly just the echo between my ears, and a pink bloody lump dropped on the red sand before me. I watched her stride quick to Tintype, wrest his hand away from where he was clawing himself, and bend, blade out, over his hunched form. I saw him relax suddenly when she straightened up, implant in hand. Buttons aren't planted deep: a little pressure and the bleeding stopped. That whispering was still there, however.

I glanced at Suicide. She was tilting her head, looking mazed.

"Hear it?" I asked.

She nodded, frowning in concentration.

"Words. *Soon.* And *hatching.* And *punishment.*" She listened a while, then shook her head. "Now just a hum."

"So not just the headmods."

"No."

Tintype untucked a little package. "Here."

White and spongy, little balls. Something hard in the middle of each. "Like this." He pushed one into each ear. Suicide and I looked at each other. The hum was getting louder, the whispers sharper.

We shrugged and put them in. The sound cut back, and faded. Still there, but still and small, like the voice of God.

"You were expecting this?" asked Suicide.

"Something like this," he replied.

We trudged on. Once, experimentally, I took a sponge half out of one ear.

DUSTALLWASDUSTAFTERANDTHESTARSTHEMERCILESS STARS

I staggered and shoved the plug back in. Tintype flashed me a look.

I walked in the quickening heat and thought some more.

You couldn't see it at a distance, but the ground was sloping up. Tintype still seemed to know where to go.

"I've been thinking," I said, close to his ear, since the buttons were out.

"Have you?" he said, with mild interest. "Then tell!"

"I'm pondering how a pensioner gets word of that rarest thing, a map to the Source. Or a Governor's pass to go sea-wise. I'm wondering how a ticket-of-leave man has the very merry little bobbins that will block that too-terrible sound. I'm wondering how you knew about the cellulose gliders.

"The Pinkertons upset you, but you're not surprised. I'd guess you figured quickly that those who sent you would send others. Not the first time a client sent two teams after the same prize.

"But what's stuck in your craw is this: you didn't expect another plant. Because that's what you are, aren't you? You never were a dinkum convict. You were to find a team and sit, pretty, until the right time came. Until your sources could find a key, or a map, or the right earplugs, or a cellulose glider."

I thumbed backwards in the direction of the wreckage. "Wonder why they didn't get the earplugs. Maybe they did, and forgot. Or something went wrong with the gliders. Or your clients have a touch of the experimental, and want to know what works, what doesn't. How many teams that tried the Never-Never had plants? There's probably another, trying from the north. Scientific method. Try, fail, fail better."

He was quiet for a long time after that.

"I'm not so smart," he said, finally.

The whispering was becoming speech as we went up and up the gentle slope. Uluru driving us mad, Johnny Roman would say.

Soon. Soon. It hatches.

My scope was stinging, and I stopped to wrest it off. Suicide helped with the fine tip of a blade. The variable-mag was becoming permanent. We must be close to the Source.

"How do your blades feel?" I asked, as she neatly dissected the nerve.

" 'Sallright," she said. "Nothing yet. That's why they're custom: the metal's too thin to register."

More speech, dropping like ripe fruit. *Cold, here. How do you live? Things grow in the cold that should not grow at all. I'll never be warm.*

I wondered if we were all hearing the same thing.

Ahead, a ridge of loose rock. Everywhere was dust in red streaks.

"Wait," said Suicide.

She was standing with fingers spread, looking at the backs of her hands. I had to turn to see her, hating not having my 360 scope.

We went back to her. Under her skin the blades were trembling.

"Back up," said Tintype, and she did. The movement stopped. He studied the ground minutely. Meantime the voice went on. *Hatches soon. The others are dead.*

Tintype was crouched on the ground. "How came you here?" he shouted suddenly. There was a pause while the whisper-speech stopped.

No one has asked in a long time.

Another pause.

I was ... exiled? Yes. A punishment. Transported. From my home I was ... thrown. Very far.

"Why?" I shouted, while Tintype grubbed in the dirt. Didn't see why he had to do all the talking here.

There was something self-satisfied in the answer. *I bred where it was forbidden. Only the Matrix can breed the Central, but I won through, I did it. They feared me too much to disseminate, but exile me they did. They threw me to the cold worlds. But they could not stop my hatchings.*

"Here," Tintype pointed. If you looked close, you could see a faint line on the ground where the little bits of ore shifted in straight lines. He dug in his toe and made a furrow in the dust, perpendicular to our path.

"You can't go beyond here, not with your blades," he told Suicide. "The mag gets stronger each step, and they'll rip out of your body. Do you understand?" She looked sullen but nodded. We went on and she squatted down, watching.

Because of the cold they fight inside me. They are all devoured, all but one. And he hatches.

We came to the ridge of rocks. And looked over.

Back Home, once, I saw the trap of an ant lion. Biggish sort of insects, they dig a hole, a funnel-shaped trap of loose soil, and ants and such who trip over it fall to the bottom where the ant lion lies buried.

This doodlebug's crib circled wide – how wide I could not tell; the slope all chunks of loose ore. One, two miles down, perhaps, was a black dot. I squinted, missing my scope. It might have been a hole. A century of Parramatta pensioners scrabbling a month would be hard-put to dig such a thing. Two century of Botany convicts with hell-for-leather Squatters on their tails, perhaps.

The voice was very clear now.

I would be Matrix. I couldn't wait. I should have killed Matrix when I had the chance.

Tintype knelt on the edge of the ridge and peered down. Hypnotic, all those rocks merging into something smooth-looking with that dot, harder to see than it should have been and the heat haze wavering. A long thin something – yellowbelly or fierce or maybe just a coppertail – scuttled past Tintype's hand and he startled back and overcomped sideways. Before I could grab him he overbalanced and started sliding down that slope of tumbled ore. He struggled for purchase but there was none.

I threw myself belly-down, digging in with my toes and grabbing for his flailing hands.

" 'Type! Superstar!" Suicide yelled from behind the barrier Tintype had toed in the sand. " 'Star! Hold him!"

"Trying to," I grunted, and the shadow of a smile shimmied over Tintype's face. "Told you I wasn't so smart. Don't let her come across," he said, maddening-calm with the long descent, that slope, that maw beneath him. Bloody rocks were wrong, too round, too slippery for what they were.

I could've killed them both, truly, yelling at me this and that while plowing in my knees and elbows and slipping in anyway.

Are you coming to me now? The voice was curious.

Then something like the wind at my back and she had me around the waist, both her wrist-blades protruding enough to root in my leathers and poke my ribs, thank you very much. I looked back and she had her knee-blades planted deep, enough to hold all three of us for a while.

You may all come. See!

"Get back, Suicide!" yelled Tintype, never mind that I was hauling him inch by inch up the rubble, his feet clawing for toehold, now she had us anchored.

But she hung on, grim as death, and I thought at first it was dinkum and the mag was variable after all when she started to scream.

I heave-hoed hard as I could and sent Tintype rolling safe past the lip of the trap. Suicide was writhing in the red sand, gashes opening down her leathers where the blades were birthing, ripped from her flesh by the mag.

Tintype grabbed her feet, I took her shoulders and we tried to heave her past the barrier. But she was spasming now, her screams a thin, shrill tea-kettle sound. She thrashed like nothing human, and a blade shot out of her, neatly skinning half my thumb.

I hung on, but Tintype got a solid kick in the chest, sending him tumbling. Coated in red dust, he staggered back. I lost my grip, and Suicide dropped. The back blade shot from her, clattering down the slope. Then one tore out of the back of her hand.

Somehow Tintype scooped her up and went running for the barrier. I followed, dodging as her hardware zipped past my head.

At the barrier he almost fell, but we caught her between us, laid her down gently as we could.

Past the leathers I saw slabs of red flesh and mottled white bone. The tendons on the backs of her hand were exposed. Beneath, her leathers, my arms, were soaked.

Tintype cradled her, holding her head. Don't do that, I thought automatically, but she didn't struggle. She was panting quickly now, like a tired dingo.

"What?" said Tintype, bending over her.

"Hatching soon," she said. "The barrier moons, all in pieces. So cold."

She looked past Tintype, up at me. "I'm cold, 'Star."

"Don't," said Tintype, but she was gone.

Tintype sat expressionless for a long time. In the twilight wind, the blood on my arms felt sticky and cold.

"Bollocks," he said at last, quiet-like.

Nine years, I never heard him swear.

"Bollocks to them all."

In a single movement, he got to his feet, Suicide in his arms. There was a terrible stillness about him.

He walked back to the pit and I trotted by his side.

"We need to get out of here, 'Type."

He ignored me. At the lip of the slope he stopped, and I tried to take the body.

"Let me take her, 'Type. We'll go back and find the mules."

Tintype snarled at me, and I recoiled. He folded himself upon the lip, with her body across his lap.

"Go away, Superstar," he said, deadvoiced. "Get as far away as you can."

Suicide looked boneless across his knees, and her shorn head in the crook of his elbow looked like a tired doll.

A smooth click and I stared down the barrel of Tintype's gun. Never knew he had a gun.

"Go, or I will shoot you, 'Star," he said, but I was fair mazed. Celluloid, fine grained, a lovely piece, really. But how did he rate a gun, forbidden to pensioners? And where did he hide it all this time?

But then. He wasn't really a pensioner, and hid everything from us.

Everything, even love.

Still, his voice was calm. "I'll start with the shoulder, 'Star, then the legs. Move out while you can."

I moved back slowly, crunching on the ore, then faster. Out of range, as I reckoned it, I stopped, and he put down the gun.

Methodically, he searched in his innumerable pockets. He took out something small, and square, and black, with a screen that glinted in the sun. Behind me and overhead, I heard the hum of gliders.

There were five of them, the same as those that crashed the Pinkertons. Tintype had something like a stylus and was manipulating something on the little black box.

I stifled the impulse to duck as the gliders hummed closer. Bollocks to them all.

Tintype, done with his fiddling about, held up the box and flashed it in the setting sun. The gliders were straight up by now, and I saw them adjust their course to center on Tintype.

He waited. He waited until they were very close.

Then he tossed the box in a beauteous parabola, arcing into the pit. The gliders, one two three four five, went straight down into the trap. He never looked round to watch them, still facing me.

The hum stopped, hiccupped like an angry insect.

And then.

A great flare, straight up like a pillar of fire. For a second I saw them both silhouetted stark black against the orange. Then the ash rained down. I did duck then; I groveled in the dirt. It was a long time before the roaring stopped.

I walked to the dimple where the pit had been, taking the sponges out of my ears. Nobody was saying anything. I was covered in red dust, half an inch thick: a creature of the Never-Never.

As far as I could see, mile upon mile of ore. And the milky sparkle of opal.

Reckoning-man and all, he had brought us to this.

Something moved, shifting chunks of earth with a clink and clank.

I decided to wait and see if it was human. But 'twasn't. Tintype was gone, with Suicide, with the clients and their gliders, with Uluru buried deep in her exultation and despair.

Something tickled my brain, and I wondered if I'd missed a headmod.

Mother?

Wings it had, which made sense, didn't it, if it was to fly between the stars? No head, but a mouth, serrated sharp, embedded in a stocky body. Nothing to compare this to: not 'roo, not goanna, not dingo, not man. Things like feet, too many, clawed like Suicide's blades. Like her, a thing made to fight. It could've gutted me with a thought.

It looked at me, eyeless, sideways-like, and cawed.

I'm cold, mother.

I stepped closer and saw things like worms crawling over its body. Closer still and saw they were pinfeathers, growing fast before my eyes.

I'm hungry, mother.

Days away the Pinkertons roasted beneath the sun, and I had no thought but to lead it there, though my 'skins were all but dry and I'd never make it. It followed me patient for half a day and then must've nosed them out, for that mouth came out of that dreadful body and hooked me up by the leathers. I dangled like a puppy while its feet beat the ground and the ground went by in a blur of dust and opal.

It ate fast, if delicately. Thought it would eat me too, but I was too tired to run when it stepped, fussy-like, towards me.

But it only settled against me, tucking its terrible feet beneath, and went to sleep.

I thought about howsome my last sea voyage wasn't half bad, and I'd rather like another.

"Well, little bird," I whispered. "Shall we go to London to see the Queen?"

Arbeitskraft

Nick Mamatas

1. The Transformation Problem

In glancing over my correspondence with Herr Marx, especially the letters written during the period in which he was struggling to complete his opus, *Capital*, even whilst I was remanded to the Victoria Mill of Ermen and Engels in Weaste to simultaneously betray the class I was born into and the class to which I'd dedicated my life, I was struck again by the sheer audacity of my plan. I've moved beyond political organizing or even investigations of natural philosophy and have used my family's money and the labour of my workers – even now, after a lifetime of railing against the bourgeoisie, their peculiar logic limns my language – to encode my old friend's thoughts in a way I hope will prove fruitful for the struggles to come.

I am a fox, ever hunted by agents of the state, but also by political rivals and even the occasional enthusiastic student intellectual *manqué*. For two weeks, I have been making a very public display of destroying my friend's voluminous correspondence. The girls come in each day and carry letters and covers both in their aprons to the roof of the mill to burn them in a soot-stained metal drum. It's a bit of a spectacle, especially as the girls wear cowls to avoid smoke inhalation and have rather pronounced limps as they walk the bulk of the letters along the roof, but we are ever attracted to spectacle, aren't we? The strings of electrical lights in the petit-bourgeois districts that twinkle all night, the iridescent skins of the dirigibles that litter the skies over The City like peculiar flying fish leaping from the ocean – they even appear overhead here in Manchester, much to the shock, and more recently, glee of the street urchins who shout and yawp whenever one passes under the clouds, and the only slightly more composed women on their way to squalid Deansgate market. A fortnight ago I took in a theatrical production, a local production of Mr Peake's *Presumption: or the Fate of Frankenstein*, already a hoary old play given new life and revived, ironically enough, by recent innovations in electrified machine-works. How bright the lights, how stunning the arc of actual lightning, tamed and obedient, how thunderous the ovations and the crumbling of the glacial cliffs! All the bombast of German opera in a space no larger than a middle-class parlour. And yet, throughout the entire evening, the great and hulking monster never spoke. *Contra* Madame Shelley's engaging novel, the "new Adam" never learns of philosophy, and the total of her excellent speeches of critique against the social institutions of her, and our, day are expurgated. Instead, the monster is ever an infant, given only to explosions of rage. Yet the audience, which contained a fair number of working-men who had managed to save or secure 5d. for "penny-stinker" seating, was enthralled. The play's Christian morality, alien to the original novel, was spelled out as if on a slate for the audience, and the monster was rendered as nothing more than an artefact of unholy vice. But lights blazed, and living snow from coils of refrigeration fell from the ceiling, and spectacle won the day.

My burning of Marx's letters is just such a spectacle – the true correspondence is secreted among a number of the safe houses I have acquired in Manchester and London. The girls on the rooftop are burning unmarked leaves, schoolboy doggerel, sketches and whatever else I have lying about. The police have infiltrated Victoria Mill, but all their agents are men, as the work of espionage is considered too vile for the gentler sex. So the men watch the girls come from my office with letters by the bushel and burn them, then report every lick of flame and wafting cinder to their superiors.

My brief digression regarding the *Frankenstein* play is apposite, not only as it has to do with spectacle but with my current operation at Victoria Mill. Surely, Reader, you are familiar with Mr Babbage's remarkable Difference Engine, perfected in 1822 – a year prior to the first production of Mr Peake's theatrical adaptation of *Frankenstein* – given the remarkable changes to the political economy that took place in the years after its introduction. How did we put it, back in the heady 1840s? "Subjection of Nature's forces to man, machinery, application of chemistry to industry and agriculture, steam-navigation, railways, electric telegraphs, clearing of whole continents for cultivation, canalization of rivers, whole populations conjured out of the ground – what earlier century had even a presentiment that such productive forces slumbered in the lap of social labour?" That was just the beginning. Ever more I was reminded not of my old work with Marx, but of Samuel Butler's prose fancy "Erewhon – the time will come when the machines will hold the real supremacy over the world and its inhabitants – is what no person of a truly philosophic mind can for a moment question."

With the rise of the Difference Engine and the subsequent rationalization of market calculations, the bourgeoisie's revolutionary aspect continued unabated. Steam-navigation took to the air; railways gave way to horseless carriages; electric telegraphs to instantaneous wireless aethereal communications; the development of applied volcanization to radically increase the amount of arable land, and to tame the great prize of Africa, the creation of automata for all but the basest of labour ... ah, if only Marx were still here. That, I say to myself each morning upon rising. *If only Marx were still here!* The stockholders demand to know why I have not automated my factory, as though the clanking stovepipe limbs of the steam-workers aren't just more dead labour! As though *Arbeitskraft* – labour-power – is not the source of all value! *If only Marx were still here!* And he'd say to me, *Freddie, perhaps we were wrong.* Then he'd laugh and say, *I'm just having some fun with you.*

But we were not wrong. The internal contradictions of capitalism have not peacefully resolved themselves; the proletariat still may become the new revolutionary class, even as steam-worker builds steam-worker under the guidance of Difference Engine No. 53. The politico-economic chasm between bourgeoisie and proletarian has grown ever wider, despite the best efforts of the Fabian Society and other gradualists to improve the position of the working class vis-à-vis their esteemed – and *en-steamed*, if you would forgive the pun – rulers. The Difference Engine is a device of formal logic, limited by the size of its gearwork and the tensile strength of the metals used in its construction. What I propose is a device of *dialectical logic*, a repurposing of the looms, a recording of unity of conflicts and opposites drawn on the finest of threads to pull innumerable switches, based on a linguistic programme derived from the correspondence of my comrade-in-arms.

I am negating the negation, transforming my factory into a massive Dialectical Engine that replicates not the arithmetical operations of an abacus but the cogitations of a human brain. I am rebuilding Karl Marx on the factory floor, repurposing the looms of the factory to create punch-cloths of over a thousand columns, and I will speak to my friend again.

2. The Little Match Girls

Under the arch-lights of Fairfield Road I saw them, on my last trip to The City. The evening's amusement had been invigorating if empty, a fine meal had been consumed immediately thereafter, and a digestif imbibed. I'd dismissed my London driver for the evening, for a cross-town constitutional. I'd catch the late airship, I thought. Match girls, leaving their shift in groups, though I could hardly tell them from steam-workers at first, given their awkward gaits; and the gleam of metal under the lights, so like the monster in the play, caught my eye.

Steam-workers still have trouble with the finest work – the construction of Difference Engine gears is skilled labour performed by a well-remunerated aristocracy of working men. High-quality cotton garments and bedclothes too are the remit of proletarians of the *flesh*, thus Victoria Mill. But there are commodities whose production still requires living labour not because of the precision needed to create the item, but due to the danger of the job. The production of white phosphorous matches is one of these. The matchsticks are too slim for steam-worker claws, which are limited to a trio of pincers on the All-Purpose models, and to less refined appendages – sledges, sharp blades – on Special-Purpose models. Furthermore, the aluminium outer skin, or shell, of the steam-worker tends to heat up to the point of combusting certain compounds, or even plain foolscap. So the Bryant and May factory in Bow, London retained young girls, ages fourteen and up, to perform the work.

The stories in *The Link* and other reformist periodicals are well known. Twelve-hour days for wages of 4s. a week, though it's a lucky girl who isn't fined for tardiness, who doesn't suffer deductions for having dirty feet, for dropping matches from her frame, for allowing the machines to falter rather than sacrifice her fingers to them. The girls eat their bread and butter – most can afford more only rarely, and then it's marmalade – on the line, leading to ingestion of white phosphorous. And there are the many cases of "phossy jaw" – swollen gums, foul breath, and some physicians even claimed that the jawbones of the afflicted would glow, like a candle shaded by a leaf of onionskin paper. I saw the gleaming of these girls' jaws as I passed and swore to myself. They were too young for phossy jaw; it takes years for the deposition of phosphorous to build. But as they passed me by, I saw the truth.

Their jaws had all been removed, a typical intervention for the disease, and they'd been replaced with prostheses. All the girls, most of whom were likely plain before their transformations, were now half-man half-machine, monstrosities! I couldn't help but accost them.

"Girls! Pardon me!" There were four of them; the tallest was perhaps fully mature, and the rest were mere children. They stopped, obedient. I realized that their metallic jaws, which gleamed so brightly under the new electrical streetlamps, might not be functional and I was flushed with concern. Had I humiliated them?

The youngest-seeming opened her mouth and said in a voice that had a greater similarity to the product of a phonographic cylinder than a human throat, "Buy Bryant and May matchsticks, sir."

"Oh no, I don't need any matchsticks. I simply—"

"Buy Bryant and May matchsticks, sir," she said again. Two of the others – the middle girls – lifted their hands and presented boxes of matchsticks for my perusal. One of those girls had two silvery digits where a thumb and forefinger had presumably once been. They were cleverly designed to articulate on the knuckles, and through some mechanism occulted to me did move in a lifelike way.

"Are any of you girls capable of independent speech?" The trio looked to the tallest girl, who nodded solemnly and said, "I."

She struggled with the word, as though it were unfamiliar. "My Bryant and May mandible," she continued, "I was given it by . . . Bryant and May . . . long ago."

"So, with some struggle, you are able to compel speech of your own?"

"Buy . . . but Bryant and May match . . . made it hard," the girl said. Her eyes gleamed nearly as brightly as her metallic jaw.

The smallest of the four started suddenly, then turned her head, looking past her compatriots. "Buy!" she said hurriedly, almost rudely. She grabbed the oldest girl's hand and tried to pull her away from our conversation. I followed her eyes and saw the telltale plume of a police wagon rounding the corner. Lacking any choice, I ran with the girls to the end of the street and then turned a corner.

For a long moment, we were at a loss. Girls such as these are the refuse of society – often the sole support of their families, and existing in horrific poverty, they nonetheless hold to all the feminine rules of comportment. Even a troupe of them, if spotted in the public company of an older man in his evening suit, would simply be ruined women – sacked from their positions for moral turpitude, barred from renting in any situation save for those reserved for women engaged in prostitution; ever surrounded by criminals and other lumpen elements. The bourgeois sees in his wife a mere instrument of production, but in every female of the labouring classes he sees his wife. What monsters Misters Bryant and May must have at home! I dared not follow the girls for fear of terrifying them, nor could I even attempt to persuade them to accompany me to my safe house. I let them leave, and proceeded to follow them as best I could. The girls ran crookedly, their legs bowed in some manner obscured by the work aprons, so they were easy enough to tail. They stopped at a small cellar two blocks from the Bryant and May works, and carefully stepped into the darkness, the tallest one closing the slanted doors behind her. With naught else to do, I made a note of the address and back at my London lodgings I arranged for a livery to take me back there at half past five o'clock in the morning, when the girls would arise again to begin their working day.

I brought with me some sweets, and wore a threadbare fustian suit. My driver, Wilkins, and I did not have long to wait, for at twenty-two minutes after the hour of five, the cellar door swung open and a tiny head popped out. The smallest of the girls! But she immediately ducked back down into the cellar. I took a step forward and the largest girl partially emerged, though she was careful to keep her remarkable prosthetic jaw obscured from possible passing trade. The gutters on the edge of the pavement were filled with refuse and dank water, but the girl did not so much as wrinkle her nose, for she had long since grown accustomed to life in the working-class quarters.

"Hello," I said. I squatted down, then offered the butterscotch sweets with one hand and removed my hat with the other. "Do you remember me?"

"Buy Brya—" she began. Then, with visible effort, she stopped herself and said. "Yes." Behind her the smallest girl appeared again and completed the slogan. "Buy Bryant and May matchsticks, sir."

"I would very much like to speak with you."

"We must . . . work," the older said. "Bryant and May matchsticks, sir!" said the other. "Before the sun rises," the older one said. "Buy Bryant and May—" I cast the younger girl a dirty look, I'm shamed to say, and she ducked her head back down into the cellar.

"Yes, well, I understand completely. There is no greater friend the working-man has than I, I assure you. Look, a treat!" I proffered the sweets again. If a brass jaw with greater familial resemblance to a bear-trap than a human mandible could quiver, this girl's did right then.

"Come in," she said finally.

The cellar was very similar to the many I had seen in Manchester during my exploration of the living conditions of the English proletariat. The floor was dirt and the furnishings limited to bales of hay covered in rough cloth. A dank and filthy smell from the refuse, garbage and excrements that choked the gutter right outside the cellar entrance, hung in the air. A small, squat, wax-splattered table in the middle of the room held a soot-stained lantern. The girls wore the same smocks they had the evening before, and there was no sign of water for their toilet. Presumably, what grooming needs they had they attempted to meet at the factory itself, which was known to have a pump for personal use.

Most cellar dwellings of this sort have a small cache of food in one corner – a sack of potatoes, butter wrapped in paper, and very occasionally a crust of bread. In this dwelling, there was something else entirely – a peculiar crank-driven contraption from which several pipes extruded.

The big girl walked toward it and with her phonographic voice told me, "We can't have sweets no more." Then she attached the pipes, which ended in toothy clips similar to the pincers of steam-workers, to either side of her mechanical mandible and began to crank the machine. A great buzzing rose up from the device and a flickering illumination filled the room. I could finally see the other girls in their corners, standing and staring at me. The large girl's hair stood on end from the static electricity she was generating, bringing to mind Miss Shelley's famed novel. I was fascinated and repulsed at once, though I wondered how such a generator could work if what it powered, the girl, itself powered the generator via the crank. Was it collecting a static charge from the air, as the skins of the newest airships did?

"Is this ... generator your sustenance now?" I asked. She stopped cranking and the room dimmed again. "Buy ..." she started, then recovered, "no more food. Better that way. Too much phossy in the food anyhow; it was poisonin' us."

In a moment, I realized my manners. Truly, I'd been half expecting at least an offer of tea, it had been so long since I'd organized workers. "I'm terribly sorry, I've been so rude. What are you all called, girls?"

"No names now, better that way."

"You no longer eat!" I said. "And no longer have names. Incredible! The bosses did this to you?"

"No, sir," the tall girl said. "The Fabians."

The smallest girl, the one who had never said anything save the Bryant and May slogan, finally spoke. "This is re-form, they said. This is us, in our re-form."

3. What Is To Be Done?

I struck a deal with the girls immediately, not in my role as agitator and organizer, but in my function as a manager for the family concern. Our driver took us to his home and woke his wife, who was sent to the shops for changes of clothes, soap and other essentials for the girls. We kept the quartet in the carriage for most of the morning whilst Wilkins attempted to explain to his wife what she should see when we brought the girls into her home. She was a strong woman, no-nonsense, certainly no Angel of the House but effective nevertheless. The first thing she told the girls was, "There's to be no fretting and fussing. Do not speak, simply use gestures to communicate if you need to. Now, line up for a scrubbing. I presume your . . . equipment will not rust under some hot water and soap."

In the sitting room, Wilkins leaned over and whispered to me. "It's the saliva, you see. My Lizzie's a smart one. If the girls' mouths are still full of spit, it can't be that their jaws can rust. Clever, innit?" He lit his pipe with a white phosphorous match and then told me that one of the girls had sold him a Bryant and May matchbox whilst I booked passage for five on the next dirigible to Manchester. "They'd kept offerin', and it made 'em happy when I bought one," he said. "I'll add 5d. to the invoice, if you don't mind."

I had little to do but to agree and eat the butterscotch I had so foolishly bought for the girls. Presently the girls marched into the sitting room, looking like Moors in robes and headwraps. "You'll get odd looks," the driver's wife explained, "but not so odd as the looks you might have otherwise received."

The woman was right. We were stared at by the passengers and conductors of the airship both, though I had changed into a proper suit and even made a show of explaining the wonders of bourgeois England to the girls from our window seat. "Look, girls, there's St Paul's, where all the good people worship the triune God," I said. Then as we passed over the countryside I made note of the agricultural steam-workers that looked more like the vehicles they were than the men their urbanized brethren pretended to be. "These are our crops, which feed this great nation and strengthen the limbs of the Empire!" I explained. "That is why the warlords of your distant lands were so easily brought to heel. God was on our side, as were the minds of our greatest men, the sinew of our bravest soldiers and the power of the classical elements themselves – water, air, fire and ore – *steam!*" I had spent enough time observing the bourgeoisie to generate sufficient hot air for the entire dirigible.

Back in Manchester, I had some trusted comrades prepare living quarters for the girls, and to arrange for the delivery of a generator sufficient for their needs. Then I began to make enquiries into the Socialistic and Communistic communities, which I admit that I had been ignoring whilst I worked on the theoretical basis for the Dialectical Engine. Just as Marx used to say, commenting on the French "Marxists" of the late '70s: "All I know is that I am not a Marxist." The steam-workers broke what proletarian solidarity there was in the United Kingdom, and British airships eliminated most resistance in France, Germany and beyond. What we are left with, here on the far left, are several literary young men, windy Labour MPs concerned almost entirely with airship mooring towers and placement of the same in their home districts, and . . . the Fabians.

The Fabians are gradualists, believers in parliamentary reforms and moral suasion. Not revolution, but evolution, not class struggle but class collaboration. They call themselves socialists, and many of them are as well-meaning as a yipping pup, but ultimately they wish to save capitalism from the hammers of the working class. But if they were truly responsible somehow for the state of these girls, they would have moved beyond reformism into complete capitulation to the bourgeoisie. *But we must never capitulate, never collaborate!*

The irony does not escape me. I run a factory on behalf of my bourgeois family. I live fairly well, and indeed, am only the revolutionary I am because of the profits extracted from the workers on the floor below. Now I risk all, their livelihoods and mine, to complete the Dialectical Engine. The looms have been reconfigured; we haven't sent out any cotton in weeks. The work floor looks as though a small volcano has been drawn forth from beneath the crust. The machinists work fifteen hours a day, and smile at me when I come downstairs and roll up my sleeves to help them. They call me Freddie, but I know they despise me. And not even for my status as a bourgeois – they hate me for my continued allegiance to the working class. There's a word they use when they think I cannot hear them: "Slummer". A man who lives in, or even simply visits, the working-men districts to experience some sort of prurient thrill of rebellion and faux class allegiance.

But that is it! That's what I must do. The little match girls must strike! Put their prostheses on display for the public via flying pickets. Challenge the bourgeoisie on their own moral terms – are these the daughters of Albion? Girls who are ever-starving, who can never be loved, forced to skulk in the shadows, living Frankenstein's monsters? The dailies will eat it up, the working class will be roused, first by economic and moral issues, but then soon by their own collective interest as a class. Behind me, the whirr and chatter of loom shuttles kicked up. The Dialectical Engine was being fed the medium on which the raw knowledge of my friend's old letters and missives were to be etched. *Steam*, was all I could think. *What can you not do?*

4. The Spark

I was an old hand at organizing workers, though girls who consumed electricity rather than bread was a bit beyond my remit. It took several days to teach the girls to speak with their jaws beyond the Bryant and May slogan, and several more to convince them of the task. "Why should we go back?" one asked. Her name was once Sally, as she was finally able to tell me, and she was the second smallest. "They won't have us."

"To free your fellows," I said. "To express workers' power and, ultimately, take back the profits for yourselves!"

"But then we'd be the bosses," the oldest girl said. "Cruel and mean."

"Yes, well, no. It depends on all the workers of a nation rising up to eliminate the employing class," I explained. "We must go back—"

"I don't want to ever go back!" said the very smallest. "That place was horrid!"

The tedious debate raged long into the night. They were sure that the foreman would clout their heads in for even appearing near the factory gates, but I had arranged for some newspapermen and even electro-photographers sympathetic to Christian socialism, if not Communism, to meet us as we handed out leaflets to the passing trade and swing shift.

We were met at the gate by a retinue of three burly-looking men in fustian suits. One of them fondled a sap in his hand and tipped his hat. The journalists hung back, believers to the end in the objectivity of the disinterested observer, especially when they might get hurt for being rather too interested.

"Leaflets, eh?" the man with the sap asked. "You know this lot can't read, yeah?"

"And this street's been cleared," one of the others said. "You can toss that rubbish in the bin, then."

"Yes, that's how your employers like them, isn't it? Illiterate, desperate, without value to their families as members of the female of the species?" I asked. "And the ordinary working-men, cowed by the muscle of a handful of hooligans."

"Buy Bryant and May matchsticks, sir!" the second tallest girl said, brightly as she could. The thuggish guards saw her mandible and backed away. Excited, she clacked away at them, and the others joined in.

"How do you like that?" I said to both the guards and the press. "Innocent girls, more machine than living being. We all know what factory labour does to children, or thought we did. But now, behold the new monsters the age of steam and electricity hath wrought. We shall lead an exodus through the streets, and you can put that in your sheets!" The thugs let us by, then slammed the gates behind us, leaving us on the factory grounds and them outside. Clearly, one or more of the police agents who monitor my activities had caught wind of our plans, but I was confident that victory would be ours. Once we roused the other match girls, we'd engage in a sit-down strike, if necessary. The girls could not be starved out like ordinary workers, and I had more than enough confederates in London to ring the factory and sneak food and tea for me through the bars if necessary. But I was not prepared for what awaited us.

The girls were gone, but the factory's labours continued apace. Steam-workers attended the machines, carried frames of matches down the steps to the loading dock, and clanked about with the precision of clockwork. Along a catwalk, a man waved to us, a handkerchief in his hand. "Hello!" he said.

"That's not the foreman," Sally told me. "It's the dentist!" She did not appear at all relieved that the factory's dentist rather than its foreman, who had been described to me as rather like an ourang-outang, was approaching us. I noticed that a pair of steam-workers left their posts and followed him as he walked up to us.

"Mister Frederich Engels! Is that you?" he asked me. I admitted that I was, but that further I was sure he had been forewarned of my coming. He ignored my rhetorical jab and pumped my hand like an American cowboy of some fashion. "Wonderful, wonderful," he said. He smiled at the girls, and I noticed that his teeth were no better than anyone else's. "I'm Doctor Flint. Bryant and May hired me to deal with worker pains that come from exposure to white phosphorus. We're leading the fight for healthy workers here; I'm sure you'll agree that we're quite progressive. Let me show you what we've accomplished here at Bryant and May."

"Where are the girls?" the tallest of my party asked, her phonographic voice shrill and quick, as if the needle had been drawn over the wax too quickly.

"Liberated!" the dentist said. He pointed to me. "They owe it all to you, you know. I reckon it was your book that started me on my path into politics. Dirtier work than dentistry." He saw my bemused look and carried on eagerly. "Remember what you wrote about the large factories of Birmingham – "*the use of steam-power admits of the employment of a great multitude of women and children.*" Too true, too true!"

"Indeed, sir—" I started, but he interrupted me.

"But of course we can't put steam back in the kettle, can we?" He rapped a knuckle on the pot-belly torso of one of the ever-placid steam-workers behind him. "But then I read your philosophical treatise. I was especially interested in your contention that quantitative change can become qualitative. So, I thought to myself, if steam-power is the trouble when it comes to the subjugation of child labour, cannot more steam-power spell the liberation of child labour?"

"No, not by itself. The class strugg—"

"But no, Engels, you're wrong!" he said. "At first I sought to repair the girls, using steam-power. Have you seen the phoss up close? Through carious teeth, and the poor girls know little of hygiene so they have plenty of caries, the vapours of white phosphorous make gains into the jawbone itself, leading to putrefaction. Stinking hunks of bone work right through the cheek, even after extractions of the carious teeth."

"Yes, we are all familiar with phossy jaw," I said. "Seems to me that the minimalist programme would be legislative – bar white phosphorous. Whatever sort of Liberal or Fabian you are you can agree with that."

"Ah, but I can't!" he said. "You enjoy your pipe? I can smell it on you."

"That's from Wilkins, my driver."

"Well then observe your Mr Wilkins. It's human nature to desire a strike-anywhere match. We simply cannot eliminate white phosphorous from the marketplace. People demand it. What we can do, however, is use steam to remove the human element from the equation of production."

"I understood that this sort of work is too detailed for steam-workers."

"It was," the dentist said. "But then our practice on the girls led to certain innovations." As if on cue, the steam-workers held up their forelimbs and displayed to me a set of ten fingers with the dexterity of any primates. "So now I have eliminated child labour – without any sort of agitation or rabble-rousing, I might add – from this factory and others like it, in less than a fortnight. Indeed, the girls were made redundant this past Tuesday."

"And what do you plan to do for them?" I said. "A good Fabian like you knows that these girls will now—"

"Will now what? Starve? You know they won't, not as long as there are lamp-posts in London. They all contain receptacles. Mature and breed, further filling the working-men's districts with the unemployable, uneducable? No, they won't. Find themselves abused and exploited in manners venereal? No, not possible, even if there was a man so drunk as to overlook their new prosthetic mandibles. Indeed, we had hoped to move the girls into the sales area, which is why their voiceboxes are rather . . . focused, but as it happens few people wish to buy matches from young girls. Something about it feels immoral, I suppose. So they are free to never work again. Herr Engels, their problems are solved."

For a long moment, we both stood our ground, a bit unsure as to what we should do next, either as socialist agitators or as gentlemen. We were both keenly aware that our conversation was the first of its type in all history. The contradictions of capitalism, resolved? The poor would always be with us, but also immortal and incapable of reproduction. Finally the dentist looked at his watch – he wore one with rotating shutters of numerals on his wrist, as is the fashion among wealthy morons – and declared that he had an appointment to make. "The steam-workers will show you out," he said, and in a moment their fingers were on my arms, and they dragged me to the entrance of the factory as if I were made of straw. The girls followed, confused, and, if the way their metallic jaws were set was telling, they were actually relieved. The press pestered us with questions on the way out, but I sulked past them without remark. Let them put Doctor Flint above the fold tomorrow morning, for all the good it will do them. Soon enough there'd be steam-workers capable of recording conversations and events with perfect audio-visual fidelity, and with a dial to be twisted for different settings of the editing of newsreels: Tory, Liberal, or Fabian. Indeed, one would never have to twist the dial at all.

We returned to Wilkins and our autocarriage, defeated and atomized. Flint spoke true; as we drove through the streets of the East End, I did espy several former match girls standing on corners or in gutters, directionless and likely cast out from whatever home they may once have had.

"We have to . . ." but I knew that I couldn't.

Wilkins said, "The autocarriage is overburdened already. Those girlies weigh more than they appear to, eh? You can't go round collecting every stray."

No – charity is a salve at best, a bourgeois affectation at worst. But even those concerns were secondary. As the autocarriage moved sluggishly toward the airship field, I brooded on the question of value. If value comes from labour, and capital is but dead labour, what are steam-workers? So long as they needed to be created by human hands, clearly steam-workers were just another capital good, albeit a complex one. But now, given the dexterity of the latest generation of steam-workers, they would clearly be put to work building their own descendants, and those that issued forth from that subsequent generation would also be improved, without a single quantum of labour-power expended. The bourgeoisie might have problems of their own; with no incomes at all, the working class could not even afford the basic necessities of life. Steam-workers don't buy bread or cloth, nor do they drop farthings into the alms box at church on Sunday. How would bourgeois society survive without workers who also must be driven to consume the very products they made?

The petit-bourgeoisie, I realized, the landed gentry, perhaps they could be catered to exclusively, and the Empire would continue to expand and open new markets down to the tips of the Americas and through to the end of the Orient – foreign money and resources would be enough for capital, for the time being. But what of the proletariat? If the bourgeoisie no longer need the labour of the workers, and with the immense power in their hands, wouldn't they simply rid themselves of the toiling classes the way the lord of a manor might rid a stable of vermin? They could kill us all from the air – firebombing the slums and industrial districts. Send whole troupes of steam-workers to tear men apart till the cobblestones ran red with the blood of the proletariat. Gears would be greased, all right.

We didn't dare take an airship home to Manchester. The mooring station was sure to be mobbed with writers from the tabloids and Tory sheets. So we settled in for the long and silent drive up north.

I had no appetite for supper, which wasn't unusual after an hour in an airship, but tonight was worse for the steel ball of dread in my stomach. I stared at my pudding for a long time. I wished I could offer it to the girls, but they were beyond treats. On a whim, I went back to the factory to check in on the Dialectical Engine, which had been processing all day and evening. A skeleton crew had clocked out when the hour struck nine, and I was alone with my creation. No, with the creation of the labour of my workers. No, *the* workers. If only I could make myself obsolete, as the steam-workers threatened the proletariat.

The factory floor, from the vantage point of my small office atop the catwalk, was a sight to behold. A mass of cloth, like huge overlapping sails, obscured the looms, filling the scaffolding that had been built up six storeys to hold and "read" the long punched sheets. A human brain in replica, with more power than any Difference Engine, fuelled by steam for the creation not of figures, but dialectics. Quantitative change had become qualitative, or would as soon as the steam engines in the basement were ignited. I lacked the ability to do it myself, or I would have just then, to talk to my old friend, or as close a facsimile as I could build with my fortune and knowledge. All the machinery came to its apex in my office, where a set of styluses waited in position over sheets of foolscap. I would prepare a question, and the machine would produce an answer that would be translated, I hoped, into comprehensible declarative sentences upon the sheets. A letter from Marx, from beyond the grave! Men have no souls to capture, but the mind, yes. The mind is but the emergent properties of the brain, and I rebuilt Marx's brain, though I hoped not to simply see all his theories melt into air.

With a start, I realized that down on the floor I saw a spark. The factory was dark and coated with the shadows of the punched sheets, so the momentary red streak fifty feet below was obvious to me. Then I smelled it, the smoke of a pipe. Only a fool would light up in the midst of so much yardage of inflammable cotton, which was perplexing, because Wilkins was no fool.

"Wilkins!" I shouted. "Extinguish that pipe immediately! You'll burn down the factory and kill us both! These textiles are highly combustible."

"Sow-ry," floated up from the void. But then another spark flitted in the darkness, and a second and a third. Wilkins held a fistful of matches high, and I could make out the contours of his face. "Quite a mechanism you've got all set up here, Mister Engels. Are these to be sails for the masts of your yacht?"

"No, sir, they won't be for anything if you don't extinguish those matches!"

"Extinguish, eh? Well, you got a good look, and so did I, so I think I will." And he blew out the matches. All was dark again. What happened next was quick. I heard the heavy thudding – no, a heavy *ringing* of boots along the catwalk and in a moment a steam-worker was upon me. I wrestled with it for a moment, but I was no match for its pistons, and it threw me over the parapet. My breath left my body as I fell – as if my soul had decided to abandon me and leap right for heaven. But I didn't fall far. I landed on a taut sheet of fine cotton, then rolled off it and fell less than a yard onto another. I threw out my arms and legs as I took the third layer of sheet, and then scuttled across it to the edge of the scaffold on which I rested. Sitting, I grasped the edge with my hands and lowered myself as much as I dared, then let go. Wilkins was there, having tracked my movements from the fluttering of the sheets and my undignified oopses and oofs. He lit another match and showed me his eyes.

"Pretty fit for an older gentlemen, Mister Engels. But take a gander at the tin of Scotch broth up there." He lifted the match. The steam-worker's metallic skin glinted in what light there was. It stood atop the parapet of the catwalk and with a leap flung itself into the air, plummeting the six storeys down and landing in a crouch like a circus acrobat. Remarkable, but I was so thankful that it did not simply throw itself through the coded sheets I had spent so long trying to manufacture, ruining the Dialectical Engine before it could even be engaged. Then I understood.

"Wilkins!" I cried. "You're a police agent!"

Wilkins shrugged and swung onto his right shoulder a heavy sledge. "'Fraid so. But can you blame me, sir? I've seen the writing on the wall – or the automaton on the assembly line," he said, nodding past me and towards the steam-worker, who had taken the flank opposite my treacherous driver. "I know what's coming. Won't nobody be needing me to drive 'em around with these wind-up toys doing all the work, and there won't be no other jobs to be had but rat and fink. So I took a little fee from the police, to keep an eye on you and your . . ." he was at a loss for words for a moment. "Machinations. Yes, that's it. And anyhow, they'll pay me triple to put all this to the torch, so I will, then retire to Chesire with old Lizzie and have a nice garden."

"And that?" I asked, glancing at the automaton on my left.

"Go figure," Wilkins said. "My employers wanted one of their own on the job, in case you somehow bamboozled me with your radical cant into switching sides a second time."

"They don't trust you," I said.

"Aye, but they pay me, half in advance." And he blew out the match, putting us in darkness again. Without the benefit of sight, my other senses flared to life. I could smell Wilkins stepping forward, hear the tiny grunt as he hefted the sledge. I could nearly taste the brass and aluminium of the steam-worker on my tongue, and I certainly felt its oppressive weight approaching me.

I wish I could say I was brave and through a clever manoeuvre defeated both my foes simultaneously. But a Communist revolutionary must always endeavour to be honest to the working class – reader, I fell into a swoon. Through nothing more than a stroke of luck, as my legs gave way beneath me, Wilkins's sledgehammer flew over my head and hit the steam-worker square on the faceplate. It flew free in a shower of sparks. Facing an attack, the steam-worker staved in Wilkins's sternum with a single blow, then turned back to me, only to suddenly shudder and collapse atop me. I regained full consciousness for a moment, thanks to the putrid smell of dead flesh and fresh blood. I could see little, but when I reached to touch the exposed face of the steam-worker, I understood. I felt not gears and wirework, but slick sinew and a trace of human bone. Then the floor began to shake. An arch-light in the corner flickered to life, illuminating a part of the factory floor. I was pinned under the automaton, but then the tallest of the girls – and I'm ashamed to say I never learned what she was called – with a preternatural strength of her own took up one of the machine's limbs and dragged him off me.

I didn't even catch my breath before exclaiming, "Aha, of course! The new steam-workers aren't automata, they're men! Men imprisoned in suits of metal to enslave them utterly to the bourgeoisie!" I coughed and sputtered. "You! Such as you, you see," I told the girl, who stared at me dumbly. Or perhaps I was the dumb one, and she simply looked upon me as a pitiable old idiot who was the very last to figure out what she considered obvious. "Replace the body of a man with a machine, encase the human brain within a cage, and dead labour lives again! That's how the steam-workers are able to use their limbs and appendages with a facility otherwise reserved for humans. All the advantages of the proletariat, but the steam-workers need neither consume nor reproduce!" Sally was at my side now, with my pudding, which she had rescued from my supper table. She was a clever girl, Sally. "The others started all the engines they could find," she said, and only then I realized that I had been shouting in order to hear myself. All around me, the Dialectical Engine was in full operation.

5. All That Is Solid Melts Into Air

In my office, the styluses scribbled for hours. I spent a night and a day feeding it foolscap. The Dialectical Engine did not work as I'd hoped it would – it took no input from me, answered none of the questions I had prepared, but instead wrote out a single long monograph. I was shocked at what I read from the very first page:

"*Das Kapital: Kritik der politischen Ökonomie, Band V.*"

The *fifth* volume of *Capital*. Marx had died prior to completing the *second*, which I published myself from his notes. Before turning my energies to the Dialectical Engine, I had edited the third volume for publication. While the earlier volumes of the book offered a criticism of bourgeois theories of political economy and a discussion of the laws of the capitalist mode of production, this fifth volume, or extended appendix in truth, was something else. It contained a description of socialism.

The internal contradictions of capitalism had doomed it to destruction. What the bourgeoisie would create would also be used to destroy their reign. The ruling class, in order to stave off extinction, would attempt to use its technological prowess to forestall the day of revolution by radically expanding its control of the proletarian and his labour-power. But in so doing, it would create the material conditions for socialism. The manuscript was speaking of steam-workers, though of course the Dialectical Engine had no sensory organs with which to observe the metal-encased corpse that had expired in its very innards the evening before. Rather, the Engine *predicted* the existence of human-steam hybrids from the content of the decade-old correspondence between Marx and myself.

What, then, would resolve the challenge of the proletarian brain trapped inside the body of the steam-worker? Dialectical logic pointed to a simple solution: the negation of the negation. Free the proletarian *mind* from its physical *brain* by encoding it onto a new mechanical medium. That is to say, the Dialectical Engine itself was the key. Free the working class by having it exist outside the physical world and the needs of capitalism to accumulate, accumulate. Subsequent pages of the manuscript detailed plans for Dialectical Engine Number 2, which would be much smaller and more efficient. A number of human minds could be "stitched up" into this device and through collective endeavour, these beings-in-one would create Dialectical Engine Number 3, which would be able to hold still more minds and create the notional Dialectical Engine Number 4. Ultimately, the entire working class of England and Europe could be upcoded into a Dialectical Engine no larger than a hatbox, and fuelled by power drawn from the sun. Without a proletariat to exploit – the class as a whole having taken leave of the realm of flesh and blood to reconstitute itself as information within the singular Dialetical Engine Omega – the bourgeoisie would fall into ruin and helplessness, leaving the working class whole and unmolested in perpetuity. Even after the disintegration of the planet, the Engine would persist, and move forward to explore the firmament and other worlds that may orbit other stars.

Within the Dialetical Engine Omega, consciousness would be both collective and singular, an instantaneous and perfect industrial democracy. Rather than machines replicating themselves endlessly as in Mister Butler's novel – "the machines are gaining ground upon us; day by day we are becoming more subservient to them" – it is us that shall be liberated by the machines, through the machines. We are gaining ground upon them! *Proletarier aller Länder, vereinigt euch!* We have nothing to lose but our chains, as the saying goes.

The Dialectical Engine fell silent after nineteen hours of constant production. I should have been weary, but already I felt myself beyond hunger and fatigue. The schematics for Dialectical Engine Number 2 were incredibly advanced, but for all their cleverness the mechanism itself would be quite simple to synthesize. With a few skilled and trusted workers, we could have it done in a fortnight. Five brains could be stitched up into it. The girls and myself were obvious candidates, and from within the second engine we would create the third, and fourth, and subsequent numbers via pure unmitigated *Arbeitskraft*!

Bold? Yes! Audacious? Certainly. And indeed, I shall admit that, for a moment, my mind drifted to the memory of the empty spectacle of Mister Peake's play, of the rampaging monster made of dead flesh and brought to life via electrical current. But I had made no monster, no brute. That was a bourgeois story featuring a bogeyman that the capitalists had attempted to mass-produce from the blood of the working class. My creation was the opposite number of the steam-worker and the unphilosophical monster of stage and page; the Engine was *mens sana sine corpore sano* – a sound mind outside a sound body.

What could possibly go wrong . . . ?

To Seek Her Fortune

Nicole Kornher-Stace

I

In the land of black salt and white honey, the Lady Explorer bartered a polar bear's pelt, a hand-cranked dynamo, her second-best derringer and three bolts of peach silk for her death.

"You stole the map that brought you here," said the witch who was waiting at the shoreline when the Lady Explorer had hacked her way out of the trees. At first the witch had said nothing, only sitting on her heels and skinning iridescent fish into an ebbing tide. She didn't watch, though the Lady Explorer did, as the sea bore each raft of scales, like chips of ice and fire in the setting sun, away to sea. To all appearances the witch expected the Lady Explorer to recoil in horror when the guts followed. The grunt brought on by her failure to flinch could have signified anything from approval to cramp.

When the witch spoke, however, the Lady Explorer glanced up from the water, startled. "I *beg* your pardon," she gasped, hand to mouth in her best well-I-never pose, while behind it her mind worked into a lather.

"It's not surprising. Seeing as the crew you fly with stole that ship as well."

The Lady Explorer froze. A sudden terror seized her in its teeth and shook. If the witch knew that, then what else could she see? That she'd been nothing but a stupid factory girl, upswept on the wave of a rebellion and rejoicing even through her fear? That she'd had to pay her way to the factory-workers-turned-airship-crew with the only currency she had? And what she'd had to do to in the end to earn their respect?

She remembered the tools in her hands, her skirt in her hands, the gun in her hands, and was ashamed.

The boy peering out from behind her hip looked up at her, one hand fisted in the sailcloth of her slapdash trousers, gauging the tension radiating off her. One good startle from fleeing back into the jungle, or perhaps into the sea.

The Lady Explorer gathered herself. *Well, I did not come here to gawk at the sights like a schoolgirl at a cathedral. I came here for answers. Before it's too late.*

She said, "I *assure* you, I did nothing of the—"

"That contraption up there tells me different."

Bewildered, the Lady Explorer looked over her shoulder to follow the witch's gaze up and up to where the airship perched with its improbable delicacy on the lip of the caldera. As she watched, it roused and settled, preening like a nesting hen the size of a four-story brownstone with bat wings and rose windows for eyes. She blinked and looked again and it was still.

Water. She needed water. And she'd eaten nothing but the hardtack pilfered from that scuttled pirate outrider for the best part of a week. Nor slept: the last scraps of dried meat and fruit she'd squirreled in the boy's bunk, then sat at the door daylong, nightlong, rifle in her lap. The crew would mutiny, and soon, she guessed, but hadn't chanced her yet. If she had to cut off her arm and roast it over the combustion engine, the boy at least would eat.

She steeled herself. Her chignon had exploded in the heat, sodden squid-arms of it slapped her face, her eyes. Irritably she shoved it back, drew herself up, set her shoulders and her jaw to hide her apprehension. She'd not come this far to be toy for some rootwitch, regardless of what she knew.

She affected the disdainful drawl the foreman used to use, days when she'd beg early leave from the factory with a migraine from the eyestrain of the close work, or a roiling in her guts while her womb built a person even as her hands built a ship. "Is that so? I see you two are great friends already. What else does it—"

"It remembers the place where it was born," the witch interrupted, her voice gone dreamy like a child's half-asleep, like some seer's in some cave. The Lady Explorer snapped to attention, for she had heard that tone of voice before. "It smelled of grease and sweat and metal there. Men and women hunched at benches, piecing up its bones, its skin. It came awake like a whale rising from the dark depths of the sea. When they set its heart in place, the joy leapt up in it, flew out of it like lightning: the discharge of it killed three men. Just fried them where they stood, like a basketful of eels. The smell—" She chuckled. "You should see your face. It remembers the taste of you, as well. Blood and bone."

Before the Lady Explorer could react, the witch seized her bad hand, held it up so that the empty finger of her glove fell slack.

Instantly the sense memory flooded her, despite the intervening years: a stab of panic as her hand caught in the struts, a snag, a drawing-in. The other workers' shouts. A sharp wet crunch.

She jerked her arm away.

"It says it never meant to hurt you."

She still felt that finger sometimes, or its ghost. Hoisting the boy to her shoulders. Hacking through brush. Burying her people. Unburying other ones. Sighting down the rifle's length. It still knocked her aim just out of true, if she permitted it, which she did not. Only by pulling well more than her weight on the crew's endless expeditions would she maintain their fragile tolerance of her own infrequent ones, and she'd be damned before she showed those bastards any weakness.

"If you know all that, then you know why I'm here. I didn't come to fence with witches."

"Did you not?" Her face cracked along its faultlines into a quiet smile. "A pity."

As the barter was brought down from the airship and the Lady Explorer disappeared inside the witch's little house, the boy drew cities in the white sand with a stick, shell-fragments for carriages and leaf-spines for streets. By now he was good at waiting. It took much longer to make a city than to have a card revealed to you, even if it was a fortune-telling card, as his mama had explained; an answering card. A card that tells you secrets. He couldn't count high enough yet to know how many secrets his mama must've been told by now. A great many, he was sure. He imagined her as a mama-shaped penny-candy jar, each secret a bright sweet bauble nestled behind the cold glass of her skin.

He picked the biggest shell-carriage up and marked it with a charcoal from his pocket: one messy-haired smiling face that was his mama, one smaller smiling face that was himself. Turning, he tossed the shell into the sea and watched as it skipped four times and sank. He knew from his mama's stories that there were cities down there too.

When the Lady Explorer emerged from the little house she looked paler, greyer, older; lighter and heavier at once. But her arms were still strong when she picked him up and swung him. "It's time to go," she said, and he rode her shoulders back into the treeline. When the jungle shut its curtains at their backs the sun went out like a lamp, so that when he closed his eyes against his mama's hair, the wet sweet smell of rot was all he knew.

The vast dark stingray of the airship stirred and lifted, and as it rose above the canopy the Lady Explorer held her son up to one of its eye-windows so that he could wave goodbye to where they'd been. Offshore, a thrashing in the water caught her eye, which her fieldglass soon revealed as a pod of dolphins harrying a shark. *My sins*, she thought, and smiled grimly down at them; *my sins*.

II

In the land of silver trees and golden fruit, the Lady Explorer bartered a case of tawny port, the captain's quarters' folding screen and rolltop desk, a filigreed sterling tea service and the airship's only drop glider for her death.

"What's the vintage on that port?" the scientist enquired, almost before the Lady Explorer, her son and two of the airship's roustabouts had unpacked all the crates. Still breathless from the climb to the laboratory, the Lady Explorer stuck a hand in blind and rifled the excelsior. It had gone damp with the temperature shift to the glass, and the bottle that she grabbed was cold to the touch and slippery. She hefted it and squinted: half because her eyes betrayed her, half to hide the twinge her back gave as it straightened. She couldn't help conflating her bones with the airship's bones: each joint gradually tarnishing, gradually grinding down from shiny brass to verdigris.

"Eighteen ... sixty-six," she read aloud, and improvised: "A fine year for the—"

"You wouldn't know a fine year if it bit you in the leg," the scientist sneered. "The not particularly well-turned leg, I don't doubt. Just look at you. Bristling at me like a mad dog. Your stance – your hands – you're utterly transparent. Rings on your fingers and engine grease under your nails. That corset's the only thing keeping your spine from snapping under the weight of that vast empty skull. Feigning at *quality*, madam, suits you ill."

Hating herself for it, she dropped his gaze. Snickering at her discomfiture, he crouched beside the crates, and as he did so a light glanced off his ankle, catching her eye. From there, a slender silver chain ran a few yards to the leg of a long table laden with flasks and beakers and the disassembled skeletons of automata. The table, she now noticed, was bolted into the floor. The skin where the chain had bitten was greenish and suppurating.

When she looked back, the scientist was staring out a window no wider or longer than her forearm at where the airship waited, quiescent, mantling a lane flanked with marching rows of pomegranate trees.

The look on his face reminded her of the look on her own, back when it was someone else's airship and she and fifty others were working themselves half dead to build it.

The sudden sympathy she found she felt slowed her reaction to a staring inutility when, beside her, her son drew a long pistol and brought it to bear between the scientist's eyes.

"Speak to my mother in that way again," he said airily, "and you'll be scraping that smug look off the wall."

"I suppose," said the scientist, "I may as well be charitable. That" – he pointed at the crates – "is utter swill, but I can take it off your hands. Perhaps it will serve to degrease the hydraulic fittings. Now then. Shall we get this over with?"

Long accustomed to this dance, her son left the laboratory before being asked to, ushered the roustabouts before him, and had the grace not to slam the door at his back. Nonetheless his gut clenched with the certainty he'd seen the scientist – who was readying some vibrant fluid in a crucible that was a clockwork raven's head, over a flame that was its heart – cast him an ugly smirk as he went out. His mother was occupied in inspecting a half-clockwork, half-organic specimen, which bobbed in its pickling jar amid threads of its own flesh and flakes of its own rust. She'd seen nothing.

The three men sat in the hall (he counted himself a man now, for his voice had nearly stopped cracking – ah, now *that* was an embarrassment he wouldn't miss!) and gambled rifle-cartridges and chores and coins upon a weathered pair of ivory dice that lived in the pocket of one of the roustabouts, the story behind the acquisition of which was subject to its keeper's whim. Today he'd cut them from the belly of a black wolf in a pinewood by a lake, along with an ell of scorched red velvet, a flintlock pistol and a mismatched scattering of bones.

"Three scapulae and five clavicles," he pronounced grandly, "but no mandibles or frontal plates at all!"

At this point the Lady Explorer's son knew the roustabout had been practicing his reading with the Lady Explorer's medical journals again (while tempering his learnings on human anatomy with a blithe disregard of the respective sizes of a wolf's mouth and stomach) and immediately decided to outgrow his long-lived fear of the roustabout's yarns.

The dice had earned him a week free of maintenance duties and a tidy heap of coins – round, ringed, hexagonal, octagonal, brass, copper, silver, lead – by the time his mother emerged from the laboratory, flushed with agitation and worrying at a sleeve. When she forced a smile and reached a hand down to help him up, he did not quite disdain to take it.

Most of the coins he left on the floor in a sudden fit of apathy. His favorite only, which he'd been palming as a good luck charm throughout the game, he pocketed. Its reverse was obliterated but its obverse bore the likeness of a very young girl with cornsheaves in her hair beneath a coronet of seven-pointed stars. The tears she wept looked oddly dark.

Leaving, he could not help but notice the utter silence from beyond the laboratory door. He cast a furtive glance over his mother but could discern no bloodstains on the skin or cloth or hair of her. Besides, he reassured himself, he would have heard the shot.

III

In the land of violet storms and crimson seas, the Lady Explorer bartered the spare canvas for the airship's wings, five phials of laudanum, the last kilo of salt and the auxiliary power supply for her death.

Her eyesight failed her in the rain, so her son read out the water-warped, mold-furred tavern sign to her: The Rotting Shark.

He hoped she also could not see the look of surprise, half-tender, half-annoyed, that he found himself wearing at this admission of her mortality. Up till now he had fancied her close kin to the automata: ageless so long as her clockwork was wound or her engine was fed.

For a moment he looked as though he was about to speak. Then, noticing her utter absorption in the door, he sighed and fiddled with his cuff instead.

The noises from within the building were what they'd by now come to expect of such places: drunken shouting, and below it, lower-keyed tones from what cardsharps and cutpurses and gunslingers took delicate advantage of that drunkenness. Someone wauled a marching song from one war or another on a flute. A crash as of a flung chair followed, and the music stopped.

In a moment, two men stumbled out the door, bearing up a dead-weight third who bled heavily from one temple.

"This time I stay with you," the Lady Explorer's son informed her.

She looked away over the rumpled crinolines of meadowland, lying as if discarded at the trackless flyblown foot of seven gangrene-colored hills. As she watched, a dark bird stooped and hammered down on something unseen in a stubbled field.

Then she shrugged and shouldered through the door.

A figure hailed them at once from a far table; they crossed the room and sat. The shape across from them was hooded, but the voice had been a girl's. When she pulled the hood back, the Lady Explorer's son nearly shouted in alarm.

The girl was two girls, bound together as in the cases of some twins he'd seen in the medical journals – but by some kind of ivy, not by flesh. Green tendrils had grown through the trunks and necks and heads of both, binding them together like a corset, hip to temple. A thick finger of ivy had crooked itself through one girl's eye, just missing the other's where it threaded through her socket, squashing the eyeball sideways but not quite bursting it.

"We were expecting you," the ivy-girls said, their voices tightly harmonized and not unpleasant. The Lady Explorer's son wondered by what perverse whim of nature the ivy's tithe had been no greater – and no less – than a certain fraction of their loveliness. The Lady Explorer wondered whether they'd ever been able to climb, or dance, or run, or keep a secret.

"From a long way off we saw you. We saw a woman who escaped the slow grind of a wretched death only to become obsessed with it, stalking it as any starving hunter stalks his prey, and wasting as acutely every time it flees his snares. A grail quest, a fool's errand, a dog chasing its tail, and yet she persists. Before we tell her fate, we would comprehend her folly."

The Lady Explorer glanced over, but her son was sitting with arms crossed, gazing back at her with defiance. She sighed.

"When we built the airship," she began, "one of my tasks was to hold the tray of wires and electrodes when the master engineer connected her controls up to her heart. I could barely hold it still. I couldn't feel my hands. The calluses from stitching wings   every night I'd go home and touch my stomach, where the baby grew" – a sidelong glance at her son, who flinched away, embarrassed – "and every day I felt it less and less. As if he was slowly disappearing. Or I was."

She flexed her fingers, staring as though she expected to parse sudden revelations from the caked grime of her gloves.

"And so all the workers bided their time until the airship was completed? Tell us, were the first whispers of rebellion yours?"

She almost laughed full in their faces, remembering how near she'd come to pissing herself when the shooting began. How another worker had thrust a gun into her hands and she'd stared at it, aware only in a vague sense of how it fired. How she'd hidden under the workbench with her belly to the wall, so the bullets couldn't reach the baby without passing through her first. How she'd stayed there until the sounds of shooting turned to scavenging as the workers loaded up the ship they'd won with anything they'd found to hand, and she was dragged out by the apron-belt and tossed aboard, a spoil amid spoils.

What she said was: "The airship's switchboard was full of dials and toggles – the only intermediary between the captain's will and the ship's. I watched the engineer set each piece into place and wondered whether somewhere inside me there was a switchboard just like hers, with dials to show all my potential fears, potential loves, potential deaths. Who knows what becomes of us in the other world? Why might we not have a choice? Might it not be that each time my death is told, that that dial stops, and where it stops becomes the truth? And if I reject the death it tells, maybe I can start the dial spinning once again."

"Until it stops."

"When someone tells a death I can accept, I'll *let* it stop. I'll keep on searching until someone does."

The girls eyed her closely. "But what the ivy tells us," they said, "so shall be."

"That's what you all say. You tea-leaf-readers, card-turners, guts-scryers, hedgewitches, table-tappers, you're all the same. So far I should've been shot, drowned, stabbed in an alley, run down in the street, fallen off a widow's walk, been shipwrecked, hit by lightning, and perished of consumption in a garret. And yet I am here and asking."

Once they'd given her her death on a folded slip of paper and she had gone her way, the ivy-girls went hooded out into the rain, watching the airship shake the water off its back like a dog, bank hard, and vanish oversea.

"Lies of omission are still lies," said one mouth, while the other one said: "She really ought to tell that boy the truth."

IV

In the land of blue ice and red lichen, the Lady Explorer bartered half of the phosphorous matches, a foxfur waistcoat, the least mildewed of the down quilts and the airship's rudder for her death.

The whaler had been stranded on the ice shelf some twenty-odd years when the airship touched down and hailed her – more as a formality than anything: she was tatter-sailed, barnacle-encrusted, glazed with ice, and the Lady Explorer half expected to see *Mary Celeste* or *Flying Dutchman* emblazoned on her stern. What was there, however, was a palimpsest of christenings: something unintelligible overpainted with *Lydia* in what looked like long-dried blood.

Someone's sweetheart, the Lady Explorer in the wan scraps of her worldliness surmised. Some woman out of widow's weeds two decades gone, and taking solace where she may. She wished her well.

For half an hour, the airship's crew signaled to the *Lydia* with flags and phosphorus flares while the Lady Explorer checked the navigational instruments against five different maps and shook her head at each of them in turn. At last, the Lady Explorer in a white rage and the crew jubilant, they readied the salvage gear.

Just as a few of the men were beginning to swing grappling hooks over their heads, and others to cheer them on, the engine-tender spotted a group of figures approaching across the shelf, each dragging two or three frozen ringed seals behind him, bound together by the hind flippers in strings like sun-dried fish she had seen once in a market on the bone-white shore of a blood-warm sea.

Later, over the last of the airship's Darjeeling, they sat around the *Lydia*'s reeking tryworks, the earthbound ship's crew and the winged one's, and the *Lydia*'s bosun read the Lady Explorer's death in the swirling oil of the trypot.

When the bosun whispered what he'd seen into her ear, the Lady Explorer set down her tea, clambered down onto the ice shelf, and began to walk. Slowly, faltering: her legs leaked strength like water through cupped hands these days, and her joints screamed every time a foot shot sideways on the ice.

"She'll come back," the bosun told the Lady Explorer's son when he hissed a curse and stood, brow creased with equal parts concern for her frailty and anger at her stubbornness, to follow. "They always do."

"How will she find her way?"

"The ghosts'll show her. Old flensing trails." The bosun pointed out across the shelf, where, some half-mile inward from the *Lydia*'s berth of ice, a vast red stain bled up out of the endless white like overdilute watercolor paint. It spread, growing tendrils that stretched out in turn and doubled back and looked, as the Lady Explorer's son's field binoculars and the last late light informed him, very like the wakes of bloody booted footprints tacking back and forth around the suggestion of some hulking shape he could not see.

"What did you tell her?" he asked at length.

The bosun's eyes went misty. "That she'd go out in a blaze of glory in a dogfight with a man-o'-war, all hands lost, and she'd plummet from the sky like Lucifer aflame."

The Lady Explorer's son sighed.

"Well, what d'you want me to have said? It's what I *saw*."

"I don't know. Something." He tipped his head back, watching as the first pale stars came out. "She's like an old man sleeping in his coffin to get used to the idea. I wish one of you would tell her something that would make her send it off for kindling and get back in her goddamned bed."

"Nothing wrong with preparing to greet the spirits on the far side of the river," said the bosun primly, picking tea leaves from his teeth with a whalebone pin.

"Not unless when you do greet them," the Lady Explorer's son retorted, "you find you have *nothing at all to say*."

Returning along a strange red path she hadn't noticed on her journey out across the shelf, the Lady Explorer found the *Lydia*'s crew trying to force the airship's rudder to fit where the *Lydia*'s once was and the airship's crew strapping a new rudder in place with an elaborate harness that put her in mind of a spiderweb. The harness was seal-sinew and her son had carved the rudder from a single block of ice with the tools they'd salvaged from the factory.

"Almost pieced back together," the grinning bosun told her as she passed the *Lydia*. "Patched the hole in her hull with some pitch off a merchantman gone astray a few years back. A few dozen more seals, and we'll have enough skin for a sail."

Her nerves were still raw from mediating the barter for the rudder, and her heart still kicked her every time she recalled how her son had come to her aid against their crew and vowed to get the ship back in the air, and though she'd tried ten times since then to catch his eye and smile, he had never looked her way.

Coming round from the prow, somewhat stung at her son's apparent scorn, it nettled her to discover that, for her part, she could not quite meet the gleaming violet placidity of the airship's regard. She made a shy-eyed gesture at the makeshift rudder, then held up her bad hand for the benefit of the airship's compound gaze. "Now," she said, finally hazarding its stare, her face unfathomable, "we're even."

The new rudder took them eleven degrees south before it began to melt. When it had shrunk from the size of an outhouse to that of a steamer trunk, then a tabletop and a sawblade, the airship's crew set her down on the water and took shifts paddling with whalebone oars, following their collective guesswork of unfamiliar constellations south.

Four days' cruising from its landing, a hunting pod of orcas surfaced around the airship and chaperoned it straight to landfall some six hundred miles on. During this leg of the journey, great clumps of kelp and cairns of fish were given to appear on deck, always at night, always when nobody stood watch, and by no agency that anyone on board could later rationally explain.

V

In the land of grey houses and grey streets, the Lady Explorer bartered the greatcoat off her back, the machete and flensing knife from her belt, the copper honeycombs and amethystine glass of the airship's compound eyes, the compass round her neck, the rainwater cistern and the shorn iron-grey length of her hair for her death.

She tired quickly here. She told herself it was the sullied air, the oppressive angle of the light, the smell of dust and gin and desiccated violets coming off the flocked wallpaper of the medium's salon. But her hands were veined and mottled, her memory and bladder failed as often as they held, and she did not believe her own lies.

She flew a ghost ship now. The crew had pooled what they had gained and kept over the years to purchase a retrofitted washbasin of an airship from the shipyard outside town, which they'd (somewhat amusingly, she thought) renamed the *Swan*. They would break the bottle on her bow within the week, and then she would take wing.

Her own airship, or what was left of it, rested in the yards, lonely as a boat in drydock, while she and her son paced the warren of its rooms like restive ghosts themselves.

In what her quest had not ransacked from the captain's quarters of the airship, the Lady Explorer's son sat her down on a rotten chaise and took her hands, more to pin her in place when he stared her down than from any outward tenderness.

Reflected in her dulling eyes he saw a figure trapped as if down a well and glaring out at the world it could not reach. With mild shock he realized that it was himself.

He forced his gaze back to her. "Look at you," he sneered. "Have your damnable dials stopped yet? You've one foot in the grave already, and what do you have to show for it? Has it never crossed your mind that none of your precious mountebanks can tell your fate any better than I can? Look here, at the scuffing on my boot. There – *that* looks like a swarm of bees, and *there*'s the river you jump into, trying to escape them. These pebbles stuck in the mud on the sole signify the rocks you forgot you had in your pockets, and sadly you drowned." He paused, trying to collect himself. "You look me in the eye and tell me that this . . ." He gestured at the room, once fine, now as though ravened at and left for dead; and at her, once strong-armed and sharp-eyed, now rotting like a windfall full of wasps; and at himself. "That any of this was worth it."

She eyed him very closely. "Do you honestly think that this – that any of this – has ever been about *me*?"

Not waiting for an answer, she shook her hands free of him and left.

In her absence, he took a deep breath, counted to ten, let it out slowly, and when this failed to have any noticeable effect on his level of serenity, he took four long strides across the room and swept a shelf full of framed daguerrotypes and conch shells and hurricane lamps to the floor. For a moment the crash appeared to satisfy him. He half turned. Then spun on his heel and punched the wall.

From the wall came a whirring and a series of reproachful clicks, and then a panel in the wainscoting slid free, releasing a bloom of mildew and two folded sheets of paper. Both were yellowed with age and buttery soft with rereading.

The softer and older-looking of the two he recognized. The words were centered on the page in a clump, outlined by a long-armed globular shape, which, in turn, was flanked by smaller outriding shapes. A few squiggles off to either side of the central mass suggested waves.

Mama,
Because you always have your Nose in your Book of Maps,
I will Hide this Letter there, Disguised as a Map. If you are

reading this, I have Tricked you, and I am Sorry, so please do not be Angry.

I met some Boys and Girls on the Beach yesterday, when you told me to Go Play while the Grown-Ups Sold some Things at the Docks. I tried to Play with Them, but they laughed at me and kicked Sand on my Trouser-Legs. They said that Real Boys and Girls live in Houses and have Pet Cats and Sunday-Shoes and Governesses. They did not Believe that I could live in the Sky and still be a Real Boy. One bigger Boy said that I must be a Gull-Boy or a Crow-Boy and my Mother a Bird. I struck him in the Nose. It bled. A lot.

Still I think I should like to Live in a House. I do not know what Sunday-Shoes or Governesses are, but I did like to Play with Jacob's Cat, before we had to Put her in the Stew.

P.S. I am also Sorry that I spilled your Ink, but I needed a Shape to draw my Coastline from. I told you that little Cora did it. That was a Lie. Please do not be Angry about that too.

The other was unfamiliar.

My darling Child,
Oh! I cannot Call you so anymore, can I, for you are a Grown Man now and I an Old Woman, and much like a Madwoman in an Attic, I fear, as far as our Fellows are Concerned. I do not doubt your Sentiments toward me are similar. Well do I deserve Them!

To my Shame, I have not been wholly Frank with You. I cannot Undo my Errors now, but I can, perhaps, patch up some few of the Holes that they have Rent between Us.

When we stole the Airship, I was but a Girl – a Working Girl of Twenty, with Engine Grease in her Hair and all over Bruises, Cuts and Scars from her own Labor. A Girl just Strong enough to stay aboard the Ship, give Birth to You, and there fight to Remain; but a Girl just Silly enough that when we Stopped outside a Town to Make Repairs, and a Traveling Circus joined our little Camp, and those of the Crew with a Spiritist Leaning asked the Circus Fortune-Teller to tell theirs, I went along.

What the Fortune-Teller told me was that our Airship would be Crippled by a Broadside with a Ship-of-the-Line and drift through Equatorial Waters, deadlocked as a Clipper on a Windless Sea, and that I would Perish of Starvation, along with most of the Crew – and my only Son.

It was in that Moment that I became the Person you have always Known me as. After a Life of Hardship, which until Then I had Accepted, I resolved that I would Fight – an unseen Enemy, and a Formidable One, and perhaps One who cannot be Defeated, it is True – but I could not leave you to that awful Fate, or to any of the Others, prescribed to me over the Years.

Because, as perhaps by now you will have Guessed, each Death that I was told was Mine – but it was not Mine Alone. I have seen you Shot, Drowned, Stabbed in an Alley, Run Down in the Street, Fallen off a Widow's Walk, Shipwrecked, Hit by Lightning and Perished of Consumption in a Garret – and it haunted me. But what Haunts me more is this: would those Deaths have been Mine Alone if I had not Sought to Keep you Close? Will my Attempts to Rescue you lead you to your Doom instead?

Though I fear I shall never have the Courage to Say it to your Face, it is my one remaining Wish that you get out, get free of this, and live your Life as best you can – and perhaps, one Day, find it in your Heart to Forgive one Foolish Old Woman, who sought to Protect you by keeping you – by keeping Both of us – Encaged.

And now I am off to Deliver this Letter before I change my Mind. Lest I give the Crew Reason to think that a Woman who has Learned to Repair a Combustion Engine in Freefall or Shoot a Tiger between the Eyes at Ninety Paces is afraid of her own Son!

P.S. It turns out I am not as Brave as I had Hoped. It is Three Months since I Wrote this Letter. I will Show it to you this Evening, upon your Return from Treasure-Hunting with the Crew, and then likely Flee to my Room like a Child from a Strange Noise on the Stair.

The Lady Explorer's son stared at the letter for some time – at the shakiness of the penmanship, the smudges from rereading, and the date at the top, some six years gone. Then he folded both letters back up together, put them back in place, and went to pack his things.

"The spirits sense resistance in your soul," the medium said to the Lady Explorer, as the table rose and sank and the chandelier flared and dulled and the curtains snapped against the panes in a gale-force wind localized specifically to themselves. After giving the Lady Explorer ample opportunity to admire these phenomena, the medium took up the mirror in which she'd read the Lady Explorer's death and swaddled it in black silk. "You're like a ship fleeing a storm with no sails, no bearings, and no port to pursue. I have dealt with spirits that did not know or accept that they were dead. You seem not to know how to be, or accept being, alive."

That evening, the Lady Explorer stood on her balcony, watching as the airship lurched, unmanned and blinded, up through the city's widow's weeds of coalsmoke toward its maid's May-wreath of sun. Once it dwindled to a crow, a flake, a mote, she took herself back inside her newly rented rooms, threading her way between heaps of pelts and boards of butterflies and oddly fleshy potted flowers that would not survive the snow.

At her desk she sat, dipped her pen, and in rusty penmanship with a quavering hand began to write:

> The Worlds within Us and without Us are the Same. In One as in the Other, We delude Ourselves that there are New Lands to discover, Virgin Territories awaiting Conquerors and Claimants, while in Truth there are only Lands to which We Ourselves have not been. Some Trepidation is natural, then, on the Final Approach to an Unfamiliar Landmass, looming with presumed Malevolence on a glittering Horizon . . .

Perhaps the airship would find itself a new batch of disheartened, wanderlustish souls to keep it company. Perhaps it would return for her, or for her son. Perhaps it would be grappled down by scavengers, flayed for parts, before it reached the sea. Or perhaps it would fly on, uncrewed and uncommanded, flaunting for the ghost-ship-hunters and the tall-tale-tellers and what children did not flee its shadow when it spread its wings against the sun – until the years dissolved it as they dissolved her, and it fell in clinker from its perch of air.

Her head grew heavy, and her pen stopped. As she dropped down into sleep she found herself smiling as she replayed in her mind how she'd returned to the airship from the medium's that afternoon to find that her son was gone, the thread she always kept tucked in the edge of the false panel in the wainscoting was on the floor, and on her pillow was a sheet of paper.

It was one of the recruitment broadsides the *Swan*'s crew had been passing around town, featuring a woodblocked airship folding her wings against her hull to stoop upon some hapless prey or other on a placid sea.

When she turned it over, penciled on the back she found the note.

I have seen Sunday-Shoes and Governesses, and I prefer the Sky.

The Ballad of the Last Human

Lavie Tidhar

This is the story of the dog Chancer, who was an adventurer and a philosopher and an occasional thief. Chancer had an airship he had liberated from merchant cats, and he was making his way across the One Continent, stopping at kennel towns and Nests, trading human relics and information and whatever else he was able to carry.

The winds and a carelessness about his choice of direction led him to the heart of the One Continent, beyond the lands of the cats and the lands of the dogs, into the heartlands where the spiders lived.

He landed his feline airship at a Web town called Ur, and began trading for silk. Chancer reckoned he'd landed himself in riches: spider-silk was rare and valuable, and here he was, by chance and luck, in the heart of the Webs. All he knew, or thought he knew, was that he was going to get rich.

Instead he met Mot.

This is the moment Mot hatched: from a silk sac hidden underground, somewhere safe and secret and forgotten. The sac opened; silk ripped. And a thousand spiderlings came scuttling out into the world. Mot remembered only flashes of that time, tiny slivers of information: a sense of immense dimensions, the glint of light on glass. And something through the glass, something strange and scary. A monster locked away, out of sight.

When the spiderlings came out of the sac they scattered in all directions. Mot, guided only by the desire to go up, followed an ancient route out of the caverns and into daylight. What he saw when he emerged was the colour blue: it lay in dazzling brightness before him, a giant, blue world bordered by a sky that mirrored it. He wove a cocoon and got into it, and he floated on the blue world until he reached the outskirts of a Web, touching the water, and climbed out and onto the Web.

That Web was the city of Ur, which sat like a diamond in the heart of all the Webs, and Mot was adopted into it, just as all his siblings were in their turn adopted by the Web communities they had each found. Spiders were born in secrecy and made their own way in life.

Since that first moment out of the cave Mot had loved the water, and most of all travelling. He hung out at the dockside of Ur, where the Web touched the water and where silken rafts and boats carried passengers and lit the skyline with gaily coloured lamps. When he grew up enough he too ferried passengers and cargo; for a time he joined a group of treasure seekers who dived into the lake in search of human artefacts.

That was how he first met Chancer.

Chancer had spent two weeks in the Web town and he was getting ready to leave. He liked the spiders he met, who were friendly and polite but also quite unsure of what to do about a dog in their midst. He could have bought enough silk to leave and go back to the lands of the dogs and become prosperous, but he didn't; he hung out in the dockside milk dens and listened to gossip, and talked to people.

He was sitting there the night Mot came in with a gang of his friends, and he allowed them to satisfy their curiosity about his presence with good grace.

So you're treasure hunters, are you? he said at last. Ever find anything worth having?

The spiderlings were competing with each other about their best finds. All kinds of obscure human relics, the purpose of which no one in fact knew, were mentioned. Chancer nodded and watched.

After a while most of the spiderlings went off. Mot remained behind.

Didn't hear you say anything before, Chancer observed over his saucer of milk. But I'm guessing you do have something to say.

Why are you asking? Mot replied. From what I hear you're buying silk, not treasures.

I like silk, Chancer said slowly. The spiderling was direct, and he approved of that. But I like treasure more.

Mot's eight eyes regarded Chancer's two.

I know of a treasure, he said.

I thought so, said Chancer, and allowed his fangs to open in a grin. And you might need an airship to move it?

I might, Mot said, and his feelers moved in a spider's grin, matching Chancer's.

When Mot and Chancer left the milk den the triple-moonlets were waning in the sky. They walked on the sand, the canopy of the Web above them forming a lattice of light and shade on the ground.

They took off in darkness, the airship rising from the web the way a bee takes flight from a flower in search of new nectar. There was a quiet understanding between them that seemed to grow through the night and through the silent journey, flying low with the ship reflected in silver and gold in the water and the light of the moonlets.

Mot, who had never before been on an airship, took to it like a cat. He wove sails and ropes into the structure and hopped from place to place, hanging directly over the water, waving his feelers in the rushing air.

When dawn arose and the sun came low over the horizon like a giant flower opening its leaves, Mot wove two fine, strong threads that fell over the side and plummeted into the water below.

They fished from aboard the ship, hauling the strange fish of that lake into the air until they landed on the deck with a wet whack.

Later, Chancer left some of the fishmeat to dry and they roasted the rest, cooking it slowly over a small coal fire.

At night Chancer howled at the triple-moonlets, and Mot joined him in spider-song, so that the ship seemed engulfed in sound.

On the third day they spotted land.

They touched down on water, and Chancer threw in the anchor and watched it fall, and fall, until at last it caught. The waters were deep, but calm.

Before them was a small sandy beach, leading to a sheltered alcove, and an opening, a chink in the mountain. They explored the beach that day, Mot scuttling deeper and deeper into the cave, his feelers moving in excitement.

It smells right, he confirmed to Chancer as they built a fire on the beach and cooked a stew of fish, pungent with the handful of herbs Chancer had plucked inside the cave. They were silvery grey, long graceful stalks of a web-like plant, and they added a rich, earthy taste to the stew.

As they finished the meal a sense of calm fell on them. They looked at the water and it seemed to form a strange, alien face, moonlight and moonshade adding to the semblance of a figure that mouthed words at them without sound.

The face stretched and shrunk with the movement of the waves; then it flared into brilliance as the stars seemed to fall in a shower from the sky, trailing threads of light into the water that joined into a giant, glowing web that covered the horizon.

What is it? Chancer asked.

Mot didn't answer. The strange face seemed somehow familiar, like a half-remembered dream. He didn't answer, and Chancer didn't ask again, and soon the night was dark again, and quiet, and they went to sleep.

The second day on shore they began to explore the caves. The deeper they went the hotter it became, and the walls grew a faint luminous fungus that seemed to them like arrows, always pointing down, down. Mot wove threads that marked their passage, trailing behind on the caves' floor. They passed in darkness and in silence, through caverns of stone aged beyond the age of the dogs, beyond the age of the cats, beyond even the age of humans.

In one of the caverns they discovered a silken sac, carefully hidden in a small opening in the wall. The sac moved, as if hundreds of tiny bodies were moving inside. They left it alone.

In another they discovered the bodies of cats, dressed in strange, metallic armour. They lined the giant cavern from end to end, standing in rows, metal weapons raised. They passed through them slowly and with care; it seemed as if at any moment the silent battalion might rise and come back to life.

In yet another they discovered human relics, strange and unknowable. There were technological artefacts there, and Mot tagged each one carefully. They decided to try and take as many as was possible back to the ship.

They walked for four days, eating dried fish and drinking water from small, ice-cold pools where moisture glistened on the walls.

On the fifth day Mot stopped, and his feelers shuddered. He and Chancer advanced slowly, and were soon in a small cavern, dark and dry and with the smell of disuse about it, as if no living thing had been inside for thousands of years.

Yet living things had been there: moving with their feeble lights through the cave they found signs of this, a few tattered threads of silk: all that remained of Mot's birth-sac.

Then Chancer's light swept over something that reflected and refracted the light back into his eyes and he growled, and Mot hissed.

They had discovered a coffin. The giant glass structure rested in the wall as if embedded in it, like amber in rock. Inside a shape was visible, strange and frightening. They shone their light into the coffin and a face stared at them, and Chancer growled again and swore: it was the same face they had seen in the water, but now it was still, and as unmoving as stone.

Then Chancer touched the coffin, and the darkness exploded into a brilliance of light.

The cavern filled with light; Chancer and Mot shrunk back, and as they did the side of the coffin began to open, and the eyes inside came alive.

The light was like a web suffusing the rock, a net cast over the darkness. Ethereal sounds, a faint, strange music, filled the air. The creature in the coffin rose and stood on two legs, its eyes on the adventurers.

Words came out of its mouth, but they were incomprehensible to Mot and Chancer. As they watched, the lights dimmed and the monster in the glass remained in the centre of an evolving web of light rays, haloed and silent.

The web of lights shifted and changed; it seemed to them to resemble a vast circular shape beyond which was a giant ocean. It was as if they were somehow caught inside a representation in light and shade of their world, and where the monster stood was the centre. The web of light ebbed and pulsed, marking mountain ranges, lakes, shores, tundra, deserts, veldt, forests, caves. At the heart of it all stood the monster, two-eyed, two-legged, tall and pale. Its eyes were the colour of the sea at dusk.

Words came to them again, heard in the mind; the monster's lips did not move.

A dog. And a spider? It sounded amused. What strange company to be awakened to.

What . . . what are you? Chancer demanded, made bold by despair.

The voice came to him, soft and caressing like a spider's silk.

You must know what you were looking for, it observed. To have come all this way, here, to the secret heart of the world . . . what treasure were you seeking, that you seem so at a loss?

Human, Mot whispered. And – Human, the voice in his head agreed. It sounded regretful.

The web of light shifted again, and in its dancing the world faded and faces appeared: there were cats there, their faces and bodies changing from one cycle to the next; there were dogs, likewise changing, a fluid movement through immeasurable time; there were spiders, a multitude of differences, divers and climbers, rock-dwellers and tree-dwellers, large and small; there were Avians there, gliding through air and roosting in vast Nests at the tops of trees. Chancer growled as the faces of other creatures appeared; those known as the Green Menace, the creatures of the swamp unseen for centuries; that strange, alien being called the Forgotten Sea, that moved like a drop of molten silver atop the Great Ocean; and others, stranger still, some familiar but many more that neither he nor Mot had ever seen.

You thought I was the treasure, the voice said, and there was mute sadness in it. But I am only the guardian of a treasure, and one that you already possess.

The light shifted, faded. In the silence the sudden sound of marching startled them. As they turned, the battalion of armoured cats streamed into the cavern until they threatened to fill it and formed into a web of their own, with Chancer and Mot in its centre.

Go, whispered the voice. The creature seemed to abate, to lose its animation. It sat back into the coffin and the glass began to close over it without noise.

Go, children. There are treasures enough, and time . . .

The light withered and was gone. The cats had cleared a space to the entrance of the cavern.

Mot and Chancer looked at each other, two eyes regarding right.

They left the cavern in silence, and their thoughts were their own.

This is the story of Chancer and Mot, and of the treasure they discovered. They traversed the path they had come, the cats following them at a distance, and on the fourth day they emerged into light.

The sun shone over the lake. On the water, bobbing gently, was Chancer's airship.

They took to the air that day, and as they flew over the lake Mot wove lines for them, and they fished in the light of the moonlets, and built a fire, and talked. Their subsequent journeys are a matter for other stories, and those are the stories that everyone knows: how they crossed the One Continent from one end to the other and how they went on, beyond the Great Ocean. There are stories that say they found the Forgotten Sea and dwelt for a time in the Isle of Wraiths; that they met and fought with the Frog Folk, the Green Menace of the swamplands; that they flew with the Avians on their inexplicable journeys across the world, and that they lived for a time in the Pole, a story made all the more fanciful by what it is said they found there.

They had discovered a treasure at the heart of the world and every day they spent it, in their exhilaration and in their joy at the world and their being alive in it.

This is the story of Chancer and Mot. And this is the ballad of the last human.

Acknowledgements

"Steampunk: Looking to the Future Through the Lens of the Past" © 2012 by Ekaterina Sedia. Original to this volume.

"Fixing Hanover" © 2008 by Jeff VanderMeer. Originally appeared in *Extraordinary Engines*. Reprinted by permission of the author.

"The Steam Dancer (1896)" © 2007 by Caitlin R. Kiernan. Originally appeared in *Sirenia Digest*. Reprinted by permission of the author.

"Icebreaker" © 2012 by E. Catherine Tobler. Original to this volume.

"Tom Edison and His Amazing Telegraphic Harpoon" © 2008 by Joseph E. Lake Jr. Originally appeared in *Weird Tales*. Reprinted by permission of the author.

"The Zeppelin Conductors' Society Annual Gentlemen's Ball" © 2010 by Genevieve Valentine. Originally appeared in *Lightspeed Magazine*. Reprinted by permission of the author.

"Clockwork Fairies" © 2010 by Cat Rambo. Originally appeared in Tor.com. Reprinted by permission of the author.

"The Mechanical Aviary of Emperor Jala-ud-din Muhammad Akbar" © 2009 by Shweta Narayan. Originally appeared in *Shimmer*. Reprinted by permission of the author.

"Prayers of Forges and Furnaces" © 2012 by Aliette de Bodard. Original to this volume.

"The Effluent Engine" © 2011 by N. K. Jemisin. Originally appeared in *Steam-Powered: Lesbian Steampunk Stories*. Reprinted by permission of the author.

"The Clockwork Goat and the Smokestack Magi" © 2009 by Peter M. Ball. Originally appeared in *Shimmer*. Reprinted by permission of the author.

"The Armature of Flight" © 2010 by Sharon Mock. Originally appeared in *Fantasy Magazine*. Reprinted by permission of the author.

"The Anachronist's Cookbook" © 2009 by Catherynne M. Valente. Originally appeared in *Steampunk Tales*. Reprinted by permission of the author.

"Numismatics in the Reigns of Naranh and Viu" © 2012 by Alex Dally MacFarlane. Original to this volume.

"Zeppelin City" © 2009 by Eileen Gunn & Michael Swanwick. Originally appeared in Tor.com. Reprinted by permission of the authors.

"The People's Machine" © 2008 by Tobias S. Buckell. Originally appeared in *Sideways in Crime*. Reprinted by permission of the author.

"The Hands That Feed" © 2011 by Matthew Kressel. Originally appeared in *Steam-Powered: Lesbian Steampunk Stories*. Reprinted by permission of the author.

"Machine Maid" © 2008 by Margo Lanagan. Originally appeared in *Extraordinary Engines*. Reprinted by permission of the author.

"To Follow the Waves" © 2011 by Amal El-Mohtar. Originally appeared in *Steam-Powered: Lesbian Steampunk Stories*. Reprinted by permission of the author.

"Clockmaker's Requiem" © 2007 by Barth Anderson. Originally appeared in *Clarkesworld Magazine*. Reprinted by permission of the author.

"Dr Lash Remembers" © 2010 by Jeffrey Ford. Originally appeared in *Steampunk II: Steampunk Reloaded*. Reprinted by permission of the author.

About the Contributors

Ekaterina Sedia resides in the Pinelands of New Jersey. Her critically acclaimed novels, *The Secret History of Moscow*, *The Alchemy of Stone* and *The House of Discarded Dreams* were published by Prime Books. Her next one, *Heart of Iron*, was published in 2011. Her short stories have sold to *Analog*, *Baen's Universe*, *Subterranean* and *Clarkesworld*, as well as numerous anthologies, including *Haunted Legends* and *Magic in the Mirrorstone*. She is also the editor of *Paper Cities* (World Fantasy Award winner), *Running with the Pack*, *Bewere the Night* and *Bloody Fabulous* (forthcoming). Visit her at EkaterinaSedia.com.

Jeff VanderMeer's books have made the year's best lists of *Publishers Weekly*, *LA Weekly*, Amazon, the *San Francisco Chronicle*, and many more, and he has won two World Fantasy Awards, an NEA-funded Florida Individual Writers' Fellowship and Travel Grant, and, most recently, the Le Cafard Cosmique Award in France and the Tähtifantasia Award in Finland. He has also been a finalist, as writer or editor, for the Hugo Award, Bram Stoker Award, IHG Award, Philip K. Dick Award, Shirley Jackson Award and many others. He is the author of over 300 stories, and his short fiction has appeared recently in *Conjunctions*, *Black Clock*, Tor.com and *Songs of the Dying Earth*, among several other original and year's best anthologies, and *Library of America's American Fantastic Tales*, edited by Peter Straub.

Caitlín R. Kiernan is the award-winning author of nine novels, including *Silk*, *Threshold*, *Low Red Moon*, *Murder of Angels*, *Daughter of Hounds* and, most recently, *The Red Tree*. She is a prolific short-fiction writer, and her stories have been collected in *Tales of Pain and Wonder*, *From Weird and Distant Shores*, *Wrong Things*, *To Charles Fort, With Love*, *Alabaster*, *A is For Alien* and *The Ammonite Violin & Others*. She lives in Providence, Rhode Island.

E. Catherine Tobler lives and writes in Colorado – strange how that works out. Her fiction has appeared in, among others, *Sci Fiction*, *Fantasy Magazine*, *Realms of Fantasy*, *Talebones* and *Lady Churchill's Rosebud Wristlet*. She is an active member of SFWA and senior editor at *Shimmer Magazine*. For more visit ecatherine.com.

Jay Lake lives in Portland, Oregon, where he works on numerous writing and editing projects. His 2011 books are *Endurance* from Tor Books, along with paperback releases of two of his other titles. His short fiction appears regularly in literary and genre markets worldwide. Jay is a past winner of the John W. Campbell Award for Best New Writer, and a multiple nominee for the Hugo and World Fantasy Awards.

Genevieve Valentine is the author of *Mechanique: A Tale of the Circus Tresaulti*. Her short fiction has appeared or is forthcoming in *Clarkesworld*, *Strange Horizons*, *Journal of Mythic Arts*, *Fantasy Magazine*, *Lightspeed* and *Apex*, and in the anthologies *Federations*, *The Living Dead 2*, *The Way of the Wizard*, *Running with the Pack*, *Teeth* and more. She is a co-author of the forthcoming pop-culture book *Geek Wisdom*, and her non-fiction has appeared in publications such as *Fantasy Magazine* and *Weird Tales*. Her appetite for bad movies is insatiable, a tragedy she tracks on her glvalentine.livejournal.com.

Cat Rambo lives and writes in the Pacific Northwest. Among the places her work has appeared are *Asimov's*, Tor.com and *Weird Tales*. Her collection, *Eyes Like Sky and Coal and Moonlight*, was a 2010 Endeavour Award finalist.

Shweta Narayan was born in India and lived in Malaysia, Saudi Arabia, the Netherlands and Scotland before moving to California. The Artificer bird was born in the story in this collection, and keeps turning back up; so far, in *Realms of Fantasy*, the *Clockwork Phoenix 3* anthology and *Steam-Powered: Lesbian Steampunk Stories*. Shweta also has fiction online in *Strange Horizons*, and poetry in *Goblin Fruit*, *Jabberwocky* and *Stone Telling*. She was the Octavia E. Butler Memorial Scholarship recipient at the 2007 Clarion workshop and a finalist for the 2010 Nebula Award. She can be found online at shwetanarayan.org.

Aliette de Bodard lives and works in Paris, where she has a job as a computer engineer. In her spare time, she writes speculative fiction: her series of Aztec noir novels, *Obsidian and Blood*, is published by Angry Robot; and her short fiction has appeared in *Asimov's*, *Interzone* and the *Year's Best Science Fiction*. She has won a Writers of the Future and a British Science Fiction Award, and been a finalist for the Campbell Award and Nebula Awards. Visit aliettedebodard.com for more information.

N. K. Jemisin is a writer who lives and writes in Brooklyn, NY. Her first novel, *The Hundred Thousand Kingdoms*, was nominated for Hugo, Nebula, Gemmell Morningstar and Locus Awards and is followed by her second book in the Inheritance Trilogy, *The Broken Kingdoms*. Her short fiction has also been nominated for a Hugo and a Nebula, as well as attracting several "Year's Best" Honorable Mentions. "The Effluent Engine" is her first attempt to write steampunk, but she kinda likes it and will write more. Her website is at nkjemisin.com.

Peter M. Ball is a writer from Brisbane, Australia. His publications include the hardboiled faerie novellas *Horn* and *Bleed* from Twelfth Planet Press, and his short fiction has appeared in publications such as *Fantasy Magazine*, *Strange Horizons*, *Apex Magazine*, *Interfictions II*, *Shimmer* and *Eclipse 4*. He can be found online at petermball.com.

Sharon Mock's work has been printed in magazines such as *Realms of Fantasy*, *Clarkesworld Magazine* and *Fantasy Magazine*, where "The Armature of Flight" first appeared. She is a graduate of the Viable Paradise workshop. She lives in Southern California with her husband, the writer and artist Zak Jarvis.

Catherynne M. Valente is an author, poet and sometime critic who has been known to write as many as six impossible things before breakfast. She is to blame for over a dozen works of fiction and poetry, including *The Orphan's Tales, Palimpsest, Deathless* and *The Girl Who Circumnavigated Fairyland in a Ship of Her Own Making*. She has won the Tiptree Award, the Andre Norton Award, the Mythopoeic Award, the Lambda Award, the Rhysling Award and the Million Writers Award for best web fiction. She lives on an island off the coast of Maine with her partner, two dogs, an enormous cat and a slightly less enormous accordion.

Alex Dally MacFarlane lives and works in London, where she collects coins and eventually plans to return to academia. Her work has appeared in *Clarkesworld Magazine, Fantasy Magazine, EscapePod, Sybil's Garage, Lady Churchill's Rosebud Wristlet* and various other publications. A handbound limited edition of her story "Two Coins" was published by Papaveria Press. She blogs at alexdallymacfarlane.com.

Michael Swanwick is one of the most interesting and unpredictable writers in science fiction today. His works have been honored with Hugo, Nebula, Theodore Sturgeon and World Fantasy Awards, and have been translated and published throughout the world. Michael is the author of eight novels and five major collections of short fiction. His latest novel, *Dancing With Bears*, featuring the Post-utopian swindlers Darger & Surplus, is published by Night Shade Books. Swanwick lives in Philadelphia with his wife, Marianne Porter.

Eileen Gunn's fiction has received the Nebula Award in the US and the Sense of Gender Award in Japan, and been nominated for the Hugo, Philip K. Dick and World Fantasy awards and shortlisted for the James Tiptree, Jr. Award. She was the editor/ publisher of the late *Infinite Matrix* webzine, and on dark nights can hear it stomping about in the attic. Gunn served twenty-two years on the board of directors of the Clarion West Writers

Workshop. She is the author of the short story collection *Stable Strategies and Others*, published by Tachyon Publications. Her website is at eileengunn.com.

Tobias S. Buckell is a Caribbean-born speculative fiction writer who grew up in Grenada, the British Virgin Islands and the US Virgin Islands. His latest novel, *Sly Mongoose*, a Caribbean Space Opera, is published by Tor and his first short story collection, *Tides from the New Worlds*, was published by Wyrm Publishing in 2009.

Matthew Kressel's fiction has appeared or will appear in *Clarkesworld Magazine*, *Beneath Ceaseless Skies*, *Interzone*, *Electric Velocipede*, *Apex Magazine*, *GUD Magazine* and the anthologies *Naked City*, *After*, *The People of the Book*, *Steam-Powered: Lesbian Steampunk Stories* as well as in other markets. He runs Senses Five Press, which publishes the magazine *Sybil's Garage* and the World Fantasy Award-winning *Paper Cities*. He co-hosts the Fantastic Fiction at KGB reading series in Manhattan alongside Ellen Datlow, and he is a member of the Altered Fluid writers group. His website is matthewkressel.net.

Margo Lanagan has published four collections of short stories (*White Time*, *Black Juice*, *Red Spikes* and *Yellowcake*) and a dark fantasy novel, *Tender Morsels*. Her next novel, about selkies, will come out in early 2012. Margo lives in Sydney.

Amal El-Mohtar is a Canadian-born child of the Mediterranean, presently pursuing a PhD at the Cornwall campus of the University of Exeter. She is the author of *The Honey Month*, a collection of poetry and prose written to the taste of twenty-eight different kinds of honey. Her poem "Song for an Ancient City" received the 2009 Rhysling Award for best short poem, and "The Green Book" received a Nebula nomination for best short story. She also co-edits *Goblin Fruit*, an online quarterly dedicated to fantastical poetry, with Jessica P. Wick. Find her online at amalelmohtar.com.

Barth Anderson is the author of two novels, *The Patron Saint of Plagues* and *The Magician and The Fool* (both published by Bantam

Spectra). His short stories have appeared in *Asimov's*, *Strange Horizons* and *Talebones*, and his story "Lark Till Dawn, Princess" won the Spectrum Award for Best Short Fiction. Anderson is chief blogger at Fair Food Fight and lives in Minneapolis with his wife and children.

Multiple World Fantasy Award-winner **Jeffrey Ford** is the author of the novels *The Physiognomy*, *The Portrait of Mrs. Charbuque*, *The Girl in the Glass* and *The Shadow Year*. His short story collections are *The Fantasy Writer's Assistant*, *The Empire of Ice Cream* and *The Drowned Life*. He lives in New Jersey and teaches at Brookdale Community College.

James Morrow is a Nebula Award–winner and the author of *Blameless in Abaddon*, *The Cat's Pajamas*, *City of Truth*, *The Eternal Footman*, *The Last Witchfinder*, *Only Begotten Daughter* and *Towing Jehovah*. He lives in State College, Pennsylvania.

Cherie Priest is the author of the bestselling *Boneshaker*. She has three other works set in the same milieu as *Boneshaker*: a novella from Subterranean Press called *Clementine*, another novel from Tor called *Dreadnought* and "Reluctance". Priest's other novels include *Four and Twenty Blackbirds*, *Wings to the Kingdom*, *Not Flesh Nor Feathers* and *Fathom*. Her forthcoming books include urban fantasies *Bloodshot* and *Hellbent*. Her short fiction has appeared in *Subterranean Magazine*, *Apex Digest* and *Steampunk II: Steampunk Reloaded*.

Margaret Ronald is the author of the novels *Spiral Hunt*, *Wild Hunt* and *Soul Hunt*. Her short fiction has appeared in *Strange Horizons*, *Fantasy Magazine*, *Beneath Ceaseless Skies* and many other venues. Originally from rural Indiana, she now lives outside Boston.

Megan Arkenberg is a student in Wisconsin, where she lives with dozens of college-ruled notebooks and a pocket watch named Juggernaut. Her work has appeared in *Clarkesworld*, *Beneath Ceaseless Skies*, *Fantasy Magazine*, *Ideomancer* and many other places. She procrastinates by editing the fantasy e-zine *Mirror Dance* and the historical fiction e-zine *Lacuna*.

Benjamin Rosenbaum lives near Basel, Switzerland, with his wife Esther and their eerily clever children, Aviva and Noah. Benjamin's stories have appeared in *Nature*, *Harper's*, *F&SF*, *Asimov's*, *McSweeney's*, *Strange Horizons* and a collection, *The Ant King and Other Stories*, from Small Beer Press, and have been translated into fourteen languages. He has been a party clown, a synagogue president, a computer game designer, and can cook a mean risotto. More at benjaminrosenbaum.com.

Mary Robinette Kowal is the author of *Shades of Milk and Honey* (Tor 2010). In 2008 she received the Campbell Award for Best New Writer and has been nominated for the Hugo, Nebula and Locus awards. Her stories have appeared in *Asimov's*, *Clarkesworld* and several Year's Best anthologies. A professional puppeteer and voice actor, she lives in Portland with her husband Rob and a dozen manual typewriters. Visit her website maryrobinettekowal.com for more information about her fiction and puppetry.

Samantha Henderson lives on the outskirts of Los Angeles, with an excellent view of the burning hills every summer. Her short fiction and poetry have been published in *Realms of Fantasy*, *Strange Horizons*, *ChiZine*, *Fantasy*, *Abyss & Apex*, *Weird Tales* and *Ideomancer* and have been podcast on *Escape Pod*, *Podcastle*, *Drabblecast* and *StarShipSofa*. Her first novel, *Heaven's Bones*, was released in 2008 and was a nominee for the Scribe Award. You can stalk her at her livejournal (samhenderson.livejournal.com) or website (samanthahenderson.com).

Nick Mamatas is the author of several novels, incuding *Sensation* and, with Brian Keene, *The Damned Highway*. His short fiction has appeared in a number of anthologies including *Hint Fiction*, *Lovecraft Unbound* and *Supernatural Noir*. His essays and reportage on politics and economics have appeared in *Clamor*, *Left Turn*, *The New Humanist* and *In These Times*.

Nicole Kornher-Stace was born in Philadelphia in 1983, moved from the East Coast to the West Coast and back again by the time she was five, and currently lives in New Paltz, NY, with one husband, two ferrets, one Changeling and many many books. Her short fiction and poetry has appeared or is forthcoming in a number of magazines and anthologies, including *Best American Fantasy*, *Clockwork Phoenix 3*, *Apex* and *Fantasy Magazine*. She is the author of *Desideria, Demon Lovers and Other Difficulties*, and *The Winter Triptych*. Her current novel-in-progress is a blend of steampunk and mythpunk, with a Lady Explorer, a fake Tarot, a workers' rebellion, a demon-possessed airship and other miscellany. She can be found online at www.nicolekornherstace. com or wirewalking.livejournal.com.

Lavie Tidhar is the author of steampunk novels *The Bookman* and *Camera Obscura*, and the ground-breaking alternative history novel *Osama*. He grew up on a kibbutz in Israel and has since lived in South Africa, the UK, Vanuatu and Laos. Other works include novellas *Cloud Permutations, Gorel and the Pot-Bellied God* and linked-story collection *HebrewPunk*.

The Mammoth Book of Best New SF 24
edited by Gardner Dozois

ISBN: 978-1-84901-373-4
Price: £9.99

Seventeen-times winner of the Locus Award for the Year's Best Anthology

For over twenty years, Gardner Dozois's compelling annual has deservedly remained the single must-have collection for science fiction fans around the world. Unfailingly offering the very best new stories of the year, it showcases up-and-coming stars alongside established masters of the genre. This year's collection includes the work of over thirty writers, including Robert Reed, Nina Allan, Kage Baker, Yoon Ha Lee, Ian R. MacLeod, Joe Haldeman, Naomi Novik, Cory Doctorow and Aliette de Bodard.

In addition to over 3000,000 words of fantastic fiction, the anthology includes bonus features such as Dozois's insightful round-up of the year in SF and an extensive recommended reading guide.

"For over two decades, Gardner Dozois's Mammoth Book of Best New SF has defined the field. It is the most important anthology, not only annually, but overall."
Charles N. Brown, publisher of *Locus*

"Dozois's definitive must-read short story anthology takes the pulse of science fiction today."
Publishers Weekly

Visit www.constablerobinson.com for more information

The Mammoth Book of Apocalyptic SF

edited and with an introduction by Mike Ashley

ISBN: 978-1-84901-305-5
Price: £7.99

Apocalypse Now?

Have the last days begun?

Humankind has long been fascinated by the precarious vulnerability of civilization and of the Earth itself. When our fragile civilizations finally go, will it be as a result of nuclear war, or some cosmic catastrophe? The impact of global warming, or a terrorist atrocity? Genetic engineering, or some modern plague more virulent even than HIV or Ebola?

Mike Ashley's gripping anthology of short stories explores the destruction of civilization and looks at how humanity might strive to survive such a crisis, including the end of the Earth.

A vaccine threatens to turn into a virus that could wipe out mankind in **'Bloodletting'** by **Kate Wilhelm**

Will the internet destroy civilization, or save it? **'When Sysadmins Ruled the Earth'** by **Cory Doctorow**

In **'Guardians of the Phoenix'**, **Eric Brown** depicts a world in the grip of climate change

How will the end come, and will you be there to witness it?

Visit www.constablerobinson.com for more information

Brave New Love
edited by Paula Guran

ISBN: 978-1-84901-601-8
Price: £6.99

When society crumbles, can young love survive?

When the young are deprived of their bright future and left to
survive day to day, what bonds remain between individuals? Can
young love survive a dystopian nightmare?

This exciting collection of stories explores the struggles –
romantically, emotionally and physically – of teenagers trying to
survive after civilization as we know it has fallen apart. The end
of our world has come, and those who live on must confront
new realities. These are compelling, emotionally charged stories
of young lives lived in desperate circumstances.

Including stories by:

Elizabeth Bear • Steve Berman
Seth Cadin • Kiera Cass • Amanda Downum
Jeanne DuPrau • Nina Kiriki Hoffman
Jesse Karp • Diana Peterfreund • Carrie Ryan
Nisi Shawl • John Shirley • William Sleator
Maria V. Snyder • Carrie Vaughn

Visit www.constablerobinson.com for more information

Zombie Apocalypse!
created by Stephen Jones

ISBN: 978-1-84901-303-1
Price: £7.99

THE END OF THE WORLD –
WITH FLESH-EATING ZOMBIES!

In the near future, a desperate and ever-more controlling UK
government attempts to restore a sense of national pride with a
New Festival of Britain. But construction work on the site of an
old church in south London releases a centuries-old plague that
turns its victims into flesh-hungry ghouls whose bite or scratch
passes the contagion – a supernatural virus which has the power
to revive the dead – on to others.

"The Death" soon sweeps across London and the whole country
descends into chaos. When a drastic attempt to eradicate the
outbreak at source fails, the plague spreads quickly to
mainland Europe and then across the rest of the world.

Told through a series of interconnected eyewitness narratives
– text messages, e-mails, blogs, letters, diaries and transcripts
– this is an epic story of a world plunged intochaos as the dead
battle the living for total domination.

**Will humanity triumph over the
worldwide zombie plague, or will the
walking dead inherit the earth?**

Visit www.constablerobinson.com for more information

To order other Mammoth titles from **Constable & Robinson** simply contact The Book Service (TBS) by phone, email or by post. Alternatively visit our website at www.constablerobinson.com.

No. of copies	Title	RRP	ISBN	Total
	The Mammoth Book of Best New SF 24	£7.99	978-1-84901-373-4	
	The Mammoth Book of Apocalyptic SF	£7.99	978-1-84901-305-5	
	Brave New Love	£6.99	978-1-84901-601-8	
	Zombie Apocalypse!	£7.99	978-1-84901-303-1	
			P&P £	
			Total £	

FREEPOST RLUL-SJGC-SGKJ, Cash Sales Direct Mail Dept.,
The Book Service, Colchester Road, Frating, Colchester, CO7 7DW

Tel: +44 (0) 1206 255 800
Fax: +44 (0) 1206 255 930

Email: sales@tbs-ltd.co.uk

UK customers: please allow £1.00 p&p for the first book, plus 50p for the second, and an additional 30p for each book thereafter, up to a maximum charge of £3.00.

Overseas customers (incl. Ireland): please allow £2.00 p&p for the first book, plus £1.00 for the second, plus 50p for each additional book.

NAME (block letters): _____

ADDRESS: _____

_____

_____ POSTCODE: _____

I enclose a cheque/PO (payable to 'TBS Direct') for the amount of £___

I wish to pay by Switch/Credit Card

Card number: _____

Expiry date: _____ Switch issue number: _____